大蛇の刃
Orochi no Yaiba

by Itoshi

Art by Aldaria

Every time when I look in the mirror
All these lines on my face getting clearer
The past is gone
It went by, like dusk to dawn
Isn't that the way
Everybody's got their dues in life to pay
I know nobody knows
Where it comes and where it goes
I know it's everybody's sin
You got to lose to know how to win

- Aerosmith

This one's for EAB - who never ceases to inspire me with
her passion, dedication and creativity for the craft.
Thank you for keeping me sane.

- Itoshi

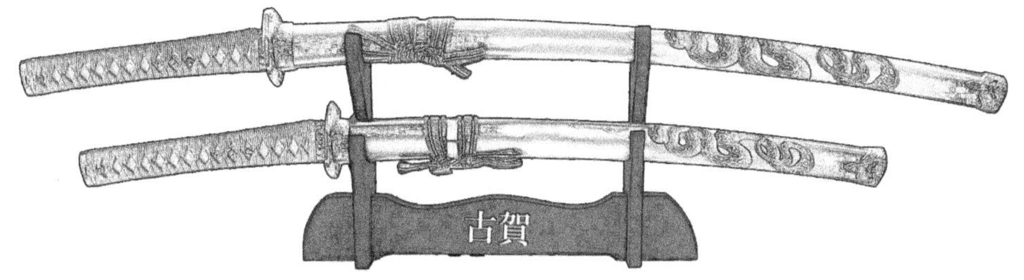

Forward

A word about language

The Orochi Series has certainly been a challenge for me to write in that it relies heavily on the expression of languages among diverse characters with varying degrees of proficiency. Sadao in particular, has a knack for many languages. He's fluent in English, Japanese, Korean, Mandarin, and to a lesser extent, Spanish and French.

In *Orochi no Kishi* - this language diversity between characters was easy to express, because it was told entirely from Mouse's POV. (Yes, it really was - and in third person limited!) So whenever Sadao and Tagata launched into Japanese, Mouse simply had to guess at what was being said via body language or else complain until someone translated for him. A lot of readers enjoyed the task of looking up what was being said during the occasions I wrote the Japanese out in *romaji* (Japanese expressed in the latin alphabet).

In *Orochi no Yaiba* however, the majority of the story is told from Sadao's POV, and Sadao understands nearly everything, regardless of tongue. I'm not as gifted in languages as he is, so it was a struggle to come up with ways to relate to the reader what the heck was going on. My solution was this: for Sadao's narrative, Japanese will be expressed in English italics with some Japanese romanji sprinkled in for effect. For other languages Sadao understands like French, I wrote mostly *in* French with some translation provided. Fortunately, I'm blessed with two editors who studied French a heck of a lot longer than I did. I'll apologize for the iffy Spanish in advance.

By far the most difficult aspect of the language game was making Tagata and Shiratori *sound* like themselves while speaking their native Japanese (in English). I had established their personalities in *Orochi no Kishi* mainly through how much they butchered their English. Tagata takes a more cautious approach to speaking, fearing his mistakes; while Shiratori obliterates his articles and plurals like he just didn't give a fuck. Which in fact, he doesn't.

This is my long way of saying let's all pretend Sadao, Tagata, and Shiratori are speaking Japanese among themselves while in Sadao's POV, even if they're not. Cool?

-Itoshi

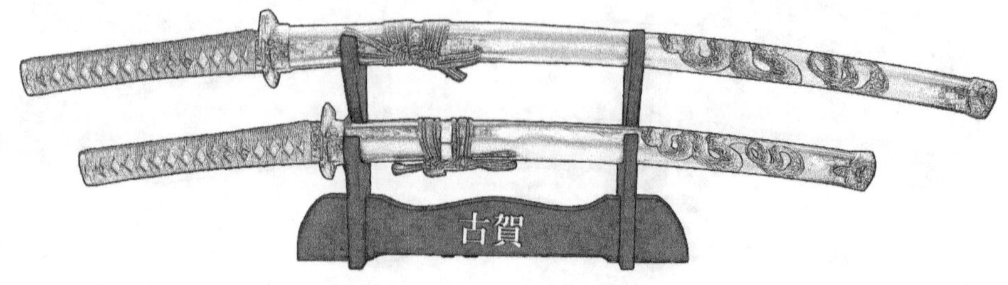

Prelude

Crossed Wires

Blythe, Arizona - Summer, 2048

"Hold still a minute," Dad said. "Let me talk to Barney, boy."

Mouse tried to hold still, but Mouse couldn't see over the counter and that made him jumpy - so jumpy that he began to bounce like a ball up and down. On each jump, he could just see the top of Barney's bald head and the cool stuff that hung from his garage roof inside. Big tools and hoses. Mouse liked big tools and hoses.

"Dad!" bounce "I ... " bounce " ... want..." bounce " ... up!"

On his final bounce he got a grubby hand around the pole that held up the sign above Barney's service window. Mouse could read! It said: trash and tr--eah--suu...

Bang! Rattle, rattle.

Mouse slipped and landed in a bucket butt-first.

"Dad! I fell down! I'm stuck! Dad! Daaaad!!"

"Okay, jumpin' bean. Get on up here 'fore you fall in something worse!"

Dad bent down and popped Mouse out of the bucket with his big Dad hands. Mouse scrambled up onto the counter with Dad's help and sat cross-legged, blowing his long fair hair out of his face.

Mouse pointed at something inside Barney's garage. "Dad! What's that big cone thing?"

Dad squinted and peered past Barney into his workshop where truck frames and engines lay about in disassembled chunks. "Well son, that's a pick-up transmission. Looks like Barney's gettin' her cleaned up."

Mouse scratched his nose. "What's a transmitten?"

"*Transmission*. It helps the pick-up change gears to climb hills and haul heavy loads. That's a big word for a little guy like you," Barney laughed, wiggling Mouse's shoe.

"I'm not little," Mouse said indignantly. "I'm four now!" He held up four dirty little fingers to prove it.

Barney pushed his cracked glasses up higher on his nose. "Well, so you are. As big as that! You'll be ready to drive in no time."

"I can drive now!" Mouse said. "Tell him, Dad! I can drive the tractor! I made dirt come out!"

"Yep, yep. The boy here is a right honest farmer. Helped me turn some garden patch over for Widow Quelle. She's teaching the boy to read, too."

"I can read! And I can count: 1 2 3 4 5 6 7 8 9 10 11 12 13 14 15 16 17 … all the way to a zillion!"

"Whoa! As far as that!" Barney laughed. "Einstein, you got here, Dill."

Dad patted his head and smiled. "Yep, sure is. Fast learner. Already reads better than his pop. 'course then I never did read no better than a cross-eyed mule in a dust storm anyways."

"Are you gonna buy a hose, Dad?"

Dad smiled and lifted Mouse up so he could sit on his shoulders. "Not today son, but we're gonna go treasure huntin' anyway with Barney's blessing."

"Treasure!" Mouse said, pointing upward as he held on to Dad's long hair. "That's what that sign says: Trash and Treasure!"

Both men looked up at the sign painted in drippy blue letters on a rusty piece of sheet metal.

"Well I'll be hog-tied, son - so it does! Little Einstein, you are."

"Yard's yours, Dill," Barney said with a nod. "Dogs are chained up in back. They won't give you no trouble."

"Good," Mouse said as Dad lumbered toward the quarter-mile-long fenced yard of rusted wonders. "'cause I ate all the bacon!"

"Did you now? Let's hope Barney caught all his dogs or I'm gonna hafta feed you to them!"

"Dad, I'm not bacon."

"Nope, but you sure are tasty," Dad said, nibbling on Mouse's bare knee through a hole in his overalls. "Mmm, fresh boy!"

Mouse squealed in delight. "Ssstoop!!"

Dad carried him halfway across the junkyard to a section where a pile of busted up TVs, radios and something Dad called "computers" baked in the sun among a briar of twisted wires.

"Let me down! Let me down!" Mouse squeaked, kicking his feet. He liked radios, even the ones that didn't make any noises. Radios were cool. He had a lot of them back in his room at the gas station.

Dad set him gently in the middle of the junk hillside. Mouse scrambled among the cracked casings, digging around until he found a radio with knobs. "Look, Dad! The dial moves! And it has an antenna! Can we get it? Can we?"

Dad chuckled. "Easy there, shopper. We've got a lot of components to search for first. And not much cash. I just bought you a used CB last week!"

"I know, Dad! But this one is blue and the dial is so big! I bet we can hear Japan!"

"I don't think as far as that. Phoenix, maybe, if we rig an extension. That old antenna's near busted in two."

Mouse held the radio tight and looked up at his Dad with his "please" face.

Dad shook his head in defeat. "All right, boy. Put it in the rucksack."

Mouse clutched his prize and climbed over to the pack Dad had been carrying. He slid the old radio into it, cinching up the top so it would be safe. Down over the hill of electronics he saw the roof of a big long shipping container. Its rear doors were open and hoses were spilling out.

Hoses!!

"Dad! I see hoses! Big hoses! Down there! Can I go see?"

Dad looked over his shoulder toward the area in question. "The radio is all you're gettin' unless you want to trade, son. Best think it over before you go crawling in there. We got rattlers out here, you know."

"I know, Dad! Always look before you grab. I know the rules!" Mouse hopped his way down the trash heap and landed with a hollow bang on the roof of the container.

"You be careful in there, you hear?" Dad said, keeping an eye on him as he sifted through wires and connectors. "You give a shout if you see anything move. Probably just mice, but we can't be too careful. Don't go where it's dark and don't get stuck in any more buckets!"

"I knooow!" Mouse slid down the warm ribbed steel from the roof to the base of the door. Hoses of all kinds were waiting to be explored where they lay along the floor and up along the walls on decaying metal shelves. Green and red and black - some skinny and some curvy - others still had clamps on them and numbers stenciled to their sides. These were hoses no one had ever bought. *Cool!*

Mouse pushed the door open wide to let in the sunlight. He stepped over the fallen rubber and rusty ring clamps as he made his way along the shelves, touching only the outsides of the hoses and peeking in to check for critters. There were plenty of spiders and webs, but none that could hurt you bad. Mouse knew which spiders were bad.

Mouse could almost see to the end of the big container, but the last few feet were still in shadow. Mouse tip-toed forward slowly to let his eyes adjust.

"You okay in there?" Dad called from outside.

"Yeah, Dad. Sheesh! Just me and hoses in here!"

"See one you like?"

"I like all of them!"

"That's the problem, son…"

Mouse did see a hose he liked - a really big one - it was almost as thick around as him. He wanted to get closer but there was an old stack of wood pallets in the way. He had to climb over them and it was hard to see. He wanted to know how long the hose was. Maybe he could make a tunnel with it for his track cars.

Mouse held on to the edge of the long shelf and used it to help him climb up onto the top of the pallets. His feet were wobbly. He took a moment to balance himself and let his eyes adjust to the gloom.

And that's when he saw it, crouching in the back corner - two hollow eyes and a mouth red with blood. Mouse couldn't understand what he was seeing. It was there and it wasn't there because he could also see his prize hose running right through it. The wood gave way under his feet. He screamed and fell, taking the shelf of unbought hoses down with him. He hit the dusty floor hard and everything went black.

Chiba, Japan - Summer, 2048

Sadao crouched in the corner of his cell as far from the light of the shuttered window as the chain would allow. He sat on his knees on the stone floor with his hands behind his back. He was methodically winding a strip of leather around his wrists to create the appearance of being tied up.

Outside, the fishmongers were starting to shout across the docks to the *itamae* who rose with the sun to get first pick of the night's catch to slice up for sushi. Sadao knew there were only minutes left. He had barely returned in time. His forehead dripped with sweat. He had to stop fidgeting soon and cool himself down. The straps would have to hold for now. Relaxing his arms, Sadao let his wrists slide down his back to the floor to pick up the knife. For a moment his fingertips couldn't find it and he panicked. He twisted his head around and tugged at the shackle that he had locked around his ankle to try to look. There, in the dull morning light, he saw the blade next to his foot. He grasped it and held the hilt behind him as his weakened muscles protested from the strain.

He wanted to scream with the effort to stay still. His heart was racing and his head swam from the relentless humidity and heat of summer. He had not been fed hardly at all this past month and his bones stuck out from his skin. Too much exertion brought on dizzy fits and confusion. He needed to focus. *Stay calm and wait.*

Sadao had wasted to little more than a sack of bones dotted with whip cuts and scabs that would no longer heal. If it weren't for the young samurai soldier who had captured him during a delivery for his master and fed him these last four days in the forest, he would likely be too weak to stand. This old friend from his English school had given him a sharp knife and stirred his withered spirit with strong words. He encouraged Sadao to rise up and take his freedom back. If his escape plan did not succeed, either way, he was dead.

He beats you and he starves you, he'd said. *Why do you obey such a master? You've let your spirit be drained for far too long. Wait until he shows you his thing, then take it from him! Take back your spirit he has stolen from you!*

Sadao realized in that moment, looking into the eyes of the young soldier, that he still had a choice. He didn't have to suffer anymore this way. There were boats always coming and going in the harbor. There was work sometimes for those willing to haul barrels in the blistering heat. There was a mouthful of dried fish, a bowl of rice and a canteen of clean water and a crude bed at the end of each day. To Sadao, it seemed like paradise.

You are a slave because you allow yourself to be a slave.

Sadao closed his eyes and focused on his breathing. This was not the time for dreaming about ships and barrels of fish. He let all thoughts leave his head. He sought the words he knew by heart and let the syllables fall from his lips.

Boku wa chikaradzuyoi kawa da,
Kawa wa ishi no ue wo nagareru,
Ishi ha kawa no chikarazuyosa to onaji youni yasashiku sodatsu
Kisetsu ga sugiru youni ishi ha koishi tonar

He had been taught this meditation at school by his instructors for focusing the mind. It had served him well for his exams. And after the schools were abandoned, it had served him while out in the jungle on patrol - when survival depended upon staying still and calm.

Time passed and the light grew stronger. Deep in meditation, Sadao at last heard the familiar key and latch give way. The metal door banged open and the footfalls of his captor shuffled unevenly along the stones toward his cell.

"Boy-san?! Doko ka?"

Sadao lifted his head and opened his eyes. His breath was even and his mind clear. He was ready.

"Koko ni imasu, Goshujin-sama!"

He could smell his master approaching before the light of morning illuminated his round hunched shape. His face was swollen and marked with sores and filth. It looked like he had slept in the streets again.

"Boy-san, you came back, eh?"

"Hai, Goshujin-sama. I am back. Remember, you sent me on a long errand."

Crack! For a drunkard, his slaps were still well aimed. Sadao's face had grown numb to them.

"Lies! You ran off! Got hungry did you? I told you, no one will feed orphan scum like you!"

Sadao sucked the blood from his lip and bowed his head.

Wait for him to show it to you, the young samurai reminded him in his mind. Sadao's knuckles tightened on the hilt of the knife.

"I am sorry, Goshujin-sama. You have been kind. You fed me just yesterday before you went to town," he lied.

The man stumbled and sat down heavily on the grimy bamboo leaf covered floor Sadao called a bed. *"I went to town ... "* the man echoed, squinting to help focus his polluted memory. The smell of his sake soaked breath made Sadao sick. He breathed through his mouth and stayed calm. *Calm like a swift clear river, laid with stones.*

"Yes, Goshujin-sama. You welcomed me home with dried fish and put me to bed. Before you went to town." Sadao moved his ankle slightly to call attention to the fact he was indeed chained.

The man scratched his matted hair and snorted. Then a crooked smile came over his face and he laughed. *"Bah! You try to fool me? If you came home yesterday, why are your shoes still in the hall?"*

Sadao's heart stopped a moment. The *geta* - he'd forgotten to put them up on the shelf in his rush to beat his master home. *"Go-Shujin ... "*

"Silent! No more lies!" His master smacked him across the mouth again, then leaned in and grabbed his neck, forcing Sadao to look into his yellowed eyes. The man got up on one knee and began to untie his soiled trousers. *"I will shut your mouth!"*

Sweat gathered on Sadao's palms and forehead. The man soon had his trousers down around his knees and his shriveled penis in his hand.

The river ... I am the river ...

Sadao bent his head to accept his master's gift. The piss stink of his pubic hairs tickling his nostrils was enough to make him ill, if there had been anything in his gut to spew. The shriveled flesh oozed into his mouth and lolled about on his tongue like a dead eel. No matter how many times he had been called upon to perform this service, nothing had ever hardened him to the utter disgust of it.

"That's good, Boy-san ... you remember your manners now," the man said, gripping his hair. Sadao had to suffer the thrust of his grimy balls against his chin. *"Ganbare. This may be the only meal you'll get this week."*

Sadao forced himself to work the man's organ between his tongue and palate. It stayed soft and useless although a foul pus seeped from the tip and down his throat.

The river flows over the stones … and the stones grow soft as the river gains strength …

"Ah, Boy-san, that is how I taught you. Shujin will reward you soon. Deeper, Boy-san … only your whore mother ever treated me better - aaaaaaaaghhh!!!"

The man screamed as Sadao bit down hard enough to feel a pop and his mouth filled with blood. His master tried to jerk himself free but Sadao's teeth were too deeply embedded in his flesh. *"Gaaagaghhhh!!!"* The man wailed and tore a fistful of Sadao's hair clean from his scalp.

Sadao spit him out and in the next second, snapped his wrists free to take his master's bloody member in hand and slice it clean off with one firm stroke of the knife. The man fell to the floor, screaming and kicking, bleeding in ribbons of gore as Sadao got to his feet and stared at the shriveled thing he held in his hand. It amazed him how small it looked in his palm - a sad little piece of rubbery skin.

"Aaaagghh!! What did you do to me? What did you do?!"

Sadao held the man's penis out for him to see. He squeezed it in his fist and let the blood dribble out onto the man's horrified face.

"… and the stones are worn to pebbles as the seasons pass, and the river flows unhindered over them."

With one more dip and swift cut of the blade, Sadao soon claimed the man's sweat-coated balls. Like furred pebbles - all such small meaningless things when held in the hand.

"You're a demon!! A demon in human form!!"

Sadao regarded his bleeding captor with a smile. His weakness was gone, his thirst was gone. All that remained was a burning hunger.

"A demon would have been better kept!" he said, kneeling before his master one last time. *"Let me show you, Goshujin-sama, how a proper meal is served … "*

Blythe, Arizona

"Don't worry, Dill," said Doc Meadows. "Your boy's gonna be fine. He's strong as an ox, that kid. Head'll heal up just fine. Just a stitch or two was all that was needed. Keep it clean and he'll be back runnin' around in no time."

Mouse lay on the doctor's exam bed with an iced bandage on his head. The sun had gone down and he could only see silhouettes of the cabinets and equipment in the lamp light. Doc gave him a little shot and he felt sleepy as he listened to the men talk just outside in the hallway. He was tired from all the crying and hugged his new blue radio to his chest and closed his eyes. He didn't want to see anymore scary things tonight.

"But, Doc, the kid was hollering his head off about some boy he saw. He says there was a skinny kid in the back of that container all bloody and hurt. He insists. But I radioed Barney. He got his dogs all over that area searchin' and there ain't no such thing! I'm worried Doc. That shelf knocked the boy's stuffin' all to hell, I'm sure of it."

"He'll be fine," Doc said calmly. "Little guys with big imaginations ... you put them in a dark place and they're bound to see anything. He got spooked is all. He's only four, Dill. He's no grown-up. I used to see a kid who'd tell me every month or so he was picked up outta his bed by a little grey man with big eyes and taken for a ride in his rocketship. He used to talk all kinds of crazy shit like that. But he's 24 now and all right in the head. Got his own son now telling him stories just as nuts. But that's all they are, just stories."

Mouse opened his heavy eyes and fiddled with the dials on his radio. It didn't have power or a proper antenna, but he believed it was working. It had to be. With a dial that big, it just made sense the signal had gone like magic all the way to Japan just like he said it would. The boy he saw didn't have eyes like his. They were dark and narrow. It was a real message sent from far away. That boy needed help, and someday he was gonna figure out how to send a reply.

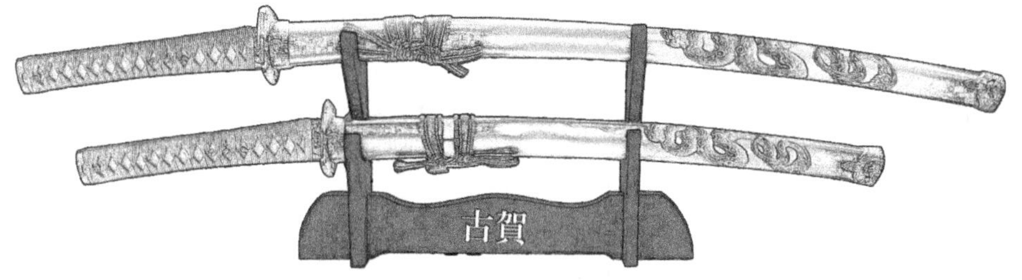

Chapter 1

The Bridge

The mist had come up suddenly, obscuring the direction of the sun. Sadao could not see more than a step ahead. He kept his footfalls steady on the slats of the bridge, careful not to make the old bamboo creak and give away their position. His sense of direction was fading with the light. The mist had swallowed up smells, sounds - and yet he knew he was not alone. There were others moving in the thick air some steps ahead and behind him - methodical and determined.

Sadao, why are you still marching?

He lifted his head to look for the source of the voice, but it was as lost in the fog as he was.

Be quiet, he whispered. *We should not talk.*

Why?

Because we will be found.

Who are you hiding from?

Sadao shut his mouth and kept marching, steadily, evenly. Sweat dripped from his brow and the weight on his back grew heavier. If he didn't focus he would fall behind and lose the others.

Sadao, yamero!

Sadao stopped abruptly. There was someone blocking the bridge. He could see the outline of plated armor wavering in the mist.

Kyouji?

Saying the name brought the man's face into focus. He stood motionless between the ropes, perfectly balanced and still as the air. The brilliant plates of his golden armor were dull in the diffused light.

We can't stop here!

You are right.

We have to keep moving. Sadao insisted, wishing to reach the far end of the bridge.

Why a bridge, Sadao? Would a wider path frighten you?

Sadao panicked; the air was closing in on him. *Let me pass!*

You carry too much weight. You can not come this way until you set it aside. This bridge will break.

Sadao scanned the mists futilely, looking for another way that wasn't blocked. Others were coming up behind him, as trapped as he was.

Go back. You are not ready. The others need to pass.

No! I promised! I would not desert this time! I am staying until the end!

No one would say you have deserted. You are an honorable man.

Sadao squinted into the mist, desiring to read the man's expression, but it remained obscured.

I want to finish this.

Someday you will. And on that day, I will come for you. Until then, we part ways.

The gold armor began to fade from his sight into the mist.

No! Wait!

Turn back before you become lost!

Where do I go? Don't leave!

Sad fool, did you forget the color of the sky?

Mid Pacific Ocean - 2073

"Kyouji!"

Sadao woke with the dead man's name on his lips. There was no mist, only the flat peeling grey paint and rivets of the steel roof of his cell. His head swam as he tossed the sweat soaked blanket from his shoulders in frustration. Sleep had only come in fits. And what little moments of unconsciousness he had gained had been filled with nightmares. His stomach lurched with the rise of the small square room. It rose up and up then fell slowly to the right, only to shudder for a moment as it tipped to the left to rise again in an endless cycle of misery.

Nausea twisted his gut and Sadao gripped the cold rim of the berth, forcing himself to attempt a sitting position. The movement was too abrupt for his injured leg and a violent stab of pain shot up his thigh and into his hip.

"Aaagh!" He rolled off and collapsed onto the rusty floor, retching. He dragged his numb leg aside to avoid soiling his jumpsuit in the foamy river of bile that snaked across the floor with each pitch of the *Hourglass* - a prison ship, deporting him back to Japan.

Kuso! Ima mou?!

Another retch pinched his gut and he pushed himself up onto his good knee to give in and surrender the remains of the fluid he'd managed to keep down for only a few hours. His arms trembled from the effort and his head spun with dehydration as he coughed up the last of it.

It was a terrible curse to be saddled with seasickness as an oyster farmer's son. His brothers had laughed at him, with his head over the side of the boat every time they went out in the wind and weather to check the floats. For forty years, Sadao Koga and the sea had been bitter enemies.

He hung his head, breathing in the stale air before attempting to get to his feet. It took a few tries, but he managed to haul himself up by the edge of the berth to brace his ribs against the sink basin. He pushed the button and a thin metallic-smelling stream of water dribbled out. He filled his cupped palm and splashed the cool water over his face, trying to rinse the stink from his overgrown beard.

Push, slurp, push… he sipped what he could from the tap slowly. He was desperately thirsty. Two days without more than a trickle of a piss worried him greatly, but he knew any more than mouthful of water would cause his ravaged stomach to revolt.

Would not be good to die here in the middle of the ocean, he mused. Not now. Even dream Shiratori agreed. Now was not the time to give in.

Sadao stood on his good leg and held onto the bars covering the single porthole of his cell. He reached through them to turn the latch and open the cloudy glass, letting the salt spray into his room. It stank, but the air felt cool. He leaned his forehead against the bars to calm his head. The stern of the ship rose and dipped against a background of white-capped waves. The view, for the moment, eased his nausea. Memories came to him of high white clouds and steep hillsides. The mists of the Pacific smelled the same as they had on the distant shores of his homeland decades ago. Now those shores were growing closer, nautical mile by mile.

The Ise Peninsula's bamboo forests could be insufferable in the summers of his youth. In his mind, Sadao could still hear the song of the cicadas, filling his ears with their buzzing chatter as he tried to sleep with his army brothers. They'd huddled together under a shelter of thin green poles and leaves, praying to not be shot in their dreams.

Ganbare! Think of the ones you protect!

He did. Closing his eyes against the endless miles of green-grey sea, Sadao opened his heart to the memory of two clear blue eyes searching for him from a closer shore. Their message had been received - *take the boat*. He had and now he stood on weak legs, clinging to the walls of his rocky cage, waiting for an answer.

It was dark when the klaxon rang out through the hallways and the alarm beacon lit up his cell, flashing in oscillating red. Guards began running up and down the gangways outside his cell, shouting orders in confusion. Sadao lay still in his berth, awaiting instruction. On the mainland, the red alarm meant a prisoner was loose and all officers were to report to their posts for further action. The prisoners were to lie down on their bellies and cover their heads so the count could begin. Sadao had no desire to upset his leg by diving to the rusty floor. He closed his eyes and waited but no instructions came.

A shot rang out and his eyes snapped open. The gunfire had come from the main deck above. Puzzled by the sounds, Sadao got unsteadily to his feet, limping to the porthole. The sea had calmed and so had his sickness to an extent, but the sudden shift from prone to vertical made him dizzy. He held onto the porthole bars and looked out.

Smoke trailed the ship, flowing from the engine exhaust towering above him along with the unmistakable flickering of fire.

Bam! Tat-tat-tat!

More gunfire sounded in rapid succession. Automatic weapons - not the common side arms carried by the correctional officers. Sadao limped to the inner door of his cell and pressed his face to the bars to see down the gangway and over the rails to the decks below. Four horseshoe rings of cells were stacked deck over deck inside the stern of the ship. Eighty half-occupied holding cells in all. Shouts from the other prisoners mingled with the thumps of boots running along the catwalks made it difficult to discern where the commotion was centered. Someone down low was shouting "Fire, fire!" and begging to be released. And then all sound became engulfed by one horrendous explosion.

Kablam!

Sadao was thrown to the floor and peppered in glass as his porthole window blew inwards from the force of the exterior blast. Shouts became screams as the ship groaned in crippled agony. Sadao joined it as he hauled himself painfully to his feet to shout at the men running past his cell. Both prisoners and crewmen alike were fleeing. The lower decks below were now filling with orange flames and the reek of diesel fuel.

"Soto ni dashite!" His shouts joined the others, all planted against the bars of their cages, waving arms and legs to gain attention from their confused captors. The ship gave another deeper boom and lurched. Sadao stumbled on his bad leg and slammed his shoulder into the bars at the front of his cell. He caught himself and looked down. To his horror, the floor beneath him was shifting, sliding to the left rapidly with each toss of the sea.

We're sinking!

Of all ways to die, Sadao desired drowning the least. Except perhaps to be burned alive and then drowned.

"Dokubou kara dashite! Let me out!"

The shouts from below were getting louder as the stern of the ship began to fill with smoke. Sadao held his sleeve to his nose and continued to yell until a pair of boots jumped down from above with a ring of keys. It was one of the guards from the higher decks, working as fast as his hands could move to turn the prisoners loose.

"What's happening?! Who's shooting? Are we under attack?"

The guard freed the inmate to his left before jamming the keys into the lock of Sadao's cell.

"Pirates! Mexican pirates!" he said. His eyes were wild with fear. "They blew up our engines!"

His hands shook as he worked the key hole. The locks on this vessel were so rusted, it wouldn't turn. He looked confused and tried another ring to the same frustrating result.

"Try a longer one!" Sadao shouted as the guard glanced at the flames rising higher from below. Men down there were shrieking as the burning fuel-topped water sloshed into their cells. Their screams were terrible to hear. "Hurry!"

The guard shook his head, close to tears. "I-I can't find one that'll work. I'm sorry! I'm sorry!" He glanced helplessly at Sadao before turning his efforts to the remaining prisoners in the row.

Sadao threw himself against the bars. "Hey! Don't leave me in here!"

There was another explosion and the ship pitched hard, throwing Sadao backwards. He swore as he landed on his ass. The resulting fireball that billowed up from the ship's bowels narrowly missed his shoes as it burst up the gangways full of newly freed men just outside. He saw the face of the guard twist in agony and vanish into the orange billows of heat. Distorted flaming human figures leapt and fell from the gangways into the rapidly rising water. Screams echoed off the walls as Sadao scrambled backwards, deeper into his tilting cell. Had he been freed, his screams would have been among them, swallowed by flame.

"Ay, amigo! Este modo!"

"Nan da?!" Sadao whipped his head around. A man was at his blown-out porthole window, just above his head, waving. He was suspended by a rope secured somewhere to the stern deck above.

"Bueno, senior Koga! Darse prisa!"

"What - ?" Sadao didn't have another moment to wonder how one of the ship's invaders had managed to blow the bars off his window or moreover, how he knew his name. His cell was leaning hard and water was beginning slosh in at the lower end, bringing the reek of fuel with it.

Sadao got to his feet and leapt for the opening, jamming himself in halfway. The dangling man lifted him up and pulled him the rest of the way through headfirst into thin air. Below there was nothing but darkness and burning sea to catch him. Arms scrabbling at air, Sadao dove 70 feet past the stern into a pool of choking flame. The surface hit him like a whipcrack across his whole body. Underwater, he paddled to right himself. Bubbles rose from his mouth as his lungs burned with the need for air. Sadao swam for the surface, watching his escaped breath expand and glow with the colors of fire as they rose ahead of him.

Hoping to come up into a patch of ocean not coated in diesel, Sadao broke surface just under the dying ship's massive rudder, now rising 50 feet out of the water it belonged in. His lungs, although rewarded with air, were now filling with deadly smoke from the pools of fire surrounding him.

Get away from the ship!

Sadao turned and swam, trying to keep clear of the fuel slicks, but his arms soon ached from the effort of towing his bad leg behind him. Sadao was once again reminded as he had been in his youth that Japanese do not naturally float. It took enormous effort to stay at the surface.

He could hear voices at some distance. Shouts, but not in panic or agony - they sounded like commands in Spanish. He splashed around, peering through the curtains of flame to try and find the source. And then he saw it, some 200 yards out, a fishing boat's hull - intact and cruising his way.

"Here! Aqui!" He tried to wave and shout but the effort only made his head dip below the surface and his mouth fill with traces of unburned fuel. Sadao choked and sputtered. His stomach once again threatened to reject its contents. His eyes were burning, blurred and unable to see. His splashing was only making the fuel coat more and more of his skin. It burned worse than the fire. Through the blurs of smoke and flame something came at him from behind and knocked into his skull.

Sadao was far under the surface when his consciousness snapped him back to life. The fading swirls of blue-black orange wavered so far over his head now. All around him was cold, dark emptiness. The cold of the sea eased his burned skin. The last gulp of poisoned air exploded from his chest as he fell deep, deeper than he had ever fallen before.

Falling with him as his useless eyes faded, was the dull glint of golden scales. A fish, he thought, as awareness drifted away.

Do you believe you are ready to finish your journey, Sadao?

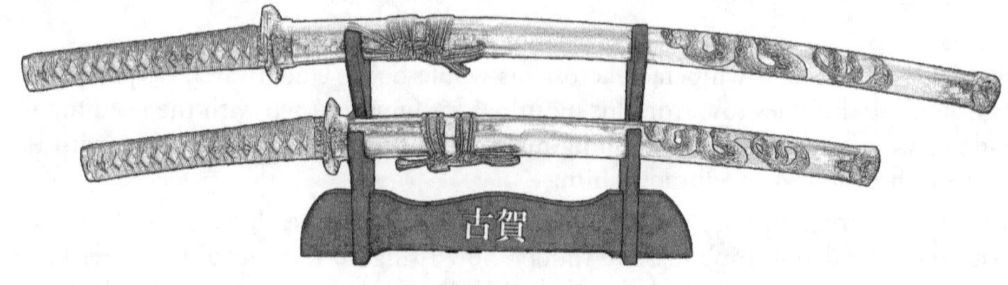

Chapter II

Gambling Man

Utah State Correctional Facility, One month earlier ...

The leg hurt.

No matter what position Sadao shifted into to try and rest, the leg throbbed and gnawed with a dull persistent ache. The hard uneven mattress and chill of the metal springs beneath it did nothing to alleviate his discomfort. Sadao groaned and opened his eyes. Morning had come anyway, casting a pale light on the same dirty walls, same dirty floor. For 20 long months, nothing had changed. Not even the squeaking rear wheel of the mail cart that now approached his cell.

"Koga! Mail!"

Sadao elbowed himself up, wincing to the only shout that morning he would have sat up for. His name was not called often.

"Koga! You gonna get your ass up, or do I have to throw it?"

"I'm up!" he barked, forcing his stiff hip to move. He shoved the leg forward with his hand and reached for the crutch. It had fallen to the floor during his long sleepless night out of reach.

"Koga!"

"*Kuso!* I'm getting up! Leg won't move!"

Henry the mailman poked his lumpy nose through the bars to investigate. He watched with curiosity as Sadao reached overhead to grab an old restraint rung to pull himself up to a standing position.

"Bastard docs did a real job on that leg, didn't they?"

Sadao made a painful limp forward. The Utah Valley's bitter cold mornings were the worst. "That is an accurate assessment. I only wish the chief of surgery agreed. He calls me his 'masterpiece'."

Henry laughed. "Nothing like prison medical services, eh?"

Sadao grabbed the bars and dragged his unforgiving leg forward to face the old man. "Butchers. Every one."

"Heard you refused another surgery," Henry said, handing Sadao a long white envelope through the bars. Sadao glanced at the sender and quickly slipped it into the back pocket of his yellow jumpsuit. "Don't know why you'd want to miss out on six weeks in a warm bed with nice smelling ladies to tend to you."

Sadao regarded the oldest lifer on the block and grimaced, shifting his weight. "Each time they cut me open and fuck with it, the damn leg gets worse. No point."

"Don't know what you did to get yerself that shot up, but it must have been a hell of a fight."

Sadao grinned despite the pain.

"Maybe someday I'll find a way to get you to tell me about it."

"Not a chance."

The old man shrugged and pushed his cart forward down the long hall with a whistle, on to the next cell.

Sadao watched Henry's retreating silhouette before making the exhausting four-step journey back to the cot. He braced a hand against the wall and lowered himself back down. *Ungh.* Sitting was no better than standing. But today the mail had come and that was worth the pain.

Sadao pulled the envelope out and read the false address at the top. It was from I. Juan Hardik from Tentpole, Nebraska. *Terrible.* Sadao smiled and tore the seal. Inside, there was a single page letter and a sketch.

Hey, Cowboy

I hope this letter gets through!! I'm not allowed to send anything of any value or bulk. I keep trying to send you braids of my new 'do but your caseworker says they keep getting stamped: UNPERMITTED. Assholes. Tagata's been braiding my head. One small tangled forest at a time. Looks pretty good. If I had a working camera, I'd share the progress with you, but I can't so here's a doodle. Lupe drew it, not bad, eh? It's my cute side. You'd be proud of our little taco - he's kicking ass in auto races. Don't worry, he hasn't crashed the Mustang - yet. I miss him in the garage but I've got a new team of rugrats to oil the chains. Some of Tagata's latest recruits from Baja. They call me Mouse-san. Darling as hell.

I tell them about you, you know? What you did for us. I tell them all the time because I want them to know. I don't want them to hear it all twisted up from somewhere else. Sometimes I think I'll go crazy if I can't at least tell stories about you. It kind of makes me feel like you're still here.

Miss the fuck out of you. Can't even eat a damn pickle without popping a boner. Don't worry. I won't cheat. I can't, I'm wearing your ASS RING. Real date killer. So hurry and bribe some goddamn lawyers and get your dick home before I fuck a fence post!

- Your 'little' Mouse

Sadao smiled and set the letter beside him on the cot and shifted his weight. He lay back, pushing the limp felt they called a pillow behind his head and dragged his leg into the least painful position. He propped up the little drawing of his braided Mouse on his stomach to study it. The sketch was of his "cute side" but it had nothing to do with the pose. It came from within and shone through those clear blue eyes. Lupe's pencil did not possess the color, but in his mind Sadao could see them, looking back at him with irrepressible mirth. It was like a balm to him, this odd little soul - come from nowhere to bring his mind and body peace.

His finger touched the pencil strokes gently. He'd missed this face more than he knew possible. By his choice, there'd been no letters, no calls, and no gifts. Until now, his only personal possessions were a few books. There were no photos to connect him to the desert and the people he had left behind except for what he kept safely hidden in his mind.

Sadao closed his eyes, breathing, letting memories come of smooth pale skin and delighted sighs. His groin stirred. *You are not the only one living in Tentpole, Konezumi,* he thought. He folded his gift and letter, slipping them inside the lining of his jumpsuit.

Sadao reached for the patchy blanket and threw it over himself. It didn't keep out the chill but it did hide him from passing eyes. He breathed deep and let the ache in his leg float to the back of his mind as he focused on memories of warm skin up against his chest and thighs. He recalled what it felt like to have strong working hands running down his back, grabbing his ass playfully.

There was always so much joy in loving Mouse - kissing his smiling mouth and licking his throat. The sounds he'd make as Sadao's hands ran over his body were so unguarded and shameless - there was never a shred of dishonesty in them. He loved to hear those sounds - to coax them out, one after the other, like music. He'd give anything to hear Mouse's voice now as he imagined claiming his mouth with a kiss.

Itoshii Konezumi, you have no idea, do you? Sadao thought, as he rubbed the fly of his prison suit. He was solid in a second. Too much time had passed since he'd last let himself loose. It was early still - there was time before the breakfast call. He unzipped and let his erection out under the privacy of the blanket. He squeezed the base a few times then began to slide his dick through his fist in slow steady strokes.

Memories came to him as he gripped the pillow - hot puffs of breath on his neck and shoulder; puppy-like kisses down his throat and chest. It excited him - the way his beard and nipples were always in peril of being chewed. He liked it that way - the exuberance, the eagerness to please. He loved the feel of Mouse's hungry mouth on his balls and dick - the tease of his teeth. But even more, he loved the twitching hole waiting to be filled beneath.

Slick precum drooled from the tip of his cock just thinking of it. Sadao caught and smeared his shaft in it, heightening his pleasure. His fist ran smooth up and down his length. He gave it an extra twist of his fingers under the head, working the loose nub of skin. He was still unaccustomed to masturbating without the silver ring - without anything. It was the one time he fought the guards in earnest, when they threw him down naked and forced his legs apart to take all possessions from him the day he arrived. They could have had taken anything from him but that and it was gone.

Sadao fought back a groan and pumped himself faster. Anger would not bring the relief he needed so he thought of the jewel's pair - still screwed in tight where he'd left it as a clear warning if anyone got close enough to discover it. It was his treasure - that pinched ring of pleasure - waiting, taunting him with tight welcoming heat.

Do you know how irresistible you are to a starving man?

He wanted to reclaim his prize - shove himself in and feed that quivering pink hole until it was brimming with cum.

Sadao tightened his grip, breath hissing through his clenched teeth, as he sank deeper into fantasy. He could imagine hot muscles molding to him as he worked himself in, feeling the inner walls throb each time he stroked his lover's dick. Fucking him, fingers digging into the sweet mounds of his ass that jiggled with each pump of his hips. The howls his Mouse would make, the sobs of ecstasy. The way he pushed his hips back against him, begging for more, clenching his dick, holding him at the very edge of release ...

"Nnnngh!"

Streams of ejaculate burst through his fingertips and hit the underside of the blanket. Sadao breathed hard through the flood of pleasure that took him, careful not to make anymore sound as he squeezed the last of it out. Then every muscle relaxed at once. His head fell back against the pillow. His hand loosened from his softening cock. He used his last moment of awareness to tuck himself back in before he sank, at last, under a painless wave of sleep.

"Koga! Up! Your lawyer's here."

Sadao blinked and rubbed his eyes. Sleep had carried him right through breakfast to midday - the first decent rest he'd had in weeks. It was a shame attorneys didn't make night calls.

Sadao reached for the crutch and forced his leg to stand him up. It was moving a little better now that the cold walls of his cell had warmed in the midday sun.

"Drop it! Hands in the chow hole! You know the drill." His favorite guard had brought full wrist and ankle chains. Pale-faced Brother Smith.

"Are you afraid I'll run?" Sadao asked, limping forward to lean his crutch against the bars.

"Less talk, more action, Koga!"

Sadao complied and turning around, put his hands behind his back and pushed them through the narrow horizontal opening so Brother Smith could fashion his metal accessories. Once his wrists were cuffed, the CO unlocked his door to drop a length of chain down his legs. He knelt and shackled the ends to his ankles. He gave Sadao's bindings a rough tug, then rose to push him forward with his club. Sadao shuffled out as best as he could with a busted hip and the heavy chain dangling between his feet.

"The kid come by to show off his new law degree?"

Brother Smith shoved him forward impatiently. Sadao was no fan of the institution's correctional officers, but this small righteous man with an overinflated sense of self-importance was especially irritating.

"Shut it. You received the best defense taxpayer money could afford."

"That is true," Sadao agreed. "What is left after The Church takes their cut ... ugh!"

That earned him a baton in the back. His jailor was a devout keeper of the faith - a Temple man. Sadao grit his teeth and shuffled with as much dignity as he could muster past the other lifelong residents of D-block.

The visitation room door was open. Seated at it was a middle-aged, heavy set Latino man in a wrinkled suit coat with jeans and cowboy boots. Sadao paused - he didn't know this man. The guard shoved him in and Sadao limped closer to the table.

The man rose and moved to extend his hand in introduction. He looked at Sadao's bonds. "Are these necessary?" he asked.

"For your safety, sir," Smith answered.

The man waved at the chains. "Take them off. He's unarmed, isn't he? I can't talk to the man if he can't use his hands."

Brother Smith frowned and relented, unlocking and removing the loop of chain between Sadao's cuffed wrists so he could bring his hands forward. The shackles remained intact.

"I'll be right outside. Ring when you're finished."

"Yeah go on, go on," the man insisted. The door was closed and secured. The man pulled a chair back for Sadao. "Have a seat, please."

Sadao sat, keeping a keen eye on this stranger. The man took the chair opposite, producing a small digital recorder, pack of cigarettes and a plastic ashtray. He clicked the recorder on. "Testing, testing…" Sadao eyed the pack of smokes and swallowed as the man checked his audio.

At last he looked up. "Mr. Koga. I have been told you like to smoke."

Sadao studied his face. Despite his casual appearance, the man's eyes held intelligence. "Are you here to extort a confession from me with cigarettes?"

"Not a confession. I need information and I have been told the best way to get Sadao Koga to open his mouth is if he has something to put in it."

"Who told you this?"

The man grinned, showing uneven teeth. "Interested parties," he said, extending the open pack to Sadao. He selected one and let the man produce a lighter for him. He leaned into the flame and sat back, enjoying his first hit of nicotine in months. His habitual brand, too. It brought back memories of the desert. He took his time with it.

"You can have a whole carton if you like. I can arrange that. Provided you return the favor."

Sadao didn't answer at first, just finished the cigarette at his own pace and motioned for another. The man complied and extended his lighter again. Sadao lit up and watched him through the growing haze. "Suppose you tell me your name and your business first."

"Of course, of course. I thought I had." He produced a badge and photo. "Name's Javier Munez, U.S. Immigration Authority. I've come to expedite the terms and conditions of your extradition."

Sadao exhaled slowly. "What extradition?"

"Ah ... I assumed the news would have reached you by now." Javier seemed puzzled.

"I don't have broadcast or communication privileges."

"Nor have you fought for them, as I read in your rather lengthy case file. No information in or out. Although you would qualify under Utah State law by now due to your spotless behavior record. Still, I assumed fellow inmates would talk."

"They don't speak to me much," Sadao said, flicking his ash in the plastic dish. It was a souvenir from a Vancouver casino. "Are you a gambling man, Mr. Munez?"

"Huh? Oh, right. The tray. Not especially. They offer good vacation packages, though. The wife likes to go now and again."

From the used suit coat to the cheap getaway holiday, Sadao believed this man indeed worked for the U.S. Government. "So am I to understand I will be granted a change of scenery soon?" Sadao asked. "I don't recall requesting one." The man did have an effective interviewing technique - boring the interviewee into asking the questions.

"Yes, and if you don't mind, I'd like to get the rest of our conversation on record."

Sadao gestured to invite him to click his recorder.

"U.S. Immigration Extradition case number NWS 338493, Koga, Sadao. Taped October 23rd, 2073 Utah State Corrections Facility in the City of Draper. Commencing interview ... Okay, Mr. Koga, please state your name clearly, age and year and place of birth."

Sadao set his cigarette down in the ashtray. "Okay, I'll play along. I am called Sadao Koga, age 40. Birthplace Toba, Japan - Mie prefecture, May 12, 2033. I am a Taurus born in the Year of the Ox, which I've been told explains my stoicism. I enjoy ramen noodles and collecting racing class Kawasakis."

"No need to offer any extra information than requested, Mr. Koga. We need to verify your birthplace for legal purposes. Nothing more."

"Let me guess - these great United States of America are tired of paying my room and board. Am I right?"

Mr. Munez shut off the recorder and leaned closer. "I am trying to save your ass, Mr. Koga. It would be easier for both of us if you would just stick to the questions. I need to establish that you are not a natural born citizen of the USA and therefore should be extradited back to your birth nation in accordance with the 2058 US/Japan Criminal Deportation Treaty."

Sadao scrutinized him. "You will find no immigration records for me."

"I know, but don't think I haven't tried," he said in hushed tones. "We both know you came in through Baja illegally at age 16 or thereabouts. Refugee of the Japanese Civil War, recruited by the Northwest Racing Division where you were trained and bred like a thoroughbred to earn massive winnings for their directors and sponsors. You enjoyed a rather impressive career from the news clippings I've gathered and managed one of their top tier teams for over a decade. We know who you are, Sadao Koga! We just need to prove it!"

Sadao was impressed with the man's candor. "Why this sudden urgency?" he asked, taking up his cigarette again. "They have 40 years, give or take, to send me to the North Pole if they choose."

"That's the part of this puzzle you are missing, Mr. Koga. You do not have 40 years - one at best!"

Sadao looked at his cigarette and coughed. "You talked to my doctors?"

"No, stubborn mules like you will live to see 115! I'm talking about your sentence. It's been upgraded to death!"

Sadao's cigarette dropped from his fingers into the tray. "How is that possible? I received one trial, one sentence. *Life.*"

"You made the mistake of committing your crime in a religious state, Mr. Koga. The Church Fathers can claim Divine Inspiration and override any sentence decided upon by the judicial courts at any moment they choose. If you had been following the news, you would know the Wasteland racing world has been under fire ever since you brandished your sword at the awards ceremony at the conclusion of the Multi-Division Overland two years ago. Your victim, Chairman Marcus Getty, has been revealed to be a monster of much larger proportions than yourself. You were protecting your people.

The media knows this, the people know this. They are calling for your release. You're no longer a murderous racecar driver, but a revolutionary symbol of the underclass. Activist groups are leading marches on the Salt Lake Temple as we speak. They are calling for your freedom. You are an embarrassment to the LDS faith, and they want to assure that you will meet your maker long before smoking ever will!"

Sadao was uncertain of what to say. He'd not heard a word about this, certainly not from his fellow prison inmates, although many tended to keep their distance. Something about his tattoo proved to work as an excellent deterrent. "How do I trust you?" he asked. "How do I know anything you say is true?"

Javier lifted his palms in a pleading fashion. "You can't. You don't. You need to go with your gut on this. Believe that I am an honest man who stands for the rights of immigrants. My family also came over the border in shadows and secrecy. But we fought for our rights and now we have a place in America."

"I don't want a 'place' in America. And I'd rather hang than return to Japan."

"There are people on the outside who want to save you, Mr. Koga. To do that, we need some scrap of evidence you were not born in this country. There is no birth record in all of Mie Prefecture of a Sadao Koga being born in 2033 or 2034 or anywhere near that date. These were pre-war years. Records were airtight in those days. The database is still viable. The Immigration Bureau of Japan denies your citizenship. I need you to tell me why."

"Perhaps I was birthed from under an old saguaro in the Great Western Desert," Sadao said softly. "The desert has been my only home."

"I questioned this myself. Thought maybe you'd invented your past in order to create some kind of mystique. But no, now that I've met you, I know. You are without a doubt a native-born Japanese."

Sadao raised a brow. "Indeed."

"It's the accent," Javier clarified.

"I do not speak with an accent!"

"It's the muddy Ls, Vs and Ws. And you clip combined consonants. If you were born speaking English you wouldn't have that. Although you try to hide it, it's still there."

Sadao stared at the ashtray and grinned to himself. "I was told many times my English was perfect. By Americans!"

"I am more skilled in this field of nationality detection than most, Mr. Koga. And I am skilled in knowing people. I believe you are a man worth saving. The question is, do you want to save yourself?"

Sadao was silent for a moment. "Who hired you?"

Javier sat back and produced a briefcase, which he opened on the table top. He took out several letters stamped DENIED. They had been opened and resealed with tape. He handed them to Sadao. "You have one point of contact left in the real world as far as I can tell. These letters were intercepted by prison authorities and rejected based on their content. Blond hair."

Sadao opened one and a thin braid fell out on the tabletop. *Mouse.*

"The return addresses are amusing: Ms. O. Horni, Ivan Dick Naou, Mstr. Bates Fouyu, Butte M. Tee, Dre Peacock, and the latest I heard was from an I. Juan Hardik. That one passed inspection, likely due to my recent involvement in your case."

Sadao snorted as he shuffled the letters, eight of them. "Clever."

"Clearly somebody out there misses you. And from the way you are handling those letters, I'm guessing you miss her, too."

"*Him,*" Sadao corrected, wrapping the braid around his fingers - soft as silk. He lifted the little coil to his nose and inhaled. Hmm, like the desert wind.

"Him, my mistake."

Sadao eyed this so-called Immigration Lawyer of the People. "Are you surprised?"

"In my line of work, nothing surprises me. Is there a legal connection between you two I should know about?"

"Meaning?"

"Meaning are there any legal records confirming your relationship?"

Sadao stroked the braid gently with his thumb. "You mean, were we married?"

"Yes, that is what I mean. If 'Mr. Hardik' here is a natural born American, we're going to have problems."

"I would be naturalized."

"Yes."

Sadao slipped the braid back into the envelope. Organizing the stack, he tucked them safely into his jumpsuit. "We have matching genital piercings and a promise. That is all."

Javier blinked. "More than I needed to know. But thank you for your confirmation."

"Samejima," Sadao said resolutely.

"Huh?"

"Samejima, Sadao. That was my birthname. I did not take my father's name until I was three years of age and invited to live in his house just prior to the unfortunate and mysterious wasting of his first wife and the sudden uncelebrated marriage to my mother. She was nineteen when she took my hand and led me into what I thought was a shogun's castle. Three stories. Tatami floors. Silk pillows. Rice paper walls painted with gold and silver foils. I thought I must be a prince to get to live in such a fine house."

Javier smiled and clicked on his recorder. "Once more, Mr. Koga. Please, for the record."

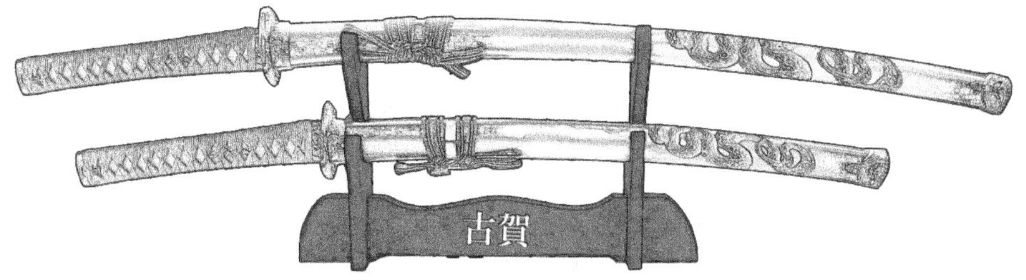

Chapter III

Races Run

Sasori Racing Camp - 40 miles northeast of Squamish,
British Columbia, Canada - 2073

The hair hurt.

Each time Tagata forced the comb through a very narrow selection of fine blond uneven hair, the roots protested where they tenaciously clung to Mouse's skull.

"Ow! Watch it with that thing."

"Do you want the head of even rows or not?"

"*A* head. A, not the.."

"But we are talking about specific head. Your head. Specific is 'the'. This you taught me."

"Yeah, but… ooouuch … fuck! It doesn't count this time!"

Tagata grumbled and pulled the comb out, picking the pulled hairs from the tines. "This English of yours - is no sense to me."

"'It *makes* no sense to me,' you want to say…and my head is even enough - just give it a rest with the pulling! I'm gonna be bald!"

Tagata sat at the end of Sadao's lounge next to a bowl of water and a hundred or two tiny rubber bands. Light colored ones for light colored hair - the first blond hair Tagata had ever styled like his own dark fall of mini braids. Below him, Mouse sat on a cushion on the kitchen floor watching his torn-out hair gather and tumble over the linoleum in the blow of the fan.

"You have uneven row because you cut too many off!"

"*Rowzzzz* plural. And sure, I'll chop myself all to hell if it means I can send Sadao a piece of me without it getting rejected."

"What do you think Sadao-sama need so much hairs for?"

"*Needs* so much hair for."

Tagata made a sucking sound with his teeth as he wound and snapped a little rubber band into place at the end of the finished mini-braid. "Now I think you make fun. Hairs is many things. Not one piece, see?" He held out a wad he'd been balling up next to him on the table. It indeed was composed of hundreds of *hairs*.

"Yeah, sure, but when you talk about it you say hair. Not hairs. This is my hair. You are braiding my hair. My hair hurts because someone keeps pulling the hairs out of my head!"

Tagata tossed the Mouse-tumbleweed in the trash and brushed off his leather pants. "This is all English I can listen tonight. Too much bullshit. Japanese, my language, was not made by crazy person with no sense!"

Mouse whirled his partially braided head around. Sure, he'd agreed to the lessons - to help Tagata gain confidence in his international communications with other racing teams - but he lacked Sadao's natural affinity for multi-language logic. English had the least of it, he was afraid to admit. But as the new Boss of the now renamed Sasori Team - The Scorpions - Tagata knew his own verbal communication was lacking.

"This coming from a guy who speaks a language with no future tense! How the heck do you tell people what you are going to do tomorrow when you can't mention the future?"

Tagata stood up. "No need there is for future language in *nihongo*. We say when we will do this thing - tomorrow, next day, later - then you know this thing will happen in future. A future ... *the* future!"

"But what if you don't know when? What if you haven't decided? Or you gotta get ready for something that will happen someday? Like putting up a tarp in case it rains?"

"When we need to prepare ahead of a thing, we say *te-oku*. I prepare ahead to do…"

"And that's not crazy?"

"What is crazy is all English words made of letter that bring wrong sound. T-h-r-o-u-g-h is throwg, not throo!"

"Maybe you're just throo with this lesson?"

"Yes, I am very throo! Without extra 'gh'!"

Mouse raised his hands in defeat and let Tagata step past him without argument. He'd learned over the last two seasons under Tagata's command that the young Boss had definite sore points of frustration. English comprehension was certainly a big one, although he was putting in his time on the books. He was quieter and more thoughtful in his decision making than Sadao, but he lacked his mentor's natural sense of people. Tagata's past as a champion racer earned him the team's respect, but he struggled when it came to correctly guessing their intentions.

Tagata brushed the remains of Mouse's hair from his sleeves and went to the sink to wash his hands. Watching his new employer's motions at the sink brought Mouse a flicker of déjà vu. It was a memory from the first night he had slept in Sadao's trailer. Granted, he was chained up under the dinette then, but as the younger taller Tagata bent to work the faucet, he could remember the sinuous lines of the eight-headed Orochi, snapping and coiling across Sadao's back as he washed the blood of a dead man's severed neck from his sword. Sigh ... good times.

"Hey, um… how's the tattoo coming along?"

Tagata flinched across his shoulders as he shut off the water and wiped his hands dry.

"*Sujibori* - lines - is almost finish," he said with a forced grin.

"You sound less than thrilled."

"*Horimono* is very painful. Take many hours. Sensei use traditional nara ink and bamboo needle. Very long. Very sharp. Not pussy American tattoo gun."

"Does it match the scorpion design on your face? I'd love to see it! Is it as big as Sadao's? His goes clear down over his ass."

"*Irezumi* ritual is sacred. I will not show to you until all finish," Tagata answered with a sweep of his hand.

Maybe his sasori didn't quite reach his butt, Mouse decided. Did clan bosses compare designs? Like whose is larger? Over his two and a half years of serving as team mechanic for the Japanese racers, Mouse had only seen two full back tattoos - Sadao's eight-headed snake and Shiratori's impressive white blind eagle. It was a crime such an amazing work of art had died along with the General. *You did set his corpse on fire*, Mouse reminded himself. Yeah, but he'd wanted it that way. *Fuck, don't get emo now ...*

"Okay, okay, I'll wait," Mouse said. Depression and worry were beginning to creep in as Tagata gathered his things to leave. It was getting late and Mouse didn't really want to be alone tonight. At least not alone in Sadao's former trailer. But then again he didn't really want to hike back up the hill in the dark to his cabin, either. Emo was winning.

"You should stay in camp tonight," Tagata said, reading his thoughts as he gingerly slipped into his red leather Sasori jacket. The fresh ink must have been sorer than he wanted to let on. "Days are more short now."

"Yeah I guess," Mouse said with a sigh. He wasn't looking forward to shivering alone in bed all winter again.

"Where is Lupe? Will he return soon?" Tagata asked. Maybe he was beginning to understand his mechanic's unspoken words at least.

"He's gone into town to see about some rotating rims. He won't be back until sometime tomorrow."

Tagata's eyes narrowed. "He should not be taking Mustang car into town. Too famous! Someone will see and follow!"

Mouse scratched his head and shrugged. Lately Lupe had been pimping the shit out of Sadao's ride. He'd taken over all his former boss's wheels, in fact - the trailer, the car, and even his starting position as the team's only auto racer. And Mouse was fairly certain Sadao wouldn't appreciate the rosary and bobblehead Holy Mother velcroed to the 1968 Obsidian's dash.

"I'm not in charge of racers," Mouse politely reminded him.

"Hmm - I will have talk to him. Send him to me when he returns."

"Sure, Boss," Mouse nodded. Tagata dipped his head in thanks and made to leave.

"Tagata-san, can I ask you something? Something personal?" Mouse was surprised he was detaining him once again, but his anxieties were getting the better of him.

"That depends. Personal for you or for me?"

"For me, I guess. I know you were closer to Sadao than anyone over the last decade and I've been wondering … if maybe he kept something from me."

"I do not think Sadao-sama kept secrets from you."

"He managed to keep the whole 'let's win this race so I can relieve the Chairman of his head and get all shot up and go to prison' plot from me."

"True, but that was only for your protection. 'I will not have Mouse involved in this.' That is what he said. Sadao-sama was very firm of this."

"*On* this, but no, I'm over that. It's just … it's been two years, you know. I send letters and I know he won't send any back to protect our location. It doesn't mean he doesn't think of me … but still, I'm worried."

"Is this the personal question you want to ask me? Does Sadao-sama still think of you? How should I know this?"

Mouse squirmed. He knew Tagata was being honest. But it still wasn't what he wanted to hear. "I know, I know. But, for as long as you knew him - did he ever 'hook up' with anyone for a while. Like seriously?"

Tagata sat on the end of the lounge to think. "Sadao-sama personal life was not my interest."

"But you must remember something? I mean, I can tell you I know he slept with women, and maybe men too, for business connections. I do know about all of that. He told me. I'm not asking about his clan boss affairs, but whether or not he had any personal ones."

"Japanese men do not bother with such details. But for you, who is worried, I will try…"

Mouse stood quietly but his heart was pounding fast.

Tagata's took a moment. "Yes, I think I do remember someone. This person I did not meet but I think Sadao-sama did make time to visit once or twice during race tour. But this too maybe was business connection."

Mouse stepped closer. "Who?"

"I do not know a name."

"Was it a guy or a girl?!"

Tagata studied him strangely. "Why does this matter?"

Mouse started pacing. "Because … like I said, I'm worried. I didn't get to spend much time with him before he was taken away. I don't know what he wants in his life. You know, like kids and stuff? I'm a guy - I have limits!"

Tagata chuckled, getting back to his feet. "You are worried about wrong things. Sadao-sama already has family, and many *musukora* - sons."

"Did he ever talk about settling down, and marriage and stuff like that?"

"No. Sadao-sama did not talk of these."

Mouse stopped his pacing and tried to hide his disappointment. "Okay, thanks."

"Mouse-san. You should not worry. Sadao-sama is what do you say? *Sutekina* - constant man. You are only companion he walked with where eyes could see."

Mouse smiled a little. "Really?"

Tagata put a firm hand on his shoulder. "Sleep well. Dream of a good life together. Maybe Sadao-sama will hear you."

Mouse reached out and hugged Tagata tightly in sheer relief.

Tagata padded his shoulder awkwardly in response.

"Thank you, thank you!"

"I do not know what I say make you this happy," Tagata said in confusion.

"It gives me hope we can pick up where we left off, when he comes home," Mouse said.

Tagata's expression remained neutral.

"He ... is still coming home soon, right? This lawyer you found, he's on it, you said?"

Tagata nodded grimly. "He is on it, as you say."

"No timeline?"

"There are many steps to make Sadao-sama free man. Some steps are ours, but many more are his. We must find patience."

"Uuugh, I'm tired of that answer!"

"I am sorry it is only answer I can give."

"I know. I know. I'm like a kid with a mountain of gifts under a Christmas tree and no idea when dawn is coming. It's making me nuts."

"I promise one little thing. Sadao-sama will be home before first snow."

"You sure?"

Tagata smiled a rare clan-boss smile that accentuated the three loops of silver he wore in his lower lip. "Maybe he will have bow and go under this tree of yours."

Mouse could only smile twice as bright and subject the poor man to another uncomfortable hug-o-thon.

Sadao's old bedroom at first glance was largely unchanged - until the drawers and closets were opened, only to find them full of air. Mouse had been moving Sadao's things out of his old trailer and up the hill to the cabin ever since its renovation was completed three weeks ago.

Mouse had claimed the abandoned cabin a quarter mile hike above the team's lakeside encampment not long after his arrival. It had great views of the pines and water. If you stood on the porch, you could just see the tops of the racing trailers and trucks parked out along the wide gravel shores below. It had taken several months of back-breaking work to repair the roof, clean out and refinish the interior of the log cabin, and to furnish it with some homemade pine furniture. The rough-hewn wood was made comfortable with stuffed cushions of handsewn bear and elk skins. Lupe and the garage kids helped, but the project had cost him most of his yearly salary and a hammered thumb or two. But now it was a real frontier homestead hidden at least 25 miles from anywhere in the heart of the Canadian Coastal Range - the precise location Sadao's cryptic map coordinates had led him and Lupe to.

Mouse opened the trailer closet and peered inside. A few heavy leather racing jackets still hung at the far end. He lifted them off and tossed them onto the bed. On tip-toes he reached up and felt along the upper shelf for anything he may have missed. His fingertips brushed against a paper box. After a few hops and grabs, he got it down. It was an old boot box. He blew dust from the lid and sat down on the bed to take a peek inside.

A bunch of yellowed papers and receipts from equipment purchases were inside. Mouse smiled. Shiratori had been the keeper of the paperwork, and by the look of the title certificates, these had been personal purchases Sadao had elected to keep secret from his bean-counting General. Yep, Kawasaki street racers - Sadao's favorites. Classics - every one - representing the very height of 21st Century Japanese engineering. It was a shame they all went up in smoke in Sadao's equipment trailer explosion - the one that had also taken the life of one of his dearest young racers.

Mouse kept digging. More papers - some were faded awards certificates. Geez, the man won a lot of races in his life. Mouse read the titles: First Place - Albuquerque Sundown, auto division; First Place - Great Salt Lake Tournament, auto division. The auto races were on top but below them were award after award for street bike city races, the kind Mouse's dad used to take him to as a kid in Phoenix. From the dates: 2050, 2052, 2053 it seemed Sadao's real fame had come in his 20s on the back of a high speed street bike. He didn't embrace the automobile until his 30s, around the time he became Orochi Team Boss. Maybe some kind of compromise had been made? Although auto racing was only marginally safer than street racing, it amused Mouse to learn that leading the Orochi team didn't keep Sadao out of the driver's seat. No wonder he'd been so willing to man the auto leg of the Overland. The man couldn't help himself.

A glossy photograph was at the bottom. As Mouse pulled it out and brushed the debris from it, his heart gave an extra thud. The young Japanese man in the photo was holding up a racing cup with a circle of flowers around his neck. Next to him was a sleek black Kawasaki ZX series by the framework - one of the most powerful racers ever manufactured. Fucker must have gone 180 miles per hour or more.

Mouse flipped the photo over. There was a date stamp at the bottom of the print from a local news outlet: August 23, 2059. Mouse did the math in his head - Sadao was … 26 in this photograph. He flipped it back over. My God, he was perfection - geared up in black leather from the waist down with a tight racing t-shirt stretched over his chest. His biceps flexed beyond the short sleeves as he held the trophy up for the cameras. And his face … holy fuck, so young. His hair was longer, held back in some kind of band and the beard ... it was long and braided, dangling from his smug chin with - was that a pearl capped at the end? That fucking sex-on-two-wheels son-ovabitch!

Mouse flopped back on the bed and cradled the photo in his hands. Jeeeesus, what he wouldn't give for a time machine about now. He'd have been the worst clinging roady ever to exist if he'd seen that hot action ride into town. His head spun and his heart pounded with lust. Had he been at that street race and older than 14, he'd have grabbed that hot stud by his chin braid and thrown his fine ass over the bike, torn the leather clean off and drilled him end to end - cameras rolling and all!

Fuck fuck fuuuuck! Mouse kicked the mattress in frustration. Tagata had better make good on his promises and get this man home to him now! No amount of crazed lotion-palmed, double-fisted fapping was gonna take care of this! He needed fucking - balls out, hair pulling, ass biting, knuckle cracking, bed breaking, fucking.

But truth was, Mouse didn't want a sweet, stay-at-home man. He wanted a fucking superhero, with titanium balls and a dick to match. Unfortunately, men of steel tended to grab swords and do heroic bloody things that got their asses locked up in prison for way too long!

Mouse groaned and gripped the photo tight. He did not handle abstinence well. He was tired of beating off to an empty pillow. No use torturing himself with races run long ago by a young Asian Adonis and his long gone Kawasaki. He set the photo down and rolled his face into the stack of racing jackets. One breath in and he was catapulted forward in time.

Mmnn ... smoky leather. This was the scent of his lover - his now 40-year-old, retired, shot-up all to hell and nearly died, incarcerated lover. Mouse moaned sadly and hugged the jackets to his chest. Lust turned on a dime into loneliness and longing. More than sex, he just wanted that man back safe in his arms.

"Do you miss me, baby?" he whispered to the jackets. "Are you thinking of me? Do you get my letters? I think I'm losing my marbles a little more everyday. I've made us a home - well, a cabin. I built it for you so you could have someplace quiet to rest and heal. I want to bring you home with me so bad.

"Tagata's lawyer says the leg is still a problem. He says you look thin, tired and in pain. I can't stand thinking of you like that. All alone, dealing with God only knows what kind of shit in that fucked up bible-thumping state prison. I want you back, baby, so I can spoil you rotten. I'll feed you, bathe you, shave you, rub your feet, suck your dick ... heck I'll even do that thing with your balls you love so much. Anything. I don't care anymore. I'm yours, Sadao."

Mouse paused to rub his damp eyes against the collar of Sadao's jacket. "I don't care that you're not that stud in the photograph anymore. I don't care how beat down or broken. I can wait forever even if it kills me. Just, don't forget your Mouse, okay? Please, baby. I can take any torture in this world but that ... "

Mouse closed his eyes and hugged the remains of Sadao's many skins. If he wasn't totally going nut-balls insane, it felt like the empty sleeves might be hugging him back.

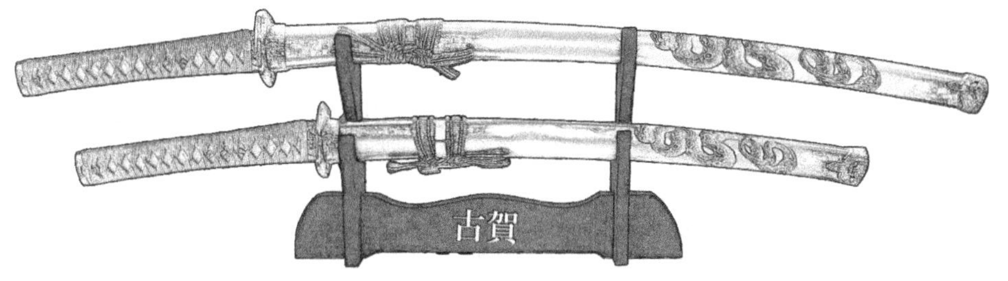

Chapter IV

Yakuza

Sadao stood in the exercise yard, leaning against the grey stucco wall to keep the weight off his leg as he watched his D-Block neighbors play a game of pick-up on a chalk drawn court. It took him a while to get out here as he didn't like to bring the crutch with him to the yard. Although no one had given him any trouble aside from a sneer or two, he didn't want to invite it either and kept mostly to himself, with the limp as much out of public view as possible.

He'd only recently been granted general population yard privileges - no doubt in response to Munez pushing the right administrative buttons for once. On warm days he took advantage of it to try and get some of the sallowness out of his skin and bring warmth back into his bones.

Shattered, they'd said. Shot in five places. The hip and upper femur were blown into 11 big pieces and assorted crumbs - most of it missing. No problem, they'd said. We can fix it, they'd said - apparently with staples and duct tape. Every time he took a step on it, it felt like the artificial ball joint would bust right through the mangled mess of bolts and mesh housing it. His post-surgical x-rays had resembled something you might see in a natural history museum complete with assorted bullet tips - souvenirs of the pinnacle racing victory he was least proud of.

The leg's support structure wasn't the only botched part of the job. The wiring was all wrong too. Nerves and veins didn't work for shit anymore. The leg throbbed, cramped and was constantly cold. Most days he couldn't feel the left foot at all. Sadao found himself glancing down just to make sure the damn thing was still attached. Walking - well, he did as much as he could stand before the pain made him want to punch a wall.

Henry entered the yard and shuffled his way to Sadao's favorite sunning spot as was his usual habit. Arthritis was his burden and he wasn't up to playing ball. No one gave the old man any trouble, either - not since he had befriended the yakuza. Henry sat on the stone steps next to Sadao and fumbled around for a box-shaped object in his sweater pocket. Sadao eyed his fumbling with great interest.

"You have tobacco?" he asked.

"Hmph. Probably stale. Some prick down on C-Block never paid up for them. After 90 days I keep the goods. It's in my verbal contract," he laughed, producing the pack.

Sadao licked his lips. "I don't have money," he said. "But I'd ask you for one just the same."

Henry sniffed the wrapper glumly. "Guess I can't smoke 'em all. Or get this dang wrapper off. Here." Sadao got the plastic ripped and seal torn before the old man could blink behind his greasy glasses.

"Got a light?" Sadao asked, with the first stick balanced between his lips.

Henry chuckled and dug around in his jumpsuit pockets - at last producing a dented matchbox. "Might as well light us both. Hands don't work no better than your leg," he said, flexing his misshapen fingers.

Sadao took the matchbox and adding a second cigarette alongside the first, expertly lit both at once. He shook out the match and let it drop to the concrete as he puffed and handed one off to the old man.

Henry sucked on it a few times and coughed. "Been years since I smoked," he said. "Probably shouldn't start up again, but what the hell."

Sadao took a long drag, his first in days and sank back against the wall, exhaling slow. *Heaven.*

A whistle blew and Sadao opened his eyes in time to stop a basketball under his foot as it came rolling at the two of them.

"Ay, Yakuza. Throw us the ball!"

The voice was rude. Sadao eyed the player as he continued to enjoy his smoke. The ball stayed under his foot.

"What the fuck is your problem? Give us the ball, Chino!"

Sadao regarded the two men. One was hispanic and the other was just pretending to be. They were covered in selfmade gangster tattoos.

"Yakuza was the more accurate insult," he said, reaching down for the ball. He held it in the crook of his arm. "I don't believe I heard either of you say please."

The latino began to swear under his breath in Spanish.

"*No seas culero, puto!*" Sadao snapped. He tossed the ball back hard, knocking the wind out of the kid who bent over groaning. His white homey laughed and caught the ball as it bounced off of his friend's gut to the pavement. "Dude, that's fucked up. Fucking Chino knows your language!"

"Fuck you, man!" the latino boy spat and in a blink the two "friends" were a blur of arms and legs. The whistle blew and a CO came to break them up.

"I see you're good with kids," Henry laughed.

Sadao smoked thoughtfully. "Used to be."

"That true, what they called you? Yakuza? Got one hell of a tattoo, I know. It's got all the Cholos talking. They say you're ninja special forces or something."

"Hmn. Interesting theory, but I didn't earn my tattoo in Japan. I was inked stateside. Doesn't mean the same thing here."

"So you weren't a ninja, eh? Gang boss, then?"

"Of a kind. Racing team."

The old man's eyes lit up. "No kiddin'? Which one? Not that I gambled in 30 years."

"Orochi."

Henry looked puzzled. "Nope ... sorry don't recall that name."

Sadao smiled. "After your time, maybe."

"What did you race? Let me guess…one of them fancy Japanese bikes?"

"Good guess. When I was younger I specialized in street racing - mostly of the marginally legal kind. My team though, our focus became more offroad than on. Motocross, open course - that was our goal. I, myself, preferred autos. But I kept my bikes, the ZRs, for years until ... "

"You kill some guy in a race? Is that why you're in here facing life?"

Sadao laughed and flicked his spent cig to the ground, crushing it with the dead foot. "No. Sorry to disappoint."

"Don't want to tell me, do you?"

Sadao eyed the pack of remaining unsmoked cigarettes in Henry's pocket. "It's not something I'm proud of, no."

"Wouldn't think so. You Asians, you keep it tight. Don't brag like these shithead kids. What a waste of life. All these dumb bastards. Look at 'em. All of them think they're hot shit. Proud of being in lockup. World's gone mad, I say." He glanced up at Sadao and noticed his fixation with the cigarette pack poking from his sweater pocket. He patted it. "Tell you what. You tell me what you did to get in here and I'll give you the whole pack, free of charge."

Sadao thought it over. "Tempting, but I'll have to decline. Not for my secrets but for doctor's orders. If I have any chance of this leg healing I have to cut the smokes. Bad for circulation. Worst sentence I've ever gotten. Electric chair would have been kinder."

The old man laughed and offered Sadao a second stick and a match anyway. "I hear you, but then I think, who gives a shit about doctor's orders? It's not like I'm ever gonna see over these walls again. Who am I watching my health for? You got somebody, Koga? Back home? Uh, where is your home?"

Sadao shrugged as he struck the match on the wall and lit up, shaking the flame out. "Never had a permanent home. Just a racing trailer. Lived in the desert mostly. Southern Wasteland territories. We traveled from competition to competition like nomads."

"Whoo, that's somethin' ain't it? All that heat? Didn't think nobody lived south of the 40 any more."

"Not many do. And we had to move north in the summer. Stayed inside during midday. Not a bad life, really. As long as the A/C worked."

"Got yourself a sweetheart back in that desertland?"

Sadao grinned. "You could say that."

"Pretty, I bet. Guys like you always get the pretty ones. Probably all of them."

Sadao laughed. "I'm not that young or swift anymore to catch all the desert rabbits. Just one."

"This rabbit got a name?"

Sadao paused a moment over his cigarette. "Yeah, Mouse."

The old man nodded. "So we weren't talking 'bout rabbits after all."

"No, we weren't. But this one is very special to me."

"Hmm ... think this 'Mouse' will wait for you?"

Sadao inhaled, let the taste of the tobacco soak into his tongue. He blew it out slowly. "I never asked him to. But I'm afraid he might try. Look - there's a favor I need to ask."

The old man looked up, curious. "Need me to smuggle in something for you? Cigarettes I can do - dunno about a whole person."

Sadao smiled, "That's not what I'm requesting. You have access to R&D, don't you? On your rounds?"

"Yeah, but only on Tuesdays. What are you looking for?"

"Something they took from me the day I was brought in - a small carved ring of silver with a black pearl. I want it back."

Henry shook his head and whistled. "Didn't they send it back to your relatives?"

"I don't have any. No home address, either. Receiving said it would wind up in the donation box."

"Dunno if I can get into Receiving storage that easy. Especially where they keep the jewelry. Odds are it's already been shipped out for smelting. But I do know a feller who cleans in there sometimes. I gotta pay him something."

Sadao flicked his ash on the ground. "I told you, I don't have money."

"Hm. It worth a lot, this ring?"

"On the open silver market, maybe a couple hundred. But to me, it is beyond value."

The old man chuckled. "I hear you. Okay, I'll see what I can do, but you're gonna owe me, son."

"Certainly."

"I get you this ring, you gotta tell me what you did to get locked up - agreed?"

Sadao stuck his cigarette in his mouth and shook the man's hand.

"Agreed."

High overhead, the shower water hissed from the rusty pipes and fell down onto his shoulders. Sadao leaned into the stream and braced his chained wrists against the concrete wall so the water's warmth could coat his head and course down his back. He positioned his legs and hip just so the water could slough off his body and land with a loud patter onto his cold foot. Sometimes, if he warmed it enough, some tingling would return to his toes.

Blindly, he reached for the soap dispenser and lathered up his hair, chest and arms. The water would shut off soon enough and he didn't want to waste the opportunity to get a proper wash in. The sink in his cell wasn't much of a bathtub. He sorely missed his trailer shower - even those days when the desert heat had cooked the water reserve tank to near-boiling.

Sadao raised his chin to let the soap rinse from his head. He could feel the ends of his hair touching his shoulders now. He'd get it trimmed if he could trust the barber not to slit his throat. Sadao shook his wet head out and took another squeeze of the soap into his palms to wash his groin. He took care to work it in and around the harder-to-reach places.

Bam! There was a sound of a club hitting the wall to his left. "Stop playing with yourself Koga, and speed it up!"

Sadao rubbed the suds leisurely under his balls with both hands and opened an eye. It was his favorite CO - the Temple's good son was ready with his stick in hand and his face too close to Sadao's proximity for professional comfort.

"I know it may come as a shock to you, Brother Smith, but some men may have more ground to cover in this area than others."

Whack! The sting of the club striking his back was a familiar one. Too bad the idiot didn't realize this was where the snake's skin was at its thickest.

"I said, 'Hurry it up!'"

Sadao didn't flinch and held the CO's eye, taking his time to rinse the soap completely from his chest and groin. Around him he could hear the other men stepping back and toweling off. "Maybe, if my speed is not to your liking, you should offer to assist."

"You ... disgusting abomination!"

Whack! Whack! Whack!

Sadao grit his teeth against the force of the blows but his gaze never left the angry little man's face.

"Smith! Hold your weapon!" Smith froze at the sound of his superiors' voice.

"I'm taking over from here. Resume your post at D-Block!"

"Aye!" Brother Smith replied sharply, holstering his club. He backed away - eyes on

Sadao's until he exited the showers.

"Excitable one, isn't he?" Sadao said.

"Can it, Koga! I'll give you 15 minutes in here alone if we don't have to do a write up. Any blood?"

Sadao glanced over his shoulder and shook his head. "Takes more than a few blows to crack this hide."

"I bet," the Captain said with a nod. "Enjoy yourself - I'll leave Edwards outside to take you back."

Sadao nodded and stuck his head back under the spray, relaxing once again. The Captain was a decent man. One of a few among a gang of thieves, who walked on both sides of these bars.

Minutes trickled by as the showers emptied out. Sadao allowed himself precious moments of enjoyment of the simple pleasure of warm water running over his injured leg. His head hung in the spray and the length of his hair almost blocked his view of the benches behind him. It was enough to convince the slight form crouched behind the soiled linen bin it was time to make his move.

Sadao flipped his wet hair aside and turned, catching the flying wrist in his bound hands and twisting the sharpened serving spoon from his assailant's grip. Clatter!

"Aaaagh! *Mierda!*" the boy shouted as Sadao kicked the weapon away and yanked him hard up against his chest. Sadao turned and slammed him into the shower wall, knocking the kid's wind out for the second time that week.

"Ugh! Gaagh!"

Sadao had him pinned - head to towel. With his fists he took ahold of the punk's neck, sliding him up the wet tiles until their eyes met and his bare feet no longer touched the floor. It was the kid from the basketball court, the actual Latino. He looked terrified as he flailed his legs and raised his hands to grip Sadao's arms.

"Even chained up, I can take you," Sadao said. "Who would be foolish enough to send a child to play a man's game?"

The kid struggled to breathe in Sadao's grip but was rewarded only with a tightening of his fingers on his windpipe and an increase of pressure as he crushed the kid's chest between his own and the wall.

"Who was it? Someone not very clever and not very smart. My guess is our Church Fathers' favorite dog. He knew exactly when the Captain was due to arrive and would likely take pity on me. And you in your bravado and need to avenge some imagined slight thought you could pull it off!"

The kid kicked at air and made choking gasping noises in response. His towel slid away to the floor.

Sadao leaned in close so he would be heard clearly over the hiss of the showers. "I would kill you right here with a twist of my arm if I didn't feel sorry for the poor sad mother who birthed your worthless piece of ass. This is not a fight you are remotely

prepared for. And against an adversary of skill and advantage you've never imagined."

"You … can't … ffng..fucking walk! Crip! Aaaagh!"

Sadao slammed him into the wall again. "You thought the leg would make me weak? You thought because you can run fast you would have an advantage? Didn't anyone ever tell you that the wounded, caged animal is also the most dangerous?"

"I-I cccan take you … Yakuza!"

Sadao laughed and crushed the kid's throat until his eyes began to bulge.

"I can feel your piss running down my leg," Sadao said and threw him to the floor. The kid scrambled and scooted away, coughing. "*Loco hijo de puto!*" the kid spat, running naked in a wet panic for the door.

"I preferred Yakuza!" Sadao yelled after him and bent to the floor to retrieve the shiv. He ran his thumb along the filed edge in curiosity. It barely scratched his skin.

Amateurs, Sadao thought and tossed it in the trash.

Lockdown.

Long past midnight Sadao grew tired of trying to pretend to sleep over the dull throb in his leg and tossed his blanket aside in defeat.

Kuso!

He got up gingerly and with aid of the crutch, went to the locker on the opposite wall of his narrow single cell. He ran the combo and opened it. There weren't many items inside, even though Munez had taken pity and deposited a few dollars in Sadao's commissary account for a few items. A comb and leather band sat in the base of the locker with a few toiletries. He used them now to pull his hair back from his eyes. Once tied and tamed, he grabbed a small LED lamp and the stack of Mouse's letters, which he kept wrapped carefully in an old pillowcase. Items in hand, he shuffled back to the window and sat on the edge of his cot on his good hip, unwrapping his small treasure.

He'd read the letters a hundred times each, every word memorized. But even so, he found comfort in just holding the same sheets of paper his lover once had in hand many months ago in another country. He also found delight in the smooth flowing shape of Mouse's handwriting. Like everything about the man, it was unabashedly playful and honest.

Sadao shifted through the letters until he came to the little drawing of Mouse done by Lupe he'd received about a month ago. He liked holding this one especially. Aside from the addition of braids, Mouse's face and expression looked very much as he remembered it. If Lupe's artistic hand was true, his *Konezumi* had proven he could hold up just fine on his own.

I did not want to be the one to break you.

Two years ago on a stage covered in blood and bullet casings, these had been the last words he'd uttered before the darkness took him. Sadao didn't know how to find the words to describe it. Not even to himself. Somehow he had moved away to a space above and behind himself. He could see the top of Mouse's head leaning over him, screaming his name. But he had felt no reaction, just a vague realization that this was his body in the vision playing out down below him as the paramedics rushed in to try and hold his failing flesh together. His limbs were lying motionless and it had no meaning, no purpose, no feeling to him. Not even the devastated agony in his lover's face could rouse his emotion.

Sadao had been taught from a young age that when the spirit leaves the body, it is reborn into a new one to live again over and over in an endless cycle of life and death. He had also been taught to believe that when we die and are reborn, those we love go with us and return to us in new forms but the connection remains. In the most bleak and painful moments of his life, Sadao's spirit had clung to this one unwavering hope. In many ways, it had been his salvation. Nothing he had ever been told had prepared him for the truth - that the process of death rendered life meaningless.

A chill draft floated down from the window and ruffled the letters. Sadao set his hand down to stop them from blowing away. As he did so, his eye caught something familiar in the left margin of the top-most letter. He held the lamp closer and scrutinized the script. It wasn't in Mouse's hand and it wasn't English either. It looked as if it had been written in pencil then erased. It was a phonetic character of the Japanese language - "te". He brushed it with his thumb, then began to flip through the rest of the the letters, looking for more. And there were more, starting about five letters back. In the same spot, scratched in pencil then erased and made to look like a mistake. Sadao read them in order: fu ne ni no te. *Fune ni notte.*

Take the boat.

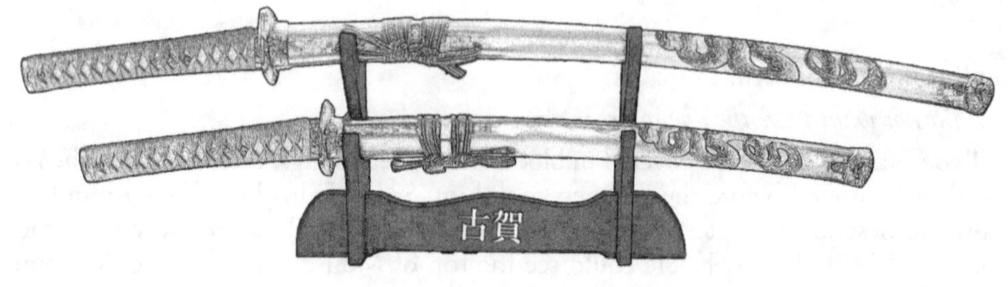

Chapter V

Fauna

"Hey man, if you're gonna sleep in my bed, you should at least get out of it before noon!"

"What?" Mouse woke with a start. He'd been dreaming hard - vivid images of water and steam filled his mind. Sadao had been there, in that wet warm place - skin on skin, breathing heavy in his ear. He didn't want to wake up. "Ungh, what time is it?"

"Time you got your ass up, Gringo!" Lupe tossed Mouse's jacket at his head. "I picked up those new snowbike skis you wanted from the Squamish Depot, too. The garage kids had to help me unload them. Nobody knew where you were. I should've looked right here!"

Mouse yawned and gathered up Sadao's old jackets. He'd fallen asleep in a nest of them, evidently. Fuck, it was 10:23 A.M. Half the daylight was gone. "Just picking up the last of our things," he said, lamely.

"You've been picking up 'things' for three weeks now!"

Lupe stepped into his bathroom and splashed water over his face and hair, combing his wind-tossed mane back into place. Being the driver of the team's only official race car, Lupe's 'do suffered from the Mustang's lack of side window glass - not the most comfortable way to drive through the mountains in mid fall. "Seriously, vato, this homemaking thing you got going - I know you want your Old Man back bad - but he's not gonna come any faster no matter how many socks you put in drawers up there."

Mouse sighed. "I know."

Lupe came out drying his face. He tossed the towel aside and sat down next to Mouse and looped an arm around him. "It's okay to say you're lonely up there, you know. You wanna stay down here with me some more, I got no problem with that."

Mouse looked sheepishly up at his best friend. The kid had grown like a pine over the last two years. Eighteen years old now and a full fledged racer, Lupe had a good two inches on him. Give him another year and he'd be taller than Sadao. Maybe he was taller already. It distressed Mouse to realize he wasn't completely sure how tall

Sadao was anymore.

Mouse conjured a warm smile. "I'll be okay. Tagata says he'll bring him home before the first snow."

Lupe squeezed Mouse's shoulder in comfort. "I know New Boss talks big, but I don't know if he's really gonna be the one calling the shots on this one."

"What do you mean?"

"You know, he's got that new lawyer guy down in Utah pushing papers and stuff. And that shit takes time."

"Wait a sec… How do you know about all this?"

Lupe shrugged. "New Boss just told me what's up. Why? Shouldn't I know?"

Mouse was confused and a little pissed. "I thought this jailbreak shit was top secret!"

"It is, man. But this new lawyer is Mexicano, like me. Tagata-san thought I should talk to him. Find out if he's the real deal, you know?"

"Having you speak Spanish over a CB channel for a few minutes was Tagata's big vetting process?!"

"I guess … "

Mouse made a hopeless sound and buried his head in his hands.

"Hey, cheer up. If it's any help, I think he's a good man. This Javier guy, he's handled a lot of tough extradition cases. High profile, too."

"Extradition?! You mean he's trying to get Sadao deported?!"

"Yeah, man. Tagata-san didn't tell you? It was that or death."

"Whaaaat?!" Mouse leapt right off the bed and grabbed Lupe by the collar of his racing jacket. "What do you mean, death?!"

His friend grabbed his wrists in defense. "Mouse! Shit man, take it easy. Those Utah Jesus freaks upgraded his sentence - some kind of political move. So this lawyer, he's got a legal counter attack to force them to deport instead - make it look like Old Boss got sent away back to Japan. But really they're gonna send him here! Jesus, I thought you knew all this shit!"

Mouse dropped Lupe's jacket and moaned. His heart was pounding in his ears. "I don't like this! I don't! It's this same Japanese secret plan bullshit they pulled on me two years ago that got Sadao locked up to begin with! Except this time they've got you in on it, too! Why the fuck didn't you tell me?"

To his credit, Lupe looked just as shocked as Mouse. "I'm sorry, okay? They only tell me what I need to know when I need to know it. I was in town picking up my rims and I got radioed from Tagata to go to a restaurant and take a call from this Javier Munez guy on a private landline."

"Where? What restaurant? Anyone could have been listening!"

"It was some taco shack halfway to nowhere on the backroads. These guys, the taco muchachos, they're a part of it. Some kind of underground immigrant network. They help sneak people into Canada out of the U.S. and Mexico who got problems. They know what they're doing. You gotta trust me!"

Mouse looked hopelessly at his friend as nausea filled his gut. "Death? Lupe, I need to go see him. What if they can't pull this off? What if they shoot him tonight?!"

"Naw, man. They're not gonna let you get anywhere near him - you know that. Besides, it's not like that. We gotta make a move for sure, but those preaching assholes are watching their backs. Javier's people are making a big public stink, embarrassing the Church and all that. He's got his people marching on the Temple calling for his release like he's some Asian El Che. He told me no way The Church Fathers are going to give up a chance to pack Old Boss back to Japan. They don't waste air fuel on prisoners. He'll get shipped out on a boat."

"And how on earth does this lawyer and his 'taco guys' propose to pluck Sadao out of the middle of the Pacific Ocean without being seen?"

Lupe looked grim. "They're working on that part."

"This all 25 of them, Aki?"

Mouse and his lead lug rat were unpacking and lining up the last of the new ski assemblies for the dirt-to-snowbike conversion that was already a month behind schedule. The snowmobile-like rear tracks had gone on the old Hondas smoothly. But the single supporting front-end ski rails the conversion kits had shipped with were not to spec, and a time-consuming reorder from Vancouver had to be called in. Mouse was up to his armpits in discarded dirt bike wheels with no working snowbikes to show for it. Tagata knew about the fitting error but the plain fact was the men needed to train now if they were going to be able to compete by mid-winter. They were a Canadian Division team now and that meant snow and ice racing as well as dirt and pavement.

"Yes, Boss," the kid said with a nod. "I measured all frame carefully. New skis will fit."

"Good," Mouse said, picking up a ratchet. "Let's try to get these bastards on before midnight."

Aki repeated Mouse's instructions to the three other mini-mechanics in Japanese and all five garage team members got to work. Aki was his new co-pilot. He was sixteen years old with a head for mechanisms, and his English ability and natural curiosity for how things worked made him a strong ally in the garage. This nimble teen had been essential in aiding Mouse in rebuilding his decimated garage crew. With Goru long dead and Lupe joining the active racing roster, Mouse had to scramble to get his nuts and bolts in a row.

Plus, most of these kids were new, fresh off the Pacific. Tagata's last recruitment run had been devastating. Lupe had gone down to San Diego with the Team Boss last summer to serve as translator. What they found lying about the docks and city slums were hundreds of starving, haunted, war-wounded children. Tagata needed only 12 new men; he couldn't afford any more. He struggled with Lupe's help to find the few teen boys whose minds and bodies had not been utterly destroyed by war, disease or street drugs.

Lupe's eyes clouded with tears recalling the scene to Mouse - the desperation, the begging. As a former street kid, Lupe's role in choosing which abandoned children lived or died had been a soul crushing task. In the end, they brought back 18 kids; 13 were aged 12 and older, and five who were aged four to seven, whom Lupe and Tagata could not stand to leave behind. Lupe's old buddy Kei adopted them into his new extended trailer that doubled as a daycare and mobile school room. He'd grown hugely fat in the last two years and served as surrogate mama for Sadao's former "little ones" and the new "even littler ones." The kiddies flocked to his round flesh like ducklings. The older ones were fed, healed and quickly assigned to camp job detail until they reached the racing training age of 16.

Mouse blew on his cupped hands to warm up his fingers before screwing the main assembly bolt in place on a Honda 440 up on a repair stand. What had once served as their fleet of Motocross bikes was now barely recognizable as snow and ice rigged winter sport vehicles. Having lived in the insufferable heat of the American southwest desert his whole life, Mouse found huddling in the garage truck's poorly heated tent extension was a new kind of suffering altogether. Even under the warmth of the standing flood lamps, fall was now well upon them and life in the high Canadian Coastal mountains meant shorter daylight hours for working in above freezing temperatures.

Should've set the damn alarm before falling asleep in the trailer last night. Now you're stuck working in the dark. Tagata's gonna chew you a new one for wasting lamp generator fuel.

Here in the mountains, the team enjoyed the convenience of a permanent camp, protected from outsiders and guaranteed by the Canadian government to be sovereign property. This was Sasori land. Sasori laws and protections were in full effect. Like an Indian Reservation, they were citizens of their own micro-kingdom, ruled by Tagata and his team leaders as long as they kicked a relatively large amount of ass for their Division benefactors. Granted, there were no probing, peeping tom chairpersons meddling in their affairs, but the price for being left alone was being alone - no pizza, no movies, no mailmen making door-to-door deliveries. As long as the weather held out, team members could make regular runs into small towns along the backroads between their lonesome lakeside winter paradise and Squamish for supplies. But once winter set in for real, they were locked off from the rest of civilization for a good six to eight weeks.

Mouse watched his breath rise in clouds from under the hood of his fur-lined jacket as he cranked the ski rail spindle into place. He could remember their first winter at the high camp with shivering detail. The unnamed lake was a mile wide green-blue oval of solitude amidst a vast evergreen forest tucked away in the heart of the Coastal Range. A desert rat who knew next to nothing about weather, Mouse had learned the hard way how to respect nature and the turn of seasons in this high brutal country. He'd nearly froze a toe off last year, rooming in Sadao's former trailer with Lupe. Snow drifts were seven feet high and a shortage of gas combined with sub-zero winds was no time to get caught low on supplies. They'd been locked up tight, trapped like most of the racers in their frozen tin can walls like a pair of ice cubes until the week-long blizzard passed and teammates came with picks to chip them out. They'd survived by huddling over a battery operated hotplate under a mass of racing jackets, and capturing snow to melt and drink as it blew into the shower through the now twice removed fan vent.

Somehow in the span of a year, the desert rat had become a mountain mole. And this winter he would be ready with his own fortress of comfort - fully stocked, fully equipped, and complete with a living, breathing, Sadao-shaped bed warmer. He almost couldn't wait for the first whiteout, provided the man actually arrived in time before the roads closed! It sucked icy rocks not being able to sail out over the ocean and scoop his love up in a fishnet, like now!

A high-pitched scream and a crashing sound snapped Mouse from his cozy cabin reverie. He looked up from his rail adjustments. Commotion was brewing outside.

"Stay here," Mouse told the teens and exited the tent flap door, grabbing a heavy flashlight that could double for a club in a pinch. It was fully dark outside and not much past 6 P.M. Most of the camp was up and out of their trailers, throwing on caps and gloves, wondering what the hell was going on. Mouse joined them, jogging through the lines of vans and trucks toward the noise.

At the center of camp stood the long illuminated mess hall tent. Steam rose from the commissary trucks' main kitchen unit. Dinner was only minutes away from being called. As Mouse made his way through the gathering of curious racing team personnel, he realized the girly screams were that of Cook-san, the team's aging resident chef. Tagata, he, and a few other team leads were arguing in Japanese and pointing to the pantry sheds and freezer units at the rear of the food truck. The double doors were thrown open and men were beginning to toss open bags of rice and flour out onto the ground. Another line of men were hauling out and dumping steaming pots of what was supposed their dinner onto the muddy ground.

Mouse rushed up to Tagata. "What the hell are they doing? That's our food!"

"Mouse! Wait!" Tagata gripped Mouse's arm to prevent him from interfering with the wasteful operation. Before he could protest, Cook-san let out another shriek as several dozen small furry critters scurried from the pipe vents and leapt for the canvas peaks of the mess tent where they slid down to the ground to hightail it back into the woods.

"The hell are those?!"

"Wood mice," Tagata said. "Very bad. Carry many diseases."

"Wood mice?" Mouse came into understanding as sack after sack of chewed open dried goods were thrown out of the pantry door and onto the ground in a hail of grains and powder. He'd chased a few mice out of the garage before, gnawing on his bungies, but the pantry was better sealed. At least he'd thought it was better sealed. He turned back to Tagata. "But ... there's mesh on the vents isn't there?"

"Removed," Tagata stated ominously.

"Removed?" Mouse glanced from Tagata's cold expression to Cook-san's tear-streaked one and back.

Tagata met his eyes. "Someone does not want Sasori team to eat well this winter."

Snowbike ski assembly and dinner were both postposed as Tagata and his camp leaders organized an all-hands clean up effort. The tainted food had to be removed by wheelbarrow, then shoveled and burned in charcoal pits. Mouse helped gather split logs from the woodsheds to throw on the bright bonfires of popping corn and toasted grains. The scent of hundreds of pounds of tainted dried goods going up in smoke made his stomach growl through the cloth rag tied around his nose and mouth - a preventive measure against hantavirus, a known killer in these climates. Even though Mouse had his own stash of food back up at the cabin, the loss of nearly all of the Sasori pantry goods did not bode well for the team's growing appetites. Worry spread fast among the young men as they watched the pantry truck turned inside out, sprayed with bleach and hosed down with filtered water pumped in from the lake.

Mouse took a break from hauling wood to check in with Lupe and his racing circle members as they took turns scraping freezing rice out of the dirt.

"Birds will get the rest, don't you think?"

Lupe coughed from behind his rag gag and shook his head. "Boss wants all this shit in the fire before dawn. Gonna be one long fucking night! And I'm fucking starved!"

"I think we're all going to be hungry sooner than we'd like," Mouse said. "We'll have to organize more hunting and fishing parties - rely on our own resources more if we have to fight mother nature like this. Tagata said the damn grates were removed, did you hear that?"

Lupe leaned on his shovel a minute, squinting at Mouse in the dark. "No shit? Who'd do something like that? Are they crazy?"

"We used to have break-ins and raids before, you know. In the desert."

"I know, but those were other teams - competitors in competition camps. Back when we used to share flat open land. We don't got no competition around here. Not until the Winter Sports Rally and that's 40 miles south! Ain't nobody knows about this camp up here at the North Pole! They hide the fuck out of that exit road."

"You see Santa out here shoveling this shit? It's fucking weird, though," Mouse said, looking past Lupe toward the mess tent. It was the only lit tent area in camp now. Fuel emergency had been called and all non-essential lighting had been shut off. The generators ran overtime to assist in the sanitation of the entire kitchen truck, from ovens and utensils to the far corners of the pantry. Fortunately, the freezer goods had not been nibbled or pissed on. Power was a closely guarded and regulated system. Unforeseen crises like this one meant the overdraught had to be rebalanced from elsewhere. Mouse was glad he'd brought a flashlight.

Mouse wanted to talk to Tagata about scheduling re-supply runs, but from his vantage he could see the Boss was busy as hell and probably not in the mood to hear suggestions from the team mechanic about matters of food. Cook-san was sitting on a pine stump, sipping tea, seemingly calmed to some degree by his sous chefs as they did their best to cook venison and canned beans over hastily constructed fire pits. Mouse moved closer to them, hoping for a swallow of anything warm when something caught his eye from across the lake.

That's weird…

He stopped and made a deviation to the water's edge. A couple of camp residents were taking note of the mysterious sight too. "*Denki,*" they were saying, pointing to the far shore. Lights.

To the best of Mouse's knowledge, nobody had any business lighting anything on the opposite shore. The team was ordered to stay in formation on the lake's eastern side and the men to stay securely in their trailers each night. The team leads had set up a system of nightly radio roll call to assure nobody was still out in the woods now that the night temperatures were dipping below freezing. Search parties were quickly organized if a man was declared missing and the children always closely guarded. Aside from the occasional wandering grizzly, the camp's only true enemy was cold. Two young men died their first year in this wilderness, freezing to death a stone's throw from camp in a whiteout.

Mouse watched the light as it flickered through the dense pines. It appeared to be stationary and powered, not burning. It was probably a hunting party that had wandered far out of their range onto Sasori land. Outsiders were nearly unheard of in their territory, but not impossible. Although his cabin on the hill above camp was fortified and his rifle fully loaded, Mouse knew he wouldn't sleep well while there were strangers in their midst. Now he had to speak to Tagata. But as soon as he blinked, the light was gone and the lake with no name was plunged back into darkness.

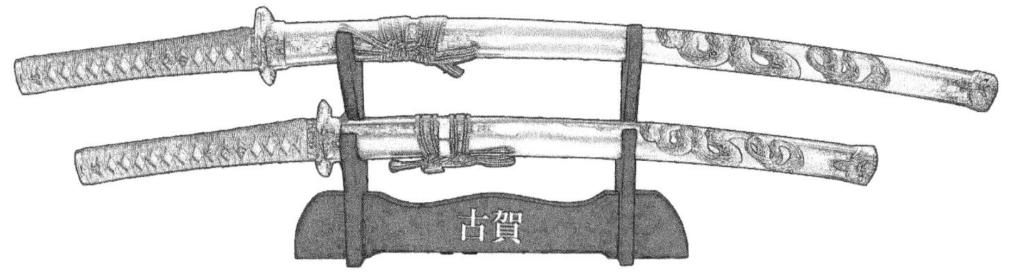

Chapter VI

Bad Translation

Dry Lakes, Arizona - 2071

Shouldn't get drunk the night before qualifiers, Sadao reprimanded himself as he lifted the square sake *masu* to his lips and tipped the cool liquor back into his mouth. He rolled its sweetness around his tongue and swallowed, all while being closely watched by Shiratori. The man had an udon noodle stuck to the front of his armor - very unbecoming. Sadao reached across the table and flicked it off with his finger.

"Hanse! You always try to cheat!"

"Lies! I am a worthy opponent!"

Sadao selected a battered lime from the sticky dinette tabletop between them and tossed it in the air. He grabbed a carving knife and threw it, with the intent to slice the fruit in two mid-air. But his vision swam and his knife flew through the lime's phantom twin, burying the blade in his cupboard instead.

"Kuso! I'm drunk, you bastard!"

Shiratori cackled at him as he refilled their wooden cups. *"Not drunk enough!"* He raised his *masu* with a big white grin and waited for Sadao to do the same.

"Fuck you," Sadao said in English and tipped his cup back. Too late now to retreat, might as well bury himself. "I have a motocross to run tomorrow!"

"Let boys run race. They are trained. They know their way," he replied with only a slight slur to his words. But if Sadao's blurred vision was semi-adequate, the General's *chonmage* atop his head was leaning a bit too far to the left. "You protect too much. Boys can not be men this way."

"I'm setting an example," Sadao grumbled. "Boys need discipline to stay focused."

"And Boss-sama need unfocus to see what mistake he is made with too much mama hen!"

Sadao's frown turned into a laugh. "Your English… atrocious! Didn't you pay any attention in school?"

Shiratori leaned forward, sweeping their fruitastic mess away with a swipe of his metal arm. He set the shiny elbow firm at the table's center, mechanical fingers wiggling. "We wrestle. I show you what real man pay attention to!"

Sadao rubbed his face with his lime-juiced hand. It stung his eyes, bringing his spinning head a little more in focus. "I'm not arm wrestling your prosthetic. I'm not that drunk!"

"I no cheat! I use no more than regular man strength!"

"Like hell you won't!" Sadao leaned back from the table, refusing to participate.

"I pay attention in school. Learn all I need. Nothing more. I know English good enough to talk to stupid Americans. They speak English no better!"

Sadao yawned - it was late. "You have a point."

"You, schoolboy, so pathetic - always do what teacher say. Do what make teacher happy. What make *oyasan* happy. Always such good boy, Sadao-kun. Always such good grades. Such waste!" Shiratori spat.

"If you're trying to anger me into wrestling you, you're failing miserably."

Shiratori's alcohol-flushed skin reddened further. "You no listen! Always you care what other man think! Make bad decision this way!"

"I do not make bad decisions! I make considerate decisions!"

"You are wrong! Tell me why camp money is always too little! You buy too many favor; you buy too many thing to make other men happy. You buy too many sad-face kid!"

Sadao picked up the empty sake bottle and threw it at a wall. It failed to break and left a dent in the paneling before hitting the floor with a lame bonk. "We are not discussing this again! I am responsible for recruitments! You have no say in this! I choose the men we need!"

"You choose men you think will tell you, 'Good job, Sadao-kun. Good grade!' Just like teacher, just like school master. Where were teacher and master when your family was killed?"

Sadao slumped back into the lounge seat. "You really want me to slam you to the floor, don't you? I'm too tired for that shit tonight!"

Shiratori regarded him steadily. "I try to teach you good lesson!"

Sadao was momentarily transfixed by his ceiling fan. It was oscillating strangely. Maybe it was the sake or maybe Mouse was plotting another escape. "Don't bother me with lessons. I'm 38 years old, my friend. I've learned all I want to know. And I know people!"

"Tell me Boss-sama, do you trust this mechanic you find in desert town?"

Sadao shifted his gaze back to Shiratori. "Mouse? Why are we discussing him?"

"You keep him too close. I think maybe you do not trust."

Sadao shook his spinning head. "No, you misunderstand. I trust Mouse. He's a pain in my ass, but I trust him! He'll prove himself and his loyalty to us tomorrow, I'm certain of it."

"If Boss-sama have trust, why is Mouse-san still guest in your home?"

"What do you mean?"

"Don't pretend I am blind. I see how he looks at Boss-sama."

"What? Murderously?"

"With desperate uncontained love."

Sadao laughed. "Go home, Shiratori. You're drunk."

"Not too drunk to see this man. You keep him too close. You will make more bad decision so his eye will not change."

"Don't say such stupid things!"

"If I am stupid, then why is that man asleep in your bed?"

"Because he has no other place to stay!"

"We have many trailers, some half full. You keep this man to yourself."

"Fuck!" Sadao set his elbow on the table and offered his hand to Shiratori, whose face spread into a sly grin. "Put your cyber-arm where your mouth is and we will see who really has a lesson to teach!"

Shiratori gladly offered his inhuman hand to his opponent. "You decide to wrestle me now, but I have already won!"

Sadao smiled. "Prove it."

Utah State Prison - 2073

Sadao shuffled up the canteen line, tray in hand, waiting his turn for a scoop of gluck they called prison food. Today's main attraction was greenish, trying to pass for creamed spinach, though Sadao doubted a naturally grown vegetable ever had anything to do with it.

"Here you are, my friend. Fresh out of the microwave!" Henry was working the serving line and he gave Sadao a hearty plop of the stuff with an ill-suited ice cream scoop. Henry shrugged. "Sorry for my aim, shortage of spoons."

"Thanks," Sadao said dubiously. The portion overran its serving well and soaked his almost edible dinner roll. *Mazui.* He'd kill for a bowl of Cook-san's *kitsune udon* about now. He wondered if their old chef was still alive. How strange to think he might be seeing him again soon.

A splat of something beige roughly in the shape of sliced turkey came next, drowned in a grey sauce. It smelled like shoes.

"Trust me, if you don't think that's the bee's knees - you're going to love the cranberry sauce!" Henry scooped up an especially big chunk of the rubbery stuff from a fresh can with a big grin.

Sadao held up a hand. "Please, don't waste it!"

Too late - the red wedge hit the plate, sending a splash of turkeyish sauce onto Sadao's worn prison jumpsuit.

"Hey, Yakuza! You gonna move your ass sometime tonight? Some of us who work for this shit are hungry!"

Sadao gladly retracted his tray before Henry could assault it with any more culinary disasters.

"Seriously, try the cranberry," Henry insisted. "It'll surprise you!"

Sadao nodded and, ignoring the insults from the Latino youth, made his way to the empty end of a table. It took some effort to force his leg to swing over the bench seat.

"That gimp Chino can't even sit for shit!"

His encounter with the shiv in the showers had started some kind of rumbling among the Latino set. Their fruitless insults were coming on with more frequency and volume now. Sadao simply ignored them. Were they in a different place, in a different time, Sadao would have had that punk's testicles tied around his neck by now. But Javier had warned him not to make any trouble for himself in the next few weeks while extradition procedures were crawling their way across desks.

"Keep your nose clean and you'll do fine," he'd said during their last call. "We need you to be ready to board ship in two weeks!" With less than a week left before departure, Sadao intended to do just that - punks be damned. Instead, he occupied himself with trying to decide which pile of dinner ooze would least likely kill him if ingested.

"Hey, look, there's room at his table! I think he needs a little company!"

An unwelcome annoyance was announcing itself as dinner entertainment. Soon he was surrounded by Shiv Boy and his tattooed pack of rejects. Sadao took a deep breath and centered his mind.

"I don't think Chino likes his dinner," one of them said. "Maybe he wants noodles."

"Or maybe he needs those sticks to eat his veggies," snickered another.

"I don't suppose any of you have ever seen a map of the East before," Sadao said, nudging his food around idly with a plastic fork. "Chinese and yakuza do not hail from the same country."

"Like fuck they don't! I seen that Kung fu flick last night! They all talking in Chinese or some shit and they all got crazy motherfucking dragon tattoos."

"It's called karate," Sadao said without emotion. "And to an uneducated eye or ear, Nihongo can be confused with Chinese, although both languages are entirely different."

"Wow, is that the truth? Guess I wouldn't know seen as I was kicked out of fifth grade to help my momma sell blow! I must of missed the map quiz!"

Sadao declined to respond and carved off a mouthful of cranberry gel. He expected it to taste like cherry soap, but what he didn't expect was the hard click of metal that hit his back molar. Thinking it was a bit of can lid, he immediately spit the bite out into his hand.

"Pwaahahha! Chino don't like his cranberry, neither!"

Sadao squished the gel in his palm and fished the metal out with his thumb. It was his ring, the silver loop and pearl he had promised himself to Mouse with. Henry had come through.

"Fuck is that?!"

Before Sadao could blink, the kid at his right swatted the ring from his hand.

"Hey!" Sadao sprung out of his calm and smashed the kid's head face-first into his food tray. Turkey and spinach runoff dripped to the floor as he wrestled the kid's arm for his jewel. He had him by the wrist and squeezed.

"Gaaaaaaoow, shit!" The kid's wrist bones popped and he opened his hand, letting the ring drop to the floor under the table. Sadao scrambled for it, but his leg was not fit for bench maneuvers and one of his opponents on the other side slid under faster and grabbed it.

"Shit! Look at that! Guess I shoulda had the cranberry myself! This thing real?" The kid put it to his mouth to make a show of biting it.

Sadao made a lunge across the table for it, but the kid jumped back too fast to grab it. "It's mine," Sadao snarled. "And if you want your hand to stay attached to your body, you'd better return it."

"Oh, I don't think so. Finders keepers, motherfucker! Is that a pearl or something?"

Some of the kid's cronies were grabbing his arm for a better look of the ring he wore proudly on his index finger. From his peripheral, Sadao noticed the guards beginning to turn away from their conversation to see what was going on at the far end of the canteen. And as much as he wanted to separate this young prick's finger from his hand and reclaim his property, he knew a physical struggle would only bring them running and he'd lose his jewel all over again.

"So you think you want to keep it?" Sadao said coldly.

"Yeah, I think it looks good on me," the kid replied, wiggling his finger.

"Then maybe you should learn how to wear it properly. It's not a finger ring. It's worn through a piercing. More specifically, when it's in my possession, it's worn through the end of my cock. It rests between my dick and my balls and I feel it every time I take a step. It's there when I piss and it's there when I bury it deep in my lover's ass."

"Fuckin-A!" The kid make a face and tore the silver ring from his finger and threw it back at Sadao. He caught it and quickly dropped it into his deepest pocket. "Fuckin' gross man, I ain't wearing no faggot ring! I eat pussy, man! I eat all the pussy!"

His pals started laughing and pointing at him, diverting attention from Sadao.

"Ah, you're a little faggot now! You got dick juice in your mouth!"

"Yeah it's like you sucked Chino's dick biting that thing!"

"I ain't got no dick juice! Fuck you! I ate your momma's pussy, twice!"

That's when the shoving and spinach flinging began and Sadao was able to slip quietly away.

The Temple's favorite son was waiting for him when he emerged from the men's room some minutes later - his hidden ring returned to its proper place.

"I've got a job for you, Koga!"

"I'm exempt from prison labor," Sadao reminded him pointedly. "Bad leg."

"If you can stand, you can clean. Henry, bring the mop bucket!"

Henry grumbled a reply from the kitchen.

"You started quite a food fight in there with your antics. Your mess, you get to clean it!"

Henry emerged from the kitchen with a mop bucket filled with water. He rolled it up to Sadao with a sorry look in his eyes. Brother Smith shoved the handle into Sadao's chest.

"I've heard we'll be giving you a nice send off soon, back to Japan. Think of this little chore as your exit ticket."

Sadao gripped the end of the mop and pushed the sloshing bucket past the annoying little man and into the now vacant dining hall. The floor was a mess; green ooze and red gel marked a trail of bad behavior from the spot he had chosen for dinner halfway to the rear of the kitchen. Sadao halted the bucket and with a sigh, dipped the mop in to get to work.

Stay out of trouble. Don't cause yourself any extra paperwork, Javier had warned. So although the hip protested with each mop and squeeze of the rinse lever, Sadao kept his pain to himself and eyes on the sticky floor.

You'll be in Canada, soon. Or the bottom of the Pacific. Either way, no more mops in your near future.

About 20 minutes into it, the rest of the kitchen crew had left. Only Henry lingered to wipe down tables. Brother Smith had become distracted by something on the TV in the common room across the hall and was nearly out of eyeshot. Henry took this as an opportunity to grab a second mop and give Sadao a hand.

"Asshole didn't say nothing about not helping out a friend," the old man whispered. "Did you enjoy your cranberry surprise?"

Sadao nodded as he pushed soggy salad out from under a table. "Much appreciated.

I suppose you've come over to collect your payment?"

"Damn straight," Henry said with a crooked grin.

"Fair enough," Sadao said, rinsing the holiday-colored vomit from his mophead. "There was an important man in my racing division - a Chairman - who threatened the members of my team, so I removed his head with my katana during our awards ceremony in front of a live audience and the local media. I took a lot of bullets to the hip and leg from his trigger happy guards. Woke up in a hospital four days later with the police surrounding my bed."

Henry blinked behind his smeary glasses. "No kidding."

"Bastard had it coming, believe me."

Henry was quiet for a moment then chuckled. "Don't folks use guns anymore? Katana - that's some kind of sword, right?"

"Japanese melee weapon. I was trained to fight in school before the war reached our village in southern Japan."

"That so? They issued you weapons with your school books?"

"Something like that, yes. But my blade had been in the Koga family for many decades. My distant ancestors were samurai class. I wonder if I will ever see--"

Bam! Click!

Both men paused in their mop talk. The dining hall doors had slammed and locked behind them. Turning about, it was plain to see that Shiv Boy and his friends had been invited in for a private sitting, and were quickly moving toward them.

"Looks like you missed a spot, Yakuza!" It was Dick Juice with a glint of long metal in his hand. "We came back to help."

Sadao's instincts told him no outside help would be coming from the correctional staff - not with Brother Smith guarding the outside doors and the kitchen's missing altered serving spoons in the hands of the prison's idle youth. The gang climbed over tables and shoved chairs out of their way as they moved into formation around them.

Two glints of sharpened metal, three sets of taped fists. Five against two, pretty fair odds.

"Run, Henry," Sadao said and upended a bench to serve as a shield.

"But- !"

"Get out of here!" Sadao yelled, grabbing the mop in both hands. Henry wisely shuffled hard for the safety of the kitchen.

Bam! Splash!

Sadao kicked the mop bucket over and creamed jelly-slimed spinach water soaked the floor in front of the advancing kids. One of them slipped and fell face first into his dinner for the second time that night.

"Vamonos!"

Sadao thrusted the mop forward and rammed the soggy end into Dick Juice's gut. The kid doubled over with a grunt as Shiv Boy danced around the mop lake to come at Sadao's left. Sadao, table shield in front and wall at his back, cracked the mop handle in half over his knee and pointed it at Shiv Boy tauntingly.

"You want this?" Sadao shouted, aiming the sharp end toward Shiv Boy's neck. The kid stopped in his tracks inches from the jagged end, suddenly not so confident. The gang balked and looked to each other for direction. "Come any closer and I'll ram this through his throat!

"Fucking get him!" Shiv Boy yelled. He jumped back from Sadao's weapon, knocking it aside, and the kids snapped out of it. Slipping and sliding, they all rushed the table fort at once.

Sadao rebounded with a wide swing and sliced one of the kid's upper arms as he made a weak attempt to drive a spoon handle into his shoulder. Sadao rammed him in the chest when his aim went wild, slamming the kid back into the wall. The modified cutlery hit the floor in a clatter. Sadao kicked it halfway across the room, before swinging back with the broken handle to give a table-climbing kid a closer shave to his chin than the punk had ever managed on his own.

"Ow!" Asshead grabbed his bloody chin and fell backwards off the table's understructure as another crawled around the far end, diving for Sadao's legs. The kid tackled him on his weak side and Sadao felt his hip betray him, sending him right down into the overturned mop bucket.

Shiv Boy and Dick Juice let out a cry of victory and the gang scrambled on top of him - pinning Sadao's dominant arm and leg. Sadao cracked the mop handle across a third kid's back, making him yelp, but Dick Juice stomped on his forearm and forced him to drop the wooden weapon.

"Hahah!" With his gang holding down a limb each, Shiv Boy sat himself proudly across Sadao's chest in victory.

Overpowered, Sadao stopped struggling and shifted his energies to a different tactic. "Are you proud of yourself?" he asked as the kid fingered the remaining shiv. "You'll get a nasty infection that way," Sadao said coldly.

"Not me, Chino. Dipped it in the hall toilet, just for you!" Quicker than he had anticipated, the kid flipped the weapon and plunged it hard into Sadao's side.

"Aaaaagh!!" The sheer pain of it was shocking. It went deep, scraping a rib. Sadao twisted his torso to throw him off but it only drove the shiv in deeper. He held his screams and tried to focus on his attacker.

"You feel that, Yakuza? Eh?"

Sadao ground his teeth. "You think a worthless punk like you can kill me? Aaagh!!"

The kid drilled the weapon in deeper, leaning over Sadao's pain-twisted face. "Not today, Yakuza. That's someone else's job. But King Go-Away says to tell you, 'Hello!'"

"What- ?" There was a sound of a match being struck back toward the kitchen and suddenly the room filled with spraying water - accompanied by a blaring red alarm.

"Get outta here, you shitty bastards!" It was Henry - he'd tripped the fire detector in the kitchen with his smuggled book of matches.

The Latinos looked around scared at the flashing beacon and all at once made a run for the auto-unlocking fire exit at the rear of the room that led to the fenced exercise yard.

"Hah haa! No match for this old fart!" Henry yelled, waving his matchbook. Any second, half the correctional officers in the prison would be rushing into the room.

"Henry!" Sadao yelled through the torrent of water. "Help me get this out!"

"Huh? Oh shit! There's my missing serving spoon!" Henry ran over to him, concerned. "Think we'd better let the docs get this. I heard it's bad news to remove a stabbing object."

Sadao tried to work the end loose but his hand slipped in the sprinkler downpour. "Henry! Grab a towel! *Now!*"

Henry reached for one of the soggy rags he'd been cleaning tabletops with before they were ambushed.

Sadao took it from him and wrapped it around the end of the spoon sticking out of his left ribcage. Men could be heard running up the halls toward them. The main door was jammed shut and COs were ramming themselves into it.

"You got that? I really don't think you should--"

"Aaaagggh!" Sadao yelled as he pulled the crude weapon clean out of his own flesh. There was a flood of blood that came out with it but the rain of the sprinklers quickly washed it off into the swill of spilled cranberry sauce. Sadao took the wet towel and tucked it into his jumpsuit to put pressure on the wound.

Henry was hovering over him, looking at him like he was either the biggest badass to ever get locked up in this shithole or else the craziest. "Now see here, we gotta let that bleed a little so's the wound don't get infected."

"No time! Henry! Listen to me! Pick up the shivs. Hide them fast! No one can know what happened in here. Understand?"

Bam, bam, bam! The double doors were being heavily rammed now.

Henry bent and picked up the stabbing weapon and tucked it into his sweater as water poured over his glasses.

"If I'm sent to the clinic, I miss my boat! Do you understand me?!"

"Yeah, yeah I got it. I got it!"

Henry was a bit slow, but he was loyal. He made off with the shivs into the depths of the kitchen while Sadao swallowed his curses and managed to get himself back up onto his feet. He tossed the broken mop handle into the trash and shut the lid just as the officers managed to bust the canteen doors wide open.

It was hell waiting for the rolling library that night.

Sadao lay in his bunk, blanket over his chest, feigning sleep. They'd allowed him a shower before lockdown. The investigating officers concluded that the oven had been left on in the kitchen with a bit of turkey grease in the pans and must have triggered the smoke alarm. This caused Henry and himself to get caught in an unplanned wash-down and an ill-timed double door lock mechanism failure. In an unrelated report, a bunch of the boys from D-block had managed to break into the exercise yard out of turn.

In the shower stall alone, Sadao rubbed a slip of soap as deep up into the wound as possible. His rib was sore, possibly torn from its connective tissues. But by some miracle, nothing important appeared to be severed. It bled some, that was a problem. And as soon as he felt the soap had done its job, Sadao spread the mouth of the cut as wide as he could stand it to let the warm water from the showerhead spray out what he hoped was the worst of the potential bacteria. A strip of towel tied tightly around his chest and a clean jumpsuit served to cover what he figured would be an old scar and amusing story someday.

Now in the bunk, he'd packed the wound with bits of a spare sock and lay as still as possible, waiting for Henry to make his rounds with the book cart.

"Hemingway always lifts my spirits," he heard the old man say between squeaks of the cart wheels as he ployed his selections to the incarcerated. "I recommend the *Old Man and the Sea.*"

"Fuck the old man! I want pussy and ass! If Hem-fuckin'-noway has a big ass bush and huge fucking tits - hand that shit over or else go fuck yourself!"

Squeek squeek squeek…

Henry had arrived with a glum look. "No appreciation for the classics tonight. Can I interest you in a little *War and Peace*, Mr. Koga?"

"More peace than war, please," Sadao said, sitting up with a grimace. "But a little Napoleonic War before bed never did anyone harm, I guess."

He stood slowly and shuffled close enough to Henry's cart to reach through the bars to take the huge tome from his arthritic hands. "Expanded edition, I see…" Sadao commented as he turned away to open the binding. Inside the hollowed-out book was a short flattened roll of duct tape and some wads of gauze. "This will help put me at ease, I think."

"I hope it's adequate," Henry followed. "Pickin's were slim on the shelves tonight."

"It's fine," Sadao said quietly, shutting the book to wait for lights out to apply the makeshift first aid properly. "I owe you a lot, old friend."

"Naw," Henry said, cheerily. "Just glad you'll be sailing home soon. Say hello to that rodent fella of yours for me, okay?"

Sadao chuckled, even though it hurt his chest to even breathe. *Mouse. I can't think that far yet.*

"Gonna miss doing you favors, though. I gotta admit, they were original."

"There's one more I need to ask."

"How's that?"

"Just an odd question. Do you know anyone in any of the outer blocks who goes by the name King Go-Away?"

Henry's bulbous nose wrinkled up. "Nope, can't say I have. Terrible nickname."

Sadao nodded in agreement. "It is. And that's why I don't think it's right."

"Hey, bookman! You gonna bring me something to crush cockroaches with tonight or what?"

Henry blinked behind his greasy glasses. "Well, that's my cue! Happy trails, Koga. Try not to cut off any more heads or else we might find ourselves neighbors again."

"I'll try." Despite the pain, Sadao bowed in respect to the old man as he wheeled away with a lighthearted whistle.

May peace find you, my friend.

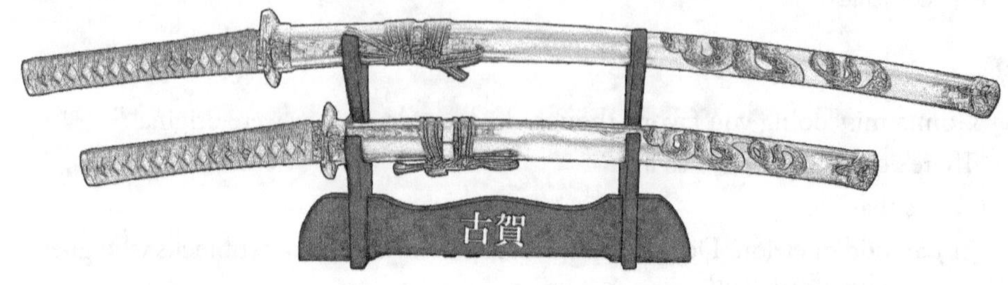

Chapter VII

La Cucaracha

Do you think you are ready to finish your journey, Sadao?

Deep under the flaming sea, the curious golden fish swam circles around Sadao's sinking body. Its plated scales seemed familiar - forming a pattern he knew.

Kyouji - won't you let me find peace?

We were taught from the first day as warriors to welcome death, not to fear it, the fish whispered. *Death is our destiny. Death is our rebirth. This is the way of the sword - an endless cycle.*

The fish swam faster under him, staying his fall. *Let me go,* Sadao thought. *I have no more strength in this fight.*

If you go before your time you will leave everyone in this world behind. Your paths will divide forever.

I failed. This is my punishment.

No! Death is not punishment! Death is a reward you are not ready to accept!

His last breath exploded out of him. In his final moments of conscious thought, Sadao felt his body still in the throbbing sea and begin to rise, stroke by stroke, swiftly for the surface.

North Pacific Coast - 2073

I'm not dead.

This was Sadao's first thought upon awaking in a strange wooden berth in the crowded hull of a small vessel, the belly of which was packed with ropes, weapons, fishing nets and… Mexicans? Several men were sitting around a makeshift table in the center of the deck; drinking, eating, smoking and generally making a lot of noise.

They appeared to be celebrating.

Sadao's nose lit up at the scent of tobacco. He worked himself up slowly through the pain to sit up. There were no portholes on this deck. They were still traveling but the water felt calm. He wasn't feeling quite as ill as he had been the prior week out in the Pacific. His shriveled stomach grumbled in curiosity as to what his companions were feasting on. They were grilling something on a gas hot plate in the center of the table.

"Hey, deadman rises! He's awake!"

Sadao nodded as a cheer went up, followed by more cracks of beer can tabs and shouts in Spanish.

"You hungry, amigo? We got tortillas, carnitas, onions, hot pepper… " The companion Sadao recognized vaguely as his prison ship porthole savior held out a beer to him.

"Water, please," he croaked on dry vocal chords. "And a cigarette."

"No problem, amigo. This man has priorities!"

Sadao gladly accepted a canister of fresh water and quickly gulped it down his parched throat. His entire body was sore from days without proper hydration and smoke inhalation - not the kind he enjoyed. His bad leg ached and his stab wound throbbed. In short, he felt like utter shit. A lit cigarette was passed his way and he accepted it gratefully. He took a drag and immediately regretted it. The coughing fit that followed nearly brought up the water he'd just managed to swallow. Even so, it didn't stop him from taking another drag.

His buddy laughed and left the table to come sit on a crate next to him, clapping a hand to his back in solidarity. "You have determination, my friend. I like that!"

Sadao exhaled more successfully the second time and gulped down more water. The nausea at least was gone for now. "You're the one who threw me out of a window into flaming water," Sadao noted. "Thanks."

"It's my job! Good thing you can swim, eh?"

Sadao smoked a moment, trying to put together what had happened to him. He remembered struggling in the water, trying not to be on fire and then… He felt the back of his head through his long disheveled hair to find a sore raised area. "I was hit… "

"*Perdón, amigo.* We ran over you with our skiff. It was hard to see in all the smoke, but we found you one way or another. Gonzales here used to spearfish in Cortez - he dove for you. You sank like a rock!" Gonzales raised a beer and drank in his honor.

"Where are we going?" Sadao asked his companion. The boat did appear to be moving at a good clip.

"North! To your people and our *dinero.* I hope this 'Tagata' has lots of money or we keep you for ransom, eh?" Sadao had the distinct impression that was no joke. He looked around and sized up his current situation - trapped in a small fishing boat hull with eight armed men with no windows or exits. All told, things were not that much different.

"Beats prison, I guess," Sadao said, enjoying his cigarette. "Hey, hombres, toss me a tortilla!"

They did and Sadao tore off a strip and popped it in his mouth along with a bit of beard. He brushed it out of the way. Between the near drowning and chronic lack of a barber, he must look horrendous. His hair had grown to just past his shoulders. He hoped Tagata had a shower and change of clothes waiting for him. Jumpsuit yellow was getting old. Sadao eyed his still-smiling neighbor. The man stank of beer and looked like he'd needed a shave for at least twice as long as Sadao had. And a pirate dental plan.

"So, pirates, huh? I didn't think there were any left willing to cross U.S. waters."

"We waited until your ship was in neutral territory. Those *gabachos* don't know shit. They just pissed their *bragas* and let us take over without a fight."

"Why'd you sink it, then? Not that I care. Ship was a horrible place."

"Eh? Don't you know? That was part of the deal. Make it look good, you know?"

Sadao shook his head. "No, I don't know. Make what look good?"

"Congratulations!" the man said, clapping his back again. "You're a dead man, amigo!"

Sadao blinked. It made sense now - the attack and sinking. Sadao hoped Tagata's new team was doing well enough to afford this operation or he'd better get used to tortillas and beer really quick.

"So we keep you hidden until your pick-up comes for you. You don't show your face to no one. Dead men don't walk in daylight. Understand, amigo?"

Sadao nodded. "Yeah, I understand."

His companion laughed and motioned for another beer. "They didn't tell you much, did they? Can't tell secrets you don't know to nobody, right?"

"I guess not." Even so, he had words for Tagata on this whole scheme. As usual, an overabundance of force was used to solve a simple problem. But then Taga always enjoyed burning things to the ground.

"See, amigo," his companion continued. "We don't do no rescue missions for just anybody. No matter what the price. But this time we make an exception, for you and the team. We like to spend a few pesos at the track! *Vivan los Sasoris!*"

The men banged the table with their fists and echoed the cheer.

Sasori - *scorpion.* That made perfect sense. Tagata had renamed the team under his own totem. It was the natural thing to do when changing divisions, but it made Sadao feel a pang of loss.

"We like this man, this new man you have - Escovado. He is one badass motherfucker!"

It took Sadao a moment. "You mean Lupe? Lupe Escovado? Our bodywork artist?"

"Yeah, with his '68 Mustang. That guy fucks up the track, man. Escovado!!"

"Escovado!" The men cheered again.

His Mustang? He really wasn't boss anymore.

Another day passed at sea and Sadao took advantage of the journey to rest, refuel and rehydrate. He checked his duct tape bandage. The salt-water soaked gauze underneath had helped to disinfect the wound. The entry point was still tender but it had sealed surprisingly well without the benefit of stitches. He poured cheap alcohol over it for good measure but for the most part, it appeared to be healing. He left it unbandaged, figuring any medical supplies the fishing boat might hold would not be particularly sanitary.

He lay in the bunk under a musty blanket, smoking and listening to the snores of his compadres. It was clear they were heading North - it was getting colder below deck. He figured they'd likely try to bring him in up through the Juan de Fuca straight past Washington and the San Juan Islands. Perhaps they'd dock in Vancouver or Squamish further up one of the Salish Sea's inlets. Either way, he was nearing freedom with each nautical mile.

Canada. Tagata's birth nation had offered the threatened Orochi team an escape route up through Idaho to a secret border crossing just north of Spokane. It was risky. If they'd been caught during their Salt Lake desert evacuation, most of the team would be on refugee boats sailing to Chiba and certain death from war, starvation or disease. In the 25 years since it began, the Japanese Civil War was still smoldering on in pockets of unrest. Clan lords now ruled the prefectures like Shogun of old. Feudalism was alive and well on those distant shores and Sadao had meant it when he said he'd gladly accept a noose around his neck before an actual deportation. The death of the Chairman in such a spectacular method had been the media and police distraction necessary to assure an entire racing team's escape from the opposite end of the salt desert. It had been Shiratori's idea - a plan he had concocted and orchestrated for months leading up to the event. Sadao regretted deeply that although they had both pledged to die in that fight together, only one of them had fallen.

It's your guilt that drives your visions, he reasoned. Why else would you see a giant samurai fish? Shiratori would never sink that low. No pun intended.

Mouse would be in Canada, too. He would have been living in Canada's high alpine region for at least 18 months now. Sadao wondered how he was liking the cold. Not much, he surmised, picturing his stubborn blond beauty wrapped up in scarves and coats cursing his head off. He regretted losing Mouse's prison letters to the sea. But as much as he ached to see him again, to hold him, Sadao felt an uneasiness. Deep in his gut there was doubt. Fear. Guilt. Feelings he couldn't quite grasp and as of yet did not have time to process.

With reunion comes healing, he reasoned. *Mouse does not need to know your uncertain-*

ties. Sadao remembered it again in his mind - the bloody stage, Mouse's screams, and himself no longer corporal, fading away, lost. Nothing he had ever known had driven fear deeper into his heart than that moment of disconnection.

I failed you, he thought, closing his eyes. *I won't fail you again.*

"Rise and shine, amigo! It's party time!"

Sadao's eyes jerked open to find his porthole pusher standing over him with a blindfold and rope. The boat had stopped.

"Are those really necessary?" he grumbled, sitting up painfully. "I'm hardly in shape to run."

"Staging, my friend. Negotiations will go better if you don't speak!"

Sadao pulled off the blanket. His salt water hardened jumpsuit was rubbing his skin raw across his shoulders. "What about a change of clothes? I think this prison-wear might be a bit obvious, don't you think?"

"Yeah, yeah, we get you some pantaloons, okay? *Date prisa!*"

The loose fitting pants were too long and covered his prison sneakers, making dragging sounds in the dirt as they walked. Sadao marched at gunpoint, blindfolded with his hands tied behind his back. The barrel of a big firearm kept nudging his back under the borrowed poncho thrown over his shoulders. It did little to keep out the chill, but at least it wasn't yellow. He hoped Mouse wouldn't be waiting at the end of this wooded trail. This whole situation was humiliating enough.

They'd docked the boat far up a wooded inlet by the sounds and smell of it. Ocean breezes carried the scent of mountain pines and ferns that swirled around his nose as he blindly disembarked. He'd been marched inland now for about a mile, winding up a trail past a river. They were deep in the woods now by the feel of the dimming sunlight. There was heavy cover and his nose caught the scent of a distant campfire, drawing closer.

"When we stop amigo, you get down on your knees and wait. No funny business!" The steel barrel in Sadao's back emphasized these guys were all business now.

"Do I look like I'm amused?" Sadao asked, marching ever forward. His hip was in no condition to climb and each limp up the path was growing more laborious and painful. He stopped a moment to take the weight off of it and was knocked to the ground with a kick to the back of his knees.

"Maybe you don't think we're serious, eh?" Before he could muster a reply, he got a piece of cloth shoved into his mouth and tied behind his head. Sadao whipped his shoulders and threw the pirate off in disgust. He earned a gunbutt in the back for that, knocking his wind out as he hit the dirt. He coughed behind the gag as two men hauled him back up to his feet. *"Vamonos!"*

Sadao marched until he sensed a break in the trees. A meadow perhaps or a clearing of some kind. Somebody fired off a shot into the air and it was answered by a return shot. Then silence until the distant sound of a racing engine could be clearly heard moving down the mountain toward them. Not just any racing engine - his racing engine. Nothing else on earth sounded like a '68 Mustang.

Buppa beeppa, buppa beeppa, buppa buppa buppa bup!

"Did my fucking car just honk *La Cucaracha?*" Sadao mumbled angrily.

Sadao's knees were kicked out from under him and the gun at his back moved to his temple.

"No funny business!" He was reminded. The Mustang purred across the open space and skidded to a stop somewhere ahead of where Sadao knelt in the pine needles. Loose rocks hit his knees and he smelled exhaust.

"Hola! Amigos!" The voice was Lupe's - lower and more mature, but Lupe's nevertheless. The pirates fired off their guns in celebration and cheers went up in Spanish amid more blares of his augmented car horn. On a good day, Sadao could understand basic conversational American-Spanish but these guys were Old Country and spoke too fast for his ears. Something about *we are honored to meet the great Lupe Escovado. Our hero!*

Shit.

What happened the next hour or so amid cheers of "Viva la Sasoris" could only be best described as a drunken pistol-popping joyride around the valley floor in his beloved automobile. At first Lupe seemed to be behind the wheel, but that soon degraded to some asshead behind the stick, grinding gears and spinning tires with overzealous amateur driving shenanigans.

Sadao growled in seething hatred for the entire planet's pirate population behind his gag. Knees going numb on the cold ground and hip screaming in pain, he shivered through it until it sounded as if Lupe had managed to park the free-for-all and was coaxing Mexico's finest into negotiation talks.

He caught, "How much for the fugitive?" and after an exclamation involving the Holy Mother from Lupe it got down to: "He's not worth that much even alive..." and "What about his cigarette bill?"

Okay, maybe they had a point there.

In the end, cash exchanged hands in a large bag-sounding thing. More celebratory gunshots were fired - enough to rouse the Canadian Forestry Division who sent out a helicopter to fly over the valley to investigate. As soon as the propellers came into earshot, the Lupe Escovado fan fest was over and pirates could be heard running for the cover of the deep forest.

Lupe tugged Sadao's gag off and gave his shoulders a shove. "Come on, Boss! We

gotta move!" Sadao pitched forward, teeth in the dirt.

"Can't! Leg is asleep!"

"Shit, shit, shit!!" Lupe hauled Sadao to his feet and half dragged him, hands still tied behind his back to the passenger's side of the car. He grabbed Sadao by the waistband of his borrowed pirate pants and stuffed him in the window head-first where his skull collided with the horn.

Buppa beeppa, buppa beeppa, buppa buppa buppa bup!

"Itai! Baka na Mexica-jin me!! Teme wo koroshite yaru!"

"Don't kill me until I get us out of helicopter view!" Lupe shouted, piling himself into the opposite window and hitting the gas.

The Mustang leaped into gear and wheels spinning, made for the nearest dark forest road. Sadao rolled around in the passenger's seat until he could sit up and work the damn blindfold off his eyes without the use of his bound hands. What greeted his vision was a purple velvet-covered dashboard accented with little white LED lights that spelled out "Escovado" along with various resident jeweled rosary, prayer cards and a glow-in-the-dark Virgin Mary with a fuzzy lamb companion.

"What the fuck did you do to my car, Lupe?!"

"Chill, Boss!! Let me get us out of this shit first! Then you can beat my head in, okay? You still see that chopper?!"

Sadao struggled to free his hands. No luck. Otherwise, they'd be wrapped around Lupe's neck. He tore his eyes away from the auto's ghastly interior and leaned his head out the window, watching the treetops whisk by. The sun was falling behind the mountain tops - soon they'd be safely in total darkness. "No! I think we lost it! Pull over!"

"Not yet, let me get us deeper in!"

Sadao popped his head back in. *"Yamero! Ima sugu!"*

"Okay! Okay! I'll stop!" Lupe seemed to still know Sadao meant business when he yelled at him in Japanese and slowed the car to a stop under a huge trio of pines. "We're parked, okay? You can stop screaming in my ear!"

"Get out and come untie me!"

Lupe obeyed. He climbed out and came over, reaching in with his belt knife to cut Sadao's bonds loose. Soon as he was free, Sadao lifted himself out of the window, took one step towards Lupe and clocked him with a solid right punch. Lupe fell back against the tree holding his bruised jaw.

"Fuck! You'd think a guy could get a little thanks for risking his neck to save his old boss!"

Sadao ignored him, his eyes were too horrified by the new paint job on the outside of the Obsidian. It was all pinkish purple now with starry swirls and "Escovado" in elaborate hispanic cursive. The racing number was changed to 33. Shit, it was like he'd been asleep for a hundred years.

"I have rims, Lupe!" Sadao yelled. "They are fucking rotating!"

"Sorry man, okay? But you've been away awhile and you know, shit changes…"

"They don't need to change this much! This car was a classic, Lupe! A rare 1968 piece of sleek black and silver chrome perfection you clearly never learned to appreciate!!"

Lupe stepped away from the tree cautiously. "Look Boss, you gotta understand. I had to trick her out a bit for the *piratas*. These guys wouldn't have been game to your rescue if I hadn't promised them a good time, you know? They're fans!"

"It's a fucking pimp mobile!"

"It's … I can tone it down, I guess…"

"Tone it down? She needs to be put out of her misery! Given a decent burial! Give me the fucking keys!"

Lupe sighed and dug in his pocket for the chain. "Here, but…"

Sadao swiped them out of his hand. "You shut the fuck up and pray I don't leave you here tied to a tree for the bears!"

Sadao shuffled stiffly to the driver's side and after a sad attempt to lift his bad leg in, had to accept Lupe's hand up to get him in behind the wheel, which was covered in some kind of pink fake fur.

"Knife!" Sadao shouted when Lupe slid in the passenger's side.

"Oh man, you gonna fuck up my ride?"

"It's not your ride!" Sadao snapped and helped himself to Lupe's side knife. Lupe whimpered in misery as Sadao cut the fluffy abomination from the steering wheel and tossed it out the window.

"Stop sniveling and show a little self-respect!" he bellowed, starting the engine with a roar and yanking down the dangling fluffy dice which he tossed out the window as they pulled out.

Lupe kept his tongue to himself as they drove out, lights off, on a dirt back road heading through the forest.

"Am I going the right way?" Sadao snapped at his reluctant passenger after a few minutes of aimless turns.

Lupe rolled his eyes. "Sure, if you want to head back to America and *prison*."

Sadao slammed on the brakes. "Then start talking!"

Lupe described a circuitous route back North through a number of difficult-to-find forgotten roadways that Sadao had to turn the lights back on in order to locate. He couldn't hold back a comment when he found a few extra flashing settings had been added to the electrical controls.

"If this car's rear-end starts bouncing, I'm putting you in the trunk!"

"No fancy shocks man, okay? She's still race-worthy!"

"She'd better be," Sadao snarled as they hit a bad pit in the road. It threw him forward against the steering column and the force he used to slam on the brake sent his bad leg into spasm.

"*Kuso!*" Sadao pressed his forehead to the steering wheel in silent agony.

"Jesus, Boss. You okay?"

"Do I look like I'm fucking okay?!"

Lupe looked extremely concerned. Maybe the kid did still have a shred of loyalty left to him. "Hang on, Boss! Don't move!"

Lupe scrambled out his window as the car sat in the middle of the abandoned road, idling.

He came over to Sadao's side and reached in. "Hey man, come here." His voice was full of worry. Sadao sighed in defeat, allowing himself to be lifted out to the ground. He couldn't stand any weight on the leg after all the abuse it had suffered that day and Lupe wrapped his arms around him, bracing him up.

"Sorry I hit you," Sadao said as the young man held him, waiting for his pain to ease. He noticed that Lupe had grown at least two feet in his absence.

"Don't worry, Boss. I'll get you back for it," Lupe said, patting his back. "Wouldn't have a race car to pimp out if it weren't for you taking a bullet for the team. And probably would have died a sack of bones on a street in San Diego, too, if you hadn't found me as a kid. Love you for that, you bastard."

"Yeah, I'm a real hero," Sadao groaned, grateful for the kid's sturdy arms. "Shit day. Just get me someplace safe where I can have a shower and a cigarette."

"You got it, Boss."

Sadao sat at the end of a motel bed in a towel, smoking and watching Lupe in the reflection of the dirty mirror, fussing about with the CB radio unit he'd brought into the darkened room from the car on a long cord.

"Fuck this piece of shit!" Lupe said, as he slapped the side of the box. The aging device sprang to life with a hiss and a dull yellow glow. Lupe began fiddling with the dials, scraping out a mini-orchestra of static.

Sadao watched the red tip of his cigarette rise to his face and temporarily illuminate his features as he inhaled. He was oddly fascinated by the visage in the mirror. It was someone who resembled himself and yet was almost a stranger. His hair hung down wet against his shoulders. His eyes seemed darker and his nose sharper than he remembered. The beard was damp and long. He twisted it idly with his fingers into a point

- not unlike how he used to wear it in his twenties, braided with a pearl. Centuries ago, it seemed.

"Fucking bands are all crossed this late at night - I can't get shit!"

Sadao finished his smoke and leaned forward to crush it out in the ashtray on the scuffed pressboard desk, sending his foreign face back into more comfortable shadows. They hadn't been able to make it all the way back into camp. The night was too dark and the car was running too low on gas. Whistler was the last real town before the final 90 minute winding alpine climb. It looked as if they'd have to rest here for the night until the town's one gas station opened in the morning.

"You need to move the dial more slowly," Sadao commented. "Use the squelch."

"I am moving it slowly!" Whap, whap. "Cheap old puta is what this is!"

Sadao turned to look at the young man, now broad shouldered and much stronger than he last remembered him.

"How's Mouse?" he asked.

"Huh? How's who? Oh, now you ask about him! Fine and probably ready to kill me if I don't get you home to him tonight!"

Sadao scooted back up against the loose headboard and fit a lumpy pillow behind his head. "You should go on. Buy fuel at first light and head back alone."

Lupe stopped his dial abuse and squinted at him in the dimness of the night light. "Are you fucking nuts, Boss? Leave you here? He'd fry me alive! We gotta get you back to camp before people start asking questions."

"Leave me the rest of the ransom. I'll get a bike and GPS - come in on an off-road route. Safer for you and the others that way."

"What rest of what ransom? Those cabrones cleaned me out of more than gas, man!"

"I've seen what you stashed in your jacket hood lining. Looked to be $6K or more. Plenty for a used bike and some decent clothes." Sadao had no intention of strolling into camp in a poncho.

"That," Lupe said, agitated, "is my hazard pay!"

Sadao laughed. "Right. Taga may have been frivolous in this venture - but he's not that generous."

"Forget it. I come back without you, I'll need twice the hazard pay."

"Mouse doesn't know you're here, does he?"

Lupe shrugged him off and resumed band screeching.

"He doesn't know *I'm* here." It was not a question.

Lupe's shoulders gave. "Okay, okay, that's fucked up, I know. But ... New Boss, he didn't want Mouse getting caught up in this. He didn't want *me* getting caught up in this. But he had no choice. Javier's compadres wouldn't make a deal for you if I wasn't part of it, get it?"

"How long have you been keeping this operation a secret?"

Lupe was not pleased with this line of questioning. "Long enough, okay? And I feel like a total *puto* for it. Mouse would give his left nut to be here right now banging on this damn box. But Tagata-san thought he'd be the first guy the bounty hunters tailed if they got any hint of survivors."

Sadao eased his head into the least uncomfortable lumps. "A lot of men died on that ship."

Lupe nodded. "A lot of murderers."

"Not all of us were murderers…"

Zweeeeeeeee! "Whoa! Hang on, bitches! Lupe Escovado has the magic touch!"

The signal, weak at first, became stronger as Lupe sent out a series of clicks to alert the receiver to turn on their descrambler set to a related code only known to members of the Sasori team. There was a long pause and he pinged it again. Soon after the second attempt an answering "ready" ping was received followed by a voice. "Lupe? What the fuck? You know what time it is?"

"Haha! 3:13 A.M., my friend! You won't believe the night I've had!"

Sadao sat up despite the pain in his leg. He forced it across the mattress to snatch the receiver from Lupe's hand.

"Hey! I was getting to you!"

"Lupe, what the hell is- "

"It's me, *Konezumi*."

Dead silence. Sadao looked to Lupe who shrugged. Static, then an answer.

"Baby…? Is that you?" His voice sounded so small, it was both sweet and painful to hear.

"Yes. I'm here. I'm out."

"But what- ? Why, How?! Lupe?!"

"He picked me up. Long story, I'm afraid. Too long for this band to be safe. I will tell you when I see you. We ran low on fuel and--"

"See me? When? Oh God-! Baby, don't move! I'll come to you. Tell me where you are! Are you safe?"

"I'm safe enough for now. You'll have to trust me on that." Scrambling noises could be heard in the background whenever Mouse took the mic. "Mouse, please. Just stay and wait for me."

"I'm done waiting, asshole! I get no word from you for two fucking years and now you tell me you're holed up with my used-to-be best friend someplace he didn't fucking tell me about and I can't come see you?! Fuck that!"

Sadao couldn't hold back a grin - so Mouse. "Listen to me, *Konezumi*. You need to wait. It's not safe yet. We have to make careful moves to bring me in."

"I can't, okay? I can't sit and wait for you anymore. Please baby, I have to see you! I don't care if you're on the moon, I'm coming!"

Although choppy with cross signals, the desperation in his voice came through like a bell.

"Shhh ... calm yourself. Mouse. Listen. I am sending Lupe on ahead," he said as Lupe gave him a "what the fuck" look. "It's better if I come in alone."

"But - !"

"I insist. If you try to come find me I'll be gone. I need time, Mouse. Do you understand?"

"Time? Why? How much time?"

"Just a little longer. I promise I will come to you. I just don't move as fast as I once did."

The line was quiet.

"Don't sulk, *Konezumi*."

"I'm not! I'm not! Fuck, why do you have to make this so hard?"

"I am sorry for that. But I promise I will come to you very soon."

" .... "

"Mouse?"

" ... yeah?"

"Be ready."

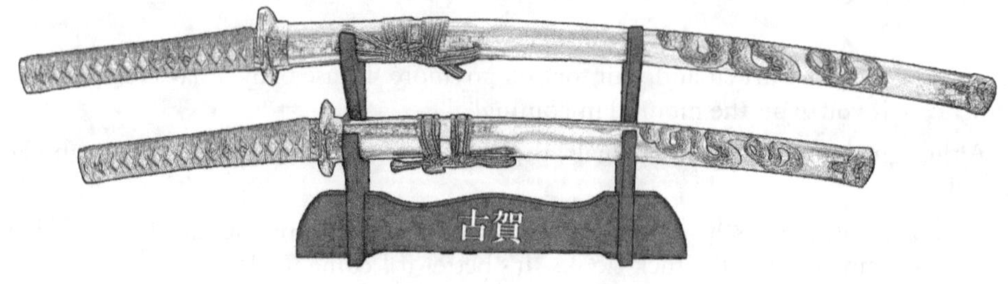

Chapter VIII

Song of the Pines

Mouse paced the cabin floor biting his thumb, which had long since turned prunish and red. He didn't have a proper watch, but he could tell by the angle of the sun that the day was growing too long for comfort. He knew Sadao would have to travel cautiously on off-road trails most the way up to avoid being seen, lest it become known he'd survived his prison ship sinking.

"Give me time," he'd said. "I don't move as fast as I once did."

Mouse played the words over and over in his head as he crossed the creaking wooden planks of their soon-to-be new home. Was he expecting too much? This little love nest he'd spent months to clean and repair, ostensibly to keep Sadao in a warm safe place come winter, was more about suiting his own desire to have a private space where they could live apart from the noise and distractions of the daily life of the Sasori team. Tagata was Boss now. Sadao would not be expected to work as hard as he once did, but what if …

Mouse stopped his nervous pacing and sat on the bench near the stove, rubbing his forehead. The little ring of silver Sadao had made for him was a constant subtle pressure against the skin between his legs. Damn that man for placing it in such a sensitive spot! He was reminded of it every time he moved and ached for its twin.

Nearly two years … who waits for someone this long after just a short affair? They'd been together, what - nine weeks? Between all the chaos and drama, did that even count as a relationship? Sadao would without doubt return to his people, but would he return to him? Maybe he had come already and had gone past the path to the cabin and headed straight for the campsite down by the lake? He didn't have a phone up here. The radio … nothing but static unless Tagata or Lupe hailed him. And they were getting tired of answering his half-hourly calls of "Have you seen him yet?"

Dammit! Weren't Japanese supposed to be punctual? Mouse rose to his feet and lifted off the bolt that secured the heavy door. He threw it open and marched out onto the porch that ran from the front to the lakeview side of the two-room rustic home. From the South-facing edge of the redwood rail, he could just see the cluster of trucks and trailers dispersed along the shoreline below. The afternoon breeze sang through the pines, carrying with it the sounds of distant voices and motorbike engines. Mouse scanned the endless treeline.

Baby, where are you? Do you miss your home? Do you miss your Mouse?

Mouse hugged himself and hitched a leg up on the railing, watching the sun slowly sink closer to the peaks of the far mountains. It was getting cooler at night now. And the days were growing shorter and shorter. Winter would be here soon and with it, the snow.

He closed his eyes and leaned his buzzing head against a post that held up the porch roof and listened to the sounds of the mountains. He faintly heard the roar of the pines, which always grew stronger at sundown, the smell of distant campfires, the bugle of an elk many miles away ... all of this he wanted to share with Sadao. Alone together in this quiet place above the bustle of camp, he wanted to do all the things he'd promised himself he'd do for him if he could just come home and now it was ...

Mouse's eyes flew open - cycle engine. Between the chorus of the trees it was there. It was coming from the upland road, not the lakeside below. His boys would be collecting the vehicles by now, and stowing the equipment for Lieutenant Lupe to come before day's end to secure the garage truck in his absence. Mouse moved from the side of the cabin slowly to the front, straining his ears. His heart was pounding so loudly it was hard to tell exactly what he heard. He moved to the front steps and waited - his breath coming in measured gasps so he could listen between them. That engine was something new, heavier - unlike the lightweight racing class bikes in camp. Only Sadao and Shiratori had moved by cruiser and the sound was drawing closer.

Soon a headlamp could be seen darting and flashing between the tall trunks of the pines until it lit the incline toward the cabin. Mouse took an uneasy step back toward his open door... just in case. But the bike, a silver and black touring Kawasaki, made the quick turn off the main trail and ran straight up his drive to stop at the foot of his front steps. The engine idled as the driver put his booted foot down to steady the bike and removed the shielded helmet. A ponytail of dark hair came to rest on the man's shoulder. Mouse took a step forward. The driver set the helmet on the dash and brushed the stray hairs back from his face to turn and squint up at the cabin in the fading light.

"Hey, cowboy," Mouse said, putting a hand on the porch post to steady himself. "Welcome to Canada."

Sadao shut off his engine and dismounted slowly. Mouse's smile faded as he could see the action clearly pained him. He watched him stretch the hip briefly before taking a step forward.

"Sorry I'm late. Squirrels."

Mouse found his smile again and rushed down the steps to bombard him with a hug. Strong arms came around him and wrapped him up tight in the scent of fresh leather. "Ohh..." was all he could manage to say as he pressed his nose to the man's neck and held him as close as he could. New bike. New clothes. Same scent. *Sadao.*

Sadao's gloved hand stroked the back of his braided head as he moved to kiss Mouse's ear. *"Tadaima, Konezumi."*

"Oh! I know that one! I know it!" Mouse said, pulling back just enough to look up into his eyes. Even in the failing light their shape and color were true - Japanese almond brown. *"O-Okaeri,* right? Tagata taught me that!"

"Very good," Sadao said, caressing his cheek. "Your r's have improved."

"I practiced…" Mouse was too taken in by the new face of Sadao to elaborate. He'd lost a lot of weight, that was obvious, but the hair - the beard. There was so much more of it. He touched the man's chin with his fingers, pawing through it like a curious child. "So soft…God, I want … mmmngh … "

Sadao's kiss was full and firm. The beard cushioned his chin as a warm tongue sought his and drank him in. The feel of being in Sadao's arms again made Mouse want to crawl right up into his leather riding jacket and build a nest for the winter. Their tongues swirled and caressed, intensifying and softening as hands wandered over bodies, saying hello. He'd never forgotten how good Sadao could kiss, but somehow it was like time had collapsed and they were back in Arizona, kissing in the desert wind.

But here at 7,500 feet, the wind was cold and the sun had dipped behind the peaks when they finally drew apart to breathe. Mouse leaned his forehead against Sadao's shoulder, giddy with happiness. His hair was more mussed than usual and somehow the back of his shirt had been pulled up and a gloved hand had found its way down the back of his jeans where it was squeezing his ass affectionately.

"Are you going to show me in, or do I have to fuck you on the stairs in front of the elk?"

"Ahh yeah, sure…" Only now was Mouse aware of the pounding bunched-up knot of dick in his jeans. He felt his way across the leather crotch in front of him and rubbed his palm over the impressive bulge there. "Jesus…"

Sadao groaned and pulled him closer. Mouse wanted to drop right there and spread in the gravel driveway. "Now?"

Sadao laughed. "Maybe we could. But it's been a long ride, I'd prefer a shower and a bed."

Mouse lifted his head, dizzy from their embrace. "Mngh, yeah, I have one of those!"

Sadao grinned and kissed his nose. "Good. Show me."

Mouse grabbed his hand and tugged him forward. Sadao came more slowly and limped to the foot of the stairs. Here he paused, lifting his arm to motion Mouse to tuck under and help him up the flight.

"Oh, sorry!" Mouse complied, lending him his shoulders and helped his lover ascend the steep flight one difficult step at a time. Sadao grit his teeth and looked as if he was getting the leg to move out of sheer intimidating will. Mouse had no idea the injury was still so difficult for him.

"Stairs," Sadao gasped as they reached the top. "Still a problem for me."

"I'll fix it!" Mouse announced. "We don't need stairs! Who needs stairs?"

Sadao looked around, amused. "Are you going to lower the whole cabin? I'll be fine. I need the practice. The view is well worth the climb."

Mouse's heart was pounding. He felt so disappointed in himself. Of all the preparations he'd made, he hadn't thought about the leg, nor realized how debilitating it was.

"Hey," Sadao said, kissing his mouth. "Forget it. Show me inside."

Mouse took his hand, adjusting his exuberance to move at the speed of Sadao's pronounced limp. He brought him into the main room and secured the door behind them, inviting him to remove his jacket and gloves.

"You can hang your things here by the door. I put up lots of hooks, see? Sorry, it's getting a little dark in here. I'll get a fire going!" Mouse rushed over to the potbelly stove and threw in a few logs. He cranked on the gas, struck a match and the pinewood stack lit up in orange hues. He closed and latched the stove door and brushed off his hands, rejoining Sadao whose eyes were following the high beams of the structure. "It heats up really fast. And it's bright! I use the top for heating water."

Mouse took Sadao's hand and pointed to the far wall, where a counter ran along under the north-facing double paned windows. "We have a sink," he said, bringing Sadao to it. "There's a hand pump for the well water," he said, giving the device a demonstrative crank. "We have an endless water supply here and it tastes amazing! Are you thirsty? Hungry?"

Sadao eyed him warmly. "A glass of water would be fine."

"You got it!" Mouse upended a mug and splashed a pump of fresh water into it, passing it to Sadao.

"Thanks, *itadakimasu*." He took a good drink and set the mug back on the counter, wiping his beard on his long sleeve. "Where do you sleep?"

"One-track mind, cowboy? Come here," he said, taking his hand again. "I'll show you the best feature."

At the opposite end of the main room was a door. He led Sadao to it and pushed it open to reveal a nice cozy bedroom dominated by a wide soft bed covered in quilts and furs, held up by a homemade log frame. The room also had a traditional fireplace and chimney made of rough cut stone.

Sadao sniffed the air. "It smells new ... did you build this?"

Mouse beamed. "I renovated it. With some help from the team. We did it Amish-style. Spent last spring and fall making a half dozen old cabins up new again. Canadian teams aren't particularly nomadic - heavy winters - which trust me, you don't want to spend in an aluminum box. Cold as fuck!"

Sadao moved through the room, taking it all in. "Where is my trailer?"

"Down by the lakeside in camp. You'll have to fight Lupe for it, through. He's an active racer now. Won an all-around in a regional competition last spring. He's a force to be reckoned with." Mouse looked aside as Sadao opened the double doors of the armoire and slid a drawer open to find his personal effects, most of the clothing-related ones anyway, neatly stowed. "He feels he earned your abandoned space after I moved your things in here with me."

Sadao found his katana hanging from a nail near the bed and fingered the silk fringe that dangled from the strap. "How strange," he said softly. He turned back to Mouse. "I always thought one day I'd like to live in a place like this. Somewhere quiet. It's perfect."

Mouse sighed in relief. "I just wanted you to feel at home."

Sadao moved to him and took him back into his arms, pressing their groins together and kissing his cheek. "I am home, *Konezumi*. I have no doubt of that. We can talk later. Now, all I want is a hot shower and *you*."

Mouse moaned and smiled. "Then, I think you're really going to like the bathroom."

Off the bedroom was one last door. It led to a pine-floored room with a toilet, washboard and shower. At the end under a big window was a large barrel-shaped sealed wooden tub half-surrounded with decking.

Sadao backed Mouse into the warm steamy space, releasing his mouth from his urgent kisses only long enough to shed both of their shirts. Strong, sculpted arms and shoulders tempted him. He crushed Mouse to his chest and began devouring his neck hungrily, taking bites.

"Ouch! Hey! Easy! Don't send me to the medic tent!"

Too long to go without hearing his voice. Too long to go without feeling the heat of his skin against his own. Sadao was so focused on taking heaping mouthfuls of Mouse, it was a minute or so before he even bothered to look around. He sucked Mouse's neck and shoulder another moment before it sank in, what was causing all the steam to rise in the room. Coals were burning in a heating bed just below the flooring. He held the face he'd missed so terribly between his hands and blinked at the pale blue eyes in wonder.

"You built an *ofero*? How?"

Mouse grinned up at him. "Oh, it took some doing, believe me. But like I said, we have plenty of water here. And wood .. and coal. I studied some plans I found in an old magazine at the Vancouver library and thought, why not?"

Unwilling to let go of Mouse, Sadao kicked the covering aside with his foot. Hot shoulder deep water awaited them. His dick tightened. "Shower," he croaked. As much as he wanted to throw Mouse in and have his way - the Japanese in him refused to soil the water.

"Here," Mouse said, pointing to the wall spigot. He cranked it on over their heads and Sadao jumped back to get out of his leather pants and boots before he ruined them utterly. Stripped properly naked now, he tossed them away at a safe distance and met Mouse under the spray.

"Wash me," he ordered as he made for Mouse's belt. He could see and feel the hard mound under his knuckles as he worked the tongue loose.

Mouse scrambled for the soap bar, lathering Sadao's chest and his own before going for his cock. Sticking straight out and hard as hell - the sensation of Mouse's soapy fist moving up and down his shaft was unbearably arousing, but Sadao didn't have the words to tell him to stop. Instead, he grabbed his young lover by the braids and kissed him, thrusting into his hand.

In another minute he had Mouse freed and stripped of his wet jeans and shoes. Fully naked, his cock was a beautiful sight - long and angular with a flushed tip. Sadao had a weakness for Mouse's pale pink flesh. He'd dreamed of it - gripping the engorged organ in his fist, stroking it, teasing it, sucking it dry. He sank to his knees, ignoring the protest from his hip and relaxed his throat to take him down in one gulp.

"Aaaaaahhh!! Oh shit! Oh shit!!!"

Sadao sucked him voraciously - all the way in and out again, swirling his tongue around the pert pink tip. He rolled Mouse's balls in his palm, wiping up trailing soap bubbles and sliding them between his thighs. He felt Mouse's fingers tangling in his wet hair, pulling it loose from its band. Eager precum oozed from his dick onto his tongue. He spat it into his hand to work the slickness up between Mouse's cheeks. He sought the silver ring and flicked it, rubbing a fingertip around Mouse's asshole, making him scream.

"Oh, fuck! Baby, slow down … it's been a while … I'm gonna … oh, GOD!"

Sadao sucked him hard and slipped one long finger straight up into his ass, right on target.

"Oh fuck, FUUUUCK!!! Aaaagh!! Aaaahh!!!"

Mouse's hips bucked uncontrollably as his dick filled his mouth with hot shots of cum.

"Oh God, oh God … "

Mouse convulsed a few more times before he pulled out and dropped to his knees in front of him, panting. "I thought I was gonna faint," he said weakly, sinking into Sadao's arms.

Sadao held him, rubbing his damp back. "Shh…just breathe."

Mouse's arms wound around his waist and kissed the orochi head inked on his chest. "Missed you," he whispered as the shower sprayed down over them. "I missed you so much. I want … " Mouse's groped for Sadao's hard dick and squeezed it. "I want all of it … can't wait anymore."

"You'll get it," Sadao promised. "Go enter the tub. I'll wash fast."

Mouse was waiting for him waist deep in the water, panting and working his cock up into another willing erection.

"No need to jump ahead," Sadao said, stepping in. He held onto Mouse's shoulder to aid him in swinging the bad leg around.

"I'll make stairs!"

"Shh! No more talk," Sadao said, pulling a steamy Mouse into his arms. He held the back of his head and kissed him deeply, rubbing his dick into Mouse's groin. They were both hard and straining against each other in seconds.

Ah! What a joy to be so aroused again, so single-mindedly focused on pleasure. Sadao reveled in it, as Mouse's strong hands ran all over his back and ass, grabbing and squeezing, moaning into his mouth. Sadao couldn't get enough of his taste. He kissed Mouse so hard it was a challenge to breathe.

"Nngh - !" Mouse's mouth wasn't nearly enough to sate his lust. He pried the man off him and spun him around, bending him over the lip of the tub facedown on the decking. He reached around and grabbed Mouse's erection in his fist, feeling the force of blood pounding through it. He bit his shoulder. "Show it to me," he growled. "Show me my jewel…"

Mouse whimpered and complied, laying his chest flat against the decking. He spread his legs as wide as he could and tilted his perfect round ass upward for inspection. Sadao couldn't resist giving those sweet buns a good slap while Mouse howled for him, encouraging him.

Smack! Smack! Smack!

Hypnotic how the flesh trembled with each blow - how well the soft and hard contours molded to his hands as he grasped and pinched. He spread the reddened globes apart with his thumbs and there it was, ring of silver and black, right where he'd left it. He looped a finger through and tugged.

"Aaaaoooowww!! Fuck!!"

"Good. Still in tight."

Mouse bucked his hips angrily. "Of course it is! I've never taken it off!"

"No one's been here but me?" Sadao said through his teeth, giving the loop of silver a twist.

"Aaaahh!!" Mouse cried out as he worked the ring back and forth, testing its security. "Jesus! No! Fuck! Been blue-balling it for two fucking years, asshole!"

Smack! Sadao leaned in and licked the back of Mouse's neck. "Good boy…"

"Oooohh…." Mouse purred as Sadao let his piercing go and began to rub his engorged cockhead over the pinched hole above it. It felt tight as hell. Sadao knew he needed to really work it open when Mouse was this excited, but the bit of pink was too tempting and his need was too great. He aimed and gave it an urgent shove.

Mouse wailed and pounded the decking with a fist as Sadao's bare tip failed to com-

plete its task. "Fucking wait! I've got lube! I've got lube!"

Sadao grabbed a handful of wet braids, raising Mouse's head. "Where?" he growled. His dick was so hard he couldn't take another moment of being denied a proper fuck. Two years without sex, without Mouse - he was a frayed rope ready to snap.

Mouse struggled to reach for a basket of bottles on a nearby shelf. He grabbed for it and the whole thing tipped over into the tub - shampoo and shave cream went adrift between their legs.

Sadao kicked the bottles around with his knee. "Which one?!" he snapped.

"I-I think ... it's blue?!"

"You've got ten seconds before I pry you open and fuck you raw!"

Mouse moaned and fumbled about for the right tube, as best he could with Sadao still holding his hair. "This one, shit!! Stop gouging me with that thing! Did you forget assholes don't self-lubricate?"

Sadao grabbed the tube in his spare hand and bit the cap off, spitting it into the water. "I told you - be ready!" Tube in fist, he jammed the nozzle up into Mouse's asshole and squeezed out half the contents before tossing it aside.

"Christ, I'm not a fucking ball joint!"

Mouse's hole drooled with gel. Sadao took him by both ass cheeks and thrust all in with everything he had. Deep flesh sucked him down, squeezing him, sending a sensation of euphoria up his dick and into the pit of his groin. He ground himself around in the hot slickness, indulging in the feel of being balls deep in a man who enjoyed the feel of him just as much.

"Oh fuuuuck, babe. So good. Shit, you feel huge ... "

Sadao drew out slowly, watching the ring of flesh purse like it couldn't let him go. The sucking sound it made with ample lube resonated right up into his balls. Instinct took over Sadao's body and all effort narrowed into one hard point.

"Grab the deck!" he shouted and began to pound.

The view was incredible - Mouse, arms-out, grabbing the wooden planks, his wet muscles flexing across his shoulders and back against each thrust, sending surges of steamy water over the edge. His perfect pink opening - round and smooth, sucking him and spitting him back out with a slick coating of lube on each pump of his hips. The globes of his ass jiggled in approval each time they collided. And the pearl, locked in snug, raked and raked under Sadao's shaft, urging him on.

Nothing in this world had ever felt half as gratifying as fucking Mouse. Sadao didn't know if it was the shape of his ass, the way they fit together, or if it was the way Mouse moaned in shameless desire; always willing, always ready for more - as if there was no end to his capacity for sex. And yet he'd waited for 20 long months, giving himself to no one. That fact is what truly set Sadao's drive on fire. This beautiful, strong willful man was completely his. No one could taste this flesh. No one could see how this back arched in pleasure. No one could watch his eyes seal shut and his mouth drop open in abandon as he took it hard up the ass. Every thrust brought out a wail of guttural joy from his lips that no one else would hear - at least not if Sadao still had a katana hanging on his wall to make sure of it!

Sadao growled deep in his throat as he increased his effort, intensifying the friction. The bath water was at high chop and sloshed all over the sides, dousing the decking and soaking Mouse's hair as he wailed between waves. Sadao braced his hand against Mouse's back and thrust downward to drill his pierced dick into Mouse's prostate.

"I - oh gaaaahhnnnghh! Babe ... harder, fuuuuuuuuck!"

It was too much - the pressure was growing unbearably thick in his groin. The urge to come overwhelmed all other thought. There would be no slow indulgence of pleasures here. A dam was about to burst and despite the protest in his bad hip, Sadao was powerless to hold it back. He fucked harder, deeper, gripping Mouse's ass, forcing him back onto his cock. Something cracked in his hip, but he couldn't stop, not for a second to readjust as Mouse's ball sac smacked wet and solid into his own. He leaned into it, the pain screaming up his leg, giving in to the demand of his rising orgasm.

Mouse was shouting something about coming so hard it was "gonna blast the finish off the wood." *Good, good boy. Come for me ...*

"I'm gonna ... Aaaaaaaaghhhhhh!!!"

White streams doused the decking, mixing with the overflow. Mouse's asshole tensed and trembled inside. He clenched down on Sadao, caressing his shaft with his jewel - his treasure, his home.

Sadao climaxed, slamming his exhausted pelvis against his lover once, twice, and again, as his cum fought its way out of his spasming cock into hot gnawing muscle. He slammed home one last time and froze hip to ass, jerking involuntarily as his dick continued to unload two years of isolated frustration. He moaned into his lover's shoulder, his body collapsing from the effort. The hip failed him as he reluctantly withdrew and he fell back into the water with a splunk!

Mouse swam to him and caught him, settling him up against the curve of the polished wood, kissing his face madly.

"Oh God, baby ... smooch smooch ... that was so good, so good ... missed you ... smooch ... oh God, I missed you so fucking much!!"

Sadao relaxed into the rising water, utterly spent as his grateful Mouse cuddled up beside him and got the water running again to refill the lost gallons.

"God, that felt so good, baby ... baby? Sadao?"

"Huh?" he'd nearly fallen asleep. *Bad form, Koga.* "Hmn, sorry. Water feels good." For once the warmth and buoyancy combined with the euphoria of release eased the persistent throb in the leg. He felt like he was floating, which in fact, he was.

"Are you okay? I didn't hurt you, did I?"

Sadao forced his eyes open. Mouse was wide-eyed and worried. His wet hair rimmed his face like a wreath. "So beautiful..."

"What?" Mouse leaned an ear in.

Sadao cupped his chin and lifted his eyes where he could admire them. "Your eyes, so blue. I'd forgotten."

Mouse dipped his nose adorably and smiled. "Really?"

"Come here," Sadao said and kissed him softly on the brow. Mouse sighed and slipped back into his arms, hugging him under the water.

"I can't believe you're here," he said. "I dreamed this so many times. I didn't think it would ever happen - ow!! You pinched me!"

"Are you dreaming now?"

Mouse laughed and smacked his chest. "No, obviously! I'm too annoyed to be dreaming."

"How's your ass? Feeling okay?"

"It feels like a science experiment - but yeah, I'm good. Suffered worse, you know. From you! How's the leg? Are you okay? You were really going all out there for a while."

"Leg will recover. Besides, I have you to take care of me now. Set my bones to rights."

Mouse beamed. "I'll set your bones, alright! All your bones! So, you really like the cabin? It's not too far from camp, you know. Just a quick downhill, um, walk ... "

Sadao caught his hand and kissed it. "I love it. This ofero especially. I haven't lain in a bath since I left Japan."

Mouse kept on grinning, a sweet shyness on his face. Adorable. "I was worried you'd want your trailer back," Mouse said.

"No," he said, looping a dripping braid behind Mouse's ear. The braids did suit him well. "I want to stay in one place, build a real home with you. Be still for a while. Nothing in this world I want more than that."

Mouse made a sound that Sadao could only describe as pure joy. He gave Sadao a fierce full body hug, wrapping his arms clear around his middle and squeezing tight.

"Ooff..." Sadao flinched in pain.

"Oh! I did hurt you that time!" Mouse sat back, feeling for Sadao's mangled hip under the water. "Does it hurt to the touch?"

"No ... it's..."

"Wait..it's over here. You've got a red mark on your side, baby!" Mouse had found his stab wound and was pawing at the tender skin.

"It's nothing," he grimaced.

"What happened to you? It feels deep ... a stab wound?! Oh my God, what did they do to you?!" Mouse flew into full hospital mode. He kicked the drain to lower the water to have a better look. "You were hit with something! A knife?"

"Shiv and it's nothing. Don't worry about it."

"But ... the entry area is all red! Was this treated by a doctor? We need to get you to

Sensei, now!"

Sadao grasped Mouse's probing hand. "I'm not going anywhere but your bed to-night. I was hit by some punks a few days before I left prison. A goodbye gift, I think. They wanted to hurt me, not kill me. The wound will heal soon."

"Oh baby, I'm so sorry!" Mouse kissed his cheek. "I'm sorry I couldn't help you! I'm sorry you were alone!"

Sadao shushed him softly, wrapping a comforting arm around him. "I'm okay. I'll be fine. I have you to look after me now."

Mouse's face softened in fearful sorrow. "What else did they do to you?"

"Hey," Sadao said, touching his chin. "I'm an old combat soldier, remember? No-body fucked with me. Not that way. I was just caught off guard a moment. You should see the other guy, eh?"

Mouse brightened a little. "I bet he's missing teeth."

"More than teeth. Don't worry, *Konezumi*. I am home. And I'm not leaving for anything."

Mouse rode Sadao's cock slowly, astride the man now properly dried, bandaged, and slathered in antibiotic ointment. Mouse had tucked him safely in bed and kissed his wounds from top to bottom before settling down onto his cock with loving lips and hands. He couldn't help it. As much as he wanted to coddle the man, he was half mad with hunger for his body. As battered as it was, it still aroused him like nothing else. He took it slower this time, sucked his dick and licked his balls until he was hard and groaning for more. They were both starved for the years of physical contact lost between them. Mouse wanted to fuse Sadao up inside him and never let him go.

Mouse took his time grinding his lover's dick up and around inside him, working out every kink of tension still left in his ass. Lube and cum still oozed from his hole on each plunge. He had a towel by Sadao's hip as not to mess the bed. He didn't want to move Sadao unnecessarily for a linen refresh.

Pleasure wound up on each merge of ass to groin, flushing his skin and making beads of sweat bloom down his spine. A fire crackled in the brick fireplace, licking the log walls with light and shadows. Everything about this moment moved him - this was his home, his bed, his man. It was all finally here, filling him up with an aching hap-piness. Sadao's eyes were on him, his hands ran up and down his thighs, guiding him. Mouse couldn't help but move his hips a little more, a little faster, stirring up ripples of excitement too enticing to resist. His thighs shook with anticipation.

"Sshhh ... " Sadao whispered. "Take it easy. Relax your ass."

"Can't," Mouse panted, squeezing him inside. "Need this. Need to feel you … "

"You are feeling me," Sadao said, rubbing his rump. "You'll feel me even more if you slow down."

"Mngh … .ahh … it's too good … you feel … so … ohhhh … ."

Sadao took his cock and gave it a firm hold at the base. Mouse felt his dick thicken in his grip; the head grew shiny and smooth with engorgement. Sadao ran his thumb over the glossy cap and up and down the trails of bulging veins with attention to detail.

"You have a fine member, if I've never told you. Michaelangelo would weep."

"Uhgghh, I thought it was all about my ass … " Mouse groaned, forcing his hips to move less vigorously, trying to roll more slowly onto his lover. The sweet throb in his groin was nearing unbearable but he wanted it to last.

"It is all about your ass. But as you're facing me, I have something new to admire and I don't want it to vanish so quickly. Looks lovely in this light. All of you. I should be so lucky to enjoy a man this well made."

"I'm sure … you've had better."

Sadao glanced up from his flesh sculpture. "You don't take compliments well, do you?"

"Your timing is not … gaah … the best … shit, I can't take this!"

"You can take it. You can take a lot. I've seen it. Built of stronger stuff than most men and twice as resilient. A rare, rare find." Sadao's fingers slid around and down Mouse's hip to the place where they were joined. Rubbing the rim of stretched skin, he hooked a fingertip in to feel himself surge in and out. A deep look of pride came over his face. "I wonder, what would have happened to you if I hadn't found you out in the desert?"

Mouse sped up his rhythm. "Uh, I'd masturbate more?"

Smack! squeeze squeeze

Not the answer Sadao was looking for.

"All alone in that garage. Miles of empty sand and weeds. Tell me you didn't feel it that day."

Mouse's poor smacked ass and strangled cock were the only feelings Mouse could process at the moment.

Smack! "Tell me!"

"I feel, um … like I'm gonna blow!"

"Look at me," Sadao snarled, tugging Mouse's ass rim with his finger. "Look down at me and tell me what you see."

Mouse's thighs were burning as he bounced faster up and down. His ass was smacking against Sadao's thighs with each effort. Mouse's vision swam with lust. But he saw … oh he saw that sensuous mouth, those keen narrow eyes, those fucking muscles and smooth skin; the dark hair falling low now over the head of the snake inked into Sadao's shoulder.

"Um ... angh ... ahh ... you're really hot?"

And the understatement of the year award goes to…

Mouse couldn't stand another second of his dick being denied release and reached down to rub his blood-flushed head. Sadao smacked his hand away.

"You don't come until you answer me!"

Mouse threw his head back and moaned for mercy. Truth was when he was this worked up he could come just with his ass. But Sadao's fist had a death grip on him and his orgasm was going nowhere but teetering at the edge, building and building.

"Please, baby ... You feel so good - I can't take it!"

"I told you, you can take anything. You're stronger than you'll ever know. So open your eyes and tell me what I want to know!"

The fire at his back was heating Mouse's sweat to the boiling point. He was fucking Sadao's dick so vigorously now he could barely catch his breath. "Oh God! No one in this whole fucking world ever did this to me, okay? It's always been you! I felt it when we met, I felt it when we fucked and I felt it between my fucking legs all these last two fucking years! I feel it, okay? I feel it! Aaaaaagghhhhh…..!!"

He must have said the magic words because Sadao's iron fist slid up and jacked him like lightning. Mouse bellowed over Sadao's matching groans and a gush of jizz shot out of him and hit the headboard, followed by another and another. Third spooge of the night, too. Christ, this man could make him come like a firehose.

Mouse slumped forward onto Sadao's chest, gulping air. Sadao held him tenderly now, kissing his arm and shoulder, murmuring in Japanese as his emptying balls shook and quieted under Mouse's oozing ass. Filled to capacity, Mouse couldn't hold on to his softening dick and it slithered out with a splurt.

"Ii ko da. Ore no Konezumi."

Mouse raised his head when the pounding in his heart slowed to a manageable level. He wiped the sweat from his brow and focused on the face of the man lying beneath him. His half-closed eyes gazed back serenely. His hair ran loose on the pillow and Mouse couldn't resist the urge touch it. He twirled a few of the still damp tips around his fingers - silky smooth. He pawed at it, pulling it through his fingers over and over, savoring the feel.

"So much hair…" he breathed. "Love it…"

Sadao smiled and reached for a braid of Mouse - running it through his fingers.

"I see we've both gone through some changes," he said softly. "Some for the better."

Mouse felt heat warm his cheeks. He was suddenly shy again. He ducked his head to let the rest of his braids fall forward onto Sadao's chest.

"Taga has a deft hand to tame this hopeless mane."

Mouse smiled. It felt so good to smile. "Thanks, you can tell him yourself in the morning."

Sadao gathered more of the braids where they coiled on his chest. "Don't talk about morning yet," he said. "Let's just have this."

Mouse took his hand and kissed it. "I do remember you, you know. In my garage, acting all puffed up and proud of yourself - Mr. Big Shot Racing Team Boss, trying to impress me. I wanted to punch that smug grin right off your face."

"I remember. I wondered who this odd little man was - to show no fear. It made an impression."

Mouse drew a finger along Sadao's dark-haired chin. "I remember you went to leave. And you said my name - *Konezumi. 'Sayonara, Konezumi'* you said, and you walked away. I freaked out all of a sudden, you know? I called you back. I didn't have an explanation at the time but it was like I couldn't bear the idea of you walking away forever."

"I wish we could have met under better circumstances," Sadao said. "I was in a desperate situation and acted out of that desperation. If I've never told you, I'm sorry. I'm sorry you lost your home."

"Forget I mentioned that place," Mouse said, pressing a warm kiss to his cheek. "It's a million miles away in another life - a life I'm glad I was able to escape. Now there's only us and this cabin. Nothing else is important to me. There's food here to last us awhile, you know. I stocked up. You, my friend, need fattening up!" He gave Sadao's prominent ribs a poke.

"Hmm, guess I lost weight. Muscle more than anything. The leg kept me from my usual routines."

Mouse sat up and pulled the blanket aside to expose Sadao's mangled hip. The skin over the hipbone below his new bandage was a puckered mass of scars. He ran his fingers over the carnage. Sadao flinched and he stopped.

"Does it hurt?"

"No, just the feeling is strange. There's numbness…"

Mouse rubbed his thigh. "Can you feel this?" Sadao nodded. Mouse tried his calf - Sadao nodded again. He moved his hand over the foot and was shocked at the coolness he felt there. He reached under the covers for Sadao's right foot and was shocked again. His foot must have been warmed by the bathwater earlier. "Your left foot is so cold!"

"Circulation isn't the best. Surgeons got a few wires crossed during reassembly."

"But … this can't be good, I mean … " Mouse rubbed the foot more vigorously to warm it. "Can you feel this?"

Sadao watched his efforts placidly. He shook his head. "Just … some tingling now and again. And pressure when I walk."

"Didn't they give you any physical therapy or … " Sadao's raised eyebrow stopped him.

"Chopper of heads, remember? Let's say I received all the treatment I deserved."

"Baby, I'm so sorry."

"Don't be," Sadao said, motioning Mouse closer. Mouse threw the covers back over them and lay his head against Sadao's shoulder, rubbing the cold foot between his toes.

"I hate what they did to you," he said as Sadao stroked his back.

"This is not the time for hate or regrets," Sadao stated simply, kissing Mouse's forehead. "We are safe now. We can rest. Reconnect."

"I like the connecting part," Mouse said, smiling. "I wanna connect some more but …"

"Hm? What's stopping you?"

Mouse felt that strange shyness take him again. "I don't….well I … I don't want to overtax you."

Sadao laughed and kissed him soundly. "There is more than one way to connect, *Konezumi*. Some methods are less taxing than others. If you are so concerned about my well being, maybe you should experiment."

Mouse hugged him. "You're going to regret making that suggestion in the next few hours or so before I'm done with you."

Sadao tipped his chin up and kissed him with a warm tongue. "I doubt that," he breathed. "Show me."

The fire was dying down but the bed was still warm. Sadao loathed to leave it to set more logs on. Unlike his prison bed, this one was wide and soft, cradling his back, hip and warming the cold leg under a heap of blankets and furs. Pain was faint, only a slight dull throb. It would be sore tomorrow - sore from a long ride and all the exertion. It had hurt to work the joint that hard but the resulting pleasures and reward of release had been worth whatever regrets may come his way. Right now everything in his life was at peace. Still and quiet. To finally be able to just close his eyes and listen to the sound of the dying fire mingled with Mouse's breathing was perfection. He felt light inside, freed.

Sadao brushed an errant braid from Mouse's nose so he could watch his sleeping face in the amber light. The soft brown brows still carried a pinch of worry to them as he slept. His quick childlike breaths matched the pace of his eyes darting beneath pale lids, rimmed with a flicker of fine lashes. Mouse had fought off drowsiness for as long as he could, but only when nestled fast to Sadao's side with a protective arm thrown around his middle for reassurance did he finally succumb. Sadao stroked his arm lightly, feeling the tickle of fine hairs under his fingertips. Such a simple thing to lie here and hold his man while he dreamed.

What a strange and amazing creature you are, Konezumi.

Bright blue eyes half hidden under a mop of blond hair. The nose, a bit too big for the face, and the thin line of lips below was wholly endearing to him. Even in midst of his own exhaustion, Sadao longed to rouse this love, smother his mouth with kisses and once again possess his body. His cock stirred at the thought. He lowered his nose to breathe in the soft crown of tangles he'd missed so desperately.

Mouse twitched and his breathing skipped. His eyes shot open, wide and frightened. His hand gripped Sadao's arm. "What? Huh…?"

"Shhh, it's okay," Sadao breathed into his hair. "You were dreaming."

"Hmm … oh, thank God," Mouse sighed, hugging Sadao's waist under the blankets. "I thought somehow I was wrong. I thought I'd dreamed this." His eyes searched Sadao's in the dimness, asking for reassurance.

Sadao stroked his cheek. "I'm here. We're here in this bed. Together. Don't doubt it. Go back to sleep, *Konezumi.*"

Mouse relaxed against Sadao with a smile, sliding his hand down his chest. "I don't want to sleep. If I sleep I might lose you. I'd rather … whoa! Again?"

Sadao chuckled and kissed his forehead. "Later. It can wait for morning."

Mouse gave his find a squeeze. "Doesn't feel like it can wait."

Sadao took his groping hand and brought it to his lips. "We both need sleep now more than sex."

"I don't wanna sleep," Mouse said with a yawn.

Sadao gathered him even closer and tightened the blankets around them. "Can you feel my arms around you?"

Mouse nodded and rested his cheek against Sadao's shoulder. "Yeah. Feels so warm. I've never been this warm up here before."

"You will feel these arms and their warmth as you close your eyes and fall asleep. And you will feel them still as you dream. I promise you, I won't let go."

Mouse's eyes drooped and he rubbed at them. "Mmkay…"

Sadao held him and whispered into his hair until his sleepy little Mouse sighed and began to dream in peace.

Interlude I
2036 - 2048

First

The Castle

Sadao had seen the castle on the island many times, walking by his mother's side to the marketplace by the docks that rimmed Toba's curved bay. The centuries-old structure had many floors and windows, with a peaked roof of stunning blue tiles atop bright white walls. It shone in the sunlight of summer, rising above a backdrop of thick bushes and maple trees.

A shogun must live there, he thought. Like the ones in his storybooks his mother read to him at bedtime. He paused to look another moment at it by the tsunami barrier, scrambling up the concrete wall for a better view. In the calm waters of the bay, fishermen were busy casting nets under a bright blue sky of enormous billowing clouds erupting over the endless Pacific.

"Sadao-kun! Come!"

His mother's voice was stern as she tugged him off the wall; her grip was tight on his wrist as she pulled him along. Sadao struggled to keep up, wondering how his mother could move so fast in her full kimono dress of pale cherry blossoms, wrapped tight with a pink obi around her slender frame. Her wooden *geta* clacked loudly along the sidewalk as they moved through the busy marketplace.

"Okaasan! I want to see the boats!" he protested. On market days she always let him stop to see the boats.

"Not today, Sadao. I explained to you. Today is very important. We must not be late."

Sweat dripped down her neck from under her elaborate bound-up hairstyle. Obasan had risen early that morning to help dress his mother and prepare a quick breakfast of boiled rice and soy eggs. His mother didn't eat. Her face was powdered and her lips were painted red. He could not remember her lips being red before.

"Sadao-kun, you must keep up!" she said with another tug. And he did as fast as his three-year-old legs could carry him. To his amazement, she tugged him past the fish-

mongers' and farmers' stalls to the gateway that blocked the path to the high bridge arching over the bay to the central island.

"Okaasan?"

"Shh! No more talking!" she asserted, pulling him tight to her side. *"Remember to bow to everyone you see!"*

The guard promptly opened the gate and gave them both a welcoming bow. *"Ir-rashaimase."*

Sadao was so stunned he forgot to bow and his mother pushed his head down.

"Please be careful crossing the bridge," the man said to them with a warm smile.

Sadao stared up at him, mouth open as his mother dragged him past the opened iron doors and onto the arched stone bridge.

The island was bigger and more beautiful than Sadao could have imagined from any storybook. What looked to be a random flush of trees and shrubbery from the marketplace was actually an expertly designed garden of cut stone paths and bamboo beds. Brass lanterns hung everywhere at every turn in the path from trees and posts. Sadao could remember seeing them lit from the shores on New Year's Eve. The whole island glowed in wavering golden light. And now he was here! There was so much to see from the shimmering orange and white carp in the ponds to the stone faces of the statues, holding brimming baskets of harvested oysters. *Shinjyu-jima*, they called this place. Pearl Island.

"Okaasan! Itai! Stop pulling me!"

"Shh!" she hissed.

Sadao's mouth opened but not to speak. They had come to the very steps of the enormous wood and iron doors of the castle. A servant greeted them at the opened door and motioned them to enter. Sadao was so nervous he stopped dead in his tracks and bowed his heart out.

"Sadao! Not to her! She is a maid!" his mother whispered, standing him up.

"You said everybody…"

"Enough! Take off your shoes and do not make another sound!"

Inside, the maid collected their shoes and Sadao and his mother stepped up onto the tatami mat flooring. Sadao gaped at the magnificence of the entrance hall - the fixtures and walls were trimmed in dark polished wood. Calligraphy scrolls and gold foil rice paper paintings decorated the walls. The scent of blossoms wafted from an artful arrangement of fresh cut flowers in a vase on the wide tokonoma.

"Master is waiting," the maid said, dropping to her knees in her kimono to slide open a large *shoji* door immediately in front of them.

Sadao gasped as his mother pushed him down onto his knees and shoved his face to the floor to show utmost respect. What he had seen in that brief moment the door opened and before his nose was pressed against the woven mats was a real live shogun in full dress, seated upon a dais at the end of an opulently painted room of tigers and lions lunging at them from every angle.

Sadao looked in panic toward his mother who knelt next to him in similar pose, her arms out, palms upon the floor in supplication.

"Who is he?" he whispered.

Her black-lined lids flickered open. And in that moment, Sadao could see her fear mirrored his own.

"He is your father, Sadao."

Sadao loved his new home. It was a big palace of many floors and windows with special hidden doors and crawl spaces he wanted to explore. But there were also many rooms and halls he was forbidden to enter and his mother was always scolding him for climbing up into places where he wasn't allowed.

"Don't wander at night, Sadao-kun! You'll wake sleeping spirits!"

There was a little room at the top of the castle he especially loved. You could only get to it if you slid open a secret door at the end of the third floor hallway and scrambled up a ladder inside. So he'd wait until his mother fell asleep to creep out of their bedroom in his nightshirt and barefeet.

No one seemed to ever come up here. There was dust on the bare wood floor and windows. They were funny windows - all triangles and squares cut into the walls without screens or glass. They were shut with locking swivel pegs but Sadao managed to wriggle them open. Through them he could breathe the night air and see the long bridge from the marketplace that led to their island. It was the perfect spot to watch for visitors. Many people came to see his father and stay in their home as guests. Some would stay for many months but Sadao was forbidden to talk to them unless summoned.

Sadao scrambled on all fours to the little square hole and peeked out. Across the angled slopes and dips of the roof tiles, he saw a window he had never seen open before. It was way across on the other side of the palace. Someone was hastily shaking out a soiled bed cover. Sadao pushed his small face into the window hole to try and see more but his forehead got stuck.

Eeeeaaaooooww!! Uuuuugggghhhhh!!

An old woman's voice howled from inside the far away room. Sadao popped his head back in and shut the panel, locking it. He was so frightened! She must be a she-demon like his mother said! He scrambled back down the ladder, through the secret panel and into the hallway. It was dark and quiet. He froze, listening. He didn't know if the demon had seen him.

It was very quiet in the sleeping house but he could just hear an Ooooohhh! far away and muffled. He ran down the hall back to his room he shared with his mother and opened their screen too fast. It banged in the frame. His mother woke.

"Sadao! Shut the door - it's cold!"

Sadao padded in and slid under the futon cover next to his mother. She was very warm and he pressed his toes up against her leg.

"Sssss! Why are you so cold!"

"I went to toilet, Okaasan."

She opened her eyes and looked at his face. *"Your cheeks are red ... and dirty! Answer me with truth! Did you sneak away again?"*

He lowered his head.

"Sadao! Show me your hands!"

He raised them slowly. She grabbed them both and examined his palms.

"They are filthy!"

Sadao shut his eyes as she slapped both his wrists. Smack! Smack!

"Go wash! Your feet and hands! This is a clean house, not a farm!"

"Hai, Okaasan," he said and slid out of bed.

"And come right back! No more wandering!"

"Hai."

Sadao opened their door slowly and peered into the hall. The *otearai* was all the way down the backstairs. It was very far and very dark. He didn't want to go alone.

"Shut the door, Sadao!"

"Hai..!"

He stepped out and taking a big breath, ran down the long hall as fast as he could. He rounded the corner and half slid his way down the narrow stairway to the lower floor landing. The tiles were cold as he peeked around the corner. Someone was already in the washroom. The blue pair of toilet shoes were missing.

Sadao backed up and hid in the stairwell, waiting. Although his father's house was very large, it only had one washroom with sinks and laundry machines. The tiny toilet closets on each floor did not have sinks, so it was always a chore to come downstairs to clean his hands and face. *What if the demon is using the sinks? Did demons need to wash their hands?*

From where he stood, Sadao could only see the entryway to the laundry room area. Inside, a second inner glass door led to the steamy covered ofero and showers. With a household full of people and servants, the round bamboo basin was kept filled and hot day and night. Sadao's mother would always send him down to bathe with one or two of his older half-brothers to make sure he cleaned up properly.

Footfalls were shuffling up the maids entrance on the far side of the house. Since

Sadao was not afraid of maids, he leaned his nose around the corner. He saw a young women with short cut hair push the outside door open with her shoulder. In her hands she carried a basket filled with the soiled bedding he'd seen being shaken out of the demon's bedroom. It even smelled like a demon!

His heart pounded as he watched the maid slide out of her house shoes and into the pink pair of toilet slippers. She pushed the laundry door open with her hip. As she went in, Sadao could see past the laundry machines to the ofero room beyond. The inner door was propped open and inside a hideous boney figure stood hunched over shivering, as an older maid washed her backside with a rag. Her wrinkled skin was ghostly white. Sadao froze in fear as the crone raised her bald scraggly head and looked right at him!

"They're killing meeee ... " The demon rasped as the laundry door slammed shut.

Scared beyond his wits, Sadao ran over the tiles and past the laundry area toward the kitchen. It was a forbidden area of the house for him, but he had to wash his hands! And he wasn't heading back to the washroom - not with a demon in there! No way! He flew through the kitchen's split curtains and came face-to-face with his father. He was standing at the stove in his elegant gold and blue robes, his long grey hair bound up high on his head. He was fixing a pot of tea.

Sadao stared up at him wide-eyed a moment before he remembered his manners. He bowed deeply. *"Please excuse my intrusion, Otousan!"*

"It is late, Sadao-kun," his father said, adding a sachet of sweet smelling dried herbs to his steaming kettle to steep. *"You should not be out of bed."*

Sadao didn't know what to do. He'd never spoken to his father before without his mother present, and then only when they were summoned to his meeting chambers. In the past nine months since they'd lived here, Sadao had only seen his father occasionally at a distance on the property; during other times, he would be asked to join him with his brothers for formal dinners with business guests. Sadao was not allowed to speak during formal dinners. None of his brothers were either, except the oldest who was newly married. Women were not allowed.

"I apologize for my intrusion. I need to wash. And the otearai is full! Okaasan said - !"

"Ah, I see. Hurry then."

Sadao bowed a few more times, afraid to look up at his father. He went to the sink and on tiptoes, turned the water on to wet a small washrag with soap. Then he sat on a stool to wash his hands and feet.

The young maid with short hair entered when he was nearly done and seemed shocked to find him there.

She bowed to Sadao's father. *"Shall I take him up to bed, Goshujin-sama?"*

"I will take him," his father said, handing the steaming kettle to her. *"Give Obaasan this; it will calm her nerves."*

"Hai, Goshujin-sama."

"Come, Sadao-kun!"

Sadao snapped to his feet and tossed the rag in the laundry bin. He followed the golden hem of his father's robes from the kitchen and down the forbidden hallways to his father's private study. He stopped at the doorway, uncertain what to do.

"Come in, Sadao. Tonight, I will permit it."

The room was lit with colored glass lamps, giving the opulent room an unreal glow. His father seated himself upon a braided cushion and invited Sadao to join him on the padded stool opposite. Sadao sat and looked nervously around. So many books - Sadao liked books!

"Now, look at me, little one. Tell me what you saw."

"Huh?"

"In the otearai."

Sadao's breath sped up. He could not meet his father's eyes. *"A demon, I think. Otousan."*

"A demon? Yes, I can see that. What did this demon look like?"

"She ... was old and scary. She didn't have hair! She saw me!!"

"Are you scared of demons, Sadao?"

Sadao felt tears spring up in his eyes. He nodded.

"You do not need to be."

Sadao looked up into his father's eyes. They were narrow and grey, half buried in wrinkled folds. His face was long, angular, unlike Sadao's more squared features. At his chin his father wore a long white braided beard tied with a pearl. In the odd lamplight he too looked like a demon. Sadao began to shake.

Demons! I live with demons!

"Sadao-kun! Do not be afraid. You are a Koga now. Do you know what it means to be Koga clan?"

Sadao looked at the ornate floor rug under his toes and shook his head.

"Do you see those swords?"

Sadao followed his father's finger to where it pointed to the weapons stand on a polished table top near the wall.

"Hai, Otousan!"

"Bring me one," he said.

Sadao got up as told and walked cautiously to the table. There were two matching swords, both encased in silver and pearl inlaid lacquer scabbards in the pattern of a snake. One long sword and one short. Afraid of dropping it, Sadao chose to take the smaller one. He brought it to his father and bowed.

"Turn up the lamp," his father ordered. Sadao obeyed and the room became much brighter.

"Good boy, now come sit beside me and look."

Sadao knelt on the rug beside his father and watched him pull the blade from the scabbard. It was very shiny and looked very, very sharp. It slid out with a hiss.

"It's new!" Sadao proclaimed, in awe of the way his and his father's faces were reflected in the curved steel.

"No, in fact. This blade is very old. Older than this house. It belonged to my father's father's great-grandfather. It is a hundred and eighty years old. Do you know what this blade is called?"

"Katana!" Sadao said brightly. He loved samurai books and movies.

"No," his father corrected. *"That is the name of the long blade. This is its mate, the wakizashi. It is worn beside the katana."*

"Wakizashi…" Sadao repeated softly. He'd heard of that, but had never seen one up close. *"Seppuku sword."*

To Sadao's surprise, his father grunted - perhaps that was his laugh. *"Very good. You know much about samurai?"*

Sadao nodded eagerly. His fear was abating now that he was focused on something he liked. *"I like all the movies! I've seen them all! Even the ones in black and white! Those are the very best!"*

"Yes, they are. Did you know while you were watching those movies that you were watching stories about your ancestors?"

Sadao was stunned. *"Huh?"*

"The Koga family are Samurai Class. Your ancestors were all samurai warriors."

"Really?"

"Someday these swords may become yours."

Sadao smiled. *I'm a samurai! A real samurai!* But something troubled him. He'd seen all the films, the bloodier the better.

"But Otousan … how does the blade stay so clean?"

His father slid the short blade back into the scabbard. *"Because, my son, this wakizashi has never known blood. Koga warriors stand strong in their battles. Never surrender. Never commit seppuku."*

"Never?" Sadao was a little disappointed. In the movies, to slit open one's own belly was the ultimate sacrifice - the ultimate show of courage - to choose death over defeat or surrender. His father motioned for Sadao to return the small sword to the rack.

Just as he was placing it on the rungs his father added, *"The katana, however, has been bathed in the blood of our enemies endless times. Hundreds of men have lost their lives to its biting edge."*

Sadao stared at it. Long, black and sleek, sleeping in its snake scabbard. He decided he did not want to see what the blade inside looked like. He heard his father's robes shift as he stood. He came to Sadao and placed a hand on his shoulder.

"We are part of an ancient and proud family, my son. Koga men do not fear demons. Come, let's return you to your okaasan."

Upstairs his mother was kneeling at the door of their room, peering out.

"Sadao-kun! Where have you been!" she said, stepping down into the hall in her nightgown, angry. She grabbed his wrist and pulled him forward just as his father reached the head of the stairs. She prepared to slap him, but her hand froze at the sound of his father's voice.

"Yamero!" he commanded. *"Do not punish him. He was in my care."*

His mother fell to her knees and bowed all the way to the floor, begging his father's forgiveness for being the mother of such an unruly, uncontrollable child.

"He is only curious. That curiosity has been satisfied for tonight. Put him to bed gently."

"Hai! Hai! Gomen nasai! Goshujin-sama."

Sadao's mother didn't raise her head or stand up until his father left the hall. Then her eyes turned angry again as she got to her feet and grabbed his hand. *"I want to beat you until you cry!"* she wailed. *"But now he forbids it!"*

"Gomen, Okaasan. I saw the demon in the ofero!"

His mother pulled him back into their room and threw herself down on the futon, exhausted.

Sadao crawled up beside her. *"A real demon, Okaasan! With real fiery eyes and long black nails!"*

She took his hand and squeezed it, laying her head down on the pillow. *"She's not a demon, Sadao. She's just an old sick woman. Pay her no attention!"*

"An old woman … but … why does she live here?"

"Sadao! Why do you ask such stupid questions?"

"But, why?"

"Because she is your father's wife! Now lie down and sleep before I decide to punish you afterall!"

She's lying, Sadao thought, laying his head on the pillow next to her. *She's my mother and doesn't want me to be scared. But I know the truth! I am a samurai like my father! I am not afraid of this demon hag! We destroy evil. She is evil for sure! I've seen all the movies! Why else would my father be serving her poison tea?*

Second

Ienaki-ko

Toba-Kontaiji Terrace English School - 2045

Sadao could not remember the first time he noticed the little boy with the dirty skin and long tangled hair among the beggars. It seemed his small thin face had just been a blur among the rest of the hungry refugee children, who lurked about in the forest surrounding their small English school. It was a private school for exceptional students, taught entirely in the English language. Tuition was not cheap; the majority of the students came from the few wealthy, influential families in and around Toba who were involved in the pearl trade.

Sadao's father felt once he had reached the age of eight and still showed no signs of becoming a proficient farmer, that perhaps his youngest son's mind was better suited to books and studies. *"My little scholar,"* he called him, *" ... should be taught the language of international commerce and prosperity."* No more nets and boats for him. This was an enormous relief to Sadao; he would no longer have to suffer the effects of sea-sickness or need to scrub the stink of oysters out of his hair and hands.

The old hag that had haunted their home with her moans passed when Sadao was five, and soon after his father had married his mother in a small private ceremony. In the years that followed, it became clear that Sadao was the new favorite among his father's sons. Once only allowed to see his father at a distance, Sadao was now requested almost nightly to come sit by his side and read to him from his lessons of the day. Their relationship had become less strained, even though Sadao still felt his stomach rise into his throat whenever his father's servants came to fetch him. His mother's attitude had eased toward him, too. He was permitted a much greater range of freedom. He was even allowed to leave the island once or twice a week to go buy treats, books and entertainment from the Toba Marketplace.

Sadao's second eldest brother had moved off the island in the last 18 months. Married now, like his eldest brother, they both had their own homes further up the mountain valley. Sadao shared the large upstairs room with his remaining middle brother,

Yasuo. Yasuo wasn't very happy about being stuck with most of the farming chores, despite being assisted by many of their father's hired workers. Yasuo was slow witted but tall and strong for his 17 years, and would often knock Sadao about when no one was watching. Sharing a living space alone with him always put Sadao ill at ease. They each had their own beds at separate ends of the long room with a shoji screen between, but that didn't prevent his older brother from slipping past it to mess with his books and notes from school and to steal his marketplace treats.

"Shit devil!" he would call Sadao. *"School pansy!"* And other nasty names. Sadao hated him - he wished him dead many times over. Occasionally, bloody and sore from a recent beating, he would visit the island's small altar, light incense, ring the prayer bell and pray to *Kamisama* to exact his revenge.

But high above the valley at the small secluded school in the bamboo forest, Sadao could relax and be himself. Curious and bookish, he was soon a favorite among the senseis who taught their young male students language, arts, mathematics, history, philosophy, physical fitness and meditation. Sadao excelled at all of these subjects until the day came when they were to be instructed in the martial arts.

It was not unusual for a country school to teach *kendo* or *karate*. In fact, Sadao had participated in both to some extent. But this was different. The new senseis who arrived at the school ordered a classroom cleared out to serve as a proper dojo. The walls were soon stripped of Shakespearean quotes and hung with armaments, ranging from bow and arrow to spear and katana - real weapons with sharp shining blades.

On his first day of war-training, Sadao sat upon his knees on the floor in his new white *gi*, head bowed in focused mediation. He was in a circle with the other school boys his age-range. Their new martial arts sensei spoke.

"What you will learn in this room is not a game or an idle exercise. What you will learn are skills for survival and protection. You will be taught weaponry, attack and defense. We will tolerate no light-hearted attitudes! We expect total focus and obedience. Anyone who shows a faint or frivolous heart for these lessons will be dismissed from the school at once!"

Sadao's eyes shot open from his meditation. He was frightened. Some of the other students began to mumble and their sensei slammed a long bamboo shinai against the wall.

"Silence! Do you not understand the seriousness of your situation? Do you not understand why you must train hard and swiftly?! You have all grown too soft! Tell me why war-training, above all, is most important subject you will learn at this school?"

Sadao wanted to speak up. He wanted to say, "Why are we in trouble? We are good students. We all work very hard at our studies!"

Someone else spoke for him, but it was not the words he wanted to hear.

"War is coming to Ise!" a small boy with a beautiful face announced. "Even now it has reached our northern borders! We must protect our homes! We must not let invaders take what belong to us and our ancestor! My family house was taken and burned!

Our things stolen and sold! I vowed revenge!"

The instructor smiled and patted the child's head. "Well spoken, Shiratori-kun. He is right! He has come to Toba with his family to live with cousins, fleeing from the northern territory. War is at our borders even as we sit here among the peaceful mountains going about our lives! Tokyo has fallen, Kobe has fallen, Osaka is on fire!"

There was an audible gasp. Most of them had not known this. Why had it taken a new student refugee from northern Ise to bring them this news?

Osaka … on fire? They could not see the large city as it lay beyond the highest peaks. But Sadao had asked his mother what the odd glow in the far northwestern sky had been the other night. It was seen off and on for many weeks. She had told him it was a lantern festival being celebrated far away. He'd believed her, even though her voice had been strange. Osaka was the largest city beyond the cloistered Ise Peninsula. If it had fallen into the hands of warlords, who would protect them from the fire reaching their homes?

Sadao tried to focus on their first awkward lessons that day - breath and balance. But, his mind was far away, imagining lanterns burning and temples going up in flames. He had not thought much about the war until now. Before, when his schoolmates or elder brothers spoke of it, it was always a problem of the weakened governments in ravaged Northern Japan, where railways and power had been destroyed by cyclones, earthquakes and tsunamis. These were the flooded cities that had fallen into warlords' hands. Refugees from the northern prefectures had found their way south into the southern cities to live in camps above the rising sea. It was always mentioned on the news when Sadao was allowed to be near a television panel to overhear it. When he would ask his father about it, he was told the fighting was far away and not to worry.

"The problems of the North do not concern us," he would say. *"We are protected here by our defense army. Our mountains are very tall - the roads obscure and difficult to pass. War will not reach our isolated communities."*

But it had. It had shown itself in the faces of the hungry children waiting outside the front doors of the school. Each week there were more - children of lost families; *ienaki-ko* they were called - the "homeless children." They lived in the slums down in the lower valley, building shelters of discarded metal scraps and bamboo under the abandoned *shinkansen* tracks. The bullet trains stopped running when Sadao was five or six. He could barely remember what they looked like whizzing by in a long blur. People huddled now under these silent rails, hungry, diseased and scarred. He was forbidden to go near them.

As Sadao gathered his books into his satchel, he could see the line of ienaki-ko through the front windows, lined up to beg from the students and senseis as they were dismissed. Their instructors encouraged the students to place unwanted lunch items in a large basket in the meal hall for the unfortunate ones. Sadao often gave away his pickles. But never his rice cakes! Those were only for him.

Today, the faces were annoying to Sadao. So many - how many more would come?

Among them was a little boy, jumping to see over the shoulders of the older refugee children.

As the bell was struck and the students dismissed for the day, Sadao hurried past the grabbing hands for his shoes in the outdoor rack. As he reached for his labeled slot, he realized it was empty.

"Sadao-kun!" A young voice rang out among the ienaki-ko. *"I have new shoes now!"*

Sadao spun around to set his eyes on the little boy. He was maybe five years old with Sadao's very own expensive leather shoes tied to his small dirty feet.

"Give those back!" Sadao yelled. *"You can't have them!"*

"Why not? You have lots of shoes!"

"Because they're not yours!"

The boy turned and ran, with Sadao running after him. He picked up leaves and dirt in his socks as he chased him down the mountain road that wound down through the bamboo forest to the harbor. The kid was fast and already a few switchbacks ahead of him. Sadao tried to cut the distance by taking a shortcut but wound up twisting his foot on a loose rock, which stopped him cold.

"Come back here!" Sadao screamed as he watched the small figure getting farther and farther ahead of him. *"Kusogaki!!"* Sadao yelled. He picked up a rock and threw it down the path, just missing the kid's fleeing head. "Fuck you! Fuck all of you *ienaki-ko!"*

"I would not call names so freely, Sadao-kun!"

Sadao knew that new voice and turned. Shiratori stood on the path just above him with disapproval in his eyes.

"Was I talking to you? I don't think so!"

"You should let hungry boy have shoes."

"Fuck you! This is none of your business! You don't know me!"

"I know you have many shoes," Shiratori said, coming closer and offering Sadao a hand out of the rocks and back onto the path. Sadao begrudgingly took it. "Small child does not."

Sadao tested his weight on his bruised foot. It hurt but he didn't want Shiratori to know it. "Go away. I don't want your help or advice!"

"I thought I would always have big house full of shoes and then one day I did not."

Sadao limped forward, giving Shiratori a glance. "Is that true? What you said in class? Your home was burned?"

"It is true. I do not lie about this. My family ran and lived in forest for many day and nights. No food. No warm clothes. We were surprise when invader come under darkness of new moon."

Sadao studied the new kid. Although he was a few years younger than Sadao, he had a very mature manner for his age.

"So what's your story, anyway? If you're homeless, how can your family afford this school?"

Shiratori walked patiently beside him, matching his painful steps. "My family is Shiratori clan - very old, very wealthy. Our cousins have been kind to give us room in their house."

"You say all of this like it happened to someone else."

"No, this happen to me."

Sadao stared at him. Impossible; not a shred of emotion crossed the kid's face.

"Bullshit," Sadao muttered, lumbering on. "If that really happened you'd at least be a little upset I would think!"

"Tears do not change fact. My home is gone. I live with many cousin now here in Toba. They have money for good school. Say my English need much improve."

"Yes, it does," Sadao agreed, still not believing a word.

"You believe that you will stay safe forever on Shinjyu-jima?"

"I never said that," Sadao grumbled. "How do you know where I live?"

He laughed. "Everyone know where Sadao-kun live. Very important place. Good for defense. It will fall first when warlord come to take Toba Bay."

Sadao had heard enough. He swung his fist and punched Shiratori square in the jaw. The little boy looked unsurprised as he rubbed his sore chin.

"Take it back!" Sadao yelled. "Take back what you said or I'll hit you again!"

Shiratori held his ground. "Hitting me, like tears, will not change fact - Shinjyu-jima is ideal stronghold."

Sadao shook his head, utterly confused by this kid. Nothing he said or did made sense. "Leave me alone!" Sadao said and walked faster to get himself home before Shiratori could say anything more.

By the time Sadao reached the stone bridge to Shinjyu-jima his feet were scraped, cut and bloody. He didn't care and dismissed the guards' offer to carry him the rest of the way.

"I can handle this myself!" he yelled in English. The guards shrugged and let him pass.

Sadao let himself in the house through the rear servant's entrance. He wanted to go clean up in the showers before anymore people could see his embarrassing predicament. The stairwell was quiet but once he descended to the washing floor, he heard a noise in the dark landing area. Confused, he hugged the wall and leaned around the corner.

It was his brother Yasuo. He had his pants down past his knees and was pushing their new apprentice maid Junko up against the wall. She was making a weird sound with her nose and cheek against the panelling. Tears were running down her face. It was bad enough Yasuo picked on him, but not a nice person like Junko! He was clearly hurting her with his "squishing."

"Hey! Leave her alone!" Sadao shouted, stepping bravely into view.

Yasuo raised his right hand and flipped Sadao off. *"Ike zo!"*

Junko cried out in fright and tried to pull down her ruffled maid's skirt which was rumpled up against his brother's belly.

"What are you doing? Stop making her show her butt to you!"

Yasuo made a growling sound and shoved Junko to the floor. She spit at him and got to her feet. Straightening her skirt, she ran past Sadao for the stairs. Yasuo pulled up his pants and turned on him.

"I'm going to fucking kill you, you little spying shit!"

Sadao darted past his larger brother for the washroom door, banging it open. No one was in the washing area but as soon as Sadao's bloody feet hit the steamy tile floor, he slipped and fell on his side, hitting his head. In the seconds it took him to recover, his brother had caught up with him and slammed his heavy body down on top of him, yelling his terrible names over and over as he hit him in the face and stomach.

"Fucking little bastard swine! You're too much of a little fag to know what's going on! What the fuck are you doing using the backstairs?! You're nothing but a begging thief!"

He yelled so loudly spittle flew from his mouth and Sadao choked on the stench of his alcoholic breath.

"Yasuo! What are you doing to your Ototosan?"

Yasuo stopped, fist poised in the air. Sadao strained to see who had come. His ears were ringing too hard and the lights spun in his vision.

"He fell!" Yasuo lied.

"Go. Now! If I ever see you near my son again, I'll have your Father send you away to the army!"

Yasuo got up and retreated, flipping Sadao off as he went. *I'll get you!* he mouthed.

"Sadao!" His mother knelt and put her arms around him. *"What did he do to you?!"*

"I hate him. I hate him! I want him dead!"

"Shhh ... don't say such things," she said, holding him close and soothing him. *"Let's get you cleaned up."*

Sadao's mother undressed him carefully and washed his wounds gently with a warm cloth while he sat on the little bamboo stool near the floor spigots, quiet and withdrawn.

"There, it's not as bad as it looked at first. But that bruise on your face will show. I'll need to tell your father something."

"Tell him the truth!" Sadao said, coming to life. *"Why does everyone protect that bakayaro?!"*

Sadao's mother regarded him sadly and didn't reprimand him for swearing. *"Because ... he is third born of a first wife."*

Sadao didn't understand why that had to be so important - but his mother's face was reminding him once again that their place among the household was never going to be a certain one.

"I hate him!" Sadao said and began to weep.

"I know," his mother said softly as she held and rocked him through his tears. *"I hate him too."*

"You lose fight?" Shiratori asked the following week during *bushido* training. Much to Sadao's current string of rotten luck, they'd been paired up together for outdoor drills soon as Sadao returned to school with faded bruises and new shoes.

"Yeah, my *onisan's* a prick!"

"I am sorry you have prick *onisan*. It is dishonorable to fight opponent smaller than yourself."

"It doesn't stop him."

"Silence! Shiratori-kun! Koga-kun! Since you have so much to discuss, why don't you both come forward and demonstrate for us the Reverse Blind Strike?"

Sadao and his partner bowed and stepped forward into the battle circle. A melon had been balanced upon a post pounded into the ground at shoulder height. Sadao and Shiratori stood side-by-side to the left of it and straightened their shoulders - focusing their breathing. They had been learning stealth attacks for tricking foes into an unexpected kill.

"Ready?"

"Hai!"

"Attack!"

Sadao was closest to the melon so he moved a step to cross in front of Shiratori. Pulling his partner's bokken from its sheath, he swung blind to the right and behind him, perfectly envisioning Yasuo's head upon that post instead of the round fat fruit. His swing was so forceful, the wooden blade didn't just knock the fruit from the post - it exploded it, coating the students and senseis with juicy melon guts.

Their instructor removed his glasses to wipe his lenses clean as the boys stood at attention to await his review. "Well done," was his only comment.

"Sadao-kun, wait!" Shiratori ran to catch up with him as he descended the hilly path heading back to town once lessons were completed for the day.

Sadao wasn't in the mood for listening to Shiratori's rhetoric that day, or any day of the week for that matter. The kid had a way of getting under his skin with all of his unwanted philosophical advice.

"Leave me alone, Shiratori-san! I don't want to talk to you today!"

"Senpai! I have something for you!"

Although Sadao was two years ahead of him in age and studies, Shiratori had never addressed him as his upperclassmen. As this was an English school, such titles were often dropped. Even so, it made Sadao pause.

"What? I don't want anything from you."

"Not even something that will help you to win against big prick brother?" Shiratori caught up with him and opened the buckle on his satchel. He took out a small flat envelope and handed it to Sadao.

"What is it?"

"Something you must handle carefully."

Sadao didn't heed his warning and flipped the top open to peer inside. There was a square piece of rice paper inside marked with vertical rows of calligraphy. Sadao pulled it out. "What does it say? I can't read ancient handscript."

"You do not need to know what it say, only what it mean. What power it has."

Sadao shrugged. "It's a piece of paper. Paper doesn't have any power! Is this supposed to be a fortune card of some kind?" Priests would bless special paper for shrine visitors to pull from wooden drawers for a small fee to reveal their fortunes. Good fortunes were kept on one's person. Bad fortunes were tied to a tree or string at the shrine and left behind to ward off bad luck.

"This is no happy luck *omikuji*," Shiratori asserted. "This is *daikyou*. Very serious. Very dangerous to carry with you. Even dangerous to touch!"

"Really?" Sadao asked sarcastically. "You believe in that superstition crap?"

Shiratori puffed up as if he was deeply offended. "Only foolish man question power of our gods!"

"Then why would you be carrying it around with you if you believe in these paper curses?"

Shiratori leaned closer. "I was going to leave *daikyou* in box for Yamada-kun to find. I hate this fat stupid kid. Always touch my books. Always open my *bento*!"

"But why are you giving it to me?"

"For your *onisan*! He need strong punishment for not obeying important law of combat! He fight dirty. This I hate, hate more than lunch poking *baka*!"

Sadao looked at the paper in his hand. It was marked with a shrine stamp he didn't recognize. "Where'd you get this anyway? I don't know this symbol."

"My *Ojiisan* is very powerful Shinto priest in Nagoya. I take this from his fortune box!"

"You stole it. It's a stolen fortune card," Sadao said, dubiously. "Wow. Thanks. This will sure scare off my asshole brother."

Shiratori cackled at his ironic tone and assisted Sadao in slipping the *daikyou* into his book bag. "You must put *daikyou* someplace close to *Onisan*. The closer it is to his body, the more bad luck he will have."

"Fine," Sadao said, eager to get down the mountain path and away from this odd kid.

"Sadao-kun, read to me from this book."

Sadao opened his book of Shakespearean sonnets and read to his father a few of the verses.

> *My mistress' eyes are nothing like the sun;*
> *Coral is far more red, than her lips red:*
> *If snow be white, why then her breasts are dun;*
> *If hairs be wires, black wires grow on her head ...*

His father listened in deep thought then motioned him to stop.

"This is the greatest writer of the English language?"

"Yes, Otousan. He is revered greatly by all English scholars." Sadao's father could understand basic English if spoken to him. But he did not speak, read or write it. His main source of English education throughout the years was satellite television. Historical war documentaries in particular.

"I do not understand this poetry. Does this Englishman think he is humorous?"

"I think so, Otousan, but we are taught that he is witty. His humor has a lot of intelligence even though he was a common, uneducated man."

"It is very uneducated to insult a woman so - one he claims to be his mistress. It is very bad taste."

"I suppose so, Otousan ... .I'm sorry to ask but can I be dismissed now? It's getting late and I have an essay to complete tonight."

His father bowed, indicating he was welcome to leave the study. As he stood up, his father suddenly took his hand and pulled him closer into the lamplight. Sadao's breath caught. Was he in trouble? His father's deeply wrinkled eyes studied his face for a moment, then let him go.

"Go study hard," he said in halting English.

When Sadao returned to his bedroom he went straight to the long mirror and turned up the light. Yes! It was still here, faint and yellow, but the bruise Yasuo had left was still plainly visible on his face. Whatever story his mother had come up with to explain his injuries, it seemed his father had taken notice of it. Something had changed in the last few days since their fight. For one thing, Yasuo was sent away on a long errand to another prefecture and his mother had taken to sleeping in the weaving room across the hall. His brother was due back sometime later that evening. So Sadao cranked up his lamp, sharpened his pencils and got to work while the night was quiet.

"Fuck these shitty sluts!!" The bedroom door slid open with a bang just as Sadao was proof-reading his final essay. Yasuo had returned. *"Fuck them! I want them all fired!"*

A window on the other end of the room flew open. *"You hear me, Otousan? I want these worthless whores fired!"*

Sadao turned off his lamp and gathered his books, sliding them under the bed. He didn't want his brother finding his essay and flushing it down the toilet again.

Bam!! The shoji screen separating their private areas came crashing down flat. Yasuo marched into his space and threw open Sadao's armoire.

"Hey! Leave my clothes alone! They won't fit you!"

"Shut the fuck up, gaki! I need something clean to wear!" Yasuo said, ripping shirts off the hangers and tossing them to the floor. *"All my clothes smell like fish! Fucking maids can't clean worth shit!"*

"They don't clean them well because you are so mean to them!" Sadao bit back.

Yasuo turned on him. *"What did you say, little puss crust?"*

"I said they don't clean them well because you are so mean and rude to them! They all hate you!"

Yasuo's face was red from drink again. Sadao could smell it as he stepped menacingly toward the bed.

"Those maids are nothing but a gang of filthy omanko - just like your mother! Your slutty mother who used her stinky omeko to fuck her way into this house and brought her puny little funya-chin with her!"

"Stop saying these things about my mother! She's a good person! You don't know anything about her!"

"You think I don't know where you two came from? I know you lived in those rat infested flats behind the marketplace. Only bastards and whores live there! You never belonged here!" Yasuo said, kicking Sadao's clothes aside and approaching him. *"You're not my father's son! You're a bastard brat your mother tricked my father into believing was his!"*

"I am his son!" Sadao yelled. *"There's a test that proves it!"*

"Your mother was a baita!" Yasuo growled, grabbing Sadao's shirt collar in his fist.

"She was not! She was a maid in this house before I was born! And she cleaned houses for the wealthy!"

Yasuo knocked Sadao down onto the bed with a shove and pinned him with his thick arms, securing his wrists. *"Is she still cleaning up shit even now?"*

Sadao struggled, ready to let loose a scream if Yasuo tried to hurt him badly again. *"No! She's a good wife and mother to our father and me!"*

"Then tell me, chisai baka. Where do you think she goes on Sunday afternoons?"

Sadao tried to get loose from Yasuo's grip but the more he struggled the more Yasuo increased his hold on his wrists. *"She goes to Temple!"*

"Hah! Is that the lie she tells you? I've seen her. She doesn't go to Temple. She goes back to the slums she loves so much and sucks cock for 5 yen a customer!"

Sadao felt fury rise in his gut. *"You're a drunk stupid jealous liar because father likes me best and gives me the best clothes! I get to go to school instead of checking the floats. He knows you're too dumb to learn anything and you stink of scum!"*

Yasuo made a guttural yell and threw Sadao off the bed to the floor. He got up and went straight for Sadao's dresser, yanking out the drawers and dumping the contents to the floor, stomping and tearing as he went.

"Nice clothes, huh? Let's see how nice they are now!"

"Yamero, Yasuo! Stop ruining my things!!"

Sadao picked himself up and leapt onto Yasuo's back, scratching and kicking with all he had.

Yasuo threw him off and grabbed his book satchel from the chair and began tearing through it, tossing out the books and papers, crumpling and ripping.

Sadao didn't hear the guards enter the room and march over the fallen screen. His ears were too full of his own screams as he beat on Yasuo's back with his fists. Two arms grabbed him and pulled him off his brother while a second guard pinned his brother down under foot and bound his hands with rope.

"Enough, Yasuo!"

"Okaasan!"

Sadao's mother had followed the men in. She stepped between the two boys and examined her son's face and hands for injury. Satisfied Sadao was not visibly wounded, she turned to Yasuo whose eyes were seething and slapped his face with the back of her hand.

"You shame our family with these antics, Yasuo!" she said, leaning over him as he lay under the guard's boot on the floor. *"I have been patient and just with you. But I won't be silent anymore! Your father will deal with you now. Take him away!"*

Yasuo shot Sadao a murderous look as he was taken away by the two men. Sadao couldn't help but produce a smile as he went. His mother watched them go and passed a gentle hand through Sadao's mussed hair.

"You won't have to worry about your brother anymore, Sadao. His drinking has gotten out of hand. Your father is moving him to the lower floor where he will be better supervised. You won't have to share this room with him."

"Really? I get the whole room to myself?"

"Yes, your father wants you to have a quiet place for study. If you're alright, let's clean up this mess and I'll inform your father of what clothing and school materials will need replacing."

Sadao joined her in picking up his scattered and damaged things. His mother picked up his book bag and began to gather up the spilled contents. *"Sadao. What is this?"*

"Huh? Oh that. I don't know - something this kid at school gave me. He took it from his family's shrine, I guess."

His mother looked over the rice paper *daikyou*. *"You shouldn't be carrying this. It's very bad luck, Sadao."*

"Throw it away! I told him I didn't want it in the first place."

She stood up and folded it carefully, placing it in her pocket. *"It needs to be burned at the Temple,"* she said sternly. *"I will take care of it. Your father would be very angry to see such a thing in his home."*

"Sorry, Okaasan. I'll try to stay away from that kid."

"I think you should. He sounds like trouble."

The following weekend, Sadao was spending a sunny afternoon looking for new pens and notebooks at the marketplace with a fat wallet. Yasuo, he'd been told, would be spending a lot more time outside of their island home handling mundane errands to neighboring towns and villages accompanied by one of his father's most trusted men.

Sadao was testing different colors of ink on a blotter when he was surprised to see his mother a few stalls away, purchasing a basket of *pan* and preserved fruits. He was about to call out to her when something stopped him.

Do you know where your mother goes on Sunday afternoons?

Sadao didn't believe a word Yasuo had said out of spite, but was curious enough to want to find out why his mother would be buying groceries at the market. This was a task normally handled by the household staff.

Perhaps it's a gift for someone like Obasan. Or an omimai basket for a sick friend, he reasoned. *No need to get excited.* But still, he found himself stepping back between the displays so she wouldn't notice him as she passed.

Sadao watched his mother pay for her basket and head back to the main street that ran along the harbor's half-moon shore. She turned to go to the right instead of the left which would have led back to Shinjyu-jima's stone bridge.

Perhaps she is going to Temple to make a donation, Sadao thought and continued to follow well behind her along the busy street. But she didn't turn for the path to the

Temple either and soon left the main road for a smaller residential side road. It was harder to follow her here without being seen. There weren't as many people about and the nearby shinkansen tracks cast shadows over the tenement buildings.

Maybe it is for an old friend who is ill. She used to live near this neighborhood when she was young. But Sadao's mother didn't stop among the crowded rundown buildings either. Instead, she stepped into an alcove and donned a strange scarf and shawl that covered her face and shoulders.

She stepped back out in her wrappings, crossed the street and passed through a break in a low fence to enter the grassy field beyond - a field that led directly to the distant tin rooftops of the *ienaki-ko*. Sadao ducked down behind an old car, his heart thrumming in his chest. *She's going to the slums? In disguise? Impossible! My mother is not a whore! She must be bringing food to the sick!* Shaking with worry now, Sadao crawled under the fence and struggled to keep up with his mother, yet stay far enough behind her to not be noticed. The grass was brittle under his feet, but a breeze coming off the ocean helped to hide the sound of his steps.

There were signs here painted on scraps of wood and pounded into the ground - warnings not to go any further or risk coming into contact with the diseased. The shrouded form of his mother pushed through the open gate of another fence and descended down a steep path into the warren of shanties. Sadao hurried down after her, not wanting to lose her in the tight turns.

People were about, hunched in the shade of the old shinkansen tracks, dirty and dressed in tattered clothes. Some reached up with their hands to his mother, but she kept her pace quickly to pass them until Sadao saw her duck under a ratty split curtain into a hovel of crumbling bricks and metal scraps torn from abandoned station signs.

Sadao held his breath against the smell and sprinted past the vagrants until he reached the same split curtain. Inside, he could hear his mother speaking with someone. To Sadao's relief, it sounded like a child.

See, she's come to help someone! Bringing food to a family with a child. I knew it!

Not wanting to let his mother discover that he'd followed her, and yet wanting to see what was going on, Sadao skirted around the rickety shelter until he found a break in the leaning walls. He ducked into the shadows and slid himself slowly between the rusty metal sheets until he was just able to peer into the interior space through a couple of boards.

There wasn't much inside. Some frayed curtains, and a few mattresses covered in old blankets; random items of clothing were about, some crates and pots. There was a child talking excitedly with his mother, who was handing him the items from the basket and giving instruction on how to open or serve them. It was hard to hear her, her voice was muffled under her shroud. She appeared to be wearing gloves now as well.

Once the basket was unpacked, his mother moved one of the curtains aside and Sadao was surprised to see there was a woman lying on another mattress inside. In the dimness, Sadao saw his mother take a washcloth and dip it in a bucket to wet it, then she began to wipe the woman's face and hands clean. The child bounced around them both, excitedly eating an apple. His indistinct form at last caught some of the light that was peeping through a gap in the roof.

Shoes! It was the kid from school - he was wearing Sadao's stolen leather shoes! *Who is he?* Sadao wondered. *Why is my mother looking after him? She passed by all the other helpless ones. Why did she come here to bring food to this one boy and his mother?*

Sadao sat in the dark and watched as his mother bathed and changed the clothes of the woman lying on the mattress, stuffing the dirty items into a trash bag. The women was clearly alive but unable to move for herself. Sadao didn't understand why. Once the woman was cleaned, with the child's help, his mother propped the women up against a rice sack so she could be fed some prepared soup broth from the basket. The process was slow but it appeared the inert woman as able to take in some nourishment this way.

Is she sick? What kind of disease does she have that she can't move for herself? Now, it occurred to Sadao why his mother was wearing a scarf and gloves - to prevent illness! Sadao pulled his shirt collar up over his nose and kept his eyes on the strange events taking place inside. As they moved to lay the woman back down, his mother shifted her to a cleaner mattress; this brought her face into the light and closer to Sadao's frame of view.

Sadao realized he knew this unfortunate woman. She was one of their maids from when he was little. She had been the shy pretty one with the short black hair, which had now grown long and tangled. She was the one who had cleaned up the old witch that was his father's first wife that night. *Had the old hag made this poor woman sick? And how was she already the mother of this five-year-old child?*

"*Sadao?!*" a high voice chirped up. "*Obasan, did you bring Onisan with you?*"

Sadao jerked back in shock and collided with one of the support poles, rattling the roof boards and causing one of them to shift. An old exit sign came crashing down behind him.

"*Sadao?! Sadao! Come out of there at once!*"

He was seen. It was too late to run. "*Hai, Okasaan!*"

"*Onisan! Onisan! See, I still have your shoes!*" the kid exclaimed, dancing around him as he crawled out into view.

His mother grabbed Sadao by the arm and hauled him to his feet. Her face was still obscured by the cloth. She dragged it partially aside as if she couldn't believe her eyes.

"*Why are you here, Sadao?! Did you follow me?!*"

Sadao lowered his head, ashamed. "*Hai, Okaasan. I was scared. Yasuo said you were sneaking into the slums and I thought -*"

"*This woman is gravely ill, Sadao! You have no protection! Here, take my scarf!*" His mother grabbed him and removed her head covering, wrapping her shawl around his head.

"I can't see!"

"Good, then no one can see you! We need to leave here at once!"

"Bye-bye Onisan. I'll see you at school!" the little boy said brightly as Sadao was dragged out under the split kitchen curtain and into the slum maze.

Half blind, Sadao had no choice but to allow his mother to drag him back up the hill away from the tracks to the field. Once there, she removed the cloth wrap and threw it aside, along with her gloves, striking his face with her hand. Her expression was flushed and furious. *"How could you be so foolish? Did you not read the signs?"*

"But, why did you come here, Okaasan? Why did you touch her body? I don't want you to be sick, too! What's wrong with her?"

"Listen to me, Sadao. You must not let your father hear a word about this, do you understand?"

"But Okaasan!"

She shook him to silence him. *"Not a word! Do you want that to be us?"* she cried, pointing back toward the abandoned tracks. *"Do you?"*

Sadao felt tears spring to his eyes. He didn't understand what was going on. Or why his mother was so mad at him. He was taking no more risk than her. *"Why does that boy call me onisan?"*

"Come," she said, dragging his arm. *"We must get back and you must be scrubbed! I'll see you're scrubbed until your skin is red and sore!"*

By the time his mother had dragged him back through the marketplace to their island bridge - more than just the two posted guards were waiting for them. There were also two men in long white coats and two nurses. All four were wearing gloves and surgical masks.

Sadao looked to his mother. *"Okaasan? Who are they?"* She didn't answer him, just looked ahead at them, her head held high and her jaw set.

"My son was not exposed!" she said. *"He is in no danger!"*

A guard touched his earpiece and nodded to the doctors. One of the guards grabbed Sadao as the two doctors came forward and lead his mother away from the bridge and back toward the main street where a van was waiting.

"Okaasan?" She didn't turn her head to acknowledge him as they lowered her head with their rubber gloves to close and lock her inside. *"Okaasan!"*

Sadao watched in shame and worry as his mother was driven away.

No one spoke to Sadao about his mother during the time she was gone, except to say she was away for a while and would be back sometime later. Sadao focused his worried mind on his school work and *bushido* training. He found studies and war play were the best way to force the memory of that Sunday afternoon from his mind. He couldn't look at the faces of the ienaki-ko, who continued to gather at the school doors. He didn't want to see the small boy's face among them, or hear him shout his name. But to his relief, the high voice was no longer to be heard among the begging hungry mouths. Sadao slid on his shoes and shoved his way past them. *"Leave me alone!"* he yelled, and ran for the path that led down to the safety of his stone castle walls.

At night, in the quiet of his bed, Sadao's sleep was plagued with visions of the little boy dancing around his dead mother's body in his polished leather shoes.

Do you like how my shoes fit, Onisan? I told you! They belonged to me!

The maid's body was sallow and covered with buzzing flies. Her skirt was pulled up, exposing her bottom. Sadao awoke cold and covered with sweat, all alone in his long empty room.

To his relief, his mother was returned to them some weeks later without explanation. Just as if she had been out for a walk and had decided to come back in before it became dark outside. She came to him while he was at his desk with his papers and threw her arms around him.

"It was Yasuo," she said. *"He tipped the guards. You have nothing to blame yourself for."*
Sadao clung to her in relief.

Life carried on more or less the same for Sadao from that day forward. He rarely came upon Yasuo alone and when he did, his older brother ignored him - acted as if he didn't exist. Yasuo was gone at sea often, or was sent to attend to tasks at business locations away from the island. Sadao was able to live and sleep in peace.

For Sadao's mother though, things had changed drastically. She moved permanently into the room across the hall from Sadao and as the months passed, she became more reclusive, quiet and withdrawn. She didn't wear her fine gowns anymore or fix her hair with elaborate hairstyles. She stopped painting her lips red and more closely resembled the mother Sadao remembered from when she used to clean homes - plain and simple. When his studies allowed, they would spend time together at the marketplace, and under guarded supervised visits with *Obasan* when she came into town. Married now, his mother's sister had young twins to care for at her husband's rice farm 20 miles north of Toba in Ise. They no longer cooked meals together or laughed into the late hours.

That winter, word came from the Coastal Patrol that Yasuo's fishing vessel had been caught in a sudden squall and swept away out to sea. Neither the boat nor his brother's body were ever recovered. But Sadao could remember hearing the scream their new young maid made when she was assigned to clean out Yasuo's downstairs bedroom.

She'd found a small wrinkled piece of rice paper under Yasuo's mattress bearing the ancient kanji script of a curse, stamped with the seal of a shrine from distant Nagoya. A *daikyou*, she said. No one could account for how it had gotten there and Sadao's father ordered it to be immediately taken to the Temple and burned in the sacred fire.

Third

Paper Boats

Toba-Kontaiji Terrace English School - 2046

"Sadao-kun! Wait, please."

Sadao paused as he was gathering his English books under his arm.

"Hai, Sensei."

Darnell-sensei, a young 24 year-old American woman, smiled fondly at Sadao as the rest of the class filed out. The students headed for their cubbies to gather their things before walking down the mountain paths to their homes. When the class had emptied, she beckoned him to join her at the front of the classroom, where a small envelope was lying on her desk.

"This is for you," she said.

"What is it?" Sadao asked.

"It's an invitation," she said, handing it to him. "Open it."

Opening it, Sadao found a letter from the Tamaki Central School District. It asked if his English School would be so kind as to send an exceptional young student to assist them with English tutoring while their instructor recovered from a sudden illness. They didn't want their students poorly prepared for end of year exams.

Sadao finished the letter and handed it back to his teacher. "I'm sorry to hear their instructor has been ill."

She smiled. "I suggested to the headmaster that you should be selected to assist them. Your English is exceptional for a boy your age and your cousins' farm is not far from the middle school. Would you like to stay with them for a month?"

Sadao nodded. He was very fond of his younger cousins. Two four-year-old twin girls. They were his Obasan's children. "I will have to ask my parents," he said.

"We already have, and they support the idea. But I wanted to ask you first before we replied to the school."

Sadao could remember visiting the little farm house surrounded by flowing green rice fields last summer. He had sailed folded paper boats with the girls in the stream that ran along the property. It was an easy simple place - not so many rules and formalities as in his father's fine home. He could slosh around in the mud all he liked and take a hose bath without getting in trouble.

"What about my exams?" he asked.

"We can arrange for you to take them at Tamaki Middle School. You'll be expected to follow a study plan of your own there while you are out of town. We can't have you getting behind, either."

Sadao smiled. "Will the students call me sensei?"

His favorite teacher nodded at him. "I think they might."

Mono no aware. This was a difficult phrase to translate into English. It was based on the zen principle of 'nothing of beauty lasts forever,' therefore it should be mourned even at the height of its youth and vigor.

Sadao stared at the wildflower bouquet sitting in a vase on his desk that a student had brought him that morning. The lush blue and vibrant yellow petals dazzled the eye now, but as time passed they would soon become limp brown shriveled memories tossed in the bin.

Mono meant 'thing' and *aware* meant 'pity or sorrow.' *Mono no aware*, a 'thing of pity.' It didn't seem right as Sadao swiveled in his chair to write it on the digital board in English and kana. He'd assigned his students a simple set of haiku translations - to try and recompose the effortless perfection of Haiku Master Basho into English phrases of equal potency. It was impossible, he soon discovered. And more often comical - English grammar lacked the feather touch of Japanese brevity. He turned back to his students' papers.

The frog jumps in a old pond, making a water noise.

He corrected the 'an' and gave the student a *daiso* stamp of good effort. Technically correct, but hilariously cumbersome. He couldn't do any better. How did one without the use of Japanese onomatopoeia describe the delicate complexity of that sound? In his mind Sadao could see the old pond surrounded by bamboo, casting tall shadows over the still water like a mirror. Then, from nowhere, this small creature jumps into the center and the spell is broken - resonating in ripples of sadness. That was *mono no aware.* English had none of it.

He packed the students' papers carefully into his teacher's organizer and stood, shutting the lights and locking the door, shouldering his pack. The halls had emptied as he left the school. The country road that led up to his uncle's farm was quieter now, although a few students still rode their bicycles lazily in the warm late spring air. The worst of the humidity hadn't quite come on in full force yet, but the clouds were starting to take on their white humongous billowing summer shapes, hovering over the flow of bright green ripening rice fields. Cicadas were starting to raise their voices, clamouring along with the laughter of the school children as he walked home.

Sadao was feeling the heat when he arrived at his uncle's modest farmhouse. The sun shone in bright bursts off the polished blue ceramic roof tiles, making him strangely dizzy as he slid open the front door.

"Sadao-kun! Sadao-kun!" His two young twin cousins ran up to him in the entry-way as he hung up his bag and tried to remove his shoes before stepping up onto the tatami. They tackled him to the floor and he had to scramble onto his knees to keep his dusty shoes from dirtying the mats.

"Chotto matte! Chotto!!" he laughed, rolling them off and kicking off his shoes to safety. Two girls, identical in every way - Miko and Kiko - pounced on his chest, knocking his wind out. *"Itai! Motto yasashiku shinasai!"*

"Kiko, I can't breathe!" he gasped, tossing her off.

"Kiko ja nai!! Miko desu! Mikoooo!"

Sadao sat up and hugged the both of them so he could see their faces side by side. The little girls held very still trying to stay stone-faced while he studied them. They were identical in every way - same hair, same noses, ears and chins. From a short distance most could not tell them apart. Neither could Sadao unless he looked into their eyes. *"You are Kiko! Little fox - trying to fool me!"*

The girls laughed and helped tug him to his feet. *"We want to make boats again!"* they said. *"You promised to help us!"*

"Okay, okay, just give me a second to recover."

Obasan was beginning to prepare the evening meal and offered the kids tea and rice crackers while Sadao showed his little cousins how to fold origami boats from sheets of decorative square paper his aunt kept in her writing desk.

"You need to make the sides match evenly," he instructed the girls. *"Like this, watch. See how I point the corners together? Good, now fold very straight."*

Their little hands needed some guidance, but with some re-creasing adjustments, they soon had five small boats ready to float. They slipped into rubber gardening shoes and ran out the back door to the stream that ran down the sloping hillside over small rocks next to the house.

Sadao set his boat - a green and blue striped one in a small eddy to test its buoyancy. It almost blew away in the late afternoon breeze, so he set a small rock in it.

"You need to give them a passenger," he said. *"Find someone to ride in your boats."*

The girls knelt in the grass to find 'people' to ride in their crafts. Once all of the flower and leaf passengers were ready, Sadao had the girls set them in the eddy and when they were all lined up, he let his hand go so they would flow into the main current together. It was a race to see which boat sailed the fastest to the bottom.

The girls jumped up and along with Sadao, they followed the boats' progress downstream. Two paper boats became tangled in reeds almost immediately. But three stayed the course and floated over the flat smooth rock 'rapids' with ease carrying their bits of leaves, rocks and yellow and blue wildflowers further downstream.

"Ganbare! Ganbare!" the girls squealed, running along the water's edge. They soon gained a bit of distance on him and by the time all three of them reached the pond at the base of the stream, Kiko was already in tears. Of the three sail-worthy craft, only hers had tipped over and lost its passenger in the pond before sinking into the algae.

Sadao tried not to smile at her cute weepy face as he hugged her in comfort. *"It's okay, Kiko. Your boat was very brave. It made it all the way down the steam, after all."*

"But, my flower died!" Her sister wasn't helping the matter by dancing around with her successful gold paper design making vrrroomm sounds in the air with its drippy hull. Blue wildflower still intact.

"Here," Sadao said, plucking Kiko a fresh yellow blossom. *"We can try it again, okay? There's plenty of flowers."*

"But it's not my flower," she whined, not wanting to be consoled while her sister was clearly the 'winner.'

Sadao kissed her tears and tickled her tummy until she forgot her drowned bloom and became distracted by a frog that had jumped into the water instead. The falling sun cast orange ripples across the disturbed pond and once again Sadao felt his head spin. But this time it didn't stop and within moments his cousins' giggles turned to screams as he collapsed in a faint by the water's edge.

Confusion. Lights and strange sounds. The light spun too fast to open his eyes for more than a second. Echoes reverberated around him ominously. It was like drowning but he wasn't under actual water. Every time he tried to fight for consciousness he was greeted with excruciating pain unlike anything he had ever known. Every muscle and nerve in his body was ravaged with burning pain. He was on fire. Burning and freezing all at once. All he wanted to do was die and fall back into oblivion.

I'm dying, please, please let me die.

There was nothing. Until the ice came. Biting cold ice. He was in a tub. Tall white windows and men and women with masks and white coats were pouring ice water over his naked body. Holding his limbs. There was a horrible sound stabbing his ears. He could taste blood in his throat. His blood. He was the one making the sound. He was screaming and had no power to stop.

Please stop, please let it stop ... stop

"He won't live. He is too old."

Someone was standing near his bedside. The pain was still there but it was almost as if he couldn't comprehend it anymore - only notice that it was there. He could notice too that his swollen hands were still attached to him as well as his throbbing feet. Red and painful. It was hard to think. He couldn't tell his eyes to open or his body to move. Or his tongue to speak.

"Don't say that. Give him a chance."

"We don't have the resources. There are others we can save. This one is too far gone. I am moving him to hospice."

"No! I won't let you do that!"

"Are you his relative?"

"No! I told you. I - I'm looking after him. He's my responsibility. I brought him here! Please, Sensei! Please! This boy is very special!"

English. Sadao wondered of all things why they would speak English. That made no sense. He must be dreaming of his Toba Mountain School - else why would he hear his English sensei's voice so clearly?

I must be ill. This was the first coherent thought Sadao fully formed and held in his mind after drifting for days in odd dreams and nightmares he didn't want to remember. He wasn't even sure if he was fully awake. There were others here. He could hear them breathing. And there was sobbing too. Quiet weeping. It seemed to be a big room - lots of windows and light. His arms and hands felt warm on the sheet. They weren't swollen anymore. And there was something dangling from his wrist - a tube of fluid. He followed it up to a bag suspended over his head dripping slowly. He watched it as his vision swam in and out of focus.

I must be in hospital. I think for maybe a long time. I must be very ill.

For the first time since his illness struck, Sadao was able to account for the passage of time. Days went by and no one came to him except a nurse twice a day and twice at night to change his IV bag and empty a plastic sac of yellow fluid at the base of his bed. It was some time before he realized that bag was attached to his penis by a long clear tube.

Where is my mother? Where is my aunt? Why don't they visit me?

He waited, day after day. He slept and woke to watch the emotionless nurse change his bags. Unable to move or speak. Unable to get answers.

One day as he lay in his bed, eyes half-open, he saw men arrive in bodysuits to come carry away patients from some of the beds. They wore protective masks and gloves. He counted as they hauled them out. Three, four, five. Large bodies. Covered in blue sheets. Adults.

Why am I the only child? Fourteen. Am I an adult? Is that why my family is not here? Why won't they come?

The men moved to the bed beside him and began to lift the limp body of the woman who had been occupying the bed beside him for some days. She must have died in the night although she had been alive before sundown. Sadao wanted the men to make sure and moved his hand, to touch the arm in the yellow suit as it moved past him.

"Oi!" The man startled. *"This one's moving!! Get the doctor! Now!"*

A man and a woman in white coats and masks came soon after and nudged his arms and legs, shone lights in his eyes and pinched his toes. He could feel all of it.

"Can you hear me?" the woman asked. *"Can you blink or move? We will watch for your response."*

Sadao squeezed his eyes shut and opened them. It took a tremendous effort.

The doctors looked at one another. *"We need to get him moved out of here. Right away!"*

They put me here to die. But, I don't want to die anymore. I want to live.

Sadao was moved to a different floor of the hospital and after a few days relocated by ambulance to a different facility altogether. He still could not move more than his left hand and blink his eyes to respond to the endless questions his physicians asked him. There were questions not only about touch and movement but of awareness. Did he know his name? Did he know what year it was? They brought out charts to point to letters, words and symbols to gauge his reactions. Therapists came to move his thin arms and legs and to help him sit up. He was fed through a tube through his nose to his stomach four times a day. It was exhausting and frightening. Sadao had questions of his own but did not know how to ask them.

What's wrong with me? Will I get better? Will I be able to walk? Talk? Where is my mother? I want to see my mother!

Answers came slowly and most of them by simply overhearing conversations not meant for him. He knew he had something called 'Nagoya Fever.' It struck fast and if the initial fever didn't kill you, progressive catatonia would. The body grew weaker and weaker until it simply shut down. Thousands were infected. There weren't enough doctors to care for them all. It took a long time but a day finally came when Sadao could hold a marker and write on a wipe pad. He asked immediately about his family. His physical therapist who visited him once a day for an hour kept evading the question.

You have been in quarantine, she said. *You have been moved to a facility too far from your home,* was another excuse. But Sadao grew more insistent because he'd seen other patients visited by relatives and even more who had long since gone home with their families once they could communicate and feed themselves. Sadao could do both now without aid.

Eventually, after another month had passed in therapy, Sadao was able to speak clearly again and use his arms and legs. His movements were shaky and uncertain. But he was determined to get better and stand up and walk out of this place to find his own answers. He grew angry at his doctors and therapists and refused to listen to them. He even tried to escape one night by wheelchair but the night janitor caught him where he'd fallen at the foot of a short flight of stairs.

Depression took him. He lay still again, refusing to eat and refusing to speak. No one could tell him what he desperately needed to know. *Where is my family?! Why won't you tell me?*

At last a morning came when Sadao woke to the feel of a warm soft hand, holding his own.

"Okaasan?!" He woke with a start. It wasn't his mother. It wasn't his aunt. It was his favorite sensei from his Toba English School. She smiled at him even as tears built up in her eyes.

"Sadao-kun, I am here," she said. "I am sorry it took so long."

"Sensei." Sadao sat up. She wasn't alone. His lead physician was standing at the foot of the bed along with a National Defense soldier holding a long sack. "Where is my mother?!" Sadao asked for the millionth time.

Darnell-sensei's tears fell from her eyes as she squeezed his hand. "She's gone," she said weakly. "So is your father and your brothers, too." Sadao stared at her like she was speaking a language he'd never heard before.

"Were they sick, too?" Sadao asked. Deep in his heart he'd known this was the most likely answer.

"No," the soldier said, while Sensei wept into her hand. "They were killed."

"What - !"

His doctor spoke up. *"Not long after your aunt brought you to the local clinic in Tamaki we had news of a terrible tragedy in Toba. There was a clan raid. One of the worst. Your family was involved. We didn't want you to know this until your nervous system had a chance to recover."*

Sadao was numb, it was like fighting his way out of the fever all over again, except the pain was somehow even worse. Too much to feel. *"My family ... all of them? Where are they? I want to see them!"*

The doctor shook his head.

"They have been cremated and placed in a family shrine near Ise." The soldier stated plainly. *"I am here to ask you questions about their murders."*

"Must he do that now!?" Darnell-sensei cried out! "The boy is in shock!"

The physician nodded and the soldier handed the long army sack over to her, and stepped out of the room. *"He will be back soon, I'm afraid. We've held them off for this long, protecting you. You've been with us a long time, Sadao-kun."*

"How long..?" Sadao asked weakly.

"Eight months."

Sadao eased his head back into the pillow and he pulled his hand away from his weeping teacher. *"Where are my cousins? My little cousins -?"*

The physician looked grim. *"Your father's family is all gone. But your mother's sister's family is still living."*

Sadao lit up at this one glimmer of sanity. *"Where? Where are they? At the farm?!"*

"No," his doctor said. *"Your aunt and uncle are with your young cousins. The twins are at a similar facility in Nagoya. The girls are recovering well and should be released soon."*

Hot tears of shame ran down Sadao's face. Miko. Kiko. *"Did I get them sick?"*

"No! Of course not. Nagoya Fever isn't transferred that way. It's spread by pollinating insects, we've just learned. Contact with infected wildflowers is the causative agent. Anyone living in the Ise countryside in the late spring was susceptible to this latest outbreak. Don't blame yourself. You saw the worst of it. Young children recover from the disease quite fast. It's teens and adults who don't make it. As far as we know, you are the oldest living survivor in all of Japan, my friend."

Sadao turned to his teacher, still unable to believe his ears. "There is something we have to give you, Sadao. Something they were able to recover from your father's home. It was found in the study, locked in a wall safe the raiders were not able to open." She leaned forward and set the army sack on the bed next to Sadao where it dented the mattress with its weight.

"What's inside of it?" Sadao asked. The thought of what it might contain terrified him.

"An heirloom, I think," his teacher said, reaching over the bed to unzip the fastenings. Inside were his father's ancient swords - the *katana* and the *wakizashi* - each sheathed in their casings of polished gold embedded lacquer.

Sadao shut his eyes and turned away. "Please leave me alone," he whispered.

His teacher sniffled, squeezed his hand and with his physician, quietly stepped from the room.

In his mind, Sadao could still hear the girls' laughter over the trickling of the stream behind the farmhouse. The tiny paper boats filled with deadly flowers were still sailing downstream to the pond where some would sink and some would float. But in the end, all would fade to dust.

Fourth

Shrine of the Frogs

Toba Mountain Pass, 2047

The rain wouldn't stop.

For three nights and four days the sky had raged, sending endless wind whipped sheets of water down over their heads and backs. Every step of their march down the mountain was imperiled by slick mud and loose rocks; it left their arms and legs bruised and bloody. Their seven-man troop had slogged their way through the patrol route for six long hours, now arriving at the watchtower platform atop the inlet cliffs to keep eye over the harbor entrance until the sun sank behind the mountain.

Sadao and his comrades crowded into the poorly assembled bamboo hut, covering their soaked heads under a stinking oil tarp left behind by the last unit. Shoulder to shoulder, shivering on the cold flat stones of the platform, Sadao watched rivers of wet mud pour down the incline from above. It rained up to his ankles, soaking his heavy boots. His feet were so cold he could no longer feel his toes moving inside. Their radio was dead - the circuits were fried by the weather. No word had come in from their senior officers for three days; no orders except the ones they had marched out with - guard the mountainside from the cloud coated peak to the shrine at the base, half drowned in the ever-rising ocean.

The sea was a vast sheet of angry grey, stretching out below them through the swaying bamboo. Giant golden frogs swam through the white caps - big and small in rows and clumps, croaking. Shiny brass skin and bumpy warts flashed in an imaginary sun. Sadao's forehead fell towards his knees.

Whump! *"Stay alert, Koga!"*

His eyes snapped open and the frogs swam off at his senpai's command - hallucinations bred from sleeplessness.

"Here, take this." His sergeant, Hirayama, held out a cigarette. *"Ashito managed to light some. Keep you awake."*

Sadao took the rain blotched cigarette and cupped it in his hands to keep it from going out. He inhaled, coughed at the horrid taste, and inhaled again. His lungs burned and the pain of it made his eyes clear some. The amphibians were gone. All that remained were the algae stained roof tiles of the sunken shrine 30 meters below the cliff's edge, beating back the ocean's onslaught.

"I used to dive here with my brothers," Sadao mumbled around the cigarette. *"We'd collect old go-en from the broken saisen box."*

His sergeant laughed. *"No need to cleanse yourself first."*

"No point. The mizuba rusted away decades ago." Sadao smiled at the memories of the deteriorating red painted *torii* - the cracked temple bells and fish-eaten ropes. It was all still down there, deep in the sea, rotting and floating away. It seemed like a hundred years ago from another life before the war - before the schools were closed, before his uncle turned him over to the Defense Army, before his long illness, before his murdered family became only shattered ghosts haunting his dreams. *"There's frogs down there,"* he said.

"Huh?"

"Big brass statues - hundreds of them. All around the place. I never knew why. I asked my father once about them, but he couldn't remember. He was very young the last time the jinja was above water."

"Here," Hirayama, said, nudging closer and wrapping an arm around him. *"Stay warm. We'll rest soon."*

Sadao nodded and dropped his cigarette butt in the racing water. It was soon washed away over the cliff and into the sea. He loosened his pack and leaned his exhausted body into the offered embrace. Hirayama was a kind man - at 17, he was also the oldest among them. He slept close to the younger ones at night, held their hands when they cried for their mothers. Sadao was not one to cry out. Who would come? No one but the enemy. He loosened the strap that held his father's swords tight across his back and let their weight sink to the ground.

He dreamt of the sun shining across the rice fields blowing in the summer wind. He was a school boy again, walking home to his cousins' farm, carrying his books in a sling. Young girls on bicycles pedaled past in their pleated skirts while the cicada hummed.

Bam! Bam!

Distant gunfire ripped him from his sleep. It was dark now and the wind was howling, whipping the tarp around them. Hirayama was on his feet motioning them to stay low and quiet. Ashito and the others were rubbing their eyes and straining to hear over the wind gusts. All of them must have dozed off. The rain had stopped.

Boom! Ratatata!

Sadao covered his ears. The shots echoing off the bay cliffs were deafening - too close.

"They're coming! We need to move! On your feet!" The troop responded, scrambling to gather their packs. *"Leave it!"* Hirayama yelled. *"Now!"*

A bullet hissed through the bamboo roof, spraying splinters. And another came, striking the mud of the steep path with a splat!

In an uncontrolled burst of panic, Sadao and his comrades ran blind through the jungle off the road and into the thick wet leaves. They fell and tumbled down the mountainside - shouting for each other in the darkness.

Swizzzst!

Bullets still came whizzing past their heads. Sadao raced after the bounding pack ahead of him for a few meters when he heard Ashito scream and Hirayama yell his name.

Under attack! We're under attack! With guns!

Sadao tripped over a root and went headfirst into the brush, tumbling around. *Stay down!* He rolled into the thick of the waterlogged vegetation and lay frozen in the pitch.

Ashito was screaming. It was like a girl's scream, terrible to hear. Hirayama called for him once more through the bamboo and there was a crack of gunfire. His voice was cut off mid-yell.

There were distant voices, barely audible over his heart's pounding. *They're all dead! Dead…!*

Forcing his lungs to slow, Sadao moved his arm over his shoulder to reach for his father's katana. The weight of the double sheath felt lighter across his back as he groped around.

No … no, no, no!

His fingertips found the katana's hilt but the paired wakizashi was gone. He scrambled around on his belly straining his eyes in the darkness, clawing the mud, but there was nothing to see or feel but dead leaves. *It's gone! My father's fathers carried it for 200 hundred years and I've lost it!*

Voices were coming and footfalls crashed through the brush. Laughter - they were laughing! Laughing that they had killed.

Anger galvanizing his strength, Sadao moved into a crouch, still low and hidden but with the long sword drawn and ready in his hands. The naked blade was held upward to slash clean through anyone who dared approach him.

Come to me now! Find me!

But the footfalls and shouts didn't come any closer. They faded with the laughter back up the mountain until there was nothing left to hear.

"Someone there?!"

Sadao snapped out of his stance at the sound of Ashito's weak voice.

"Ashito! I'm coming!"

"Hurry!"

He marched back up the hillside in the dark listening for his injured comrade's cries under the wind. Sadao found him, a limp red mass of limbs fallen at the foot of a cherry tree.

"Ashito! I'm here! Stop yelling, I don't know how far our voices travel."

"Koga ... I'm sorry!" The boy was gripping his left side where blood was pouring through his fingers. *"Hirayama - he's ..."*

"I know," Sadao said, checking Ashito's pulse at his neck. It was weak and his skin was cold. *"That can't be helped. Show me your wound."*

Ashito grimaced, *"It hurts..."*

"Easy..." Sadao moved his locked hands away to get a better look at the damage. In the dark, everything looked black with blood. Ashito coughed up a spray of blood and a pink rope of intestine exploded out of his side. Sadao jerked back in shock.

"Is it bad?"

Sadao's head swam and nausea twisted his gut. *"Yeah,"* he managed.

Ashito's eyes screwed shut. *"I'm sorry ... so sorry ..."*

"Hold your breath in," Sadao said. He cleared his mind and pushed the loose coil of gut back up into the gaping wound, holding his hand firmly over the torn mass of skin and muscle. His eyes darted around in the dark for something to bind it with. But there was nothing - Ashito's pack had been left behind at the watchtower along with his own.

"I'm sorry too, Ashito ... I should have stayed awake ... I should have been a better soldier! I should have ..."

Ashito's eyes, white and sightless stared up at the canopy of leaves. He was gone.

"Gaaaghh!!" Sadao got to his feet. Arms slick with mud and blood, he reached behind his head and grasped his father's legacy in both hands and tore the sword free from its sling.

Swllliinnngg! The strap snapped and the camouflage scabbard flew away into the vegetation. He swung the weapon hard, slicing an unsuspecting bamboo shoot clean from its stalk. It gave a sharp snap that fed Sadao's fury as he swung and severed another. He put his back to the corpses of his friends and ran to the uphill path with the taste of blood in his mouth.

Screaming and swinging he ran, slaughtering the vegetation in his path. He retraced his coward's journey back up mountain, air rasping his lungs, until the shot-out roof of the watchtower came back into view. Someone was there in the dark with a dim lantern, hunched low, rustling through their forgotten supplies. The figure was so focused on gathering their spoils, it failed to hear Sadao's approach. He could still feel the satisfying pop of the bamboo in his teeth. He wanted to hear it again.

"Sadao...?"

"Who's there?!" Sadao demanded, marching forward, blade raised high.

"I found it, Sadao. The small sword, see?" The thief held up the dropped wakizashi.

It was the same boy, a little older now, a little taller and thinner. He wore the colors of the enemy clan on long dirty coat sleeves that trailed over his grubby thieving hands. Sadao's old leather shoes, now a size too small and full of mud and holes were still tied to his feet with twine. He had a sack with him - already stuffed with his dead friends' possessions.

"Put it down! It's not yours!"

"But I want it," he said with a whine, clutching the weapon in his floppy sleeves. *"It's mine, too! You have the big one already!"*

Shouts in the distance. A child's whine carried very far. *Let them come!*

"I said, it's not yours!!"

He swung the katana into the support post of the tower and dove forward onto the child who kicked and fought him for the wakizashi, squealing…

"It's miiiiiiine!!"

Sadao used his weight to wrestle the kid under him. He got an arm up under the boy's chin and they fell backwards onto the stones, legs kicking at each other.

"Miiiiiiinnneee!!"

"Itai!!" The little shit bit his forearm. Sadao punched him hard in the gut and the child cried out in pain, dropping the sword.

Bam!! Bam!! The bullets were coming again. Down from above, whistling through the forest.

Sadao flipped the kid under him and grabbed the dropped sword. Holding the boy down with his bleeding arm, he turned the short blade's point inward and aimed it at the screaming gaki's throat.

"You want this?! So much you'll scream out for it in a forest full of guns?! Wearing the enemy colors? Did you think it would stop their bullets?!"

"O-oni - s-san … "

"Don't ever call me that!!" Sadao screamed at the child's frightened face. *"I am not your brother!! My brothers are dead!! Their children are dead!! My mother is dead and my father too!! Everyone, dead!! I will never be anyone's brother again!!"* He pressed the tip of the sword into the kid's throat, right into the hollow where the scratch of the razor tip began to draw blood.

Sadao's breath was a seething growl, bloody spit flew across the boy's face. His small eyes were wide black pools in the flicker of the lantern and in them, Sadao caught a faint glimpse of himself. His skin covered in gore, his face twisted in rage. And all the child's eyes reflected back was the same misguided, undesired love.

"O-oni - s-sa -!"

The crunch of a child's severed throat is nothing like a bamboo stalk. The hollow

pop and crack does not come. The young leaves reaching up for the sun do not fall to the forest floor in a satisfying rustle. There is no sound but a deep sucking void.

Bam!! Bam!! Rattttatttt!!

Airborne, with his father's loosened katana in his hands, Sadao dove from the edge of the watchtower platform 30 meters through the air toward the water. Under the waves of the sea, the bullets sang a softer song. Their bubbled traces made odd reflections across the faces of the hundred brass frogs, dressed in seaweed, sitting peacefully in the depths of the angry sea, waiting for dawn to light their hidden world.

"Where is he?! Where is the boy?!"

"He's upstairs. He's not well. Please don't…"

Smack!

His aunt's scream was short and soon muffled. Her weeping was drowned out by the sounds of his uncle's heavy feet stomping up the wooden stairs to the children's room. Sadao lay on the futon alone, shirtless, smoking a cigarette and moving as little as possible.

His uncle's red bald head was at the door.

"Okiro!" he shouted.

Sadao did not respond.

"You're a traitor to this family! Abandoning your post! You shame us with your cowardice!"

Small puffs of white smoke rose to the ceiling where the twins used to light the candlebox at night and make storybook figure shadows with their hands. He wondered if they had candle boxes in the sanitorium. He should send them one, he mused, as he killed the butt in an ashtray that used to sit on his uncle's desk. The smell of the man's breath was directly above him. Sake - Imperial Label. Somehow, there was always money for that.

"Answer me! Lazy, worthless bastard child! How will you pay for your room and board now?"

Sadao said nothing and reached to bring a fresh cigarette to his lips - the last of the pack. Eyes on the ceiling, his hand groped lazily for the lighter.

Wham! His uncle's foot came down crushing his forearm.

"Answer me!"

Sadao looked to his fingers, twisted into a claw on the other side of his uncle's dry heel. The pain of it was incredible. He watched in fascination as the blood drained from his fingers and the skin went pale, pale as Ashito's face.

"If you won't work - if you won't fight - you will be sold!"

There was a tingling, just a bit in the very tips of his fingers - a dull throbbing that became a widening, spreading release as if the hand that had once held his murdered father's smallest sword was no longer there.

"Fine," Sadao said and his hand was freed.

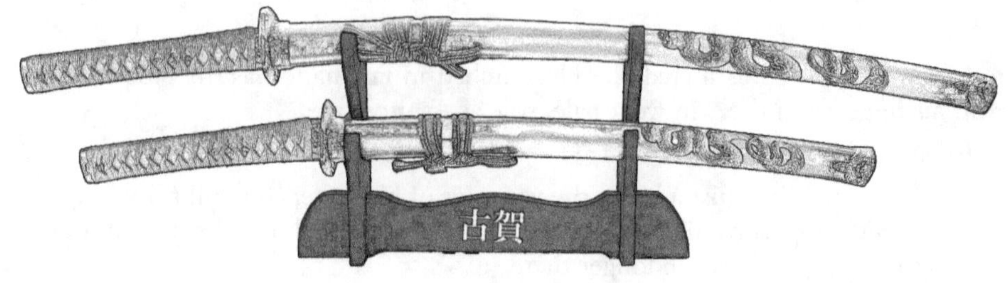

Chapter IX

Shinjyu

Sasori Lakeside Camp - 2073

Mouse woke to a cold bed. His eyes shot open the moment he realized it. The sheets were turned back on the opposite side of the bed and a towel rested over the bedroom chair.

He sat straight up. "Sadao?!"

"In here, *Konezumi*."

Sadao's voice and the scent of his cigarettes emanated from the main room, as did a rapid conversation in Japanese over the radio. He was talking to Tagata.

"Taga says you're late for work!"

"Fuck work!" Mouse shouted back. "I'm beat!"

More Japanese followed as Mouse wrapped a blanket around his nakedness and joined Sadao at the kitchen table next to his pot of green tea and cereal bowl, which had clearly become Sadao's new ashtray.

"I see your breakfast routine hasn't changed - tea and cigs. I eat out of this you know," he said, peering into his abused pottery. Sadao grinned and flicked in a line of ash as he leaned in for a kiss.

"Have some tea."

Mouse grabbed a spare mug and poured from the kettle as Sadao continued his conversation. It sounded lighthearted until the topic shifted back to team business.

"Yes, of course. I'll make sure Mouse can still walk down to camp, pants on. We'll see you at the lake soon."

"It is good to hear your voice, Sadao-sama. You have been missed by many."

"I've missed everyone, too. It's good to be home," Sadao replied and signed off, setting the radio receiver back on the shelf.

"I'm surprised you're up so early," Mouse yawned. "I thought I wore you out."

"Leg was bothering me. Needed a hot soak. Your ofero is perfect for that - helps the muscles to unlock. Not a luxury I had in prison. I'm sorry I left you. I didn't want to wake you up."

"S'okay. I'm just not all that thrilled about having to re-insert you into the real world so quickly."

"Don't pout like that. Or you'll find yourself even later for work."

Mouse raised a brow. "Really? That's all I gotta do, push out a lip to get you to stay?"

Sadao ditched his cigarette. "Maybe…"

Mouse let the blanket drop and settled himself across Sadao's lap. He bent and kissed his lips. Warm hands ran down his back and cupped his ass.

"I didn't know you could be seduced so easily."

"Been locked up a long time, remember?" Sadao said, kissing his collarbone. "Nothing but memories of you and the desert to comfort me those long dark nights. Tortuous."

"Aahh…" Mouse had an insta-boner and Sadao's palm found it, stroking firmly. "I thought you promised Tagata I'd still be able to walk."

"I'll carry you," Sadao said as Mouse rubbed his answering bulge through his jeans. They kissed with growing intensity until Mouse's ass couldn't take being empty anymore.

"God, I want you so bad," Mouse gasped as Sadao fingered his asshole. "You could fuck me a week straight and it'd still not be enough."

"We don't have that much time," Sadao said, as Mouse dug into his fly and pulled out his dick - rock hard and ready to please. Sadao grabbed Mouse by the ass and heaved him up onto the table, sloshing the mugs. Mouse lay back on the spilled tea and spread his legs, rolling back his hips to welcome Sadao's tongue to open him up. Though admittedly, he was pretty loose at this point.

The sun was bright in the main room. It must be 10 A.M. or later, Mouse mused, as Sadao buried his face between his cheeks. The sounds of hungry slurping filled the room. *Paradise … I live in nirvana now.* Sadao's fingers gradually replaced his tongue, stretching the rim and flicking the pearled ring making Mouse squirm. Sadao lifted his face, bent Mouse over in half and buried himself all in.

"Uuugh!" Mouse moaned. "Fuck, you feel enormous! Did your dick get bigger in prison?"

"Perhaps," Sadao said, moving in for a kiss. His beard smelled of musk. God, Mouse loved it when Sadao really dug in like that. Getting eaten before a fuck was as romantic to him as a kiss on the mouth.

The table creaked with each thrust, scooting a bit across the floor. More tea sloshed out of the barely standing mugs, wetting Mouse's braids in warm liquid. His hands gripped the table's surface, trying to stabilize himself for Sadao's benefit. The man was all over him, hands and tongue - nipping, pinching and sucking his shoulders and chest, groaning with the thrill of it.

His ass was so full and hot, Mouse wound his legs around Sadao's torso, wanting to bring him even closer. Sadao responded by pounding harder into him, making Mouse wonder if the nails he'd used to construct the pinewood table were long enough to hold up to their passion.

Eek. Crack. Eek!

Note to self - build all furniture with load-bearing sex stress in mind. Shit, he just couldn't get enough. Mouse wrapped his arms around the man's shoulders and urged him on and on and -

"Fuck!" Sadao shouted. All at once he reached a full stop, palm braced on the table. Mouse blinked in confusion. His head was swimming with thwarted pleasure as Sadao pushed him off.

"You okay, babe?"

Sadao was frozen, head down in a grimace. Gingerly, he brought himself up to a more upright position. His dick loosened and slid out of Mouse's ass. *"Nngh! Kuso!"*

Mouse scrambled to sit up. "Babe?"

"Leg…" Sadao said with effort. His fingertips were white, gripping the table's edge.

"Shit!" Mouse scrambled off the table and brought the chair back around behind Sadao so he could sit down. The man was in agony. "Oh my God, baby! What I can I do?"

"Just…don't move me," he stammered, sitting bare-assed in the chair with his jeans down around his ankles. His erection took on a decidedly downward incline.

"Oh God, I hurt you! I'm so sorry!"

Sadao sat, eyes screwed shut, fighting the pain. Mouse knelt beside him, stroking his arm. "Babe, I'm so sorry."

Gradually, Sadao's breathing deepened and he opened his eyes. "Maybe … we should be getting you to camp."

"Not if you can't move, shit! I knew I overtaxed you! You need to see Sensei! I'll hail him!"

"No!" Sadao shouted as Mouse began to rise. "It's a cramp. It will ease in a moment. Just give me a few seconds."

Mouse stood up and touched his hair. Sweat stood out on the man's forehead. He'd never seen Sadao in pain like this.

Your greedy little ass did this, moron. Poor man had his hip all blown to shit and you fucked for 6 hours straight last night and expected him to jump through hoops this morning? On the breakfast table for crissakes? What's wrong with you?

After several long minutes, Sadao began to relax. "It's passing. Go grab a shower. I'll be fine."

Mouse rubbed Sadao's shoulder. "I'm glad, but make no mistake, Sensei's going to be on your reunion tour this morning."

Sadao nodded and motioned for Mouse to clear out so he could pull his jeans back on.

By the time Mouse had showered and dressed, Sadao was able to stand and walk again. He motioned Mouse back under his arm for the descent of the stairs and most of the quarter-mile walk down the hill to the lakeside. As worried as he was about Sadao's leg, Mouse really didn't mind playing the role of human crutch, as the duty involved a lot of snuggly closeness and stolen kisses.

You were only companion Sadao walked with where eyes could see, Tagata had said, and that didn't appear to have changed one bit as they came into view of the camp trailers and trucks. Mouse was a little walking bundle of happiness as they ambled along arm in arm. *Yep, that's right, people - got my man back!*

Lupe was the first one to spot them moving slowly up the shoreline path toward the garage truck. He gave a shout that turned heads and all at once, team members began to realize who this hobbling long-haired man was, limping into camp with Mouse's assistance.

Young men abandoned their various activities and ran forward to greet them with shouts of "Boss!! Boss!! *Okaeri!!*"

Tagata emerged from between the rows of trucks and tents and gave a shout of his own in their native tongue and the men echoed it across the camp - calling for assembly. Racers and workers alike ran to the open space near the mess hall tent pitched near water's edge.

"Sadao-sama, your presence honors us," Tagata said in English, perhaps for Mouse's benefit, as the men moved aside to let him through. "We thank you for your hardship and struggle. Please excuse my poor efforts to lead this team in your absence," he said and bowed deeply before the team's former Boss. Sadao loosened his hold on Mouse to return the gesture, although bending at the waist clearly pained him. Tagata deepened his bow accordingly. Mouse had learned in his years among the Japanese team members that this signified status - to lower your head below your predecessor's. He would always be Sadao's inferior for the remainder of their lives, even if Sadao was retired.

"Enough formality, Tagata-san," Sadao said, straightening up. He motioned the tall young man to come to him for a very un-Japanese hug. Mouse lowered his eyes, as did the rest of the men, to allow them this display. He could hear Sadao give the man a whisper of confidence for his ear alone. Then the moment passed and they separated. "I would not have trusted my team to anyone else," he said. "But my time has passed. The Sasoris are in capable hands and will remain so. Carry on as you have. I am pleased to see many new faces among those I've missed." Sadao beckoned to his old crew. "Come here, let me see you all."

The assembly of racers moved in to take their turn clapping Sadao's shoulders, bowing and shaking his hand. "Old Boss! *Okaeri!*" Lupe got excited too and ran forward to give Sadao another welcome-back hug. "Old Boss! Old Boss!" the men started to cry out, following Lupe's lead.

"Perhaps we need to come up with a better title for me than 'Old Boss,'" Sadao said amid the excited men.

"Yeah, what do we call you now?" Lupe wanted to know. "You've always been Boss to me."

Sadao exchanged an amused look with his successor. "Tagata-san is Boss now. Maybe you should all call me *Oyaji*."

Tagata looked dubious. Lupe grinned too as more men stepped forward to take their turn welcoming Oyaji home.

"What does o-ya-whatever mean?" Mouse asked Lupe, who still knew ten times the Japanese he did. Two years in camp with these guys and he hadn't picked up a whole lot other than basic mechanical terms necessary to guide his garage crew.

"Oyaji," Lupe corrected. "It means, 'Old Man.'"

"And that's better than 'Old Boss' because...?"

"It's what they used to call Yakuza godfathers. I think he's trying to be ironic."

Oyaji it was then. Mouse stood aside to let the seasoned racers, then the newer racing team members, make their hellos and introductions. Many of them had not been old enough to join the active roster when Sadao left. Now they were tall strong men, bowing to the mentor who had first guided them in their racing skills.

Sadao greeted the new nervous trainees, too. "You were all so much smaller last I saw you," Mouse heard him say in English. It was touching to see these teens with their bold tattoos and piercings be so tentative about approaching Sadao. Some couldn't make the hard steps forward without showing their emotion and shed a few tears when Sadao made a point to speak and touch each one of them. Their Oyaji had become almost mythical. Two years did change a lot when it came to the young.

Mouse turned his head when he heard children's laughter. Sadao followed his gaze to see Kei waddling up the path with his ward of some dozen or so kidlets aged five to eleven behind him. Sadao exchanged a quick glance with Mouse.

"I know. There's a lot more of Kei to love," Mouse said with a grin.

"Indeed," Sadao said under his breath as he stepped forward to attempt to embrace his former teen assistant with both arms - neither of which managed to meet on the opposite side. "Kei," he said softly as the large man immediately began to weep in his arms. Sadao held him a moment saying something about "doing well in watching over his sons." Kei nodded, wiping his round red cheeks and motioned the excited children forward. Sadao was all at once pounced upon and Mouse had to steady him as he knelt in the dirt to allow the boys to climb all over him, demanding hugs and tickles.

"Ta-kun!" Sadao exclaimed, lifting one of them up onto his knees. "*Ookiku natta ne?*"

The child had been barely five last Sadao had seen him. Now he was two feet taller and about to turn seven. "I miss-ed you," the kid said, shyly trying out his English skills.

Sadao touched the child's cheek. "I missed you, too. Very much." Little Takeshi threw his arms tight around Sadao's neck and refused to let go. "*Ii ko da...*" Sadao whispered, kissing his head. Sadao took his time nuzzling all his little ones who had been old enough to remember him from before. But there were five children who remained standing nervously a few feet back from this strange man their classmates were going nuts over. "*Kinasai*," Sadao said softly, inviting them to approach him. "Tell me your names."

The kids looked to Kei first, who encouraged them. Two of the boys stepped forward first, identical twins. They bowed and gave their names in shy voices. "Twins," Sadao said in wonder. "Our first pair. Forgive me, it will take me some time to tell who is who." When the two boys looked confused he repeated himself in Japanese, to which they said a few polite words and ran off to join some of the other kids on a nearby rope swing. The last two children wouldn't come forward at all.

"*Daijyobu*," Sadao said and Kei stepped forward to put a gentle hand on the back of each child to ease them closer. One kid took off straight for the swing in fright. But the other, a little child in a baseball cap with a dirt-smudged face, refused to budge and clung to Kei's thick leg stubbornly with a little frown.

"*Oiede*," Sadao said. "*Boku wa yasashii hito da.*"

"Go on," Kei said, nudging the child a step forward. "This one knows English well," he said.

"Is that so? You must be a very clever little boy," Sadao said, holding out his hand. The child looked to be around six years of age with delicate features and big dark eyes.

The little kid glared at him and tugged Kei's leg. "Sensei! Tell him!"

Sadao looked up confused. Kei seemed uneasy and started to stammer. "Well ... it's complicated..."

Sadao held out his hand, and the kid took another step forward, frowning. He reached up to pat the nervous child on the head and the tiny thing jerked back so fast the oversized ballcap tumbled to the ground, revealing a fall of straight jet black hair. Sadao's eyes widened and he gaped up at Kei. "This is a girl-child!"

"Duh!" the little kid said, insulted. She picked up her cap and planted it back on her head. She turned to look up at her sensei. "You said he was a smart man!"

"Um, well yes he is," Kei said with a nervous smile. "He's just surprised, like we all were when ... we realized ... uh ..."

Sadao's eyes tracked directly to Tagata, who gave him a "What was I supposed to do?" shrug. Clearly this child's real gender had been unknown to mostly everyone, including Mouse - who had assumed all the new rugrats from the San Diego docks were male. A rumble of concern echoed through the gathered crowd. Mouse elbowed Lupe, who had been on the recent recruitment expedition. "Didn't you know?"

His friend shook his head in shock. "Looked like a boy to me," he whispered back. "His ... *her* hair was shorter then."

"You didn't check?"

"I didn't look under the hood, okay?"

"*Namae wa nan da ka?*" Sadao asked the little girl, who was doing her best to puff herself up to the hundred or so staring men and boys.

"My name," she said with a pause to emphasize her preference of English, "is Jiro."

That caused more mumbling among the audience.

"Jiro is a boy's name," Sadao said. He was still on his knees so his eyes met directly with hers. "If you want people to know you are a little girl, you will need to have a girl's name."

The little thing looked at her shoes. She was dressed head to toe in boy's clothing. "No," she said. "My name is Jiro!"

"It's what we've been calling her," Kei offered. "She won't tell us her real name."

"If you will not tell me your real name," Sadao said. "Will you let me give you one?" he asked. "One that is proper for a girl?" The child seemed to brighten at this notion and nodded. "Come closer, little one."

She let go of Kei's leg and walked more confidently up to Sadao. He reached out and this time she allowed him to tip her cap up so he could see her face better.

"You have very fair skin and large dark eyes. They remind me of the black pearls I used to polish when I was young. I think I will call you Shinjyu."[1]

The girl thought it over a moment, then broke into a shy smile.

"You like that name?"

She nodded.

"Shinjyu it is."

"Can I go play now?" she asked with a look up at Kei. He excused her and she ran for the tree swing, now being tugged at by six kids at once. "Move it!" she yelled. "It's Shinjyu's turn!"

With his lap now empty of children, Mouse helped Sadao back onto his feet. "That was something you don't see everyday in this camp," Mouse said in his ear.

"I will be having words with Tagata about this," Sadao assured him.

"A little late now, don't you think? Those kids came in two months ago."

"There's a reason we don't have women here. And he knows why."

"She's not a woman, Sadao. She's a little girl."

"She won't always be," Sadao said, moving with Mouse's help through the dispersing crowd toward the man he intended to speak with.

---

1 *pearl*

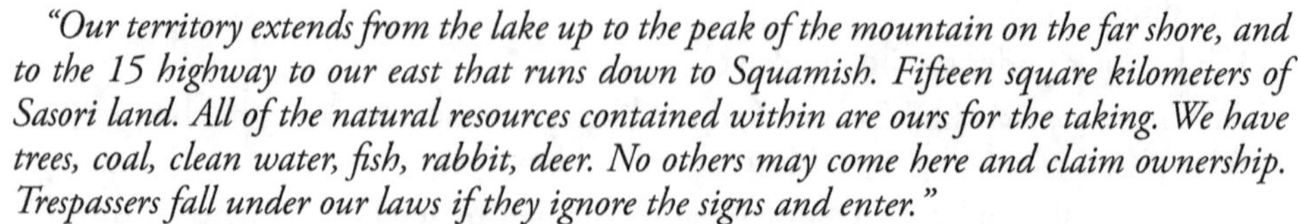

"Our territory extends from the lake up to the peak of the mountain on the far shore, and to the 15 highway to our east that runs down to Squamish. Fifteen square kilometers of Sasori land. All of the natural resources contained within are ours for the taking. We have trees, coal, clean water, fish, rabbit, deer. No others may come here and claim ownership. Trespassers fall under our laws if they ignore the signs and enter."

"English, Taga. You need practice," Sadao said, accepting a cigarette from his former Captain.

Tagata sighed and placed a fresh ashtray on the pinewood table between them. He settled himself opposite Sadao in a matching Adirondack chair. "I hate English. Stupid language," he said, offering Sadao his silver lighter.

Sadao lit up and relaxed into the chair, blowing smoke toward the tall tree tops. The recline of the handmade chair was well suited to his hip, which only became comfortable at certain angles. "It's a language that you will need to master if you're going to be successful in this country."

"I know this," Tagata answered, forcing the proper "th" sound through his teeth. "Does not mean I have to like."

They smoked in the warm sunlight on the open deck that extended from the front of Tagata's A-frame cabin by the lakeshore. It, and three other similar structures given to high ranking racing officers, were within a stone's throw of each other and a quick jog to the main camp. Construction equipment and spare building materials were stowed under tarps to wait for the winter months to pass into the next building season.

"You have shown remarkable improvement. Your pronunciation, especially."

"This Mouse teach me. When he is not working, he help me to learn the right way to move my tongue for English."

"I'm glad to hear you two have been getting along."

Tagata smoked a moment. "He is good man. Loyal. Work very hard. I like this man now, I think."

Sadao chuckled to himself. "Time does heal wounds, as they say."

"Who say these things? Always English, there are words having too many meanings. Give to me many headaches."

"Give it time, Taga. Soon you will begin to dream in English. This is when I knew I had truly grasped the language, when I began to speak in my dreams with a foreign tongue. Even when I dream of Japan now it's often in English."

"My dream, all Nihongo! This way I know what dream people talk about!"

Sadao smiled. "Fair enough. You've done well here. You have many accomplishments to be proud of. These cabins are quite comfortable. The men seem to be well adjusted to mountain living."

Tagata shook his head, taking a drag. "We lose some first year. Two die in ice storm. Soon, twelve others desert our camp. We do not see again these men. It is big loss to the team. We did not have full roster first year of competition. Very bad."

"Which men?" Sadao asked, shocked.

"They belonged to the one who has passed."

"Whitebird men?"

"Yes. They leave first spring. No word. Just gone."

"That is unfortunate," Sadao said. "You could not have prevented that, I'm afraid. There were some who continued to openly defy my orders after the joining of our teams. Only the will of the one we lost could restrain them."

"*Shou ga nai desu ne?* There is no good word in English to say about this."

"No, there isn't."

"Also, I must tell you, Kinjo was gone from hospital last year sometime."

"Gone? You mean he escaped?" Sadao asked, disturbed.

Tagata snorted. "Now you know why English is bad for me. No, I mean he was healed so hospital sent him away."

"Where did he go? I banned him from ever returning to the team. Not just for Mouse's safety but for the safety of all racers!"

"He was sent back to Japan. Deported."

"Good. He won't be missed."

"I agree. He always was fault of many fights. It was good thing, what you did - to ban him."

"I was told by my lawyer he attempted to file assault charges against me. But that only led to Utah authorities discovering his illegal status. I never did learn what their final decision was against him."

"It was on news some night. He was put on boat. Miyagi told this to me."

"Miyagi? So we still have one of The General's former men among us?"

"Yes, but the rest - they are gone."

"Probably for the best," Sadao said and Tagata nodded his agreement.

They smoked for a while in a comfortable silence until Tagata asked, "Sadao-sama, what is it that you plan to do now?"

"Hmm, for the first time in my life, I have no plans. And for now I would like to keep it that way."

"But there must be something Sadao-sama desires?"

"If there is, then I don't know about it," Sadao said, crushing out his cigarette. "If I plan anything it is to rest. Read my books, carve a little. Keep Mouse happy. I owe him that much."

"Rest is good plan," Tagata agreed.

"Prison wasn't kind to me. I feel as if a part of me died there. I'm feeling old, Taga. Tired. Worn down to the bone."

"If you forgive me, Sadao-sama does look thin."

"Didn't have much of an appetite in prison," Sadao said, pulling out another stick. "I still don't. Food takes too much energy to consume." Tagata offered his lighter again.

"You must come to lunch next hour. Cook-san will make you favorite food."

"Maybe," Sadao said, inhaling. "I need to get accustomed to eating regularly again, to sleeping again. I slept very little in lock-up. Pain and cold were constant companions."

"Sadao-sama will enjoy good rest in mountains, I think."

"Only if my leg and Mouse will allow it," he said with a grin.

Tagata looked puzzled.

"I have a lover twelve years my junior, Taga. Not a concern before the leg injury. But now, compared to him, I feel like an old man with a trophy wife half my age."

"Trophy wife? What is meaning?"

Sadao laughed. "Marry someone your own age. That is my advice."

"Marry? This I have no time. Not even girlfriend time. Team Boss does not have these things."

"I'm afraid that's true. Personal time was something of a luxury," Sadao said, flicking ash. He envied Tagata's ashtray, something Mouse's cabin sorely lacked. "But maybe that will change now. Maybe I can learn to be a good husband. If I had one regret in prison, it was that I had never made time for a family."

"You have family," Tagata said, gesturing toward the busy camp.

"I do, but I feel like I've missed an important chapter in my life." Sadao said, somewhat surprised at his own words. "I don't know. Could be just middle-age talking."

"Does Sadao-sama desire children?" Tagata asked.

"No!" Sadao coughed. "Absolutely not! I can barely take care of myself! Besides, my lifestyle doesn't warrant an easy path to fatherhood. My little ones are enough. Speaking of which, this girl-child - you know this is a concern."

"I know," Tagata said. "This is difficult problem. I did not know until Kei confess to me this secret. He did not want anyone to know for long time. He love this girl very much. Does not want her sent away."

"The longer you wait, Taga, the harder it will be. On her and on Kei. You know she can not be allowed to grow up here. A racing camp is not a place for women."

Tagata smoked thoughtfully. "I will ask Canadian authority what is best."

"She needs to be adopted out to a good home. Under no circumstances should she be sent back to Japan!"

"Of course not. I will take care of it."

"Good," Sadao said, leaning back into the chair and closing his eyes. It was nice for once not to be the one who had to take care of everything. The sun was warm on his face as it passed through the pine boughs. He let his cigarette burn out in the ashtray as the scent of evergreen and the sounds of camp lulled him to sleep.

"Hey! Tell Old Smokey he needs to get his ass down here and come eat!"

Sadao jerked awake. "Eh?"

Tagata was still sitting beside him with a wry grin. "Trophy wife is come for you."

"I'm relaxing!" Sadao shouted back at Mouse, who was coming up the path as the lunch bell began to ring.

"Cigarettes and tea do not equal a well-balanced diet! Hop to it!"

Old Smokey groaned and forced himself to sit up. "See? No sleep."

Tagata rose and helped him up. "I ask Cook-san to make you special *katsu-don*," he said. "Fill your belly again."

Mouse took over as human crutch as they headed into the middle of camp for chow time. Sadao had to admit the familiar tables, chairs and scent of steaming rice billowing out of the kitchen into the main tent was comforting enough to put him in the mood for eating. Mouse served him and made careful count of how many times the chopsticks rose to his mouth.

"Hey, less chat, more chewing!" he'd snap whenever Sadao's attention would wander into conversations with passing crew members and mess hall staff, who stopped to say welcome back. "You're not leaving this table until that bowl is empty!"

"Mouse, realize my stomach has shrunk to the size of an egg thanks to prison cuisine and a week of my gut turning inside-out at sea! Not even half this bowl could fit inside me anymore!"

Mouse picked up the *ohashi* like he was an errant toddler and scooped up a glob of curried rice and spun it in a circle. "Does this have to be an airplane heading for the hanger?"

Sadao grunted and took the chopsticks back. "I can feed myself!"

Tagata tried to stifle his smile at the scene but wisely kept quiet.

Two thirds of the bowl made Sadao feel ready to pop. He wanted to get up and move a bit to aid his digestion.

"I'll go to Sensei later this afternoon," Sadao said, limping at Mouse's side on his own power as they exited the tent. "Let me stretch a bit. You need to get back to the garage."

"Not until I drop you off at medical myself. I don't trust you."

"I want to walk."

"No. Not unless I'm with you."

"You can't watch me every second of every day!"

"Try me! You need supervision! You're a hot mess right now!"

"Very flattering."

"Yeah, but you're my hot mess!" Mouse said, stroking his overgrown beard and kissing him right there in the middle of the bustling camp. Sadao couldn't resist returning the embrace, parting his lips for a deeper kiss, and allowing his arms to encircle his wonderfully bossy other half. Somebody whistled. *Let them see*, he thought, savoring Mouse's tongue. *We've earned this.*

Blue eyes looked fuzzily into his own when they parted. "Oohkay," Mouse said dreamily. "You win. Let's go for a short walk. There's something I need to show you, anyway."

Mouse took Sadao's hand and led him off the main camp path up into the woods along a partially overgrown trail. It wasn't far but the way was secluded. Soon they came upon a long pine building with a slanted roof and a painted front. Sadao brushed some deadwood away to reveal an indigenous motif of thunderbirds and beavers.

"What is this?" Sadao wondered.

"It's an old Squamish tribal longhouse. It was already on the property when the team took it over. Used to belong to a long deceased Indian medicine man, they told us. We wanted to use it for a school room for the kids but - I dunno, something about the place gave everyone the creeps. So we use it for storage," Mouse said, removing a key from his chain for Sadao to take from him.

"Why are you giving me this?"

Mouse looked awkward. "What's inside belongs to you now, I think."

Sadao was confused since nearly everything he owned from his old trailer was stowed someplace in the cabin, and his bike collection had been destroyed years ago in the equipment trailer fire. He took the key and unlocked the padlock on the sliding wooden door. It was dark and smelled musty inside; there weren't any windows. He took a few tentative steps in.

"I'll get the lantern," Mouse said, lighting a kerosene lamp behind him.

Sadao waited for the lamp to light up and the shadows to retract. No wonder children were scared of the place - they were surrounded by what appeared to be ghosts on stands lined up along the walls along with other tarped crates and boxes. Sadao went to the closest ghost and lifted the covering - it was eighteenth-century samurai armor and weaponry. Shiratori's.

He didn't speak for a while, just went around the space, remembering the odd armaments his old friend had collected and worn with pride throughout the years. Even his white winged cruiser and favorite street bike were stowed in here, well preserved from the elements.

"Where is his golden armor?" Sadao asked softly. Mouse was close behind him, lighting his way.

"Um, he was cremated in it," Mouse said tentatively.

Sadao looked at him. "Did you see to that?"

Mouse's eyes were bright in the dimness. He nodded.

"Thank you," Sadao said.

"The trailer - we repurposed it," Mouse explained. "The equipment end is Kei's schoolroom now. We tried to assign someone to the living quarters but none would stay overnight until we moved all this stuff out. Even now, the living quarters changes hands every few months. Haunted, they say."

"That doesn't surprise me," Sadao said, looking at the sum of items. "The man never liked sharing his things. Still, it's a shame to have it all gathering dust. I'll think about what should be done. But for now, you'd better get me to Sensei and you back to the garage before Tagata starts hailing you over the camp intercom."

Mouse liked Sensei's new assistant. For one thing, he spoke English. And with Sensei getting up there in … years? centuries? the team needed a fully trained medical back-up. His name was Michi, 21 years old from the Vancouver Medical Academy. He knelt at Sensei's side by the futon as Mouse helped Sadao undress from his hip down.

Sadao rested with his hands behind his head while Sensei and Michi prodded and poked at Sadao's stab wound, the left side of his hip, and leg scars. It was hard for Mouse to look at all the damage in the full sunlight that filtered down through the medical tent roof. It reminded him too much of the blood-soaked stage and Sadao turning pale in his arms.

Michi took portable X-rays and soon brought out the developed images for everyone to see while Sensei took a prodding stick and dragged it along Sadao's hip and leg area, asking for responses. Although they spoke only Japanese, Mouse could tell Sadao was explaining the areas where he felt numbness, pain, or nothing at all. Sensei and Michi listened intently and asked Sadao many questions, pointing to the X-ray evidence before Mouse had to butt in.

"So, what's the deal? Can we fix him?"

Michi blinked behind wire-rimmed glasses. "This injury is not fixable," he said simply. "Too many surgeries performed by improperly skilled surgeons. He has a lot of physical damage and scar tissue."

"I can see that. But what about his pain and this cold foot? We can't do anything?"

Sensei asked Sadao a pointed question, to which Sadao groaned and was reluctant to answer. There was some argument between them and Michi joined in, backing Sensei up. Mouse looked between all three of them. "What the hell are you all talking about?"

Michi spoke while Sadao continued to argue with Sensei. "This leg can not heal unless Oyaji agrees to give up smoking."

Oh, God ... no wonder he's bitching.

"Smoking causes the blood vessels to restrict and will only aggravate the poor circulation to the left foot. If he does not take proper care, he may lose it."

Sensei was getting impatient with Sadao's protest and so was Mouse. So he smacked him on the thigh. "Hey, asshole! Listen to your doctor! Your party days are over! You gotta quit and I'm gonna make sure you do!"

"I'm not arguing with you too right now!" Sadao snapped, resuming his Japanese. He sounded like he was trying to bargain with Sensei, who was hearing none of it. The cigs had to go.

"Also, smoke stops the path of *chi* - vital life energy. We can help *chi* to flow with acupuncture and massage to help improve movement and ease pain, but Oyaji must cooperate with us. Right now he will not tell Sensei how much he smokes."

"Oh, Jesus, I can tell you he smokes like a chimney! Always has. I'd say ... pack a day? More, when he's stressed."

Sadao glared up at him. "I do not! I'm a social smoker!"

Mouse glanced heavenward for strength. "You're in some serious denial, bud. I've got a cereal bowl at home full of ash from your breakfast! They've built colleges in your name thanks to your tobacco taxes."

"Fine!" Sadao said. "I'll cut back!"

Sensei murmured something to Michi to pass to Mouse. They were done trying to talk to Sadao about it.

"Sensei wants to know if he can trust you to monitor smoking cessation treatment."

Mouse nodded. "Of course. I won't let him get away with shit. If he's gotta quit to get better then he's gonna *quit!*"

Sadao held his tongue and glared at the canvas ceiling.

Soon after that was settled, Sensei went into his pharmacy to prepare something herbal and Michi spelled out the plan for Sadao's 12-step program, although there were far less steps. The rules were simple - no cigarettes or tobacco products ever again. Remove them from the home, yada yada… Discourage social interactions around other smokers (Tagata? *Right.*) Sadao would be given nicotine infusions twice a day which he could administer himself, etc. And he was to return to the clinic twice a week for acupuncture and bodywork, which would be followed up with a physical therapy routine.

"You getting all this?" Mouse said with a look down at Sadao, who was being handed a steaming mug of tea by Sensei.

Sadao answered with a grunt as he sat up to drink.

"This tea Sensei prepares for him has muscle relaxant and pain reduction properties. It is very effective and very safe. He can take up to three cups a day to help with pain and stiffness. But it will make him sleepy, so he should not take if he will be operating motor vehicles or machinery."

"Got it."

"Now we will wait for him to relax and begin first acupuncture and bodywork treatment. We would like you to observe so you can help with massage at home."

Mouse grinned at Sadao, who was finishing his last gulp of magic tea and settling back down on the futon on his stomach as instructed. "If it means I get a decent nap, I'm for it!"

Stripped naked, Sadao was snoring peacefully and well on his way to resembling a hedgehog before they were done sticking long needles into him. Michi explained in a quiet voice the network of the body's meridian system and how an injury as severe as Sadao's required redirecting his *chi* through stimulation to re-establish vitality that would bring healing. Sensei's hands were no longer steady enough to apply the needles but he observed and spoke softly to Michi about his work, which he was obviously well trained in.

After the needles were removed and Sadao was dead to the world, they began the bodywork. Sensei had prepared a salve, and Michi demonstrated how to apply it to the mangled skin and muscles on Sadao's left side. He warmed up the tissues first then applied deeper and deeper pressure, encouraging the connective tissues to loosen and relax. His muscle and bone had been blown all apart and there weren't enough square inches left of sinew to tie him all back together. This is why he suffered pain and cramping. With proper time, treatment and exercise he should feel improvement, they assured him. They did not recommend more surgery.

"Mouse! Attention Mouse! You are requested to report to the garage immediately!"

"Ugh, crap. I gotta go, Sensei Michi. Got a pissed-off Team Boss and too many untuned snowbikes. Take care of Mr. Grumpy for me, okay?"

Michi gave him the thumbs up and Mouse stepped out into the afternoon sun.

No sooner had Mouse jogged over to the garage when he was hailed on the CB by one of Tagata's assistants and asked to hurry his butt over to a race planning meeting at the Boss' cabin instead. Mouse was sweaty and out of breath by the time he opened the door to the two-room cabin and found it packed with the Sasori A-List racers and runners up. On the wall next to the sizeable fireplace, Tagata had nailed up a large map of Mt. Garibaldi's 9500 foot peak 20 miles northwest of Squamish. Mouse tried to nudge his way towards the front so he could get a better view. He spotted Lupe and came up beside him to bump knuckles.

Tagata and his route planners were pointing out various marked trails from Garibaldi's summit down through a succession of valley trails to the Alice Lake finish line. It seemed they were strategizing the best navigation route for the 25-mile Downhill. "Seemed" being the operative word since the whole lecture was being conducted in Japanese.

"Uh ... hey, excuse me but if you called me over for a reason, I'm gonna need some subtitles or else I might as well go back to getting oily."

"Mouse-san," Tagata said, beckoning him forward. "We need you to settle argument."

Mouse came forward and situated himself in front of the big map. "We uh, talking about the big Downhill, I take it?"

"Yes. Very popular event. Much money will be bet on this race above all in Winter Rally. We must not disappoint. We must pick route best for speed and traction on icy trails. Nakagawa favors direct approach - to go east from summit to follow ski run to mid point, then take riverside trail to junction before we turn to Alice Lake meadow flats to finish." Tagata traced the route with a capped pen as he spoke. Nakagawa was his older captain, one of Sadao's more mature veterans. He was 28 - two years older than the Sasori Boss himself. It was evident Tagata maintained a lot of respect for him.

"And you?" Mouse asked Tagata. "What do you favor?"

Tagata's mouth curled at the corner. "I think many team will start with safe ski run solution. Trails are groomed every day for tourists. Only close for Downhill. Good, safe solution."

"Yeah. But it seems to me if you took off in the opposite direction - west through the crags, traversed to the second sister summit and descended on the hiking trails there, you'd have less twists and turns to get you down to the valley and to the finish," Mouse suggested. "After the traverse, it's practically a straight shot. You could bury the throttle and Hail Mary right through most of that shit. It's more dangerous of course, narrower, more chance of drifts and rocks, but hell, safe don't win!"

Tagata nodded. This was the answer he was looking for. "I agree."

Nakagawa pardoned himself and made a heartfelt rebuttal in Japanese, which Tagata listened to carefully. Nakagawa marked a long diamond shaped area about 1000 feet below the second summit and circled it. There was a grumble that echoed around the cabin.

Mouse was puzzled. "What's the big blue diamond all about?"

"*Sukima*," Nakagawa said ominously.

"Eh?"

Tagata tapped his chin for the word in English. "Crack in ice," he said. "Very big crack."

"Oh, shit, there's a *crevasse* on that side? Are you sure?"

"Ice above 8500 feet does not melt in summer. Start of race will be on forever-ice, you say…"

"You mean glacier? Holy crap. That's dangerous no matter what! Even with a snow-pack! How big is this crevasse?"

Tagata verified this with his captain. "Four to six meter wide."

"That's about 15 feet! That's pushing it for a jump. Can you go around it? It's long isn't it? That would really slow everyone up."

"There is only two choice. Go around. Go through."

"Through?" Mouse asked. Are his English prepositions slipping? "How do you go through a giant ass hole in the snow?"

Tagata took the red pen and marked a path-shaped double line over the center of the blue diamond. "Ice bridge," he said. "Always there."

"But is it safe? How wide is it?"

Tagata separated his arms. "Four of my arm wide."

"Like six feet or …"

"Eight, I think," Tagata said, looking to Nakagawa who nodded. "At widest point. Six at most *semai* - narrow."

"But … Christ Almighty, you'd have to have epic traction if you're going to hit a target that size over ice at speed."

"This is why we ask you to settle debate. Can snowbike aim for ice bridge or not?"

Mouse scratched his head. "I … dunno, really. Never tried to cross a glacier on a snowbike before. I mean, we installed the multi-terrain drive trains and all that. You let me spend a little more for the concave spike treads, so that's some hard core traction but … these are light-weight racing class kits, not heavy long train rescue bikes! I thought we'd be dealing with snow mostly."

"We will, but not for start of Downhill race. It can not be helped."

Mouse turned his head to look at the proud faces of the men in Tagata's assembly. They were prepared to jump on their machines and take whatever risks were necessary to assure victory - Lupe's among them. Their totem tattoos and glinting piercings sent the message that none of them wanted to take the pussy way out.

I'm gonna send Lupe and his buddies to an early ice grave if I get this wrong …

He turned back to face the team leaders. "Jesus, you gotta let me think this one over. We've gotta get these machines on some real snow with some real men on them. I've got to consider weight, weather conditions, moisture ratio ...”

Tagata nodded. “We will make two different plan for route. And when we know all possible things - then final decision we will make.”

It was dark when Mouse slipped back into the medical tent some hours after sundown. Unlike the active season, Sensei only had one patient. And he was laying on his belly tucked in blankets, face cradled in a pillow, sound asleep. Mouse smiled and knelt beside him, brushing strands of hair back from his face. He leaned in and gave his temple a soft kiss.

“Time to get up, baby. I need to take you home.” Mouse said, stroking his cheek fondly. He really didn’t want to move him - the man needed the rest. Moving him back up to the cabin would re-strain the leg. But night was falling and Mouse knew he could feed and keep Sadao much warmer up the hill. Mouse nestled down next to him when Sadao didn’t stir. He looked so beautiful in the lamplight. Eyes shut, lips parted slightly, he looked like a fine bronze cast of reclining Buddha - the serene skinny one. Mouse hugged him tight in a surge of love.

“Unmpf...” the Buddha spoke. A sleepy eye opened, to investigate his attacker. Mouse bombarded him with kisses to his nose, face, cheeks, lips. “Ngh...why are you slobbering me?”

“Because ... *smooch smooch* ... you’re too damn cute!”

“I’m not cute. I’m fierce. Men tremble when they hear my name,” Sadao grumbled, pulling the blanket higher around himself.

Mouse kissed his burrowing head. “I tremble, but for a completely different reason. You need to get up, sleepyhead!”

“Let me be. Tired....”

“You already slept half the day away. I need to get you back up to the cabin before it gets too cold.”

“Don’t want to move,” Sadao protested. “Leave me here.”

“Nope, not a chance. Want you back in my bed. You can sleep there.”

“That’s the problem...” Sadao mumbled into his pillow. “You don’t sleep.”

“Not when there’s this much man at arm’s reach!” Mouse squeezed his ass in proof.

“We need to talk about your sexual demands on me,” he said, trying to sit up. Sensei’s brew was still making him groggy.

Mouse helped steady him. “Just want you to keep me warm tonight, baby. That’s all.”

Sadao yawned hugely. “Can I get that in writing?”

Mouse stood and half-lifted Sadao to his feet. "Nope. You've got to trust me. I'm aware of your limits."

"Sure you are," Sadao said, slipping an arm around Mouse's shoulder as he stepped into his boots. "You'll try anything to find a way to get me erect."

"Your penis doesn't lie," Mouse said, with a kiss. "It wants me 24/7 whether the rest of your body agrees or not."

"Very true," Sadao said, drawing a finger down Mouse's cheek. "My fate I suppose, to be cursed with such an attractive mate."

Mouse felt his face heat up. He pinched Sadao's arm. "Less talk, more walk, bucko."

Later that night, naked between the blankets with a fire lighting their bedroom, Mouse felt all his promises fall away as he coaxed Sadao to once again fill the relentless ache between his thighs.

"I'm sorry," he whispered, taking him inside. "I'm so sorry…I need … "

"Shhh … *Konezumi*. I'm here."

Mouse clung to his lover through the hours as the fire died down and the night deepened around them.

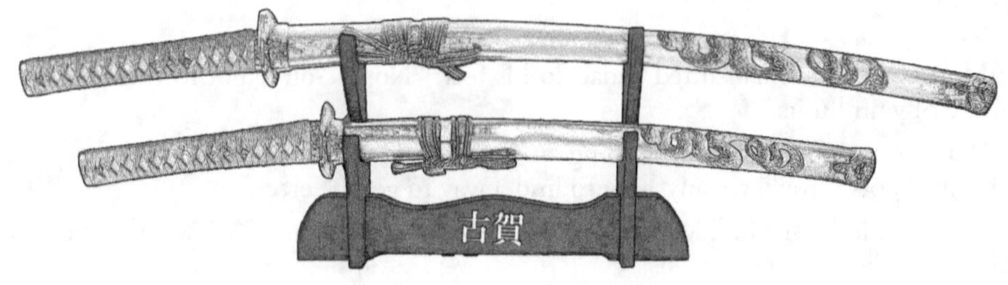

Chapter X

Gimmie Shelter

Mouse gave Sadao exactly 72 hours to prove to him he could control his tobacco consumption. When the cereal bowls still managed to fill themselves up with ash by the time he got home from the garage each evening, he knew he needed to make good on his promise to force the issue. So he got up early, grabbed the trash can from under the sink, and went around the cabin dumping.

He snuck into the bedroom on tip-toes around the sleeping puff-dragon to try to grab a half smoked pack Sadao had left on the bedside table. No sooner had his fingers surrounded it, Sadao opened an eye and brought his hand down over Mouse's.

"Where are you going with that?" Sadao asked, face against the pillow and hair all mussed.

"You don't need it. So I'm throwing it out!"

"No, you won't. They're expensive. I told you. I'm cutting back."

"Not that I've seen yet! Besides, that's not what Sensei said."

"It's what I say," Sadao growled, refusing to let go of Mouse's hand.

"Look, I can't be late again for work - I'll ration you."

Sadao released his hand and let him open the box. Mouse picked out three cigarettes and set them neatly on the bedside table and made a quick exit for the front door before Sadao could get up and find his pants.

"Hey! Get back here! Three?! Is this a fucking joke?"

"Breakfast, Lunch and Dinner, babe!" he said, shutting the front door and running for the path down to the camp with the trashbag.

After an exhausting morning of adjusting carburetor air flows to suit their elevation on the snowbikes, Mouse grabbed a spare bucket and jogged down to the training track on a cleared section of shoreline to grab Lupe for a quick lunchtime fishing trip. Lake fish had become the staple protein of the camp. Teams would take their turns going out with nets to fill the kitchen freezers, but Mouse still liked to grab a pole and tackle and head out in a small two man boat from the dock to chill on the calming emerald blue waters whenever he could. Sunrays fanned down into the deeps as they floated along, sending Mouse's mind adrift.

"Hey, you still in there, gringo?"

Mouse stirred from his reverie. "Huh?"

"Your head, it's a million miles away," Lupe said, steering the engine to move them to the far shore.

Mouse smiled. "Can't stop thinking about last night. God, we just couldn't stop touching each other. Even when we were too exhausted to fuck anymore. I wanted to let him sleep, but we just kept kissing until someone popped another boner."

"Ugh, I don't need the play-by-play," Lupe said, covering his ears. "Glad you got your old man back, but give us single guys a break with the details."

"Like you can talk! I've been walking around with swollen nuts for two fucking years while you bragged about getting all kinds of action at the races!"

"Yeah, when it's racing season! Off season, I'm totally fucked. I ain't seen pussy in months! Be glad you like dick, man. Cause that's all we got in this camp!"

"We have the Winter Sports Rally just around the corner, you know. All kinds of snow bunnies come out for that," Mouse offered.

"Yeah, but I gotta ride snowbike. No Mustang. The Mustang's what gets me laid, bro!"

"Well, you're going to have to fight Sadao for it now that he's back. By the way, what did he say about your 'redecorating?'"

"He punched me in the face first chance he got!"

"I told you!"

Lupe made a motion over Mouse's shoulder. "Catch that tree root, will you?"

Mouse swiveled and caught the first wet clump of roots that floated past them. He hung over the bow and tied the rope fast before grabbing his pole and jumping off onto the wooded shore. Mid-lake casting hadn't done them much good - too warm. Mouse thought they might have better luck in the shade on the far shore where the fish liked to settle in the shallows. He and Lupe ambled along until they spotted a splash in the water under the shade of the trees.

"This will do," Mouse said, settling down on a log. "Hand me the tackle box. These mountain trout love those yellow garlic puffs."

Lupe scrunched up his nose as he unscrewed the pungent can and handed it to Mouse.

"So, how's the old man doing, anyway? Sensei give him a clean bill of health?"

"Not exactly," Mouse said, impaling a three pronged hook with little yellow balls. "His stab wound has healed okay, but the bad news is, he's gotta quit smoking. Like now. He's got real circulation problems in the left leg and foot."

"Jeez. Can't think of a time Old Boss didn't have a cigarette in his hand."

"It's not going to be fun," Mouse admitted, casting out. His line sang and the weighted hook plopped into the water, sending ripples out over the calm surface. "We've already gotten into a fight over it just this morning when he caught me confiscating his stash."

Lupe snorted.

"He seems to think he can cut back but I know better. My Dad was dying, coughing up chunks of his own lungs, and he still wanted a fucking cigarette. If a terminally ill man can't quit, I know it's not going to be easy to convince an injured one to do the same. Good times, ahead. But, I'm up for it. Mr. Grumpy's not gonna wear me down that easily."

"He's lucky to have you," Lupe said, tying off his line weight and setting out his own cast. "He needs to get his weight up. Dude looks rail thin."

"He's been through a lot," Mouse agreed. "More than he lets on. I'll fatten him up, though. No worries. As long as I can catch some fish today. I've got special plans for dinner - lots of calories! The man never could cook for himself. You wouldn't believe how empty his fridge used to be."

Lupe laughed. "Well, it was always full of beer. That, I remember! Still is."

Mouse smiled. He knew if anyone could get that man set to rights, it was himself. He intended to take no prisoners when it came to Sadao's health and longevity. He had lifelong plans for him, despite himself.

"Whoa! I got one!" Lupe shouted. "What the fuck do I do?"

"Okay you got 'em, now just reel back in slowly ... nice, nice. Give it a little tug. Get that hook in good."

"Shit, he's a scrambler!" Lupe said, getting to his feet to battle his foe.

"Keep reeling nice and even. I'll get the net!"

Mouse put his pole down and hopped up, grabbing the hand net just as Lupe's first catch came sailing out of the water in a shower of droplets and flashing scales, splashing them both.

"Got him! Yeah, bitch! I got your ass!" Lupe exclaimed.

Mouse laughed at Lupe's mannish pride. Using a multi-tool and a glove, he grabbed the slippery beast in the net and worked the hook out of the fat trout's lip.

"Get the bucket will ya? We'll keep him swimming until dinnertime."

By the end of the hour, they managed to haul in six rainbow spotted "bitches." They hurried back to the boat, well aware their lunch break had gone on a bit too long. Mouse was handing Lupe the equipment from shore as he readied the boat when something odd caught Mouse's eye. He stood up and took a few steps back inland to get a better look. Something was flapping back in the woods.

"Hey! We gotta get the fuck outta here or Boss will skin us alive! Take a piss back at camp!"

"Not pissing!" Mouse shouted back, moving into the trees "Just gotta look at something…"

It was part of a bike tarp, left hanging from a tree branch. Mouse pulled it down to investigate. *That's weird. No one rides bikes on this side of the lake, no trails.* He took a few steps further through the brush and stumbled upon a small clearing and remains of a campfire. There was some trash about, too. He bent down to kick aside some fallen leaves and found an empty gas can. He picked it up and was suddenly taken back to that night the mice had invaded their pantry; when he and a few others had seen a light on the far shore.

Who the heck's been camping out here? Mouse wondered. *Some kids?* Tagata had instituted a nightly mandatory roll call ever since they'd lost a few men in an ice storm last year, soon followed by a 12-man walkout. No camping was allowed outside the western shore boundary. As far as he knew, there hadn't been any new missing men or teens.

Were these the fuckers who quit last year?

His toe bumped something odd. Mouse bent to check it out. It was green, rubbery and half buried in mud. *Is that an eye?* He pulled it out with a stick. The fuck is this creepy shit? It was half of a Halloween mask shaped in the visage of a cartoon frog.

"Hey, gringo! How about I leave you here and come back tomorrow so I don't get my ass fired?!"

"I'm coming! Jesus Christ!" Mouse yelled, dropping the rubbery frog-face and taking the gas can with him.

"It's one of ours," Mouse said, setting the empty can down on the workbench for Tagata to inspect.

Tagata looked it over. It was scratched and dented. "How do you know this? Just regular can. Any gas station in Canada you can buy."

Mouse screwed the cap open and sniffed. Although it was long gone dry, a few fumes lingered. He offered the can for Tagata to take a whiff.

"So? It smell like gas."

"It smells like *our* gas," Mouse said pointedly. "I use a high altitude stabilizer on the garage's stored fuel so it won't lose potency in cold temperatures. It's an old Mouse family recipe. I mix it myself. Smells like grape bubble gum."

"I smell no grape," Tagata said. He looked concerned but doubtful. "How would Sasori can be left behind at campsite on far shore? We take count every night. No man missing."

"I know but, I saw a light across the lake about a month back. I'm sorry I forgot to tell you about it."

"What light? On South shore? You saw and you think not important to me?" Tagata and he may have buried the hatchet some years ago, but the young team boss had no tolerance for slacking.

"Jesus, okay, sorry. This was the night of the Hanta Virus panic. You were a little busy. We all were! I saw a light over there. It wasn't moving. A few other men saw it too and then blink! It was gone. I guessed lost hunters or something."

"Lost hunters would not have Sasori gas." Tagata turned and laid out a series of orders to his lead men, who had followed him into the garage.

"Hai Boss! *Kashikomarimashita!*" They bowed and moved out quickly.

"We search South shore. See if any more missing can," he said, pointing to Mouse and his mini-crew. "You keep count of everything. Can, bolt, chain, all of it! I want to know who is stealing and having secret campfires!"

"You got it, Boss," Mouse said, turning to his own men. "Okay Aki, get the boys counting again. I'll try to pull supply logs from last racing season, see what matches up."

Mouse headed for the rear lockers where he secured his bookkeeping. Truth was, he'd lapsed somewhat on the bean counting since Shiratori no longer screamed down his neck about it. Other than during the racing tour months, Mouse didn't feel the need to ward against thievery. They were 30 miles from the closest rival team camp over a mountain range full of bears - not exactly easy pickings as the flat empty desert had been.

He spun the locks and pulled out his clipboards. Gas supply was still closely monitored. But the odd 2-litre can? Not so much. Anyone could have taken it anytime in the last 18 months or more. Figuring out this mystery was gonna suck.

It was getting past seven when Mouse called it a day and sent his garage boys off for the night. They'd tallied everything and Mouse could not make any account of the cans. They weren't a high priority item. Custom motorbike parts were recorded painstakingly by part and serial number, but a disposable gas can? Who gave a fuck? Mouse wasn't even sure how many they'd actually bought to date or how many they should still have lying about. He could think of a half dozen times in the last few months where someone came by asking to borrow gas cans so they could take them out for training missions when they needed extra fuel.

No, cans weren't regulated but gas was. So Mouse made a stop out at the fuel truck on his way home and spoke with the guys who kept up with the gas draw figures. Flipping through records, no one could pinpoint when or if 2-litres or less had gone missing at some point. The average evap rate could account for more than that. So it was more or less a hopeless investigation. Mouse hoped a shore search would turn up more answers. He'd told Tagata about the tarp, but much like gas cans, they were passed around pretty loosely as well. Anxious to get back to Sadao - who had made no appearance in camp at all that day - Mouse shrugged off the gas can caper, grabbed his bucket of trout and hoofed it uphill in the dark.

Mouse could hear the radio blaring long before he reached the top of the hill. Inside, after wrangling the door open around his fish, he found Sadao laid out on the sofa. His left foot was propped up on a stool and an arm was flung over his eyes.

Mouse's "Helloooo! I'm home!!" was barely audible over The Stones.

Sadao didn't budge. He was ignoring him.

Mouse set the trout bucket on the counter next to his cereal bowl. It was carrying the ash remains of three dead butts. A little 'fuck you' offering from his roommate. Mouse sighed and dumped the contents into the sink to rinse it. He was determined to make Doc Meadows' beer battered fish, biscuits and slaw tonight - if he didn't go deaf first. He reached over and clicked the radio off.

Sadao came instantly to life. "I was listening to that!"

"Half of Canada was listening to that! And I can't yell at you over Jagger!"

"Turn it back on!"

"I need radio silence tonight," Mouse said, opening his cupboards for flour and spices. "I'm making a special dinner - just for you, I might add. Not that you're putting me in a mood to cook."

The sofa grumbled something in Japanese. It didn't sound nice.

"Besides, if I have to hear 'Stairway to Heaven' one more time…"

"It's a classic!" Sadao barked. "Far superior to your hillbilly trash."

You're a classic, Mouse thought. He poured four fish into the sink and started rinsing. "Rascal Flatts is not hillbilly trash. Did you smoke anything else today?"

"No!"

"Nevermind, stupid question."

"What does that mean?"

Mouse ran the pump and looked over his shoulder. Sadao was lying there, glaring at the ceiling.

"You seem tense."

"Of course I'm tense! I'm not allowed to listen to music in my own home!"

"Oh for fuck's sake…" Mouse caved in and flicked the radio back on just as Jimmy Page's A-Minor melody began to carry over the scratchy reception. Lovely.

Sadao kept his grumpy to himself over the next hour of "classics" and conceded to be assisted off the couch and over to the table by Mouse's shoulder and arm.

"You want the stool brought over?"

"No."

"What about a cushion?"

"No."

"You know any other words tonight?"

"No."

"Fantastic."

Sadao sat and waved Mouse off when he tried to scoot in his chair. In another minute he had crispy golden fish, chopped slaw and hot biscuits with butter and honey all laid out on the table. Sadao didn't wait for him to begin gnawing on a tail.

"Did you make tea?"

"Of course."

"Where is it?"

"Hold on a minute, Archie."

Sadao gave him a look as he brought the pot over and poured for his sunny other half.

"Who's Archie?"

"Nevermind, just eat."

"What's this stuff?"

"It's coleslaw," Mouse said, taking a seat.

"What's it made of?" Sadao sniffed a stab of salad suspiciously.

"Cabbage and raisins. Stop picking at it, you need the iron."

Sadao took a bite, made a face and reached for the honey.

"Hey, it's already sweet! Jeez, don't ya'll eat cabbage in Japan?"

"Not if we can help it!"

Sadao wolfed down a trout and a half, most of the biscuits and a few forced bites of slaw before he spoke again over his tea. "Thank you for dinner."

"Oh! So he does still have manners!"

"Not for much longer!"

Mouse sat back, exasperated. "Look, babe, clearly you're not doing very well by just lying around all day. You have to get up on that leg and move."

Sadao gulped his tea and set his mug down with a firm tonk. "I'll move when I'm ready."

"Sure! But before the snow comes in, I think you should take advantage of the good weather and come down to camp with me in the mornings."

Sadao shook his head.

"Why not?"

"Don't feel like talking to people."

"I get that, but will you come down at least to see Sensei? I think his treatments can really help you."

Sadao looked as if he was thinking it over.

"Will you? For me?"

Sadao paused a moment, then nodded.

Later, in bed, when the lamps were off and the fire burning, Sadao scooted close to Mouse under the blankets and kissed his cheek.

"I apologize. I was terrible tonight."

"No arguments here. But at least I got some food in you," Mouse said, rubbing his full belly.

Sadao sighed and began to stroke his hair. "It was delicious. You're a wonderful cook."

"Thanks."

"And I'm sorry I called your music hillbilly."

Mouse snorted and kissed his chin. "It's a little hillbilly," he admitted.

"I think you're right. I do need to move a little. Get outside."

"Some fresh mountain air will do you good, you know."

"I'm having difficulty with some things, not just smoking … I don't know how to explain it."

Mouse hugged his tummy. "S'okay, baby. I understand."

Sadao tipped Mouse's chin up and kissed him. "Thank you. You're the only one who does."

Mouse smiled up at him. "Didn't you know? That's my job."

Sadao regarded him thoughtfully for a moment then moved deeper into the bed, rolling himself into Mouse's arms so his head came to rest on his chest. Mouse was amazed by the gesture. It made his heart pound as he held this beautiful, aggravating man, stroking his hair until he fell asleep.

As it came to be in the days that followed, Sadao would come down to camp with Mouse on warm mornings and spend his afternoons either lounging at Tagata's with a book or fussing around up in the longhouse. Mouse wasn't sure what he was doing up there exactly, but it seemed to help get his mind off smoking - which he still did to some extent. Can't hide the scent from your lover, after all. But it seemed he was making an effort to take better care of himself and that made Mouse happy. Plus, he was eating regularly again and was starting to put some of the lost weight back on his bones.

One afternoon, Sadao appeared at the garage with Shiratori's street bike in tow. His face was sweaty and his hands dirty from the effort to push the thing out of the woods to the lakeside.

"What's up?" Mouse asked, handing Sadao a clean rag to wipe his brow and hands. "You brought the bike down."

"Need to make some room up there," Sadao said as explanation. "Maybe you can get this thing running again. Or else use it for parts. No point letting it just sit in the dark."

Mouse paused a beat. It appeared there was something more Sadao wanted to say, but wasn't going to. Shiratori was not a subject he liked to discuss. "Okay, I'll get her polished up, see if the pistons still pop, sure."

Sadao nodded, "Thanks." And then he was off, limping back up toward the pines.

A week later, the weather turned suddenly, announcing the end of autumn and beginning of winter. A chilling mist hung over the lake until well past noon. Sometimes Sadao would idle his cruiser down to camp once it warmed up and sometimes he wouldn't. He began missing his appointments with Sensei. There were even days when he didn't seem to move at all, except to the bath and the bed and back again. Mouse knew it was due to stiffness and pain triggered by the weather, but Sadao refused to take his medicinal tea during the day. Made him too loopy, he said. So Mouse let him be, but with trials coming in under two weeks, he'd been too busy to check up on him every day. And when a particularly damp series of days hit, Mouse was lucky to see Sadao out of bed at all, although he was able to get up long enough to leave dirty dishes in the sink and laundry on the floor by the time he got home.

Sex had dwindled to the occasional blow job and only if Mouse walked up to him with his dick out and pointed at it. It had to suffice for now. He knew it was too painful for the man to move his hip or to take his weight bouncing on top of him. So Mouse would get him comfortable up against some pillows, straddle his lap and put his mouth to work.

Mouse stood outside the mess hall, stomping his feet and blowing into his gloves waiting for sun-up coffee service. Pulling back to back 12-hour days for five days straight, he and his garage team had managed to get the whole fleet of snowbikes fully fitted, tested and tuned in time to meet Tagata's trials deadline. Unfortunately, someone forgot to tell the weatherman. Despite sub-zero temps in the morning and evenings, and ice networking itself determinedly across the lake, not a single snowflake had fallen to date and it was already mid-December. Usually, they were up to their armpits by now in drifts. Snowbikes needed the real deal under their treads to run. Dirt would tear them up, so for the time being, everyone was cooling their heels - make that freezing their heels.

"Ah, fuck!" Lupe exclaimed, lining up with Mouse. "They don't got water boiling yet? Did they have to chop it out of the lake?"

"I should have made my own this morning," Mouse grumbled. "But I didn't want banging pots to wake Sadao up. He's been having a hell of a time sleeping lately - too cold. I found him dozing in the tub around 3 A.M. last night."

"Thought you two were keeping cozy up there while the rest of us bastards shiver in our long johns all night. Why the fuck didn't I rank a cabin?"

"Give it time," Mouse said, bouncing in place to keep warm. "Grab up a few more trophies. I just hope we get some snow soon so the whole team doesn't come in last place like a pack of noobs. Anyway, you have nothing to be envious of inside our love nest. Mr. Grumpy hasn't been in any kind of mood for romance. I'm lucky to get a hand job most days."

Lupe snorted. "Is the honeymoon over?"

Mouse shrugged. "It's the weather. Fucks up his leg. And he's just stubborn as a goat about moving on it. He wouldn't even come down for his appointments this week. The muscle relaxers make him too blurry-headed to read, I guess. Which is all he does now - reads or blares that fucking radio. I swear I'm gonna go deaf."

"If it means I get a break from listening to Kei blubber into the CB at me from the kids hall one more night, I'm gonna ask to trade places."

"What's up with Kei? If anyone in this camp is a happy camper in this weather, it's that man."

Lupe shook his head. "He's losing his shit, you know. That girl kid, Shinjyu? I guess Tagata's been talking to some social worker in Squamish about her. They want him to turn her in so they can put her in foster care or some shit. It ain't right, man."

"Foster care? That's Tagata's solution?"

Lupe shrugged. "I only repeat what I hear. Hey! Windows are rolling up, about fucking time!"

The conversation about their female misfit was soon forgotten as they pushed forward for a steaming cup of Joe. Mouse and Lupe grabbed their share and headed for the garage truck. Lupe wanted to get the Mustang out after its last tune-up for a drive test.

"I hope your old man comes back down soon before it snows," Lupe said as they ducked into the garage's tent extension. "He said he was going to observe my performance driving - give me some tips and stuff. I've never had a real good coach on auto. Tagata's a genius on bike but only Old Boss knows auto racing."

Mouse opened the retina scan lock and peered into it. "You make those changes he wanted?"

"Yeah, I did! Most of them, anyway. He said he wouldn't get in the car with me otherwise. I'm not changing the paint job. He's gotta live with that! And Santa Maria, she protects me, you know!"

The scan registered green but the door failed to open. Mouse rebooted it and leaned in to try again. "Just do me a favor, Lupe. Don't wreck it with him in it. Roads are getting icy mornings and nights now."

"Oh nice! You don't give a shit if I get banged up!"

Mouse gave the stuck door a heave to break the early morning icy seal. It groaned and started to move. "You don't suck my dick."

"Really, gringo? It's come to this? What's a man gotta do to get a little protection around - *whoa!*"

Both Lupe and Mouse jumped aside as a large furry creature wobbled past them and out the way they were coming in.

"Oh, fuck!" Mouse yelled, hitting the lights. Inside, a chubby fuzzy mammal convention was in progress. "Lupe, grab the broom! We gotta get these things out of here, now!" Mouse hit the emergency button and all ramps engaged at once, clearing the way for most of the little buggers to make an easy escape. Their little toes chattered on the metal flooring as Mouse ran after the wobbly stragglers with a tire iron. "Out! Shit! Lupe, get that one!" Lupe gave a girlish scream as it ran past them both and out the back ramp. It appeared to be the last one.

Lupe was backed into a corner, holding the broom handle looking terrified. "What are they? Beavers?"

"Marmots! Shit! How the hell did they get in?" Mouse looked around for obvious entrances. "They get in through the vents?" He hopped up on a chest and banged on the ventilation grates. They were solid.

"Mouse, hey! I think this is where they got in!"

Lupe was leaning over a wheel well set into the floor that had been opened for roller testing the Mustang. Only now the roller was detached and had fallen below the truck floor to the ground. Mouse peered in the hole. "The fuck happened here? These rollers weigh a hundred pounds!"

"The axle give out?" Lupe wondered.

Mouse scratched his head. "Maybe..." He stood up and looked around. Rubber chunks of chewed up hoses and wires were scattered around the floor with bits of Marmot scat. Mouse raised his head to look up - the row of snowbikes were leaning this way and that into each other on the storage gangway. "Aw fuck, they ate the treads?!"

Mouse scrambled up the ladder. Sure enough - treads were lying about in various stages of chewed. Several more showed deep bites and claw marks. Mouse banged his forehead into the topmost ladder rung. "This can't be happening, this can't be happening …"

"What kind of animal eats snow treads?" Lupe asked from below.

"Don't ask me why these furry fuckers eat hoses and shit! They just do! Fuck Darwin! Now I gotta order more treads! Tagata's gonna kill me!"

Fortunately Mouse's life was spared due to the team boss being currently unavailable. Tagata was out with his officers scouting possible training grounds at higher elevations where snowpack was never fully purged in the summers. So after pronouncing the Mustang sound - turns out these marmots had no taste for vintage belts - and sending Lupe on his way, Mouse made a point to jog up the hill at lunchtime to use his long-range radio to call down to Squamish for snow tread replacements.

Mouse unlocked the cabin door and swung the board securing it. A telltale whiff of tobacco lingered in the main room. He walked around, sniffing until he found Sadao just outside on the porch lying in the lounge swing in the sun under a blanket, reading a book and puffing away. And by the looks of the ashtray, for most of the afternoon. *Jesus!*

Mouse threw the porch door open and marched right up to him. "What the hell do you think you're doing?"

Sadao took the cigarette out of his mouth and exhaled a small cloud of piss-off in Mouse's direction. "I like to smoke while I read. Deal with it."

"And what did Sensei say to you about smoking?"

Sadao flicked his ash into the light breeze. "Sensei smokes too."

Mouse stood over him, exasperated. "And so did my father and so does half the camp, but none of them ever had disabling gunshot wounds! Fuck! Is this what you do all day up here?!"

Sadao threw off the blanket and sat up in the swing, crushing out the cigarette. "I am not disabled!"

"No, you're just a pig-headed asshole who thinks his body is made of steel!"

"I do not think that! But it is a simple fact - when I read, I smoke!"

"Then you'll need to learn to read without it!"

"I can't read without a smoke any better than you can piss lying down!"

"Oh, god. You're gonna bring that up?! Are you twelve? We're talking about your health here! Something I happen to have a vested interest in!"

Sadao sank back down, rubbing his eyes and grumbling while Mouse worked up a head of steam.

"You think this shit doesn't matter? You think this is a fucking game? Something I do to annoy you? I held your goddamn hand while you bled out on that stage and felt it go cold! Do you think I ever want to have that experience again?!"

Sadao dismissed him with a wave of his hand. "That won't happen."

"Like hell it won't! You're not superstar teenage Sadao driving a racecar off the side of a cliff like a jackass anymore. You're my 40-year-old goddamn husband and I expect you to live to see 98 or better! Are we clear?"

Sadao shook his head. "Fine." He picked up the ashtray, which looked like one of Tagata's, and in his rush to stand up he stumbled and Mouse had to steady him.

"Fuck!" Sadao yelled and hurled the tray across the deck; it hit a log post and shattered to the ground.

"That was mature."

Sadao looked away. "I know what I'm doing ..." he grumbled.

"Look at me," Mouse ordered.

Sadao refused.

Mouse grabbed his chin by his overgrown beard and forced his head to turn. "I said, fucking look at me!"

Sadao conceded but his expression was stern.

"This is serious. I know how serious it is and so do you. You are one enormous stubborn sonofabitch. But I'm not going to keep pretending I don't smell tobacco on you anymore. No more cheating! You mess with me, I'm gonna mess with you, you got it?!"

Sadao didn't answer but his eyes narrowed.

"I've waited 28 years to find my happiness. And I'll be damned if I'm gonna stand by and let you ruin that for me! For us! Now look me in the eye and tell me you don't care. That you'd rather be an asshole then take this - *us* - seriously!"

Sadao's nostrils flared. "I take us seriously."

Mouse searched his eyes. "Do you?"

"Of course I do!"

Mouse let him go with a shove. "Then show me!"

Sadao gathered himself and started to limp away.

"Where are you going?!"

Sadao opened the cabin door. "I'm showing you!!" he shouted. "You coming?!"

Mouse didn't know what he was up to and followed him back inside. Sadao limped to the coat rack and pulled down his riding jacket. He turned it inside out and showed Mouse the inner lining where it met the arm seam. "See this," he said. "Unzips right here - hidden pocket." He opened it and turned the thin material inside out. Four white tubes of poison fell out onto the floor.

Sadao tossed the jacket aside and walked across the main room to the bedroom.

Mouse, mouth open, followed him. He watched as Sadao went to the fireplace and pushed against what he didn't know was a loose stone. It slid aside to reveal a cubby hole - inside was a half-smoked pack. Sadao dragged it out and threw it to the ground. Behind it was another one unopened, and he threw it down too before replacing the stone and crushing the sealed pack underfoot as he walked across the bedroom floor.

"There's more?" Mouse asked. Sadao didn't answer but made his way out the backdoor to the shed that held their bikes.

He went to his new cruiser and pushed a button Mouse never knew about under the glove box - out fell another half-smoked pack. He chucked it to the ground too before exiting the shed to hobble out to a spot under the pines where there was a small stack of wood. He kicked the wood pile so the logs fell away and out tumbled a small avalanche of butts.

Mouse was beyond words. He just stared at Sadao and his ash mountain of shame in disbelief. Sadao sank back against a pine tree. "So it seems, I'm a bigger jackass than you thought."

"Jesus, why didn't you tell me?"

"I am telling you."

Mouse sighed. "Is there more?"

"At Tagata's but you knew about that, I guess."

"He's your fucking supplier! He doesn't give a shit about this, does he?"

Sadao smiled sardonically. "He's in the same boat I am, as they say. But fifteen years younger - and single."

Mouse went to Sadao and put his arms around him. Sadao, to his relief, did the same. "I'm sorry," Sadao said. "I didn't want to disappoint you."

Mouse looked up at him. The poor bastard was sorry - and ashamed. Fucking adorable. "I'm here to help you, baby. Not punish you."

Sadao nodded and kissed his temple. "I know."

"You can't do this alone. No one is asking you to. It's impossible."

Sadao's eyes looked past him to the treeline. "It's hard for me. I'm too used to being on my own."

"But you're not anymore, okay? For better or worse - you got me, right?"

Sadao hugged him tight. "It's going to get a lot worse before it gets better. That I can promise you."

"I don't care about that. I'm used to you being a dick. But as long as you stay honest with me, I'm prepared to deal with it, okay?"

Sadao bent his head and kissed him. "Okay."

Mouse gave him a smile. "Come on, you asshead. You've got a mess to clean up."

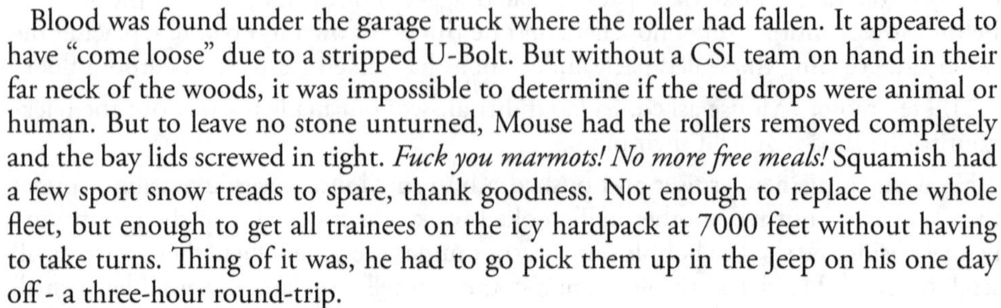

Blood was found under the garage truck where the roller had fallen. It appeared to have "come loose" due to a stripped U-Bolt. But without a CSI team on hand in their far neck of the woods, it was impossible to determine if the red drops were animal or human. But to leave no stone unturned, Mouse had the rollers removed completely and the bay lids screwed in tight. *Fuck you marmots! No more free meals!* Squamish had a few sport snow treads to spare, thank goodness. Not enough to replace the whole fleet, but enough to get all trainees on the icy hardpack at 7000 feet without having to take turns. Thing of it was, he had to go pick them up in the Jeep on his one day off - a three-hour round-trip.

Determined to get down the mountain and back up before sundown, Mouse left right at sunrise with a kiss to Sadao's sleeping forehead. He drove slow on the dirt road that led to the highway to prevent spinning out on the icy patches. Even with 4-wheel drive and snow tires on the vehicle, morning ice was a dicey game of steering and acceleration skill. He rounded a corner in a half-assed drift when something caught his eye in the rearview. The shock of it made him hit the break and the Jeep slid right up against a big tree trunk. Whump! *Oh, that's gonna leave a dent.*

Mouse looked in the mirror again then whipped his head around to try and make sure he'd just seen what he saw. Yep! There it was moving into the woods about 50 feet behind his skid. Dark hair and bare arms. Mouse popped out of the Jeep and scrambled up the embankment into the trees.

"Hey!" he yelled out when he'd lost sight of it. "Who's out here? It's freezing! I've got a Jeep!" Mouse stood still a moment catching his breath that burst out of his mouth in small clouds. "Where'd you go? I won't hurt you. I'm nice!"

He heard a rustling off to his left then a whine. Oh shit, it's a kid! "Hey, buddy. It's cool. I'm Mouse. I work at the camp down the road. Where are you? Are you okay?" He moved forward slowly towards the muffled sounds, keeping his voice low and friendly. "I'm a mechanic, you know? I like to work on cars and bikes. If you're hurt, I can help. I'm really good at fixing things."

Mouse scanned the brush with his eyes but wasn't seeing anything until he got too close and the kid stood up and ran. "Whoa! Wait!" Mouse ran too, too afraid he'd lose the little thing in the woods. He soon caught up to the fleeing form and made a dive to catch him. The kid shrieked and kicked him in the nose. "Ow! Hang on! Hold it - wha? Shinjyu? What are you doing out here?!"

She stopped fighting him and burst into tears, wrapping her arms around his neck. "Waaaaaaaaghhh!!" she wailed in his ear. She was dressed in simple boy's clothes - plain sleeves and jeans. Her arms and face were freezing. Mouse unzipped his coat and wrapped it around her, trying to warm her up.

"Shhh ... sweetie, it's okay. I've got you. You know me, right? I work in the garage. I'm Kei-sensei's friend and Lupe's friend. Right? You know me. It's okay."

Between her jaw chattering wails she was trying to say something. "Shh ... honey. Slower, I can't understand you."

"K - Kei-Sensei says I-I hafta go away because I'm a girrrrll!!" she sobbed into his shirt. "I don't wanna be a stupid girl! If I was a boy I could stay!!"

"Sweetie, hang on. Who says you have to go away. Kei? No, Kei loves you, honey. We all love you. No one is sending you away…" *Shit! Lupe was talking about this. Foster care? Jesus, they just sat her down and told her, Sorry kid, no penis, you're out?*

"I wanna stay!! I don't want the bad men to come and take me! I don't want the bad mennnn…"

Mouse stood up with Shinjyu still tucked into his jacket and began to walk back to the road. "Shh ... shh ... . Let's go back to my Jeep. Get you warm. Then we'll straighten this out, okay? No bad men are taking you anywhere."

In the Jeep wrapped in his coat and thawing in front of the running heaters, Shinjyu told him Tagata, Kei and some man from "the town" had come to talk to her that morning. Something about finding a new family with new brothers and sisters. A real headjob they did on her.

"It's because of my stupid hair! It got too long and then I wasn't a boy anymore!" She yanked at her hair, tearing out a clump.

"Whoa!" Mouse caught her hand and rubbed it between his own. "No ... no honey. Look at me." Shinjyu looked up at him with wet eyes. "We are going to fix this, okay? You and me. I'm going to take you back to camp and let Kei and Boss know that you are going to stay with us forever whether they like it or not, understand?"

Her mouth drooped into a frown. "You promise?" she asked.

Mouse smiled at her. She was the saddest, cutest thing he'd ever seen. "I promise, sweetheart. A Mouse never breaks his promise."

His trip to Squamish delayed, Mouse drove back into camp and pulled up in front of the school trailer. Shinjyu sat straight in the seat next to him, her little face set and ready for a fight. He got out and opened her door, taking her into his arms. "Remember my promise," he whispered.

Kei burst out of the school trailer's rear door followed by the remaining members of his flock. "Shinjyu?! Oh, *yokatta! Yokatta!*"

Shinjyu lept out of Mouse's arms and up into Kei's where a tearful reunion took place ringed with excited, jumping kids. There was commotion behind them and Mouse saw a group of men give shouts of relief and come running out of the forest. It looked like they'd been searching for her in the woods around the lake. A call went out across the camp and soon they were surrounded with greatly relieved Sasori members.

"Where did you find her?" Kei snuffled, coating her with kisses. "We looked everywhere!"

"I found her halfway up the exit road to the highway! She ran across the road behind my Jeep; I could have missed her if I blinked! How the hell did she get up that far?"

Kei wiped his face. "She got out sometime during breakfast. She ducked out of the tent. It was crowded in there today. I turned my head and she was gone. I was sick with worry."

"I don't wanna gooo! Mouse says I don't have to leave - tell them!"

Tagata chose that moment to break into their circle. He looked to the girl then to Mouse and placed his hands on his knees and bent over in a moment of sheer grateful-ness. Mouse knew he couldn't take losing another one to the elements. Especially not a small child. "You found her?" Tagata asked for clarification.

"Yes, she was running away from you and your hairball scheme to have her fostered? Are you nuts? Do you know what happens to those kids?"

Tagata straightened up. "You and I and Kei-san will have discussion. This is not for children to hear."

Mouse held his tongue while Kei called for his assistants to watch the children and they walked back to Tagata's cabin up the path to have it out. Mouse was spitting nails by the time the door shut behind them.

"Are you both out of your fucking minds?! Do you know what happens to foster children? They get kicked around from home to home until they run away and live on the street. Something Shinjyu is prepared to do right now! That little girl is fucking terrified thanks to you two!"

Kei wrung his hands. "I don't want her to go! I said, she can stay with me. We will move to a town. I will raise her! She will be my daughter! But ... " he looked to Tagata. "They said I am not old enough. And unmarried. And my other ducklings ... " Big tears dripped down from his eyes.

"Girls can not grow up in camp. It is the rules," Tagata stated plainly.

"Then change the goddamn rules, Tagata! You're Boss - make an exception! That poor thing would be a bear snack right now if I hadn't seen her!"

"She is too old for Canadian family to adopt. I ask all the right people. They recom-mend a good home for her, where she will have brothers and sisters."

"Where she will become lost in the system! That tough little pint of kid already sur-vived a war. You and Lupe picked her up and promised her a forever home. Now you do this?! You want to take her away from the only love and security she's ever known? You've seen her with Kei! She adores him!"

Tagata held his stance. "We do this because it is best for Sasori team."

Mouse faced him off. "That's bullshit! Sadao wouldn't have made a decision like this."

"This is Sadao-sama decision," he said without emotion.

Mouse was struck dumb. "You expect me to believe that?"

Tagata looked aside at Kei, who only wrung his hands faster.

"I don't fucking believe either of you! That's not the Sadao I know! The man who made himself a shooting target so not one of his precious babies could be taken away? Have you both lost your minds?"

"You ask Sadao-sama what is his opinion about this girl."

Mouse blew past Tagata, heading for the door. "I will. I certainly will! But no matter what the fuck he says, I'm going to say one thing right now and you'd better believe I'm serious. You send that girl away, I go with her! End of story. You can ask Sadao what his opinion is of that!"

Mouse slammed the cabin door behind him and marched to his Jeep. He got in and threw the vehicle into reverse and sped out in a hail of mud for Squamish.

It was a few hours shy of sundown when Mouse returned with his replacement treads. He parked the jeep at the foot of his front steps. Radio volume was up again - higher than usual. It was Zeppelin marathon Friday on CROQ. Pissy rate would be through the roof. Mouse took a few breaths to brace himself before getting out and mounting the steps.

The levee's gonna break for damn sure if I find that asshole smoking!

Sadao was seated on the couch fuming without the aid of tobacco. Thankfully, he made the move to click off the radio first in order to shout at Mouse.

"Where have you been all day? I wasted a second trip down to the lake today looking for you!"

"I told you, I had shit to do in town, didn't I?"

"I assumed it would be a town in British Columbia! I was radioed to come down and settle the aftermath of your tantrum first thing this morning!"

"Tantrum?! Hey, I stuck one out for that little girl! I caught her running away, Sadao! She could have frozen to death! How dare you tell Tagata to send her away! My face nearly fell off when he told me you were behind it!"

Sadao sat with a sour expression. "You done?"

"Yeah, I'm fucking done," Mouse said removing his coat. He stood in front of Sadao, hands on his hips. "Well what do you have to say about it? I'd like to know why as a former refugee yourself you'd think it was the best plan to tear that little thing away from the only home she's ever known. Can you answer me that?"

"Women do not belong in racing camps. It is a distraction and a danger!"

Mouse rolled his eyes. "Danger my ass - I work with these kids too, you know. She's six! If she's raised alongside them it won't be an issue. She'll be little sister to them."

Sadao closed his eyes but his jaw held firm. "I did not appreciate you speaking for me on this issue to Tagata. You were out of line."

"Give me a break. I lick your butthole and everyone knows it!"

Sadao's eyes flew open. "They don't have to know everything! You should be pleased to know your desertion threat made Tagata change his mind. The girl stays, a ward of the team. Against my advice!"

"Oh, thank God Tagata found the balls to stand up to you," Mouse said with a huge exhale. "It's about time he did. Besides, you know I wouldn't leave this place without you. I wasn't looking forward to hauling you out tied up in the back of the Jeep."

Sadao eyed him, silent.

"Here, I brought you something to brighten your stellar mood. Consider it a peace offering."

Mouse tossed a long thin box into his lap. Sadao rattled it. "What's in it?"

"It's a gift. I rode all the way down to Squamish and back for it, so don't throw it at anything," Mouse said, joining him on the couch.

Sadao gave him a wary glance. "Why would I throw it?" he asked and opened the box. A long hollow thin glass and metal device lay inside with a selection of attachments. Sadao lifted the device to his nose for closer scrutiny. "What is it?"

"Technically it's called a nicotine oral delivery system. But commonly it's known as a glass cigarette."

"It's a toy," Sadao said, putting it back in the box and pushing it aside. "I'm a little old for those."

"It's not child's play - it's a highly sophisticated device designed for stubborn assholes like you!" Mouse said, pushing the box back toward Sadao. "It satisfies the addiction without killing you. Or at least not killing you as fast! It's a much better choice for people with circulation issues."

Sadao rubbed his forehead. "I'm on infusions already. Three, sometimes four times a day."

"Yeah and a fat lot of good they're doing you. You're grumpy as ever. I think this might be more helpful - if you'd try it. Here," Mouse said, opening the small bag of liquid filled vials. "I'll show you how to load the -"

"Have you gone deaf? I said I'm not putting that toy in my mouth!"

Mouse looked back at him but tried to keep his cool and reached for the box. "It comes in a bunch of flavors. I bought several -"

Sadao grabbed Mouse's wrist hard, stopping him.

"Ow!" Mouse yelped, wrenching his hand free and shaking it out. "What the fuck was that for? I'm trying to help you!"

Sadao didn't answer but got up off the couch and went for the door, yanking his jacket down off the rack.

"Oh, that's just great!" Mouse snapped, following him. "You're gonna be a dick and just leave, is that it?"

Sadao pushed the latch and limped out onto the porch, making a beeline for his cruiser. He was easy to catch. "You're not going anywhere, Mister!" Mouse said and made a grab at his arm.

Sadao whipped his arm free so hard it knocked Mouse back off his feet. His ass hit the pine decking with a whump! *The fuck is this shit?* Mouse scrambled back up, pissed as hell. He tore past Sadao descending the stairs and threw himself over the front end of Sadao's bike.

"Get off!" Sadao ordered.

"Not a chance. I'm not letting you run off to Tagata for pity. You're gonna stay and deal with me!" Mouse was straddled over the front wheel, ready for a fight. Sadao mounted the bike and strapped his goggles to his head. Ignoring Mouse, he fit his key in the engine and started it up.

"Get off!"

"No!"

Sadao engaged the clutch and gunned the engine. Mouse refused to budge.

"If you let go of that clutch, my balls go flying. I don't think you wanna do that!"

Sadao flipped his goggles down over his eyes and cranked the throttle harder - engine roaring in threat.

"Really? What kind of pussy do you take me for?!"

The engine screamed and smoke billowed out of the exhaust pipes. Mouse just held on.

"Fuck!" Sadao yelled and shut off the key. He dismounted while Mouse laughed in victory only to have himself grabbed by the back of his pants and lifted straight up off the wheel. He lost his grip on the handlebars and shrieked as he was thrown for several feet. He came down hard up against a rocky surface, striking his chin.

Mouse rolled over with a groan but it went unheard over the roar of Sadao's bike tearing off into the shadows.

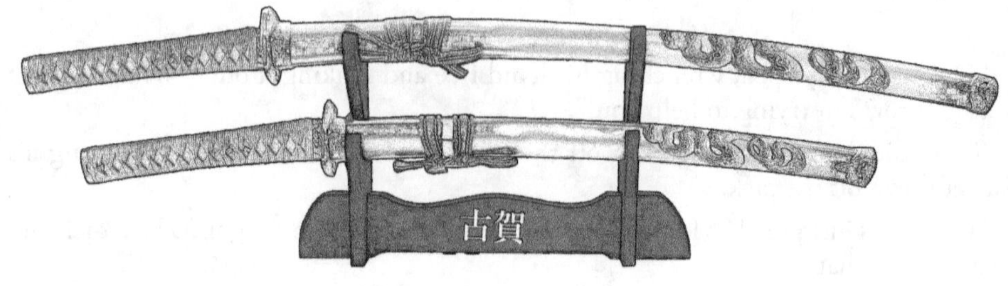

Chapter XI

Snow Warning

A storm was coming. First new snow was due to drop by midnight, said the weatherman on the radio. Mouse sat in the main room of the cabin with ice on his chin, thumping his foot nervously on the floor. The pines were howling outside the windows and dancing in dark waves under a cloudy muddled sky.

Come on asshole. Where are you?

The dull throb in his chin was punctuated by every thud of his heartbeat. Nothing worried him more than the thought of Sadao out there someplace alone. What if he got lost? What if he ran out of gas? Mouse wished against sanity the Chairman and his annoying tracking cameras were still in use so he could at least spot him on a map.

You gotta give him his space, Mouse reasoned. *He's never had to deal with something like this. He's confused and in pain right now. Like a bear with his leg in a trap. He's more pissed at himself than you.*

Mouse looked at the ice towel. Bleeding had stopped. Not a really big deal but the hit he took would leave a mark for certain. He wondered how he was going to explain it. Fell off a bike? Mouse didn't ride a motorcycle normally. He got around by foot or by Jeep. Mouse knew Sadao hadn't meant to hurt him. The man just lost grip on himself sometimes. *Shit, I sound like an old talk-show rerun.*

Just then the sound of Sadao's bike became apparent between the sweeping roar of the wind. Mouse heaved a huge sigh of relief and steadied himself for whatever attitude was going to walk in through the door. He heard Sadao take the bike back around to the shed and store it. Then his lumbering steps came around the porch to the front door. The key went in, then the board slid up and the cold wind blew in with his errant lover. Mouse stood up, tossing the towel aside on the table.

"Before you ask, I didn't smoke!" Sadao said, securing the door. "I just went riding to cool down before I - "

Sadao stopped halfway across the floor when he saw Mouse's bruised and torn chin in the glow of the stove. His face paled as he came closer and touched his cheek. Mouse winced.

"Did I do this?" Sadao asked.

Mouse turned his face away. "Who else?"

"When?"

"When you threw me ten fucking feet, asshole!"

"I didn't mean … "

"Like fuck, you didn't!" Mouse yelled, shocked at his own anger. "I've had enough of your abuse for one day. You can can sleep on the goddamn couch tonight!" Mouse walked away and slammed the bedroom door behind him.

That went well.

After Mouse got in bed to try and sleep a little, there was a quiet knock on the bedroom door.

"Go away!"

"Can I pee?"

"No!"

"You expect me to hold it all night?"

"I expect you to know where the front door is!"

A moment later Mouse heard the door open and the wind blowing into the front room. There was a bang or two, then a hardy slam. *Great, he's pissing off the deck into my wood pile.*

There was shuffling and coughing soon after the door closed again. Not so nice words were uttered in Japanese as the sink pump whined. Must be dead cold out there. Mouse stared at the log ceiling. *Fuck.* He grabbed a heavy blanket off the bed, opened the door, threw it into the main room, and slammed it shut again.

There, that'll show him! Show him I'm a pussy. With guilt.

Sleep finally took him. When Mouse woke, it was to a room full of sunlight and trees dusted with snow. The clouds had cleared and he sat up and peered out the bedroom windows. *Whoa.* About five inches of newborn white covered the ground and tree boughs. Mouse hoped it would hold. His stomach growled suddenly, interrupting his winter-wonderlanding. Someone was cooking and for once it wasn't him.

Mouse took a quick shower and got dressed before opening the door to the main room. Sadao was bringing hot plates of steaming food to the kitchen table. He glanced up.

"Just in time," he said. "Hungry?"

"You made breakfast," Mouse commented, coming over and taking a seat. "Badly."

"I'm no chef," Sadao said, setting down two plates of runny eggs, chunks of hard potatoes and over-grilled toast. "But I'm doing my best. I figure I owe you that."

Mouse sat and picked up his fork and dug in while Sadao brought over the tea and poured for them both. Mouse watched him while he chewed and swallowed with the aid of a hot gulp.

"It's edible," he commented. "I'll accept your culinary apology."

Sadao took the chair opposite and picked up his fork, pushing the eggs around. "You shouldn't," he said, taking a tentative bite.

"I know, but I'm hungry."

Sadao glanced at his face while he ate. "Looks sore."

"Oh, it hurts, alright. Every time I move my mouth. So you can keep feeling guilty all you want. Bruises take weeks to heal."

"I feel terrible, if you want to know. Worse than ever."

Mouse scoffed at his comment. "You've bruised me plenty of times."

"And you, me. But I want to say to you that I'm done. No more violence. If I ever touch you again in anger, you can leave. I won't ask why."

Mouse licked his fork. "Don't say that kind of shit. I'm not some helpless battered housewife. You piss me off for real, I'll cut your dick off in your sleep."

Sadao nodded solemnly. "I'd probably deserve it."

"Seriously babe, I know you're going through some tough shit. I'm not keeping score right now. I was pissed last night, but you get a pass for attempting to fry me eggs," he said, taking another big bite. "It's too salty, but it reminds me of the last time you cooked for me in that ghastly pink farmhouse while I was tied to the bed, remember?"

A grin teased Sadao's lips. "I do."

"Clearly, our relationship is not normal."

"You're right, it's not. But I'd like it to be."

Mouse chuckled. "Good luck. That's all I can say."

They ate quietly, talking idly about camp matters, back in step once again. Mouse helped Sadao get the dishes over to the sink. Sadao came to him as he pumped the water and put his arms around him from behind, holding him. Mouse lifted his wet hand to stroke Sadao's arm in forgiveness.

"I'm sorry," Sadao whispered, kissing Mouse's cheek tenderly. "You're the most precious thing in this world to me."

Mouse kissed him back and smiled. His whole body felt warm. "I know. And you can prove it by washing up the dishes, too," he said and handed Sadao the washrag.

"You okay?"

"What happened?"

"Did you fall off a bike?"

"Does it hurt?"

The questions kept coming that morning. Mouse wished he wasn't working so hard loading snowbikes up on the flatbed with Aki and the boys that he could stay comfortably wrapped up to his nose in a scarf.

"Slid down the icy steps, hit my chin."

That was the story and he wasn't about to elaborate. Bikes needed to get hauled up to the Meadows where Tagata's snowplow crew was hastily piling up hills and jumps for the team to train on. The snowfall was a blessing, but as the late morning sun beat down on them and temperatures rose, it didn't look to hold for very long.

Mouse and his boys tied down the last of the repaired fleet and waved the 22 retrofit, last-minute retreaded machines goodbye as the flatbed drove off to meet the team waiting in the snow. Mouse hoped he could get the garage closed up quickly enough that afternoon so he could drive up to the Meadows himself to watch his work in action. That was if he could get Sadao out of his garage. The man had been puttering around in there since early morning, looking for odd tools and asking odder questions. He needed a bike repair stand for one. But no, he didn't want to use it in the garage but up at the longhouse. No, he didn't need any help; he'd carry it up there himself. Then there were questions about electrical hook ups and spare bulbs.

"Babe, you want me to come up there and help you run wire? I'm pretty damn good with electrical."

"No," was the reply. Sadao wasn't angry - he just didn't care to elaborate as he measured out a spool of coated copper wire.

It's keeping him busy and on his feet, Mouse thought. *Can't ask for more than that.*

"Ay, gringo! Good job with the car, man," Lupe said, ducking into the tent. "She purrs like a kitten - whoa! What's up with your face?"

Mouse sighed. "You're only the 28th person to ask me that today."

Lupe came closer and touched his chin. *Why did they all have to touch?* Mouse winced.

"Did you get hit? Who hit you?"

"Look, I wasn't hit." Mouse said defensively. "I was, well - I slipped on some ice and …"

Lupe's face froze in shock. His head whipped directly to Sadao, who was rolling trimmed wire into a loop.

"That *cabron!*"

Before Mouse could move, Lupe had cleared the width of the garage and welcomed Sadao with a helluva right hook to the jaw. Bam!

Sadao was so unprepared for the punch he stumbled backwards into a stack of spare tires, ass-first.

"Lupe!" Mouse shouted, rushing forward to restrain his friend before he busted anymore of Sadao's face.

"Pendejo de mierda!" Lupe spat, his hand still formed in a fist.

Sadao wallowed in a tangled nest of bike tires, licking at his cut lower lip. *"Mexicano Loco!"*

"Lupe! What the hell?!" Mouse shouted, pulling his friend back. He'd never seen the guy get this violent before.

"Fuck him! Nobody messes with my brothers or they deal with Lupe. You got that, *chingada madre?*"

"Yeah, I got it," Sadao said, extracting himself from the nest of rubber rings. With Mouse's help, he got to his feet and reached for a clean rag to press to his lip. "Right across the mouth."

Lupe was still fueled up. "Maybe I give you another, huh?"

Mouse pushed Lupe back. "Chill it, bud. Seriously. It's fine! We worked it out, okay?"

Lupe turned to him. "Ain't nothing okay about this. Nobody beats on my brothers!"

"I'm not beaten! For fuck's sake. He apologized. We're cool! We're cool!"

"Lupe's right," Sadao said, leaning against the workbench and dabbing his lip. "It's not okay. I deserve it. Go ahead and give me another if you want."

Lupe lunged but Mouse shoved him aside in time. "Knock it off! Holy crap! I'll take care of it myself!" He went for Sadao and added to Lupe's bruise with a powerful taste of his own knuckles, right in the same spot. Pow!

"Fuck!" Sadao yelled, grabbing his chin.

"Omae! Nani wo yatteiru n da!" Tagata had entered just in time to see his predecessor getting sucker punched by his lover. *"Yamero!"*

Sadao groaned, blinking back stars. "Fine! Anyone else want to line up and take a hit?"

It took Tagata another moment to take in the scene. But from Mouse's bruise to Lupe's fury and Sadao's bleeding face, something clicked and the Sasori Boss burst into laughter.

Mouse sucked on his knuckles. "I think we're good here. Back to work, boys!"

Just about the last thing Sadao wanted to do that afternoon was climb into an enclosed space with a hot headed Mexican who'd just knocked him flat on his ass. But he'd made a promise to Tagata that he'd take Lupe driving, and seeing as he was down in camp and Lupe was present with the Mustang keys in hand, there was no getting around it - not if he wanted to prove to Mouse that he was taking steps to get his shit in order.

"Why don't you two make up by making good on the performance coaching," Mouse said, pushing them both out of the garage exit ramp together. "Go do race car driver shit. I want to get up to the track!"

Sadao grumbled but allowed Mouse to help him slide in the passenger's window of the purple Pimp-O-Ride. It was only slightly less blingy than the day of his rescue. No fuzzy dice, anyway.

"I promise I'll try not to drive Old Boss off a cliff," Lupe said, waving goodbye to Mouse as he climbed in behind the wheel.

"I thought we had decided against the name, 'Old Boss,'" Sadao grumbled.

"Listen, *pendejo*," Lupe said, jamming his key in the ignition and roaring his beloved to life. "You don't know. You were not around after the award ceremony. When they took you up in that chopper all covered in blood, we both thought they were carrying away a dead man."

"So did I." Sadao said without humor.

"It was two, three days before we heard you were still alive. I was with Mouse, man. Those three days. I took care of him. He was like a ghost - wouldn't eat, drink, nothing. That man loves the shit out of you. You're his heart, so you'd better treat him like it!"

"I admit, I fucked up. I've promised to keep it together. I told him he can leave if I ever forget."

"I'm watching you, man. You'd better not forget. Or I put you back in that chopper, you got me?"

Sadao regarded him carefully. "Yeah, I got you."

"Good, now let's drive!"

Domestic disputes for the moment settled, Lupe took them out at a conservative speed on the back road to the little used regional highway that circuited Sasori territory from the north end of the lake to the bald mountain in the south.

Once on the sunbaked pavement, the concern of ice was over and Lupe hit the gas, showing his Old Boss what he'd learned over the last two years in his absence. Sadao didn't speak at first, just let Lupe fall into the rhythm of navigating the gentle sweeps of the meandering highway. His grip was steady and his shifting well tuned to the rev of the Mustang's 5-speed racing engine.

Although Sadao didn't want to admit it, as the cold wind blew into their goggled faces, Lupe was a natural behind the wheel. *Probably should have let the kid train at*

16, he mused. But then, who would cover their bodywork? Tagata wasn't as much of a stickler for artistry as Sadao had been. Stenciled numbers spray painted in random colors seemed to suit his successor's more utilitarian needs.

It's not your team anymore. Not your concern. They have a new rhythm now, a new leader. Just as you designed. The focus now was on the future and the life he wanted to mold for himself, if he didn't fuck it up majorly first. Sadao's jaw throbbed as reminder to him of his obligations. Who knew Mouse could swing a punch that hard? *Kuso!*

"Your eyeline is a little too conservative. But I'll assume that's due to road conditions," Sadao said over the wind. "Take us up a grade. I want to observe your shifting."

"Hai!" Lupe replied and turned off for a steeper climb.

Sadao could hear Mouse's mechanical genius in the timing of the engine's shift in the high altitude. Fuel was a fine potent grade and the air compressor was boosted to overcome the lack of oxygen at 7,500 feet. There was some snow here remaining on the roadside and Lupe took that into account as they took turns at a more moderate speed. The rock walls took on a higher incline to their right as they climbed with an increasingly steeper and more perilous drop to their left.

"I'm not taking her over 60 here!" Lupe shouted. "I promised Mouse I wouldn't drive this baby off a cliff with you in it! Whether we lived or not, I'd be a dead man!"

"Understood! I'm looking for technique, not speed!" Sadao shouted over the wind. "When we clear the treeline, find a place to turn around. Then you can show me your downshift work!"

"Kashikomarimashitaaaa!"

Sadao wasn't sure if Lupe's use of respectful Japanese was meant to be ironic or not. Either way, it was a step up from being cursed out in Spanish. The kid didn't used to give him so much lip. Not before Mouse came along. He was right - everyone did know he licked his butthole. Well.

Lupe pulled into a snow-blocked sideroad when they were at level with the timberline. Bright white vistas opened up all around and the camp-side lake could be seen below as a small bluish oval half hidden in the forests below. Beautiful - if not bone-chilling cold. Sadao tucked his gloved hands into the pockets of his thick-lined leather jacket.

"Mouse didn't bother to fix the heater?" he asked Lupe as he slowed the car into a three-point turn.

"She was a desert racer, remember? Besides, New Boss doesn't want any money spent on non-essential parts."

Sadao shivered in his seat. "I'll talk to him about it. Hard to steer if your hands are frozen!"

"Are you cold?" Lupe asked with a shrug. "Guess I'm just too hot-blooded to feel it!"

"Very funny. Get us down before I ice up!"

"Hai, hai! Whoa!" Lupe hit the brake suddenly, throwing them both forward.

Buppa beppa! Buppa beppa! Buppa buppa buppa bup!

"I thought I told you to disable that fucking horn!" Sadao shouted, overcoming his impact with the safety straps. Good to know they worked, but his ribs were still a little tender from his farewell knifing in jail.

"You see that, Boss?" Lupe asked, pointing up the snowed-in sideroad.

"See what?" Sadao grumbled, adjusting his restraints so they didn't sit right over his scar.

"Snowcat tracks," Lupe said, putting the Mustang in park and climbing out the window to go investigate. There was a fresh path of flattened wide-treaded snowtracks leading up the steep incline and disappearing into a narrow cut between two rocky peaks about a hundred feet above.

Sadao groaned. He really wanted to get back down to lower elevations and warmer air. He leaned his head out the window. "I'm driving back down without you if you don't get back in this - *Oi!*"

The seat was trembling under his ass and it wasn't just the good old rumble of 8-cylinder combustion. Snow was trickling down the mountain towards them, gathering speed and growing into bigger and bigger snowballs.

"Lupe! Run!"

Lupe saw what was coming a second before Sadao did and was already clearing the short distance between himself and the driver's window in a mad sprint. He grabbed the window trim and swung himself back into the driver's seat. Throwing the car into reverse, he spun them around just as the first of the hefty snowballs began to slam into the driver's side of the car, blasting snow through the open window and into their eyes.

"Get us out of here!" Sadao hollered with ice in his teeth. Lupe slammed into first gear, spinning the rear wheels a heart-stopping moment before they caught hold, accelerating them forward onto the main road. Sadao watched with wide eyes in the rearview as half the mountainside came down the incline and exploded over the section of cliffside road they had just been parked on. "Keep going! Keep going!"

"I am! Shit! Never seen nothing like that up here!"

Lupe took them back down to the valley as fast as was reasonably safe and pulled over into the grassy dirt so they could unstrap and start bailing out the car's interior of snow and small rocks. Lupe opened the trunk and got out some rags so they could wipe down the dash and seats as well - clearing all evidence of their near burial.

By the time they finished, Sadao was breathing hard and leaning against the front fender, waiting for his heart to slow. He looked to Lupe. "Under no circumstances does Mouse need to know about this!"

"Hai, Boss!" Lupe exclaimed. No argument there. "Calm Sunday drive this was for sure! Fuck me!"

Sadao looked back up at the peak they just descended in two minutes flat without a single skid. "How the fuck did you learn to downshift like that?"

Lupe laughed. "Watching you! Mouse and I found your training videos from 20 years ago! I studied every minute of 'em! Even the outtakes, which were funny as hell!"

"I thought I threw those out!"

"Good thing you didn't, or we'd be snowmen right now! Dead ones!"

Mouse didn't need to know what happened up the mountain at the far fringe of Sasori territory, but Tagata certainly did. Sadao waited back at the A-frame cabin until he returned from the Meadows' first training day.

Tagata was surprised to find him lounging in front of his fireplace. *"Sadao-sama! Why did you not radio me?"*

Sadao got to his feet somewhat unsteadily. Too much exertion today left him feeling exhausted. *"We need to talk. It seems we are not alone in these mountains."*

Tagata made tea and they sat near the fire speaking in low voices. Sadao told him what had happened up on the high road - what Lupe had seen, the snowcat tracks and the large shudder before the mountain began to fall.

"Avalanche was deliberately set? Why?" Tagata asked.

"Lupe tells me no one else uses that road but him for training the Mustang. The motocross riders use the dirt tracks near camp, is this correct?" Sadao asked, sipping his tea thoughtfully.

"Yes, and today all Sasori snowcats and plows were accounted for up at the meadows since the snow fell last night. It is a new training ground for us this season due to the late snowpack."

"Canadian Forestry Service. They do not come into this area?"

"No. Not unless we request their assistance."

"You should hail them tomorrow at sunup to be certain but I can already predict what they will say. Also, the campfire Mouse found. Your men searched the far shore thoroughly?"

"Yes, we found no other evidence of intruders. I thought maybe these were hunters. But why the Sasori gas can?"

"I suspect the marmots that got into the garage last week were also no natural occurrence."

"Ah!" Tagata lit up with a sudden thought. *"Before Sadao-sama came to camp we had wood mice invade the food storage! Everything had to be thrown out and rebought. All these events were very costly for us. Yet, it seemed like nature was angry at us."*

"It's more than just nature, Taga. There is a competition approaching. Like before in the Southwest, cross-team sabotage is always a threat."

"Until now, we had not seen evidence of this. But now, my eyes are open. We must secure our camp. No one goes in or out!"

Sadao sat back and stared into the fire in thought. "Maybe ... this enemy is already among us," he said in English.

Tagata stared at him a moment, turning this notion around in his mind. "I trust all my men," he said succinctly. "No one is traitor."

"What about the one who stayed behind?"

"Eh? Which one?"

"The last of the Whitebird men. Miyagi."

"But he is only one who stay loyal. He come to me after his friends leave. He say - he beg to me - keep him. He did not want to go. Many tears. He show me his whole heart. I believe him."

"I would have felt the same, but ... evidence is proving otherwise. Whoever is behind these attacks, they know Sasori routines and have access to Sasori resources. I fear an insider may be sending communication to others who want to see us fail."

"But why sabotage Sasori team? I do not understand. What is bad for Sasori is bad for traitor, too. The men who left us. No sign of them. I read all the trade report. None have come to be bought by rival team. It is like they - what do you say - walk off earth. What do they have to gain if Sasori fail? Revenge? For what? We give them good home. Good racing team."

"We don't know all the reasons yet. But we will need to remain highly vigilant. It is important Taga, that you bring only your closest men into this knowledge. Set tighter perimeters and exit privileges, but do not let more than a few know why. Bad weather is a good excuse. As I understand we are in for several more inches of snow tonight and through the week." Sadao gestured to the high pointed windows of Tagata's cabin. Snow was beginning to fall across them as the winds swirled through the trees.

"Sadao-sama should stay here for the night," Tagata suggested as Sadao began to rise from his chair.

"No, I need to get back home."

"Then I will drive you," Tagata said, getting up and reaching for his coat.

"Taga," Sadao said, staying his hand. "I need to learn to get about on my own. It's a 15-minute walk for me at most. A little snow won't hurt me."

Tagata looked concerned, but helped Sadao into his jacket nevertheless.

Sadao leaned into the blowing snow, keeping a keen eye on the porchlight of the cabin perched on the hill above him. The wind had picked up suddenly and bit at his exposed cheeks and nose. *Stupid to go out without a proper scarf,* he mused. This wasn't Arizona anymore. He knew he could have weathered out the storm in the comfort of Tagata's cabin, but he was anxious to get home to Mouse. He didn't want him to worry needlessly.

The leg was stiffening in the cold and he had to drag it along like a dead tree. Damned nuisance. The left foot had lost all feeling during his trudge uphill and he had to constantly glance down to know where he put it. It slowed him but he kept his movements steady and methodical - using muscle memory to keep up the pace. If he slowed, he took the risk of not being able to move the leg at all.

The light atop the hill grew steadily brighter and closer until he reached the foot of the porch steps. He grabbed the icy rail and leading with his good leg, hauled the dead leg up step by step. A gust came through and blew off his hood, the wind screamed in his ears. He went to grab it and lost his footing on the ice. Wham! Sadao ended up facedown on the deck, with snow in his eyes and nose.

Sadao swore and got himself up by the stair rail, coughing and brushing chips of ice from his beard. Just three more steps and it's over. He unlocked the bolt and lifted the latch. He lumbered in and secured the heavy door behind him. Flickering auburn light and the scent of firewood revived his senses. He removed his coat and shook the snow off over the entry grate before hanging it on the hook next to Mouse's.

Sadao grabbed a kitchen rag and wiped his face, neck and hands dry. The room was warm but it would take time to bring any heat back into his extremities. He didn't think he had energy left in his cold stiff muscles to fill the bath. He crossed to the bedroom door and went in. The pile of blankets and furs on the bed was breathing slowly. Among them, a tangle of gold hair and braids stuck out between the layers. Here was the remedy to his condition.

You sleep like a bear in winter, *Konezumi.*

Sadao undressed from head to frozen toes and shivering, found a parting in the wooly nest and burrowed his way in toward the warm ball of Mouse snoozing at the center.

"Hmngh….Huh?! Hey…! Fuck are you doing? You're freezing!"

"I know," Sadao said, winding his limbs around him. "You're not."

"Gaah, watch it with the hands - you'll give me frostbite."

"Shhh. You'll lose heat shouting like that." Thighs proved to be the perfect cozy spot to slide between to warm up cold fingers.

"Oh God! Not there! Now I won't ever have kids!"

"Warmest nook you have. Share it," Sadao said, spooning up and warming his face in Mouse's messy hair.

"Sssss, your nose is an icicle."

"Stop fidgeting," Sadao mumbled against his shoulder as he relaxed into blissful warmth. "I do the same for you."

"That's because your lazy ass doesn't work and you're home in bed ahead of me. Wait, why are you home so late?" Mouse eyed the window as reason flooded back into his sleep startled brain. "It's dark! It's storming --!" He wriggled in Sadao's grasp to glare at him despite his grumbling protest. "What the hell were you thinking?"

"I thought I'd get home and settle into a warm bed with a sleeping spouse, not a protesting harpy!"

Mouse snorted out a laugh. "Harpy? Is that the best insult you could think of? You must be cold," he said, touching his face. No, poking it. "Your cheeks are red as a beet! Where was your scarf?"

Sadao sighed into the pillows, closing his eyes. He was desperate for sleep regardless of Mouse's levels of peeve. Mouse's hands moved over his body, conducting a physical exam under the covers.

"Your ass is cold. How long were you walking in the wind?! Even your dick is barely lukewarm. You freeze that off, we're done, mister!" The hands moved lower down over his hips to his legs - rubbing and squeezing. Sadao was already beginning to drift off when he lost awareness of Mouse's touch.

"God! Baby, your leg is so cold! Shit, your left foot is ice!" Mouse threw back the lower set of blankets exposing his feet. Mouse made a sound that didn't sound good. "Babe, look!" he said, shaking Sadao's rump.

"Eh? Let me sleep. It will warm up…"

"No it won't! Sadao, it's blue!"

"It's always blue…" Sadao murmured, half gone.

"Jeesus!"

Sadao's last shred of fading awareness was of the sound of pots banging in the kitchen and the groan of the old pump.

"Fuck ow!" Mouse swore as he dribbled hot boiling water from the kettle over his fingers in his hurry to fill the water bottle. Nineteenth-Century cabin heating sucked when it was below freezing out. He was shivering even this close to the stove. He hadn't bothered to throw anything on in his rush to bring life back into Sadao's foot.

"Of all the goddamn stubborn pig-headed …"

Mouse screwed the cap on tight and set the kettle back on to boil. He'd force some tea down the man's throat somehow but right now the foot needed emergency action.

Dammit! Why doesn't he care? What'd the leg ever do to him?

Mouse wrapped a dry rag around the hot rubber and dashed through the cold room and back into the cozier bedroom, kicking the door closed. He sat on the end of the bed and lifted the blankets. The foot was a sickly shade of green now. Better than purple blue, he supposed. He folded the hot water bottle directly over it and wrapped it up snug around his ankle with the towel. Sadao made a snorting sound between snores but didn't wake.

Pig-headed, exhausted and frozen. Why? Dammit!

Mouse wanted to smack the sonofabitch he was so pissed. Didn't he know? If the leg went bad it could kill him. At the very least it would have to go. And that wasn't the kind of surgery easily performed in a clinic tent. How do you explain admitting a dead man into a public hospital?

Mouse sighed and crawled back under the covers and wrapped his arms around Sadao as best as he could, rubbing warmth into his thigh. He watched his face. Sadao was out cold. Hardly the ever vigilant gang boss he'd remembered trying to steal a knife from in years past. It seemed forever ago. Sadao's hair had pulled loose from the leather band in the wind, leaving it to cling onto the ends of a few loose strands. Mouse reached over and pulled the last of it free, letting his hair fan out over his shoulders.

"What can I do?" he asked softly, running the soft dark hairs though his fingers. "What can I do to make you see what you're doing to yourself?"

Another soft snore was his only answer.

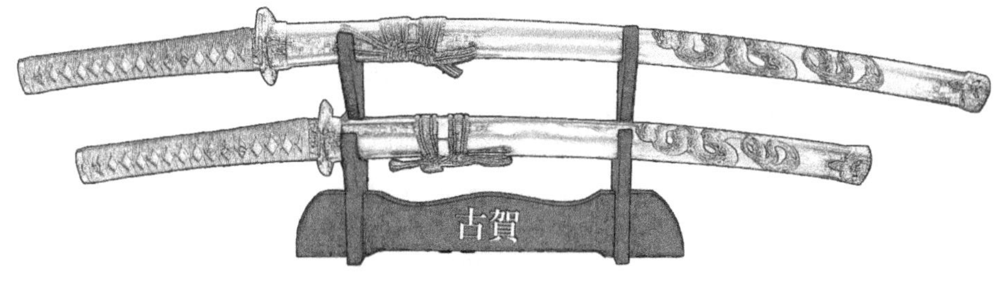

Chapter XII

The Babysitter

Mouse pulled up to the children's schoolroom trailer in his Jeep with a Santa hat on his head and Aki riding shotgun with a red nose tied to his face. He honked the horn and gave a hearty Hohoho! Kids tumbled out the back of the trailer - lessons were over for the day. It was party time!

The kids ran up and began jumping anxiously, peering into the back of the Jeep. It was loaded up with sleds Mouse and Aki had made from the rejected snowbike front skis and spare wood.

Mouse called out names in a jolly voice as his reindeer assistant handed down the matching hand-painted personalized sleds for each of the kids. Ten in all, with an extra in case one broke.

"Santa Mouse!! Santa Mouse!!" They squealed as they hugged him and flopped down into the snow on their new rides.

"Come on kids! Let's head for the hills!" Mouse said when his jeep was empty. All of them, Kei included, wobbled through the fresh snow, pulling their little sleds and making their way up the trail to a nearby slope at the end of the lake.

It wasn't quite Christmas, but then the Japanese didn't really celebrate the holiday, anyway. A man in a red cap with toys and cake was pretty much all the Christmas they knew. Mouse promised Kei he'd bring them all something special - wear them out, stuff them with cake and let them all nap in front of the fire in Tagata's cabin. Tagata had been less than thrilled about the idea, but he paid the price for having the largest living room and a table suitable for serving punch.

"Yamete kudasai!" A young man shouted, blocking their path. It was one of Tagata's newly instated security guards, Miyagi.

"Hohoho!" Mouse shouted. "Ye won't be stopping the children from having a go at the fresh snowpack, will ye?"

"Who is 'Yee'?" Miyagi asked. He didn't look amused, nor familiar with Christmas at all. "This area is out of bounds."

"Hohoho! You must be on Santa's naughty list!" Mouse sang as the kids and their sleds surrounded the confused sentinel.

"*Ano basho ha tachiiri kinshi deru.* It is forbidden. Go back at once!"

Mouse pulled off his hat and stepped right up to the guy. "Look buddy, I got ten kids here who want to sled for an hour or so a few hundred feet beyond your ridiculous border! We aren't going to cause any trouble."

The young man held firm. "If you do not listen, I will have to report you to Tagata-san!"

"Really?" Mouse laughed. "Yeah, you go right ahead and do that! Report us for sledding!"

"Yeah! Report us for sledding!" One of the kids shouted as a snowball nailed the guy right in the nose. Woooomf! A second later, snowballs were flying from everywhere and Miyagi ran off for safety.

"Onward!" Mouse called. "Our hill is in sight! We have defeated the abominable snowman!"

"Yaaaaay!!" The bigger kids made a run for the hill and were already diving down it, shrieking in excitement as Mouse and Aki helped the littler ones haul their sleds up the short hill. They got their little bottoms aimed in the right direction, steering ropes in hand and with a push, sent them sailing down the hill into Kei's arms, or legs as the case may be.

"Santa Mouse, I need help!!" It was Shinjyu, she'd insisted on carrying her sled up herself. She was the last one to make it to the top of the hill.

Mouse rushed to her aid and set her sled down firmly in the snow. "Okay, honey, hop on up!" Shinjyu climbed on and Mouse set the ropes in her gloved hands. "Hold on tight!" he said and gave her sled a little push.

She screamed in a high pitch as only a girl can, and tore down the hill, fast as a rabbit. So fast she managed to steer herself right around Kei's legs, a seriously crafty undertaking. And then she kept right on going and going…

"Oh, shit! Aki! Hand me the spare sled!!" Rudolph to the rescue, Aki had the sled in his hand and with a huge leap forward, Mouse dove belly first, legs flying behind him down the hill after his escaped wee elf.

Steering by rope, he too, narrowly missed Kei's massive legs and with a *thuwoof,* was soon airborne over a shallow ravine that had taken Shinjyu a few feet down with it. He landed on his liver, and went into a barrell roll, coming to a dizzy stop right in front of Shinjyu's sled, which was stopped by his ass. *Ow!*

"Yay! Let's do that again!" Shinjyu yelled, hopping off her sled and hugging Mouse's head as he tried to sit up.

"Ugh, um … ow, let's not. You went crazy fast on that thing!" Mouse tucked Shinjyu under his arm and flipped her sled over to feel the rails. "Did these get extra wax or something?"

"You've saved me twice!" she exclaimed.

"I have! I think you owe me a little help by now."

Shinjyu nodded. "I can help! I can help you fix things!"

Mouse picked her up, as well as their two sled ropes, and started trudging back to the hill. "Hm, you're a little young still to help me in the garage…"

"I can fix anything," she assured him. "Kei-Sensei says I'm his very best helper because I'm the only one who can find lost shoes and stuff. Boys lose *everything!*" she said, rolling her eyes.

"You know," Mouse said, coming to a slow realization. "There is something you can help me with. Or rather someone."

"Who? Is it a boy? Because boys always need lots of help!"

"Yeah it's a boy. A big boy. But, I think you can handle him."

"Did he lose his shoe?" Shinjyu asked.

"Kind of … how would feel about babysitting for me a few days a week after lessons?"

"Will I get paid?"

"Sure!"

"Cash?"

Mouse looked her in the eye as he crunched through the snow. All business, this girl.

"We can negotiate a rate."

Shinjyu nodded. "Good. It's a deal."

Sadao drummed his fingers against the ofero's pine decking. He'd slept well past midday and after a leisurely breakfast of tea and soy eggs over rice, he'd indulged himself in the bath. Steam rose from the heated water, clouding the windows. Mouse wasn't due back for hours. He reached up and slid the window open a crack, letting in a cold breeze. Then he lifted a loose board at the back of the tub unit and slipped out an emergency cigarette and matchbook. He lit it and sank back into the water, taking in a really good drag - the first in days. Absolute paradise.

I won't smoke the whole thing. Flush the evidence. No harm done. Mouse won't cut my dick off.

Reasonable plan, he thought - until he heard the front door bang open.

Kuso!

Tssssst! He doused it in the bathwater but the smoke cloud wasn't exiting the window fast enough. He was still fanning it when Mouse walked in.

"Nice, I'm gone a few hours and you're up here smoking like a locomotive."

Sadao sat up. "I had one drag! One! I haven't smoked in three days!"

"Correction, *hadn't*," Mouse said, unimpressed with his track record. "Get your pants on. We have a guest."

"What? Who? I don't want to see anyone!"

"Tough shit, cowboy. Saddle up! Vacation's over!"

Sadao had no idea what Mouse was up to but he got dried, dressed and opened the bedroom door.

Shinjyu was standing there, hands on her tiny hips, glaring up at him.

"Mouse says you've been a bad boy!"

"What?!"

"Too much smoking! Too much laziness! You need a babysitter! You need Shinjyu!"

Mouse stood proudly behind the tot with a grin a mile wide.

Sadao was speechless, his finger remained pointed at the girl in question.

"I've hired a caretaker to look after you while I'm working. I'd listen to what she says, she's a real hardass."

"You," she said poking his thigh, "need fresh air and exercise. No more sitting on your lazy butt! Get your shoes on! We're going outside! Now!"

"Wait … Mouse?! You can't just leave her with me all day! Shouldn't she be in school?"

Mouse looked over his shoulder as he made for the door. "School's out. And I think you need a new hobby. Trust me, this little lady's got plans for you. I made sure of it. She's on my payroll."

poke poke

"Let's go! I'm gonna make you work! No more time for smoking!"

Shit.

"Not so far ahead!" Sadao shouted as Shinjyu's small frame grew smaller on the path ahead.

"Come on!" she whined, skipping along the snowy wooded trail. "You're soooo slow!"

"I'm older than you!" Sadao snapped, but hobbled faster through the snow, using a cane he'd recently carved to help his busted hip swing the dead leg forward. He didn't want her getting out of sight.

Shinjyu ran and hopped in circles around the tree trunks as he struggled to catch up. She sighed extravagantly. "Why do you walk so funny?"

Sadao lumbered to a stop in front of her and stared her down while she hopped on one foot. "Why do you?"

The girl stopped her hopping and stared right back up at him. "I'm six! What's your excuse?"

"I was injured!"

"I knew a boy who was born with no legs at all and even he was faster than you!"

"I didn't know this was a race," Sadao grumbled.

"It's not - it's just walking," she said, stomping one foot down then the other, making the frozen pine needles crunch under her snow boots. "See, like this! One-two! One-two! Now you, you do it like Shinjyu!"

"I think you were a drill sergeant in a former life," Sadao sighed and tossed the cane aside. He set his fists at his sides and forced his spine to straighten. Like a good soldier, he tried to follow her example. At least for a few steps or so up the path. Until the popping in his hip and accompanying pain made him slouch back over to favor his good side, panting.

Shinjyu looked enormously pleased with herself and bent to pick up his cane. "Good job! Mouse said you could walk normal if you wanted, but were afraid to try."

"Afraid?" Sadao questioned, grasping the handle of the hand-carved cane. "Who says I'm afraid? It hurts is why!"

The girl twirled around and resumed skipping forward. "No pain, no gain! Come on, slowpoke!"

"Slowpoke, huh? I'll show you a slowpoke!" Sadao said and began, to the best of his ability, to haul ass.

By the time they got to the edge of the half frozen lake, Sadao's leg muscles were throbbing and his brow was coated in a fine layer of sweat. And still the kid skipped in circles around him. Her energy was boundless.

"We made it! We made iiiiit!" she sang.

"I'm going to sit," Sadao announced and used the trunk of a dead pine to lower himself to the ground. *Nnnngh!* Fuck, it hurt to move this much. He shifted his hip into a less uncomfortable position and leaned back against the dead wood. There was a chilly breeze coming in off the lake. He closed his eyes a moment to catch his breath.

It got quiet and he opened them. Shinjyu was standing directly in front of him, dark little eyes burrowing into him. "How old are you?" she asked.

Sadao set his cane close by and wiped his forehead on his sleeve. "Forty."

She cocked her head in a way not unlike someone he used to know. "Are you a grandfather?"

Sadao's eyes got bigger. "Absolutely not! I'm not even a father!"

She laughed. The more annoyed he got, the happier it seemed to make her. "Then why do they call you Oyaji?"

"Oh, that," Sadao said, somewhat relieved. "I used to be boss. Now Tagata-san is team boss. It's not appropriate for the men to call me the same. Oyaji is what they used to call Yakuza leaders -"

"I know! I know Oyaji! They are bad men. You are not a bad man, are you? So you must be very old."

Sadao chuckled at her reasoning. "Some people think I'm a bad man."

Shinjyu tossed her hair out of her face. "Then they're stupid!"

"Some people might agree with you on that, too."

"Do you know how to catch fish?" she asked, jumping to the next subject.

"Lake fish? No. But I used to lay traps and nets when I was your age. In the ocean."

"I want to catch a fish and eat him!" Shinjyu said, throwing a rock over the water where it cracked through the thin ice and sank. "Will you help me?"

"Sure, but I think you'll have trouble if all you use for bait is rocks. Mouse has a pole. He should take you fishing sometime and show you how to use it."

Shinjyu shrugged and bent down to pick up another rock, tossing it in the water with a plunk.

"Is Mouse your boyfriend?"

Sadao blinked. The conversation was moving far too fast for him. "Yes, he is. Why?"

"I *told* Takeshi Mouse was your boyfriend but he said I was stupid. Boys can't have boyfriends, he said, but *he's* stupid."

"Well, he's young," Sadao offered. "He maybe doesn't understand yet. You shouldn't call him names."

"I told him Mouse is like the mama and you are like the papa because you have a house and are always hugging and stuff."

Sadao paled. "Stuff?"

Shinjyu sat down in the snowy gravel and began organizing rocks in a circle. "Everybody saw you kissing ... *everybody*."

Sadao tried to hide his grin. "Sorry, didn't realize we had such a wide audience. We've missed each other a lot. When you miss someone, you want to kiss them."

"Oh, I know that! But boys are so lame. They think kissing is yucky."

"They'll like kissing once they get a little older."

Shinjyu looked up from her rock sorting and before Sadao knew it, she'd hopped over and planted a peck on his cheek. Then she ducked her head shyly and scampered away.

"Hey! What was that for?" Sadao asked, laughing.

Shinjyu giggled and ran and hid behind a nearby boulder.

"I know where you're hiding. I can see your shoes!"

She shuffled enough to retract her feet from his view.

"I still know where you're hiding! I can hear you giggling."

Her little head popped up from behind the rock. She wore a silly frown.

"Why are you frowning now?"

"Because you know where I am!" she whined.

"I need to know where you are. I don't want you getting lost. Come back here."

Shinjyu stood and kicked dejectedly at pebbles as she sauntered back to him.

"But if you know where I am, then you won't miss me! And if you don't miss me, you won't want to kiss me," she said sadly.

Sadao smiled up at her in her pout. "Give me your hand, *hime*."[1]

She held out a wet gravelly hand. He brushed a clean spot free and brought it to his lips like a gentleman. "See, I did miss you."

She lifted her chin up proudly and swirled her hips like she'd just won a game.

"Now hand me a few of those rocks you gathered and I'll show you how to skip them over ice."

By the time they worked their way back up to the cabin, the sun was going down and Sadao felt like he'd run a marathon. Took some effort to get up the steps, but once inside and despite the soreness, he did acknowledge there was somewhat better movement in the hip.

Shinjyu was tired too and getting cranky. She scampered into the kitchen and began nosing through the fridge while Sadao collapsed on the couch with his leg on the stool.

"I'm hungry! I want some cheese!" she said, her voice echoing inside the appliance.

"Okay, you may have some but not too much. Mouse will be home soon to cook dinner. He doesn't like cooking for stuffed kids."

Shinjyu brought out the whole plate and set it on the table with a clank. She lifted the cover off and made to grab a slice with her hand.

"*Yamero!*" Sadao barked.

The girl looked up, startled.

"Look at your hands."

1		*hee-may* - "princess"

Shinjyu looked at her hands, confused.

"They are brown. Go wash them. And get a proper fork. We are not dogs."

Shinjyu sighed and dragged a chair over to the sink. She climbed up and lifted the pump, but her small body didn't weigh nearly enough to force the handle down to produce water for washing up.

"Gnngh, it won't go! It's stuck! I'm hungryyy!"

Sadao sighed and considered which was the less painful option, getting up off the couch, or listening to the child whine. He lowered his leg off the stool and attempted to sit up. Pain unlike any he had felt in weeks shot up his leg to his spine. "Aaaaghh!"

"It won't gooooo! I want cheeeesee!! Noww!!"

Sadao fell back on the cushions, seeing stars.

"I'm hungryyyy!! It won't goooooo!!"

"Donaru yamenasai!! Ningen wa te de tabenai!!" [2]

She went dead quiet. Sadao lifted his head and blinked at her through the waves of pain. Her face drooped as she looked down at her dirty hands. She closed them into fists and her lower lip began to tremble.

Sadao's heart cracked right down the middle. "Shinjyu, *gomen* … "

Her eyes shut and her little chest heaved in a huge breath. "Mmmwaaah ahhh ahhh!!"

It was the most pitiful sound he'd ever heard. "Shinjyu… "

"Waaahaaahahahh!!"

"Nakanai de …. Shinjyu, gomen. Ore wa baka da." [3]

She couldn't hear his apologies over her crying. Sadao bit down and forced himself to stand. The hip was locked and he had to drag the leg to try and get closer to her. She was still on the chair and he was afraid in her sobbing she'd fall right off and hit her head on the edge of the table. He grabbed the counter for support and lifted her down with one arm. She clung to his leg and bawled and bawled.

"Youu voice is ssscary!!"

Sadao was helpless in knowing what to do. With his boys, he'd pick them up and toss them in the air a few times until they quieted. But as far as he could remember he'd never scared a child to tears before. He felt like the lowest form of life on earth.

"Shinjyu. I'm sorry. I didn't mean to yell at you. *Honto ni baka da."* [4]

Her little hands were gripping his thigh painfully tight through his jeans as she soaked his kneecap with a fountain of tears and snot.

---

2   *Stop yelling! Humans don't eat with their hands.*

3   *Don't cry. Shinjyu, I'm sorry. I'm an idiot.*

4   *I'm truly an idiot.*

"Oyaji wa baka ja nai! Shinjyu wa damena ko nano!" she wailed.[5] It was the first time she'd spoken Japanese to him. And what she said crushed the remains of his heart to dust.

"No, no … Shinjyu is not a bad girl. Hime, come here."

She gulped back a sob and held her thin arms up to him. He lifted her so her rump was seated on the counter and he could see her puffy red eyes and tear streaked face. Sadao pumped the water into the stoppered sink and dipped a wash rag in. He wrung it out and gently wiped her face clean then one little hand at a time, reassuring her over and over she wasn't a bad girl.

"I am sorry, little one. I have been among boys for too long. I've forgotten how to talk to a lady. Maybe I am a bad man after all. Although, I try not to be."

Her crying had quieted some so he broke off a chunk of cheese with his hand and gave it to her to munch on. She ate it quietly, not meeting his eyes.

"Bad men say Shinjyu is not a good girl. Bad men always say …" she said in a whimpering voice.

"Shhh … no, hime. They are wrong. Shinjyu is a good girl. A very good girl," he said, brushing her hair back from her eyes. "A very beautiful little girl."

Her eyes got bigger and she met his gaze. "Really?"

Sadao sighed in relief. It looked like they were still friends. "Of course. And I promise not to shout at you ever again. Can you forgive me?"

She nodded her head and reached for him, climbing up into his arms for a hug. He held her close. Her small frame was so light it was like holding a silk pillow. Right where her chest met his he could feel the furious beating of her heart. Her soft black hair caressed his cheek while she burrowed her face in his neck, hiccuping through the remnants of her tears. Instinctively, he began to rock her slowly in his arms.

"Shhh ... Shinjyu-hime ... little princess - don't cry anymore. It's okay, shhh ... "

Footsteps came up the stairs outside. Soon Mouse was poking his head in the door.

"Did you start dinner without me?" he asked as he took in the scene.

Sadao shook his head and gestured to the plate of cheese. "Shinjyu was hungry."

The girl lifted her head. "Mouse!" she said brightly and reached out a grabby hand for him with a big smile. Sadao felt a pang of jealousy as she left his arms in favor of Mouse's. She giggled as he took her up and twirled her around in the air.

"Whoo! How's my babysitter? Wait, was she crying?!" Mouse brought her to his hip and touched her face. Shinjyu pressed her lips together and pointed at Sadao accusingly.

Mouse was aghast. "What did you do?!"

"I … may have shouted a little too loudly at the girl."

---

5   *You're not an idiot! I'm a bad girl.*

"May have?" he looked to Shinjyu.

She nodded her head solemnly. "He's scary."

"I said I was sorry!"

Mouse and the girl both regarded him with disgust.

"She was crying about food, I asked her to wash her hands, the pump stuck, my hip seized - "

"I don't care if your fucking leg fell off. You don't shout at a 6-year-old girl!"

Sadao scrambled for a defense … and had none. "Don't use that language around her."

"Oh! My language? At least I don't make little girls cry with my words, Mr. Etiquette."

"Yeah, Mouse doesn't have a scary yelling voice!" His princess chimed in.

Sadao swore under his breath and limped his way out of the kitchen of punishment.

"I heard that! And so did she!" Mouse said, making a show of covering her ears. "She understands Japanese, you know! Even the bad words!"

"I'm taking a bath! Cook something!" Sadao barked and slammed the bedroom door shut.

Sadao soaked in the tub with a damp towel over his eyes. The hot water was slowly easing the muscle spasm in his thigh. His stomach growled loudly and he wondered why he wasn't hearing cooking sounds. Maybe the other two planned to starve him to death.

After what seemed close to an hour, Mouse came in with a paper box and chopsticks from the camp commissary.

"I didn't cook," he said, taking a seat and setting the box on the tub decking. "Shinjyu wanted to go home so we ate in the mess tent. The curry's cold by now. Probably resembles an internal organ, but I figure it's what you deserve."

"I told you, I apologized," Sadao said, lifting off the towel and opening his dinner. He snapped the *ohashi* apart and shoveled in a bite of gluey *katsu*. He glanced up at a wholly unsatisfied Mouse as he chewed. "Alright, I admit, I may have a little anger problem."

"Little?" Mouse scoffed.

"Medium-sized," Sadao corrected.

"Try medium-large, bucko. You disappointed me today. Shinjyu really wants to help you."

Sadao chewed and swallowed. "I know. And she did. I'll make good with her. I'm thirsty - go make me tea."

Mouse cleared his throat.

"Please ... go make me tea, my beloved spouse who is always right in all things."

"Better," Mouse said and clopped Sadao on the back of the head as he got up.

"*Itai!* Does every part of my body have to hurt?"

Mouse came back with a steamy pot a few minutes later and poured for both of them, passing Sadao a mug.

"*Arigatou,*" he said graciously, giving Mouse a nod.

"You're welcome. By the way, Shinjyu told me she managed to get you to walk with her all the way to the gravel beach and back today. I'm impressed."

"You should be," Sadao said, sipping. "I'm paying for it now."

Mouse nodded thoughtfully. "I think half your problems would be solved if we could ease the pain factor some - allow you to move better and give you a chance to retrain the leg."

Sadao stabbed at his rice. "If you're referring to pain medication, forget about it. Don't need to get hooked on pills."

"I'm talking about a small regulated amount."

"No," Sadao said resolutely. "Out of the question. I'm having difficulty enough with tobacco. If you haven't noticed."

"Speaking of which, Shinjyu told me you didn't light up today. I'm even happier about that."

Sadao gave him a look as he shoveled in another bite. "I'm not going to smoke near a young child."

"Then congratulations, you're half a day clean. And to celebrate, I'm going to make your second cup Sensei's special brew. Lube your ass up and rub you down good."

Sadao made a sound. "As long as that's all you do. I'm in no shape for bedroom gymnastics."

Mouse smiled evilly. "All you gotta do is lie there, baby."

"For now, let's just accomplish first finishing my dinner then getting me out of this damn tub."

It took some clever shifting and hobbling but Mouse managed to get a parboiled Sadao out of the water, dried and onto the sheet-protected bed. He'd lit a good fire to keep the bedroom warm for the event - purely for medical purposes.

Sadao lay on his stomach with his face in a pillow, already half asleep. Mouse climbed up behind him and gave his ass a smooch.

"I said no extra services," Sadao mumbled into the pillow.

"You don't want the Happy Ending? I'm gonna take it slow until you pass out before I get into the real deep work," he snickered.

Mouse dipped his fingers into the salve Sensei had provided and allowed it to warm and melt between his hands. "I think you're gonna like this!"

Mouse started with the good thigh and ass cheek. He smeared and worked the healing goop into the muscles of Sadao's lower body that had to do double work for the side that was busted.

"Mmmfph…"

"Feel good?" Mouse asked, already feeling a wee tingly just from hearing the man moan a bit.

Sadao nodded and his eyes closed followed by a long sigh.

Mouse took his time with it, using pressure and stretching the way Michi had shown him. Within ten minutes or so, Sadao was out cold - something Mouse found completely adorable.

"That's right, babe. Puddy in my hands."

Mouse planted a kiss on Sadao's other ass cheek and taking another dip into the salve, began to work on the bad side. At first, he ran the medication over his scarred areas. Then slowly, as the muscles and tissues warmed, he began to add pressure.

Sadao made a disagreeable sound in his snoozing and Mouse stopped a moment, just caressing his good side until he heard the man grunt and relax into a deeper sleep. "Sorry, baby. Gotta do this right."

Mouse scooted up and straddled the bad leg so he could really began to work into the left hip and buttock. Everything about the area felt wrong. The scarred skin was tight and pulled in odd ways. The underlying tissue felt like chopped steak instead of fine firm muscle. And the tendons that had been spliced and rerouted were like hard steel cables all wound up too tight. No wonder Sadao felt so much discomfort in this area. It was amazing he could walk at all.

Mouse tried not to let what he felt under his healing hands upset him. But it was little wonder the guy was grumpy. Mouse did his best to not fear making it any worse and followed Sensei's advice to a tee, adding ever gradual deeper and deeper pressure to every gnarled up inch of damaged sinew. He worked the hip, butt and thigh until his own arms ached. From there, he moved down the leg to the calf and foot which, as always, felt unnervingly cool.

His hands, fingers and thumbs slowly worked warmth back into the foot. He used the chi method he was taught to encourage better blood flow all the way down to each toe. He hoped it wasn't just a bunch of hoohah. As a final step, Mouse brought in towels he'd warmed in a cake pan on the stovetop. He wrapped the foot, leg and hip in toasty terrycloth before wiping his healthy skin clean of excess oil. Lastly, he took a washable blanket and sheet and wrapped the rest of Sadao up in it like a burrito.

Sadao was voicing a good snore by the time he'd cleaned up and got himself ready for bed. Mouse slipped in under the covers next to mummy-Sadao and kissed his forehead goodnight. "Sweet dreams, cowboy. I hope I did some good tonight."

●————————————○————————————●

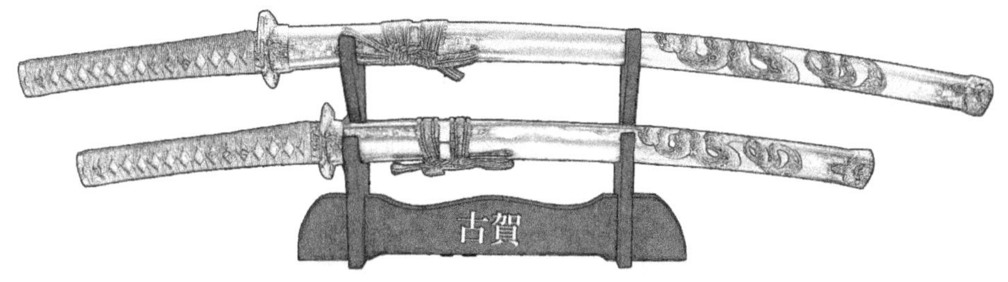

Chapter XIII

From Ashes

When Mouse woke it was Sunday. The team was up in the meadows practicing and since the garage truck couldn't fit up the narrow road to the training track and the team had a full flatbed of primed snowbikes, Tagata granted him a day off. The first in a month. He intended to enjoy it thoroughly, whether Sadao agreed or not.

Mouse rolled and nuzzled his love, still wrapped up like a burrito - his swaddled sleeping baby. Smooch smooch.

Sadao groaned and tried to roll away but the blankets stopped him. He opened an eye. "Why am I bound up?"

"Remember?" Mouse asked, brushing his long hair from his face and planting another kiss. "You got the full spa treatment last night. How do you feel?"

Sadao worked an arm loose and used it to circle Mouse. "Good, actually. Feels like I slept for a week." His eyes tracked the progress of the sunlight on the cabin's log ceiling. "Is it noon?"

Mouse kissed his mouth softly. "Not quite. Tagata gave me the day off. I'm all yours today, baby."

"Hmm…" Sadao worked his other arm loose and brought Mouse in close for a proper kissing. Mouse couldn't help moaning into Sadao's mouth when he felt his tongue. It had been forever since Sadao had made a move on him. He must be feeling good. Mouse enjoyed the velvety feel of his lips until his dick got too hard to ignore. "Uh ... babe, I don't want to push you but, if you keep kissing me like that I'm gonna explode."

Sadao nibbled his chin. "So am I."

"Really?" Mouse tore open his Sadao burrito to find a big hot pepper waiting for him. "Oh, damn! I want that!"

Sadao smiled, kissing his cheek. "Go get it, then."

Mouse shimmied quickly down the bed. He grabbed a helping of warm fresh Sadao buns and gobbled up the main attraction.

"Ahh…go easy on me," Sadao said with a twitch. "Just woke up, you know. Extra sensitive."

"Gmnh ... you need to pee?" Mouse asked.

Sadao groaned as Mouse stroked him root to tip. "Too late for that. Too hard. Need to finish me off first." He shut his eyes and pressed his nose to the pillow with another grunt as Mouse licked him up and down, enjoying his flavor. Mouse felt his own cock straining against the fly of his undershorts and slid them off before they got sticky. Soon as his legs were clear, he dove back in.

"God, you taste so good, mmmfgh!" Mouse wanted to suck him off nice and slow, really torture the poor bastard. But Sadao pushed his groin against his face, urging Mouse to take him in deeper, allowing his dickhead to slide all the way in and nudge the back of his palate.

"Ah, like that.." Sadao breathed. "So good."

After letting Sadao get a few full fucks from his mouth, Mouse backed off and teased the ring of silver locked in just under the man's engorged head with flicks of his tongue.

Sadao wound his fingers in his hair, still trying to fully control the situation. Mouse wasn't having it - this was his game. He squeezed the base of Sadao's cock and shifted lower in the bed to lick his sac. His balls were so warm and loose they practically fell into his mouth. Mouse sucked them in one by one, giving them a good polish.

"Nngh!" Sadao punched a pillow and Mouse glanced up, letting a soaked testicle go with a plop. Sadao was panting for relief. Precum ran freely from his tip, drizzling onto the sheet. "Need to come," he gasped, as if that wasn't obvious.

"Mnn, I know - it's been a long time," Mouse said. He ran his thumb just under the slit and a fresh gush of ooze leaked out. "You must really be backed up." He smeared the slippery wetness under Sadao's balls and around his asshole. The man gave a grunt of approval and arranged himself to allow Mouse more access. Face down, thighs spread, ass up.

Whoa! He doesn't usually do that!

Mouse leaned in and gave Sadao's tenderest dark spot a sweet kiss, a lick and then another. His mouth watered as he dug in and worked him over fold by fold. So fucking hot and tasty. Mouse slid the tip of his tongue in and out nice and slow, feeling the rim quiver. *That's right, baby, Mouse knows where you live.*

"You want me to give you more?" Mouse asked, as he slipped his thumb inside Sadao to confirm his question. The man tensed up and hissed, the head of his dick dripped with impatience.

"Was that an okay ... or a ... "

"Don't ask, just do it!"

Oh yesssss! Mouse scrambled up onto his knees and slid his hands around Sadao's hips, adjusting him carefully. Now would be a really shitty time for a leg cramp.

"Should I get a pillow under you?"

"Stop screwing around and fuck me!"

Okay, that answered that question. Mouse shimmied up on his ass and laid his dick right up against the most exquisitely made butthole in the history of humanity. He squeezed his dick out over it, wetting it with gentle thrusts.

Sadao buried his face in the pillow, letting out a sound that made Mouse's balls throb. Hell with it, he needed this too. He spread the shiny ring of flesh with both thumbs and nudged himself in.

"Ahhh!" *Oh God oh God oh God!!*

Tight tense heat gripped him. It'd been so fucking long since he'd had this man, Mouse forgot how powerful the feel of it was - taking him. He tried to be gentle, just easing himself in, but instinct took over as his cock was sheathed in heat.

"Ah, shit ... ! Baby, I'm sorry, you're just too ... Oh, God!"

Sadao came up onto his elbows, arched his back and tightened his butt to shut him up. His way of saying *I can take it! Let's do this!*

Mouse grabbed Sadao's good hip and let himself go. After a few thrusts, Sadao's rim opened and rounded out smooth for him, allowing Mouse to sink in deeper. He backed himself out and plunged in again with an appreciative moan. A wave of *Oh fuck yeah!* shot from his dick right up his spine. Mouse had been dying for a good solid fuck. Oral sex skimmed off some of the steam, but deep down there was an ache that had been building for weeks. With Sadao's hip out of commission, he wondered why it took him so goddamn long to just mount the man. Sadao certainly didn't seem to object!

The fuck was solid and lasting, building up nice and full between them, making them both pant and moan encouragements. Sadao had managed to leverage his working hip and leg to provide a solid point of impact for Mouse to thrust up against. The satisfaction meter was off the chart. This is what Mouse had missed - the affirmation of their bond on the end of each thrust.

Smack! Smack!

Sadao growled and bit the sheets as Mouse brought it on. Ripples of pleasure shook down his tattooed back to the snake tail coiled over his trembling ass. God help him, Sadao really did like getting nailed. As long as his friends didn't find out.

Too late, baby! They know you're whipped.

"Ah, fuck, babe. I can't..!"

Sadao lifted his head and turned to watch. His eyes tracked across Mouse's bare chest to his fluff of blond hair trailing from his navel to the point where they were joined. Sadao smiled and began clenching his cheeks on each pound.

"Jesus! Stop doing that! You're gonna make me pop!"

"That's the point, isn't it?"

Mouse wasn't in any frame of mind to debate who the fuck was pleasuring whom. It was all he could do not to blow up the second he gave a shred of thought as to what was happening. *I'm fucking the holy shit burgers out of Sadao Koga right now. This fine, hot, sexy piece of prime ass is all mine. Look! My dick is buried in it right … right NOW! Oh, crap nooo nooo! Why did I go there! Baseball! Think about baseballlll!*

"Ahh, baby, sorry, I'm gonna … oh shiiiiit!"

Sadao bucked him back hard. "Show me!" he barked. "Let me see it!"

Mouse yanked himself out and slammed his throbbing cock between Sadao's ass cheeks and one huge shudder later, unloaded his balls all the fuck over his back, whitewashing his tattoo.

"Uhhh….guuuuhhhnnnghh … ahhhh…"

When Mouse could see again, he witnessed Sadao beating himself off onto the sheets, cum glazing his knuckles as he teased out each burst. There was a lot of it, forming a puddle of spunk right where Mouse slept.

"Shit, good thing it's laundry day. I think we wrecked this bed." Rivulets of cum ran down Sadao's inked skin and added to the splatter art they'd produced together. "I pity our maid. Oh, yeah we don't have one. Fuck, we need to plan for this shit. I'll be doing the wash for days."

Sadao slid onto his belly and tugged Mouse down with him. "Planning takes all the fun out of it," he said, with a kiss to Mouse's nose. "You're a great fuck, you know? Thought I was going to lose it the first time you slid in."

"No shit?" Mouse felt a blush fill his face. "Me too. We really need to fuck like this more."

"No argument," Sadao said, grabbing him up for another deeper kiss, squeezing his ass.

"It's gonna snow again tonight," Mouse said, nuzzling his spunky man. Ick, wet spot was already getting cold!

"Then we'd better get down to Squamish right away."

"We're going out? Really?"

"Want to get Shinjyu something nice. Something better suited for a girl than dirty jeans and old track shoes."

Mouse smiled. "I think I might have competition for your affection. I'm jealous."

"I'll get you something nice, too. Hm … if you pay for it, I guess. Stone cold broke at the moment."

Mouse pinched his nipple. "Unemployed bum! What am I now, your sugar daddy?"

Sadao smacked his ass. "Absolutely. Now let me up, daddy. Need to piss."

● ———————— ○ ———————— ●

After breakfast and a bath, Mouse wanted to get them on the road down to Squamish as soon as possible to beat the snow that was predicted to begin falling after sundown. During winter, the sun didn't stay up for very long in Canada. They would have made good time if Sadao hadn't insisted on wearing his goddamn sexy-as-fuck lace-up leather chaps - ostensibly to keep his legs warm. But when Mouse was required to get down on his knees to help lace them, things soon took a detour into the performance of other services. And so a pair of blow jobs later, they were finally out the door.

When they first hit the exit road, Tagata's overzealous border patrol officer, Miyagi, stepped into the lane with a shotgun, blocking their way.

"Oh, Jesus, not this asshole again," Mouse said, stopping the Jeep and cranking down his window.

"Exit pass, *kudasai*."

"Exit pass? I don't have any pass. I'm going shopping in Squamish. It's my day off!"

"You must have pass!"

"What's this about?" Sadao wanted to know.

"You don't know about this bullshit?" Mouse said, turning to his passenger. "This is harassment - Tagata's got some kind of control game going on. They even busted me and the kids for sledding!"

Sadao shook his head, annoyed. He leaned over Mouse's lap to chew Miyagi out in Japanese. They argued a moment until Sadao gave up and pulled the drive stick into first gear. "Get us out of here," he said. Mouse hit the gas, leaving Captain Power Crazy in the slush. He fired his shotgun in the air in defiance as they sped off.

"What the fuck did you tell him?" Mouse laughed.

"I told him I'm the only exit pass you need."

"Damn straight!"

"What size do you think she is?" Sadao asked, thumbing through a circular rack of clothes. Long winter sleeves of cute pinks and purples whirled by for the fifth time. In truth, he had no clue what little girls liked. He'd never bought anything for a woman under age 20.

"I think she's about a 6, I'd say," Mouse said, coming out of the dressing room in another pair of ill-fitting jeans. "Usually the size matches their age. She's little, though. I'd go for a 5." He pointed Sadao to the right section.

"Thanks."

"Do you think these jeans make my ass look big?" Mouse presented his rear for inspection.

Sadao eyed the body contours in question. "Your ass is fine. Legs are too long."

Mouse slumped. "I know. Short is a curse. I can cut them off at the bottom, though. If you want my advice, I'd get Shinjyu something she can climb trees in. That girl's a real monkey."

"Is she?" Sadao was envious of Mouse's familiarity with the girl. His cheek tingled at the memory of her innocent kiss. One thing he was sure of - he wanted to earn more of them. "What about these?" He held up a pair of girl's jeans with little mushrooms and daisies sewn onto the fabric.

Mouse's face lit up. "Perfect! Oh my God, those are adorable! Get her some sweaters too, and good girly boots! She's a tromper, that one!"

Sadao nodded and using his cane, moved on to the sweaters folded in a rainbow of hues on a nearby display table. He had to admit, cutting smokes for a week had gradually lessened the pain he usually felt when applying weight to the mangled hip. Maybe there was something to Sensei's advice. Even so, he'd still gladly walk through boiling iron for a cigarette about now. Instead, he ran his hands over the sweaters to redirect his focus. He wanted to get Shinjyu something warm and soft, remembering how small and light she'd felt in his arms. Like a little doll. She needed extra protection from the elements.

By the time Mouse had found a short stack of reasonable jeans, Sadao had selected five pairs of tough girly pants, four long-sleeved knit shirts in various colors and patterns and three sweaters - blue, red and yellow with matching boots. And a dress - a warm long-sleeved light purple and pale yellow striped knit dress with matching leggings.

"Oh! She's gonna look so cute in those! Let's get her a hat too, and some mittens!" Topped off with a scarf and assorted accessories for keeping little hands and heads warm, the total at the cashier came to nearly $400.

Mouse glanced at Sadao, who was requesting each of the clothing items be wrapped in tissue paper and inserted properly into the shopping bags.

"You couldn't have picked something from the sales rack?" Mouse asked, opening his wallet and counting out the bills. "This kid's going to be spoiled rotten before she reaches ten!"

"No babysitter of mine is going to be dressing like a street orphan. I have a reputation to keep," Sadao said, handing Mouse the bags to carry. "I want to stop at the jewelers, too. Need some supplies."

Mouse frowned. "Do I need to remind you I'm on Tagata's payroll now?"

Sadao grinned at him as he limped toward the doors. "Maybe sugar daddy needs a second job. Looks like they're hiring at the gas station."

"That's not funny! If anyone needs a second job in our home, it's you, Sir Couch Potato!"

Once outside, Mouse nudged Sadao to remember to put on his sunglasses and annoying ballcap - his idea of a disguise. Squamish's shopping district was more crowded than usual. Vacationers were beginning to arrive for the winter game events, due to begin in two weeks. The Winter Sports Rally was among the main attractions. Although the competing teams were mostly Canadian and Northern U.S., it would not be unusual for Northwest Division personnel to turn up. They would rent out the local cabins nestled in the surrounding hillsides. Sadao had to remind himself periodically that he was, in fact, a dead man walking. His body was reportedly being picked apart by crabs at the bottom of the Pacific.

Shopping wasn't nearly as fun as he'd hoped at the jewelry store.

"Well, how much are those gonna cost?" Mouse whined. "Do you really need 22-karat gold? Can't you get silver instead? What about plated? It's cheaper!"

Mouse hovered at his side, asking annoying questions while Sadao picked out the jewelry settings and findings he needed for earrings and rings he wanted to make. Mouse had moved his worktable and swivel chair in from the cold shed, and set it under the large windows near the stove in the front room so he could work in adequate light. All his jewelry, gems, pearls and carving tools had been safely kept for him in little labeled boxes. It was time he began using them again, to help redirect his mind and lower his stress. If only he wasn't financially chained to his spendthrift spouse.

"Because, I don't think any of those boys are gonna tell the difference between a few carats. You can't even read the stamps on these bands without a magnifier!"

"Mouse! Please, I know what I need," he said firmly, nodding permission for the jeweler to start ringing him up. "They're not all for the boys," he added.

"You're making the girl jewelry now, too? Jeez, you must really want to win her over. I'm jealous."

"There might be something in here for you, too. But at the rate you're annoying me, don't place any bets on it!"

That shut Mouse up. He sighed and handed his wallet over to Sadao with a look of defeat. "I put out for brake pads too, you know," he grumbled. "Guess I won't be picking up any of those today!"

"Much harder to personalize brake pads," Sadao said, pulling out the last of the bills. "Besides, consider this an investment in my health. I'm less likely to smoke if my hands are busy."

Mouse took his wallet back and turned it upside down, shaking out the nothing that was left in it. "You're not an easy man to keep. We're going to need to discuss your allowance."

Sadao accepted his packages and receipt from the clerk and leaned in to give Mouse a kiss on his cheek. "You always knew I didn't come cheap."

After a quick deli sandwich lunch - paid for in loose change found in the Jeep - Mouse had to make one more stop before they pulled out of town.

"Hang on a sec. Stay low!" he said, parking on a side street.

Sadao slouched down in the seat. "Why?"

"I need to grab the mail!" Mouse popped out of the Jeep and jogged across the street to a small postal office.

We have mail?

Soon he came bounding back out with a handful of letters. Mouse slid into the front seat, shut the door and flipped through the mail.

"Tagata, Tagata, Tagata … Lupe - there's a pirate flag for a return address… a catalog from Barney's Trash 'n' Treasure … oh!" He stopped on one letter and flipped it over. "This is for me! From Blythe!" Mouse tore the letter open excitedly, eyes tracking across the hand-written letter inside. "It's from Gloria … she says…" Mouse's face slowly fell, then paled as his eyes read slower. His hands began to shake and Sadao reached over to touch his thigh.

"What is it?" he asked, softly.

"It's Uncle Fred…" Mouse's face clenched in grief as he finished the letter and tears fell from his eyes as he shut them. He didn't need to say the rest.

Sadao slid over the seat and put his arm around Mouse to comfort him as he wept. The sound of his open sobs against his shoulder moved Sadao deeply. Mouse was a man who loved with his whole heart and grieved with equal capacity.

"Shh…" he eased him, rubbing his back as his emotion poured out of him. "It's okay … he knew you loved him. That's not something you hide."

"He raised me. B-but I never went back … I never saw him … after…" His words were hard to hear through his choking tears.

Since I took you away from them, Sadao thought. *I stole you from everyone who ever loved you. I couldn't help myself.*

"Shh … *Konezumi.* Don't say that. He did see you. More often than you think."

Mouse raised his wet face and snuffled. "Huh?"

Sadao wiped the tear trails from his flushed cheeks. Mouse had never looked more beautiful to him than just then. "He saw you on the news. In the reports. In the photographs. Don't tell me he could tear his eyes away - that anyone from your town could turn away. You're a part of them."

Fresh tears welled up in his sweet blue eyes. Mouse threw his arms around Sadao and hugged him fiercely. "Thank you…" Mouse whispered. "Thank you for giving me this life."

Sadao crushed him to his chest, burying his face in Mouse's shoulder to hide his relief.

Sadao dozed off on the drive back up the mountains to camp. It was beginning to get dark and snow was starting to fall from the skies in light puffs. Mouse flipped the lights on and drove steadily up the winding highway. Sadao was dreaming of watching the snow fall from his upstairs bedroom in his father's magnificent house when Mouse shook his knee.

"Babe? You awake?"

"Hm?"

"Need you to watch the road behind us a sec."

Sadao yawned and sat up. The Jeep's blaring heater was making him too warm and sleepy. He turned it down. "Why? What's wrong?" he asked, looking in the rearview. Other than the road going dark and the snow starting to fall faster, he didn't see anything.

"I think someone's following us."

"What? Where?"

"Just, I think this SUV has been on us since leaving Squamish. It's white. Big fancy thing."

"Could just be a high roller moving in. Lots of cabins and resorts up here."

"Yeah, that's what I thought at first but we're past Whistler now - almost to the camp's secret route turnoff. Not a lot of traffic comes up this far and even at that, it's mostly just hunters and hermits. No one that drives $150,000 automobiles."

Sadao turned to look out the back window. He watched the road snaking off behind them, and Mouse was right! There was a pair of headlights about a fifth of a mile behind them.

"Try speeding up. See if you lose them," Sadao suggested. Mouse accelerated and after about a mile, it became obvious the SUV did too.

"They still there, hanging back?"

"Yes. I'm afraid they are," Sadao said with growing concern. He didn't want any strangers or snoops knowing what exit they took to the camp. "Pull off at the next turnout and kill our lights."

Mouse took them up another mile or so and made a sharp right turn onto a side road that led to an offseason campground.

"Take us a few feet in," Sadao said, watching the rearview. "There!" He pointed to a small depression in an area next to the road that was hidden by trees. Mouse bounced them over the ditch and soon as Sadao said "Kill it!" he shut off the lights and engine.

"Think they'll see our tracks?" Mouse asked.

"Not sure. It's pretty dark. Road is icy; we might be okay."

The large white SUV made the turn on cue, tires skidding a moment on the uncleared road. It continued past them into the fresh snow and looked as if it would continue, until they saw the brake lights came on.

"Shit," Mouse uttered. "Now what? Fuck, I don't have my rifle."

"That's your solution? Shoot first, ask questions later?"

"Fuck yeah, it is! If it means some bounty hunter is after you! Shouldn't have taken you into town! Stupid decision!"

"Shh! They're turning around. Get down."

Sadao and Mouse slid low in their seats and watched as the headlights approached slowly, then passed, much to their relief. They both craned their necks up in time to see the vehicle turn back onto the main highway, heading back down the mountain.

"They're going back! Why'd they do that?"

"Who knows," Sadao said. "But I don't think a bounty hunter would drive such an obvious vehicle. I think it's safe to continue. Let's get to Taga's, let him know what we saw."

"These are all mine?" Shinjyu asked, staring wide-mouthed at all of the shopping bags laid out on Tagata's main room floor in front of the fire. Mouse had run over and picked her up at the kids' hall where they'd been having bedtime stories with Kei. He didn't want the other kids to get jealous so they did their unveiling at The Boss's cabin.

"Sure are, honey," Mouse said, sitting on the carpet with her and dumping a bag of sweaters over her head. "Girl clothes for a very special girl!"

Shinjyu squealed with glee and rolled herself like a dog through all of Sadao's careful tissue wrap. "Thank you, thank you, thank you, Mouse!"

"You need to thank Oyaji, too. He picked all these out, just for you," Mouse said with a wink at Sadao, who was seated on the couch sipping warmed sake with Tagata. The Sasori boss looked a little surprised and confused at their shopping spree. He mumbled something to Sadao in their language and Sadao shushed him, his eyes completely focused on Shinjyu.

"A dress! Can I put it on?" Shinjyu asked, picking up the knit dress.

"Sure, honey. Let me help you." Mouse helped her out of her old shirt and on with the long-sleeved dress. She kicked her old pants off too and scrambled up on her feet, twirling around and around, and bouncing to make the skirt fly.

"A dress! A real dress! And gloves!" she peeped, grabbing up a pair and wriggling her hands into them.

Mouse caught her around the middle and gave her tickles. She laughed in a pitch only a small girl can hit and tumbled head-first into an empty bag. She came up laughing with it on her head, and picked up another to put over Mouse's head. Mouse hugged her bagged head and whispered into the paper. "Go give Oyaji one, too."

She got on her socked feet, bag-blind with arms out and stumbled in the general direction of the couch, colliding with Sadao's knee.

"Oi!" he said, smiling. He set his sake aside and reached down to bring her up into his lap.

"Boo!" she said, lifting her bag off and placing it on his head like an odd square crown.

"Thank you, Oyaji!" she said with a big bright smile. "I like my dress! It's purple!"

"It is," he said, smoothing her static charged hair. "I'll get you more if you like them."

"I like dresses! I used to have lots and lots but this one is the very best - it spins!" She wrapped her purple striped arms around his neck and kissed his chin. "Look," she said and hopped off his lap to demonstrate. Sadao watched her twirling form with warm eyes.

Jesus, and here I thought I had him whipped. Gotta step up my game! Mouse thought.

Seeing Shinjyu happy and Sadao's eyes melt like that helped ease the pain of losing Fred. Sadao's words had brought him a lot of comfort. *I hope you can still see me, old man. See how happy I am.*

Mouse helped Shinjyu put on a fashion show for the bosses while they discussed in low voices the occurrences that had been happening in and around the camp. Mouse overheard in their mix of English and Japanese something about no further signs of the snowcat tracks or the gas can campers having been discovered on Sasori land. Sentinels were guarding exits and keeping close watch on camp staff and racers alike. Tagata had even summoned Miyagi and his team on radio so he could alert him about the latest mystery of the white SUV.

Shinjyu was taking applause from all three men, bowing in her daisy mushroom jeans, yellow sweater and knitted cap when a knock came at the cabin door. Miyagi came in with his shotgun on a strap around his shoulder. He was not pleased to see Mouse and Sadao and a little girl lounging about his Boss's home.

"I have list you ask for," he said, bowing to Tagata.

Tagata took the paper and read it over. "Is this a joke?" he asked sharply.

Sadao got up and held out a hand, requesting to read it himself and Tagata handed it over reluctantly.

"So, the following Sasori team members have been reported breaking boundary rules," he read aloud. "Lupe ... not surprising. Kei ... okay, somewhat surprising. Mouse..." Sadao glanced quizzically at him.

"Guilty!" Mouse called out, raising his hand. "Lock me up!"

Sadao's eyes tracked back to the paper.

"Oyaji ... well, that would be me. Shinjyu...hm ... disobedience must be contagious." His eyes rolled to Tagata who was face-palming. "And a list of the rest of the Sasori team members under age ten," Sadao said, thrusting the paper back in the sentinel's hand. "I guess we can all sleep safe tonight."

Horrified, Tagata shoved his guard in the chest and began berating him in Japanese. He chased him back out the front door of his home, and relieved him of his shotgun.

"I will make change in guard assignment," he assured Sadao. "Camp will be safe. Garage will be safe. Racer will be safe! No things will keep us from success in Winter Rally!"

Sadao was reluctant to return Shinjyu to the kids' cabin. But Kei was happy to take her sleepy head into his arms and tuck her into bed among the snoozing boys while they put her new clothes away. She looked like a little dark-haired angel to him, sleeping with her mittened hand tucked under her chin. She'd insisted on sleeping in her new soft sweater and jeans. Sadao bent and kissed her forehead before taking Mouse's hand and wishing Kei goodnight.

Outside, the snow was still falling peacefully without wind. Soft and quiet, the snow clusters scattered the surrounding camp lights and muted all sounds. It was like being stowed away safely in cotton. Today had been a good day for him, but not so much for Mouse. His weeping was still fresh in Sadao's memory as he guided him past the kids' hall up to the path that led to the longhouse.

"Where are we going? It's snowing? Aren't you tired?"

"There's something I want to share with you," he said, as the painted Squamish Indian thunderbird and beaver heads came into view. The snowfall made the ambient lights of camp glow far into the trees.

"You cleared away the brush," Mouse noted. "Wow, it's beautiful! You can see the whole mural now!"

"Wait until you see the inside," Sadao said, unlocking the door and sliding it open. He reached in and flipped a switch that lit up the whole interior from a row of suspended lights.

Mouse's eyes were wide as he took Sadao's hand and stepped in. "You ... oh my God! Look…! Sadao, you made a shrine! For Shiratori-san!"

Sadao nodded, proud of his hard work. "I hoped that if I gave his soul a proper place to live, he'd stop haunting his old trailer and give our living racers some peace."

Mouse spun around slowly, noting the carefully cleaned and dressed suits of samurai armor now displayed with honor upon their stands along each wall of the longhouse. His eyes followed the glint of polished steel and black lacquer sheaths of each and every one of their fallen comrade's weapons - katana, chest plates, helmets, longbow, spears, bokken, shinai. In the center of it all - upon a dais and supported by a modified repair stand - was Shiratori's magnificent white cruiser, polished to brilliant perfection.

Sadao took Mouse's hand and led him toward it. Before the motorcycle was a wide set of steps with a row of red cushions. On the highest step before the dais was a large incense bowl filled with sand, burnt candles and ash that had once belonged to the General.

"It's still not finished," Sadao said. "Floor needs smoothing before I unveil it to the team. But I thought you might find some comfort in offering a prayer to the one you've lost. It's brought comfort to me in my life to be able to speak to those who have gone on before me."

Mouse's eyes were wet as he looked up at him, nodding. "What do I do?"

"Kneel here," Sadao said, and together they knelt beside each other on the cushions. "Take a candle and light it and place it in the offering bowl."

Mouse selected a thin white prayer candle from a long wooden box and held it toward Sadao and his waiting lighter. "So that's where your lighter went," he said with a smile.

"Figured I'd find a better use for it," he said, lighting their candles. Mouse followed him in placing the candles securely in the sand. Sadao lit a stick of incense in a tray, blew on it, and let the curl of scented smoke rise up through the handlebars of the cruiser toward the track lights. Sadao rang a small brass bell then clapped his hands loudly three times, making Mouse jump. "Ring the bell and clap three times," he said. "Let the spirits know you are here. They like to hide."

Mouse rang and clapped and looked to Sadao in wonder. "Now you pray," he said, pressing his hands together and Mouse followed. Sadao closed his eyes and deeply inhaled the scent of the incense. "Pray to let them know you are thinking of them. That you seek their wisdom and guidance. Pray that they will light your way when it is time for you to join them in the next world."

The shrine was as still as the air between the soft drifts of snow falling outside. In the brightness of Shiratori's legacy he and Mouse knelt together, breathing and listening for answers in the quiet.

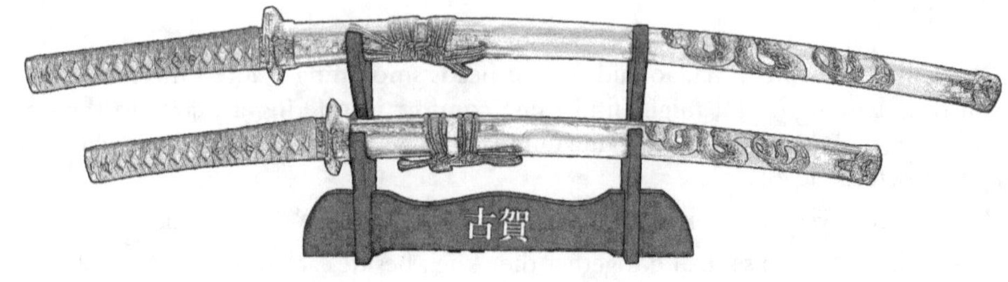

Chapter XIV

Under the Ice

"Aw, you shaved your beard! Dang it, I was getting used to the mountain man look."

"That's exactly why I trimmed it," Sadao said, exiting the bathroom in a towel and pausing to check his neatly buzzed chin in the bedroom mirror. "Didn't want to be mistaken for Sasquatch."

Mouse laughed and threw more logs into the hearth. A nice blaze was going, warming the room perfectly. "Fat chance of that. You're virtually hairless. Smooth as a baby."

Snow was falling almost every night now, building up the snowpack. The team's snowplow fleet was busy from dusk to dawn, keeping the exit road clear and the trails up to the meadows training area accessible. Tagata was pushing his riders hard, making them prove their worth on the backs of the snowbikes in cold bright sun or flurry, as evidenced by all the repair welds, fender dents and belt replacements Mouse had been tasked with lately. There were only four days left before the team would migrate down the mountain to Squamish for the Winter Sports Rally. And Mouse's decision whether the team should tempt the crevasse route on the downhill was still open to debate. Fresh snow provided excellent traction, but their meadows training area lacked an underlying base of ice.

Sadao had spent most of the day with Tagata, going over his roster and rankings based on last season's stats. He'd almost not made it back before the snow and wind made the hill climb impossible, despite his mobility improvements. Mouse had stood out on the porch in the blowing wind with a searchlight and pulled his cold ass in the front door. He marched him straight to the bubbling tub, ready with hot tea and reprimands. Properly soaked, cleaned and shaved now, Mouse was anxious to take advantage of his thawed snowman as well as the blazing fire.

"Don't get dressed yet," Mouse said, motioning Sadao to join him on the rug at the foot of the bed in front of the fire. He was happy to see Sadao was still keeping his hair long.

Sadao smiled down at him, and slipped off the towel to finish drying his hair before tossing it aside. "It's warm enough in here, I guess." He reached over the bed and pushed down a few pillows and blankets.

Oh, fuck yeah! There went the towel and pillows! It's on!

Mouse stripped out of his shirt and jeans in ten seconds flat. "We'll likely get snowed in tonight," he said, reaching out a hand to help Sadao down onto the bear fur rug. "Won't need to get up so early. Maybe we won't need to get up at all … "

"I sense your plan," Sadao said, lowering himself carefully using Mouse's shoulder and the edge of the bed. "But then, nngh, I'm retired. You're the one who needs to set an example for the team youth."

"I got your example right here," Mouse said, throwing his arms around his shoulders and hugging him tight. *Mmmmnn …fresh naked Sadao.*

Sadao welcomed his embrace as they sank down into the pillows, kissing. Mouse ran his hands all over the man's back and ass, stroking and squeezing. He let Sadao get a full taste of his mouth before offering up his neck to the torture of tongue and teeth.

"Mmngh," Mouse moaned with each nip and suck. Sadao was nibbling him a bit harder than usual. "Afraid you're gonna leave marks one of these days…"

Sadao took his time mouthing Mouse's throat before he paused to answer. "You're already marked by me," he said, reaching down to slip a hand between Mouse's thighs to finger his small prize. The ring of silver tugged at Mouse's tender skin and made his hips buck in response. "Anything more would be excessive."

"You could tattoo your name all over my body. I wouldn't care," Mouse whispered, stealing another kiss. "I want to belong to you. I want everyone to know it, too."

Sadao held his face and kissed him with a slow tongue. "I think the secret's out."

Mouse giggled and squirmed in delight as Sadao's mouth worked lower down his neck to his chest, where he spent his time entertaining each nipple. "I could pierce you here," he said, nipping the nub before moving lower. "Or here, perhaps." Mouse twitched as his belly button was licked and nibbled. "Or maybe even … "

"Aaaaahhhh!" Mouse's whole body stiffened as Sadao swallowed his cock. "Oooohhh, please … not there. No needles… I'm too … oh … ohh … ahhhh … "

Sadao took him all the way in, giving him a nice deep suck. Mouse moaned and writhed against the rug, gripping the pillow under his head. The feel of the soft fur against his back and ass paired with the movements of Sadao's mouth was too much. His hips moved in rhythm. "Aaaahhhh … "

Suddenly, Sadao raised his head and let Mouse's dick slide out and drop against his belly. Mouse looked down in confusion, panting. "Why'd you stop? Jesus, that was incredible!"

Sadao dipped his head to kiss the tip of Mouse's dick. "Sorry, got carried away," he said, moving into a kneeling position at Mouse's feet. He winced as he settled himself.

"You okay, babe? You want us to move to the bed?"

"I'm fine," Sadao said, leaning back to pull open the nightstand drawer. He grabbed the lube before scooting back down to Mouse's groin area. "Show it to me," he said.

Mouse spread his legs in response. Sadao looked his posterior over carefully, moving his legs to get a good look around. Then he lifted his balls and checked underneath in a very unsexy way. "What're you doing? A pelvic exam? Just stick it in!"

"You need to let me take care of your body properly. And that means taking a look once in awhile."

"Fine! But not in the middle of a fuck!"

"We'll get to that," Sadao said, squeezing lube onto his fingers. "I need to make sure you stay fit to bear the force of my lust."

Mouse laughed and opened his legs a little wider. "I bear up just fine, thanks. Ohh … that's … ahhh …mmmn … "

Slick warm fingers massaged his ass and balls, getting the area nice and moist. Mouse sighed and relaxed into it. From his manner, he could tell Sadao was in no mood to rush. Even if his cock was poised and ready for action.

"Uuuunngh…." The soothing fingers slowly worked their way up inside him, twisting as they went - a nice slow grind. Mouse moaned in pleasure; he wasn't sure what got him more worked up - the technique or the mere idea a part of Sadao was inside him. "Ahhh.."

"The sounds you make when I touch you… there's no other sound I enjoy to hear more," Sadao said, admiring his finger work. "Nothing compares."

"Ahh … are you just going to yap all night or … nnnngh…"

Sadao leaned over him and kissed his mouth softly. "There's a storm building outside, you said. We might not leave the cabin for days."

Mouse bit his lower lip and rolled his hips back, trying to entice the insertion of more Sadao parts. "That's great as long as those days involve your dick in my ass. Fuck … need your … cock … "

Sadao smiled and sat back, getting his bare ass more settled into the rug. His fingers retreated and his knuckles teased the eager ring of loosened muscle, making Mouse cry out in frustration. "I like hearing the urgency rise in your voice. I take a great deal of pleasure in knowing I am the only one who hears you this way. Turns my cock to iron."

"Mmnngh … " Mouse lay splayed across the rug, back arched and hips pumping his neglected erection into the warm air. Sadao's fingers toyed with the ringed pearl under his balls, making him crazy.

"Fuck, please … what do I need to do here?"

Sadao didn't answer, just gripped the base of his own dick. "My pearl, my treasure … " he breathed. His gaze stayed fixed on Mouse's ass as he lubed himself up, until his flushed tip shone and overran with moisture. Mouse drooled - it looked so good, red and engorged.

"Oh, Jeeeeezus … guh … I gotta …" Mouse slid his hand down to his own cock for some relief. He couldn't just lie there anymore, humping air while Sadao did *that*. Precum soon coated his fingers, making the feel of it amazing. "Ahhh … oh … God, why does that feel so good?"

"Because you and I share a connection," Sadao said, working himself overhand, flicking his own pearl ring with his forefinger. "And I want to see how far you can go if I offer no assistance."

No assistance? Really? Where were a charged set of batteries when you needed them?

"I think you just enjoy torturing me … uh … Christ I need something up my ass …"

Sadao cocked his head as he jerked himself faster, his free hand held Mouse's ass cheeks apart for a better view. He rubbed the pinched hole with his thumb. "I wonder what you did to relieve yourself while I was gone."

Mouse's dick throbbed at Sadao's words and his face reddened. "Fuck! Whattya think I did? I beat off!"

"Show me," Sadao said sternly. His eyes were intense with arousal.

"Ugh … I am!" Mouse's excitement was growing just as quickly as Sadao's but the plain fact was he was so hard up for it, he really did need something in his ass. "Shit - !"

Sadao gave his butt a sharp smack! "Do it!"

"I … gotta …"

Smack! Squeeze, squeeze … Smack!

"Ahh … shit!" Christ, now he'd have a red ass to match his face.

Sadao stroked himself faster. His mouth curled in enjoyment and his breath came in rasps as he took a perverse thrill in making Mouse's cheeks jiggle with each impact. Smack!

"Fuck you! Okay!" Mouse closed his eyes and lifting his leg, reached around the back of his thigh to shove in a finger. "Gaaaaah … ahhh!" Despite the contortion, the moment the digit went in he felt his pleasure intensify. But even so, his asshole begged for something bigger, more forceful.

"That's good," Sadao purred. "I wondered what position you'd use. I imagined many."

Mouse worked the solo digit harder for his audience, gritting his teeth and jerking his dick while Sadao caressed his stinging buns in encouragement.

"In my cell, alone, I'd take myself in hand, thinking of you … pleasuring yourself."

Mouse stretched and twisted his arm to work himself more forcefully. The deepening of Sadao's voice combined with the embarrassment were unbearably arousing. And yet, he just couldn't quite … fap fap cramp!

"Aaaaghh!!" Mouse gave up. He collapsed in a heaving heap and rubbed the pinched muscle in his forearm. "Fuck, I can't! I can't!" He elbowed up to glare at his lover. "You wanna see me squirt? You gotta cowboy-up!"

"Come here," Sadao barked. He grabbed Mouse by the arm, pulling him up and dragging him across his lap sideways. A strong arm wrapped about Mouse's shoulders and Sadao's mouth came down on his, swirling his tongue while his fingers went up inside his hole and found its target. Mouse spit out Sadao's tongue and screamed.

"Aaaaaaaaggghhhh….!"

Mouse forgot how strong Sadao was in his upper body. He was pinned solid up against his chest while his ass was getting worked in a punching motion. It was hard, merciless - making Mouse wail with excitement. At last, he was getting nailed with an intensity he hadn't felt since before the injury. What Sadao could no longer deliver with his hips he could more than make up for with his well aimed fingers.

Mouse reached for Sadao's dick and jerked him as best as he could while screaming. "Aaaaaaaaagh…..God, oh God, oh Godddddd…!"

Sadao was relentless, keeping his rhythm constant. The incredible heat and stiffness of Sadao's hard-on made Mouse's ass clench up around the wedge of fingers splitting him apart. *Fuck, is his whole hand up in there?*

"Don't bear down yet!" Sadao warned. "Fight it!"

Mouse tried. He tried to relax, but the pressure and intensity were too much! He gasped and shuddered around Sadao's fingers, wanting them deeper, fighting the urge - demanding his muscles to try to resist. But the lust in Sadao's eyes and the bulging shaft of veined flesh in his hand brought all that effort to a quick end. "Oh, shit! Oh, shit! Ohhhhh shiiiiittt!"

Mouse lost it. A heap of cum shot out of him and up Sadao's chest. Powerful expulsions of wound up lust sprayed all over the man whose fingers had just delivered the hard raw fuck he'd been craving.

Sadao's fist came down, covering Mouse's grip. "Nnnnngh……!" Sadao's eyes screwed shut as his balls convulsed. He grabbed Mouse by the back of his head and forced his face downward. "Catch it!" he ordered.

Mouse, delirious from his own release, took a second to follow his command. He dove for it, his lips forming a seal over the end of Sadao's cock. Sadao let go and unleashed a powerful gush into his mouth. Mouse drank it all down in gulps, spurt after spurt. It was four hard contractions before the flesh began to soften between his lips. Mouse couldn't stop licking it as Sadao deflated into satisfied moans. It was the most delicious hunk of meat he'd ever known. His spent dick leaned to the side and fell over in gratitude.

"Damn," Mouse said, when he could speak. "You came hard."

Sadao wiped the sweat from his forehead. "Needed to …" he said, leaning over to catch his breath. "For once without the fucking leg interfering!"

Mouse rubbed his thigh affectionately as he calmed. "Babe, you know I'll gladly switch up with you."

Sadao squeezed his hand. "I know. And don't think I won't take you up on it, but I need to be making you scream to achieve full satisfaction."

"I scream when I'm fucking you, too."

Sadao smiled and brought their faces together for a kiss. His tongue was sweet. "Not the same thing, *Konezumi*. I have a terrible ego to feed."

Mouse grinned against his lips. "Won't argue with that. Did you really beat off in prison to the idea of me fingering myself?"

Sadao unfolded his legs and stretched out on the rug next to Mouse, pulling him close. He kissed his hair. "Afraid so."

Mouse hugged him happily. "So did I but in my fantasy, I showed up at the prison disguised as a guard and backed my ass up against the bars when no one was looking."

Sadao's eyes widened. "Don't tell me these things now!"

"Why not?"

"Because I'll have to fuck you again!"

Mouse smiled. "That's the plan, cowboy. I want you to fuck me until we don't know what day it is anymore."

"It's Tuesday."

Mouse punched him in the arm.

"Okay, okay!" Sadao laughed. "Ardent incessant fucking is coming ... Just need a minute to catch my breath."

"You been feeling okay?"

"Yes! Stop asking me this. I will inform you if my condition changes!"

"Jeez, you're sure grumpy for a guy who just spooged his brains out."

Sadao sighed and relaxed. "I apologize. I know I'm not easy to deal with."

Mouse cuddled him, laying his chin on his chest. "I don't mind. I knew you were an asshole the moment we met. But I was a sucker for you anyway."

Sadao chuckled. "No one's ever been able to tolerate me for long, nor me them. It's amazing to me you've held up this long."

"You've never been in a relationship before like this, have you?"

Sadao snorted. "Been in plenty, but none like this, no. This, I want to protect," he said, caressing Mouse's face. "I want to honor you, make you happy - simple things that I've never had the time or desire to do before. So I apologize if I keep fucking it up."

"You're doing just fine," Mouse said, kissing him. "Most days I'm so happy I think I'm gonna pop."

Sadao smiled, treating him to a longer kiss. "That's good to hear." His lips were near his ear. "*Itoshii, Konezumi.*"

Although Mouse's knowledge of Japanese was still spotty, the sweetness in Sadao's voice said everything he needed to know.

"Your beard got little!" Shinjyu exclaimed as Sadao picked her up in his arms after school lessons were over the next day. She patted his chin with her hands and giggled. "It's all tickly!"

"It is, hime. I trimmed it."

"Why did you make it little?" she asked, curious.

"This is what I used to look like before I let it get long."

"You look funny now," she said with dead honesty.

Sadao laughed. "Well, don't tell Mouse that. I'd like to think it makes me look more responsible."

Shinjyu hugged him, pressing her cheek up against his little beard. "It's fun to hug now," she said. "I don't care if you look funny."

"Good," Sadao said, nuzzling her back and making her laugh from the feel of shorter hairs on her cheek. "Have you decided where you'd like to babysit me today?"

"I wanna go see the racers! I wanna see them make big jumps!"

Sadao thought it over. He supposed they could talk Mouse into letting them borrow the Jeep for a few hours. He didn't want to transport the girl to the meadows by bike at her age. "Why don't you take me to lunch first?" he said, putting her down and taking her hand. "Then we can ask Mouse for his keys."

"Sure," she said, pulling him along through the snow. "But you have to drive, okay? My feet can't touch the pedals."

Sadao squeezed her hand. "Good idea."

Shinjyu was part of their daily routine now. Mouse would get up early and head to the garage, leaving breakfast warming on the woodstove in the main room for him. Sadao would get up at his own pace, eat, bathe and get himself together in time to walk down to the camp by noon to pick up Shinjyu for lunch and some kind of an adventure. When it got too cold or the girl got too tired, he'd walk her back to the kids' hall and return her to Kei for dinner and bedtime. Babysitting him a few days a week had become four days a week, then five, and now he made it a point to make sure they spent a few hours together even on Mouse's days off. He honestly couldn't let a day pass anymore without seeing her face and holding her tiny hand.

"Come on!" she said, tugging him. "I want to be first in line so we can go see the racing right away!"

"Easy, hime, I don't run through snow very well!"

"Don't blame snow! It's soft! Move it!"

Her persistent drill sergeant manner kept Sadao from slacking off on his physical therapy requirements. She didn't take any excuses and her energy and spirit were infectious. No matter how sluggish he felt crawling out of bed, by the time he got himself dressed each day, Sadao found he could hardly wait to step out into the Canadian winter to go fetch her for their special afternoons. Some days they went to the lake. Other days they helped Mouse in the garage. Sometimes they went with the boys sledding or hiking on short trails between the camp and the exit road. No matter the distance or destination, Sadao found each day a little easier to manage - less pain, stiffness, lethargy - and most importantly, less desire to sneak cigarettes.

Sadao was steadfast in his promise to never smoke near children. But after returning Shinjyu to her keepers, he'd sometimes find himself in the company of Tagata and that meant tobacco was within easy reach. Mouse always knew when he slipped so there was no point denying it. Instead, he'd come clean the second Mouse came home and started sniffing his hair and clothes. He'd be grilled, lectured, assigned cleaning duties or other punishments, then kissed and cuddled and encouraged to try and do better.

And he was doing better, but Mouse was no longer the only reason.

"Tell Cook-san I don't like pickles, Oyaji! He'll listen to you!"

"I will remind him," Sadao said as they got in line waiting for the mess tent to open for lunch hour.

"Hey! Is that my favorite babysitter?!" Mouse was coming up the path and hastened when he saw Sadao and Shinjyu in line. The girl bounced up into Mouse's arms for a squeeze and twirl. Mouse set her on his hip and leaned into Sadao for a quick kiss. "Make that favorite babysitter and baby!"

"Ugh ... do you have to kiss *all* the time?" Shinjyu whined. "It's so embarrassing!"

"You don't mind if I kiss you," Mouse said, leaving a peck on her cheek.

"That's different! I'm not a grown-up!"

"What? You mean somebody passed a kissing ban for grown-ups? That's news to me."

Shinjyu frowned. "Where I come from, grown-ups don't kiss! Ever!"

"Hm, I don't think I'd like this place," Mouse said teasingly.

"No, you wouldn't! There's too many rules! You would be in trouble all the time! I was in trouble all the time, so they sent me away!"

Mouse and Sadao exchanged a quick look. Not a lot was known about Shinjyu's origins. And if asked, she refused to speak about it. If pressed she'd become upset, so they'd decided to let her tell her own story when she was ready. From what Kei and Sadao could gather, she'd lived in some kind of guarded household in Japan with "Bad Men" who were angry with her a lot. Sadao figured it might have been some sort of clan stronghold where it was not uncommon for the children to be looked after by servants. But how she came to be on a boat bound for San Diego was the real mystery.

Children from wealthy clan homes were not generally thrown away.

"And tell Cook-san I want ice cream! Bubble gum ice cream with real gum in it!"

"It's too cold for ice cream today, honey. Brrr!" Mouse shivered. "I'm hoping for warm bread pudding, mmmmm ... "

Shinjyu turned her nose up. "Bread pudding sucks!"

"Shinjyu, that is not nice language for a girl," Sadao said sternly.

"But Mouse says it! He also says as--*smmpf!*"

Mouse covered her mouth with a big nervous grin. "Kids ... "

"I told you to watch your tongue around the girl, didn't I?" Sadao said under his breath.

"She's gonna learn it somewhere. Might as well learn it from the best," Mouse said as he set Shinjyu down.

"She doesn't need to grow up to curse like a mechanic!"

"Not a mechanic! I'm gonna be a racer!" Shinjyu proclaimed, running around their legs with an invisible steering wheel. "Vroooom!!"

Mouse beamed as Sadao held up a finger to silence him. "Don't encourage her."

"Who me?! I'm just the potty mouth. I'm not the one with dozens of trophies gathering dust in the cabinet."

"I'm going to need your keys."

"Huh?"

"The Jeep. I promised Tagata I'd get up to the meadows to watch exercises today."

Mouse's nose twitched. "And ... Shinjyu?"

"She's coming with me."

"You are a barrel of contradictions, you know that?"

"Aware," Sadao said, holding out his hand for the keys.

"Vrooooom!! Skreeeeeech!!"

"Seriously," Mouse said, removing the Jeep keys from his ring and handing them over. "I'm taking this moment to say, 'Don't blame me if the girl becomes a triple cup champion!'"

"Don't be ridiculous. Far too dangerous!"

"What's too dangerous?!" Shinjyu demanded to know, frowning up at Sadao.

Sadao didn't answer, just picked her up and kissed her forehead. "Be good, and I'll make sure you get ice cream today."

The girl grinned. "With real bubble gum?"

"Yes, hime. Real bubble gum."

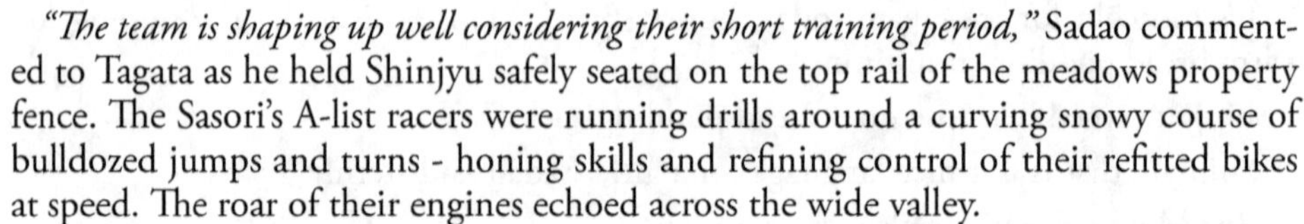

"The team is shaping up well considering their short training period," Sadao commented to Tagata as he held Shinjyu safely seated on the top rail of the meadows property fence. The Sasori's A-list racers were running drills around a curving snowy course of bulldozed jumps and turns - honing skills and refining control of their refitted bikes at speed. The roar of their engines echoed across the wide valley.

"The men still need much work. They have speed but lack refinement on turns and landings. I hope this weather stays calm, or they will have to face heavy snow for the freestyle drills," Tagata said, looking up at the cloudy sky. He was always quick to point out what details could be improved upon.

"It takes time for a racer to learn his bike's balance and shifting thresholds," Sadao noted. *"They've not had these modified vehicles in their grips for long."*

"They go super fast!!" Shinjyu squealed, pointing. Lupe gave Shinjyu a wave as he zoomed past. "Lupe is the fastest! I like him the best! Can I watch the real races, Oyaji? Can I?"

Tagata grinned. Sadao gave him a look as he adjusted Shinjyu's scarf. "The children will not be going to the Rally, hime. You'll have lots of important studies and games to play with your friends and Sensei Kei."

"No!!" she said, kicking her feet in the air. "I wanna come with you and Mouse! I wanna help cheer for the Sasoris!"

A pack of snowbikes flew by in a roaring blur of white, dusting their winter coats and gloves with a snowy mist.

"Pblblt! I got snow in my mouth!" Shinjyu complained.

"Racing is for grown-ups, hime. But I don't think I will be leaving camp either with Mouse."

"No!! That's not fair Mouse gets to go see the big race and we don't!"

"Mouse works the big race. He does not enjoy the spectacle. He is very busy in the garage and he can't look after you."

"Oyaji - you will not come to watch?" Tagata asked, leaning in to avoid her ears.

Sadao lifted Shinjyu down from the fence and let her run up onto the nearby snowplow - safely parked and locked down. She clambered up into the driver's seat and yanked on the knobs, pretending to participate in a snowplow event. "Rooom! Vrooom! GET OUT OF MY WAY SLOW POKES!"

"It's not good for me to show my face among the racing public, Taga," he said, following the young girl stiffly through the snow with the aid of his cane. *"I'm still lying at the bottom of the sea, remember?"*

"I suppose this can not be helped, but Sadao-sama will be much missed. For me it will not feel like a true race without your presence."

Sadao smiled at Tagata's sincerity. *"I'll admit, I'm tempted. But I'm not entirely certain that we weren't followed out of Squamish by that mystery car when Mouse and I went into town."*

"Does Sadao-sama have an idea who it was?"

Sadao shook his head. *"I don't. But it was unsettling just the same. I stay reminded that my presence here puts the team in jeopardy."*

"Jeopardy? This is not something Sadao-sama truly believes?"

"Our location is always kept in close secret, I know. But if anyone were to spread rumor of my survival, I have no doubt the Utah Elders would put a large price on my head. Bounty hunters would think nothing of invading every inch of these mountains. I think perhaps that white vehicle may have been such a person. Although, they weren't very stealthy."

"My sentinels have seen nothing more of it. The exit road is closely guarded and the route hidden. No cars, no trucks have come since."

"It needs to stay that way, and better if I lie low. I'd hate to be the cause of any security breach."

"I do not think Sadao-sama needs to have this concern. The Sasori team will protect you as you have protected them. We are all one family."

Sadao bowed to his former captain. *"Thank you. I will consider your invitation."*

Soon after Tagata called in his men for evaluation, Shinjyu grew bored of the motionless snowplow and wanted to walk over to a nearby frozen pond to see if the fish were still swimming. Sadao followed her as she skipped through the drifts in her heavy coat, striped dress and mushroom pants to kneel at the edge.

"Don't walk out on the ice!" Sadao warned. "You might fall through."

"Duh, I'm not stupid!" she replied, peering out over the frozen surface. She picked up a long dead branch to try and scrape the snow off the surface. "I can't see down."

Sadao joined her and tapped at the ice crust with his cane. It held solid. "I think your fish are frozen," he said. "You'll have to wait for spring to catch them swimming."

Shinjyu sighed. "I wanna catch one now!"

"I'll ask Mouse if we can use his poles. The south end of our lake is still not quite frozen over."

Shinjyu's head popped up to look at him. *"Haha* had fishing poles. But she said I was too little to use them. But I'm big now, right? I can fish now like a big girl!"

Sadao watched her face intently. This was the first time she'd mentioned her mother. "How old were you then, when your mother told you you couldn't use her poles?"

Shinjyu shrugged and raised her hand to show a measurement. "This big," she said.

"But then she went away and I didn't see her again."

A familiar pain ran through Sadao's chest. "What about your *Chichi?*" he asked softly, using his cane to kneel down in the snow. "Did he have fishing poles?"

The girl shook her head. "No, just a lot of guns! Lots and lots of them! *Chichi* had a really big room with lots of animal faces on the wall. It was scary. I wasn't allowed to go in the gun room."

"My father had a room I wasn't allowed to go into either, his library."

Shinjyu was digging at the edge of the pond now, uncovering frozen blades of grass and pulling them up with her mittens. "What's a lbrary?"

"*Library* - It's a room with lots of big bookcases full of books. I used to sneak in there to practice reading other languages besides Japanese. *Chichi* caught me one night and I thought I would be scolded but instead he asked me to read to him in English."

Shinjyu squinted up at him. "He didn't give you a spanking?"

"No, he just made me take more lessons. 'I have many hard working sons,' he said. 'But you will be my scholar. No more fishing for you. Study hard! Make us proud,' he said. And I did study hard, for a while at least."

"That doesn't sound fun! I don't like studying. I want to fish and sled instead!"

"I used to fish all the time with my brothers, but the sea waves always made me sick. I wasn't much help to them. I was glad to give up nets for books."

"When did your parents die?" Shinjyu asked, scooping up a mound of snow into a white dome.

Sadao helped her scoop snow to keep her engaged enough to keep talking. "Why do you ask me that?"

Shinjyu shrugged. "Because nobody here has *oyaasan.*[1] They all died or went away."

Together they began to trim the snow dome with little blades of frozen grass. "My parents died in the war," Sadao said. "When I was fourteen. So, I left Japan and came here to have a new family. How about you? Did your parents die in the war?"

The girl kept her eyes on her snowdome, slow to answer. "The Bad Men told me *Haha* died but I don't believe them. They lie. They lie to make me sad." Her degloved fingers worked faster to punch more blades of grass into the dome, like they were making an arctic hedgehog. "Why did *Chichi* bring the Bad Men and make *Haha* go away?"

"I don't know, little one," Sadao said. Tears were springing up in her eyes and as much as he wanted to know who she was and where she came from, he couldn't bear to see her upset. He got to his feet. "Let's go see if the racers are done talking."

She lifted her arms so Sadao could pick her up. She clung to him shivering, but it had nothing to do with the snow. He wrapped her up tight in his arms and pressed his

---

1   *"parents"*

lips to her soft cheek. "There are no bad men here, hime. I promise. We can all stay here as long as we like, be our own family."

"You won't go away?" she asked, against his shoulder.

"Never."

Her hand clung tight to his jacket collar. "But ... I'm afraid *Chichi* will get mad again and get his guns and make you go away like *Haha*!"

Sadao's breath caught. "Hime ... is your father still alive?"

She raised her head and looked Sadao dead in the eyes. She nodded slowly.

"Where is he? In Japan?"

She looked over the surface of the frozen pond and pointed to the treeline.

Sadao whipped his head around half expecting to see someone. "Do you see him?"

"No. Not now. But sometimes I see the bad men. They come at night from the tall trees and look in my window when I'm sleeping. They always try to scare me!"

Sadao watched her eyes intently. She looked into the pines behind them as if searching for something hidden. Kei had told Sadao she would wake him every so often with nightmares.

"Shinjyu, are you sure the bad men are real? We are very, very far from Japan. Maybe this is a bad dream you had."

She scrunched up her face. "No! No! I told Sensei it's not a dream! I see the bad men! They come out from the trees and shine their lights in my face and wake me up! They want to take me away like *Haha!* I know they are looking for me. But I won't let him find me! I'll be a boy and hide again!" She buried her face in his neck, crying. "Don't let him find me, *Touchan!*"[2]

He held her tight. "I won't, hime. No one will take you from me, I promise!"

"Look, I made fishies!!"

Sadao looked up from his book. Shinjyu had been sitting on the floor drawing quietly near the warmth of the stove with some colored chalk on butcher paper while he rested his leg up on the stool. She held up a large drawing of blue swirls with little brown and black finned globs swimming about.

"This is the mama and this is the papa and these are the little babies!" she said excitedly, getting to her feet and bringing the drawing to him. Sadao held it up between his hands while she pointed out the nine little fish offspring. "And that's a baby, and that's a baby, too!"

---

2   *"daddy"*

"They're very well drawn, Shinjyu," he said, admiringly. "You're a good artist. They look alive."

"And I wanna catch them and eat them!"

Sadao laughed. "I promise we will take you fishing very soon. Go set this on the table, hime, so Mouse can see when he gets home."

Shinjyu had clung to him for safety after her proclamation at the meadows earlier that day. Sadao carried her about, trying to cheer her up as the team resumed maneuvers but she stayed shy and didn't want to leave his arms. After an hour or so his leg regrettably grew too painful to support both of them, so they came back to the cabin early to have some tea and crackers with jelly. She was unusually quiet, so Sadao got out the chalk and paper for her and asked her to draw what was on her mind, but all that came out were fish.

"Whatcha reading?" The girl asked, climbing up onto the couch.

"Are you all done drawing?" Sadao asked, lifting his arm to welcome her to snuggle up next to him. She laid her soft little head against his chest and poked at the book he held in his hand.

"What's that say?"

"It says many things. Can you read it?"

She shook her head.

"Can you try for me? How about this word?" He pointed to "monkey."

"Unh-un," she said with a shrug.

"Where you taught to read English?" Sadao asked.

She shrugged again.

"Let's try something else," he said, reaching for the coffee table. He didn't have much of anything for children but he did find a small book of Buddhist poems in Japanese.

He settled them both under a blanket and flipped to an easy page. It was a meditation on the falling snow in winter.

"How about this?" He asked and pointed to *yuki* - the kanji for "snow". "Do you know what this means."

The girl yawned and tucked her toes up under the blanket. "Nope," she said. "Read it to me. I like that better."

"Okay, but next time I want you to read to me."

She didn't answer him but as he read the words in Japanese her long lashes began to droop. She reached for the ends of his long hair, wrapping a coil of it around her fingers and popping her thumb in her mouth so his hair rested under her nose. This was something Sadao had never seen her do before. She suckled quietly as he finished the poem.

He began another and watched her as he read softly over the crackling of the fire until her suckles slowed and her thumb dropped from her sleeping mouth. Sadao was mesmerized - he didn't dare to move or make another sound if it might wake her. Her thin pink lips were parted and tiny puffs of air caressed his skin as she breathed. Sadao touched her cheek - fear exhausted children. He knew this too well. At that moment, he vowed nothing on this earth or beyond would ever come to harm this child again. Not as long as air still moved in his lungs and blood still pumped through his veins.

When Mouse got home that evening, he opened the door to find a very tuckered out pair of Japanese asleep on the couch. Sadao lay on his back shoeless and snoring with the little dark haired princess sprawled across his chest. Her tiny hand was wrapped up in the ends of his long hair. They looked so comfortable, Mouse felt a pang of jealousy. He tiptoed around them and went into the bedroom for a bath.

When he came back out to start dinner, Sadao's eyes were sleepy but open. He motioned Mouse over and he accepted the kiss from his lips. Mouse set a hip on the back of the couch and drew a finger along her hair.

"How long have the two of you been out?" he asked softly.

"Hmn, a few hours, I think. My leg is numb, but I don't want to move her."

"You hungry?"

"Starving. The girl will need dinner, too."

Mouse smiled and started to get up. "I've got enough, don't worry."

"Mouse…" Sadao stopped him with a hand on his wrist.

"Yeah?"

"I don't want her bunking with the boys anymore. It's not safe."

"Why? They're well supervised."

"By more boys, yes. She needs better protection. Better guidance. Kei has a lot of children to look after. You know she got away once already."

Mouse was confused. He'd never heard Sadao say one bad word against Kei or his care of the camp children. "And you're suggesting what, exactly?"

Sadao nodded toward the far wall just outside their bedroom door. "We could set up a small bed for her over there. It's stays warm enough if the stove is lit. I'll chop extra wood for it."

Mouse sat back down. "Sadao … you know what you're saying, don't you? We move her in here, there's no going back. Have you asked her what she wants to do?"

"She called me *Touchan* today - 'Daddy.' She was shy about it, but I think her heart is being honest. And so is mine," he said, caressing her sleeping cheek.

Mouse quietly took in the moment. In his mind, he saw this day spreading over years and into decades as Shinjyu grew into a woman and an incredible warmth filled his chest. Tears sprung up and he squeezed Sadao's hand. "Okay, we do this then. I'll make a call out to Squamish tomorrow - see about getting her a proper bed. And she'll need a chest for her things and maybe a small armoire..."

Sadao smiled. "Good. Better go get dinner started, Mom."

Mouse lifted a finger. "I'm not Mom! Mouse is fine. Just fine!"

Sadao grabbed his finger and kissed it. "Understood ... Mouse-mom."

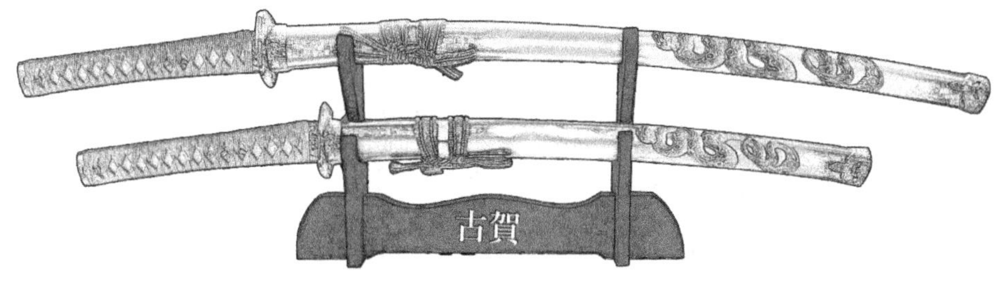

Chapter XV

Golden Voice

Sadao waited until Mouse was freed from the garage for the day to join him in picking up Shinjyu from school. The snow was still thick on the ground from the previous night's snowfall but the clouds had cleared, revealing an icy bright sunshine. Sadao shivered in his leather leggings, stamping his boots to keep warm until he saw Mouse emerge from the garage. He rushed to catch up with him for their short walk to the kids hall.

"You're here early!" Mouse said with a warm kiss.

"Of course, it's an important day."

Mouse hugged him tight and nuzzled his cheek. "You ready for this, Papa? Last chance to back out and stay single!"

Sadao gave Mouse's ass a squeeze. "Haven't been single for years."

"Ha! Two years maybe, if you count prison time!"

"I do," he said with another kiss. "Did you think I was unfaithful in prison? Slim selection."

Mouse's face lit up as he tugged Sadao's hand. "Come on, Daddy, let's go get our daughter!"

"Mouse, too?!" Shinjyu exclaimed as she bounded out of the trailer at lesson dismissal and ran up into Mouse's arms, giving him a fierce hug that made Sadao's envy rise. "Am I babysitting both of you today? I'm gonna charge double!"

Mouse laughed and winked at Sadao. "Not today. You get the day off. We have surprises instead."

"I love surprises! Is it more spinny dresses?"

"More than that," Mouse said, kissing her nose and giving Kei-sensei and the little boys a wave. "It's up at the cabin. I'll race ya!"

Mouse set her on the ground and the two of them charged off through the snow.

"Hey! Wait-! Some of us can't move that fast!" Sadao shouted, limping through the snowpack to the start of the uphill trail. Mouse and the girl were already a third of the way up to the cabin. He struggled along after them with his cane, cursing himself for not insisting they bring the Jeep down. Despite his effort to hussle, Sadao soon found himself breathing hard and working up a sweat hobbling uphill. Climbing anything still proved to be exhausting.

Fuck, I'm out of shape!

By the time he reached the crest of the hill, Mouse and Shinjyu were laughing and swinging in the porch glider. "About time, Speed Racer!" Mouse shouted.

Sadao panted his way to the base of the cabin stairs. His hip throbbed in pain at the thought of ascending them. "I'm going to be even slower if you two don't come down and help me!"

"Yeah, yeah, let's go help the gimp, Shinjyu…"

"Don't call me that!" Sadao huffed as Mouse lent him his arm and they both took the first big step up. Soon he felt the pressure of Shinjyu's little hands on his ass, pushing him from behind.

"Move it! Move your butt! I want surprises!!"

Inside were a number of boxes - some big, some little - that had arrived earlier that morning in the back of Mouse's Jeep.

"Oh! Big ones!!" Shinjyu squealed and tore into the plain paper wrappings. The first one she went for was a large chest with a simple lock on the front. "It says my name!" she said, pointing. "In Japanese!!" 真珠

Sadao eased himself down onto the couch and pointed at the engravings with his cane. "I carved the kanji myself for you. So everyone will know whose chest this belongs too."

"What's in it?" she asked with wide eyes.

Sadao reached into his pocket and produced a key. "Open it and find out."

Mouse knelt beside her and helped her figure out how to turn and lift the lock. Together they opened the lid. Inside were clothes, shoes, nightgowns, slippers and more dresses with long "spinny" skirts. Shinjyu's mouth dropped open as she pawed through the selection. She pulled out a small brush and mirror set too, looking into the reflection with awe.

"It's like what princesses have!" she said. "Is this a magic treasure box?"

Mouse gave her a snuggle so both their faces reflected in the mirror. "It can be whatever you want it to be."

Her lip pushed out. "And the boys can't break it?"

"No, honey. This is your special princess treasure box. No boys allowed!"

"Look!! Fishiiiiies!!!!"

Mirrors and dresses forgotten, Shinjyu uncovered an aluminum pail in the back of the chest filled with little wooden puckered fish faces. She pulled it out with both hands and turned its contents over onto the floor. An avalanche of hand carved and stained fish tumbled out over the floor in various sizes.

"Mouse, look! There's so many!"

"Here, you'll need one of these," Mouse said, fetching her one of the two accompanying poles from the bottom of the chest. Each short pole was strung with twine and tied to a ringed magnet at the end. He put the pole in her hands and untangled the twine so the magnet hung free. "Try to catch one!"

She sucked in her upper lip and focused, hovering the weighted magnet over one of the fish until it wiggled and snapped up to connect with a magnet embedded between its fish lips.

"I got one! I got one!" she cried, jumping up and down. She reached and pulled it off the end of her pole and dropped it in the bucket with a bang. "That's fun! Look, Oyaji! There's big ones and little ones! Just like in the lake!"

"There's two bigger ones, actually," Sadao noted. "The rest are their babies, same as your drawing." He pointed to her framed chalk illustration, now hanging over a large sheet-covered object to the right of the fire stove.

"What's that?" she asked. "Is that for me, too?"

"Yes, hime," Sadao said, with a smile toward Mouse. "Everything new in this room today is for you."

Shinjyu scooted her feet through the swimming floor fish until she came up against the big object. With a quick look back toward Mouse and Sadao, she yanked the sheet off to reveal a white framed girl's bed with pale flowers painted on the posts and a nice thick mattress fitted with soft warm sheets and blankets.

"It's a bed!" she said. "A princess bed! Is it my bed? Can I sleep in it? All night?!"

With Mouse's help, Sadao stood and together they lifted her up and sat her down on the new bed between them.

Shinjyu looked at them both expectantly. Sadao reached for a small box on the nearby table and handed it to her.

"This is for you," he said quietly. "Something very special for a very special girl."

Shinjyu was a little uncertain so Sadao helped open the box in her hand. Inside was a small silver pendant fitted with a black pearl.

"Whoa!" she said as Sadao held it up to show her, then fastened it behind her neck. She stared down at it in surprise. "It's so pretty! Is it really mine? To keep for forever?"

"Yes, hime. It is yours to keep for forever. Every member of my family wears a black pearl from Shinjyu-jima where I was born. Mouse and I want you to be part of our family. And to live with us from now on as our daughter."

Shinjyu held the pendant in her tiny hand, looking up at the both of them in wonder. "You mean ... it's not pretend princess? I can be a real princess? I don't have to go back to the boys after dinner?"

"No," Sadao said steadily, trying hard not to look at Mouse's wet eyes. "This is your home. For as long as you want it to be."

The little girl's lip trembled a moment, and her eyes took on a far away look that concerned Sadao. "Can I call you Touchan?" she asked shyly, looking up at him.

"Of course," Sadao said softly, stroking her cheek. "I would like that very much."

"Touchan!" Her small face filled with joy as he wrapped her up in his arms, kissing her warm cheek. He pressed his face to her's, feeling her little tears. Her hands clung tight to his shoulders. "Give Mouse a hug too," he rasped, before her sweetness would unravel him altogether.

"Mouse!!" she squealed, hopping over into his arms. "Don't cry! It's happy time!"

"I know, I know! I'm just an old softy!" he said, burying his damp face in her hair. "I'm just so happy we can all be a family together!"

Sadao breathed deeply; his throat burned. He was envious of Mouse's ability to show his emotion so easily.

"But Touchan," Shinjyu said, bouncing on Mouse's knees. "If we're all one family, where's you and Mouse's black pearls? Don't you have a necklace, too?"

"Ah…" Mouse's red-faced look of panic sent Sadao into a fit of laughter that soon grew contagious. A tickle fight ensued, followed by more unwrappings of children's books and activities. Shinjyu was soon far too engaged with her hand-carved fishes, coloring books and new clothes parade to remember her question.

Mouse made an easy spaghetti dinner for their first new family meal, Shinjyu's favorite. The girl was hungry - she ate two plates and drank three glasses of milk. Sadao wondered where on Earth she put all that food when he could barely finish one modest serving.

After dinner, Sadao gave her spaghetti face a bath while Mouse popped cookies in the oven. He dried her off in the bedroom and got her dressed into one of her new warm pink nightgowns that hung right down to her toes.

She jumped up and down on the big mattress while Sadao changed into a dry shirt. By the time he fitted the pullover on over his head the girl was already in trouble.

"Shinjyu - *abunai!*" Sadao shouted just in time to stop his daughter from pulling down his katana from where it hung from a hook on their bedroom wall.

She looked up at him with big moist eyes. Her mouth was set in a pout. "You said no more yelling!"

"I didn't yell, Shinjyu. I was warning you of a danger," he said, reaching over her head to adjust the dangling sheathed weapon. "Swords are not for children."

"Is it a real sword?" she asked, watching him rehang it higher up on its woven cord.

Sadao looked down at her where she stood on the bed, index finger in her mouth. Curious.

"Yes, hime. It's very sharp. Very real."

"But ... I wanna see."

Sadao thought it over. He figured better to satisfy her curiosity than risk her examining the blade on her own. "Okay, but you need to sit down calmly on the bed for me." Once she was seated, Sadao took the sword down and sat next to her.

"Hands together, please."

She nodded and folded her little hands in her lap.

Sadao carefully pulled the blade from its scabbard and laid it gently against his knees. The sun was setting outside the window behind them and the angle of the light set the polished blade afire.

"Whoa!!" the girl exclaimed. "That's so cool! Where did you get it?"

"This katana has been in my family for many generations. It's very old."

"Older than you?"

"Yes, hime," Sadao laughed. "Even older than me. It belonged to my father and his father's father. And even his father before him, too."

"That's cool! Do you kill people with it?"

Her question gave Sadao pause. She was always asking him the oddest things for a little girl.

"A katana is a very sacred weapon. The warrior who carries it must respect the power it holds. He is a conduit for the spirit of the blade. Look how the light defines the mastery of the swordsmith." He rolled the katana back and forth; the honing pattern simmered in a wave down the middle from base to angled tip, bisecting the spine from the outer edge.

"It's like waves!" she said. "Like the lake when the wind blows."

"Very good. That is what the blade pattern represents. It divides the hard and soft steel like air and sea, oil and water, darkness and light. It is a delicate balance that its master must learn to respect. It is a knife's edge path between right and wrong - life and death. A warrior must always keep this balance in mind when he carries this sword."

"Can I have it someday?"

Sadao reinserted the katana in its scabbard, snapping it shut. "You will have to be trained. You must earn the privilege of carrying a sword. In ancient Japan, only certain families with birthrights would be allowed to carry katana. Do you know what they were called?"

"Samurai!"

"Good girl, that's right."

"Are you a samurai?" she asked, as he stood to rehang the sword well out of her reach.

"No. Not really. But I am a swordmaster. I studied very hard from when I was about your age."

"I wanna study sword! I wanna be a samurai!"

He smiled and picked her up from the bed, kissing her forehead. "You can be anything you want. As long as it doesn't involve boys or high speeds. I'll carve you a bokken and we can practice together. Would you like that?"

Her whole face lit up. "Yes, Touchan! I wanna sword. I want one now!"

"How about a cookie instead?" Mouse was at the door, oven mitts on his hands. "They're done!"

Shinjyu kicked her legs. "Put me down, put me down! I want cookies!!!"

Sadao let her go and she dashed past them into the main room, where a steamy plate of snickerdoodles awaited.

"Careful, sugar-pop. Blow on them - they're hot!" Mouse called after her before turning back to Sadao. "Did I hear her ask if you killed someone with that thing?"

Sadao nodded solemnly.

"How'd you get around that one, Papa?"

"Diversion. I think it's time I do train her - guide her spirit away from her past darkness into a lighter place where it belongs."

"To sunbeams and daisies? Good luck. That kid's got fangs like her Touchan."

"I do not have fangs," Sadao asserted. "But I do want a cookie."

"Better hurry up," Mouse said, clearing the doorway. "She's got a head start on you."

Later that night, Sadao and Mouse sat on Shinjyu's new bed to tuck her in and listen to Sadao read a story from one of her new books about Canadian forest animal families. Shinjyu listened very intently, thumb in her mouth. She made it a rule to point out every mommy and daddy squirrel, elk and swan and to count all of their babies carefully before Sadao was allowed to turn the page.

"We have a forest family too!" she said. "You're the daddy," she said pointing to Sadao. "And you're the Mouse!" she said, giving Mouse's belly a poke. "And I'm the baby! Except I'm not a little baby anymore - I'm a big princess girl! Next page, Touchan!"

She was asleep before they finished counting the ducklings. Slowly and carefully, Sadao got up and tucked the blankets around her while Mouse threw another log in the stove trap.

Sadao kissed his new daughter's soft head before taking Mouse by the hand into their bedroom and dimming the outer room lamps.

"I guess we leave this open now," Mouse said, only partially closing their bedroom door. From their room, they could see the top of her head and long dark hair asleep on the pillow just outside.

"Come here momma Mouse," Sadao said, beckoning him to their dresser. He reached in and pulled out a small box hidden in a sock. "I was saving this for our first anniversary, but seeing as Shinjyu's already brought it up, I thought now would be a more appropriate time."

"What did you do? You made me something?!" Mouse asked, beaming as he opened the box. Inside were two small silver ear cuffs, set with a black pearl each. "Earrings?"

"They fit on the edge of the ear."

"One for you and me?" Mouse asked dreamily. "Shit, I love it when you make us jewelry!"

"You're already bound to me," Sadao said, fitting one of the cuffs on Mouse's ear and turning his head to allow Mouse to do the same for him. "But these are pearls everyone can see. I want Shinjyu to know who her people are and to be proud of her family."

"You're a hopeless romantic, you know that?" Mouse said, blushing. "I love it! I love our home! I love our little girl and *God* how I love -"

Sadao touched his lips and leaned in to kiss his mouth softly. "I know, *Konezumi*. Everything's perfect now."

Mouse hummed happily as Sadao gathered him close for a slow tender kiss, tongues gently caressing between warm lips. Mouse moaned into his mouth as their kiss lingered and their groins brushed, causing a very natural reaction between them.

"Mmmn ... damn, I guess we have to be responsible now, huh?" Mouse asked, breathing heavy.

Sadao laughed and kissed his nose. "Somewhat, yes ... let's give her a night to settle in at least."

Mouse shivered in his arms. "I'm gonna need a shower then," he said gently pushing them apart. "A real cold one!"

"So Gringo, how's fatherhood?" Lupe asked Mouse the next day as he entered the garage truck fresh from the snow fleet's last training day. Mouse, Aki and his lug nut team were finishing up the packing and tie downs for the garage truck's relocation to Squamish early the next morning.

"It's awesome!" Mouse said, sliding down the deck ladder to show off his new earcuff to Lupe.

"Whoa! You two get married again?"

"Sorta," Mouse said with a grin. "Sadao wants us to be a real Orochi family, complete with matching jewelry we can wear on the outside. Shinjyu's got this adorable pendant. She absolutely loves it, thinks she's a princess. We've had to remind her not to strut too proudly in front of the boys. I cleaned out my bank account buying her furniture and new things, plus some new games and books for the boys. We really need to win some fucking races next week or I'll be feeding our new daughter trout and crackers. Hey, Aki! Throw me some more bungies!"

Lupe caught a wad of hooked ropes as they flew in from the outside where the garage kids were collapsing and rolling up the tent extension. "Where're these going?"

Mouse took half of the bungies from Lupe and went to the opposite end of the truck. "Take those and hook the drawers together like a chain from that end. Keeps them from flying open when you take those high-speed mountain turns!"

"Got it! I hope we can roll out tomorrow before the next storm. Weather report says more snow is due to fall after 6 A.M. Driving this bitch over a snowed-in pass isn't my favorite gig, man!"

"We'll have her ready. Don't worry! You can roll at first light!"

Lupe and Aki were assigned to get the garage rig safely down the mountain to their sea-side inlet encampment outside of Squamish by tomorrow afternoon. Mouse would spend one last night in the comfort of his cabin family before he had to leave in the Jeep to join the team for the duration of the Rally.

"I'll be honest, Lupe. I don't like the idea of leaving Sadao and Shinjyu up here without me."

"Huh? What? They're not coming down?"

Mouse hooked the last of the drawers and met Lupe in the middle, where he lowered his voice. "Sadao's concerned about being recognized. A lot of sponsors and chairpeople will be in attendance from the Northwest Division. Even though we'll be buried neck deep in Canadian Division fans, he's worried. He doesn't want anyone spreading rumors he's alive."

"It's cold as fuck now. Can't he just wear a ski mask or something?"

Mouse shrugged. "I dunno. Someone followed us out of Squamish last time I took him down to shop. We don't need any more unwelcome traffic coming up here."

"Nobody's found the exit road yet, have they? They hide that motherfucker pretty damn good. I've missed it like eight times and I know where it is!"

"According to Tagata's sentries we're still good. I mean, I know there's gonna be plenty of soldiers staying behind and monitoring the area but that cabin is kinda far up there. I'm trying to talk Sadao into staying down here at Tagata's with Shinjyu, Kei and the kids until we all get back."

"Yeah, why doesn't he do that?"

Mouse sighed. "It's Sadao. Doesn't want to give up his tub."

"You spoil that man, vato!"

"Believe me, you have no idea!"

Ninety minutes later, Mouse and his team high-fived it for the night. Mouse accompanied Lupe back to his trailer on his way toward the cabin trail. The sun was setting behind the treetops, casting long shadows in the snow.

"So we've got 20 good bikes and 4 alternates, right Gringo? Sounds like plenty to me. You'll be kicking it in a lawn chair with a warm beer this Rally."

"Hah! I wish. Thing about snow racing is all the unseen hazards. I'm not so worried about the circuit races and trick jumps and all that. It's the Downhill I'm most concerned about - for you guys and the bikes and that bullshit crevasse. I've studied Tagata's course map inside and out. Lots of potential for buried rocks and trees, no matter what route you choose. But I hate to say it - if you guys are gonna have any chance of crossing the finish line first, you've got to take that shitty glacier route.

"You think we should just jump it?"

"Ah, depends on the snow pack up there. Tagata says he'll take us up the night before to check it out. But I'm worried the drive trains just aren't long enough to guarantee enough traction for a 15-foot jump."

"So I guess we gotta take that ice bridge, then."

"It's what my gut tells me. But it's gonna be a bitch to hit at 50-plus. One degree off and you're heading for the center of the earth. The cold center!"

"I can do it. Don't know about some of the others, though. Between you and me, some of these younger guys don't have the huevos yet."

"Well, they'd better hatch some huevos if they don't want to find themselves wedged into an ice canyon for eternity."

"Ah!!" Lupe covered his ears. "Don't need to remind me, man! I got enough to worry about with asshole rivals banging my ass off the trail and into a tree. Don't gotta get my heart pounding over all that dark ice grave bullshit, too!"

"Sorry, bud. Just talking like a concerned teammate," Mouse said, patting Lupe's back. "I've geared up those bikes to handle just about anything. You've got the best frames and treads Tagata-san was willing to buy! You can handle a little ice."

"Fuck me! You'd better have tricked my ride to handle everything! Like Bigfoot and shit!"

"Hey, it's me. I've always got your ass!"

"Yo-! Anybody home?"

No answer came as Mouse hustled in the cabin door, shaking snow from his hair. He was freezing from the walk up the hill and the interior was nice and toasty, thanks to a bright fire roaring in the stove. He shut the door and a quick look down confirmed that his husband and daughter were home; Sadao's and Shinjyu's boots were both accounted for, as well as their coats.

Mouse got out of his own snow gear quickly and went into the bedroom - it was empty as well. But Sadao's jeans were left on the floor, along with his shirt. Mouse picked them up as usual and knocked on the bathroom door.

Splashing came from inside and giggles. "Mouse is hoooome!"

The bathroom door banged open and a very naked, very wet little girl ran out and hugged his legs.

"Shinjyu? Why are you naked? Where's your dad?"

"Touchan's in the ofero! Can you come too?"

Mouse stepped in and through the steam, he saw Sadao pouring a bucket of hot water over his head as he sat naked on the washing stool. He slicked his long hair back and looked over his shoulder at Mouse.

"Ah, you're home. What's for dinner?"

Mouse stood there stupidly, holding Sadao's clothes. Shinjyu scampered across the slatted floor and jumped back into the tub. Sadao got in more slowly, supporting his hip as he slid himself into the steamy water. Shinjyu splashed around him, squealing.

"Now we can have a family bath! Family bath tiiime!!"

"Easy, hime, don't knock all the water out," he said before turning to Mouse. "You look cold - get in."

Mouse paled. "Uh ... maybe I should get dinner ready - ?"

"It can wait," Sadao said, welcoming Shinjyu to crawl up onto his submerged lap. "It's below freezing outside and the water won't stay warm forever."

"I want Mouse to have bathtime too, Touchan!" the girl whined, tugging at Sadao's hair. "Why won't he get in? Make him get in!"

"That's okay - I'll clean up later, honey." Mouse glared at Sadao, pointing to his discarded pants and nodding to Shinjyu as a silent show of his distaste.

"Stop being so prudish and come join your family," Sadao ordered.

"Yeah," Shinjyu echoed. "Don't be poodish! It's bathtime. Bathtime is fun!"

"Families bathe together in Japan," Sadao said, relaxing against the smooth wooden frame as Shinjyu lept off of his lap and into the water after a small washrag. "Encourages bonding."

"We're not in Japan," Mouse said through his teeth as he dropped Sadao's clothes on the floor in exasperation. "And where I come from, boys and - excuse me, men, especially - don't bathe with little girls!"

Sadao reached for his hand. "You are not in America anymore, *Konezumi*. You are in the mountains in a private cabin on sovereign soil forty miles from nowhere. Who cares who you bathe with or not?"

"But … I care … it's…"

Shunjyu popped up laughing with the towel over her eyes. "Mouse is afraid I'm gonna see his pee-pee, right Touchan?"

"Oh, God … " Mouse turned to leave, but was caught fast by his wrist and thrown head over ass backwards into the very place he was trying to avoid. He scrambled for a foothold and came up coughing hard. "What the fuck was that for?!"

Sadao frowned at him. "It amazes me the vulgarity you'll freely express in front of our child, and yet the idea you may be unclothed in her presence terrifies you."

"Of course it does!" Mouse said, pawing the wet hair out of his face. "That's not how I was raised!"

Sadao sighed in defeat. "Fine, bathe in your clothes. I don't care. But next time, ask yourself why you would build a Japanese bath for your Japanese family if you did not intend to use it in a Japanese way!"

I did, Mouse thought. *Just not with a little girl in tow!*

Shinjyu was tugging at Mouse's wet sleeve. "Clothes don't belong in the tub! Off! Off! They're dirty!"

"She's right you know - pollutes the water. You should shower first, too. Very rude to step into a shared bath without cleaning yourself first."

"I - I was thrown in!"

Shinjyu was pushing him. "Go! Wash up first! Yuck!"

Mouse gave in and hauled his wet self up out of the bath and over to the shower. He made a point to turn his back to them before stripping off his sopping clothes and washing off. To his horror, he could hear Shinjyu laughing.

"Mouse's bottom is cute, Touchan."

"Yes, hime. It is."

"Stop talking about my a - backside!"

"Why not? It's as charming as the rest of you. No need to be ashamed."

"What's asaimed mean?" Shinjyu asked.

"It's an emotion I hope you'll never feel, hime. It's when you don't feel comfortable being in your own skin."

"Hey," Mouse said, shutting off the water and placing a wash towel around his hips. "I don't have one single problem with my skin!"

"Then drop the towel and get in."

"I'm … working on it!"

Mouse inched himself over and carefully rotated his legs into the tub, with the towel firmly in place.

Shinjyu was busy playing fetch with the washrag as he lowered himself and towel into the water. The heat did feel exceptionally good after his long walk in the snow.

"Did you get the garage packed today?" Sadao asked with closed eyes.

"Yeah, it's good to go down tomorrow with Lupe and Aki."

"I wanna go down tomorrow too! I wanna see the big race!" Shinjyu whined.

"We've discussed this," Sadao said with a sigh, indicating this was the umpteenth time he'd had this conversion that day with their daughter. Mouse hid a grin as his muscles relaxed into the warmth. Day one as a full-time father and Sadao's exasperation was already kicking in. "You have important lessons and events to attend with your classmates. Kei-sensei has lots of fun things - "

"But I wanna see racers!!" Shinjyu wailed, water dripping down her upset face. "I wanna seeee. Mouse will take meeee!" She splashed over into his arms, sticking her tongue out at her beloved Touchan.

"I can't take you down with me either, sweetheart. I have to work the whole time - I never get out of the garage. You wouldn't be able to see anything fun."

"Touchan doesn't work! He's lazy! But he won't take me! Ugh!" Shinjyu said with an angry splash of her fists that roused Sadao from his attempt at calm.

"*Sakebanai de, Shinjyu!*" Sadao's voice was firm but not unnecessarily loud.

"No yelling!" Shinjyu shouted back and burst into angry tears. "You suck, Touchan!"

She buried her face in Mouse's chest and let loose a howl loud enough to wake the hibernating grizzlies.

"You can deal with her and her fantastic word choices," Sadao said under his breath, getting out of the tub. "I've had enough."

Mouse held their little ball of wet frustration as she sobbed. He tried hard not to laugh as Sadao toweled off. "Tough day, Papa?"

Sadao grumbled something in reply as he tucked a towel around his waist. "She needs to learn she can't have everything her way all the time."

"Yes I can!" Shinjyu wailed, hugging Mouse tighter.

"I think she can hear you," Mouse laughed, stroking her hair as she gasped and sniffled against his chest. He couldn't help but coddle the poor little thing. Frustration was an emotion Mouse had been well acquainted with growing up. "Shhh… calm down ... " he said, but as he bent to kiss her head something odd caught his eye. He could see at a part in her long black hair that there was some kind of blue symbol marked on her head.

Sadao saw Mouse's eyes change. "What is it?" he asked under her wails. Mouse pointed to the back of her head and Sadao leaned in close to take a look. He parted her hair slightly with his thumb to inspect the odd markings.

Shinjyu shook away his hand. "Don't touch me! I'm mad!"

Sadao shot Mouse a silent warning with his eyes that made his skin prickle.

"Let's get you out and dried off, honey. Are you hungry? I'm making mashed potatoes and sloppy joes!"

Her red-rimmed dark eyes brightened. "Yum! I like sloppy joes! Can I help make them?"

"Of course, sweetie. Here, let your daddy dry you off," he said, lifting her out. She went into Sadao's arms willingly now, jabbering about food. Racing was, at least for now, forgotten and forgiven.

After a late dinner, Sadao got Shinjyu ready for bed, nightie on and teeth brushed while Mouse cleaned the dishes. Then all three of them snuggled up in the big bed for stories from one of Sadao's old Japanese fable books. He first read in Japanese, then translated into English for Mouse to follow along. They were stories about magical raccoon dogs and a young maiden who could take the shape of a swan. The fire flickered and the gas lamp glowed as he turned the pages. Shinjyu lay between them, eyes on the book with a thumb in her mouth. By the second short story she was out with her nose to Sadao's ribcage, breathing softly.

Mouse felt a bone-deep happiness watching Sadao stroke her long black hair. Except for the fact he was parting it slightly to reveal the hidden mark.

"So, what does it mean?" Mouse asked softly. The suspense had been killing him.

Concern etched Sadao's face. "I'm not certain. The kanji written here are 'kin' and 'koe'. It means 'gold-voice'."

"Family name, maybe?" Mouse offered.

"Not one I'm familiar with," Sadao said, gently parting and stroking her hair. "Japanese surnames are generally references to nature. I think this is a clan marking for members of a particular self-named group - not likely a nice one. Post-Civil war Japan has been largely ruled by modern Shogun, claiming land and resources by force. The same way my father's island was taken - families slaughtered or forced into exile."

"Maybe her family was exiled," Mouse said. "Maybe they died and she was abandoned at the docks."

"Perhaps," Sadao said. "But there is something that bothers me. Something I never told you about my time in prison."

"What?" Mouse asked, alarmed.

Sadao pressed a finger to his lips. "Shh! Don't wake her." Mouse clamped a hand over his mouth and nodded.

"When I was attacked, the little shit that shivved me said something odd. He said, 'King Go Away says hello.' I couldn't follow what he meant. At the time I wrote it off as the random name of some punk in his posse. But this mark Shinjyu has, if you flow the words together like a name, it can be pronounced, 'Kin-goe.' I think my attacker was just mispronouncing this clan name tattooed on her head."

"Huh ... " Mouse said, thinking it over. "How on Earth could Shinjyu be connected to some random brats you tussled with in prison?"

Sadao smoothed the girl's hair, covering her tattoo. "That is what I keep asking myself. She talks about 'The Bad Men.' She thinks they are coming for her."

"I've heard her say that, too. Do you think they're real?"

Sadao looked puzzled. "At first I felt it was nightmares - memories of her troubled past, but now I'm not so sure. She seems convinced she's seen these men come out of our woods and look in her window at night with flashlights. She thinks they are sent by her real father, come to take her back to Japan."

"Agh, that's creepy as fuck. Really? He's still alive, you think? Is that why you moved her up here?"

"Part of it," Sadao said, bending to kiss her head. "It's hard to tell if there's any reality to her fears. Unlikely her parents survived, I think. Anyone who would have troubled themselves to mark her like this wouldn't have abandoned her. Truthfully, I just couldn't bear it anymore when she wasn't with me. Like it was with you," Sadao said, looking at Mouse. "I tried to keep you separate - as I must do with all my boys, give each an equal part of my attention."

Mouse blushed. "You don't pick favorites…"

"Right…but I failed in that with you and now it is the same with her. I can't stand the thought of her being frightened or harmed. And if it is possible someone is looking for her … "

Sadao was becoming unusually emotional. Mouse reached out to take his hand. "It's okay, Papa. What you're feeling is normal. Of course you want to protect her from danger. We both do." It was unbearably sweet to see Sadao so overcome with love for his new child.

Sadao nodded. "I passed from this world that day, you know … on the stage."

Mouse's heart began to pound at Sadao's sudden turn of subject. "Really? You remember that?"

"I saw it. I saw my body dying and you -" Mouse squeezed his hand, urging him to continue. "I saw you bent over my body, screaming for me … Shiratori was there, standing somewhere off at a distance. He was waiting for me…his spirit. There was a bridge. I was supposed to go -" Sadao's eyes were distant with the memory and his grip was tight on Mouse's hand. "I couldn't go - I knew if I left then, I'd never see you again. For as long as my spirit wandered from life to life, I would be alone."

"Sadao…" Mouse stroked his hand, coaxing him back to the present. "It's okay, baby. I'm here. Shinjyu's here. We're a family now. We stay together, okay?" Sadao shut his eyes as Mouse kissed his forehead. "You can let that go now. You came back to me; that's all that matters. And Shinjyu, she's like a gift. A gift for both of us, for getting through those horrible times. Do you believe that?"

Sadao breathed and opened his eyes. "Yes."

"It's okay to admit that we need people. And it's okay to want them close as we can stand it. I'm gonna follow you forever, you bastard. Haunt your soul. You're stuck with me and the girl - that's a done deal."

Sadao leaned over Shinjyu and kissed Mouse soundly. "I want that very much."

"I think Shinjyu's opened up something in you that's been locked up too tight for too long. And it's all bursting out now. And that's okay, baby. It's a good thing - a beautiful thing. You need this; she needs this. Together, you can heal each other."

"I don't want her to know a single moment of the kind of childhood I had. I fear she's seen too much violence and sorrow already. I wish I'd been there the second she was born."

"Sadao, the way she came into this world is how she came to you - to us. And it matters more because you share a similar history. She's young now, but she'll grow up to value that. Our past is what shapes us into who we become as adults and how we connect to each other."

"I don't want to imagine her grown up. I can't think about that yet."

Mouse kissed his hand. "I know, Papa. It's hard - she's your baby. And you want her to stay that way. Your pearl. She's like that jewel in your tattoo - wrapped securely in coils and viciously protected. I'd hate to be her first boyfriend."

Sadao's eyes popped wide open. "No boys! Never!"

Mouse laughed. "Oh, God, poor things. They'd better learn to run fast. Kill the light, Papa. She can sleep with us tonight. It'll keep those evil boys away!"

The jungle was hot, moisture dripped from the bamboo leaves overhead. The pack on his back was heavy and the strap holding his father's swords bit into his shoulder. They'd been marching for hours in the oppressive heat, following each other's footsteps in the mud. Sweat coated his skin and his clothes hung damp from his limbs. Exhaustion was making his vision swim.

March! Ichi, ni - ichi, ni!

Hault!

They were stopped and Sadao ached to drop to his knees in the dirt and sleep.

Sadao! Get up! He's here. Following again!

Nan da?

His platoon stood frozen in a line, looking back down the mountain's winding path. Sadao - who was last in the line - turned to follow their eyes. Below, in the thickness of the scrub, movement could be seen rustling the bushes.

If he keeps following, he'll get us killed!

Sadao knew what to do. He dropped his pack and drew out his father's katana. Down the path he went, stepping soundlessly with the hilt in his grip until the rustling stopped. He stilled, listening ... until he saw the leaves move again.

Zzzzingg! Zzwwwingg! The blade cut through the air and the leaves, sending shreds of foliage and blood flying. He heard a child's cry. Not a boy's cry. A girl's - Shinjyu's. Panic shot through his gut as the frail voice whimpered in pain. He panicked, diving into the brush after her cries.

No ... no ... no...!

You missed, the voice said.

The cries stopped and Sadao got up and whirled around. Behind him was the boy - the same boy who stole his shoes. His face was blue and his eyes bloodshot. His father's wakizashi still lay thrust deep into his throat. Blood gurgled from his lips as he spoke.

Look, Onisan ... I still have our father's sword!

Sadao burst awake from his troubled sleep, breathing hard. The fire had burned down to a dull glimmer, casting long shadows across the roof beams. Mouse lay snuggled up at his left side breathing deeply while Shinjyu slept with her arm across his chest on his right. He touched her hand - it was soft and warm. He stroked her hair and kissed her forehead, moving her over his belly to lie against Mouse. The two of them reached for each other in their sleep and kept dreaming, unaware he had slipped out of the bed. He stood and reached high up on the bedroom wall for his weapon.

Shivering with cold, he threw a blanket over his shoulders and tossed more logs on the fire in the bedroom before angling the door open to peer into the front room. The stove was still burning - a warm orange glow was flashing in the steel trap, casting huge shadows on the walls. Outside, the wind blew snow flurries past the windows that faced the lake and the distant camp lights below. Sadao pulled out a chair and sat - staring out into the fall of white, watching and waiting - mindful that his razor sharp katana lay across his lap ready to draw in a moment's breath.

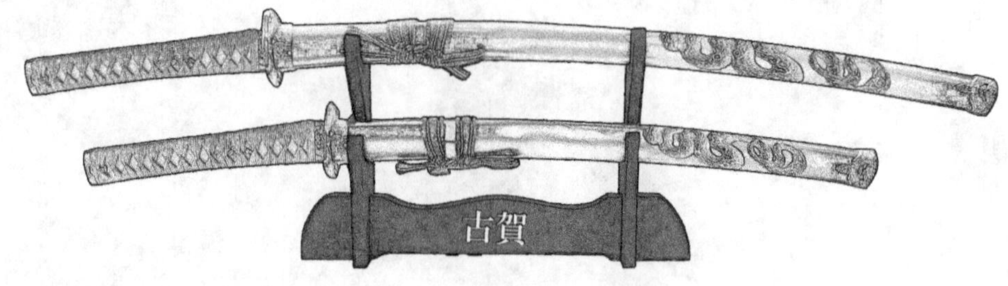

Chapter XVI

Mon Mari

The following afternoon, Sadao received a knock at the cabin door. Generally, when someone wanted to get his attention, they'd use the radio. But it was tea-sipping, leg-resting, blanket-cozy couch time and that meant radio was off!

"Who is it?" Shinjyu was in school and Mouse was down in camp getting last minute tools and supplies packed into his Jeep. He would be relocating down to Squamish early the next day to support the team for the duration of the week-long event. With childcare now becoming a full-time commitment, Sadao savored these few quiet moments by himself.

There was a muffled reply outside the heavy door - not a voice he recognized. The temperatures had dropped below freezing and he no longer left the windows open even a crack. If he did, the cold would seep in and his leg would seize. "Go away!" he yelled. "*Ikeyou!* Mouse and Shinjyu are in camp! *Daremo inaindakara!*"

The knocking only got louder. *Kuso!*

Sadao tossed the blankets off, lifted his leg from the cushioned stool and growled through the pain. It was not a good day for hopping up for guests. He hobbled across the floor, musing if it was worth the agony to go back to the bedroom first so he could greet the persistent knocker with the edge of his katana. He slid the bolt back and threw the door open. "What?!"

The face that greeted him in a fur-lined cap and scarf was so unexpected it took him a moment to speak the right name. *"Gisette? Que fais-tu ici?"*

"Oh, mon dieu! Mon dieu!" she cried and fell into his arms. Cold red lips pressed against his face as she kissed him from cheek to cheek. *"Sadao! C'est vrai! C'est un miracle!"*

Her kisses were so vehement she risked knocking them both over backwards. Sadao gripped the door frame and tried to calm her. "Gisette, it's okay. Calm down - I have trouble enough standing for one."

On the porch behind her stood two of Tagata's guardsmen with rifles. A large expensive white SUV was parked at the base of the gravel driveway flanked by two snowbikes.

"Oyaji - anata no tomodachi dashou?"

"Yes, she's an old friend. You can leave her with me."

The men bowed and returned to their vehicles.

"Impossible! On m'a dit que tu étais mort!" Gisette cried, petting his face and kissing his lips again. "I thought I would be dead too! They shot at my car!"

"Gisette! Please," he said, separating her from him with a gentle but firm hand. "It's okay. We have to guard the road."

"When I saw you in town, I thought I had gone mad! 'It can't be!' I said. 'He is gone. *Il s'est noyé!'"*

Sadao patted her shoulder. "Yes, reports of my death were somewhat exaggerated. Will you come in? It's freezing this time of day."

"Yes-yes! *Merci!*" The former nightclub-singer-turned-heiress trotted inside wearing a pair of high-heeled snow boots and a mink-lined jacket. Sadao shut and bolted the door - the last thing he wanted was for anyone else to see her here. *When was the last time we met?* he wondered. *Sometime during The Overland?* It didn't completely surprise him she'd sniffed him out - dead or no. As his chief benefactor throughout his racing career, Gisette always had a way of finding him when he least expected it.

"Would you like something warm to drink?" he asked. "Your hands were very cold."

"Oh yes, please! That would be lovely, darling. Is this your home?"

"Yes," Sadao said, limping to the kitchen and working the pump to fill the kettle.

"It's quite rustic, isn't it?"

"It's quiet," Sadao said and set the kettle atop the wood stove. He opened the trap and threw in an extra log. "Coffee or tea? That's all we have."

"Whatever you like, darling. I don't mind."

"Tea then. Please sit. There's not a lot of furniture. This will take a few minutes. No electricity, no microwave."

Gisette removed her scarf and sat at the end of the couch opposite Sadao's stool. She caught his hand as he limped past. He stopped, her eyes were wide with concern. "What did they do to you?" Her hand moved to hover over his mangled hip.

"I was shot. Bullets turned my pelvis to dust."

"That is what the reports from Utah said, but the latest was that you'd died on that horrible prison ship! Drowned, they said. At the bottom of the Pacific. I cried for days to think of it!"

Sadao squeezed her hand to reassure her. "I'm fine, I didn't drown. I didn't die. I'm here, back with the team where I belong."

Her eyes grew wet with relief. "Thank God for that, Sadao. Thank Him and His angels you survived!"

"I would, but no one must know I'm here. Understand this, Gisette. No one must know. Not the racing Chairs, not Canadian Immigration - no one! I'm still a fugitive of the United States, were I alive in their eyes."

"Then they can go to hell! You are a hero, Sadao. Everyone knows this. You should request asylum! Canada will protect you as they have protected your team! I can contact - "

"No one, Gisette. I beg you to listen. I want no part of any laws or governments. I just want to rest," he said and lowered himself to sit beside her, lifting his leg onto the cushion for some relief.

"*Mon dieu!* You are in such pain! You should not be alive only to suffer this way! Please darling, let me help you. I know surgeons - many, the very finest in my country."

"No one!" Sadao barked. "Especially not surgeons. I'm this way thanks to their care. I want nothing more to do with doctors or hospitals. Sensei is looking after me now."

"That old man? Your witch doctor? What can he do?"

"He's given me the first real glimpse of some relief from this injury is what he's done. There are more methods of healing in this world than cutting a man open and sewing him back together!" He was shouting. Sadao took a moment to calm his voice. "I'm sorry, but I've already had this argument many times with many people. It's my leg, I'll make my own decisions about it."

Gisette tugged at the strap of a small bag she wore over her shoulder. She unzipped it and pulled out a cigarette, sticking it between her thin red lips. She fumbled around for a lighter and lit the end with trembling fingers, taking a nervous puff. "I apologize. This is just, too - too much."

Sadao sighed. "I know. I'm sorry too. I wasn't up for visitors today. I wish you'd called."

Gisette blew a disgusted puff of smoke above her head. "How would I call? You have no number, no phone! No address! No existence!"

"Ridiculous request. Forget it - Kettle's about to squeal."

"You, do not get up!" she said. "I will do it. Hold my cigarette!"

Sadao took it from her and studied the ring of lipstick around the filter. It looked delicious so he shrugged and took a drag off it. Place already smelled of it, so what would be the harm?

"Bring an extra mug for the ash," he said. "Tea tin is on the right end of the counter."

She returned shortly with three mugs. Two with steaming water and steeping bags, and a third for the ash Sadao had caught in his hand. He thanked her and brushed away the grey matter from his palm.

"Ridiculous to live like this - without power or even a basic ashtray," she said, resuming her seat and blowing the steam across her mug. "If you wanted a cigarette you could have asked. I suppose you don't have any of those, either."

"I don't, actually," Sadao said, taking a hot gulp. "Trying to quit."

"Ha! Sadao Koga without his pack-a-day habit? That I have to see."

"I was smoke free for two weeks until you dropped by," he said, crushing the butt of her former cigarette into the improvised ashtray. "Circulation in the leg is bad. Smoking makes it worse. Don't tell Mouse I cheated a little, okay?"

"Mouse? Who? Wait -" Gisette's eyes flickered across the main room to the crowded boot and coat rack. Then, she turned her head to look into the single bedroom, and to the small flower covered bed by the stove behind where they sat. "You don't live here alone," she said, stunned.

"No, I don't."

"But - Mouse, that name… that was your mechanic. And there's toys by that small bed. Does a child stay here?"

Sadao grinned. "Our daughter, Shinjyu. She's at school."

"School! What? Your daughter?! From when?"

"From since I gave up the smokes. Adopted, of course. She's six. Angel of my heart."

"You're seriously raising a child with him, the mechanic? That… unkempt desert person?" Her voice no longer possessed enough shock to hide the disgust.

"His name is Mouse. *Mon mari.* I'll ask you to show respect for the members of my family."

Gisette's mouth formed a perfect "O" of surprise. Not the first time he had seen it that way. "I don't…" She stopped herself and took a painful sip of hot tea before setting it aside and reaching into her purse for a new cigarette. "Well, you always were a fickle man," she said as she lit it.

"Gisette, I expected you to be the most understanding of my old friends."

A flicker of a smile crossed her lips. "So, 'old friends,' is it?"

"Yes," Sadao said motioning for another stick. "That is how I would like to think of you. Fondly."

"Could be worse, I guess," she said, offering her lighter as he leaned into the flame. "Still, you can't blame me for shock. I never took you for a family man. Or family men, either."

Sadao coughed. "Your memory must be slipping. I never planted my flag on either hill."

"No, but then I assumed you were just young."

"I haven't been young for a decade or more. Open your eyes, Gisette. This is who I am. And for once, I am happy."

Gisette looked away, clearly not filled to the brim with acceptance. "I guess a lady shades her eyes from things she doesn't want to see," she said wistfully.

"Shades?" Sadao laughed, flicking ash in the mug. "You used to beg to watch, if memory serves."

"Well, I was young once too!" she snapped. "Still, by morning I always thought of you as the lone wolf, strutting away from his latest kill."

"Even a strutting wolf doesn't wish to die alone. I tried it once. Didn't care for it."

"We all die alone, Sadao. Each and every one of us," she said bitterly.

"Gisette - you have a home. A husband. You're not alone. You of all people."

"Hah! A husband? I haven't seen Clive in a year. He took off for Japan for his studies. He's so happy chasing your Nagoya Fever around he hardly remembers to call. You think you know my life, *mon ami?* You think I look forward to my golden years beside a husband who will hardly look my way unless I'm contagious? Where do you think I will be at 50, 60?"

"Same as you are now, as you've always been," he said with a smile. "Madame Gisette Hawthorn, heiress to the largest private estate in Alberta."

Gisette's lips pinched together a moment. "At least I have a microwave oven," she said, flicking ash. "Where's your trailer? Did they confiscate it? If it's impounded, I can claim it. My accountant will have my copy of the pink slip."

Sadao grinned. She was never a subtle woman. "I still have it. It's parked in camp and occupied by one of our racers - Lupe Escovado. You'll have to fight him for it."

"I didn't come to fight anyone. I'm making a point you used to live better when you let me take care of you."

"I'm a big boy now. I can take care of myself."

"I hope so, Sadao," she said and crushed out her cigarette. "Because right now you're not convincing me. Where on earth did you find this child to adopt, anyway?"

"She came in with the last round of Baja recruits. Someone hid her away good - disguised her as a boy. We didn't even realize she was female until months after she arrived."

"You aren't seriously considering bringing up a child in a place like this are you?"

"Yes we are. She's very happy here with Mouse and me. We're a family now, Gisette. We are whole. I've found my home at last and don't intend to ever leave it."

In the end, Sadao would call her unlikely visit pleasant, if not strained at moments. His unexpected guest soon grew tired of hearing about the Sasoris, snow, prison food and funny things Shinjyu says and began to check her watch. It made him nostalgic in a way. He had always known her to be a single-minded woman.

"I must get going, darling," she said, patting his knee. "The Sponsors' Committee has me packed to the gills with meetings this week. I doubt you've heard or care anymore, but there's a new 'mystery team' causing all sorts of problems with the Rally event schedules."

"What mystery team? If I don't know about them, then Tagata doesn't know either. He keeps me well informed. I do still care greatly about racing and the welfare of this team, you know."

"Hah! Apparently, he doesn't keep you up to date half as well I as used to, if you haven't heard about this gang of marauders!" she said, getting up and taking the dishes to the sink. "No, no, you sit!" she demanded with a wave when he tried to follow her. "It's rather curious, they claim no nationality or clan affiliation whatsoever. Completely neutral! No division affiliation! They have all the latest gear and equipment, too. Brand-new custom designs. Can you imagine what kind of billionaire they'd need backing them? No one's talking of course - some marketing scheme, I suppose. Tacky, but effective. We know next to nothing about the racers either - they wear masks."

"Masks?" Sadao asked, getting up anyway with the aid of his cane. "What kind of masks?"

Gisette dried her hands on the dish rag and tossed it aside with a shrug. "All kinds from what I've heard - lucidore, Halloween, kabuki, various animals. There's even a Richard Nixon!"

"Americans?"

"That's just it, darling - we don't know. They entered the Rally minutes before the final deadline with all the right paperwork and a lot of fake names. They don't even have a team name! So we've decided to call them The Masked Marauders. They race in purple and grey camo colors. Atrocious. Whoever they are, they know how to work the system. The Chairs and Sponsors claim they don't know who's funding them, either, but I suspect some of them are lying. That ridiculous old Chairwoman Baker knows where they're from - I'm convinced of it! Maybe you can squeeze something out of him ... *her* ... like you did for your team charter back in the day."

"Let's not get into airing old laundry, Gisette. I'm retired from those sort of team negotiations. Besides, she's a hundred years old now. And I'm 'dead!'"

Gisette laughed and stepped forward. She put her hands on his face, stroking his beard, and kissed his mouth in a much more reserved manner than she had begun. "Thankfully not. I will let you know if I hear anything more. And I promise you, I will keep your secret. Sadao Koga will stay safely buried at sea."

Sadao hoped for once she was sincere.

"Smoke?! The fuck?! Do I have to pull your babysitter out of first grade to watch over you again?"

"Calm your fury. I had a guest."

"A guest?" Mouse asked, shutting the door and hanging up his coat. "Who?"

"Old friend. I guess she saw me that day down in Squamish. She's our mystery SUV driver, anyway."

"Wait a minute. *She?!*"

"A female human, yes."

"This human have a name?"

"Of course, Gisette."

"The French bitch from that awful tent dinner thing two years ago?"

Sadao leaned back against the couch. "Yes, the French woman from the awful tent dinner. I've known her for years."

Mouse set his hands on his hips. "I bet you have!"

"She's harmless."

"Is she? Do I have to go sniff the pillows? No wait, I'll sniff something else."

Sadao presented his chin for inspection. Mouse leaned over him and gave his beard a whiff. "Okay, you pass*snmff.*" Sadao grabbed him and smothered his mouth with a fervent kiss.

"Believe I'm loyal to you yet?"

Mouse eyed him. "I guess. You *smoked*, however. Nice one, blaming your 'friend' then trying to hide it with toothpaste."

"Damn," Sadao grumbled. "It was just one!"

Mouse rolled his eyes. "Sure."

Sadao pulled him down onto the couch and kissed him again, more thoroughly this time. "Shinjyu still busy?" he asked, giving Mouse's ass a squeeze.

"Yup, until 7 tonight. She wanted to have dinner in camp with her friends. Aki is bringing her home. First light tomorrow, I gotta leave - make sure Lupe didn't hit a log and dump everything ass over tea kettle in my garage!"

Sadao nodded toward the bedroom. "One for the road?"

"You're randy for someone who just spent his afternoon with a woman."

"I'm happy," Sadao said. "And I'd like to thank you for that. Properly."

Mouse grinned. "Lead the way, cowboy."

Naked, front to back, Sadao moved himself rhythmically inside Mouse's body. It was quiet - their heavy breathing and the thick sucking sound of their joined bodies disturbed the room's stillness. It was the good slow fuck they'd not had the chance to indulge in since becoming parents. A quickie in the shower or a frantic over-the-workbench afternoon lunch break was becoming the norm. It was nice to have the bed again; to take the time to find the right position so he could use his good leg to pump with some ease.

Mouse's ass was warm and relaxed, sending waves of rising pleasure between their fused bodies. Sadao licked and nibbled Mouse's tender neck, while his fist circled his cock, stroking smoothly.

"Engk!" Mouse squeaked. "I can't …"

"Shhh … you can," Sadao murmured in his ear. "You are. You don't have to do any-thing. Just feel me."

Mouse, he had come to delightfully discover, could be coaxed into an intense pro-longed orgasm if he stayed still and fluid in his arms. It was a challenge for Sadao to get Mouse to do anything he requested when out of bed, let alone in it. For a bottom, Mouse was a hard man to pin down, as evidenced by the squirming of his hips.

"Fuck! I cannn't…! Let me move. I - I need to move…"

Sadao tipped his chin up for a kiss. His tongue lept out to taste his but Sadao only sucked it softly. "We're not doing this your way."

"But…" Mouse tried to squirm out of his grasp so Sadao punished him by pausing his thrusts. He reached low and gave Mouse's balls a nice rub with his thumb. They were slick with impatient ooze. Mouse raised his adorable nose and moaned helplessly.

"Will you behave?" Sadao asked.

Mouse nodded furiously. His hair fell over his forehead and stuck to the line of sweat on his brow. "Please - ah! Oh God, God …"

Sadao moved again, holding Mouse's leg up over his hip as they fucked. The lever-age allowed him to pull his cock all the way out before sinking it slowly back in. He indulged himself in the feel of Mouse's asshole resisting his engorged head, then releas-ing under the pressure and sucking him up in hot slick muscle until his pearl buried itself deep down. Mouse's matching jewel intensified his excitement as it rolled slowly up and down his shaft.

"Uuugghhh…"

The moan was unearthly. His lover was passing the point of reasoning. Mouse's head tossed against the pillow, eyes shut tight while his ass and thighs shook uncontrollably in anticipation. He'd taken Mouse into a state where the body took over the mind's will. And still Sadao fucked him deep, slow, even.

"Uuuuuuuggghhhh…"

It was time. Sadao took Mouse's cock back in hand and worked it steadily, urging on his climax. Mouse arched his back and his ass opened up even more. Sadao felt like his balls might get sucked in too. There were times he wanted this man to swal-low him whole. The thought of their bodies merging somehow beyond their physical limitations brought him to the brink of orgasm. Sadao bit into Mouse's shoulder to hold himself back.

"Aaaaaaaaaagghhhhhhhhhhhh!"

Mouse's cry went on ragged and loud for a long time before the first pump of his dick shot into Sadao's fist. It came on sweet and thick, again and again. He gave in and thrusted into his own climax. Pleasure rushed through his veins as he freed Mouse's shoulder to give a shout of his own. He plunged full-in, surrendering to the pounding release, filling his lover up to the brim. "Ahh…!"

Long still moments passed with nothing but the sound of their breathing and wind in the pines outside. His jaw ached from biting into Mouse's flesh. He kissed Mouse's ear and watched himself slide out of his ass in a drizzle of white. He caught it with a small towel - cleaning up the worst of it - before gathering a boneless Mouse to his side. He wiped the cum from Mouse's abdomen and kissed his sweaty forehead.

"See what happens when you listen to me?"

Mouse's eyes fluttered but fell shut again when they failed to attain focus. "Mngha, gahnh…" Tongue didn't work yet, either.

"Here, roll to your side. Let me see your shoulder."

"Hmngh..?" Mouse rolled with a lot of help, clearly feeling no pain.

Sadao kissed his pale shoulder where the skin was dented and red, but not broken. "I lost control, too," he breathed into Mouse's ear. "You make me forget myself."

Sadao licked the wound smooth, then ran his nose along Mouse's shoulder and neck, inhaling deeply. "I love the smell of you after sex. The chemistry you release - I can't get enough of it. Mmn, on your arms too. Everywhere, a feast for my nose." Another advantage to fucking Mouse stupid was the lack of resistance once the main act was finished. Sadao lifted Mouse's arm and inhaled the musk gathered in the pale shock of curls underneath.

"Mmm, like wine."

Snap! The arm came back down, nearly severing his nose.

"Stop huffing my pits! Explain to me who this woman is to you. Is she a former friend, lover, what?" Mouse was determined to get answers, no matter how thoroughly he was fucked.

Sadao sighed and dropped his chin to Mouse's shoulder. "Both, I guess. But that's all in the past."

"How far in the past?"

"Far enough! I have no interest in fucking that woman, if that's what concerns you. She has nothing I want or need."

"There's something she wants from you, I bet. How the hell did she find you? We ditched that SUV miles back from the camp road. Did you invite her over for tea?"

"How would I invite her? Over our coded CB radio?"

"Yeah, on the booty call channel!"

"Oi! Can we return to the Gisette-free afterglow. I was enjoying that -!"

"Was she your girlfriend?"

"Of course not, she's married!"

"Mistress then?"

"Why does it matter?"

"Because she showed up at our front door unannounced after it took us two years, a sunken ship, a bag of ransom and a buttload of Mexican pirates to get your ass out of trouble last time! What if she goes to the police?"

Sadao rolled into his back. Hip pain was returning. "She won't."

"How do you know?"

"Because I know Gisette! She's shocked I'm alive and settled down with you. But she'll recover."

Mouse sat straight up. "Are you saying she's shocked to find out you're into dudes?"

"I was clan boss for eleven damn years - I was into everybody! Just not for very long. But not anymore. I made a choice, *Konezumi*. A promise. Every old hole I ever fucked could walk through that door and it wouldn't make me change my mind! We are a family! This is the life I want!"

Mouse hung his head. "Yeah, I know. I'm sorry. It just bugs me is all. And worries me - for your safety of course."

Sadao motioned Mouse back to his side and kissed his hair. "Believe me, trust me. All that matters to me are the ones who live under this roof. I will protect you both to my last breath. If she was any kind of threat, I would have run her through with my blade on sight."

"I wish you had. But ... you did fuck her once, right?"

Sadao groaned. "A hundred years ago, yes. Did you want a full account? Dates and locations? I am too tired to remember these things. They serve no purpose to me now."

"No it's okay. It's just ..."

"What? You're pouting. You need to tell me this thing that's troubling you."

Mouse looked up at him with big blue worried eyes. "Do you miss boobs?"

It was so unexpectedly adorable Sadao burst into laughter. "Not especially, no. Is that why you're worried? Because you lack certain endowments?"

Mouse reddened. "I guess that was a stupid question."

Sadao lifted his chin gently. "Look at me, *Konezumi*. I like *you*. I don't care what body you came in. Although, this one is very appealing."

Mouse sighed in relief. "Thank God."

Sadao kissed him - too sweet for words, this man. Mouse's arms wrapped around his neck and Sadao kept the kiss going until he felt the tension leave Mouse's shoulders.

"Gisette said something odd today - that I was fickle. But I don't believe that is the right word."

"I don't know what that's like. Sleeping with a woman, I mean," Mouse admitted. "I never did or wanted to really."

Sadao stroked his cheek. "I didn't know that."

"There weren't many women around when I was growing up. Those that were, were really old. I didn't feel like having sex with anyone until men started coming around the garage."

"How old were you when it finally happened?"

"Hm, you mean my first time? Sixteen. Fred was in town and this hunk of a tow truck driver stopped in for an oil change. But, I don't think we ever got around to that."

Sadao smiled. "Sixteen, huh? You must have been a catch. I wish it had been me. I'd have been so good to you - sweet young American boy, curious to know what it's all about. I'm envious of your towman."

"Hah, don't be. He wasn't all that. Asshead was 50 miles down the freeway before I woke up."

Sadao gave Mouse's buns a squeeze. "His loss. You have me beat, by the way. I was eighteen."

Mouse's eyes got bigger. "No way! But - you won that huge race when you were -"

"Seventeen, that's right."

"But you hadn't ... didn't you have fans?"

"Of course, but sex was not part of my game back then."

"Is that why you had so many lovers? Like a game?"

"No, not a game. *The* game. When you don't have money to throw around in this industry, a willing cock is prime advantage. I made good use of it."

"I guess," Mouse said glumly. "I didn't have that kind of advantage where I came from."

"Look," Sadao said, lifting his chin. "This isn't a contest. I don't want you to worry about my past. I did what I had to. What matters is, I don't have to live that way anymore. I don't want you to doubt yourself. I chose you for a reason."

Mouse relaxed and snuggled against his chest. "I'm glad you chose me, but I'll probably never understand why."

"Hm, how do I explain this to you?" Sadao said, stroking his back. "No one before that I knew intimately was trustworthy. They came to me because they wanted something from me. Or else I needed to get something from them. You are not like this in any way. You ask me for nothing."

Mouse giggled. "Really? I ask for your dick. A lot."

"That is understandable."

Mouse punched him and Sadao caught his fist and kissed it.

"The thought of you warms me through, *Konezumi*. You are a bright fire at the end of a long dark journey. All my hope and comforts lie in this bed we share."

Mouse's eyes brightened. "I like that answer," he said, rolling to his back and raising his arms up over his head. "You may snort me now to your content."

Sadao wasted no time taking advantage of his offer.

Steam rose from the bath and coated the windows as the light of the day faded behind the trees outside. Kei had radioed - Shinjyu had fallen asleep in the kids trailer. He asked if she could stay over with the boys. Mouse was glad. He was enjoying this unplanned evening of closeness with Sadao, and loathed to have it end before morning. He closed his eyes and relaxed into Sadao's arms. Sadao was seated behind him in the warm water, arranging his wet braids so they wouldn't drip into his eyes.

The only sound was a slow drip coming from the shower tap. Until Sadao made a sound in his throat that sounded like a private laugh.

Mouse opened his eyes and smiled. "What's funny?"

Sadao kissed his damp head. "Not so much funny, but ironic. I was thinking about how much a man's fortune can change so drastically."

"What's ironic about it?" Mouse asked, the heat of the water was making him pleasantly drowsy. He wanted Sadao to tell him one of his bizarre Japanese fables. "Does it involve bells?"

"No, not like that. I was thinking of the choices I made as a child and the choices I made as a man. How those decisions brought me to so many seemingly hopeless ends, that somehow didn't end but shifted and bloomed into something else unexpected."

"You'll have to use some proper nouns because I'm not quite following you."

"When I was a boy, I thought my life's path was very clear - study hard, please my father, become a teacher, marry and raise children on a small farm of my own with a house of white walls and a blue tiled roof."

"A teacher? Really? You?"

Sadao chuckled again. "It seemed a well lit path. I adore children, you know. And I loved teaching them, for a brief time."

"I can't picture you at the front of a classroom with chalk in hand wearing a white shirt and tie. Can't picture you with a fat country wife, either! That's where you grew up, right? In the country?"

"Yes, Toba. Seaside town. Very sheltered place. Famous for pearls," he said nostalgically, touching Mouse's ear cuff.

"I love it when you tell me about the pearl farms and your island. Sounded so beautiful. Wish I could have seen it."

"I wish you could have too. I wish I could take you back to that time before the war to watch the fishing boats sail out into the bay from the top of the tsunami wall. But it's all gone, I've been told. Burned to the ground, they say. I got out before the worst of it. I'm grateful for that. My memories of my birth town are unscathed. I didn't ever want to leave.

"Yet, my choice to leave Toba and teach school up in Ise in my early teens was the choice that kept me alive. I chose to desert the army when war came, and then I chose to escape to America on a boat. Soon after I also chose to become a racer - a good one. And lastly, I chose to become a team boss…"

"And then you chose to kidnap me!"

"Yes, fatal decision, that one."

Mouse nipped his arm in disapproval.

"Why do you always hurt me?!"

"Only when you deserve it. Which is often!"

Sadao took a breath and drew Mouse a little closer. "When I was in prison I had a lot of time to think. For the first time in my life there were no choices to make. No distractions. I thought my cell was a final one. I did not imagine an escape. Being alone with myself I was forced to consider the whole sum of my life - and the thought of it was not comforting. I realised I had many regrets."

"Regrets how?"

"Leaving you behind for certain. I felt that I had betrayed your faith in me by not informing you of our plans during the Overland. The outcome was not as I expected, either."

"Did you expect to escape to Canada with the others?" Mouse asked, a little confused.

"I expected to die. But that was not the ending fate had for me."

Mouse didn't know how to answer, except to give Sadao's arm a reassuring squeeze. He didn't want him to flash back to his near-death experience again.

"In many ways, you and Shinjyu have cleared my conscience of those regrets. The largest one being that I'd never quite made it to that valley farm with the blue tiled roof."

"Am I your fat country wife?" Mouse laughed.

"Yes," Sadao said with a kiss. "But not one who wears aprons and plants rice, thankfully."

"I'm glad we managed to find a way to have a child…" Mouse said, looking up at Sadao. His gaze was at the far window, the one that faced toward camp. Concern narrowed his brow.

"Alright, let me dry off and I'll go down the hill and pick up Sleeping Beauty for you."

Sadao's face brightened. "Will you?"

"Sure, Papa. Whatever will put that stupid grin back on your face is worth losing a little extra private time for." Mouse said, kissing his cheek.

"Thank you. I feel uneasy when she's not here."

"Just give me one last good smooch and I'll be off."

"Simple enough request," Sadao said and leaned in to deliver.

Shinjyu was wide awake and restless by the time Mouse woke her and carried her back up the hill to the cabin.

"I'm hungry!" she demanded as soon as they got in the door.

"I want a bath!" she declared soon after finishing her crackers, milk and cheese.

"I want bedtime stories!" she announced after Sadao got her bathed, dried and in her nightgown while Mouse cleaned her plates and the crumb-covered table.

She certainly thrives on our attention, Mouse mused, as he watched her crawl across the couch to Sadao as he flipped through a pile of her books.

"Boo!" she said, coming up under his arms.

"Boo to you too!" he said with a laugh. All the light was back in his eyes now that she was home. "How about *Ranger Bob and the Big Bear?*"

"That one's dumb!" Shinjyu proclaimed, fussing with one of Sadao's shirt buttons. She didn't look sleepy in the least.

Sadao yawned. "Very well, how about - "

"How come you smoke?" she asked abruptly. Although Mouse had opened a kitchen window to air the place out, the room still smelled slightly of Sadao's earlier "social" cigarette.

Sadao didn't miss a beat. "Because I was a naughty kid. I didn't listen to my parents. Now it's a habit. It's hard to break a habit, but I'm trying," he said with a glance toward Mouse.

She got his top button open and was now trying to push it back in, with her tongue sticking out the side of her mouth in concentration. "I know you were bad and smoked today because I wasn't with you."

"I'm sorry, hime. I was wrong. It wasn't your fault. I'll try harder not to."

"But Kei-Sensei says smoking can make you sick. I don't want you to get sick, Touchan. 'cause I'm little and if you get sick I can't pick you up and put you in bed and give you chicken soup."

Sadao turned his face away from them both and took a couple hard breaths. He held his eyes shut a moment, then gave her a hug so fierce she squeaked.

"Touuuchan, you're squishing me!"

"Sorry, hime," he said softly, loosening his grip. He took both her hands in his so she'd look up at him. "I want to make a promise to you."

She smiled. "A pinky promise?"

Sadao nodded. "Yes, a pinky promise."

She held up her tiny finger and he linked it in his. "I promise you and Mouse that I will never touch another cigarette again for the rest of my life. And my lives beyond this life."

Shinjyu giggled and shook his finger vigorously. "Cool! Let's play fishies!" she said, jumping out of his lap and heading for her treasure chest to grab her pail of wooden fish.

"Pinky promise, huh? I guess I didn't try that," Mouse said, coming over.

"Where's that damn vaporizer of yours?" Sadao mumbled, wiping a tear from his cheek.

"Oh, the 'toy'?"

"Yes, the toy," he grumbled. "I've decided that it's about time I grew up."

It was another hour of tickles and pillow fights before they managed to wear Shinjyu out enough for her to fall asleep between them in the big bed.

So much for her princess bed … Mouse thought sleepily as his eyes drooped closed over the view of his lover and their child curled up next to him asleep. The glow of the fire danced over their cheeks.

It's gonna really suck heading down to Squamish tomorrow without them, Mouse thought. He couldn't remember a time when he'd felt more complete. His heart hurt to think they'd be apart for over a week.

God? Can you spare an angel or two to keep an eye out for them? This cabin is sorta far from the others staying behind down by the lake. And my pig-headed husband won't budge. So I'd really appreciate it if you'd keep them extra safe for me. They're my whole world, you know. I don't care about anything else. So do me a solid, okay?

Oh, and uh, say hi to Uncle Fred and my Dad. Tell them they did me right. I know compared to some I had a pretty rough start, but if I'm good enough to belong to Sadao and Shinjyu, then I'm thinking those ol' boys knew what they were doing raising me up. And I'll do the same for our little lost princess here, I promise! And… if Shiratori is up there too, somewhere, in a tea garden yelling at people in robes, tell him thanks from me too. I know he can kinda be a dick, but we wouldn't be here without him. He took a bullet for all of us. A bunch of them. Give him a shiny cloud bike with wings or something.

Mouse yawned loudly.

He'd like that.

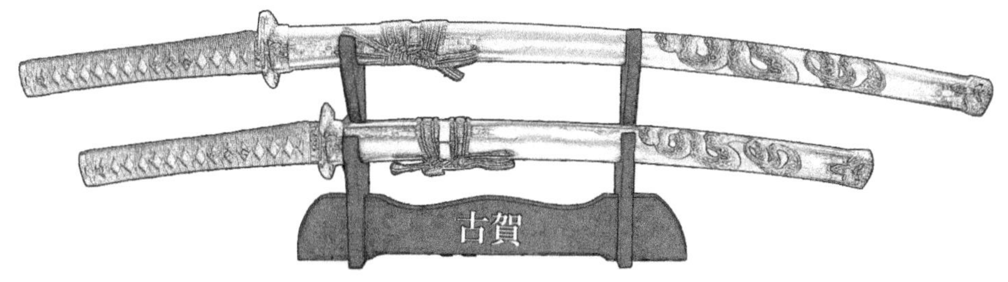

Chapter XVII

Lies Unspoken

The next morning Mouse rose before dawn, dressed and shook Sadao awake briefly next to their sleeping child to give him a kiss goodbye and a lecture.

"There's toast and eggs for breakfast if you want to make them. Shinjyu needs to be at school 9 A.M. sharp every day or Kei gets pissy. Don't forget to brush her hair! It takes a while. She doesn't like it pulled. Her clothes just came back from laundry but they're still in the bag and will need folded. Dinner … fuck it, eat at mess. Cook-san is coming to Squamish but his sous chef is staying behind for minified camp service. He's lazy as fuck so that means no sunrise morning coffee service or breakfast beyond sticky oatmeal. I don't recommend it. You'll have to make your own tea and wash out that kettle and dry it so it doesn't rust! Wipe the floor after the bath, okay? We don't want mold. And run the pump before bed so the pipes don't freeze. Don't get into any trouble while I'm away, okay? And for fuck's sake, don't smoke! Babe…? Did you get all of that? Sadao?"

Sadao pulled the pillow over his head. "Please leave…"

Sadao did haul his ass out of bed some hours later and somehow, dragged a sleepy Shinjyu up into a sitting position. As it appeared sleepy girls lacked bones; it was struggle enough to get her boots on over her pajama bottoms, her tangled hair stuffed in a cap, and a sweater and coat pulled over her shoulders. He limped her down the hill with a banana to school by 9:23 A.M., which earned him a daddy-fail scowl from Kei.

After a miserable breakfast of oatmeal glue and ice-cold tea, Sadao shivered over to Tagata's cabin in the wind to have a last minute chat before the team Boss moved down the mountain to Squamish.

"You know when they inked me, I didn't get a leather strap between my teeth."

Tagata laid on his stomach on the rug in front of his lit cabin hearth, grimacing through the pain. A double row of tiny ink-dipped needles at the end of a long bamboo stylus was being pounded into his skin with razor sharp precision.

Despite his advanced arthritis, Sensei, with Michi acting as his assistant, was laying

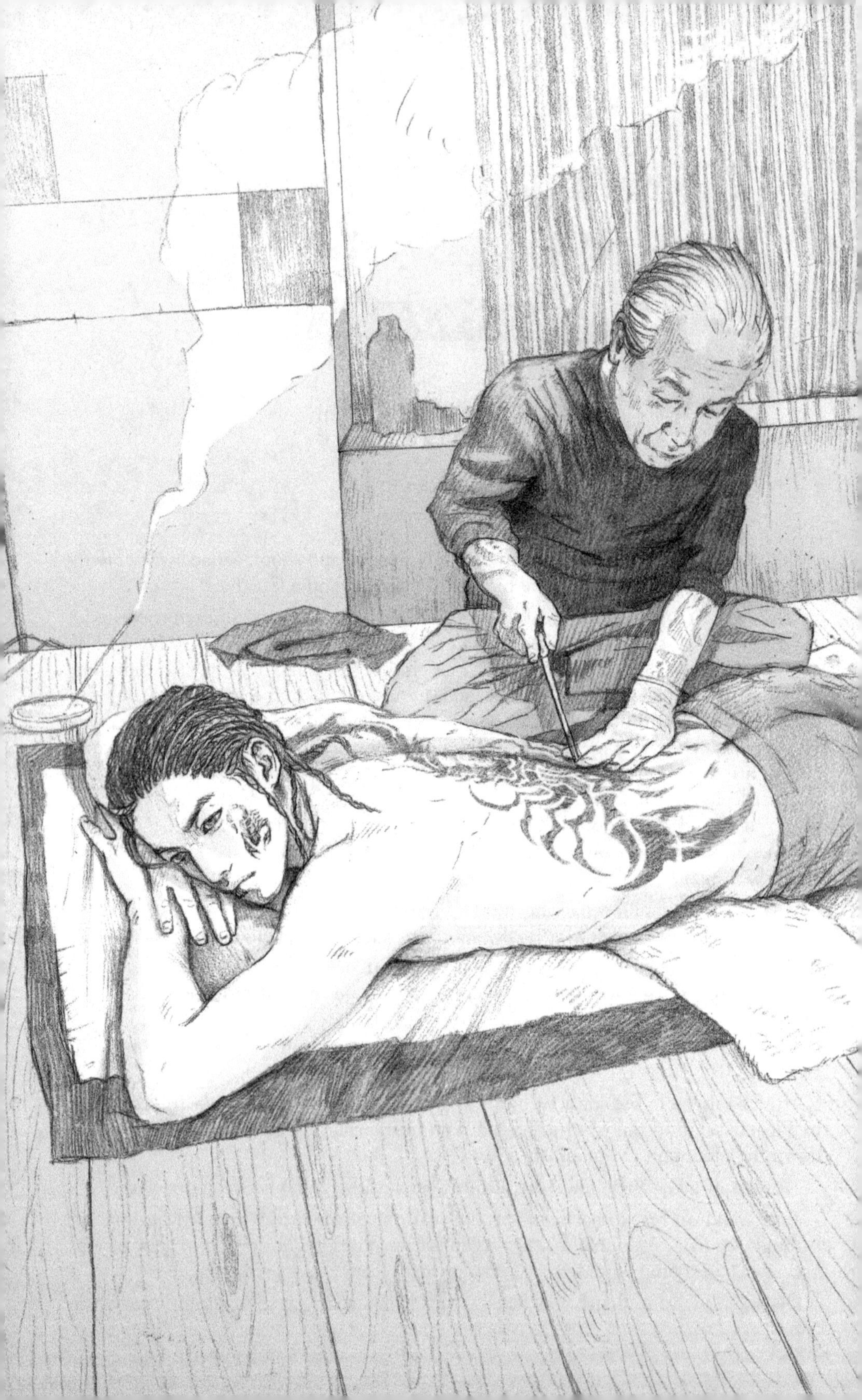

in the color now - the reds and blues that accented Tagata's primarily black-shelled sasori. The design was impressive - a fierce sinuous scorpion descended down Tagata's back, head up and claws out. The stinger wrapped around his left shoulder ending in a deadly point over his chest as was traditional.

Few in camp knew of Sensei's hidden talent. He was former yakuza, born to a Kansai clan 60 years before the start of the civil war. He had been trained in the ancient art of *tebori* by his father, who would later die of a heart attack in his 40s. As the story went, Sensei altered his career path, rolled down his tattooed sleeves and left Kyoto and gang life to attend medical school in 1990s Tokyo. But now, a hundred some-odd years later, his craggy hands still balanced the bamboo *nomi* on his outstretched left thumb as his right hand jabbed the needles in rhythm to Tagata's grunts.

"Dekinai darou?"

"Ppblt. Urusai zo!" Sadao's former captain spit out the strap and gave Sadao a rare flash of anger that matched his pain. *"Don't talk if all you have to say is biting words! I am in enough pain as it is!"*

"You should have opted to take the gun. Much faster and only half the agony."

"I don't cheat!" Tagata spat. *"Pain is necessary for this transformation!"*

"Omaetachi, damarinasai!" Sensei hushed them as if they were children. He dipped his needles in the red ink well held ready by Michi and resumed stabbing the hell out of Tagata's lower back.

Sadao grinned in pure enjoyment. His inking under Sensei's patient hands over a decade earlier hadn't been any easier on him. Not with Shiratori standing over him, relishing his misery. The Whitebird Boss had been first to decorate his flesh in such a manner when he was awarded his own team the same season as Sadao. He'd envied it - the blind shrieking white eagle, talons out, diving in to kill. He wanted a body tattoo of his own immediately - a bigger, more complex one. He chose the Orochi of legend - a serpent of many heads and tails requiring a million needle-stabs in his skin. The pain and swelling had gotten so bad, they'd kept a bucket near his head for the retching nausea it had brought on. He could still remember Shiratori's cackling, ringing in his ears each time they had to stop and wait for him to dry-heave.

"Payback's a bitch," Sadao said, knocking back a cup of warmed sake. "Be glad our fallen comrade isn't here to toss snide comments at your misery as he was for me. I'm being much kinder. Look, I'll pour you another cup."

"Sensei, chotto matte kudasai," Sadao said, asking the kind doctor to pause his torture long enough for Tagata to drink.

Sadao held the cup out to his lips and Tagata swallowed it in one gulp. "Ah-! You'll get me drunk!"

"Be glad you can get drunk. I couldn't keep anything down for more than a minute through my ordeal!"

"I have Rally to start tomorrow. Must rise early. Be sharp-headed!"

"Then I suggest you hold back on the coloring until after the event. You still have many hours to go. You'll need sleep. If you can sleep."

Tagata sat up while Michi cooled his bleeding skin with ice-filled gauze. *"I wanted to finish irezumi before our competition but it has taken longer than I planned."*

"I won't tell anyone," Sadao said, smiling. *"Unless you plan to lead your men naked. Which I don't recommend. It's hovering around 10 this week in Squamish. With a storm front moving in."*

"Your jokes are not funny," he spat, reaching for a cigarette.

Sadao laughed - it was amusing to see Tagata so out of his normal composure as to tell him in plain Japanese to essentially fuck off! The click of the lighter and crisp burn of cigarette paper set his mouth watering. With reluctance, he reached into his coat pocket for the thing Mouse had bought him.

"Omocha ka?" Tagata asked as Sadao flicked the glass cigarette's switch to on and puffed cautiously at the vaporous tip.

Ugh, it tasted like candy. "No, it's not a toy!" he snapped, wiping the vapor from his nose. "Something Mouse got me so I'll stay faithful to doctor's orders - more or less." Sensei mumbled in agreement; he wasn't thrilled with Sadao's solution but accepting of the trade-off for now.

"Tabako wo yame nakucha ikenaino?" Tagata asked, doubtful as he inhaled his cigarette that Sadao ever intended to really quit for good.

"Have to quit if I want to keep the leg. Which is impossible, if I'm going to keep company with you, so … 'toy' it is."

Tagata laughed and immediately regretted it as the resulting pain shot across the tormented flesh of his back. "Fuck!"

"Seeing as we're both equally miserable, let me distract you with some news. As you know, I had a visit from an old friend yesterday."

"Yes, your friend should not come onto Sasori property without proper clearance," Tagata said, pointing at Sadao with his smoke. "She is lucky she is not dead!"

"She didn't know. She was looking for me, however. She caught sight of us in town last month and tried to chase Mouse's Jeep up the mountain. Who knows how long she searched but she got lucky." The sickly sweet taste aside, Sadao did recognize the satisfying sensation of nicotine hitting his brain. *Not bad. I might survive this and keep my promises if I can get Tagata to stop laughing and Mouse to buy a flavor with less pink on the label!*

"I keep men watching highway for many weeks. No sign of white SUV until yesterday. None! And she come right to hidden exit!"

"She's not a threat to us, Taga. She's one of my oldest friends."

"How could she be so accurate?"

"Women's intuition. She's a bloodhound when it comes to locating me."

"This bloodhound woman cost me many bullets! How does she find you? How?" Tagata's anger was more directed at himself for letting one slip through their finely masked turnoff.

"Don't worry - I have asked her to say nothing and to not return this way. If she wants to reach me, she can use the long range channel." Tagata eyed Sadao with disapproval. It was clear this breach of security picked a deep bone with him. "I gave her her own access code," he explained. "Only myself and your chief operator will understand it."

"She must be important woman to Sadao-sama. *Gomennasai* for my misunderstanding."

"She's assisted me countless times in the past. And on this visit, she gave me some very interesting information."

Sadao relayed the circumstances of the new masked team scheduled to appear in the competitions sight unseen. This did nothing to brighten Tagata's mood.

"How do we know their reputation? Their skill? Their weakness? This is very bad news!"

"Easy, Taga. Not all competitions can be anticipated. Not all enemies can be predicted. You've trained your men very well. Your roster choice is expertly designed. There is no more planning to be done - your men know how to compete. Masks will not block them from their victories. They will fight for every win."

"But this woman say to you they have new equipment! Custom made. Mouse has worked very hard with snowbikes, but it can not be as good as this!"

Sadao gripped Tagata's undecorated shoulder. "You have worked very hard. Trust your men. And most importantly, trust your mechanic! You have the best."

The teachings of the way of the sword always began with the draw. With his bare feet planted firmly on the cold polished floor of the longhouse, Sadao gripped the katana's sheath in his left hand with the covered blade pointed upward. He focused on his breathing until his mind was quiet. In his head he heard his sensei from childhood yell, *"Nuke!"* Sadao drew straight out, as if to knock an opponent senseless in the gut with the hilt's end cap. A swing of his arm and wrist completed the move with a lateral cut, swift enough to slice through the belly and disembowel the enemy in under a second.

The honed blade sang and swished through the cold air of the longhouse. Smooth and fluid in his hands, Sadao worked his ancient weapon through the routine he'd first learned atop a mountain terrace at the age of 12 with a wooden bokken in his unscarred hands.

Methodically and trusting to muscle memory, he performed the *Hachi kata* - mastery of the eight ways. One move for each mark of the compass - a lunge, a strike, then a sharp pivot and retreat. *Shomen'uchi*, a downward cut to the head - Swish! *Yokomen'uchi*, a downward cut to the side of the head - Shling! His arms swung high for the overhead strike and following its deadly path, braced himself and dipped for the guard. At the end of each cycle - the blade was returned to the scabbard bound to his hip for a satisfying click and bow. His old masters' voices sang in his ears-

The sword that saves man also kills man.

The katana is a tool of death.

To master a sword is to be at peace with death.

To have no fear of what lies beyond this world.

To die and to be reborn again is the way of the warrior.

Do not resist its path.

As Sadao guided the blade's spirit through its practiced pitches, cuts and swings, visions of the Overland ceremonial stage passed through Sadao's focused mind - the gunshots, the screams, the way the katana had felt in his hand as the blade cut through Marcus Getty's thick neck. Blind Reverse Strike - his partner in the act had known instinctively how to stand without the use of his mechanical arms so Sadao could perform the cross step, draw and lateral strike as easily as if they were knocking a melon from a post.

"We must rely on the will of the blade," Shiratori had said, sharpening his Whitebird engraved sword on a diamond hone that final night together in his trailer. He insisted his ancestral katana be the weapon used to defeat their enemy - even if it would not be drawn by his own hand. *"I will be asked to remove my limbs before I reach the stage,"* he said pointedly, drawing the shimmering steel through a soft cloth to bring its cut to a high shine. *"I can not wield it. This I trust you only to do."*

He held the naked razor's edge out to Sadao for him to grasp. He could remember the bite of it even now as his grip embraced the wrapped leather hilt of his father's katana. The steel was sharp and warm in his hand. One slight move from Shiratori and his fingers would have dropped to the floor.

"Our minds are one," he'd said as they knelt in prayer at the small altar in Shiratori's trailer. *"Our wills are one. We are committed to take this life in exchange for our own. I ask my ancestors to guide the blade in your hand as if it were my own."*

Sadao released the blade and bowed deeply to the man he swore to share his last battle with.

"Do you still fear death?"

The whispered voice broke the flow of Sadao's movements. He lost his balance on his weak leg, and dropped the katana to the floor. He came down hard on his mangled hip - sending rockets of pain shooting up his spine.

"Aagh!"

With his back to the cold floor, Sadao's breath raked hard through his chest. Stars flew past his eyes. The muscles of his upper body and thighs shook from the effort he'd been exerting on a frame grown soft from lack of training. The leg had moved for him but the pain of it now that he was out of trance was unspeakable. The impacted hip joint throbbed nauseatingly - bile threatened to rise in his throat.

Sadao struggled to sit up, cursing through his agony and failure. The voice had been unexpected.

I'm hallucinating.

The glare of the track lighting shone brilliantly off of the waxed chrome and white airbrushed feathers of the cruiser parked in splendor upon the altar. The smoke from the incense he had lit coalesced into the shape of a helmeted man astride the empty seat with ghostly hands reaching for the handlebars. Sadao rubbed the sweat from his eyes.

"Kyouji?"

He rose awkwardly and limped to the base of the altar, clearing the phantom smoke with a wave of his hand. The spectre vanished into the bitter air.

I'm pushing too hard.

The deep meditation of his workout must have unlocked a long buried question in his mind. Did he fear death? Followers of *bushido* were steadfast in their belief of endless life - one world after another and therefore, had freed themselves of the fear of failing flesh. You could not achieve the highest honors of sword mastery without accepting mortality.

Sadao clenched his teeth and forced his hip to allow him to kneel at the cushioned base of the altar. He shut his eyes, and focused on the place deep in his heart that was burdened with so much doubt he rarely acknowledged it. He breathed slowly and allowed visions to flow through his mind unhindered. In them he saw Shinjyu's smiling face, laughing; felt Mouse's lips on his own whispering devotion; Tagata vowing to keep his men safe and to honor his legacy; the distant faces of his young twin cousins, running to him and knocking him over with kisses; his mother in her pink and red sakura kimono, taking his hand and leading him to their island home; the faces of his older brothers and their wives and small children, drinking sake together around a low table, his father's deeply folded eyes gazing down upon them in approval.

"I do not fear death for them," he asserted to the empty room. "I would die for any of them."

Still the visions came - he kept his focus on his breath to let them come. Deeper into his mind he reached for the visions he most wanted to keep buried - black velvet curtains, Mouse's sweet face twisted in grief, his arms covered in blood, shouting his name; Shiratori standing beside him in glimmering golden armor, reaching down to take his hand and lift him away from the unspeakable pain; the bridge he had walked upon with many others, stretching for miles into an ever growing mist. There was a weight on his back - the pack he had carried down the mountain paths of Toba with his father's paired swords, struggling to keep up with Shiratori's effortless steps along the bamboo planks.

"Wait! I can't move as fast!" Sadao said, aloud.

Shiratori turned to look back at him through the mists. *"Why must you cling to these metaphors? They serve no purpose here. Let your burdens go…"*

The bridge melted under him into the vision of a burned and destroyed house. He struggled through the rubble of fallen shoji frames and blackened tatami, burnt scrolls and books, crunching under his steps. Charred fabric lay across the floor. Inside the tattered folds were bodies burned beyond recognition, twisted and broken - their bones exposed and lying in unnatural poses. Smoke rose sickly from their empty eye sockets. *Okaasan? Otousan?*

I don't want to see this! Don't show me this!

Against his will, he pressed on past the rooms of the dead until he came to a place with cool tiles under his feet. Steam billowed from a lit doorway. He pushed it open and entered. Inside was an old ofero, covered and intact. He reached for the bamboo lid and slid it aside.

The ofero water boiled with the stench of cooked rotting flesh. The naked body of a small body floated among the bubbles - swollen and blistered. It rolled in the boils until the face was exposed. It was the boy who had stolen his shoes - pale eyes open and bloody skin peeling from his sallow face. The hilt of his father's wakizashi remained buried in his throat. The boy looked at Sadao with bloody eyes and moved his mouth, trying to speak but the blade blocked his voice. Sadao reached for it and pulled on the hilt as the exposed metal burned his hands. He tugged harder, and the body rose with the blade, dripping, jostling the steaming water, making it overflow as he tried to shake the hilt loose. The movement caused another, larger body to rise to the surface. Mouse's corpse bobbed up on its side, face half burned away, his blue eye was boiled white by the water. Beside him, facedown, floated the smallest body of the three with long black hair trailing in the water, revealing the tattooed kanji for Orochi on its seared skull.

"Chigau!" Sadao cried out, snapping back into consciousness. He was shivering in the cold. His breath was coursing out of his lungs in clouds. He lifted his stiff leg and got to his unsteady feet, kicking the incense bowl over with a curse. It clattered to the floor, dumping a cloud of ash. "I don't accept these visions of death! This does not bring me peace! Go back to the mists! You're wasting your spirit on me, Shiratori-san!"

Did you forget about him, Sadao? The little boy with your shoes?

Was this his own mind's voice? Or another's?

"He died at sea," Sadao said to the empty room. "With Yasuo."

Is that the lie you still tell?

Then in his right ear, clear as a bell, Shiratori's voice spoke, *"Nuke zo!"*

The crack of the main door exploding inward killed the electric lights in the room. Sadao dove ahead of the flying splintered wood and rolled to the spot his katana had fallen. He took it in hand and crouched as the roar of motorcycle engines burst into the room in a cloud of exhaust. The headlamps blinded his eyes as Sadao instinctively drew back to put the wall behind him.

It's a raid!

Rubber wheels spun on the polished floor as five dirtbikes quickly filled the space. There was shouting in Japanese. *"I have him cornered! Get the bike off the stand! Seize the wall weapons! All will be returned to their rightful place with us!"*

Sadao's katana flashed in the xeon beams as he kept his guard. *"Who are you?! Why are you desecrating this shrine?"* As his eyes adjusted in the riot of lights, Sadao realized all of the raiders were wearing Halloween masks.

The one who was shouting orders to remove the room's displays dismounted his bike, drew a handgun, and pointed it directly at Sadao's head as he stepped toward him. Behind him one of his men had managed to short-wire the Whitebird cruiser's starter. The old engine cleared its throat and bellowed as the headlamp lit up.

"These are sacred artifacts!" Sadao shouted under the shadow of the gun. *"All who touch them and remove them from this shrine will be at the mercy of the Gods!"*

"Do you at last believe in Shinto, Sadao?" the man with the gun asked. With his eyes now adjusting, Sadao recognized the rubber visage of the 37th President of the United States.

"Who are you?" Sadao shouted, stepping forward. The gun went off and Sadao ducked. The bullet whizzed past his left temple, grazing it and struck the wall behind him, halting his steps.

"The next step you take will be your last, bakayaro!" the assailant shouted. There was an odd metallic ring to his voice. It seemed familiar, yet Sadao could not place it. Blood ran into his eyes from the cut on his forehead. He wiped it away to see the walls around him were nearly bared. The brilliant white light of Shiratori's cruiser cleared the room and rode out ahead of the pack into the snowy forest.

"There is a lot of hatred in your voice. It is familiar to me. Identify yourself!"

"I have a gift for you," Nixon said, ripping a small sack from his waist and throwing it at Sadao's gut. It bounced off of him and hit the floor. The gunman backed away now and remounted his bike. *"Everyone out!"*

The bikes throttled up with Shiratori's stolen weapons strapped to their backs and the leader took one final spin around the room before wheeling close to Sadao's side. He pointed his gun at his forehead.

"Kingoe says 'Hello'!"

The bike's rear wheel spun before it caught on the polished floor and the marauders raced off into the shadows of the pines.

Heart racing and dazed, Sadao poked at the sack that was left behind with his sword. It contained some objects. With a flick of his blade, the sack was torn open and the contents tumbled out onto the floor into the altar's remaining candlelight. It was a pair of old, cracked filthy leather shoes. The heels were worn smooth with holes at the toes where a child's foot had once grown through it and had been held on with twine.

The memory struck Sadao like a wave of cold steel.

See Onisan? I have your leather shoes! See how well they fit?

Interlude II

2049 - 2071

Fifth

Fresh Blood

Gastown District, San Diego, California - 2049

"Give those back! Hey! Stop! Thief! Thief!"

Sadao ran down the potholed street, turned a corner and ducked into a shaded alley full of loose tin siding and cardboard. He ducked down behind a garbage can and waited for the shop manager and his clerk to dash past, yelling all the various ways they were going to cook him slowly over a fire pit.

Not today, he thought, zipping his jacket up higher around his catch. He waited a few minutes until he could no longer hear the men shouting and snuck out. He ran back the way he came, taking an opposite turn to head for the faded green of the old Gaslight District's waterfront park. Here, between the dock rails and the bare trees, he found his doorway of sorts and slipped into a loosely grouped arrangement of army surplus nets, firepits and canvas. Just as he did, he was grabbed from behind by the collar and shaken until his oranges spilled out from under his jacket onto the ground.

Sadao spun and took a swing at the unexpected invader. But his arms were too short to make contact with the chest of the very tall man who'd caught him.

"Stop struggling. I'm not here to arrest you for stealing," the man said. Sadao looked up at him, breathing hard. He was a white man, mid-thirties, built like a tank and wearing a racing jacket.

"I don't steal!" Sadao corrected him, trying to shake himself loose. "I worked for them hauling trash and they didn't pay me."

The man let Sadao go so he could take a step back to look up at him.

"You sure you're a grocer? You reek of fish."

Sadao straightened his jacket and shook out his sleeves, insulted. "I do not!"

"Let me see your hands," the man said, making a grab for Sadao's wrist. Sadao tried to step back but the huge man's reach was impressive. He was hauled forward and his wrist turned to expose his palm. "As I thought - dock worker, more like. You have the rope burn marks to prove it.”

Sadao wrenched his hand free and bent to pick up his fruit. “What the fuck do you want? Oranges? I don’t give blow jobs, so if you’re here for sex, go fuck yourself!”

The man laughed at this and bent to help Sadao gather his spill. “I’m not here for any of that. Some friends of yours recommended I hang around and wait for you to show up. They said you spoke excellent English and they were right.”

“What do you want my English for? Plenty of people around here speak it. Better than me.”

“Have you heard of the Northwest Racing Division?” the man asked, pointing to the logo on his cap.

Sadao shrugged as he stuffed the last of the fruit back into his jacket, as well as the ones picked up by his guest. “I guess.”

“You watch the races?” he offered.

“Sure, on my ‘air’ television. What the fuck do you want? I need to deliver these.”

“Don’t let me stop you,” the man said, stepping aside. He proceeded to follow Sadao around as he meandered through the refugee camp, depositing an unexpected orange gift into the grubby hands or tent flaps of his fellow residents. When he was done, he crouched down to run his hands in a public fountain that ran in cascades along the north end of the park.

“Are you going to follow me around all day?” Sadao asked, tearing the peel off the one orange he left for himself with dripping fingers. He took a bite of the exposed flesh as he eyed the man.

“You look hungry.”

Sadao chewed and swallowed, taking another big bite of juicy flesh. “Get to your point or get the fuck away from me. You don’t belong here.”

“All right, all right. I just needed to check you out a bit first. See if you had it all together. Some of these people around here are missing a few marbles, if you know what I mean. I’m a recruiter. I’m looking for able-bodied men between the ages of 16 and 18. I’m guessing you’re somewhere in that range?”

Sadao shrugged. “Recruiting what, bookies? I don’t do that kind of shit, either. I work for a living.”

The man grinned down at him, clearly amused. “We have charters to build a new series of teams in the Southwestern states - Arizona, New Mexico areas. We need good solid young men willing to work hard and drive hard. I’m inviting you to a recruit-ment party. Some of your neighbors are already there: TJ, Little Fry, Boka ... ”

Sadao stuffed the last of the orange pieces into his mouth and spit a seed on the ground. The guy was right - he hadn’t seen any of those boys around on his orange calls. “I don’t have any racing experience. Never even driven a car. Don’t know what you think you’d get out of me,” he said, splashing water on his face to wash off the juice.

"We train our men. It's better if you've never driven before, in fact. This way we teach you to do it right. All the job requires is strength, cunning and a fierce heart, which you seem to have in spades," the man said, handing him a card.

Sadao stood up and took it. "I'd expect to be paid every Friday, in cash. Or I'll collect the wages myself," Sadao said, slipping the card in his pocket.

"Of course."

"When's this event?"

"It's going on right now until sunrise tomorrow. I can take you."

"I'm not getting in a car with you. I'm not that stupid. I'll come in my own time."

The man nodded. "Suit yourself Mr. …?"

"Koga."

He man dipped his head. "Mr. Koga. I hope you will grace us with your presence soon." And with that he walked away back toward the waterfront.

Sadao slid the card out, it had the recruiter's name and number and an uptown address. Maybe it was worth a look.

The walk uptown took about 20 minutes. Sadao stuck to the shadows of the abandoned condo towers until the right block came into view. There was a large tent pitched across a vacant lot next to the neighborhood clinic. There were a number of young men hanging around, eating grilled bacon dogs and drinking beer. His mouth watered - it smelled delicious. The Northwest Division logo was flying between two posts. It looked like a block party but without all the heroin addicts.

Sadao jogged across the street and went up to the guy at the gate and showed him the recruiter's business card. He was waved toward a line of tables where they took down his name and gave him a number and a couple tickets for food.

"Sadao! Over here, yo!"

It was TJ and a few of the boys from the park. Sadao joined them and was soon squeezing ketchup over a fat steaming dog with a cup of beer in his hand.

"Ain't this the shit, man?" TJ said. "They gonna send us to fucking New Mexico, give us fancy bikes and bitches and shit. We gonna be on one of those racing channels! Pussy-heaven!"

"Is that what they told you?" Sadao asked, chewing his bacon-draped dog, wondering idly if it was drugged. Either way, he intended to eat it.

"Hell, yeah. We've got our badges and everything!" TJ was visibly drunk and not making a lot of sense.

"Badges?"

"You don't got a badge yet?" he asked, flapping a stamped metal tag that hung from his neck. "Did you pass the exam?"

Sadao swallowed a mouthful of beer. "No, I just got here. Exam? What kind? Math?"

TJ laughed. "You know for an Asian, you sure are fucking stupid. Medical exam, genius. They want to make sure you don't got AIDS or ass worms first. They'll call your name, make you bend over and cough, all that shit!"

That explained the clinic. Just then a trio of dudes strolled out of the clinic doors, flapping yellow slips and hooting in excitement. The intercom scratched to life, calling out a series of numbers. Sadao's was among them.

"Hurry your ass, bitch. And don't show them that rash on your balls!"

Sadao killed his beer and flipped off TJ and the boys as he tossed the empty cup in the trash. He hustled up to the doors and handed his number to a clinic nurse. She led him and five others into a locker room with showers. They were to strip, clean up, grab a towel and wait along a line of benches outside for their appointment.

Sadao sat in a towel watching his hair drip on the floor between his bare feet for an annoying amount of time until a door opened and his name was called by a nurse.

"Sa-day-o? Koga?" she read, squinting.

"It's pronounced *sah-dow*," he corrected, annoyed.

"Okay, Mr. Koga," she said pertly. "Dr. Hawthorn will see you now."

"About fucking time," he muttered under his breath as he walked passed her into the exam room.

The doctor was waiting inside, taking notes on a clipboard bursting with papers. He looked to be in his mid-thirties, sandy-haired with wirerims. He glanced up as Sadao hopped up on the table in his towel, swinging his legs.

"Hullo, Mr. uh.. Koga, is it? I promise this won't hurt too much."

"Good, because I only had time for one beer," Sadao said, sitting up straight as the doctor swiveled over to feel up his chest and throat glands. His fingers were cold.

"I'd like to get a quick medical history from you if I can, Mr. Koga."

"What do you want to know? I'm as healthy as anyone around here."

"You live in the camps?" he asked, taking Sadao's pulse and looking at his watch.

"Yes."

"Do you smoke?"

"Yes."

"How much?"

"A few, when I can get them."

"Do you drink?"

"Yes, same deal.

"Drugs?"

"No. Not into that shit."

"Good," the doctor said, thumping his chest. "Okay, lie down for me, please."

Sadao scooted back and the doctor got up from his stool to hover over him. "Open the towel, please."

"What? Fuck no!"

The doctor sighed. "It's a general health check, Mr. Koga. I've seen a hundred naked men today. You won't surprise me."

"Like hell," he said, but untucked his towel anyway as the doctor snapped on gloves and proceeded to push his limp dick around and squeeze his balls.

"Are you sexually active, Mr. Koga?"

"No."

The doctor looked at him dubiously. "How old are you?"

Sadao looked at the ceiling. "Sixteen."

"I'm going to mark you down as a 'yes' on that one to cover our bases."

"I said the answer is *no*."

The doctor lubed up his fingers with a tube of gel. "I need to do an internal exam. Please spread your legs for me."

Sadao sat up. "Fuck this. I'm done! I told you, I don't screw! And if you don't want to believe me, you can fuck yourself and the North-whatever division!"

"Sadao," the doctor said, calmly pronouncing his name right. "Whether or not you care to join the Division, wouldn't it be good to know if you're healthy? We can treat almost anything these days with a few shots or pills. Free of charge."

Sadao glared at him, letting his words sink in. In truth, he hadn't had a blood test since he was eleven, a few months before…

"Sure. Stick your hand up my ass, whatever," Sadao said, lying back down and assuming the position. He shut his eyes as the fingers went in. Dr. 'I see a hundred dicks a day' was in and out before he knew it. Much to his relief.

"Thank you, Mr. Koga. Now you may sit up and I'll listen to your lungs and heart."

Sadao wrapped the towel back around himself and coughed and breathed deeply on cue while the stethoscope roved over his chest.

"Jesus … what happened here?" the doctor asked as he moved to listen to Sadao's organs from his back. His fingers traced the reddish whip scars left over from Sadao's less fortunate days.

"What do you think happened?" Sadao snapped. "Life happened!"

"Sadao … we treat more than just illness here. If you feel you want to talk to someone we can -"

"I don't think so! Just take my blood and get this shit over with!"

The doctor nodded. "Certainly. I'll send the nurse back in to take the draw and to give you some standard immunizations. Have you been immunized since entering the U.S. - I'm going to assume - illegally?"

"No comment," Sadao said, wishing he could cover up more than just his ass and legs. "I had shots when I was a kid - I don't remember what."

"Well, I'm sure you missed your boosters. We will get that covered today. No worries. Uh, since I am also assuming you came from Japan, can you recall if you were immunized against Nagoya Fever or not?"

"No, but I had it."

This stopped the doctor in his tracks. "You had Nagoya Fever? You're certain?"

"Yeah, I'm certain. Nearly killed me. But I had it!"

The doctor opened a drawer and pulled out a rubber mallet. He knocked it about Sadao's muscles and tendons, checking reflexes, asking him to follow his finger. "Astonishing. You show no loss of muscle tone or coordination. Did you suffer any mental incapabilities?"

"No. I was weak for a while, but I recovered."

"How old were you when you became sick?"

"I think twelve or thirteen. I'm immune now, aren't I?"

"Yes, you would be. Amazing. If you don't mind, I'd like to study your antibodies from the blood sample we'll take. Extraordinary."

"Sure, I guess."

The doctor picked up his clipboard, made a note and shook Sadao's hand gratefully. "I do hope you will join up with us, Mr. Koga. It would be my pleasure to study you. Natural survivors of Nagoya Fever over the age of six are a very rare find."

"Thanks?"

"I'll go get the nurse," the doctor said with a grin and left the room.

Fifteen shots and a yellow slip later, Sadao was cleared to join the team if he so wished. The party was scheduled to run all night. Whoever was still sober enough to stand up and get on the bus to Tucson Boot Camp the next morning would certainly not be back to slum it around the San Diego docks anytime soon.

Sadao sat back in a sagging canvas chair, looking up at the smoggy stars, smoking a cigarette while his friends lit fires in the oil drum trash cans and puked beer into the late hours. Sadao was drunk too, but not completely dead of thought.

Arizona? New Mexico? Wasn't it hot as hell there? It was bad enough in San Diego in the summers when the temperatures hit 110 and hung there for months. But here, they were on the water where there was some relief. Surrounded in filth and desperation, but it was a desperation he knew. He'd managed just fine here.

Sadao flicked his spent butt to the ground and crushed it under his boot. There were holes forming in the leather soles. No money to replace them either. He reached into his jacket pocket for another cigarette and paused to look at his palm. It was scarred, like the other. Hard labor - very little compensation. And tents leaked during the rainstorms. How much longer did he really want to sit around in this dump?

He heaved himself up out of the chair and took a few stumbling steps to the registration table, bracing a hand on it to steady himself. The Division rep sat up, yawned and rubbed his eyes.

"Made a decision?"

"Fuck, yes. Give me a badge. I'm in."

Sixth

Rivals

Sadao looked out over the Sonora Desert through waves upon waves of heat. Ripples of confused air rose in layers between the tall centuries-old saguaro cactus - a spiked botanical testament to determination.

Sadao had none of it. Sweat dripped down the back of his neck into a steady river down his spine. His mouth was dry and his head pounded inside the snug-fit padded helmet. The sun goggles over his eyes pinched his nose while the chest protector - fastened to plates on his back and shoulders - bit into his ribs. Even his hands oozed with sweat in the stinking used gloves he wore to grip the handlebars of the beat-up dirt bike leaning heavily against his booted right leg.

"Listen up, you slackers! These are 65-year-old Honda CRFs! Real single cylinder gasoline four-stroke engines. Not your usual battery-powered bullshit. These babies are the tough workhorses of the Northwest Division. They've seen a lot of action and will kick your ass into the dirt faster than you can burn out their gears! You're going to learn how to tame these wild bitches today. But I know half of you think you already know all the shit from your classroom training. Well, I'm hear to tell you, you don't know jack until you've put one of these dust devils between your legs! So listen up, ladies! I'll tolerate no bullshit from anyone, you hear me?"

Their drillmaster was an American. He was a big man, muscular, with a wide jaw and dark skin. He wore only half the equipment the trainees did and had the advantage of carrying a Camelbak strapped to his back that he took frequent sips from. Sadao was dying for a swallow of something wet, as well as something long and heavy to knock this *bakayaro* across the face with. He knew this was the American way, to insult your subordinates into submission, but it made his Japanese pride seethe. He gripped the handlebars and growled into his chin guard.

"These bikes are tough, but if you fuck around with them, they'll fuck with you, understood? Each one's worth about 18 grand, more than all of you pussies will earn in your first year combined. So we're going to do this by the book! You got me? I can't hear you?!"

There was a mumbling reply.

"Now, pop that bitch into neutral, shitstains! Get a grip on that front brake and swing onto your mounts."

Sadao swung his leg hard in anger - but not high enough to avoid catching his shin guard on the rear fender of the bike. Before he could recover his balance, his standing leg slid in the rocky dust and the motorcycle tipped with it, landing over on top of him. Wham!

"Unnghh! Kuso!!"

Laughter resounded through the shielded heads of the young men around him as he scrambled to get himself out from under the 150 pound machine. A shadow loomed over him, calling him a dumbass as a pair of dark gloved hands lifted the bike up and off of him. Then he was dragged back up onto his feet by his elbow pad.

"Do it again," the drillmaster ordered. "You gotta swing that boot higher than you think!" He kept his other hand on the front wheel, steadying it as if Sadao were a toddler and not a 16-year-old pissed off teen.

"I got it!" Sadao yelled, gripping the handles once more and securing the brake. "You can let go!"

"Kickstand's down, maggot!"

More giggles.

"Fuck!" Sadao kicked it back up into place.

"You got it in neutral?" The man barked.

"Yes!"

"Doesn't look like it to me. Check it!"

Sadao looked down through his sweat blurred goggles and stomped in the general location of the tiny shift peg. He missed, swore, and kicked it again. No click - it was all the way down.

The drillmaster clocked the side of his helmet. "That's first gear, dipshit! You start up that machine your first time in gear, you'll piss your pants flying over the handlebars! And those are some expensive fucking pants! Now get your ass up on the motherfuckin' bike!"

The row of 18 young men to either side of Sadao had all managed to mount their rides without incident. He was being made an example of. Sadao wished for the thousandth time he'd never even thought about leaving San Diego. He'd traded the cooling breeze of the sea and his freedom to become a landlocked prisoner in the middle of the most unforgiving region of the United States - the Arizona wastelands.

All he did now was follow orders - Wake up! Shower! Piss! Eat! Listen! Clean this! Mop that! Study! Study! Eat! Sleep! It was like being in the army all over again. Except instead of guns they had pens and paper, memorization of racing terms, rules, organizational charts, motorcycle mechanics, anything but learning exactly what they came to do - get on a damn bike. Until today. Sadao had been shuttled around to so many dorms and classrooms he had no idea who his current teammates even were. And therefore no clue who to punch in the face later for laughing at him.

Sadao gripped the brake, swung his leg higher and this time his ass came down dead center on the seat with a satisfying bounce. He set his right boot down on the far side, gripped the clutch with his left hand and clicked his shift peg up into neutral with his toe as they were shown in the videos. He could barely feel the peg move through the heavy reinforced boot that had just saved his ankles from being crushed under the bike. Fuck, that gear click was hard to find. No wonder he'd missed it.

"Now you got it!" The man stepped back so all the boys could see him.

"Now that you have your asses on these babies, find your killswitch and click it to RUN!" There was a chorus of clicks. Sadao found his switch with his left thumb and flipped it up. Easy.

"Good! Now press start and let's hear those engines purr!"

Sadao stamped down on his rear foot brake for extra measure and pressed START with his right thumb. Nothing. Not even a click. He looked down to make sure his engine switch was indeed set to RUN and clicked START again. Still nothing. He whipped his head around, much to his relief, a few of the others were having the same problem.

"Okay, okay, shut them off!"

All engines immediately died.

"Who here couldn't get their bike to start? Show me hands, asswipes!"

Sadao had no intention of raising his hand. But some young men to his far right did and they were now receiving extra directions. The drillmaster was pointing to something at the center of their dash. The thick helmet muffled Sadao's hearing, something about "Choke knob."

"You must pull choke, hard up!" Sadao whipped his head to his left. The young man beside him who had been laughing at his failures earlier was now speaking softly to him.

"What?!"

"You bike is not run for long time. Must pull choke! Here!" The gloved hand pointed to his own bike's dash. Sadao looked down. - he had a similar button. He popped it up with his fingers.

"Next time, this will help bike start. Do not forget to push down later. Engine will get too warm!"

The voice next to him sounded eerily familiar and spoke English with a Japanese accent. But under the shades and padding of the helmet, Sadao could not identify him.

"Dare da?" Sadao asked. Who are you?

There was a low laugh. *"Omae no teki da, bakayaro!"*[1]

"Okay, let's do that again, ladies! Start your engines!"

With the choke engaged, Sadao's Honda growled to life and the seat padding under his ass trembled with the engine's powerful vibrations. The feel of it was unexpected. It felt like a beast, chained up and ready to leap. His fingers instinctively formed a tighter grip on the front brake.

"Now if you listened to me and put your fucking bike in neutral, these devil's aren't going to throw you when I tell you to roll back on that throttle! Nice and easy, let's hear those engines!"

Sadao loosened his grip on the brake and when he realized his bike wasn't going to fly forward, he took the throttle in hand and rolled his right wrist back slowly.

Grrrrrooooaaaawwwwwww!!

Sadao's heart pounded along with the roar of the machine. All at once, he forgot the heat and the thirst. His whole focus centered in on this wild creature of metal and rubber under his control, awaiting his orders. The thrill of it was not unlike the feel of a girl's skin trembling under his wandering hands. He rolled the throttle back and forth, entranced by the sounds and vibrations the bike made at his command. His dick swelled with the pounding pistons between his legs. Sadao had never once in his life driven a combustion powered vehicle. This monster wanted to move, and he wanted to move with it.

"About a quarter turn is what you want!" Their drillmaster yelled over their combined engines. "Turn that bitch back a quarter and hold it steady!"

Sadao decreased the throttle and popped his choke back in. The bike quieted some and its shudders softened. He didn't like that and coaxed his bike to kick its roar back up so he could feel it deep in his balls.

"Now pull in your clutch all the way!"

Sadao's left hand moved to his clutch handle and pulled it all the way back flush with the grip.

"Hold that clutch hard! And tap your bitches into first gear! Full down!"

His blood beat in his ears as Sadao stamped down on the shift peg. CLICK! In gear.

"Careful now, both feet down on the dirt to keep your balance, noobies! Hold that throttle a quarter back and let that clutch go about halfway just 'till you feel her start to kick!"

Sadao knew once that clutch was released, all the power he was giving his mount would transfer immediately into forward thrust from the back wheel. Speed and distance was all he could think about. He dropped his boots to the ground and gave her a little more gas, feeling her thud and shake, hearing her roar. He set his sights on the distant shimmering saguaro and let the clutch go all at once.

---

1   *I'm your rival, idiot!*

Next thing he knew he was ass over head in the dust on his back, rocks in his shirt, several feet from his bike, which had just thrown him like a wild horse. His fellow trainees were pissing themselves, bent over in hysterics. Even the drillmaster was laughing his ass off as Sadao struggled to sit up in all his dirt-scraped gear. He peeled off his helmet and threw it to the ground.

"Fuck this!" he yelled, crawling to his feet and walking away. "Fuck all of this!"

"Hah! I told you little bastards - these bikes will teach you long before you teach them who's boss! Let that be a lesson in how *not* to release a clutch! Go take a water break!"

Sadao scuttled across the desert dirt to the equipment trailer parked at the edge of the compound and kicked on the hose. He poured the warm water over his pounding head until it cooled enough to take a long long drink. Soon he was surrounded by thirsty men and somebody shoved him and yanked the hose loose, spitting out precious water across the hot pavement. Sadao turned on his booted heel and made for the trailer ramp. Someone was following him.

"Sadao-kun! *Chotto!*"

Sadao ignored the voice and proceeded to strip the insufferably hot gear from his arms and chest.

"You quit too soon! Sadao-kun!"

Sadao blinked into the hot sunlight. A small Japanese teen stood at the entrance to the trailer, holding Sadao's discarded helmet under his arm as well as his own. He tossed the dirty helmet at Sadao's feet. It rolled up to his boots and Sadao kicked it aside.

"How the fuck do you know my name?"

The young man laughed and came closer into the shade where Sadao could see him more clearly. *"You do not remember me?"* he asked in Japanese.

"I don't," Sadao said, stripping out of his sweat-soaked jersey and collapsing onto a bench seat to try and kick his boot buckles loose. "Why should I?"

The younger teen stepped past him and opened a cooler. It contained iced sports drinks for their pending lunch break. He tossed one at Sadao and after selecting one for himself, unscrewed the top and sat down beside him.

Sadao drank half the bottle down before wiping the sweat from his eyes. Realization hit him and he knew exactly who this was. It was precisely the last person he expected to see here in the middle of nowhere. "You've grown, Shiratori-san. I did not recognize you. *Gomen.*"

Shiratori cackled in a very familiar way and drank down his cooled drink all at once while Sadao looked him over. His voice had changed, too. "Why the fuck did you leave Japan? I thought you were happy there, marching in circles."

"I left for the same reason you did, to find my freedom!" Shiratori eyed him unnervingly, from his eyes to his naked belly and back. *"You've grown too, Sadao-kun. But not*

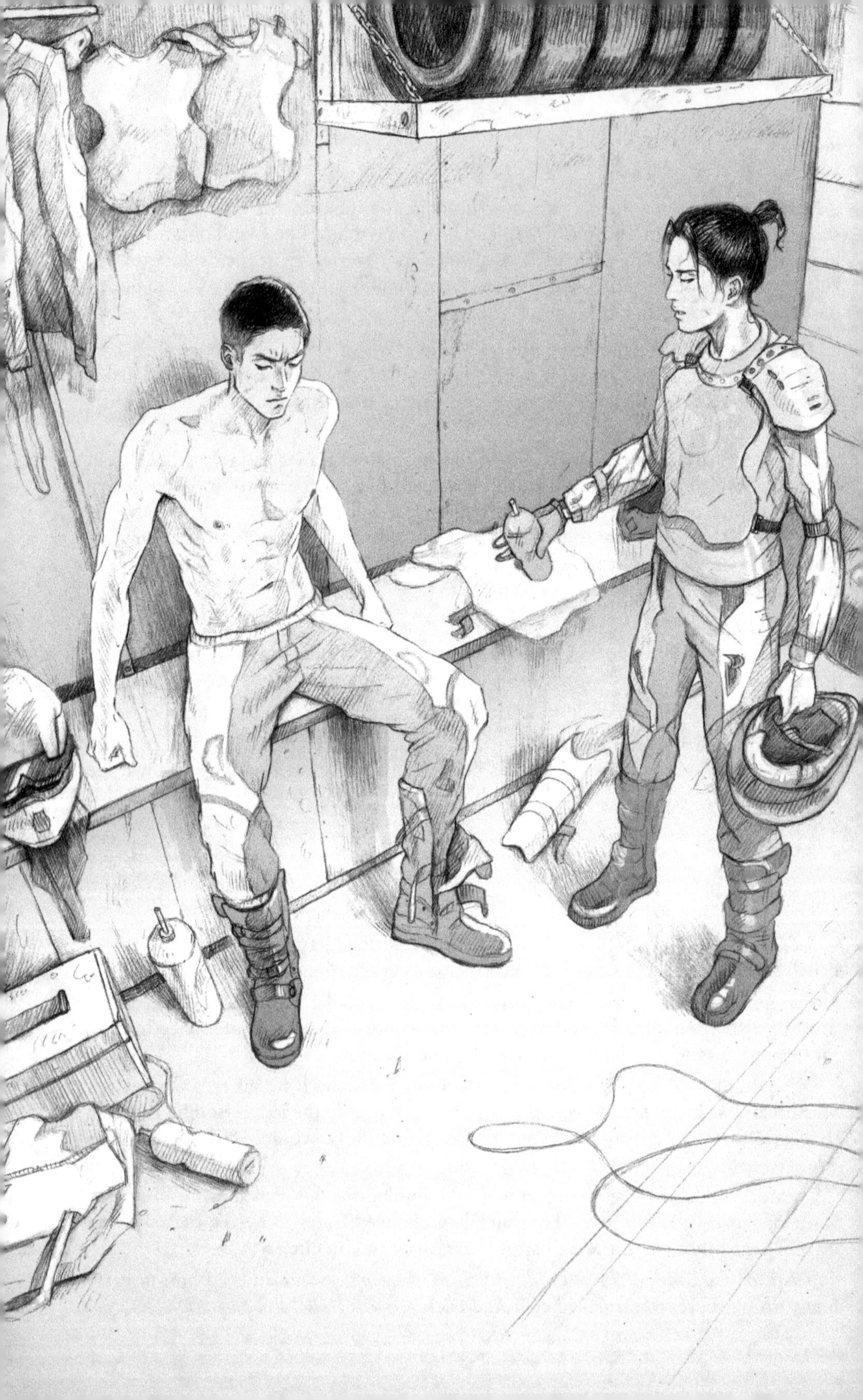

much different from before. You still have your heart set on giving up!"

Sadao sighed and stopped fussing with his boots and left the buckles half snapped in. "I didn't say I was giving up! I'm sick of being made an example of! Those bikes are heavier than they look!"

Shiratori was still studying him. "You are too impatient. Run before you listen. Your pride will not bring you new skills."

"I came in here to get away from lectures!"

Shiratori smiled at him, showing his white teeth. It was always a little creepy when he smiled but somehow Sadao found it endearing - perhaps because Shiratori was from his homeland. Even if it was a home he had fought so hard to escape.

"Sadao-kun, why did you join the Division? There is no freedom in this place."

"For the same reason you did, I suppose. To find something worthwhile doing. Living on the streets leads to nowhere. I was sick of it, just as I was sick of the war back home."

"I did not come here to escape war. I came here to fight a new war."

"What new war?" Sadao asked, finishing off the rest of his drink with a stretch. His spine hurt from getting smacked to the ground. He was hot, sore and in no mood for riddles.

Shiratori lowered his voice. *"You do not see what is happening here? What these men want from us?"*

"They want to cook us alive in this desert."

"No! They want us to do their fighting for them. Why do they recruit only foreigners? We are a different kind of soldier in a different kind of army now. They want to train us to go to war on their war machines. Fight hard for them and make them rich!"

Sadao nodded. *"Of course, I'm not a complete idiot. I didn't exactly walk into this blind. What's your point?"*

"I plan to beat them at their own game," Shiratori said with all sincerity. *"You should think of doing the same! Keep your head down and obey! Work hard, race hard. And when the time comes, we will strike them under their own belly!"*

Sadao groaned. *"I'm tired of war. I'll be happy to just have a bed, food and water."*

"You were always so willing to let another man own your spirit! Soon you will be on your knees again! Begging for it!"

Sadao reached out and grabbed Shiratori by his chest guard and shoved him back into the wall. *"Urusai! I don't bow to anyone! Never again! I'm not that scared little boy tied to your tree anymore!"*

Shiratori laughed and pulled Sadao's hand off of him. He got up and placed his helmet back on his head. *"We will see I think, how much cock you will suck before you find your spirit!"*

"Get out!" Sadao snarled, moving to stand. All at once, he remembered why he disliked this little man. Fuck him and his war-lust. All Sadao wanted in the world right now was another shot at taming that bike. He bent and snapped his boot buckles back in, picked up his gear and pulled the shirt and armor up over his head. He shoved his hands back into the nasty gloves, ready to go fight another round.

The drillmaster worked them hard that day, on and off the bikes. They ran drill after drill of starts and stops, gear shifting and braking, running over obstacles, and steering through cones. They learned how to climb hills and how to make dead starts. Despite the heat, Sadao kept his head cool and his ears open. He followed orders one after another, doing as he was told when he was told, while other men took headers into the dirt. Step by step the bike began to respond more and more to his commands. He learned how to maneuver her weight under his own and steer her expertly in the right direction at the right speed.

At last when the sun was beginning to sink orange and red in the distance, the drillmaster let them go free to ride around the training grounds until dark. Astride his bike - with the wind whipping against his arms, the clutch moving smoothly from gear to gear, gaining speed and control - Sadao felt his spirit rise. As the desert dust kicked up behind them, Sadao ran his mount hard, roaring fast and free toward the saguaros at the edge of the horizon.

Northwest Division Emerald Mountain Change Station - Rocky Mountain National Park, Colorado - 2050

Sadao pulled into the Emerald Mountain Change Station at 18 minutes past noon during the 28th hour of the Rocky Mountain Overland. His 5,500 foot descent had taken less than 20 minutes, passing eight vehicles on a road barely wide enough for one. He swung himself up and out the driver's side window through the cloud of smoke pouring out the back of his shuddering Nissan GT-R.

"Jesus hell, Koga!" the pitmaster yelled, fanning smoke. "You ride the fucking brakes all the way down the grade?!"

"Fuck, no!" Sadao snapped, ripping off his helmet and tossing it aside before unzipping the sweat-soaked front of his jumpsuit. "It's the clutch. Utter waste of steel! I told Boss it needed replacing!"

"We replaced it twice already this season! You gotta learn how to shift!"

Sadao stepped close to the man and threw the remnants of his busted safety harness down onto the oil stained garage floor. "I know how to shift better than anyone in this whole fucking Division! You see this pathetic excuse for an H-strap? I could have been thrown out the fucking window on a hairpin and rolled halfway to Boulder! I'm sick of dealing with your refurbished, second-hand, amateur bullshit!"

"Top gear goes to top racers, Koga! You wanna bruise my face for that? You're a yearling!"

"A yearling who's holding second in the Division, Jack!" said the timekeep. "He's in seventh overall! Stop pissing him off and let him get changed for the next leg!"

The pitmaster backed off, feigning innocence.

"Time?" Sadao shouted, heading for the locker room.

"You've got 17 minutes! Let's make it count!"

Day two. He'd been behind the wheel of that squealing Nissan hunk of crap for 8 hours straight - no break for him or the car. Sadao banged the men's room swinging door open, stripped his jumpsuit down to his hips, and pulled out his dick for a long, gratifying piss. He leaned his head against the cool tile wall to try to breathe and re-focus.

Anger will get you nowhere fast. Concentration is everything. Forget the shitty gear box, forget the pecking order. You want that trophy? You're going to have to bleed for it! Then maybe they'll take you seriously!

His attempt at focus was shattered by the sound of a car screaming into the garage bay outside. From the smell of it, the vehicle at his tail was at least twice as much on fire. Must be another rookie, he mused. He tucked up and went over to the sinks to splash handfuls of water over his head and bare chest.

Twenty minutes was the break time they were allotted between vehicle changes to assure the proper donning of necessary so-called safety equipment suited for their next chosen mount. A long arduous trail ride was next, and for it Sadao had scraped up enough patron donations to purchase his own Kawasaki KLX - one of the finest 20th Century offroaders ever built. With five-speeds, full-sized wheels and lightweight chassis, the bike would be his best chance at gaining a lead. Thankfully, their chief mechanic knew Japanese combustion engines - a rare find in modern day America. There wasn't much he could do about the asphalt leg in terms of vehicle; it would take years of winnings to finance his own race car. But for the mountain downhill grind into Estes Park, he knew the game was his. Seventh wasn't so far back he couldn't overcome it.

"Koga! You done holding your dick? Let's suit up!"

"Ready!" he shouted, entering the lockers. Two team assistants had his boots, pants and jersey ready for him to strip and walk into. Sleeves and legs on, one pair of hands got to buckling his heavy boots while the other fit the lightweight chest, shoulder and back armour over his head and cinched him in.

"You want help with the arm pads and helmet?"

Sadao shook his head. "I'm good. Leave me. Need time for my head to cool down."

"You got it, man." The dressers picked up his auto jumpsuit and made their way out. Sadao sat down on the bench and ripped open an energy bar and took a bite. It tasted like chocolate dirt, but there was plenty of time to fill his belly after the clock ran down and the finish line at Lake Estes was in sight.

He finished off the bar and got up to go over to the snack table for a sports drink. He'd already downed so many in the summer heat of the Rockies, he was pissing neon green. But he knew once on the back of the bike, there'd be no hands to spare for unscrewing caps. A small tube delivering 18 fluid ounces of water fastened to the handlebars was his only option for the next 6 to 8 hours. So neon lime it was.

"Haiyaku shinasai bakadomo! Isoge!"

Sadao nearly choked on his beverage - he knew that voice. He took his final swallow, burped and peered around the row of lockers to confirm what his ears had detected. Sure enough, it was Shiratori, barking orders at his attendants who were unable to understand a word of it.

When did he enter this race? Sadao wondered. *How did he enter this race? And why is he second behind me in the Division?*

Watching both the clock and Shiratori's progress, he waited until the little man chased off his befuddled assistants before making himself known. "Shiratori-san! Where did you come from?"

"I came from Ise, baka!" Shiratori said, ignoring his meaning as he brushed passed Sadao to make his snack of champions selections.

"You're not even old enough to qualify!"

Shiratori raised his chin to stare Sadao in the eye. *"I am! I just turned 17 last month!"*

"No you didn't! You were three years behind me in school! I'm 17! You're 15 at best!"

"This is not your concern!"

"It is if they catch you cheating!"

Shiratori's small perfect face tightened into a mask of barely contained fury. *"I do not cheat!"*

"It's cheating if you lie about your age! Your name wasn't even on the Division starting roster! I read it end to end!"

"I am first alternate for my team! Our lead driver met with a no-fault accident coming over the summit. Racing markers were moved by idiots and he hit a big wall! He can not continue! I am his replacement!"

"That's not legal!!"

"I am the team alternate!" the little man shouted. *"I am legal! Non-fault accidents are open to alternates! Maybe you still need to study the Division rule books!"*

"Koga! We've got ten minutes!"

"Coming!" Sadao shouted, turning his back on Shiratori and grabbing his helmet and pads. "Maybe you think being fresh will give you an advantage, but I'm already 15 minutes ahead of you! I have my own bike now - a KLX! I'll trust you won't try to break the mandatory 20-minute window to try and catch me!"

"I NO cheat! I NO cheat!" Shiratori shouted as Sadao fitted his goggles and helmet over his head, drowning out the little man's screams.

Ninety minutes later, Sadao found himself pushing his prized Kawasaki back up a steep wooded hill to the lip of the clear-cut track, swearing to himself. Idiot bystanders had fucked with the regional trail markers as well, sending him right up and over a short drop into a bed of ferns. Fortunately, neither himself nor the bike were seriously damaged, but his lower lip was cut, filling his mouth with blood. He sucked the bitterness from his teeth while laughter rang out from the woods nearby.

"Assholes! You'd better not let me catch you!"

Shouts, whoops and the sound of running were all he got in reply as he spat blood in frustration, trying to get the heavy bike to roll up over a fallen branch. "Fuck!"

With a final shove, he was back up on the narrow dirt track - one of a dozen or so crisscrossing the mountainside. The Rocky Mountain Overland was a key checkpoint race. Between these checkpoint stations, set some 25-50 miles apart, each racer was able to choose his own path from point A to B as long as they were recorded properly by the checkpoint timekeepers.

Should have stuck to your gut feeling and stopped reading the signs, he reprimanded himself. He brushed the sticky fern-seeds from his seat and climbed back on. He restarted the engine and it growled back to life. He lowered his helmet, set the clutch, cranked the throttle and resumed his course. Not ten feet further he heard the sound of a bike catching up behind him. He sped up, keeping ahead and watching the twists in the trail until his tailgater's front wheel nudged his rear, sending him into a wobble.

As Sadao gripped his handlebars and fought to stabilize the bike as Shiratori flew past him in a streak of white - single gloved finger in the air.

Bakayaro!

Sadao shifted up and gave close chase in the rocky dirt, but not vying to pass. He let his rival take the brunt of any debris that might be in the road and course correct for him. He watched the little cheat's tail twist and turn and when the rear wheel bounced, he bucked his front end up and over, allowing the Kawasaki to safely leapfrog the obstruction.

"That's right, Shiratori! I'm watching your lead! Keep speeding up and you'll end up in a ravine!"

No doubt Shiratori was deaf to his shout over the whisk of the pines flying past them in a green and brown blur. Soon, the trail narrowed and instead of aiming off onto a wider path, Shiratori turned onto a less maintained route.

What is he doing? Sadao wondered, matching his jumps and dips. Is this trail more direct? Maybe ... but he's taking a risk. If we hit a big enough rock or log at this -

Wham!!

A pine branch Shiratori had just passed swung back into his face, flinging Sadao right off the back of the bike. Ass in the dirt, Sadao watched his bike continue to race itself about another 50 feet before hitting a stump and stalling.

"Fuck! Fuck! Fuck!" Sadao kicked at the gravel. So much for his lead! Now even Shiratori was ahead of him and that asshole hadn't even run the first half of the race!

Stop being an idiot and get up! Sadao scrambled to his feet and ran for the bike and got back on. *Cut through the woods! What do you have to lose?*

Without questioning whether or not this was a boneheaded idea, Sadao stopped using the trails altogether and followed his compass dead west toward the Fall River checkpoint.

Although the extra height of his wheels allowed him better ground clearance, his bike still kicked and whined as he ground it down through the fern beds. It sent his gut full-force into the handlebars every time he caught an unseen chunk of nature, knocking the wind out of himself and slamming his nuts into the gas tank.

Sadao was seeing stars by the time he'd bushwhacked his way into a less forested area. Here, the hillside leveled out a bit, wasn't so steep. Soon the forest floor turned gravely and course, kicking up stones behind him. He descended westward, for the next hour or so until he realized the loose dirt under his wheels was becoming damp, then wet. Soon there was about two inches of water running down the center of this makeshift trail.

Riverbed! The next station is at the edge of the Fall River. This stream must dump into it. *As long as it stays shallow, I'm free!*

Sadao shifted into fifth and let her ride. The thick tread of his tires was well suited to water riding, provided it didn't get too deep or the sides of the embankment too steep. The river bed grew wider mile by mile, smoothing his way and allowing for the powerful speed of his bike to make up for lost time.

Hah! Those fools up in the woods dodging stumps, I'll make it in ahead of all of them!

Somewhere among the self-congratulations he was awarding himself, Sadao wondered why - if this riverbed was so convenient - hadn't his team leaders sent them down this course to begin with? Why stick to the mountain bike trails at all? Did they know this stream was here? How could they not? But there were no other tire ruts in the muddy bed other than his own.

Fuck, I'm brilliant...

Yet not so brilliant to abandon course before the riverbed took a turn and suddenly deepened and narrowed, transforming the wide trickle in the center of the track into a much steadier rush of shallow, but swift moving water. Before he could slow or rethink his strategy, he felt the water spilling through his spokes, propelling him forward.

It's okay, it's okay. I can still jump the bank when I need to … I can … oh fuck … water …

The turn of the Fall River Sadao had been waiting for was indeed right ahead and about 60 feet lower than he'd counted on and dusted with billows of watery mist.

… falls … .

Sadao tried to brake and slow the bike but the sides of the canyon had closed in and his boots were in the current. If he tried to stop his forward momentum, he'd be torn off the pegs and the bike and he would go over the edge.

Might as well go over as one. Bleed for it!

Sadao cranked his throttle full back. The rear tire spun, catching nothing but serving as a water wheel that propelled him forward. Water sprayed behind him as he soared out over the cusp of the falls by some 20 feet, his momentum taking him over the rush of the Fall River's rapids and certain drowning to land nose down with his front wheel buried in the soft sandy earth of the far shore. Sadao was pitched into the air, and rolled head over tail into the sand. He came to a stop at the side of the change station barn, surrounded by a flock of chickens and reporters, flashing cameras and kicking up feathers in his face.

"Holy fuck! Get him up!"

"Is he alive? Who is he?"

"Northwest Division, holy fuck! He's one of ours! Carry him if you have to! He's in first!"

Dizzily, Sadao could remember being hauled to his feet, dragged to a four-wheeler, hands set to the handlebars and told to go for broke into the final canyon leg. Four and a half hours later, he found his way out of that canyon and onto a streetbike bound for the lakeside, far in the lead with no one to catch him except the helicopters that circled behind him, vying for footage. They blocked out the setting sun, casting hulking shadows over the endless flowers and arms that circled his neck with amazement and adoration.

He was led to a stage bloody, dizzy and breathing raspily with a rib through his left lung. Sadao Koga, age 17, the first and last rookie in racing history to win a multi-division Overland race - by jumping a 60-foot waterfall and rapids, on a Kawasaki KLX, no less.

I don't cheat, he thought, holding up his cup and grinning through the pain. *I just beat them at their own game.*

Seventh

White Gold

Alberta, Canada - 2051

The Northwest Division's New Year's celebration was held in the largest private home Sadao had ever seen the inside of. He'd been invited into several flying mini homes before and after Division races - huge converted Chinook helicopters filled with fine glass fixtures and brushed leather lounges - but this? That anyone could call it a home was a gross understatement. It was more like a palace. He had no idea during that impromptu visit - scraped off the streets of the San Diego slums - that the latex fingers shoved up his ass happened to belong to one of the wealthiest men in North America - Dr. Clive Bennet Hawthorn. Team asshole inspections were a voluntary service he sometimes provided as chief sponsor of the Northwest Division teams. A dual citizen of both Canada and America, Dr. Hawthorn's primary residence occupied the better part of 12 acres overlooking the Canadian Rockies of Alberta.

Sadao stood out on the polished marble veranda looking over the balustrade into the 250-foot drop below. A manufactured stream ran through the ballroom; it dribbled over faux stones bisecting the inlaid wood flooring and exited through a hidden channel, where it spat back out into its parent river diving off the cliff's edge into the misty depths below. His vision swam from more than just a half dozen Sapporos.

"Get your drunk ass away from the edge, Koga!"

Sadao turned and steadied himself against the stone rail to belie his inebriation. *"Nani?"*

"English, you Elite Class asshole!" It was their team captain, Robert Alvarado, come to slap his back in congratulations for making Best in Show in the Tri-Division Championships earlier that week.

"Thanks," Sadao said, warmly returning the hug. The captain had come with several other team members in tow to share a smoke and admire the early evening view.

"Was getting way too fucking hot in there," Alvarado said, joining Sadao in leaning against the stone rail while he lit up. Inside, the ballroom was ablaze with circling crystal lights and live amplified music. A modern jazz fusion group was performing, headlined by the doctor's fresh, new second wife - a 22 year-old leggy French Canadian brunette named Gisette. Her voice rang out like a bell over the trombones and saxophones.

"You don't dance, do you Koga?"

"No," Sadao said, watching the young man flick ash over the balustrade into the waterfall below. He was too buzzed to smoke despite the enticing scent.

"Too bad. There's a shit ton of sweaty tits to rub up against in there. Place this big - a bunch of the guys have already snuck off to other floors to go nail some pussy in a toilet somewhere."

"Is that right?" Sadao said, glancing up at the stars that were beginning to come out. They spun a bit and he blinked to settle them.

"You know, I can't get a beat on you, Koga. You race like a motherfucker, but when it comes to getting laid…"

"I don't mix business with pleasure," Sadao explained, nodding toward the so-called hot pussy bouncing about in flashy gowns on the opposite side of the two-story windows. "Too much trouble."

Alvarado laughed, and a few of the others butting into the conversation joined in kind.

"Look man, you don't even have to try. Since that Overland win, you've got babes knocking on your trailer door 24/7. I've seen 'em. You've just landed your third Gold Cup! All you have to do is walk in there, point at some chick, flip your hair and that bitch will be on her knees, lips around your dick in ten seconds flat!"

Sadao shrugged at this. "What's the point? That's masturbation with assistance, not much else."

"Maybe Sadao-kun want better conquest, eh?"

Fuck. Shiratori stepped out of the flickering lights surrounded by some of his cronies. He'd been drafted to a rival team under the same division. They weren't truly competing against one another in the black and white sense. But for individual accomplishments and season win points, he was running neck-and-neck with Sadao in many of his specialty events, namely auto and street bike racing. The gaki had even managed to get himself promoted to Team Captain - a position Sadao coveted himself, but had remained out of reach.

Sadao detached himself from the wall and stepped up to the little man. "Shiratori-san, I didn't know nineteenth-century armor was back in style," he said, gesturing to his rival's odd costume. More and more, the junior captain was showing up in plated samurai gear with paired swords. "Did you misunderstand the meaning of 'black tie required?'"

"I dress for battle!" he said, raising himself up to his fullest diminutive height. "Every day, I am ready to fight!"

"I thought we left Japan to escape battles of that kind," Sadao grumbled. "It's not something I want to remember or celebrate." In his peripheral vision, he could note both team groups half circling around them. The racers who hadn't cooled their blood with an air-headed horny patron were salivating for a fight. Sadao had no desire to encourage it. "I have no quarrel with you, Shiratori-san. I'm honestly too drunk to give a fuck about whatever point you're trying to make."

"My point is great warrior desire challenge. There is no glory in hunting helpless prey."

Sadao rubbed his eyes. He really just wanted to sink into a pleasant fog of intoxication, find an overstuffed couch in a quiet corner somewhere and pass out until dawn. But now he had a dick waving contest to diffuse and possibly only one way to resolve it. "You are right, Shiratori-san. I don't enjoy an easy win. Nothing worth having comes easy, as they say."

Shiratori's eyes sparkled in the growing darkness and a smile spread across his finely sculpted face. "Then you choose for me my target and I will have her at my feet before the moon is set behind the mountain."

Sadao felt a small thrill of interest tickle his mind. Not so much at the prospect of getting laid in the next few hours, so much as choosing a target for Shiratori he was certain to fail at attaining. He turned to observe the hundred or so patrons swirling about the ballroom. "That one there, in the dark green coat."

The team members squinted into the spectacle to see who Sadao had fingered for Shiratori's fingering.

"Wait - hey you mean that old dude? The one by the doorway?" Alvarado was aghast. "He's like bald! And a man! Can you even pick a man?"

"Shiratori-san did not specify gender requirements," Sadao confirmed, grinning at his rival. A mumble of concerns went through the racers. All eyes fixed on Shiratori to see what he would do. The little man didn't blink an eye.

"I accept," he said. A whoop of disgust went up.

"No fucking way, dude!"

"I'd puke before I sucked that old sac!"

"Silence!" Shiratori snapped and his teammates held their tongues. "Now I choose for Koga-san," he said with a victorious grin. Without even turning to look, he pointed directly at the stage where the beautiful young French-Canadian chanteuse was singing her heart out.

A gasp rattled through the men.

"No - no Koga! Don't do it, man! Don't!"

"That's Dr. Hawthorn's wife! You'll get kicked out of the Division!!"

"I accept," Sadao said without a blink. The men tried to grab his attention, talk him out of it if they could. But the game was on and the knowledge he had already won was difficult to hide. Shiratori may have thought he was being clever but Sadao knew something he did not. Of all the knocks and invites from patrons he had received in the past year, Gisette Hawthorn's had been among them. He'd politely declined out of respect for his physician, but now that the gauntlet had been thrown, he realized he was more than up for the challenge. Her tall slender form had turned his head on more than one occasion. Fucking her would be rather enjoyable he imagined.

"How do we prove our victories?" he asked his armored opponent.

Shiratori cocked his head at the crescent moon. "We return, this spot in two hour when moon is set. With proof indisputable!"

Sadao bowed deeply to his rival and Shiratori did the same. Each man entered the ballroom at opposite ends to approach their chosen prey.

It wasn't hard to get her attention. All Sadao had to do was approach the stage, look up and catch her eyes with his own. She was mid-song but he could hear her voice rise in pitch slightly under his steady gaze. Two minutes later, she announced a break for the band and with a coy smile in his direction, exited the ballroom. Sadao met her with two flutes of champagne in the sitting room adjacent to the hall, where the singer had set up her private staging area complete with refreshments, ample seating, and a makeup station with mirror.

She accepted a glass from him and sipped it, leaving red lipstick stains on the rim.

"*Bonsoir, Mademoiselle* Hawthorn," he said warmly. "You sounded lovely tonight."

Gisette tossed back her mane of tight brown curls and laughed. "You are a cruel, cruel man, Sadao Koga! But I thank you for that. *Merci* - and it's *Madame*, by the way. I am married, as you well know." She drank off half the glass and grabbed an open bottle of water instead, casting herself across her reclining couch and kicking off her heels as she drained it.

"I do," Sadao said, hitching a leg up on the back of her lounge. "But I'll note that you took my offer of a quiet drink regardless."

"And have ignored all of my attempts to offer you the same previously. I wonder ... " she said, wiping the sweat from her neck with a cocktail napkin and tossing it aside. " ... if you aren't up to something peculiar tonight."

Sadao grinned and finished off his glass, setting it aside on a carved jade table. "Why would you think that?"

She nibbled at her polished fingernail. "I know a few things about you, Mr. Koga. For one, you are devastatingly consistent. Something changed your mind tonight about me and no - don't act as if you don't know exactly why you've come bearing bubblies and bedroom eyes all of a sudden. I know this is some game you're playing and you might as well fess up to it if we are going to become friends."

"Friends," he said defeatedly. "I hadn't considered that."

"Don't get me wrong," she added with a calculated grin. "I fully intend to make use of your lovely cock tonight - possibly well before my hour-break is up - but I don't mince words when I say friends. My interest in you is not an idle one and it goes much deeper than your pants."

Okay, Shiratori's gauntlet was well and truly thrown down and accepted by the lady as well. But this interest of hers … that concerned him a lot more. "You know about me, huh?" he said cautiously.

"That's better," she said. "Now you look at me as if I'm really here. A woman with a purpose and not some idle lay for you to go brag about to your teammates. Smell your finger or some other childish proof of conquest."

Sadao suppressed his discomfort. He'd entered a hornet's nest without realizing it and with the addition of the champagne, it was all he could do to pull his half-drunk wits together to match this woman whom he had grossly underestimated.

"Oh! You do not know how much I am enjoying this!" she proclaimed with a luxurious stretch. "The elusive Sadao Koga come to lap at my toes!" Her white sequined sleeveless gown slid a bit and Sadao could see the side of her breast and nipple through the gap in the armhole. Hers were a rich red that stood proudly erect. His dick stiffened despite himself.

"So you want to humiliate me, is that it?"

She smiled and stroked his arm suggestively. "Hardly, darling. In fact, I want to build you up into a state of self-confidence you've never known. You see, being the team physician's wife has its advantages. I like to do my homework on the racers I become invested in."

"What kind of homework?"

"History. I know you came here a refugee of the Japanese Civil War. From a small village, Toba, I believe. A pinpoint on the Pacific map. You escaped as a stowaway on a ship and scrabbled about for a living in the San Diego camps, where my dear husband first met you during the day of your recruitment. You had a few mild venereal diseases he cured with a range of shots but yet, you insisted you were not sexually active. So that can only mean one thing - rape. And when paired with your whip scars, I would guess you were indentured like so many unfortunate -"

Sadao stood up off the couch. "My medical records are a private matter!"

"And they are kept private, I can assure you of that," she said, sitting up. "Even my dear sweet husband doesn't know I've seen them. But as it would turn out, we both share a common interest beyond racing after all - you."

"What are you talking about?!"

"Nagoya Fever," she said. "It's been the main subject of his private research for a decade or more and you, my darling, are his favorite case subject. When I've come to tuck him in at night from where he's fallen asleep over his copious notebooks, I've seen perhaps a file or two he would normally keep locked in his safe."

It was coming together now. Sadao had been more than happy to give Dr. Hawthorn extra blood samples on numerous occasions, along with a gradually more detailed back history. He'd never mentioned, however, the particulars of his past childhood slavery situation. Gisette was far more than a pretty face to have put all of that together so succinctly.

"You are an exceptional man, Sadao Koga. Not even 20 years old yet and with five world records, three Gold Cups, a notorious rookie win, and now the newly crowned All-Round Champion of the Division. Everyone wants you to give them your personal attention and yet you turn them all away."

"I don't need their money," Sadao said bitterly. "I earn enough on my own. I don't want to owe anyone anything!"

"That is what I surmised," Gisette said softly. "You don't trust anyone, do you, Sadao?"

He didn't answer her - just kept his eyes on the moon outside the window, slowly descending toward the horizon.

"Let me be your friend - your confidant. Let me help you achieve the independence and security you desire. I already have everything I need. I won't ask you for anything more than to share in the celebration of your success."

"Hah!" he spat, turning back to her. "You will want something, someday. It will come. And if you do build me up to these heights of self-sufficiency, I'm certain it won't be without a fatal flaw somewhere in the patchwork of your schemes! One pull and you'll take me down!"

All she did was reach out to him and his anger with a hand - steady and confident. Her husband held a sizeable interest in the Northwest Division. Sadao knew with his wife at his back, there really would not be any mountain too high for him to climb. Shiratori may have been granted a captain position, but what of Team Boss? Did he really intend to drive a bike over hazardous terrain well into his 80s? Sadao had become accustomed to racing money and celebrity. He didn't ever want to go back to stealing oranges and pissing in the bushes.

Sadao took her hand and let her lead him around to sit beside her on the couch. She played with the braid of his beard, winding it about her fingers. He closed his eyes and leaned into her chaste kiss; he could smell her perfume and sweat. "Shall we make racing history ours, Sadao?" she whispered. Her breath was warm on his cheek; he remembered the peak of her nipple under her gown, rubbed red by the sequins. He ached to feel it between his teeth.

"Nngh!" He grabbed her by the curls and buried his tongue in her mouth, devouring her taste. Tongues lashed against each other as he kissed her so ferociously, she was flushed and panting with wide eyes when he released her. Without another word, she reached behind her dress and drew down the zipper while Sadao pulled her sleeve off to reveal the pert nipple standing up proud from her small teardrop breast. He bent and fastened his mouth to it, sucking hard, flicking his tongue around it, wanting to drive it even more erect.

"Good," she panted. "Let it out. You're safe here with me. I know you've been holding back for so long…"

He heard her, but his desire was too powerful to stop himself from pulling down the rest of her dress while he lapped the salty sweetness from her neck. He crushed her breasts in his hands, pinching the rock hard nipples over and over while she gasped and moaned. He knew there was no finesse to his lust. And if there was a shred of truth to what she was saying, there didn't need to be - he'd seduced her months ago.

Mouths fused, his fingers worked their way up under her skirt and found her there - drenched and throbbing. He buried two fingers deep in her folds and rocked her swollen clit with his thumb. His dick pulsed at the realization she'd been singing all night without panties.

"Aaah!" she cried into his mouth. "Too much, too much!"

Sadao paused. Both of them were breathing hard and sweat beaded their skin. He slid his fingers out and spread them across her kiss-swollen lips. She rolled her eyes shut and sucked her own taste from his fingers, grasping at his crotch to try and release his own demanding member. Before he knew it they were both on their feet, stripping the clothes from each other in a frantic need to be skin on skin. She helped him undo his buttons and no sooner did his shirt hit the floor, she placed a finger on his lips.

"*Attendez s'il vous plaît.* There is something I must give you before we close our deal."

"What?!" he panted. His hard cock tested the seam of his half unzipped dress pants.

She stepped the rest of the way out of her gown and trotted naked to the dressing table. She opened a series of drawers and pulled out a small white jewelry box. She cradled it in her palm and brought it to him with a smile. "This." she said, smiling with her lipstick askew.

"What is it?" he asked. "I don't need gifts."

She took his hand and placed the box in it firmly. "This, I will insist you accept."

He eyed her strangely and opened it. It was a small ear cuff. Simple but polished to a high shine. He took it out of the box and examined it. "Silver?"

She took his hand and led him to the mirror. "White gold," she said, sitting him down in her dressing chair and kissing his earlobe. "My signature precious metal." She took the jewelry from his hand and slid it snug around the edge of his ear. It snapped into place perfectly.

"I want my champion to wear a token from his queen," she said, kissing his cheek. "It will be our secret, but I will see you with it everywhere you go and know you are thinking of me and our bond."

He turned his head and it caught the light, dazzling in the reflection. She knelt naked beside him running her hand up his chest, meeting his gaze in the mirror.

"You are so beautiful, Sadao. I don't think you realize how many people seek your companionship. All the women in the Division ask about you. What do I know?

What can I tell them?" She slipped her hand up his bare back, feeling the criss cross of faded scars. "I tell them nothing. We are not so different, you and I. I was abandoned to a Quebec orphanage by my father. I was so young I don't even remember his name. I knew hunger every day. My voice saved my life and gave me a new one, just as racing has saved yours."

Sadao reached down and touched her face. "I want to believe you," he said, tangling his fingers in her curls. "But right now if we don't fuck, I'm going to explode."

Gisette smiled brightly. "We can't have that!" she said and unzipped him the rest of the way, helping him out of his pants and shoes. Seated naked before him, she wrapped her long fingers around his cock and gave it a much needed stroke, eliciting a moan from his throat. She didn't need to know this was more or less the first time he'd ever let a woman freely pleasure him. Especially not one who knew what she was doing. Her curly head dipped to take him into her mouth.

"Aah!" Wet heat enveloped him, expertly working his aching shaft between her pursed lips and tongue. She swirled her way up to the tip with a quick suck that made his thighs shudder, then down again with persistence. Watching her in the mirror - bobbing on her knees with the long shapeliness of her spine and round buttocks rising and falling in the glow of the table lights - was going to shoot him over the edge before they even got started.

"Enough!" he snapped and pulled her up by her arms. She stood over him - she was a tall vixen. Even standing without heels, she had an inch or so on him. He liked that. "Turn around. Sit back against me," he said tightly. "I want to watch my cock going up your snatch in the mirror."

Her eyes took on that wild look again. She dove into his lap and spread her long legs across his thighs, arching her back up against his chest like a cat. His dick was up against the soft mounds of her round ass. She tilted her head back to catch his mouth, sucking in his tongue. He kissed her hard again, losing himself in her taste and scent. His hands worked her breasts, squeezing them, pinching those stiff jutted nipples to her wails of delight. Suddenly, she rose up on her toes and slid herself back and down onto him so fast he was buried to the hilt before he remembered something.

"Ah! Gisette - ! Wait!"

But it was too late. She was in motion, working her hips. Her labia was spread wide in the mirror, peeking out from her shock of brown curls. She swallowed him, drowning his dick in throbbing pleasure. Thrust after thrust, he drove up inside her, aiming for her G-spot. He could see her wetness growing thicker along the length his cock with each rise and fall of her hips.

Fuck, he wasn't going to be able to take it! She moaned his name and ground her hips, writhing and gyrating, grinding him up inside her. Her juices dripped down over his balls, sending him over. He gave in, pulled her head back by the curls and bit her throat to try and tamp down his own scream.

"Nngh!!" He shot hard up into her, the force of it jerking his ass up off the chair.

She thrashed even more, forcing his spasms to strike her deep inside where she desired it the most.

"No, no, no!" she cried when he froze in ecstasy. She grabbed his hand, pressing his fingers to her clit.

"Aah!" Half-blind from his own climax, he dipped up their combined fluids and rubbed his fingers rhythmically around her hot nub. And still she rode him, spent but still erect up inside her. Catching his breath, he found himself able to better aim and quicken his fingers.

She arched up hard and froze, blinding him with her hair and deafening him with her scream.

"Aaaahhaaahahh!"

If there was anyone in the adjoining hall, they'd be calling the police by now.

Her orgasm lasted a long time - wailing at the ceiling while he stroked her rapidly through it. When her cunt finished convulsing, they were both breathless, soaked with sweat and drenched in spent fluids. His fingers were so slippery with her moisture, he wasn't entirely certain who'd produced more.

"So now will you tell me why you came to me tonight?" She asked, slumped in his arms with his softening dick still inside her.

"Shiratori challenged me to seduce you."

Her face glowed with post-coital satisfaction. "The little samurai man?"

"Yes, him."

She laughed and kissed him once more sweetly. "Send him my thanks."

Sadao took in her flushed face proudly. "I will.. but we were reckless."

"Mnnn ... don't worry, my darling," she purred, sliding up off of him so she could wrap her long arms around him fondly. "Clive won't mind."

Sadao was puzzled. "That's not what I meant. We didn't use anything."

She nuzzled his neck. "We don't need to. I know you can't get me pregnant."

Sadao stiffened and shoved her off his lap. She fell on her ass to the floor below him; he stood and grabbed a wad of napkins to wipe his groin and thighs.

"Why does this anger you?" she asked calmly. "You know I've read your medical records. Do you think I would bet my future on a champion I knew next to nothing about? Your loyalty to me is very important. I can't have my favorites knocking-up half the patrons!"

Sadao finished cleaning himself and reached for his pants, shoving them back on. He was so angry he couldn't speak.

"Darling ... "

He pulled on his shirt. Outside the moon was getting dangerously low. He didn't look back at her until every last one of his buttons were fastened. When he turned she was still a rag doll of loose limbs on the floor, looking expectantly up at him.

"We need to get something straight," he said, fixing his collar. "My past, and any other private details you stole about me, goes no further than this room!"

"Sadao, there's no need to be ashamed. What happened to you was - "

"No further!"

She looked stunned. "Fine. But realize, neither of us had anything to be proud of before we arrived here. This is a different world. Your secrets will be safe with me."

Sadao stepped closer to gaze down on her. Naked and flushed, she looked like a startled animal. "I will trust you're a woman of your word. But believe me when I say I give my trust only once. If you break this promise between us, I will know about it. And I will make sure you never forget it!"

Her eyes widened again. Her nipples stiffened once more over the excited beating of her chest. Her lipstick streaked mouth turned up at the corners.

"I believe you," she whispered.

Shiratori and company were waiting at the balustrade on schedule. The rush of the waterfall was now only a hidden roar in the darkness below. The little man's polished black armor looked slightly less polished, but his white grin gleamed in victory.

"I have won!" Shiratori declared, producing a men's old fashioned monogrammed handkerchief from his obie for both teams' members to inspect. The men tossed it around between themselves, laughing and shouting, none wanting to hold it for very long.

"Ugh, it smells like ass farts!"

"Fuck, Captain, that's gross as hell!!"

Eventually the cloth was passed to Sadao, who took the edge of the thinning overwashed fabric between his forefinger and thumb. It stank of cum.

"How do we know you didn't just steal this thing and jerk off into it?" asked Alvarado, gratefully relieving Sadao of the object. He sniffed it suspiciously then bent over to dry-heave. He tossed it back to Shiratori, who caught it and held it up proudly.

"My *seieki* does not smell of old cheese and fried egg!" he insisted. "Only old man smell this way!"

"We both saw Captain Shiratori take the old man upstairs and into the bathroom!" vouched one of his loyal men, pointing to another team member from Sadao's side, who nodded his verification. "This spooge is legit!"

"But ... hang on, weren't you supposed to fuck this guy or something?" Alvarado was always a stickler for details.

"Koga-san did not specify how green suit wrinkle man was to be conquered. Only proof!" Shiratori insisted.

"I think that only half-counts. But good effort for making an old guy squirt. You might need to ice your wrist!"

Shiratori's hand moved to the hilt of his sword.

Sadao bristled. "This stinking rag is proof enough."

His samurai rival took a step closer. "Where is your proof, eh?"

Much like Shiratori had done before in naming his target, Sadao merely pointed toward the stage where a very flushed, recently redressed Mrs. Gisette Hawthorne rushed up to the microphone. She hastily gave apologies for her tardiness to the bored audience and her confused, vamping musicians.

"Holy shit, Koga …" Alvarado said in amazement. "Woman can hardly stand! You nailed that bitch into next week!"

Sadao couldn't resist a smug glance in Shiratori's direction. Both the mini old-fart fucker and his chorus line of lackies were silently amazed.

"Fuuuuck … you idiot!" Alvarado punched his arm. "You're gonna get our team into some real serious shit now, Koga! You were supposed to bang her quick, not send her into orbit. She'll be after your dick for the rest of her life!"

Sadao recoiled and rubbed his upper arm. Alvarado packed a lot of power when he was pissed. "It's nothing to worry about," Sadao insisted.

"Yeah? What the fuck am I gonna do when the good doctor finds out?! He'll pull our funding for sure! He'll pull all of your private sponsors, too! Asshole! Why'd you fucking do that?! Jesus Christ, she's looking this way, too - all starry eyes! Fuck!"

Sadao caught his second hit by the wrist. "I said it's nothing to worry about. She won't bring trouble."

Alvarado ripped his hand free. "She'd better not, or I'm holding you personally responsible!"

"And you'll do what? Dismiss me?" Although the young man was taller than himself, Alvarado's anger dimmed and his shape seemed to shrink in the shadows. He knew without Sadao, there was no team.

"Better watch your ass, Koga," he mumbled.

"I see no proof here!" Shiratori exclaimed, breaking up their argument. "Stupid sing-song woman is tipsy from drink, no Sadao-kun monster-dong!"

"Yeah, Koga! Where's the goods?"

"Show us some curly pubes, man!"

"Didja get her panties?!"

Sadao paused. He had thought the moment she opened her little jewelry box, his proof would be the band of white gold now affixed to his ear. But now in light of Alvarado's reaction, he realized it would be far more prudent to keep their bond a secret. He dipped his head forward to allow his long hair to drape more fully over the ear cuff.

"Here," he said, holding out a hand to Shiratori. "Smell my fingers."

Eighth

Brass Ring

Sadao stood at the top of a short bulldozed hill in the center of the training field, waiting for his recruits to gather themselves and their bikes at the foot of the packed-earth rise. The boys were taking their time - gunning around in the dirt, showing off. They were five hours into their first day on the backs of some beat-up Honda CRFs. These were the same overworked training bikes Sadao had cut his teeth on a decade ago. The sun beat down hard on his cap-covered head. He wore only minimal safety equipment. The boys, however, were geared up head-to-toe in sweltering padded body armor to prevent broken limbs each time they pitched off their rides. Like his prior stone-headed teenaged self, plenty of them had tasted dirt well before noon.

"Shut off your engines and listen up!" he shouted. "I'm about to teach you the most important lesson you'll ever learn in open course racing - how to recover from a hill stall."

There was audible grumbling. Some shielded punk mumbled, "More pussy work." It generated a laugh among the assembled brats, eager to be set free to race around like assholes now that they'd passed basic start-up, steering and braking drills.

"If you want to live long enough to get your first taste of pussy, I'd suggest you shut your smart-ass mouths and listen!" His voice was sharp and loud. "These bikes outweigh you all by 50 pounds. Gravity is not your friend! Soung, drive your bike up to this line." Sadao dragged out a mark just below the crest of the hill with his boot. Soung, a lightweight, 16-year-old Korean boy, gunned his engine and did just as he was instructed. When he hit the mark, Sadao grabbed his handlebars and held his bike in check.

"Shut off the engine!" The bike died. "Grab the handbrake and put your boots down."

The kid was so small for his age, he could only drop one leg to the ground well enough to make traction. He was on a 2/3rds size dirt bike too. *Who found this kid?*

Sadao wanted to know. *He'll be dead or dismembered before he sees his first year-end rally.* Sadao looked him straight in the eyes. "Now hold steady and do exactly what I say!"

The moment Sadao let go of the handlebars, the kid panicked and his hand lost grip on the brake. His bike began to tip and roll. *Kuso!* Sadao leapt forward and caught the machine before it had a chance to follow the kid to the ground. Soung came up coughing and dusty from his unplanned trip to the ground while his peers got a good laugh in.

"Shizuka ni shinasai!!" Even though only a quarter of the assembled punks were from Japan, Sadao's sudden use of his native tongue got their traps to shut tight. They knew he was serious now.

"That could have been any one of you! Mark my words - when the gun fires for real, no one will be there to catch you! A broken arm or leg means you'll be sitting out the season in the medical tents and fed scrapings from the bottom of the kitchen pots! These six months of training are the last free meals and warm beds you'll know until you prove yourselves on the tracks! Now pay attention before I stop giving a fuck about your thankless necks!"

Sadao steadied the handlebars and motioned Soung to remount. The kid looked terrified but got on, waiting for instruction.

"Good, now leg down and grip the brake. Trust me, you won't go anywhere." The kid nodded nervously and held on as Sadao slowly released him and stepped back. "Okay, you're on a steep incline and your bike just stalled. Can any of you recall from your class training what you do next?"

Silence.

"Anyone?!"

Fuck. Bakayaros, all of them. But honestly, did you truly absorb any of the book learned skills once the exams were gathered?

"Soung, tell these empty-headed idiots what to do."

"Umm ... turn the wheel?"

"Good, yes! You remember which way?"

Kid shook his head.

"Hard left. Hold the brake, dismount and release it slowly. Watch what happens."

The kid slid off gingerly and with a death grip on the handbrake, cranked his wheel hard.

"Loosen it a little at a time - follow it."

Wide-eyed, the kid did as told and let the bike slowly turn and backup around his right hip.

"Good, see this? Soung is allowing gravity to work for him. Stop when the bike is perpendicular to the track." The bike was now below the kid but braced against his right side - well balanced and in no peril of tipping and dragging the kid down the hill with it.

"Now, you grip the brake again and crank your front wheel hard right, hard left. Again! Hard right, hard left!"

Soung did as he was told and drew amazed reactions from the kids as the bike magically worked itself into a downhill aimed trajectory. In another few seconds, it was pointed perfectly downhill.

"Now mount it, release the brake and coast back downhill to safety!"

The kid smiled in success and rolled to a gentle stop in the midst of his incredulous peers.

"Well done. Now Everett - drive on up to the same mark!"

Whoop! Whoop! Whoop!

An alarm howled over the desert floor from the main compound. Chow time had come sooner than Sadao had expected. "Alright, break! Get some food and stay out of the direct sun. Be back at 4:30! We work until dark!"

Sadao walked back down to his own mount and rode in along behind his charges until they were safely off the fields, parked and headed for the canteen.

A familiar statuesque form was waiting for him by the equipment trailer. She rushed out to greet him among the hungry youth. Long thin arms wrapped around his shoulders and a small kiss met his cheek.

"Gisette! I didn't know you were coming into Tucson today!"

Her red lips stretched into an excited smile. "I like to come by unannounced. Gives me a chance to watch you in action, Commander!"

"Ugh, tough day," he said, matching her steps toward the dining hall. "Pig-headed brats think they know everything!"

Her laugher peeled out like a bell. "Sounds familiar!"

"I wasn't half that idiotic. I respected my trainers!"

"Ha! You suffered more than your share of breaks and bruises in your salad days, my darling. I've seen your X-Rays. Your only saving grace was you got better at it."

"Hm, so what brings you into headquarters? I wasn't aware of any Sponsor meetings."

"Oh nothing too special, my dear Sadao," she said, taking his arm at the canteen door. "Let's get you your lunch, then I'll elaborate over the break."

After mess, Gisette led Sadao back toward the residential trailer lot, as was customary for her unannounced visits. But she soon steered him away from his usual parking spot and covered his eyes with her hands.

"Keep to the left. Don't peek," Gisette said, skittering along in the gravel behind him, holding her hands over his eyes.

"Cheat at what? Not landing directly on my face? I can't walk like this!"

"Oh hush! It's not much further, darling. Turn just here ... good. A few more steps...and stop!"

"Can I open my eyes now?!"

"Yes!" she said, flinging away her hands.

Parked in front of them was an 80-foot black and silver racing trailer rig fused to a living space, which was further joined by a full length detachable equipment trailer.

"Surprise! *Tanjubi - ome - daito* - something I think I'm supposed to say," she laughed, kissing his cheek.

"*Tanjyoubi omedatou,*" he corrected. "It's my birthday? Already?" He looked to his watch - May 12. *Shit. I'm older again.*

"Happy 27th, my busy Sadao!"

"I had no idea it was today. What is this, Gisette? A new training trailer for the team?"

"No, silly. It's for you!"

He looked at her. "You're kidding."

"Not one bit, my sweet. I hope you like the colors - I had it custom painted to match your style."

"Gisette - that's ... do you know what these cost?!"

"Um ... yes I do," she said, searching through her purse and pulling out a set of keys. "In fact, I'll be making some payments on it for a few years to come. But no worries, both of our names will be on the pink slip once it's paid in full."

"I -" He had no words.

"Here," she said, laying the keyring in his hand. "Open your gift."

Shaking his head to make sure he wasn't having a flashback hallucination from that celebration party back in 2053, Sadao climbed the steps and unlocked the main living entrance. Inside, he was hit with a blast of soothing air conditioning and that unmistakeable new vehicle smell. He stepped in and turned to give her a hand up, then shut the door behind them.

"Why did you do this?" he asked in disbelief, dragging his fingertips along the untouched countertops and fixtures.

"I thought our Division Training Base Commander could use some fresh wheels."

"But it's ..." His voice was lost as he wandered through the dining lounge, kitchen and into the wide pre-furnished rear bedroom; it was complete with a fully outfitted queen bed, matching bath, shower and laundry. " ... so much..."

Her arms wrapped around his middle and gave him a friendly squeeze. "Nothing but the best for my favorite champion!" she said proudly, kissing his chin. "You've earned this. We've earned this!"

Sadao slid his arm around her and pulled her close for a long sincere kiss. Gisette's heart fluttered against his chest. Her hands were warm on his arms. He released her lips and brushed a loose strand of curls from her cheek. "I love it," he said. "But you shou-"

"Shh! No more protests!" she laughed, touching his lips. "Instead be thankful you have such a generous benefactor - oh!"

Sadao scooped her up and threw her down on the freshly made bed. He knelt over her, pushing her down into the soft cool linens. "How about I show you just how thankful I really am," he said against her temple.

Her lips parted and her breathing quickened. "No protest…" she whispered. Sadao pulled up the end of her skirt and slid his hand down between her thighs to run a finger along the inside trim of her panties. This touch lingered at a spot of moisture that had already gathered in the center of the silky fabric.

"How long has it been, Gisette?" he asked, tracing her cleft through the damp fabric while she shuddered.

"Since lunch, I think - !"

Sadao laughed against her throat. "I meant since I last gave you a proper fuck."

"Ah-!" Her whole body jolted at the nip he gave her lower lip. He hooked his finger around the edge of the offending fabric, pulling it aside. Her wetness coursed out from between her lips as soon as he parted them. With gentle fingertips he explored her fold by fold as they kissed, rubbing his thumb against her pulsing clit. She broke from his mouth with a moan and tossed her head. Her curls came unbound from her hairband and tumbled over the new pillows. "A month or more … ," she whispered. "A month or more with anyone …" she admitted with another long moan.

Poor needy thing. Her engorged clit throbbed as he rolled it between his finger and thumb. "We'll need to remedy that," he said, kissing her lips lightly.

She gasped and her hips rolled, drenching him again. She was always so responsive to him, so tuned to his caresses. There was never a lot of guesswork with Gisette - just pure effortless pleasure.

He pulled down the collar of her blouse until her nipple popped free from her small lacy bra. He toyed at the erect nub with his tongue. He knew just how to wind her up - with small tight circles around the most sensitive points of her nipple and clit. Her back arched and her moans grew more steady and needful as her fingers tangled in his hair.

"*S'il te plaît, Sadao…*" she purred.

His dick was a solid mass in his jeans, eager to satisfy her; to just let go and thrust mindlessly into the wetness he was exploring with his hand. In truth, he hadn't felt pussy in a good long while himself. There weren't a lot of women to be had in the middle of the Sonoran Desert. He was fully intent on the idea of christening his new bed, but a gift this generous required a proper thanking. He kissed her mouth, sucked on her thirsty tongue and then sat up. He pulled off his shirt and slid down to the end of the bed, draping her legs over his shoulders. She moaned his name - begging in French and English - as he settled in-between her thighs and buried his face in dark silk-rimmed heaven.

Sadao sat up cross-legged beside Gisette's nude languid body on the thoroughly rumpled bed. He was pleased to see the thick mattress and solid frame could hold up to a proper nailing. He reached to the floor for his jeans and pulled out a pack of cigarettes. Her eyes were closed and she wasn't quite breathing calmly enough to speak, so he lit one and took his time enjoying his first smoke in his new domain.

After a generous meal of her flesh under his tongue, they'd gone two rounds of hard, intense fucking. At 30 now, Gisette was well into her sexual stride. It took more effort then he remembered to wear her down with his dick. *Was a good plan to ease her through warm-ups with my tongue*, he thought, as he wiped the residual slickness from his braided chin with a damp washcloth from his new sparklingly clean bathroom. It took concentration and proper pacing to bring her off through seemingly endless screaming, sheet-pulling orgasms. Seeing her laid out like the blissful dead gave him a glowing sense of victory, despite the ache in his knees.

She stirred by the time he lit his second smoke, flicking ash into a cocktail glass he'd grabbed from the lounge.

"Light me one," she said, lifting her head.

He did and set it between her lips. She took a drag and exhaled in a long sigh.

"Feeling properly thanked?" Sadao asked.

"Yes…" she said with a smile. "Well worth my travel efforts."

Sadao grinned. "I suppose I don't get around as much as I used to. Headquarters is not a nomadic establishment. However, the upgrades are worth the ball and chain I'm discovering," he said, indicating his new surroundings.

She smirked at him. "Don't get too proud. Training Commander is certainly a coveted position, but you haven't caught the brass ring just yet. We still have some hurdles to leap."

"What kind of hurdles?"

"Chairman Baker." She dragged herself up to lean back into the pillows. Time for serious business talk now that the fucking and gifting was out of the way.

"Chairman who?" Sadao asked, blowing smoke up toward the ceiling. *Excellent ventilation system*, he noted. Smoke was sucked right out in seconds. He wouldn't have to wash his curtains so often.

"Baker. He's a Canadian real estate mogul from Victoria BC. He's been appointed new chair of the Northwest Draft Committee. I'm sure you've heard - there's been talk of changes. Some of the top shareholders are displeased with the imbalance between the western and eastern teams."

"I've heard. What does this have to do with me? Trainers have no say in the draft lottery. Teams are all hydrated from the top down."

"Which is why there's such poor balance. What Baker is proposing is eliminating the draft altogether - leaving recruit selections to the racing team leaders themselves. With the shockingly fresh idea that maybe racers know racing better than fat old men in reclining chairs."

Sadao was caught off guard. There'd been no public word of this yet. "What's our move?"

"Simple, darling. You're going to pay our new chairman a visit and convince him to give you authority to choose your own men ... for your own brand-new, hand-picked team."

Sadao grunted. "Is he going to pay my trading fees? I'm on a fixed Division salary now. I don't have nearly that level of buying power - even with my savings. Which is why the Division suits always handle it."

Gisette fondled Sadao's knee with her toes. "What did they pay for you, darling?"

"Me? Nothing. I was a desperate teenager. A few beers and bratwurst and I was eating out of their hands."

She laughed. "You were indeed a diamond among rocks. But I think there might be more out there. We just need to find them…maybe among some of the fresh boys you've been barking orders at all spring."

Sadao sat and stared at her through the vein of smoke rising from between his fingers.

"You've got to be fucking kidding me."

"I'm not."

"This year's brats barely know how to find the gear pegs!"

"Then you'll find some who can."

"Forget it! It's a ridiculous idea! Say I go back to Baja with a few thousand in my pocket and rescue some of these poor kids off the boats before they get hooked on needles. There's no guarantee they'll amount to anything! It costs money to clothe and feed dead weight!"

"Not if you train them properly…"

"I have serious A-List racers to coach for competitions! I don't have time to babysit!"

"Serious racers who were also lost boys once. Just like you. What difference does it make if they're handed down to you by your superiors or hand-picked by yourself? You would at least have the opportunity to evaluate them eye-to-eye - look for that hidden spark."

Sadao killed his cigarette. "And if they prove to be nothing more but hands and legs with hungry mouths?"

Gisette leaned in close and stroked his short beard. "Then you'll have the foundations of a camp staff. They will be utterly loyal to you, darling. Trust me - some of them will prove to be gems. You rescue them from poverty, they'll be yours for life. They'll bless you with a devotion no bought-and-sold racing dog will ever give you."

She had vision - he'd give her that. But ... if these boys failed at the track, he'd be laughed out of the wastelands. Sadao wasn't sure he was willing to put his whole career on the line like that.

"Look," she said, taking his hand and kissing it. "I can give you $500,000 to buy a few trades to boost your odds if you'd like. But don't forget, you'll need to get this past Chairman Baker first."

"You just bought this trailer! Where's all this money coming from?"

"Dr. Hawthorn has a few holes in his pockets he hasn't noticed quite yet..."

"Fuck! Gisette, he's going to notice soon enough!"

"That's my problem, darling. Not yours. I can handle my husband."

Sadao rubbed his forehead. He hadn't been prepared for any of this today - not even the arrival of his 27th year. In three more years he'd be 30 - ancient for a racer. It had been a hard decision last year to leave the active roster for a more prestigious, safer but justifiably more frustrating job as Training Commander. How long did he want to put up with teen attitudes and thankless hot shots? If he were boss of his own team, he could compete as he liked and still enjoy a small fortune in winnings; assuming he had racers under his wing who could win.

"So ... where do I start?"

"Well, as I said, you can start by paying Chairman Baker a visit..."

"And ... what? Play poker with him for a team charter? I don't know anything about this man."

Gisette tossed her head back and laughed. "Darling, you are so dense sometimes. Do I have to draw you a diagram? I said, pay him a *visit*. He's quite handsome for his age."

Sadao groaned in realization of what she was suggesting. "Forget it."

"Why?"

"I don't fuck men," Sadao said, lighting another cigarette. "I'm not gay."

This only brought on more fits of giggles. "Gay is not a prerequisite for success!"

"For me it is!"

"My dear Sadao, sometimes I wonder where these fatalistic notions come from. Certainly not from the man I used to see crossing finish lines far ahead of the pack in a blur of smoke! Is your winning spirit cowering now? When you are so close to the victory you've coveted for years! Your own team, Sadao! Certainly, you can overlook a few inconveniences in the bedroom to secure this deal."

"That's easy for a woman to say!" Sadao interjected. "You don't have to perform! You can just lie there!"

She leaned forward and stroked his spent penis. "So can you..."

"I said forget it!" he yelled, shoving her hand away.

"Oh! Oh, darling, I'm sorry - I didn't think …"

He got up and took his ashtray glass with him, pacing the bedroom.

"There has to be something else," he insisted. "Something this man wants - other than my ass. Because *that* is out of the question!"

Gisette lay back on the bed sheets, her hands empty. "Chairman Baker is worth 2.8 billion, Sadao. You can't bring him a 50-year-old bottle of Irish Whiskey and expect him to remember your name the next day. Men are simple beasts. This is the only truth I know."

Sadao leaned against the doorway, smoking thoughtfully. He watched Gisette stretch across his new bed, nipples pointed at the ceiling. His dick stirred at a sudden thought.

"Do you think he would consider three for dinner?"

Gisette sat straight up, mouth agape. *"Mon Dieu!* Sadao Koga, you *are* still a champion!"

"Is this supposed to impress me?" Sadao asked his companion as he peered out the windscreen of Gisette's large rented SUV. They were stopped at a light, waiting to turn into a parking structure, as fierce rain fell in sheets across the lamplit streets of Victoria, British Columbia. Chairman Baker owned most of the harbor waterfront properties on the east end of the city. Tall colorful steel and glass high-rise buildings shone brilliantly in the scattered rain through the swish of the wipers. But it wasn't the audacious architecture that irritated Sadao's sensibilities; it was the giant inescapable red steel *torii* gate erected over the adjoining courtyard of clubs and restaurants - all flashing in 1990s retro Tokyo neon.

"Hush, Sadao. Remember to let me make all the proper introductions before you shatter the mood with your unfailing charm," she said as the light changed and they drove into the shelter of the garage. Gisette stopped at the valet stand and they donned raincoats as they exited the vehicle. Gisette handed over her keys, and the two of them ducked under a shared umbrella to brave the rotten weather among the fellow dining patrons trotting past the dripping Katakana lettered lights.

"Most of these signs aren't even spelled correctly," Sadao noted. "Don't they know most of Japan lives without electricity now! Tokyo is under 30 feet of ocean!"

"I'm certain the city planners would be thrilled to receive your creative input, darling. But for now, let's focus on our goals for the evening. One piece of paper, two small signatures and a new team will be in your hands."

"I wish it was that simple," Sadao grumbled, grasping Gisette's gloved hand as she led him around the flashing puddles and into the foyer of a busy high-end sushi restaurant called - literally - Fish Good Face Eat.

An Asian woman dressed like a geisha bowed to them and asked if they had a reservation.

"Certainly," Gisette said with a generous smile. "Chairman Baker is expecting us. Tell him Gisette Hawthorn and company have arrived."

"Oh, of course. How many in your party, please?"

"Futari dake shikainai-ze!" Sadao said irritatedly. The hostess blinked in incomprehension.

"I'm sorry…?"

"Two!" he clarified.

The hostess bowed again. "Just a moment, please. I will inform the Chairman."

Gisette placed a firm hand on Sadao's chest. The buttons of his pressed suit coat dug into his ribs. "Please, Sadao. Control yourself."

"He hired a Korean hostess and doesn't even know it! I'm not touching the sushi here."

"Why all this hostility against a man who's set on helping you!"

"Set on helping me for a very particular price!"

"You need to calm down. We discussed this. Just follow my lead."

Sadao fiddled in this overcoat pocket for his cigarette pack - he didn't find it. He glared accusingly at Gisette.

"I cleaned out your pockets at the airport - no smoking. I told you, it's the law in the public districts here!"

"Great. Can I drink?"

"Yes darling, of course."

"Perfect. I plan on getting roaring drunk before this night's half-over!"

Their Japanese-impaired hostess returned shortly and led them upstairs to a row of shoji screen-enclosed *washitsu*-style dining rooms. The "geisha" opened one of the unoccupied tables, and they were invited to remove their raincoats and shoes and step up onto the tatami. The lighting and decor were a fairly decent replica of the *Muromachi*-era dining rooms Sadao remembered visiting as a child when his father had business in town. The intimate space had shaded lamps, hand painted scrolls, and even an artfully designed flower vase set into a shallow *tokonoma*. The low central table was surrounded by four *zaisu*-padded chairs. Their hostess informed them the Chairman would be joining them shortly, as she shut the sliding screen.

"Oh look, darling! We get to sit on the floor! How fun!"

Sadao assisted her into one of the seats. "Now how do I place my legs? I never could figure this out properly."

"They're designed for sitting on your knees. Very uncomfortable for long periods. I was relieved to discover Americans actually attach legs to their furniture!"

"Oh, Sadao." Gisette looked up at him with pleading eyes. "Please try to be patient tonight. You can roar about all you like in your American leather and denim in the desert dust once this deal is closed. Of all people, I'd think you'd enjoy a little remembrance of your homeland."

Sadao folded himself cross-legged into the seat next to her and loosened his coat buttons and tie a few pegs. Sadao hated ties but Gisette had insisted on dressing him like a mortician tonight. "All I want to remember of my homeland right now is the taste of sake and beer!"

Gisette looked heavenward. *"Mon Dieu, moi aussi."*

They didn't have long to wait. Their screen shuddered open and a pair of pre-filled wine glasses were served to them by the sommelier, who quickly bowed and retreated.

Sadao lifted the glass to his nose and made a face. "Ume. Plum wine - disgusting!"

"Oh, I think it smells wonderful." Gisette took a sip, licked her lips and took a longer sip. "The taste is delightful, too! So sweet!"

"I got sick once on cheap plum wine as a teenager," Sadao said. "Never again."

Gisette drained her glass and reached for his. "More for me, then."

She managed to down most of the second glass by the time the doors slid open once again, revealing a man of average height with short brown hair dressed in a finely tailored dark-grey suit.

"Thank you for waiting," he said, removing his shoes and stepping in with a smile full of perfectly straight teeth. "I'm Chairman Reid Baker." He held his tie and leaned over the table to shake his guests' hands before he settled himself upon a cushion. Baker had fine high cheekbones and a fit build that belied his age. Sadao had to begrudgingly admit he was a decent-looking man for someone in his mid-forties.

"Commander Koga, it is a pleasure to finally meet you. I have followed your career for many years. I was heartbroken of course to hear you had retired from racing last year, but pleased to know our Division headquarters' trainees are in fine hands."

Sadao bowed his head in calculated respect.

"I was at the edge of my seat in my Chinook when you jumped that waterfall in the 2050 Rocky Mountain Overland. A stunning success! I predicted you would prove to be one of racing's greatest stars - and I was not disappointed. Many of your career records I'm sure will hold for decades to come. I'm not ashamed to admit I was overjoyed to receive Madame Hawthorn's request to finally meet with you in person."

"And we are overjoyed to meet you too!" Gisette said brightly, while pinching Sadao's thigh under the table. Sadao cleared his throat and nodded in kind.

"Thank you for meeting with us, Chairman," he added. "I believe Gisette informed you of why we're here tonight."

The Chairman beamed. "Of course, of course! You desire a team! Why not? It's the pinnacle achievement of any racing career, isn't it? Of course, we've had many applicants as you know," he laughed. "Decisions can't be made too quickly. So let's take our time tonight and enjoy the harbor nightlife! What do you make of our establishment, Commander?"

Sadao wished to all Gods he had a drink or five down his throat before now. "It's … homey."

"It's just stunning!" Gisette beamed. Her face was flushed pink from the wine. "Sadao was just remarking to me about how fine and authentic the furnishings were!"

"Wonderful!" the Chairman said, clasping his hands together. "The decorator and I did exhaustive research into both ancient and pre-civil war Japan. If you noticed in our foyer we have an exact replica of 'Catching a Catfish with a Gourd' by Master Josetsu from the 14th Century. I insisted that the artist use the same ink mixing processes and paper treatments. All handmade, of course, with authentic gold leaf. We spared no expense."

"I can tell," Sadao remarked.

"And, of course, our food and libations are equally authentic. I hope you don't mind - I asked our head chef to prepare a special meal for us this evening. A real honest-to-goodness Japanese *kaiseki* dining experience - ten courses! I helped develop some of the secret sauces myself and - oh! What did you think of our plum wine, Commander? It's imported!"

"I detest *umeshu*," Sadao answered. Gisette went for his balls but he arrested her hand just in time.

"Ah! A shame I didn't know. What would you prefer? Ask and it will be delivered!"

"Sapporo - ice cold. And keep it coming."

The Chairman picked up a small bell on the table and rang it. The door slid open immediately. "Yes, Chairman?"

"Sapporos please, for myself and the Commander. In the freezer, glasses - the tall ones," he said and then turned to Gisette, who was looking oddly bleary eyed. "And for Madame?"

"Oh my … I'd die for another glass of that … um … " Her eyes rolled back in her head and she pitched head-first against the table. Bam!

"Gisette!" Sadao lifted her head and patted her cheek. She was out cold. "Gisette? Gisette?!"

Sadao looked to the Chairman who looked to the waiter. "Fetch some ice water!" he ordered and the waiter fled, slamming the shoji door abruptly.

"Is she alright?" the Chairman asked, getting up.

"I don't know," Sadao said, pressing his thumb to her wrist. "Her pulse is very fast. She feels warm. Warmer than usual."

"There's a flu going around you know," The Chairman offered, crawling to her side and laying his own hand against her cheek.

"We were in Arizona until yesterday!" Sadao said. "I hardly think it's a virus. Gisette? Can you hear me? Help me lay her down."

Sadao lifted Gisette from the chair and set her a few feet away on the mat floor, while the Chairman placed a spare cushion under her head. Her eyes fluttered open a moment and she mumbled something incoherent. Sadao leaned in closer.

"Embrasse-moi ... " Her hand groped for his face as if in a trance. Then her eyes rolled shut again and she was out.

"Uh-oh."

Sadao glared at the Chairman. Guilty was written all over his face. "Uh-oh, what?"

Chairman Baker was nibbling his thumb. "Well, I think it's one of two things. Either she's allergic to wine or maybe she has a slight sensitivity to ... uh ... "

Sadao grabbed the Chairman by the tie and brought his face to his own. "She's not allergic to wine, *bakayaro*! You dosed the fucking wine, didn't you?"

The Chairman looked completely gobsmacked. "I - uh ... may have asked my sommelier to - you know, to help us all feel more comfortable. Gisette said you might be reluctant. I swear it was only a drop or two ...Oogh!"

Sadao nailed him in the gut with his left fist. The Chairman bent over gasping, just as the waiter slid the door open with a pitcher of water.

"Call a doctor!" Sadao yelled, grabbing the pitcher from the hapless waitstaff who couldn't tell who was in more distress - the fainted woman or the bent-over Chairman.

"No!" the Chairman coughed. "We're fine! Just shut the door!"

Sadao ignored him and grabbed one of the wine glasses, wiping it out with a napkin. He filled it with water and, supporting Gisette with his arm, tried to get some of it between her lips. The liquid went nowhere except down her chin and onto the tatami.

"You don't have to worry," the Chairman said, finding his voice. "She'll just sleep it off. She got too much of it, I think. I tried to guess her weight and yours ... "

"Well, she's not going to sleep it off here!" Sadao said, getting up and lifting her into his arms. "Open that fucking screen or I'll kick it open!"

The Chairman waved his hands in defense. "No-no please. Just listen to me ... I didn't mean any harm to her. Honest. She'll be fine in a few hours. I was just really looking forward to closing this deal with, uh... you. Really looking forward to it." He stood there with the cheesiest smile on his awkward face.

Sadao was stunned - this asshole was outright begging and blocking his path. "Is this supposed to impress me? That you'd use such low tactics to get me to comply?"

"I don't know what I was thinking! She said a few things about being concerned you might not be totally game on this ... and that's fine, I get it! She said you might need some encouragement, but -"

"Out of my way!" Sadao said, shoving him aside. The Chairman fell back on his ass and immediately went into his coat pocket and pulled out an envelope.

"Look! I've got it! I've got it right here! The charter! I brought it along and everything!"

Sadao turned around. With Gisette still in his arms, he watched as the Chairman took the paper and a pen out of the envelope slowly and set it on the table, palms up in supplication.

"See? All it needs is signatures - yours and mine and the deal's done. Just … don't leave yet. Please."

Sadao looked at Gisette's flushed face and then at the contract and pen. *Fuck!* He gritted his teeth and with care, laid Gisette's head back down on the cushion and covered her with his suitcoat.

The Chairman knelt next to the table, looking almost as flushed as her. Sadao lunged for him, pinned one arm behind his back, and shoved him face down on the tabletop next to the paperwork. "Sign it, *kusoyaro!*" he growled, pressing his cheek into the polished cherrywood.

"Yeah, yeah! I will! I will! But uh … what about your end of, you know … the deal?"

"The deal's off! I'm calling the shots now, Chairman. If you want your arm still attached to your body, I'd suggest you pick up that pen and start moving it!"

"Well, I thought maybe we could, you know, have those beers and uh…."

"You forfeited your lingering erotic evening when you decided to drug your guests!" The realization whipped through Sadao's mind that he was going to have to close this deal stone-cold sober. "Did you really think I would want to fuck a sad pathetic piece of waste like you?"

"Well, to be honest, no …" The man's words were slurred due to the fact he could only move half of his mouth, the other side being slowly engraved into the woodwork. "That's why I spiked the drinks, you know. Make it fun! Win-win for everyone!"

Sadao tightened his grip on the man's arm and pressed his weight down on him until he heard his ribs pop. "Does this feel like fun to you?! Playing with people's lives?! Is this how you get off?"

There was a pause. "Kind of?"

"You make me sick - people like you!" Rage filled Sadao's mind. He leaned in close until his beard dangled against the man's flushed cheek.

"Your money - your entitlement! Your pandering to your own self-imagined world! Did you really think I would be impressed by your fake bullshit?! You know nothing about the world I live in! Now do something that will impress me and sign!"

The Chairman screwed his eyes shut and shook his head.

Sadao raised his head a few inches off the table and slammed it back down. "Sign!!"

"You - you know you can't kill me, right?" he panted as blood began to leak from his nose. "I'm … a very important man! People in the Division would be really pissed off!"

"That doesn't mean I can't bruise you end to end!"

Sadao lifted the man's head again and slammed it down harder, making the remaining wine glass topple over. Nothing more came from the Chairman except more blood and a moan - a moan that had no place in this scenario. Sadao bent down and groped the prick's crotch. He was hard as a rock.

"You've got to be fucking kidding me!" Sadao spat, releasing the Chairman like he'd just touched a corpse. The Chairman slumped back against the table, still on his knees. He was grinning strangely and wiping the blood from his face in awe. "This is exactly what you wanted, isn't it?" Sadao confirmed.

The Chairman looked at his reddened wrist in fascination, turning it over, admiring the bruises Sadao's fingers had imprinted in his flesh. "Whoa … " the creep said. "Do you think you could give me a scar?"

"*Kuso!*"

Sadao smacked the asshole across the face and he fell facedown on the table again with another rapturous moan. Sadao pulled his finely tailored pants clear down off his hips with a yank, exposing his pale ass. "You'd better have prepared for this, because I'm not going in bare!"

The slimeball raised a finger and pointed to the flower vase with the tasteful arrangement. Sadao grabbed the porcelain and smashed it against the table's edge. A packet of condoms rolled out - a lot of them. Not a new roll, either. This wasn't the Chairman's first dance at this ball. Sadao tore one off with his teeth and ripped it the rest of the way open. He unzipped. The blood was roaring in his ears as he unrolled the latex down over his shaft. He didn't stop to wonder about when he'd gotten hard himself. But he was--very. An asshole was an asshole and if it was asking for an angry fuck, he was more than in the mood to bring down the punishment.

He worked up a mouthful of disgust and spit into the man's hairy crack. "Now Chairman, I'd suggest you grab that fucking pen!"

What his restaurant patrons must have thought, hearing the commotion coming from inside those translucent paper walls. The moans, the curses, the smashing of glass, the cracking of wood and through it all - the raw screams of Chairman Reid Baker's unbridled ecstasy.

Sadao shoved himself in with one furious thrust and proceeded to nail the bastard up against the table. One of the legs gave way and whole surface collapsed, sending the servingware and soy sauce tumbling to the tatami floor. The Chairman's arm began to bleed from an errant glass shard. He shouted cries of joy as Sadao gripped his ass cheeks and slammed his cock into him over and over until the man collapsed flat like his replicated furniture. Prone, the Chairman had to fight to keep air in his lungs under the onslaught with pathetic cries of uh … ugh..ughh - ! And the more he gasped and struggled, the more Sadao wanted to make him grunt like a pig.

"Get up!" Sadao lifted him up by the back of his expensive suit, ripping off part of the collar. He forced the Chairman's hips up and pressed his bleeding nose into the floor.

"Beg for it!" he barked.

"I ... oh! No! Don't stop..mm ... more... please!"

Sadao smacked his toned white ass. Wham! "Please, what?!"

"Ohh ... please, fuck me ... harder!"

Smack! "Your asshole knows how to address me better! I have a title! Use it!"

"Yes!! Commander! I'm sorry, Commander! Please ... More!!"

Sadao jerked his sweaty head up by the hair. "More what?!"

"More ... pounding up my ass ... grab my dick! Make it squirt!"

Sadao shoved his head back down and resumed pummeling his hungry asshole. The stretched rim was swollen and wet from the friction. "I'm not touching your filthy prick! That's your problem!"

Sadao could see the man make a fumbling attempt to reach down and rub at the end of his drooling rod. It jutted out from between his thighs, dripping into his underpants bunched around his knees. Sadao grabbed his hand and pinned it behind his back while he delivered a barrage of steady bruising thrusts that made the pathetic jerk wail.

"Aah ... I gotta... come ... ohh I need it, please let me touch it!! Please Commander!!"

"Not until you sign!"

"I-I will just ... I gotta come, please! Oh! It's so hard, it hurts!"

Sadao smacked him on the ass. Four hard blows made his suffering dick drip with precum. "I said fucking sign the charter! You don't come until you do!"

"I will, I will ... can't reach it ... ohh, more, yes ... ah! Hit me! Pull my hair - oh!"

Smack! Sadao hit him again and with his dick still buried ball's deep in the asshole's rectum, he reached over for the fallen charter half-hidden under the broken table. He grabbed it and shoved it under the Chairman's gory nose. He pulled his hair up. "Where's the fucking pen?"

"Oh your cock... so good ... keep going ... I got another one in my ... oh, for fuck's sake ... don't stop now, Commander!"

"Another pen in your what? It's not in your ass! That, I can verify!"

"Jacket - !"

"Grab it! Put it in your hand! You sign and I'll jerk you until you bust a nut!"

The Chairman reached for his ripped jacket pocket with his fingertips. Face to the floor, he rolled a new pen out and twisted it open with his teeth. "See, I gow wit!"

Sadao smacked his ass again, eliciting another moan.

"Get writing!"

The Chairman - bruises, scrapes and all - dragged the paper close to his chin and transferring the pen to his left hand, scrawled his signature on the correct line.

He turned his blood and tear-streaked face to Sadao and offered him the pen with a look of total desperation. "Now you?"

"Nnngh! Scoot forward!" Dick still embedded, Sadao pitched himself over the simpering freak and added his own signature directly above his.

Done - it's done! Elation shot through Sadao at the realization that through all the absurdity and violence, both had somehow found their darkest dreams realized.

Still gripping the back of the Chairman's head, Sadao took the charter and stuffed it into his front shirt pocket - that was somehow still intact.

"Mmm… nnn…" The asshole's asshole was still quivering. "I - I still have to ratify it, you know … deliver a declaration to the board and … then the land partitioning and …"

Smack! "Shut the fuck up! We finish this then, in grand style!"

Ears to the paper walls, the horrified dinner guests in the room adjacent had no idea the owner of their dining establishment was not only the source of all the commotion, but also about to make an unscheduled appearance. His bloodied head, torso, and full frontal erection came bursting through the authentically painted rice paper wall, spurting a big helping of extra special secret sauce all over their *agadashi* tofu and baked *mochi* appetizers.

"Excuse us," Sadao said, dismounting his spent and battered steed. The Chairman melted into the carnage, moaning in bliss as Sadao found his feet in the splinters of wood and ripped paper. He stood proudly over his kill, unrolled the condom and tied off the filled end in a neat pearlescent ball that he tossed aside. Tucked in, zipped and buckled, he retreated into their trashed *washitsu* - now perfectly resembling the war-torn country he had left 19 years prior. He collected his inert date and left without asking for the check.

Three hours later, Sadao sat in an opulent chair in an open silk robe looking out the windows of his Grand Victoria Hotel suite. He'd finished off most of a six-pack of Sapporos by himself and had smoked just as much as the boat lights swayed and slurred in the stormy harbor below. On the table next to the ashtray was the Team Charter - a little stained and rumpled, but nevertheless 100% legal. And irrefutable. If the Chairman survived his fuck, he knew there would be many new horizons ahead for former Commander Sadao Koga.

"Well worth the sacrifice," he said smugly, and reached forward to pull out another cigarette. Something odd suddenly caught his eye outside the window. The building across the way was taking a pounding in the windy rain and yet, now there appeared to be someone with long drenched hair crawling about on the metal roof attempting to repair a broken antenna. It looked unspeakably dangerous! Sadao rose to his unstable feet and stepped over to the window for a better look.

Lightning flashed and Sadao rubbed his eyes against the glare of the strike that remained burned in his retina a moment. By the time it faded, the roof across was abandoned. No one there at all - no wet man. And odder still, no antenna. Just your garden variety air conditioning unit. Sadao rubbed his pounding forehead.

"Fuck, I'm drunk."

The bedsheets stirred and Gisette raised her head. "What…? Where am I?"

Sadao turned. There was a proper pink color now in her cheeks. "The Grand Victoria," he said, moving closer. "Suite courtesy of Chairman Reid Baker."

"Oh … I must … did I drink too much?"

"I think so." He sat on the bed next to her and touched her shoulder. "Look."

"What..?" She blinked and squinted at the paper in his hand. "Oh! Sadao! Is that it? You got it!"

Sadao smiled and kissed her head. "Not in a small part thanks to you."

"Oh darling. I'm so happy for you! Are you happy?"

Sadao set the paper on the nightstand carefully, smoothing it flat. "Yes."

"But I forget … did you wind up … uh…"

"Yes."

"Really? You went through with it? Did you like it?"

"No."

"Not even a little bit?"

"No," he asserted, kissing her cheek. "I told you, I'm not gay. I am however, drunk as fuck right now."

She giggled and made room for him next to her in the bed. "Good, I'm dreadfully tired too. Let's sleep in tomorrow darling, shall we?"

Sadao slid in under the covers against her warmth. He laid a loose arm around her and closed his eyes, letting inebriated exhaustion take him under. He was happy - happier than he could ever remember feeling.

"Yes. Let's sleep late."

Ninth

End of the Road

---

50 miles west of the California/Arizona Border - 2063

"I know what you're looking for, boy, and I got it right here," the man who had introduced himself as 'Edgar' said, grabbing his crotch proudly. Mouse eyed the hearty bulge from over the top of his room-temperature beer. They sat across the table from each other in a sparkly red booth while a neon Coke sign buzzed over their heads in time with Aretha on the jukebox wailing for 'respect'.

The afternoon was getting late and Mouse didn't want Fred to worry about him. So despite the slim pickings out here at Sam's Diner on the dusty I-10 junction, Edgar was gonna have to do.

Mouse slung back his beer and killed the remainder in two gulps. "Fine," he belched. "Where's your cab?"

Edgar drove an 18-wheeled red Peterbilt with plates from New Mexico, Arizona and California, and titty girls on the tire flaps.

"So you do the southwest wasteland run?" Mouse asked, accepting a hand up into the cab.

"Sure do," Edgar drawled, drenched in redneck pride as he scooted over into the driver's seat and dropped the sunshade. "Got my old lady back in Albuquerque. Navajo gal, sells turquoise necklaces to tourists stopping for a crap along the highway."

"I really don't need any more conversation," Mouse said, yanking the door shut. He was tired of talking. "Let's do this."

"Whatever you say, boy."

Mouse was tired of talk. He was tired of Edgar's talk, especially. The man was about as intelligent as a road apple with an ego that could barely fit in the bed of his long hauler. But he smelled nice and his cab was clean. No visible signs of knives or duct tape. A picture of his 'ol lady and baby was propped up on the dash in a handmade silver frame. Guy seemed legit - just another prick on the road looking for a blow.

Mouse crawled across the hump and undid the guy's jeans. His thick ruddy cock popped right out, eager for a suck. Ooh, one of the fat-heads. Mouse ran his thumb along the prominently sculpted ridge of the man's mushroom cap. Mouse loved sucking fatties and swallowed him down.

"Ahh ... that sure does hit the spot…"

Mouse tuned him out and tuned in to the feel of his tongue running over the pulsing flesh between his lips. He gripped him at the base and sucked him in deep, drawing his tongue along the ridges and veins. Edgar tasted absolutely delicious.

"Ooh that is mighty fine … "

Too bad this special treat was attached to such a loudmouth. If Mouse wasn't so goddamn hard up for it, he'd have left this guy in the dust with the beer tab and spun the pick-up back home to Blythe - 68 miles south of this shithole.

Mouse hated this. The drive, the standing around pretending to order something, the small talk with men he had next to nothing in common with. Trying to suss out if they were gay or just bored, or seconds away from punching him in the face. But truth was nobody had broken down lately within 20 miles of his garage. It'd been two months, three weeks and six days since his last fuck. His horny ass was wound up so tight he didn't care who he hooked up with, as long as they had a dick and didn't smell like cow.

"Ugh ... fuck boy, that's so good. You gonna make me blow … aagghh!!"

Edgar erupted deep in his throat and Mouse drank him down spurt by spurt while his own dick thudded in envy. The taste and smell of spunk was only making him more nuts for it. He licked Edgar clean between squirms, then shifted back into the passenger's seat and got his own cock out. His shoes, pants and underwear all hit the cab floor. No pussy-footing here. No sir. It was fuck time.

Edgar checked Mouse out thoroughly with a satisfied smirk on his face. "You got a nice long one, don't ya?" But he didn't come any closer - just sat there slumped back against the driver's door, limp and happy.

Mouse gripped himself. "You gonna return the favor?!"

"Ah, suppose," Edgar said as he leaned forward, flipping his family photo face down on the dash. Then he punched an access latch that opened up into his sleeping compartment behind the seats. "You wanna climb on up and do this proper?"

Mouse's cock dripped in approval. "Fuck, yeah!" No shift-ball bruises tonight!

Edgar stripped out of his clothes too and crawled on up after Mouse. Mouse wriggled on a Native American blanket-covered mattress. It smelled freshly laundered. Ah, for once he could go face down in trucker bedding and not pass out from BO.

The man laid down beside him and passed a rough-skinned palm over Mouse's chest. If it weren't for the lack of greymatter between his ears, Mouse might really go for a guy like this - sandy hair, green eyes, freckles. Built like an ox, Edgar's body was all muscles and soft red curly hair. Mouse moaned a bit as his fingers explored Edgar's hard chest and belly. Oh, he loved freckled skin. Well honestly, he loved any skin as long as it was all male and on top of him.

"Don't get too soft on me," Edgar warned. "Told you I got an ol' lady."

"I know that!" Mouse snapped. Geez, can't a guy have a little fantasy for a moment? And oh, was his imagination running fast. In his mind, he had this guy he'd just picked up in a $5 diner - sexy, sweaty, and humping all over him with his big fat dickhead rooting its way to paradise. But Edgar didn't move that fast. He seemed too pleased to just lay there and watch Mouse pant and twitch under his wandering hand.

"Been a while for ya, ain't it?"

"Yeah! So? Hurry up and touch my dick - fuck!"

"I'm gonna get there ... whatcha say your name was? Chipmunk?"

"MOUSE! It's MOUSE already. Shit, who needs names? Aagh!"

Edgar laughed and squeezed Mouse's not-so-little-problem in his fist, giving him a solid stroke that drew a guzzle of precum out of the tip.

"You sure are an anxious critter, Mouse." Edgar said as his palm scooped up the goop. "We'll getcha where you need to go. Now are you a suck n' run kinda guy, or do you like it deep and hard?"

Mouse squirmed and moaned a bit. "Deep - hard ... God!" Edgar was using his wet palm to slicken Mouse's balls. Oooooh, that felt good. Mouse opened his legs and presented his ass for similar treatment. Edgar got the clue and began rubbing damp fingertips around his hole. Mouse shuddered in anticipation.

"Now, don't get me wrong here, boy. I ain't no fag or nuthin'. It's just ... there's things the wife won't do in bed, you know? And she'd go at me with pruning shears if I ever hired a professional gal at one of these here truck stops. I figure, men - you know - she ain't even gonna think of that. So when she says, 'Edgar-bear you been steppin out on me?' I says, 'No, honey I ain't fucked no women but you' - an' it's true!"

"That's ... thoughtful…ahh!" Mouse gasped as Edgar slid a nice thick index finger up his ass.

"I ain't no liar! That's fer damn sure."

God, please shut up!

"Now you want it from the front or the back?"

"Don't care ... just want it!" Why so many damn questions? Wasn't it obvious he'd take it anyway he could get it and twice?! But then if he flipped over, maybe the doof would stop talking. But then he couldn't stare at his abs and ... "Oh shiiiiiittt!"

"Hehee! There you go. Edgar's found your funbuzzer!" Edgar did have his number - right up under the pad of his probing finger - all wound up and screaming for cock. His fingertip smooshed it around, making Mouse's dick twitch. "It's tense as hell up in there, ain't it?"

Mouse pushed himself up on his elbows. "Edgar, for chrissake - get a clue and fuck me!"

Edgar looked stunned. Mouse stared back at him as his blood pounded in his ears. *Shit, did I piss him off?*

Edgar blinked and nodded. "Sure, that's cool." He got up on his knees between Mouse's thighs and, giving Mouse's balls a little lift up, took his fat still-erect dick in hand and began to go for the goal.

"Aagh!" Mouse threw his head back as the tip of Edgar's crown pressed up against his stubborn hole. Edgar felt wide enough to get stuck between his pelvic bones. Mouse squirmed, trying to ease himself around it but for whatever reason, the anxious ring of flesh just wouldn't give it up. Dammit, was he gonna be able to take this guy?

"Mngh, feels like a mighty tight fit," the genius said. "Hang on, think I got something for that."

Something? Mouse opened his eyes in time to see Edgar pull a tube of lube and a small plastic-wrapped shoehorn out of his overnight bag.

Mouse clamped his legs shut. "The fuck do you think you're gonna do with that?"

Edgar shrugged him off as he ripped open the plastic. "Gets feet in shoes, don't it? Don't worry - it's clean. Stayed at Motel 6 last week."

Mouse covered his eyes. Last thing he wanted was a hunk of plastic going up his asshole. But dammit, he was so far beyond ordinary horny right now he was afraid it might actually get him off.

Edgar sat there, fat-headed dick poking straight up as he unwrapped his solution, befuddled by Mouse's reaction. "Maybe I just better suck you, you think?"

"No!" Mouse shouted, braving his situation. Edgar jumped. "Sorry, I'm just a little … *frustrated* right now. Hell with it. Do whatever you gotta do! But I don't wanna watch!"

"Suit yourself!"

Mouse flipped over and buried his face in Navajo fuzz, presenting his ass for… whatever male-gynecological experiment was about to take place. He felt the cool lube getting squeezed out around his butthole like it was toothpaste. Then the probe was introduced, eased into the curve of his ass with a finesse that made Mouse force himself not to think about where dweebus might have learned this skill. There was a tugging sensation, then heat - tremendous heat and pressure.

"Aahghh!!" Mouse wailed, but not entirely in pain. Getting opened up and stretched always felt good but this was amazing. "Ohhhh shiiiiitt!!" He forced himself to relax into it. You got this! You got this!

"Hehee, it's a biggin' ain't it?"

"Fuck yeah," Mouse panted. Just then he felt a "pop" as his muscle ring closed over the edge of Edgar's massive cockhead, and the sticky shoehorn hit the blanket next to his elbow with a thud. Job done well.

"We gotter done, boy!" Edgar declared with a thrust that pushed the flesh of his fat dickhead right up into Mouse's so-called funbuzzer.

Mouse let out a cry so loud it was answered by a far-off coyote.

"Holy hell, boy! You better pipe down or they'll call the cops on us!"

"What cops?" Mouse hissed as Edgar pulled back to give him another thrust. "Been no law around here for a decade."

"Good thing, I guess," Edgar chuckled. "Seein' as you ain't hardly legal age."

"I'm eighteen!" Mouse snapped. And for once, it happened to be true. Fred had given him an extra tank of gas for his birthday and he'd used a quarter of it just driving out to this armpit rest stop.

"Yep, that's what they all say! Hang on boy, I'm takin' you for a ride!"

Mouse dove for a mouthful of blanket to bury his screams as Edgar grabbed his hips and got busy. His ass was so full it burned with the heat of his thrusts, although the lube was doing its job to keep things going smoothly. Mouse bit blanket until his jaw ached and then, oh Lord in heaven… the burn up his ass eased into pure melting pleasure, radiating out through every inch of him - ass to fingertips. "Uuuughhh … ."

Mouse's eyes rolled up into his spinning head. Edgar's ample dick was shooting him right off the planet on rocket 'damn!' He howled into the blanket with each pound; his hands gripped fistfuls of bedding so he could take it even further by matching Edgar's thrusts with a reverse buck of his hips as the man pummeled his flesh into pudding.

"Feelin mighty fine now, ain't ya?"

Mouse spit the blanket fuzz out of his mouth, nodding his head furiously. "More …" Mouse gasped and spread his knees wider, tilting his ass so Edgar's thrusts would shove Mouse's drippy dicktip right into the fluffy blanket motif below. Mouse forgot himself and howled at the dual sensation. His needy dick all rubbed up in soft damp blanket fuzz, his ass pounded raw and hard. This was what it was all about - the drive, the gas, the humiliation. All for 15 minutes of mad rut leading up to a bone-deep release. If he could do it himself, he would. But he couldn't. No matter what masturbatory configuration Mouse had come up with on his own, nothing short of a real man with real hard muscles and a real hard dick could truly get him off.

Pathetic is what you are, his brain decided to inform him.

Lecture me later! I'm trying to get laid here!

"Ohhh, Jesus, boy, you got one hell of an ass! I ain't felt nuthin' this tight since I done fucked a sprinkler hose last summer!" Edgar, in his own brimming ecstasy, was nailing him so fast now the whole cab was rocking and squeaking right along with their ball-smacking fun.

"Shut the fuck up! Both of you!!" Mouse screamed. "I'm gonna shoot!!"

Edgar amazingly sprang into action and pulled a lightning-fast reach around. He gripped Mouse's dick and gave it a rapid tug and twist so perfect, it made Mouse come so hard he heard it hit the blanket. "Aaaahgh … aaaahhh … ohh … God … fuck … shiiit…"

Mouse fell onto the bed as the plug powering every muscle in his body got pulled at once. He was half-aware of Edgar making a similar vulgar tribute to the Holy Father before pulling out and hosing down Mouse's backside. Dude sure worked up a load, seeing as he'd filled Mouse's mouth less than 20 minutes earlier.

Edgar collapsed beside him, gasping for air. "Jesus - hell! That was good! I ain't got no feeling in my legs!"

Buttered on both sides, Mouse couldn't make his body work well enough to flip out of the wet spot to face him, so he mumbled into the sticky blanket. "Wanna go again?"

"Fuck, yeah! Night's still young!"

Mouse felt as light as a bag of helium as he slid out of Edgar's cab to the pavement. He smiled up at the man who'd just banged the stuffing out of him for three hours. For a guy who "wasn't gay," he sure knew how to fuck a guy who was.

"Wish I could buy you a late dinner," Mouse said happily.

"Naw, kid. I should be thanking you. Sorry, I got to get up to Gallup by dawn. Don't feel right just leaving you here."

"S'okay," Mouse said. "I know my way home."

"Hey listen," Edgar said before shutting the passenger door. "I'm gonna be back this way next month, on the 10th in fact. If you wanna hook up again."

Mouse beamed in the dark parking lot as trucks poured slowly in and out. Lights passed over him, scattering shadows that made him look a lot taller than his compact 5'6". "I'd love that. I'll be here!"

"See you then, kid!" Edgar said with a nod and shut the door. His engine growled to life as he turned on his lights and rolled out with a farewell honk.

Mouse waved him off until his taillights became flickering pinpoints on the dusty horizon. *Maybe he's not so dumb after all*, he thought. *Thirty days ... I can do that.*

Mouse gave himself the day off on the 10th that following month and told Fred he had plans to visit an old friend in Bridesfall. He hit the empty freeway early, with a dick shaped bulge in the front of his jeans and a shoehorn shaped one in his back pocket. He arrived at Sam's diner a little after 10 A.M. Nobody came by that day but himself and Sam, hanging around the diner counter until about 5 P.M., when long haulers started driving in for supper and a beer.

Mouse had finished three beers and was feeling fuzzy and depressed as he watched the sun go down over his third plate of pie crumbs.

"Well, think I'm gonna call it," Mouse said, tossing Sam some coins.

"Sorry, Mouse. Not your night, I guess."

"Sure isn't," Mouse said with a forced smile.

He was halfway back to the pickup when he heard a familiar engine approaching from the frontage road. Dust billowed up as the 18-wheeler's lights turned into the diner lot, but Mouse could still make out the California, Arizona and New Mexico plates.

Woot! My ride's here!

A huge smile crossed Mouse's face and he jumped up and down with a wave.

Edgar's truck blared a greeting honk and the brakes hissed as he pulled her into one of the overnight slots.

Mouse shook his head. *You dumbass, did you think this guy carried a stopwatch?*

But his admonishment was silenced as both doors of Edgar's cab opened at the same time. A Native American woman stepped down from the passenger's side, reaching up as her husband handed her their sleeping baby wrapped in a papoose.

Shit. Shit, shit!

Mouse hung back in the shadows and watched as the pair headed for the diner. Edgar walked proudly with a protective arm around his family. The man turned his head and looked back Mouse's way a moment. He made a shrugging gesture and opened the door for his wife and child, where they became bathed in the light and drone of the jukebox. Then the door closed.

Mouse turned and darted back to his pickup, got in and cranked the engine. He backed out squealing in a hail of dust and tire rubber, leaving behind a few skid marks and a cracked plastic Motel 6 shoehorn.

He floored it up and out the frontage road, merging onto the dark highway. He headed south as fast as his father's old wheels could spin, cursing himself, Edgar, and the whole goddamn world in general. It was 20 miles or so before he cooled down enough to maintain a gas-reserving speed. Both windows were down and the hot desert wind blew his hair around his face, wiping his tears. He swore for the hundredth time to himself this would be his last trip to Sam's - the very, very last! Nothing but a waste of gas spent on bad lays and bad pie.

It's not his fault, you know. He didn't lie to you. He just … has people. He has family. They come first. Nothing you can do about that.

Mouse had family too, back home in an old broken down town on the border of nowhere. He knew they were there - Fred, Doc and the others - keeping a light on for him in the Iron Horse Saloon whenever he needed company. Mouse transversed the empty miles now, hurrying back to that place - the only place where he knew he belonged. He clicked on the radio to silence the loneliness, but all he could find as the knob turned was static.

Tenth

Sand and Fire

Racing Camp Corral, Outside Phoenix, AZ - 2066

The wind had come on hard after midnight and worsened throughout the night. Sadao slept fitfully between gusts that shook the trailer from end to end and made the metal walls rattle with each blast of sand.

Crash!

Something broke in the kitchen, but he was too exhausted to bother to go check on it. Whatever it was, it could be swept up later. He rolled in the bed with a curse and came up against bare skin. Sadao opened his eyes. The young man in the bed next to him was lying on his side, head buried in Sadao's favorite pillow. He was fast asleep, oblivious to the war nature was waging against the aluminum walls. The wind storm had come on too quickly for Sadao to justifiably send the rival team's top drag racer home to his proper encampment after their lust was spent.

Sadao regarded his slumber with envy. He figured that with all the energy he'd put into wearing the young champion down that night, he'd feel half as much fatigue - enough to sleep through the pitch and rattle of his own trailer. Maybe he could at least steal back his pillow. Sadao reached out a hand and began to tug…

Beep! Beep! Beep!

Shit. The satellite phone called to him from its charging cradle in the other room. Sadao sat up and swung his legs to the floor, flipping on the low table light.

"Hmm?" The sleeping prince opened an eye. "What's going on? Storm getting worse?"

"My phone," Sadao explained, getting up and rustling on his pants. "You don't need to get up."

The young man stretched under the sheet with a yawn. The light cotton slid down his sculpted chest to his hip, revealing a hint of hip bone. Sadao admired the kid's flawless pale skin, accented with tattoos of Native American totems on his chest and arms. To be that young and primed again… still, he'd managed to fuck his fair share of the champions throughout their touring season - particularly the lighter-skinned Americans. No one sucked cock better.

Beep! Beep! Beep!

"Fuck that's loud!" The favorite pillow was now being used to muffle his bedroom companion's ears.

"I'm getting it!" Sadao said, leaving the room and reaching for the howling unit on the shelf next to his lounge. He grabbed it and pushed the "Talk" button. *"Dare ka?"*

"Boss?" It was his watchman.

"This better be important! Do you know what time it is?'

"It's 3:48 A.M., Boss, but the wind has grown strong. It's ripping off the storage tarps and tearing apart the supply sacks."

"Are you tying them back down?"

"Hai, we are doing our best, Boss. Fujiwara is waking more men."

"Then why are you calling me? Are you expecting me to tie better knots? Captain Takayama is on active duty tonight! Get him to find more rope!"

"It's not just the rope, Boss, it's …"

"It's what?"

"Boss, can you see out your east windows?"

There was something eerie in his watchman's voice. Sadao set the phone down and leaned over to the kitchen window - the only window facing east in his current parking arrangement.

The light outside was a sickly orange color that lit up the kitchen interior as Sadao unscrewed the blinds. Gusts of sand obscured any view of the distance.

Sadao grabbed the phone. "What is it?!"

"Boss, the Shiratori camp is on fire."

Kablamm! Bamm! Boom!

The kitchen window shattered, sending glass across the stove and sink. Sadao covered his eyes with his arm just in time to deflect the shards.

"Kuso! Sound the alarm!"

Sadao stuffed the phone into his back pocket and skirting the worst of the glass in his bare feet, entered his bedroom and flicked on the main lights. The man was sitting up now, eyes wide.

"The hell is going on out there?"

"Explosion," Sadao said, pulling on his shirt and boots. "In the Shiratori camp! It sounded like a bomb went off!"

"Jesus! Want me to come with you?"

Sadao grabbed his keys and jacket. "No! Stay here until I know what's going on, um …"

"Jim."

"Right. Jim. No need to put everyone in harm's way. I'll be back. Stay near the radio."

"Okay…"

Sadao was out the door in the next second and hit with a blast of air that flung the trailer door out of his grip.

Slam!

He had to brace a boot against the frame and pull with both hands to get it shut again. He hoped "Jim" had sense to put on shoes before wandering into the kitchen. He hadn't had a chance to tell him about the glass.

The red light of the eastward camp lit his way to his cruiser, parked and covered at the rear of his equipment trailer. He loosened the tarp and it immediately flew off into the night. Sadao felt through the sandy gusts for his goggles and strapped them on. Next he tied a bandana from his saddlebag around his nose and mouth. He mounted, started his engine and rode off toward the light and smoke.

The Shiratori camp was marked out a quarter mile from the Orochi Team's banners in the midst of the Sonoran Desert. Unlike Tucson, there's wasn't a tree or even much cactus to speak of this far north. Sadao gunned his engine and drove into the shifting waves of sand and smoke. From what he could tell, the fire was spreading fast - unusual for such barren terrain. He shut off his bike when the heat became palpable and approached the rest of the distance carefully on foot.

The Shiratori team was in utter chaos. Fire raged from the north to the western end of the camp - trucks, vans, tents, trailers, and even men were on fire. The wind was propelling the swirling flames from one tent to the next, carrying the screams. Team members were running about shouting to each other through the smoke. Engines roared as men tried to drive their remaining rigs out of the path of the carnage and deeper into the desert. Bodies were being pulled out and dropped in the dirt as the able men ran back in for more possible survivors.

Stunned by the incredible sight, Sadao reached for his bike CB and radioed his Captain.

"Takayama! There's been a catastrophic explosion of some kind. I can smell fuel! Load up the flame retardant pumps and get them over here! Send someone to wake Sensei and have him prep Medical - oxygen, burn dressings, everything. And get every spare man you can find over here now in trucks and vans! We need to help move the injured! I'll call in the choppers! Wake the whole camp! These men are dying!"

Sadao dialed the Provisional Government's emergency line. It wasn't manned at this hour but his distress message was recorded as "Received." Who knew when or if the meager local disaster services would respond. Just as he signed off, two black figures came into view dragging a body between them out through the billows of smoke. Sadao tightened his bandana and ran in toward them. Both of the young camp members were near collapse themselves as Sadao shouldered their fallen comrade and hauled him out to safety for them. The two boys followed after and collapsed in the dirt coughing. Sadao looked at their faces in the red light. They were coated in soot and suffering from smoke inhalation, but they weren't burned badly. However, their friend was little more than a crispy mass of blood.

"Stay together! Help is coming! Move if the wind shifts the smoke this way! Are there more survivors on this end of camp?"

One of the kids nodded and pointed toward the tip of a large flaming canvas enclosure that could be seen pitching red embers into the whirling wind. Sadao verified with a hand gesture - the kid couldn't speak between coughs. Beyond, in the darkness to the west, Sadao could see a battalion of lights moving toward them. His team was coming.

"Keep an eye on those lights!" he told them and ran back into the chaos toward the burning tent. Sadao bent low amid the smoke, choosing his path carefully around vehicle carcasses and smoldering tires, attempting to find the least hazardous path. He held the bandana close around his mouth and took shallow breaths. The scent of fuel was coming from the north end of camp along with the wind. Vehicles could be heard trying to start but failing in the oxygen-sapped air. The lights were out as well, making his path difficult to see.

Sadao's head spun and he got down further onto his hands and knees, crawling toward his target. He reached the edge of the large assembly tent's weighted moorings and ducked under. The roof was on fire; orange flames were working their way across the canvas between support poles, lighting the ropes and pulleys as it went. Moans and screams could be heard inside, nearly invisible in the choking smoke.

"Anyone! Can you hear me? Shout if you can hear me!"

"Here!" Someone gasped.

Sadao bent and dashed forward, grabbing the man by the arm. His leg was trapped under a fallen scaffold. Sadao slid his hands under both of the man's arms and pulled back for all he was worth. The man hollered but his legs slid free, one clearly smashed and dragging along at a sickening angle.

"Anyone else in here?!" Sadao shouted as he hauled him back toward the flap.

"I don't think so!" the man shouted and began to cough. "Most got out I think!"

"Hang on - I'm going to lift you!"

The man was bigger than the kids and it took Sadao a few attempts between gasps of toxic air to get him across his shoulders. Overhead there was a snapping sound and a flash of yellow light. Too late to find anyone else, Sadao dove for the canvas wall and rolled both himself and the injured man out before the main support gave way, taking the rest of the tent down with it in a cascade of snapping wood and rope. Sadao dragged the casualty as far as he could before dropping him a moment to catch his breath and cough out his lungs. To his horror, he could hear screams of other victims still trapped inside.

"There was nothing more to be done," the man gasped. "The fire - it came so fast!"

"How?!" Sadao asked.

"Our lights! One of the main power lines gave in the wind. Fell onto the fuel line ... it went up in flames before anyone could do anything. Boss - he ran first into the fire."

Sadao didn't ask the poor man any more questions. He dragged him fully out of the smoke and into a ring of bikes where the Orochi team members had just set up a tri-age station for the wounded on the upwind end of camp. Sadao handed the wounded man over to his men. Sensei was there among them, pointing out who should be loaded up onto the trucks first and sent immediately over to the Orochi medical tents.

Sadao saw his captain among the rescuers, dispensing water and cool cloths for burns to those waiting in the dust for assistance.

"Has anyone seen Shiratori-san?"

"Sorry, Boss," Takayama answered. "No one has seen Shiratori-san alive. They say he ran into the fire as soon as it began and was lost in the explosion. It is not believed he made it out."

"I'm going to look for him! I need to be sure! Keep monitoring the rescue efforts. I called in the emergency but I don't think there's anyone available to fly in at this hour - fucking worthless!"

Assured Takayama had things well in hand, Sadao mounted his bike and began to circle the conflagration, now being doused by his team's full arsenal of fire retardant canons. The dowsers were mounted onto the backs of two massive flatbeds, each work-ing an opposite end of the camp. Foam now floated through the air as well as sand and ash, coating Sadao's face and goggles with black munge. Some of the smoke was beginning to blow off in the fierce wind, and Sadao was able to ride slowly around the perimeter to attempt to identify the area of the main blast. He found it soon enough but the 8-foot crater and surrounding blackened area was too hot and flammable to risk entering. There was nothing to be searched in this area anyway - everything had been blown to bits no bigger than a pebble.

Sadao continued his search, asking every survivor who could speak of the last known whereabouts of their leader without luck. After an hour or more, the fire had been contained and the smoke had cleared to a point that several members from a num-ber of assisting teams were able to enter the wreckage to search for survivors. Sadao brought out a few unconscious injured to the edge and radioed their location before hurrying back in. The longer he searched, the more Sadao became convinced he was looking for a dead man. And still no choppers had come.

Hours passed, and with it came the dawn and the calming of the winds. It became apparent what had caused the fire - a 40-foot lighting rig had come loose from its cables and landed directly on top of the main fuel line. The weight severed it and set off a chain reaction that blew up the three main fuel reserve tanks, resulting in the blast Sadao had felt inside his trailer.

The trailer! In all the madness, Sadao had not thought to look inside the burnt and twisted white feathered rig Shiratori called home. He wasn't sure anyone had, namely because so many had witnessed him vanishing like dust into the explosion. Sadao made his way over the hot smoldering debris until he reached the one standing end of Shiratori's living quarters. The trailer walls were still steaming and dripping with foam, so he wrapped his soot-coated bandana around his hand to open the main door. Wisps of smoke still lingered inside. Shiratori's collection of weaponry was thrown all over the floor. In the middle of the pile lay a suit of armor, and Sadao felt a chill roll over his sweaty skin as he picked his way closer to it. The burnt and twisted armor had a head.

"Shiratori-san? Shiratori?!"

Sadao dropped to his knees and cautiously turned the armor over - a man was inside of it. His face was black as night and his arms - one of them was gone and the other … It was hard to see what was left of it, other than a mass of charred bloody flesh. Sadao pressed his ear to Shiratori's soot-coated face.

"Shiratori-san!" When no discernable breath could be felt, Sadao pressed his fingers to the blackened flesh of the man's swollen neck. Sadao thought he could detect the faintest flutter of life.

At the triage, Sadao's captain and his remaining men stood in shock to see the Orochi Team Boss bring an armored corpse out of the steaming wreckage, just as the sun began to rise over the horizon.

"Is he alive?"

"I don't know," Sadao said. His hands shook as he passed the carcass of the man he'd known since middle school over to the waiting rescuers. Takayama called for Sensei, who was inspecting the next wave of injured. The old man came over swiftly and examined the charred body lying on the desert floor. Sensei felt his chest and throat as Sadao had.

"Is he breathing?" Sadao asked.

"Yes," Sensei said. *"But his pulse is very faint. He has lost his arms and much blood. I can not save this man."*

"I don't accept that!" Sadao said. *"He has a strong heart! Help him, Sensei!"*

The old man laid his hand on Sadao's arm. *"We have limited resources. There are others we can save that are not so far gone."*

"This is the only one that matters," Sadao said. *"I order you to treat him!"*

Sensei regarded Sadao a moment. *"Okay, get him on the truck!"* he said, nodding to the team members.

Sadao turned and left Shiratori in their hands while he rushed back to his bike. He lifted out the satellite phone and called the only number he was certain would answer. It rang several times before he heard her voice.

"Gisette, It's me. I need to speak to your husband."

Dr. Hawthorn looked as exhausted as Sadao felt when he entered the waiting room adjacent to the main burn unit of the Vancouver University Medical Center. Shiratori had been undergoing skin grafts and wound care for the past five days in the ICU.

Sadao stood. "How is he?"

Dr. Hawthorn motioned for Sadao to resume his seat and pulled up a chair opposite.

"I'm going to be honest with you, Mr. Koga. It's not good. Usually by this phase of treatment we expect to see the patient's vitals improving steadily - day by day. But in the case of your friend, he's not responding as well as we'd hoped. We've replenished the fluid loss and kept him under pure oxygen since the day he arrived. His blood tests indicate no lingering infections but his kidneys are starting to fail. I don't believe there's much more we as physicians can do for him."

Sadao studied the older man. "So you're just giving up?"

Dr. Hawthorn reached out and squeezed Sadao's hand. "I never give up on my patients, Mr. Koga. I'm just saying there comes a point when the patient has to make a decision to get well. I think your friend is walking a fine edge. Perhaps you could help him in making this decision."

"How?"

"I'm going to break protocol and let you in to see him. He's under a pressurized tent. I don't think he'd even be able to hear you. But, at this point, it's the best course of action I can recommend."

Sadao entered the room alone dressed in a hooded white cleansuit and booties. A single chair had been brought in next to the tented bed. Sadao sat down on it and peered through the clear plastic shroud encasing the hospital bed. If he hadn't been told by the nurses and the nearby patient chart this was Kyouji Shiratori - his former schoolmate and lifetime rival - he wouldn't have believed it. Somewhere under the pumps, tubes and bandages, there was a shell of a man wandering somewhere between life and death.

Instinct made Sadao want to reach out and hold the man's hand but there weren't any left. Just a half digit or two remaining on his left wrist, wrapped now in layers and layers of bandages. He'd lost an eye, Sadao was told. And they weren't sure he would be able to see out of the second. Ran right into the fire, they'd said. He was always the first into battle, and in battle was where he most wanted to die.

"Listen," Sadao began with a breath. "I don't think you can hear me, so I'll say these words to make peace with myself."

The room was warm and lit with the morning sun.

"I never liked you," he admitted. "You were always butting into my business. And your overbearing sense of self-superiority made me want to break your face on more than one occasion. I wanted to be rid of you, but you were always trailing me, showing up when I least expected it."

Sadao watched the digital display monitoring Shiratori's vitals beep and pulse along.

"When I was young, I wished you dead many times. I prayed I'd never have to see your face or hear your voice again - because then I wouldn't be judged. I wouldn't be accused of doing less than what was most expected of me. I was so tired of your ... advice.

"But when the fire came, something drove me to find you and save you from yourself. I know what you were trying to do. Somehow you kicked and crawled your way back through the fire to your trailer so no one would find you. But this time, I was the one who arrived unexpectedly and hauled your destroyed body out of that place before it was too late."

Sadao leaned closer and looked at the mummified man inside the shroud. "I want you to know what it feels like to be brought back from the brim of self-extinction by a will that's not your own. That day in the jungle - tied to that tree - whipped and starved, I prayed to be killed by you and your men. I didn't want to exist anymore as I was. I wanted to pass from this world of horrors and hope for a better life in the next. But you prevented me, you self-righteous bastard. You wouldn't allow me to take the coward's way out of my shame and suffering.

"So listen to me, Shiratori-san. I've pulled every contact, every trick I have to bring you kicking and screaming this far. I know you are much too vain to ever want to live without hands, eyes or that pretty face of yours you admire so much. But it's time for me to get my revenge - my time to return the favor to you. You want to die? You can't die - not until you've earned it."

Sadao stood up and took a long thoughtful look out the window. It was a bright, clear windless day in Vancouver.

"I've come to the realization that you and I are tied by invisible strings," he said at last. "Always have been and neither of us has the power to break them. But I won't sit here another moment and pity you. You're doing that well enough on your own."

Sadao turned and left the room and never returned.

Eleventh

Tarnish

Park City, Utah - 2071

Her cunt was a taut rim of pulsing moisture, swallowing his dick on each plunge. She'd waxed, giving him and whoever else stopped by this tour full view of her labia and clit - red and swollen with excitement. Her scent was high tonight - he could smell it on his hands, on his face, ground deep into his beard and groin. Her pink tipped nails dug into the mattress and her long brown curls spilled across her small peaked breasts, obscuring her face as Sadao thrust up into her.

As his pace quickened, Gisette's screams grew more raw and wild. *"Plus.. plus.."* she gasped as the air was forced out of her lungs. More…

Sadao pulled out and flipped her over onto her hands and knees. The pinch of her asshole beckoned as he continued to pound her cunt from behind. She wasn't the only one who needed more. He spit in his hand and wiped it clean across her other entrance. His thumb then followed, tugging at the opening, softening the folds.

"Ah oui! oui!"

As quick and solid as he'd been giving it to her, he knew he wouldn't come any time soon unless he fucked her there as well. The feel of her pussy was too wet and loose to overcome his distracted mind. Slick with her juices, he pulled out and laid the head of his cock up against her rim. He pushed himself in with his thumb.

She braced underneath him, purring with approval as he nudged his way in inch by inch. Ahh ... this was the feel he was seeking - gripped by tight, hot muscle. He'd licked, fingered and fucked her through four or five orgasms already - now was when he'd get his.

"Ooh mon cher ... c'est très bien ..."

He didn't want to hear her anymore - her voice was another kind of distraction. Sadao reached down and plunged his fingers into her mouth. Her eyes rolled shut and she bucked her ass back onto his dick, forcing him in fully. She was game to whatever he desired, anxious for him to seek pleasure from her however he wished.

The Wasatch mountain peaks stretched across the picture windows of her rented redwood summer palace. The plush elegance of the bedroom furnishings wrapped them in luxury. The lush pale rugs and furs were accented by his crumpled black riding pants and boots. His cruiser was parked diagonally across her driveway outside. His goggles and gloves were thrown somewhere out in the hall. Her panties and bra lay like lacy roadkill near the bedroom doorway, where he'd torn them from her body. Yet somehow, as Sadao slammed himself into Gisette's ass - with her screams echoing off the high-peaked ceiling - he still felt utterly lost.

"Aahh, Sadao … ."

"Sshhh!" He hushed her with a sharp tug of her curls. She wailed in delight and spread her long slim legs wide across the mattress. She lowered her head, inviting him to crawl down over her and cover her hands with his own. He growled with lust in her ear as the pleasure at last intensified in his groin; his climax was imminent as long as he didn't think about …

… blond tangled hair and flashing blue eyes filled with anger. Powerful hands - rough from hard work - forming a fist to connect with his face.

Your beard smells like cunt, you asshole!!

He'd had it coming to him. But right now, that was all he wanted to do - fucking come already and free himself from the rapid confused thoughts buzzing his head. He had a job to do. Focus was all and lately he'd had very little of it.

This is who I am. This is what I do!

"Nnngh … " He thrust into her with such force that the bed groaned in protest. He grabbed her shoulder and pushed her down flat, spread out like a marionette. He wanted to nail her so hard they'd fall through to the floor. He wanted to think of nothing but her body - her ass, her tits, her skin. And to forget those muscular shoulders and thighs, the round firm globes under his hands - pink from his strikes and pinched from his grip as he fucked that perfect, beautiful … .

"Aaaghh!"

Sadao shouted his release, forgetting himself at last in the rush shooting up his cock, emptying his mind into …

"Sadao … *Mon Dieu!*"

He collapsed across her slender back and slid out of her. White guzzles of cum ran from her reddened orifice.

"Sorry, I came in you," he said, rolling off her, panting for breath.

She smiled, her lipstick askew from his ravenous kisses and her neck and shoulders marked with bites.

"That's going to show," he said pointing to a bruise rising on her throat.

"*Bon,*" she said, reaching for her cigarette case. "I like wearing you out in public.

My battle scars."

Sadao wiped the sweat from his forehead. "Sorry if I was too rough. Tough couple of weeks."

"I could feel that. All the way in my bones," she said with a satisfied stretch that rattled her bracelets. "And all the way through seven orgasms - hardly complaining, darling."

"Seven to one - somewhat unfair I think. Light me one of those," he said, closing his eyes, gratefully numbed for the moment.

She laughed lightly. "I seem to remember a time when those scores were switched."

He heard the click of her lighter, and felt the warm exhale of her breath as she parted his lips with her tongue to set the tip of a lit cigarette between them. He caught it and sucked in deep, blowing smoke toward the high ceiling.

"Another life ago ... "

She lay next to him, quietly feeding him the cigarette between her own puffs. Her fingertips lazily traced the contours of his chest.

"Tickles," he said with a twitch. She pinched him instead. "*Itai!* I preferred the tickling!"

"You are still too stressed, my darling - after all that. You should stay tonight. I'll give you a bubble bath. This room has a marvelous jacuzzi tub. It will relax you even more," she said, kissing his shoulder. "You can sleep late. I won't wake you. I'll have Claire make you breakfast tomorrow any way you like."

"Can't," he said, taking the last drag and depositing the spent cigarette in the ashtray she offered. "There's too much left to do. I didn't even have time for this."

"Surely you can rest a few hours away from that madness. The heat is terrible this year down in those horrible salt flats. The air is much cooler here in the mountains. Please Sadao, for your own sake. You look exhausted."

"Haven't been sleeping much." Sadao gestured for her to light him a second stick. She did and took the first taste of it herself, bending to his lips to blow the smoke gently into his mouth.

"That is why you need to let me take care of you again," she said with a kiss. "You haven't called me in weeks."

"Been busy," he said as an excuse.

"Isn't your staff capable of anything? Surely by now you shouldn't have to look over every detail yourself."

"My staff is the problem," Sadao said, exhaling.

"Is Shiratori giving you headaches again?"

Sadao scoffed. "No, for once. It's one of the new men. Unfortunately, an essential one. Pain in my ass."

"Oh really? I had the impression from Marcus things were going swimmingly with your senior staff."

"I've had to keep a close eye on this one," Sadao said, feeling oddly relieved he had someone he could discuss the main source of his stress with. "He disobeys every rule I have. He's defiant, rude, unpredictable … I can't get a grip on him no matter what I do."

"Haven't you tried disciplining him?" she asked.

"I chained him to my fucking table. He still managed to get loose."

Gisette crumpled into a fit of giggles. "Chained him? Darling, he's a man, not a dog. You are using the entirely wrong approach. There must be something he wants - you only have to coax out what it is, then dangle it in front of his nose." She rose then and rubbed her stiffened nipple under Sadao's nose to demonstrate. He sucked it in momentarily, then popped it back out with a nip of his teeth.

"I tried that too. Disaster."

She looked puzzled. "What do you mean, darling? Tried what?"

"I fucked him."

Gisette sat partly up to gain better focus on his face.

"Excuse me, you mean to say you slept with this key member of your team who was causing you so much distress?"

Sadao rolled his eyes and crushed out his smoke. "That's exactly what I mean. Now I can't even speak to him and we have less than a week left to get four machines primed for the Overland. Even the sand buggy isn't ready - let alone the fucking Mustang! Shiratori says he's tearing out the seats now! I have no idea what I'm going to do! But I'm not going to get it done by lying around here!"

"Sadao…!"

He sat up suddenly and reached down for his pants and began shoving them on. Anger was filling him up again, threatening to spill over. If an epic fuck in the lap of luxury wasn't going to curb his foul humor, bubbles and mimosas certainly weren't either.

"Why on Earth would you want to jeopardize your team this close to a race, Sadao?"

Sadao stood up and reached down for his shirt and jerked it on over his head. "I'm asking myself the same thing. Terrible mistake - one of the worst I've ever made. *Kuso*, where are my keys?!"

"Is this why you're so angry? Under the marble table, darling. That's not like you. You don't normally diddle your staff. You didn't think this would make him more docile, did you?"

"Of course not! I'm not a complete idiot!" His heart was pounding with fury again. Fucking Mouse was a mistake; coming here to Gisette for solace was also a mistake. He hadn't been able to do one single thing right ever since that man came into his camp.

Since you kidnapped him and dragged him into your camp.

"Then why would you do something that foolish, Sadao? You know I have investments in this race. If you wanted sex you could have come to me! Have you lost all your sense?!" Gisette was cross with him now too.

He glanced at her - she was covering her bruised and tormented body with half of the stained sheet. She looked disgusted with him. Sadao gripped his keys tightly in his hand and they bit into his palm. There would be no sleep for him tonight.

"I don't know," he said at last, and threw on his jacket. "It just happened and now I'm paying for it! I'm sorry I troubled you tonight!"

Sadao left her there, silent and confused in her disheveled bed to collect his gloves and goggles from the hall. He stepped into Gisette's guest bath to wash her scent from his hands and face. He needed to go back out into the vast darkness to the salt flats, where the root cause of his distress waited to be confronted.

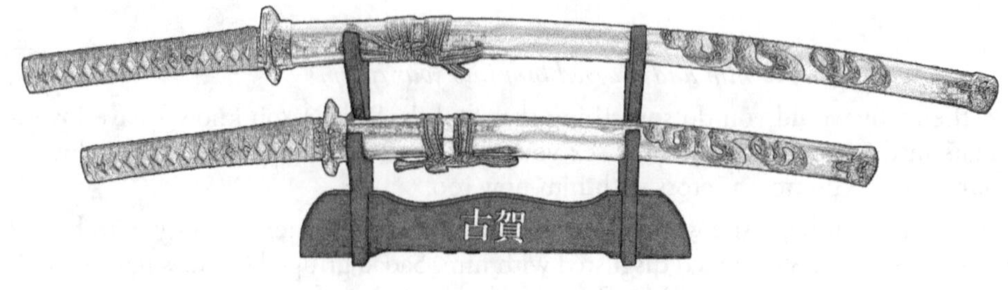

Chapter XVIII

Crevasse

"Where is he?! Let me through!" Mouse arrived at the Sasori portable medical tent just as Kei - and the other team members who had responded to the emergency alarm - had gathered at dusk to help unload a whimpering truckload of cold, confused children.

"Is he in the tent?" Mouse demanded, pushing through the agitated spectators.

"Mouse!!" Shinjyu's high-pitched voice rang out through the commotion and Mouse turned to work his way toward the pile of kidlets. The little girl ran to him and jumped up into his arms squeezing his windpipe.

"B-b-bad men! The bad men came and hurt Touchan!" she wailed. Her face was cold with tears.

"Shh… it's okay, honey. Your Pop is made of pretty tough stuff. He'll be fine. Let's go see him! Hey, move it! Little girl wants to see her Daddy!"

The crowd made way for them and Mouse slipped into the tent in time to witness Michi-sensei on his knees sewing up Sadao's oozing temple with a curved needle and thread. Tagata was there too, speaking in rapid Japanese to Sensei who was observing his intern's skill.

"Touchan!!" Shinjyu screamed. She kicked herself out of Mouse's arms and ran to her father lying on the medical futon getting mended. He caught her under his arm and hugged her to him, soothing her as she sobbed into his belly.

"Touchan ha daijyoubu dakara, hime. Nakanai de kudasai…"

"B-but he's putting string in your face!" she cried, looking like she wanted to clock Michi in the head with something heavy.

"It's like when your favourite dress gets a rip in it and I sew it back together with some thread, sweet pea," Mouse explained, kneeling beside them both and giving Sadao's hand a squeeze. "He just needs a little fixing up is all. Don't you? Jesus, you forget how to duck?"

"A-s-s-h-o-l-e-s had a g-u-n to me," Sadao explained, spelling it for Shinjyu's sake.

"They broke into the longhouse while I was training. Took all of our old friend's armaments and the Whitebird cruiser!" Sadao grimaced as Michi finished tightening his last stitch and snipped the end.

"Did you get a look at them?"

"Masked."

"Masked? Masked how?"

"Halloween prank, not so funny," Tagata explained, kneeling down to speak to both of them. "Maybe Sadao-sama not tell you yet about new mask mystery team."

"Masked mystery team? The heck? Is this the Twilight Zone?"

Sadao shifted up onto his elbow, rubbing Shinjyu's back while Michi cleaned the blood from his face with antiseptic gauze.

"Get all the blood off!" Shinjyu demanded. "I want Touchan pretty again!"

Mouse bit down a smile. "It's a little too late for that, honey. Your Touchan's got some mileage on him."

Sadao shot him a look.

"Team raid crimes should be reported to Racing Officials!" Tagata insisted, getting back to the issue at hand.

"Absolutely not!" Sadao said. "The Officials won't issue penalties without evidence! Our camp has no publicly known location and no known victim! I do not exist! They planned this. They waited until the camp cleared out before raiding the longhouse. I don't think they expected to find it occupied."

"Thieves know where we live. Have known this for long time. Somehow they move when we can not see them. I take extra roll-call to be sure none are among us."

"They're Japanese, oddly," Sadao explained to Mouse. "From Kansai - they spoke partly in a dialect of the Kyoto - Osaka region except for the leader. As I told Taga his voice was familiar, but odd sounding."

"Odd how?"

"Like it was disguised with an amplifier. Hard to tell under the rubber."

"Shit, I just thought of something!" Mouse said. "That day I found the gas can on the far lakeshore, I also found part of a cartoon frog mask. I thought that was weird as fuck. I'm sorry if I didn't mention it sooner! I thought it was just random trash."

Tagata nodded solemnly. "We have been watched. They have sneak in and out of camp many time - under many nose!" The Sasori Team Boss' use of American slang was improving to the detriment of his pluralizations.

"Sadao says they had a g-u-n," Mouse added. "Can't you rightfully request that their camp be searched for illegal weapons?"

"They won't be stupid enough to leave their firearms lying about," Sadao said.

"But the weaponry. All of the General's stuff! Where'd they put all that?"

"On a boat probably," Tagata reasoned. "Far from Canadian shore now."

"But why would they want that stuff? If they have you-know-whats, a bullet is far more effective than a seventeenth-century spear!"

"It doesn't make sense," Sadao agreed, somewhat dismissively as if the subject was one he wanted to avoid. Mouse watched his face for clues but Sadao wasn't giving anything up.

Whatever it is, he's not gonna say it in front of Tagata. Bizarre.

"Let me through… damn you, apes! I have every right! Oh, my darling! My darling!"

Both senseis and patients turned to see what sort of rabbit-furred commotion was barging her way in through the tent flaps.

"Oh, my poor Sadao!" Gisette cried, rushing to his side. She knelt to inspect his taped-up sutures. "What did they do to you?!"

"He's fine," Mouse said with a cough.

Her eyes shot up at him. "Is he? What did they sew him up with? Fishing line? He needs a real doctor!"

Fuck, déjà vu … is this what it felt like for Sadao when Marcus was screaming about Kinjo's knife work on my balls? Yeah, but I hadn't been fucking the Chairman off and on for two decades.

Sadao removed her hand from his forehead, gently. "Calm down. I'm all right, Gisette."

"Oh, brother…" Mouse moaned to himself.

"Mouse! Mouse!" Shinjyu had pulled back from her father when the wailing woman rushed in. She held her hands up for Mouse to bend down and pick her up.

"Hey, honey. It's okay. She's just an old friend of Touchan's."

Shinjyu shook her head and buried her face in Mouse's hair like she was trying to hide. "I don't like her!" she whispered. "Make her go away!"

My thoughts exactly, kid.

Sadao accepted Gisette's assistance as he got up onto his feet. It was obvious his bad leg was causing him more discomfort than usual.

"Oh, Sadao! Your hip is still so troublesome! You must let me call the University Hospital! We can airlift you to the best surgeons in Vancouver!"

"I'm fine, Gisette," he said firmly. "I'm just stiff from training. Been working it too hard. I was cut. That is all."

"But they attacked you! With guns and knives! I heard the alarm! They should be arrested!"

Tagata stepped forward now. "How? How did you hear Sasori alarm? It is private signal!"

"I told you, Taga," Sadao said, slowly pulling on his coat. "I gave her her own code on the general band. The alarm is set to call all frequencies."

Tagata didn't say anymore, but his expression spoke volumes as his eyes crossed Sadao's for answers and he wasn't getting any he liked.

Whoa, maybe Tagata really has grown a pair … this won't end well. These two fall out, I might have to pump Squamish Gas after all!

"If we're done here, Senseis, I need to help Kei find these kids temporary quarters," Sadao said, reaching for Mouse's shoulder to help him get his boots on. "It was a long cold ride for them in the covered truck. They need hot soup and a warm bed!"

"But we must tell The Council at least!" Gisette insisted. Tagata raised his chin in silent support.

"Absolutely not!" Sadao bellowed at the both of them. "The last thing the Sasoris need is Council members nosing all over their land! I'm fine! It's done! Focus on the race tomorrow!"

"But Darling…" Gisette said, sadly pawing his arm.

Sadao patted her hand. "Later, Gisette. I have children to care for right now. They're tired and frightened. We will talk later."

Mouse gave her a farewell grin as he tucked himself under Sadao's arm to help him limp out of the tent.

In an effort to find the kiddos housing, every trailer was evaluated for spare beds - much to the chagrin of the Team's active racers who were hoping to use their private spaces for post-show recreation. It would be difficult to entertain private guests with a pair of five-year olds bouncing on your upper bunk. But the safe evacuation of the children from the minimally staffed camp meant there were no trucks and drivers left up mountain to haul the kids' sleeping trailer down to Squamish. Racers had to deal or hold it until spring competitions.

"Can I ask you something?" Mouse whispered to Sadao, as they finished zipping soup-filled yawning, half-pints into sleeping bags on the overhead bunk of Sadao's old trailer. Tonight it would be home to Lupe, Sadao, Mouse and three little ones - Shinjyu and the boy twins.

"What is it?" Sadao whispered back, rubbing the boys' backs as Mouse stroked Shinjyu's head to sleep.

"Earlier when Michi-sensei was patching you up, and before your ex made her grand entrance, if I read you right it looked like there was something about your attackers you didn't want Tagata to know."

Sadao's brow twitched in surprise.

"What on earth wouldn't you tell Tagata? Especially when they attacked his camp?

He's really not happy with you right now, if you've bothered to notice."

"Shh…! Let's get these little ones off to dreamland first. It's a long story."

After the children nodded off, Sadao went into his old kitchen and pulled a dusty cask of sake from behind the partition between two kitchen cupboards.

"Really? You're gonna drink?" Mouse asked, taking a seat in the lounge. "It's …only 5:30 in the evening."

Sadao uncorked the cask and popped it into the microwave on low. "I'm drinking because I can't fucking smoke!"

With the shades turned down and the space heater running, Sadao brought the warmed sake and two glasses and sat opposite Mouse. He poured for them both and took a few sips before he began to talk.

"I have something to show you," he said, and opened his hastily packed overnight bag lying in the booth next to him. He took out a small sack and laid it on the table, pushing it toward Mouse. "You've asked me before to tell you something about myself that no one else knows."

Curious, Mouse opened the tie string and looked inside. The smell of something dirty and leathery hit his nose. He pulled the objects out cautiously. "Are these shoes? Really old kid's shoes? Ick."

"Once, they were very fine shoes. The very best my father could buy."

"Your father? You mean, these were yours? You've had them all this time?"

"No, they were stolen from me when I was a schoolboy in Toba, 30 years ago if a day. They were returned to me this morning, during the raid. Their leader threw this sack at me and said 'Kingoe says hello.'"

"Ah … fuck!"

"Don't wake the kids."

Mouse clamped his lips shut, picked up his sake glass and knocked it back, motioning Sadao to pour more. "You've gotta get me at least buzzed before I can sit through this one. What the hell is going on?! King go-what's-his-fuck is back to get you? Seriously? With shoes?!"

Sadao emptied his cup and poured for both of them again before he gathered himself to speak. "I'm not fond of recounting my early years, but I think it's time you came to understand a few things about my past."

"I live with you. I do your laundry. I fall asleep to your snoring. I doubt there's anything that's going to surprise me."

Sadao's eyes stayed on the table but his gaze was far away. "I lied to you once."

"Hm? When? It better not be about that French bitch!"

Sadao grinned mirthlessly. "No, not about her. It was about my brother - my youngest brother. I told you he died at sea."

"Yeah, so…?"

"I've told that lie so many times even I have a false memory of it. I can see it even now - my mother on the shore waving goodbye to him and my third brother, Yasuo, as they sailed from the harbor on a fine spring day under a flutter of sakura petals."

"You didn't give me that much detail. You just said their boat sank and they drowned."

"I invented that story - like I was designing a fucking postcard. It wasn't a fine spring day. No one waved anyone goodbye. Yasuo died in a squall one winter offshore miles away, unseen. And my youngest brother - he never even met my third brother that I know of. He never lived in my father's house with me or my mother and my elder brothers. I did not even know his name, this youngest one. But one day he came to my English school to beg and stole my prized leather shoes from my cupboard and I murdered him for it."

Mouse blinked in the dimness. "Did you just say murder...? The fuck are you talking about? How could you murder your own brother? Did you even know he was your brother?"

Sadao poured another cup and knocked it back in one big gulp. "He was only six or seven years old. He had a different mother - one of my father's many mistresses - but I knew he was my blood. He called me *Onisan* - big brother. Followed me around like a stray pup. He lived with his ailing mother in the slums. No money, no education. He was a beggar child who would call out my name as I was leaving school every day, hoping I'd throw him scraps.

"One day he stole my shoes and ran off with them. I had to walk home barefoot. I was embarrassed by him. I threw rocks at him and called him names to chase him off. Then one day I'd had enough and killed him. Stuck my father's wakizashi in his throat to stop his screams ... he kicked and kicked and I dug the blade in until he stopped."

Sadao eyes were hard on him now. Mouse was silent, heart thudding for several moments. "How old were you?"

"Fourteen. Old enough to know exactly what I was doing that night in the jungle."

Mouse sighed in relief. "Oh! This was during the war! Of course! You were fighting and there was confusion ... "

"No. I was not confused. He wasn't attacking us. He only wanted our food and clothes. I knew he was my brother. I knew he was desperate - helpless. His mother was likely dead by then and he was forced into thievery. He was a little child alone in a forest full of bullets and I murdered him for vanity. So he wouldn't call me brother anymore. So I wouldn't have to feel that shame. I spent many years burying these facts and decorating them with false memories. But lately ... I've been seeing his face again ... "

"What?!"

"In dreams," Sadao specified. "Odd ... somewhat, prophetic dreams."

"But ... why now? Why did those guys fling the shoes at you? The masked idiots are all young guys. They weren't in your war jungles, were they?"

"No, that's impossible. I'm thinking whoever is funding them, this Kingoe, is likely someone who knows what I've done. A witness maybe from a rival clan… Or an heir, perhaps."

"From a million fucking years ago?"

"The last time I saw these shoes they were on the body of my dead brother. Murder has no statute of limitations in Japan."

Mouse shivered and tried to shake it off. "I'm far more concerned that this asshead knows you're alive. And worse - how to find you! So … let's say somebody found your old shoes and wants to give you shit about it now? Here? In Canada? Why?"

"Dark deeds create dark shadows. They fester and grow like old wounds that won't heal. This shadow has crossed an ocean and three decades. It's high time I dealt with it."

"But … you said your whole family was killed in the war … so who … who is left to give a fuck?"

Sadao slammed his fist on the table. "I give a fuck!"

"Jesus…" Mouse half jumped out of his skin. He looked overhead at the kids still snoozing peacefully in their bunk. "I don't get it … I know it must have been horrible … but it was war, Sadao. And you were a child, too!"

"I was old enough to know what I was doing, even if I was not very skilled. I've gotten very good at killing over the years. You've seen me do it."

"Yeah, when my head was on the line! Or when your babies were facing a long painful death in the Japanese war zones! These are honorable acts of justice! You've said so yourself!"

"Not every neck I've cut has been justified. I think it's time you understood that."

Mouse opened his mouth in silent exasperation, then shut it. "So … you want me to slap you, call you a bastard or something, Sadao? I'm not going to do it. There's a hundred different reasons why you've drawn blood over the years - survival being the main one!

"I know what kind of shit life you had as a kid - it's carved all over your back for crissakes! I've seen the scars - they're faint but they're still there. And you know what? The night before he died, Shiratori sat right there like you - pouring sake - and told me all about that time his army goons had tied you to a tree; that you'd been beaten and raped by some sadistic slave master. And some bullshit about giving you a knife and telling you to 'Go eat his penis.' And if that's not fucked up, I don't know what is!"

"I didn't eat anyone's penis."

"Well, see … there's a plus!"

"I cut it off with his balls and shoved it down his throat until he choked to death on his own viscera."

"Okay, great! And I stole a Bible from the Bridesfall Church and used it for toilet paper one summer because the town had run out! There, we good? You wanna dredge up more bullshit while we're at it? What about the asshole who tried to kill me in the field that night near Williams? You want me to shed a tear for him? Or that ball-happy fuck, Kinjo?" Mouse sat back, grabbed the sake bottle and took a long burning shot. "Fuck!"

"I've spent most of my life running from my past," Sadao said after some thought. "I was foolish to think I could just stop and settle quietly into domestic life. My history of blood is endangering the team and the children. It's time we all stopped pretending that I'm rotting quietly at the bottom of the sea."

"So ... how do we start? A coming out party? Do we buy you a tiara? Christ, Sadao, I have final equip fittings tonight and track inspections bright and early tomorrow. I don't have time to deal with your past fuckups!"

"Exactly."

"Exactly ... what?!"

A whine came from the upper bunk, breaking the silence. One of the boys was whimpering. "Shit ... I'll go settle him down," Mouse said, getting up. "We talk about this some other time! Okay?"

Sadao didn't answer, just poured himself another drink and swallowed it silently to himself.

"Am I close enough?" Mouse shouted over the strengthening wind as he backed his 4-wheel-drive Jeep slowly up the east side of the Garibaldi Glacier while craning his neck out the window.

"It's good! Park that shit, gringo!" Lupe was at his rear bumper giving out hand signals. The morning had dawned cloudy and cold for the team's pre-race track inspections. A storm was due to arrive by nightfall and Mouse very much wanted to get off the summit and safely back seaside, snug in the trailer with Shinjyu and Sadao by dusk. They'd been out in the Jeep since dawn, working through lunch to finalize route decisions for the Downhill based on current snowpack and trail conditions. Mouse's stomach was rumbling as they were about to lower the Sasori team boss down into the bottomless pit.

"Are you sure my ass isn't hanging over that crack? Looks too close!"

"Crevasses in mirror may be closer than they appear!" Lupe sang. Mouse set the hand brake and double checked he was in "Park" before exiting the Jeep. Outside the wind was painful, blowing ice shards off the upper glacier into his face. *Fuck, I miss the desert!!*

Here at the level of the traverse between peaks that they were daring to take as their downhill route in order to cut the distance to the finish, the snow had built up nicely over the ancient ice flow, providing adequate tooth for the snowbike treads to keep steady on. The only problem was the 100-foot-long maw of icy death cutting across their path to victory. It looked more ominous than Mouse had expected - like a big blue-black grimace, jagged and hungry for human sacrifice. He wouldn't go any closer than ten feet from the edge where Tagata and his men were leaning over and kicking snow and ice rocks into the abyss.

Ugh… I'm getting dizzy just watching them. Fuckers fall in, they're on their own! Mouse wasn't afraid of heights really, just holes.

"You sure about this, Boss?" Lupe asked Tagata. He was securing the Boss's climbing harness to a series of ropes attached to a set of heavy-duty locking carabiners clicked into the Jeep's cable winch.

"I will be good," Tagata assured them, tugging on the ropes. "This, I have experience! To climb ice was favorite activity when I was a boy. When the waterfall freeze - I like to climb, too. Many times."

Mouse's brain screamed: *This is a bad idea!!* But he reminded himself that among all of the team leads, Tagata was the only Sasori who had grown up around snow. It was hard to imagine the Sasori Boss had once called the Canadian Rockies home after his parents immigrated from Hokkaido when he was young. He was also one of only a handful of Sasori racers who could ski. He'd taken the lifts to the mountain peak, while Mouse spun his snow tires up the summit's ice-coated forestry access roads with Lupe and the others shivering in the canvas-covered back. Mouse regarded Tagata's snowboard set upright into a snowbank.

"If this storm comes in before we're finished up here, we may all need that board to get down!"

"I will not take long," Tagata insisted, swinging his ice ax and stabbing it into the snow just above the lip of the crack. "Keep hand on the winch. I will shout up or down!" And with that he took one big step backwards over the abyss, kicking the toe of his crampon into the crevasse's inner wall. He sent chipped ice flying and down over the brim like one of those frozen waterfalls he was so fond of.

Mouse shivered. From his vantage, it looked like Tagata was being slowly eaten alive. *I can't watch this! I can't!*

"Set loose the cable - slow! Lupe, watch and signal Mouse to run the winch!"

Mouse moved into position next to the motor and reluctantly pressed the switch down with his gloved thumb. Lupe gave Mouse a "thumbs down" each time Tagata requested more line. Soon, his head disappeared below the edge of the brink. Mouse pushed his hood up over his head to dull the eerie sounds of the wind moaning as it swirled into the maw after Tagata - probably the first person to descend into the death gash on purpose.

Soon Lupe motioned him to stop the line and lock it down. Mouse shut off the motor with a sigh of relief. He'd run out about 50 or 60 feet of cable so far. Hopefully, this would be deep enough for Tagata to observe the thickness of the crevasse icebridge;

it ran dead center over the gap at about six-to-eight feet wide and 60 feet across the depths. Each winter for the past seven years, the Canadian Geographical Service had reported a thinning ice pack for this region. It was important to know how thick the icebridge really was from all sides. And more importantly, if it could handle a six-man team running motorbikes over it in succession. Vibration was a great concern if sizable cracks were present.

"Can he see anything?" Mouse asked. He could hear Tagata shouting information from down in the pit but couldn't make out his words over the wind.

"He says: 'Ice looks good. Narrower at the lower end underneath, but good. No large cracks!'"

Mouse breathed a huge sigh of relief. "Okay, great! Can we bring him up?" He was anxious to get this inspection over with. The wind was causing Tagata's weight at the far end of the line to swing and skitter the exposed cable across the ragged edge of the ice lip.

"Okay, yes! Boss has given the signal to pull him in!"

"Okay, raising up slow!" Mouse flipped the motor switch to "Up" for wind-in but nothing happened. The winch hummed but the cable stayed put. "Shit!" He shut it off, banged at the side of the roller and switched it back on again. Same thing - a hum and nothing else. *Fuck fuck fuck....*

"Boss says bring him in, gringo!"

"I know, but this thing's jammed!! The reversing gear is probably frozen!" Mouse went belly-flat in the snow to try to look underneath the mechanism. Sure enough, there was a shit ton of ice caked on under there from their icy road trip up the mountain. *Tagata's gonna skin me alive!!*

"Gringo!"

"I know! Tell Boss he's gotta hang on a sec while I try to chip some of this shit off!" Mouse got to his feet and opened the Jeep's door, grabbing a screwdriver from his glove box. Dropping back in the snow on his knees, he started to chip away at the front bumper's undercarriage.

"Don't you got a welder or something?" Lupe asked, coming over and leaving the other men to watch over their dangling leader, who was barking orders from the depths.

"Arc welder? That'll melt the damn gears together for good! And I'd need electricity! No, what I could use is like a match or some hot water."

"What about your coffee thermos?"

"Drank it."

"Maybe a lighter?"

Mouse looked up at Lupe, whose shadow was blocking his light. "Confiscated and destroyed...I have a tobacco addict at home! Ask Tagata's crew!"

Mouse kept chipping while the team leads searched their pockets and packs for something warm. All the while they shouted down to Tagata, who was getting as tired of dangling in the wind as Mouse was of chipping and clicking. There was a shout and Mouse glanced up in time to see a glint of silver fly up out of the crevasse and into the snow. Lupe picked it up and ran it over to him.

"Good thing Boss comes prepared!" he said, flicking Tagata's lighter and producing a long steady flame. Mouse took it gratefully and after some well aimed heating and screwdriving, he got the frozen gears to switch over into reverse.

Tagata popped back up out of the hole in record speed. Not pleased in the least with the delay, he marched up and snatched the lighter out of Mouse's hand.

"All equipment must be in top condition!" he yelled at Mouse while his men assisted him out if his climbing gear. His cheeks were red and raw from the ice flurry he'd been subjected to down below.

"I know! And it is! The racing gear is! The Jeep is … fuck, I'm sorry, okay? I'll treat the bumpers and winch with saline spray when I get back to the garage. I didn't know you'd be going miles into the ice! I didn't plan for that!"

"We must plan for everything!" Tagata shouted, looking to all of his leaders but especially to Mouse. "Every possible condition! Every possible outcome! This event, we can not fail!"

Mouse headed straight for the shower when he returned to Sadao's old trailer just before nightfall. He was sore, half-frozen, and embarrassed from getting bitched out in front of everyone at 11,000 feet. Despite his hunger, he elected to skip dinner in the freezing mess tent and stood under the steaming spray, thawing himself until the hot water gave out. He hoped there were still some stale crackers and a can of soup or two somewhere in the corners of the kitchen as he stepped out to meet a towel rack - filled with nothing but lint.

Christ, did no one pack towels?! Fuck this day!

He dripped across the rear bedroom floor and opened the dressers to try and find something absorbent. Socks? How would he explain rubbing a handful of Lupe's racing hosiery all over his body? Might not be appreciated. *Let's see, kitchen might have napkins …*

Mouse flung open the bedroom door to streak toward the stove, when he realized he wasn't alone in the trailer after all. A woman was standing just inside the front door, as shocked to see him as he was her.

"Mon Dieu! Si vulgaire!"

"Whoa!" Mouse yanked open the closest drawer and pulled out an oven mitt to hold over his … muffins. "How'd you get in?"

"How?! I have a key of course!" she said, holding up a small keychain with a rhinestone-rimmed strap. Gisette - in his space. Again.

"Can't you at least knock?!" Mouse asked, heart still pounding from the surprise. "I was taking a shower!"

"I can see that," she said with an air of disgust in her voice. "I would have called. But none of you carry portable phones and the satellite connection is down due to the storm."

"I'm sorry but ... this is a men's trailer! For racing team members only!"

"And I suppose that's why you keep the girl here with you, is it?"

"Huh?" Mouse backed slowly toward the bedroom, dripping. "Just ... hang on while I put on some damn pants, will you?"

He shut the door and scrambled about for his clothes, which were scattered around the bed. He grabbed a pair of jeans and jerked them on, irritated. *Who the hell does she think she is?*

"I have a key" ... really? What the fuck? Who gave her one? Sadao? Shit, asshole better have an explanation for this one.

When Mouse emerged, drying his hair on a t-shirt, the woman was still there. She was sitting on the couch, jangling her keys impatiently.

Mouse stood in the kitchen where he could drip with less clean-up. "I, uh ... don't know who you think is going to show up anytime soon. Sadao is off with Tagata at mess - I'm not expecting him until much later.

"Then I suppose I'll just have to wait for him," she said casually.

"Not here!"

"Where do you suggest I go? There's a storm blowing in down from the peaks. They've closed the I-39 pass. I can't make it back up to my cabin until morning at best."

"Great, so why don't you go get a room in town? You're rich, aren't you?"

"Because there's this big event going on, perhaps? Rooms are a tad overbooked?" Gisette spoke to him like he had an IQ of 5.

"Oh."

"Oh, indeed. And seeing as I own this trailer, I came here. I wasn't expecting to be treated like a vandal!"

"Maybe you haven't heard, but Sadao's moved on. Lupe Escovado, my best friend, occupies this trailer now. It was assigned to him by the new team boss - Tagata! It's been his since Sadao-"

"I know what happened to Sadao! You don't have to recount it all for me," she said, getting up and removing her coat and hanging her purse on the hooks by the door. "I purchased this motorcoach for my very good friend, a very long time ago! I never gave any team leader permission to possess it or to reassign it!"

"You can't stay here," Mouse protested. "We're full up!"

"This coach sleeps ten! You have five at most occupying it presently. Half of them children! It won't be pleasant, but we can at least make do." She began to stroll about, taking note of which bunks were occupied by how many sleeping bags.

"I said, no."

Gisette flicked her nails at him. "I'm sorry...who are you? Exactly?"

Mouse felt his face flush. "You know exactly who I am!"

"Ah, that's right. The mechanic," she said, dismissing him as she began to clear space on the pull-out couch.

"Hey!" Mouse snapped, moving forward to take her arm. "Don't mess with our stuff! I'm going to have to ask you to leave!"

She whipped around, eyes flashing. "Don't you dare put a hand on me! What makes you think you have the authority to put me out in the cold?!"

"I'm Sadao's goddamned husband is what! And this trailer is no longer your property to just come in and take over!"

"Oh, 'husband' now is it? How quaint. Tell me, are you two married? Legally? Here in Canada? Was it a spring wedding with white tulips? I don't recall seeing the announcement in the society pages. Or was it in the United States, perhaps - ankle deep in the cactus and cow poop before he gathered the notion to chop up his boss and get himself locked away? Such nasty business, racing. How did you two ever find the time?"

"He promised himself to me," Mouse said, using every ounce of decency he had not to punch her pert face.

She laughed. "Oh did he? With some fancy jewelry no doubt. Tell me, did he fit it with a shiny black pearl?"

Mouse lowered his head so his hair fell over his earcuff. "Ah…that's not … "

"Oh darling … did you really think you were the first to get a pretty pearl? He keeps a drawer full of them! It's how he controls you, don't you see? Makes you think you have some special place in his envious life. He's been decorating his lovers for years. One pearl at a time. They just come and go and come and go. Sometimes, he even takes the baubles back and regifts them!"

"Fuck!" Mouse grabbed her by her sleeve. "You're jealous and trying to piss me off!"

"Oh! My ... we touched a nerve. I am sorry to bring you the bad news. But you see ... I've known him practically his whole life, darling. I taught him everything - how to win, how to fuck, how to get everything he's ever desired. You're just his current phase. An odd one, that's for sure," she said looking him over. "Poor creature. Did you honestly think you were in this for the long haul?"

"You don't have any idea what I have with him."

"Don't I?" she laughed. "I've had this same conversation a hundred times with a hundred of his dalliances. They all told me the same thing. I didn't know. I couldn't possibly understand how special they were to him. They all made the same mistakes as you, don't you see? They tried to own him. Tried to tie him down. And he enjoys that possession for a while, oh, yes he does! It gets him excited - all that fawning devotion. Strokes his raging ego. But sooner or later the stroking starts to chafe. He tires of the same old pathetic routine - sex, tears, threats - nothing lasts. And when he's finished, when he's used you up, he always finds his way back to me."

Mouse knew what she was trying to do and he wasn't about to fall into it blindly. "He's changed."

"Has he? After four decades, you think a man like that can shake off his stripes? No one I have ever met in my life is as stubborn and consistent as that man! You really believe a nobody from some forgotten desert town like you is going to hold his eye forever?"

Mouse thought it over a moment. "Yeah, I do."

Her lips grew thin and she tried to shake his hand off. "You offer him nothing - no money, no position, no advantage whatsoever!"

"That's right. I don't."

Gisette froze, staring at him.

"That's what makes you and I different," he continued, letting her go. "He's over it. The fame thing. He doesn't need you anymore. He just wants a home."

Her eyes grew wide. "He came to me while he was with you! He fucked me while he was having you - just before The Overland he told me! He said it was a mistake! A disaster, sleeping with his mechanic before a race! He was disgusted with himself. He came and fucked me all night just to get the memory of you out of him!"

"I know," Mouse said with a shrug. "So ... how'd that work out for you?"

"What? What do you mean?"

"I'm not with Sadao because he's a saint. I'm with him because I understand him."

She was panting now, her hands shook as she straightened her blouse. "You don't understand anything. If you think you know him so well, then tell me why he's worn my white gold cuff every day for twenty years where everyone could see it!"

"Oh, about that. He doesn't wear it anymore. Hasn't for a while."

"You lie! I saw it last week up at your pathetic love cabin!"

Mouse went over to the coatrack and took up her purse and jacket, bringing them to her. "His hair is longer now, kinda falls over it. But if you lift his mop up you'll see it's a bit different now. Looks just like this one," Mouse said, lifting up his own hair for her to see. "Maybe he regifted it. Added a pearl."

"Impossible!"

"Look, this place is kind of a mess. Socks and kid crap everywhere. Why don't you go hang out at the Squamish Ski Lodge for a bit. Have a drink or two. I'll let Sadao know you stopped by."

"I…uh -" Mouse wrapped her fur coat around her shoulders and gently guided her out the door. The wind was blowing pretty hard but he could see her SUV was parked just a few yards away.

"Don't worry, I'll have him shoot by the lodge and say hi!" Mouse said with a jolly wave and shut the door, locking it with the inside bolt against her stunned face.

Bitch.

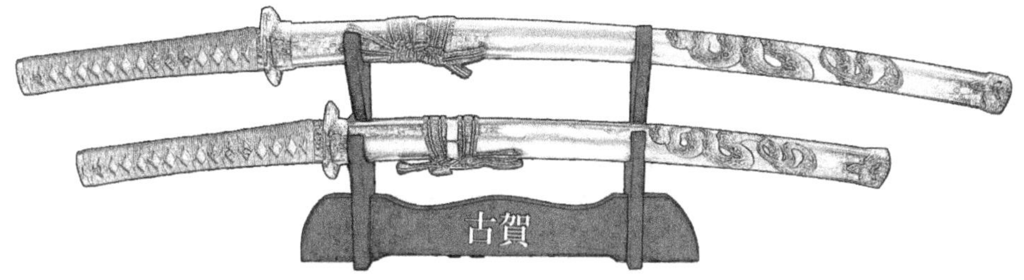

Chapter XIX

Bait

Sadao found Gisette right where Mouse had sent her, the Squamish Ski Lodge Lounge - several glasses of wine into an open bar tab.

"Oh! Darrling…" she drawled with pink cheeks and blurry eyes. "I can barely recognize you in that awful ski mask! Oh!"

"That's the idea," he said, dragging her out of the booth. "Now be quiet while I ring you out."

He paid her tab with her own bank chip and escorted her from the lounge and into an elevator. He pushed the top floor. Gisette hung on his arm, pawing at his chest.

"Where are we staying tonight?" she murmured in his knit-covered ear.

"Taga's room. He cancelled an 'appointment' tonight for you. You should thank him next time you meet."

"Oh! Is he coming too? I don't know if I'm up to handling you both but …"

The elevator doors opened and Sadao held her up until they got to the room. He beeped in the code from the front desk and led her into the small suite. Soon as he secured the door and pulled off his mask he was thanked by a ringed-palm across his face. Smack!

"How dare you?! " she cried, only half as drunk as she'd pretended to be. "You ungrateful bastard! How dare you insult me like this?"

"Insult you? I just saved you from having to sleep in the lobby! Fuck!"

Her face was flushed. "You gave my precious metal to him! My white gold! That was our promise, Sadao! You promised to wear my standard forever!"

"Oi … you mean the earring?"

"Of course I mean the earring! Don't play stupid with me!"

"Gisette, the prison took that when I was admitted. They took everything off of me! I wasn't able to get it back. Did you think-?"

"He's wearing it!!" she wailed, throwing another hand at him. Sadao caught her wrist this time and led her over to the sofa.

"Gisette, please calm down," he said, sitting her down. "It's not the same one. It's silver. It's ... not what you thought."

She looked up at him and gulped back a sob. "Silver?"

"Yes. I made them last month from Navajo silver. It matches mine, see?" He removed his pearled cuff for her to inspect. She turned her head.

"I don't want to see that, either. I thought you were still honoring me - our memories - all this time. Even when you pretended to be dead to me. Unspeakably cruel!"

Sadao put the earring back on. "I am sorry, Gisette. I'm sorry I didn't contact you sooner. It caused you a great deal of distress I didn't consider. I apologize."

"But why?"

"You know why. I have a family now. I'm a fugitive. They're harboring me. I have them to consider first."

"I thought I was your family!" she blurted. "You and I were as close as any two siblings I have ever known! We never lied to each other this way. Not once in 20 years. I trusted you with everything! Only you knew all my secrets!"

"We were never siblings," he said softly. "And that is the problem."

She pressed her eyes shut, and tears ran down her face. "Of *course* that's the problem. I never imaged in a million years you would change this way. A family? This isn't you. It can't be!"

Sadao sat down beside her. "A man can change. I had many lonely days and nights in prison to consider the whole sum of my life and I didn't like what I saw. I vowed to make things different if I was ever given the chance."

"So you just fell into the first opportunity that stumbled into your bed and said, 'This is it'?"

"Gisette - " There was a warning in Sadao's tone she chose to ignore.

"Because I don't understand it any other way! He told me he has no hold over you whatsoever. No advantage! He is nothing, Sadao! A simple, unrefined, uneducated, un -"

"Gisette! Enough!" Sadao gripped her arm to silence her.

"Haa!" she gasped in shock and he released her immediately.

"I'm sorry."

"You should be sorry. After everything I've done for you, given you, sacrificed for you! And now you want to throw it all away for throw pillows and finger paints? Do you know what your legacy has cost me? And I don't mean in dollar bills!"

"I understand you're hurt and angry…"

"I am *beyond* angry. I am beyond hurt! I don't think there is a word I can say that can describe how I feel! That somebody could just come along and destroy every shred of what we built together! What we spent decades building together side by side! If only I had known what a fool you would let me make of myself that night at the Chairman's dinner! You never refused me before! I was so hurt I cried for days!"

"Mouse and I weren't together then. I wasn't making idle excuses. I just … wanted to go back."

"So when did it start with him? How did it start?!"

"That's not your business, Gisette."

"I guess I do know when. It was after the Dry Lakes Motocross. I knocked on your door, did you know that? I knew you had someone in here. I could hear it - I could hear you. You've never sounded that way before. Is he really that talented in bed? Is it his cock, Sadao? That's the only thing I could never offer you. I've seen it, you know. Impressive for such a small man. He must have fucked you well with it-"

"I said *enough!*" This time the rage in his voice was enough to silence her.

"Fine…" she said weakly. Tears were building again. "I suppose it isn't my business to know how he came to be so precious to you. Or how I came to be nothing but someone you wanted to forget."

"I never said I wanted to forget you, Gisette. And you are far from being nothing to me. But you have to accept that for us to stay friends, some things have to change."

"They already have. Drastically. Starting with you pretending to be dead to me."

"I said I was sorry for that. I promise I won't pretend to die again without warning you first."

She seemed to soften at this and blinked through her tears. "Fair enough. What else? What other conditions do I have to accept to keep you in my life?"

"There are no conditions. Only that I ask you kindly to respect the members of my family. And our privacy."

She nodded and began to fish around nervously in her purse.

"Please don't smoke."

Gisette pulled out tissues instead and dabbed her eyes and wiped her cheeks. "I wasn't…" she whimpered. "So there's to be no more smoking, no drinking, no laughing, no coming by unannounced, no insults directed at … what is he exactly to you? He said he's your husband, of all things."

"We're not married. Not in the legal sense. But I do think of him as my spouse."

"Good, so I don't have to bring over a belated wedding gift next time, I guess … oh…!" Her hand pressed tight to her chest as if she felt a sharp pain.

Sadao leaned closer to her. "Are you alright?"

Her eyes flew open. "*Mon dieu! Non, non,* I am not alright! I am falling to pieces! How can you just expect me to stop my heart from beating? How can you expect me not to care about you!"

"Don't be so dramatic. I never said we had to stop caring about one another."

"You didn't?" Her lips were reddened from her tears. She looked so young just then. Like a small child after a tantrum.

He touched her chin. "No. But - we can't be lovers anymore. I want that to be clear."

Her hand came up to cover his softly. "You love him that much?"

"I made a promise to him, Gisette. I intend to keep it."

She shut her eyes and leaned into the curve of his hand. "He doesn't know how lucky he is to feel the warmth of your arms about him anytime he wishes."

"I also didn't say you couldn't feel my arms around you from time to time," Sadao said softly and she fell into his lap, pressing her lips to his cheek.

"Merci, merci ..."

Sadao held her gently, comforting her as she wept against him - wept for the end of a race he had stopped running two years ago.

"I'm sorry," he said, holding her as she shook. And he meant it.

When she'd cried herself out, Sadao carried her to the bed and put her in it, removing her shoes. She sleepily begged him to stay as he covered her in the blankets and gently declined.

"I need to get back to Shinjyu," he said. "She's been very protective of me since the raid."

Gisette nodded and closed her eyes. Like himself, she knew what it felt like to be an orphan and how important it was to stay close to those who loved us. When she fell asleep, Sadao slipped out and clicked the door closed behind him. He was about to put the ski mask back on when he heard a second door click further down the hall followed by the sounds of footfalls on the metal stairs.

That's a little too convenient, he thought and hurried to the emergency exit door. He opened it in time to peer down and see someone descending rapidly below him.

"Hey!" he yelled and the distant figure froze, glanced up his way, then increased the speed of his escape.

"Wait!" he shouted. *Shit! Why stairs?*

Sadao gave chase but the bad leg was not in favor of haste when it came to bending and shifting his weight under the weak hip. He tripped and stumbled into the handrail which gave him an idea. Instead of using his injured hip to walk, he'd use it to slide.

Scheeeeech! The rounded rails weren't stealthy, but they did allow him to slide and gain a little distance. A few more floors and he might just ... Thud!

The 5th floor hallway door banged shut below him, followed by a distant beep and the rumble of the elevator.

I guess I was gaining better than I thought!

Sadao slid himself to the 5th landing, limping through the pain. He cursed his lack of mobility and shoved open the heavy door, lumbering toward the elevators. He rounded the corner just as the doors were closing on a descending car. He launched himself at the narrowing opening and got a hand in. The rubber bumpers closed, pinching his fingers. He felt a whump! of pain as the elevator's lone occupant delivered a kick to his knuckles from the inside. He wrenched them out.

"Fuck!"

Sadao spotted a red emergency button and hit it. The elevator doors flew open, stopping the car a few feet below the level of the floor. A blaring alarm fired off. The person trapped inside looked up him, breathless and terrified. Sadao recognized him immediately. It was Tagata's bumbling sentinel, Captain Shotgun, who also happened to be the last of the remaining Whitebird men, Miyagi.

"I can explain!" he begged, holding up his hands as Sadao sucked his bruised knuckles. "I can explain everything!!"

"You have something you want to say to me?"

Miyagi shook in his racing boots as Tagata leaned over him in the frugal lamplight of his trailer. The storm had come in full force as predicted after nightfall. The driving snow blasted the outer metal walls of the trailer, causing it to pitch and rock like a boat. The wind had forced them to shut down the camp's main electrical generators (a lesson learned from the Whitebird tragedy), plunging the trucks and trailers into heavy shadows.

Sadao had radioed the Sasori Boss to come to the Ski Lodge immediately with his strongest men and to bring a truck and some rope; which was now being used to secure Miyagi's wrists to the arms of a wooden chair. His ankles were bound together as well. Unless he sprouted wings, the kid was not going to flee out into the storm or out from under the equal chill of Tagata's gaze.

"B-Boss - I - can explain! I - I did not wish harm on our team, I swear to you!"

Tagata glanced ruefully at Sadao who sat at the end of the table nearby, icing his sore hand. With Mouse, Lupe, Shinjyu and the twins safely huddling up warm and cozy with a loaded rifle in his old trailer a few yards up the shoreline, he was anxious to see what further truth Tagata would be able to pull out of this kid. From the look of his trembling, the boy was about to piss himself with fright if he didn't hyperventilate first.

"Why are you spying on Oyaji and his friend? Why were you in the Ski Lodge when you

have no business there?"

"I was told to go! I had no idea why! They didn't say, only that I was to follow this French woman. They gave me a photo. I - I don't even know who she is!"

"Show me the photo," Sadao said. The kid made a jerk with his neck indicating it was in his jeans pocket. Tagata reached around behind him and pulled it out, handing it to Sadao after a brief look. It was a press photo of him and Gisette celebrating at the finish line of one of his old auto competitions - probably from a decade ago. He had his arm around her, waving at the cameras. *Fuck, we look young.*

"Where did they get this?" Sadao asked, although he suspected it was in the public domain.

Miyagi shook his head. *"They didn't tell me … "*

"Who is they?" Tagata spat, coming nose-to-nose with the kid. *"Why do they ask you to be a spy?"*

Miyagi looked to Sadao, pleading for sympathy. Sadao kept his gaze neutral. This was Tagata's interrogation. *"Answer your Boss,"* Sadao said.

"It's those guys who took off last year - remember Ryota and Toma and those other guys from Osaka?"

Tagata stood up straight. *"The deserters? The Whitebird men? That's only 12 - we've counted at least 26 in masks."*

"Yeah, they have more now, but it's them! They've come back as a team. They wanted me to leave with them last season but I said no! I don't want to! I like it here! This is my home. I'm a Sasori now! But they've come back now and they have all these new bikes and high end gear that they wear and their own team boss and -"

"Who is their Boss?" Sadao demanded. *"Who is their sponsor? Young deserters have no means to start a team!"*

The kid looked pale. *"Their team leader… he comes … from Japan and he brought these guys from Kansai back with him. But - I never see his face. His voice is … I don't know how to say."*

Sadao stood up and approached.

"It's distorted. On purpose. I heard him speak. He's the only one who is not Kansai. How do they know him? Who sent him? He's young like the others."

Miyagi had tears about to break in his wide eyes. *"I don't know! They don't tell me anything! He came from Japan but he's different from us! I -"*

Bam! Tagata had drawn a short throwing knife from his braids. It flew across the trailer and embedded itself into the chairback next to the kid's head.

"Tell us what you did!"

"Boss! Please forgive me! They make me do things for them! They say the Sasoris are going to be defeated, disbanded and I'll have nowhere to go! I'll be sent back to Japan! I was scared!"

"Did you give them permission to enter our camp when you were sentinel?!" Tagata demanded.

"No! I'd never!"

"How did they come in? Attract the vermin to eat our food and damage our garage and to take that which was sacred from the shrine of their fallen leader?!"

"I don't know! I don't know!"

"I know," Sadao said. *"They probably used our older CB codes and frequencies from their first winter here. They remembered the general location of the lake, if not the exit road itself. If they were hiding on the far shore as Mouse discovered, they could have listened in on a lot of conversations at short range. They were Sasoris and Orochis once, but not before they were Whitebird men. It was before you came to us, Taga, but many of them believed I had disrespected our General, made him bow down under me when I merged our teams. Our old friend's Kansai boys were never fond of me.*

When he was struck down after the Overland, they felt I'd sacrificed his life for a team they were only adopted to. I heard one of the longhouse thieves say - 'All weapons will be returned to their rightful place with us.' They feel they are the heirs to our fallen General's legacy."

"Bullshit!" Tagata spat. *"They are deserters! Traitors of our many kindnesses!"*

"And now a recognized chartered team you must compete against tomorrow," Sadao added.

"How? How are these shit-devils a chartered team? Who gave them this honor? Who gave them their bikes and equipment? Their Canadian competition licenses? None of this is free. Our friend is dead! Who gave them the ability to oppose us? Who is their sponsor?"

Miyagi just sat, head down and trembled.

"Speak! Answer me!"

"I-I don't know, Boss! I don't! They don't say his name to me ... "

Tagata reached for his braids to heighten his threat, but Sadao intervened. *"Tagata-san, - a word, please."*

Tagata relented and they stepped a few feet aside to whisper while keeping close watch on the spy.

Sadao touched Tagata's arm to calm him. *"This boy doesn't know anything. There's no reason to harm him..."*

"Harm him? What about the harm he has done to us?! His sneaking and lies have lost us vital money and time!"

"He's being used by them - a pawn. I believe him when he says he doesn't know who's funding their team. He babbled at me for a long time until you and your men arrived to carry him out. They made him believe the Sasoris were about to become a memory. They intimidated and frightened him. He thought he had no other choice but to comply! These were his former brothers and he's not made many new friends among his Sasori peers."

"*I know this,*" Tagata answered stiffly. "*But he is still Sasori - he swore to protect and serve the Sasori banner! Do you forget, Sadao-sama, how we deal with traitors?!*"

Sadao regarded Tagata respectfully. He was right. As Boss there could be no exceptions when it came to disobedience and betrayal. A Boss who lets his men undermine him is no boss. But this was also no man.

"*This is your team,*" Sadao affirmed. "*Punishments are your determination and no one else's. But please consider Miyagi's age and position. Save your wrath for those who have truly earned it.*"

"*I am sorry, Sadao-sama!*" Tagata said. "*But this is not for you to settle.*"

"*Of course, do as you feel is best.*"

"*I will decide what is to be done with Miyagi after the Rally is over and we have our victory. But until then, he is my prisoner.*"

"*Very well.*" Sadao nodded and turned to leave.

"*Sadao-sama…*" Tagata's voice gave Sadao pause. "*I will also order all CB codes changed at once.*"

"*Of course.*"

"*No one but Sasori leaders will have access to these codes or be permitted on our properties. This includes friends of Sadao-sama and our camp here in Squamish.*"

Sadao regarded Tagata a moment. In the shadows, the young man's face looked much older than his 26 years. Sadao lowered his head in a bow. "*As you wish, Boss.*"

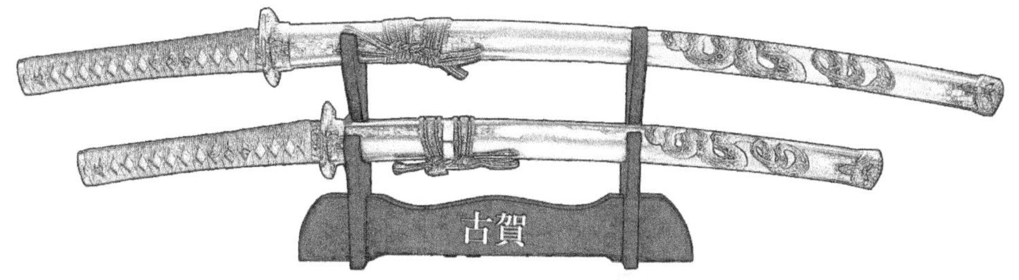

Chapter XX

Hooks, Lines, and Sinkers

The morning of the opening ceremonies of The 17th Annual Winter Sports Rally dawned bright and clear. The temperature had fortunately stayed cool enough that the previous week's snowpack was still in fine shape - ideal racing and trick jump conditions. Mouse was much relieved as he stood ankle deep in the stuff, sipping a hot coffee, watching the teams roll out under their banners amid cheers from the crowds assembled around Alice Lake's shores. This year's turnout was substantial. The betting booths were already boasting long lines and fist fights from over-eager gamblers. The Sasori Team stood to take on a generous share as long as no more marmots, wood mice, or fuck what else? Grizzlies? invaded the closely guarded garage truck.

"Hey, there's our guys!" Mouse shouted, jumping up and down like a teenager. Aki and his garage kids matched his enthusiasm, shouting, whistling and spilling coffee on the white trampled snow.

"Lupe!!" Mouse cried out when he saw number 33 roar past. Lupe raised a hand and waved first to him and the garage geeks, and then a few feet around the curve, gave a special salut to a man holding a child, wrapped up to his nose in a thick scarf.

Sadao? Did he sneak out after all?

"Hang on guys, I gotta check something out," Mouse said. "Meet you back at the garage at 10 sharp! We should be ready for the first busted fenders by then. We don't fix this shit the second it comes in, Tagata will kill us. Me first!"

"Hai! Mouse-san!" They yelled as Mouse eased his way through the crowd to the fence-line where Lupe had directed his salut. Sure enough, it was his husband and child dressed like Eskimos. Mouse came up from behind and gave Sadao a poke in the ass that made him jump and Shinjyu squeal.

"Yabai!" Sadao snapped, from inside his layers of wool.

"Yabai yourself. Thought you were sitting this one out. Safely!"

"Touchan! I wanna go higher! I can't seeee!"

Sadao grumbled but lifted the girl up onto his shoulders anyway. "No one will know me in this getup," he said, burying his nose a little further to disguise his face. Sunglasses over his eyes did the rest.

"I knew it was you in two seconds, flat! So did Lupe!"

"That's because I promised the girl she could watch Lupe in the freestyles this morning if she ate her breakfast and didn't kick while I was putting her boots on!"

"Already caving into her demands with bribery, eh? That's a slippery slope, babe. She'll have you well trained by age seven!"

"Shh...! Here come the mystery riders..."

"And now let us introduce the newest addition to the Rally, the - uh - anonymously named team in purple and grey camo - the a ... I guess some call them the Mauraders!"

The so-called team gunned their snowbikes into the circuit for their drive-by. Sadao had heard right - they did have top-of-the-line custom machines unlike any Mouse had seen before. This was no junkyard chop job - Japanese combustion engineering was alive and well it seemed far off across the sea. The imported state-of-the-art bikes shone with fresh new paint and chrome as they whizzed by. *Lucky sons of bitches.*

"Looks like there's at least 20 of them competing," Mouse noted.

Sadao nodded. "The maximum allowed for each competition. They have a wide set of skills. Each one of them is scheduled to compete in nearly every event. From freestyle to downhill. From what Tagata and Nakagawa have observed, they're all at the top of their game."

"But no one's seen their faces yet, not even in trials?"

"No. They keep their helmets on. And when not competing, they don those ridiculous masks."

"Just do me a favor today, babe, and stay out of sight, eh? I don't need them throwing anymore used clothing at you."

"I won't. The girl and I are going to stick to the heavy crowds and call it a day before the sun goes down."

"I want a racing bike, Touchan! I want a shiny one!"

"No, hime. Bikes are dangerous."

"I don't care! I'm brave and I can go fast! Fast like on my sled, right Mouse?"

"That's right, sweetie! You go faster than anyone. Still can't figure out why ... maybe I'll make you a go-cart this spring and let you tootle around camp."

Sadao jerked his head toward Mouse. Even through the shades, Mouse could feel the heat in his gaze.

Mouse leaned in. "For fuck's sake, a go cart's top speed is like 4 mph! She'll be fine!"

"No racing!" Sadao snapped. "You will obey me in this!"

"I wanna race, Touchan! I wanna go-cart! Vroooom!"

"If you never let her have any fun, she'll grow up to resent you..." Mouse sang in his ear.

"We will discuss this later!"

Says the man who had his fun removed at birth. "Umhmm...sure."

"Jesus Christ! What the hell happened to these bikes? You run over a whale?"

They weren't even half a day into the scheduled competitions, and already bikes were coming in bloody.

"All we ran over was lunch, man," Lupe said, gingerly pushing his ride up to the back of the garage truck where Mouse kept a hose rolled up. Snow trails of brownish-red followed Lupe and four of his teammates through the snow as they rolled their befouled vehicles into a line for dousing. "We came back from the taco trucks and this sticky shit was everywhere."

"Taco trucks?" Mouse asked over the rumble of the water pump and his stomach. "When did we get taco trucks?"

"Since fuck - I don't know! Some *puto* decided he'd get one over on us while we were grabbing some carnitas! It's elk blood or some shit."

"Let me guess," Mouse said, cranking on the hard spray and starting to do what clean up he could 30 minutes before their next starting gun. "You didn't park in direct view of your bikes."

Lupe and his teammates looked at each other and mumbled. "Those were some sweet ass tacos, though ... shit."

The spray-down rinsed off the worst of the mess, which from what Mouse's nose could tell, was indeed some kind of animal ooze. Hunting was a daily routine for most of the Canadian mountain dwellers. Between their leavings and ample road kill, anyone could have been fucking around with a spare liver - most likely some drunken fans of the one of the out-of-town teams.

Aki and the garage kids grabbed some rags, and together they did their best to try and rid the seats and handlebars of the ick, but there was no time to toothbrush out the nooks and crannies.

At 2:30 P.M., Mouse and Aki had all four Sasori competitors mounted on their christened vehicles and aimed at the starting gate. The snowbikes looked presentable, if not a little stinky by the time the gun fired, and Lupe and company sped out over the freshly tamped down snowpack for the first lap of the 15-mile lakeside trail race.

After subjecting the poor garage gang to carnage clean-up, Mouse decided to let the poor things out into the sunlight and actually see their hard work in action for a change. He locked up the truck and drove the kids the short distance to the track in the Jeep.

Tagata should be out over by the lodge, anyway. If we stick to the treeside, we'll be out of sight. No lazy race gawking here - nope nope!

Aki and company made a run for the deer fence behind the ticketed bleacher sections. They climbed up to the top to see over the backs of the heads of the several thousand spectators, who had invaded Squamish for this very popular three-day weekend event.

Mouse climbed up right beside them and sat atop the high fence, holding onto a tree trunk for balance. Lake Garibaldi was a beautiful emerald-blue simmering in the sunlight. The new snow sat heavily in the pine boughs, dazzling with reflected light. The rumble of the anxious crowd of fans, punctuated by bullhorn announcements of the racers' names and teams, made him ache for the old days when he'd climb stone walls and fences with his dad to get a free peek at the action.

Fuck, forgot the sunglasses. And sunscreen! Who thinks of these things when it's 30 degrees?

Bang! The starting gun fired and the snowbike engines came to life, growling for dominance as the racers took off for the far end of the lake. Once they cleared the horseshoe-shaped cove, they entered the trees to disappear from view for a few seconds before emerging again.

"Look, Mouse-san! Here they come!"

Come they did. Bursting from the thickest part of the forest, the leaders shot out of the shadows in a flurry of racing colors and snowy ice trails. Mouse could detect the engine whine of two Honda 450s among the pack. As they rushed past, Mouse spotted numbers 26 and 33 - Lupe and Sato!

"Whooooo!!!" he shouted along with his lug-rats' "Ganbare! Ganbare!" His heart pounded with as much excitement as it had when watching daring young men tearing up the desert sands in his youth. The 40 or so competitors began to spread out after the second lap. But the leading pack that contained their teammates and a few others in rival colors stayed pretty close, neck-and-neck until the final lap. Mouse and the boys saw the leads cut as close to the lake's share as possible to gain an edge, Sato coming dangerously close to falling in.

Shiiit - don't fall, don't fall ... I don't wanna dredge the lake for parts ... But Sato held the deep angle he was in and made the corner, accelerating out of the horseshoe turn and into the trees at least a full second ahead of the runners-up.

"Whoa! Sato! Sato!" The boys and Mouse began to chant. "Ganbare!!!"

"Hang tight, they'll be coming back out into view in just a ... the hell?"

Bikes shot by for the checkered finish but neither Sato nor Lupe were among them. Mouse stood up on the fence edge and held a hand up to his eyes to dampen the glare. Was he snowblind? The flag fell and the announcer called it for the Wolverines 1st, and their friends the Masked Marauders - in 2nd and 3rd respectively. Mouse and the boys looked at each other in confusion as the remainder of the racers exited the forest cover and cleared the finish in a hail of snow flurry and exhaust. As their engines cooled, Mouse could hear one still running in the thick trees just beyond.

Worried, they all climbed down off the fence and Mouse tossed the Jeep keys to Aki. "I'm going in to see what's up. I'm betting one of them fell and took out the other. Radio the emergency band for some back up. We could have a broken bone or two."

Aki nodded and the kids took off running for the four-by-four.

Mouse tromped through the snow down to the lake trail, trying to edge closer to the cleared racing track, carving a white sinuous line through the tall trees. Soon he found a break in the deer fence and slipped through.

"Lupe! Sato!!" He cupped his hands and shouted, trudging forward toward the sound of the bike engine. Soon he saw it, tipped on its side and idling on the edge of the track. Mouse ran up to it - 33 was on the front number plate.

"Lupe!!" he screamed.

"Shhh…!! Gringo pendejo!" Lupe's harsh whisper spun Mouse around. On the other side of the track there was a short drop into a frozen stream bed and in it were Lupe and Sato, and Sato's bike. The two men were sitting motionless in the snow, backs up against the embankment. Lupe's hand was over Sato's mouth, muffling his screams, as a river of blood ran from his torn leg.

Wide-eyed, all three men watched in shock as the largest cougar Mouse had ever seen tore off another chunk of elk-blood flavored leather from Sato's bike seat, chewing with relish.

"Hang on guys," Mouse shout-whispered. "I got a plan!"

"Sensei says Sato's leg will be fine. The cuts are deep but they did not tear any vital tendons or veins." Sadao translated for Mouse's benefit.

"That's what you get for almost beating me to the finish!" Lupe joked, trying to lighten the dark mood that had descended on the medical tents since the casualties of the 15-mile circuit race were hauled in via Mouse's Jeep. He was thinking of painting a red cross on the doors for all the rescue missions it had performed to date.

Lupe's cuts and bruises were declared superficial but cleaned and dressed for good measure. He was very concerned for his friend, however, but hid it well behind his good humor.

"Sato-san here nearly won you a first-prize, Boss," Lupe quipped at a truly dour Tagata. "If he hadn't stopped to admire the wildlife."

"How can you make jokes?" Tagata said. "We now have one less racer. One less bike!" He looked to Mouse for verification.

"Sorry, can't fix 'eaten.'"

"How on earth did a mountain lion manage to catch a speeding snowbike?" Sadao wanted to know.

Tagata, being the resident Canadian, answered. "We hear stories of this kind. Kid on snowtrail alone, riding, never come home. Next summer they find only skull. Big cats think, this is a deer or elk running. No hunting here is allowed for cougar. They are not afraid of humans."

"The bikes were doused in some kind of animal blood not half an hour before racing time," Mouse reiterated. "The scent must have…"

"There's three thousand screaming fans, man," Lupe said, getting serious for a moment. "Not in that exact part of the forest, but close enough. These cougars looking for takeout or what? I thought that fucker was gonna eat the whole bike! Then us!"

Sadao turned to Mouse. "How did you chase the beast off?"

"Blasting my 'hillbilly music' from the Jeep's stereo, maybe? And some honking. Definitely honking."

In truth, Mouse had no real clue what drove the animal off its prey. As soon as the Jeep came into view and Mouse backed slowly toward it and into the driver's seat for a good round of *Life is a Highway*, the cougar lifted its head, growled and ran off.

"We're being deliberately targeted," Sadao said, stating the obvious. "They've been making their attacks look like natural events since the start. It's too convenient the Marauders placed only after eliminating our men."

"We must warn the whole team to watch for dangers everywhere. Natural and unnatural," Tagata said.

"Actually…" Mouse offered. "You should warn them to watch out for tacos."

The remaining Winter Rally first-day heats ended cougar-free at 4 P.M. since sundown came early each night. Despite being down one snowbike and rider, the Sasoris had managed to place first in a handful of circuit and hill-track competitions, but the real moneymaker was the Downhill, scheduled for the next afternoon. A first or second place in that race meant the team could chill well into next summer with plenty of fat bellies and warm cabins.

After Mouse locked up the garage and double checked all the equipment as being accounted for and under guard, he shot back to the Sasori campsite, hoping to catch dinner with his peeps. He pulled up to Sadao's old trailer close to sundown to find Lupe firing up the outdoor grill. Sadao and Kei had the antsy children down by the inlet shore dangling handmade poles with baited hooks and lines into the water. Mouse's fishing equipment had been spread out across a picnic table and picked through. So far, it looked like the mini-fishermen (and girl) had been successful at catching little more than algae.

Sadao was struggling to assemble an actual professional pole, but his lack of sportsmanship was evident as he cursed at the tangled wads of fishing line he was making.

"Geez that's pathetic," Mouse said, taking it from him and cutting the rat's nest away with a multitool. "Let me string it for you. It goes like this through the wire loops, see? Then, I like to tie a jig on to hold the line at the end so it doesn't unthread itself and spill off the spool." He held the threaded line with his thumb and searched through the tackle box for an appropriate lure.

"You can give me that," Sadao said, annoyed. "I can at least tie a fucking knot."

Mouse laughed and handed the pole back to him with a proper sea-bait jig shaped like a fat sardine. "I'm just excited to see you attempting to catch dinner with your own hands. Very manly."

Shinjyu stamped her foot angrily at the water's edge next to them, making splashes. "Bad fishies! Why won't you eat your worm? Come eat your dinner, now!"

Mouse smiled as he picked up a second adult pole and prepped the line. It was an unusually calm evening, the sinking sun was casting the fresh snowpack on the mountain cliffs above them in a brilliant red orange. By midnight the second leg of the blizzard was due to move in, bringing back the bone cracking cold. The whole team was hoping the impending weather would clear by the following afternoon's much anticipated Downhill race.

"Kicking at them will only make them swim further out, honey. You need to be quieter. Wait and let them come to you and your worm."

Shinjyu set her mouth and glared up at Mouse like he'd just said the stupidest thing ever. "I don't like waiting!" she said and stamped off to pout. She sat herself down on a wide flat rock next to her prized fishie bucket, plopping stones in it and grumping to herself.

Tink tonk tonk ...

"She brought her little bucket? How cute is that?"

"She insisted," Sadao said, attempting to aim the line through the loop in the jig. "Even though I told her it was too small to hold a real fish. Now her collection of wooden carp are in peril of being devoured by the trailer's seat cushions."

Mouse strung his line, watching Shinjyu make shapes with her collected rocks in the gravel shore. They looked to be shaping up into stick figures of their family. One of the twin boys, equally frustrated with fishing, bent down to try and help.

"No! Give me that! You're doing it wrong!" she yelled. "These are my rocks!"

"Shinjyu, honey, you need to share," Mouse said, finishing his pole prep in expert time.

She rolled her eyes at him. "I don't have to share rocks - there's plenty!"

Mouse grinned and glanced at Sadao who was still absorbed in his knot tying. His face carried a very similar expression to their daughter's - vexed. "You know, she's a lot like you."

Sadao glanced up from his focused attempt to wind the line properly. "How is that?"

Mouse shrugged. "I dunno. Something in her manner. How she doesn't like to be told what to do."

"No child likes to be told what to do."

"Of course not, but she's got your 'Don't even try to fuck with me' face when she complains. Very similar. I think she has your mouth, too. It's nearly the same shape - have you noticed?"

Sadao didn't respond, just brought the jig to his teeth to cut the extra line and swore when the knot he'd labored to produce slipped clean off the eyelet.

"Here, let me. You'll go blind trying to tie that in this light," Mouse said, sticking his cast pole in the rocky beach sand.

"I'm not blind," Sadao grumbled, but passed his pole to Mouse nevertheless.

"See? That's the look! The 'Sadao is displeased' look. Are you sure you two aren't related?"

"We're both Japanese."

"Well, duh, I know that!" Mouse expertly re-threaded the jig and started the knot. 'It's more than that. I can't explain it other than to think she's maybe your long-lost daughter. After all, we don't really know where she's from or how she got here. Maybe -"

"Impossible."

"How impossible? You admit to having more lovers than you can count. And I'm sure you were careful, but who's to say you didn't get really drunk one night about six years ago."

Sadao snatched the pole back from Mouse who had just managed to tie the lure on. "Hey! We got hooks, here. I need these fingers!"

"I said, it's impossible!" Sadao unlocked the bail, preparing to cast. "I'm sterile," he said more softly and swung his arm, letting the line fly.

Mouse blinked in shock as the weighted jig sailed high out over the water and plunked back in about 40 feet out. "Nice cast ... " he mumbled.

Sadao's shoulders relaxed some as he took pride in his fishing prowess. He clicked the bail and brought the line in slowly, coaxing the little sardine to flap and spin through the water.

"Good," Mouse said. "Nice and even." They were quiet for a few moments.

"Shit ... " Mouse said at last. "That explains a few things about you."

Sadao grunted in agreement.

"How did you ... how do you know? Did you get tested or something? Were you trying to start a family at some point?"

Sadao was watching his line but his mouth turned up at the corner. "Plenty of women wished they could, I have no doubt. What better way to acquire a man's attention and loyalty than by producing his child? It was a source of private amusement for me for many years to observe their schemes. Some really put in a valiant effort."

Mouse made a face. "Spare me the details. Give me the science."

"There's not much science involved. Just bad luck. I've had more than my fair share, starting at age 14 with Nagoya Fever."

"What's Nagoya Fever?!"

"Shh! No need for Shinjyu to overhear this conversation."

Mouse looked over at their daughter. Shinjyu was busy singing songs to her little rock people. Fish, for now, forgotten. "Okay, so you had a bad flu and - ?"

Sadao had finished reeling in his line and was setting up to throw out again, picking algae from the jig's hooks. "It was a little more than that. Nagoya Fever killed a fifth of the population of Japan in 2046. Myself nearly included. I was teaching an English class in the country when I fell ill. I don't remember much. It came on fast but when I woke I was in a sanitorium under the care of nurses, unable to move or speak."

"Holy shit! You've never told me about this!"

"It never came up before," he said and cast. The line sang as it flew over the rippling water.

"So what happened to you?" Mouse asked, swinging out a line of his own. It didn't fly as far as Sadao's. The man had amazing upper body strength.

"I got better, slowly. Regained the ability to walk, talk ... But I was told I'd probably never be able to father children - an unfortunate side effect of the fever."

"I guess..."

Mouse watched as Sadao placidly reeled. He got the feeling this confession had taken some weight off of him.

"But you got checked out at some point, right? To confirm?"

"I received a full medical review upon my recruitment into the Northwest Division. I mentioned it to the team doctor and he ran some tests. So yes, my condition was confirmed."

Mouse sighed, somewhat in relief. "And here I was worried you'd want to dump me someday for a partner who can give you kids."

Sadao smiled. "That doesn't mean we can't keep trying."

"That's not funny!" Mouse said with an irrepressible grin. "And don't forget I'm still viable! Maybe ... "

Sadao raised his brow. "With your fear of women? I don't think we'll ever have the pleasure of finding out."

"I'm not afraid of women," Mouse grumbled. "I just don't want to get near one naked."

"It's really not that bad, you know. Not much of a difference."

"To you maybe! To me it's miles apart! Yecch!"

Sadao grinned. "I guess we're different in that way."

"Yeah, little bit. Can we switch the subject please?"

"Sure, but realize, my condition isn't exactly common knowledge. Even Taga doesn't know."

Mouse nodded. "I won't blab. I like knowing secrets about you no one else knows. Even if they suck."

Sadao took on a forced neutral gaze.

"Ah, geez … . Who else knows? Shiratori knew? I guess."

"Don't speak of the dead. It's impolite. But no, not him, either."

"Sorry. But if not your closest men then … Oh fuck no. Really? Not *her?!*"

Sadao reeled in and recast. Not denying it.

"Aargh! What the hell is it with that woman? You told her? In confidence?"

"Absolutely not," Sadao said, irritated. "It was never a subject of conversation between us. I make a habit of keeping personal facts personal."

"Trial and error then. She caught on after a while and clenched up a sample for the microscope."

"Don't be vulgar. It was none of those things. Gisette knew before we ever met. Her husband was the team physician."

"How convenient for her! Sheesh! How long are we going to be living in her shadow? Seems like she pops up at every turn. In our trailer even. When I'm naked!"

"I should warn you - she'll be popping up again. But this time I've asked her to bring extra towels."

"Huh?"

"I've asked her to come stay in the trailer with us this evening so she doesn't get caught in the storm again trying to get home."

"You did whaaaat?!"

"Calm yourself, *Konezumi*. It's only for a short while. The Sponsors' Ball is tonight. They always run late and her husband's out of the country. Those *kusogaki* are tailing her and I don't want her staying by herself in a secluded cabin halfway up the mountain!"

"Hang on - didn't our fearless leader just lay down a mandate about guests in camp? Don't tell me you got Tagata to make an exception for your ex!"

"He didn't."

"Fuck me, you two are gonna blow up one of these days and I don't want to get caught in the crossfire! I like this job!"

"You don't need to be concerned about it."

"Please tell me she's not sharing our bed?"

"I got one! I got a fishie!!" Shinjyu shrieked, interrupting their bed assignment debate. She was jumping up and down, holding her driftwood pole while a fat little salmon tugged at the hook, wriggling in the shallow shore water. "I wanna eat him!!"

"Yuck! Fish is gross. Can I be excused?"

"You've not even had three bites," Sadao said. "You can have a few more before bed."

Shinjyu looked up at her father with her 'try me' face and pushed her plate away.

"Yumm ... I'll eat it, Jyu-jyu!" Lupe offered, reaching for her plate. "I love ocean fish! We made some bitchin BBQ grilled salmon tonight, yo!"

"Lupe!" Sadao barked, pushing the plate back toward Shinjyu. "Your language."

Mouse snorted around his mouthful of green beans and rice brought in from mess. Their oddball extended family dinner around the trailer's dinette was quite the evening entertainment. Once he'd gotten over the shock of the pending Gisette sleep-over, he'd managed to hook three fat salmon in addition to Shinjyu's and Lupe's two. Despite his casting skills, Sadao failed to reel in anything - except ex-girlfriends.

Sadao looked to his watch as he forked up a small bite of fish for Shinjyu, who sat next to him with her lips firmly closed. "You'll need to leave soon," he said to Mouse.

"Huh? Leave where? It's blowing like ... heckers out there."

"I need you to pick up our final guest," he said under his breath.

"Ah ... fu ... udge-crackers! Why do I gotta do it?"

"Because it won't appear unusual if you're driving the Jeep back toward the ski lodge. It's near the garage truck. She'll be waiting in the lobby."

"Fine - you're coming with!"

"I can't," Sadao said, trying to nudge a flaky piece of flesh between Shinjyu's tightened lips. She was smiling. Nothing she enjoyed more than torturing her father. "Only two fit in the cab."

"I'll go, gringo. No need to get bent about it."

"No," Sadao said, firmly. "She doesn't know you."

"Well, she doesn't know me, either!" Mouse protested. "Better yet, she hates me!"

"I spoke with her," Sadao said, giving up and eating the smooshed piece of fish himself. "She won't be rude this time."

"Uuuugh…" Mouse moaned, rubbing his face. "Fine, but I won't make the same promise!"

"So … ah … you come to Squamish often?" Mouse asked, peering through the snow-blown wipers as they picked their way back into camp in the dark. The camp's outer lights were shut down again for safety. He'd already had to make a lame excuse for the Sasori guards on the way out - something about needing some tie downs from the garage to combat the wind. Outside, the windchill had dropped the temp to -2 °F.

Gisette was lying across the seat next to him in her ball gown, half-covered in a tarp. "I attend every year, but not usually in an oily sack!" she answered crisply.

Jesus, I'm gonna get Sadao for this one. Making me small talk his ex-bitch while hauling her expensive butt around. Asshole's gonna pay. In sex!! I'll make him do the weird stuff! Twice!

"Does this … car have to smell so vile?"

"It's a Jeep," Mouse answered lamely. It did have cougar-slobbered bike parts in it earlier. "It's an equipment hauler. You know … for sporting events."

"And you couldn't have sported in some air freshener?"

The air would be a lot fresher in here if you weren't breathing it!

Mouse hit the brakes suddenly in response to a flashlight beam in his eyes. Gisette rolled off the seat onto the even less air-freshened floor. She cried out something in French.

"Keep down and quiet! Someone's here!"

Mouse rolled down the window, letting in a swirling cloud of snow. Just his rotten luck, it was Tagata, his Captain and some of his A-Team out on a stroll. "What are you guys doing out here? It's freezing - below freezing!"

"We are heading in," Tagata explained, wrapped head to toe in snow gear. "We have come from the Marauder's camp!"

"The camp? Why did you - Oh! Did you raid them?"

"Shh! No. Perimeter is guarded and set with many trip laser. We watched with night vision until snow was falling. We saw a large truck leave camp with something inside, covered."

"Could be their Downhill vehicles. Getting them to the summit early, maybe?"

"No. We do not think this was bikes."

"Did you follow it?"

"We went by walking to be silent. We did not bring our snowmobile to chase trucks."

"Ah, I see. Well… gee it's getting cold, I'd better…"

"I want Mouse-san ready with me first light to go from bottom to top of mountain, look for sabotage!"

"Okay, yeah, good idea. But uh, who's running the garage then?"

"Aki is good. He can take care of bent wheels with his team. I need you and this Jeep!"

"Got it. Got it. Well, I'll pick you up at your trailer, first thing, then."

"Don't be late!" Tagata gave this last final warning before retreating into the blustering snow with his men and vanishing.

So much for getting a solid eight hours...

Thud! His ankle was struck. "Ow! What?"

"I want out of this freezing, stinking bucket you call a Jeep, now!"

Yeah, you're welcome too, lady.

Mouse got her untarped and into the trailer a few minutes later, unseen.

Soon as she set eyes on Sadao, she launched into a tirade. "I can not believe you let this man behind the wheel! It's freezing outside and I nearly died of-"

"Shh-!" her ex-boyfriend silenced her with a finger to his lips. "Children are asleep," he said. Sadao was lying back on the extended sofabed, with the twins and Shinjyu cuddled around him. From the size of the stack of picture books at his elbow, it had taken longer than usual to get them to settle down. Lupe was already snoring softly in a sleeping bag in the lounge. "Mouse, help me get them up into the bunk. Gisette, you can take this bed."

"Oh - " she said, setting her bag down on the floor. The sight of Sadao surrounded by the little ones had taken her completely off guard. She clammed up and kept off to the side until Mouse and Sadao had finished tucking the kids up into their bags.

"Well, I'm calling it," Mouse announced and made a beeline for the back bedroom, shutting the door behind him but leaving it unlocked for Sadao. Despite his better judgement, he sat on the edge of the bed and got undressed silently, tuning his ears to what was going on in the other room. Gisette was being quieter than her usual drama-filled speech but she still sounded upset. Sadao was answering her in a calm subdued tone. He wondered if this whole situation was as uncomfortable for them as it was for him.

Best not be a nosy-nelly, he thought, and went into the bathroom for a much needed shower.

By the time Mouse exited the bath, Sadao was in bed, lying on his back shirtless, hair loose, with the lights turned low and his eyes closed. One perfectly biceped arm was tucked behind the pillow, exposing a dark tuft of manly pit hair. Fuck, he looked delicious.

As he dried off, Mouse was reminded of the first time he saw the full of Sadao - in this bed, drunk and naked to the world. No chopsticks needed this time! Mouse dropped the towel and slid in under the blankets next to him. He nudged Sadao with his nose to get him to lift his other arm so he could snuggle up to his chest.

"I knew you weren't asleep," Mouse said with a kiss to his cheek. "Just faking it."

"I'm not faking anything," he said. "Just trying to set an example. No fooling around tonight. We have guests."

"But - I'm horny!"

"You're always horny."

"Can't help it," Mouse grumbled. "Here we are back on our old bed ... nice and cozy. I finally get to be snowbound with you and yeah, just my luck we have company. All of the company. I promise - I'll be super quiet."

"You'll be quiet if you're sleeping."

Mouse tried to close his eyes and relax with his semi, but visions of Sadao's butt danced in his head. "Nuts. Can't sleep when I'm wound up. Come on, babe," he said, reaching for Sadao's cock under the sheets. "Not even a little?"

Sadao caught his hand and brought it to his lips for a kiss. "No."

Mouse sighed and collapsed against his inert lover. "Sucks to be me, I guess. I finally get this super hot man all to myself and he has no sense of adventure."

"There's adventure and then there's rude. If we fuck, you'll start screaming and the whole trailer will come unhinged. Imagine trying to sleep through that! Lupe has to race tomorrow."

"It's not my fault," Mouse pouted. "Your dick feels too good."

"It's a curse."

Mouse gave him a little pinch.

"*Itai - !* Do I have to send you out to sleep with the kids?"

"No. I'll behave. But I'm not sleepy. You'll need to talk to me to get me to wind down."

"Talk? About what?"

At all costs, Mouse did not want to bring up the French Canadian elephant in their living room.

"Hmm ... tell me about your mother."

Sadao was surprised by the request. "My mother? Why?"

"Because I want to know you better. They say you can tell a lot about a man by the way he talks about his momma."

"My momma, huh? That was a very long time ago. I have to think of what to say."

Mouse nudged him. "Liar. You just don't like to show your soft underbelly."

"I've been training again," Sadao insisted. "My belly is not soft!"

Mouse yawned and walked his fingers up his not-quite-so-soft belly. "Get talking or the tickle fingers come out."

Sadao groaned. "Okay then, I guess you could say my *Haha* was an average sort of woman -"

Mouse chuckled. "Your *'Haha?'*"

"Yes. That is what we call our mothers when we speak of them."

"It's fucking adorable! Is that what you called her when you were little?"

"No - I called her *okaasan* like all respectful children in Japan."

"Ah ... I'm dying of cute," Mouse laughed.

"May I go on? Or do you need resuscitation?"

Mouse wiped a giggle tear from his eye. "I'll live, wee Sadao!"

"*Haha*, as I was trying to say, was an average woman - long black hair, slender. I guess you could say she was attractive."

"What was her name?"

"Her name? Hana. It means flower."

"Nice. What kind of momma was she?"

"Hm ... attentive. Kind, but not terribly patient. She was always quick to correct me. Apparently, I was not very good at following rules."

"Always the rebel, huh?"

"Always. I didn't leave her side in the early days. We shared a bedroom until I was six. I don't remember much else about our first home. I know we lived with her sister, my *obasan*. She and *Haha* were very close - I have memories of them cooking meals together and laughing very loud into the night. They lost their parents young and had to struggle together.

"I can remember a sense of not having much, but *Haha* always made sure I was clean and fed. We'd pass through the market in the mornings before her working hours to buy me a little treat I'd receive later if I was good. She cleaned houses in those days before we were invited to move back into my father's estate. I would explore the homes' gardens until she was done. I spent a lot of time in the dirt. She'd be angry with me - slapping my dirty hands and washing me in the garden hose so we could walk home not looking like transients!"

"I'm dead! I just died of adorableness! Little chubby cheeked Sadao with his dirty hands waiting for a cookie!"

"Rice cracker, more likely."

"Did you love her?"

Sadao raised an eyebrow. "I'd be a fiend if I said no. Of course I loved her. She was my mother. Her life was hard enough and when I came along it became twice as hard. She did her best for me. She was barely seventeen when I was born."

A sappy grin spread across Mouse's face. "What's your favorite memory of her?"

"Memory? I really liked those rice crackers … "

"No, you know, a moment or something. Something special."

Sadao's brows twitched. He was thinking hard. "She could play the koto," he said thoughtfully. "But for whatever reason she no longer had her own instrument. Then after her marriage to my father, he bought her one and then she could play it again and often. I remember her sitting out in the gardens on warm days plucking under the shade of the cypress. I loved that sound. You could hear it all over the island."

"God, that sounds beautiful … " Mouse mused. "The only instrument my dad played was a Jews' harp and fuck if that wasn't annoying!"

"Your turn now. Tell me about your father."

"I can tell you he was an ornery ol' cuss. Man's man. Desert born and bred."

"Was that English? I have no idea what you just said."

"You were absent the day they taught Western slang?"

"Evidently."

"My dad was tall, strong, big hands - a little rough around the edges but he was really great with me. I didn't get his height, though. Like your mom, he took me with him on all his odd jobs. I got cookies! Old ladies loved me. They'd entertain me while dad fixed whatever was broken."

"His name?"

"Dill."

"Odd name."

"Short for Dillon."

"Ah."

"Best memory I have of him is carrying me on his shoulders at the junkyard. We'd trek all over that rust dump looking for spare parts he needed or things I could play with. Nothing was better than finding an old radio to mess with. I loved radios. And fans. Had a thing for fans. Don't know why. I had dozens. He taught me everything I know about engines and electrical - made sure I got an education, too. If you'll remember he couldn't read much. He drank a bit. Got in a fist fight now and again. Fred was always home to look after me when he went off to the bars, but no matter how much mischief my old man got into, he was always home in time to make me bacon and pancakes for breakfast. Even when they made him sleep it off in jail. He'd say, 'I told Sheriff Billy - you gotta let me out early so's I can go feed my boy!'"

"Sounds like you two got along well."

"Oh yeah, I loved the hell out of him. Just killed me when he died. He was my world!"

"I would have liked to have met him."

Mouse laughed. "Oh shit, he'd have punched you for sure!"

"Why? Do you think we wouldn't get along?"

"No, no ... it's just, he was always very protective of me. Wanted to make sure I was being treated right."

"Ah, you're saying I don't treat you right?"

"I'm saying you have your moments. And if you had one of those moments around my dad you'd be dogmeat!"

"What did he like to do besides drink?"

"Oh, he had lots of dad hobbies like classic cars, bikes - racing of course, when he could afford the gas to take us out to see them. We'd sleep in the back of the pickup in the roady camps. Hell of a time!"

Sadao looked amused. "I didn't know you were a roady. How old?"

"About from age six to twelve I guess - we'd follow the local teams around."

"You probably saw me."

Mouse nodded sincerely. "Very likely I did but you know - we rooted for the locals. Didn't really get to know the foreign rosters."

"I wasn't on strictly foreign teams then. We were mixed. I was traded quite a bit. Hotshot - didn't take orders well. I pissed off a lot of team captains."

"I bet you did. Say - how did you wind up with your own team, anyway? Did you just move up the ranks?"

"Not exactly," Sadao said. "I didn't play well with others. I could race like hell but no one really wanted to put me in charge. This made me angry for a long time. Lesser racers I felt were given higher ranks. I was like a wild mustang no one wanted to put a saddle on. You might find this hard to believe, but I had a really bad attitude in those days."

"Had?"

Sadao gave him a look. "You want to hear this story or not?"

"Go on ... badass racing boy."

"Eventually, I realized my mind and body weren't going to hold up against the newer recruits forever. Hard racing is murderous on the body - especially off-road. It was taking longer to heal from injury. I was ... getting older. My rank was slipping. I needed another answer to gunning for finish lines every month if I wanted to stay in the lifestyle I'd become accustomed to."

"So what did you do?"

"I quit the active roster," Sadao said with a wistful sigh. "Got a training job at head-quarters dealing with even younger hotshots who were even bigger assholes than I was. It tamed me down really quick. I had to learn how to manage personnel - I had to learn patience."

"How old were you when you stopped racing full time?"

"Twenty-six. I missed it terribly of course. The division job paid fairly well, but without winnings, I was falling behind financially. Couldn't quite afford to entertain as much …"

Mouse nudged him. "I bet, Don Juan!"

"I did alright."

"So how'd you get the team?"

"I'm getting to that. Policy changes were handed down a year or so later. Division heads were at last willing to let team leads manage their own recruitment. You might say I was first in line when they started issuing new charters - with some key financial backing of course."

"Who?"

"You know who."

"Aw fuck … *her?* Our squatter?"

"You might not like me mentioning *her* - but without *her* money I wouldn't be lying with you in this bed right now! I'd still be in the middle of Tucson training brats how not to flood their fucking engines!"

"Okay - geez! Sore spot. Forget it."

"Anyway, after some negotiations, I got the team. I had enough capital to buy equipment and used trailers from headquarters to set up a small camp out near the abandoned airfields. I even had enough, thanks to you-know-who, to buy a few trades from other teams. More assholes nobody wanted to hold onto if they could get a decent price for them. I probably don't need to tell you our first three years of competition were disastrous. That is until the young ones I had hand picked and raised from youth began to reach racing age. Then everything changed. No more arguments. No more dissension and attitude. At last I had boys who would listen! They believed in me and I believed in them. That is what has made all the difference."

"So the wild mustang was finally broken, eh?"

"No - not completely. That happened some years later."

"Years? Really? So what finally wrangled you in?"

"Terrible fate. Worst of all fates. I fell in love."

Mouse was speechless as Sadao leaned in close to kiss his mouth.

"You've ruined me," he said softly. "I'm an old swayback trail horse now with a lame leg!"

Mouse slapped his chest. "Shut up!"

Sadao pulled Mouse over on top of him where his dick lay thick under the sheet between them. Mouse smiled but Sadao pressed a finger to his lips.

"When did you know?" Mouse whispered, beginning to rub up against him through his underpants.

"When did I know what?"

"That you were in love with me, idiot!"

"Did I mention names? Ow! Okay, easy on the old horse - it was when you left me! I was a fucking wreck! No one had ever made me that miserable before!"

"You deserved it."

"Agreed. But I knew something had changed in me. I didn't want to do this all alone anymore."

"Hmm ... too sweet," Mouse hummed, licking Sadao's chest.

"So when did you know?" Sadao asked as Mouse nibbled a nipple. "Since we're on the subject."

"Jesus - second you walked into the room! My dick said, 'I want a piece of that!'"

Sadao laughed and hugged him. "You couldn't stand me."

"Not when you were tying me up to beds and tables and robbing me blind - no. But I'd still have fucked you."

"Good to know..." Sadao murmured, pulling Mouse up into a nice tongue-filled kiss. "But when did your reckless lust become something more?"

Mouse took Sadao's hand and pulled it down so he could reach around his cheeks and finger the ring embedded in his ass. "This ... was everything," he whispered, grinding against Sadao with more fervor. "No more talking. I want to feel your love - nice and hard - all the way up inside me."

"I swear to you - no sounds from your mouth or the bed or we stop!"

Mouse stuck out his lip.

"Fuck! I'm gagging you and we're moving to the floor!"

"Time to ride the wild mustang?"

"Yes."

Naked, with his back to the cold floor rug, Mouse lay panting and shivering while Sadao searched Lupe's dresser for tieable objects. He pulled out a long-sleeved jersey and used the arms to bind Mouse's wrists up over his head and around a leg of the bed. Next, he selected a do-rag and tied it behind Mouse's head to gag his mouth.

Sadao's expression was stern as he limited Mouse's ability to squirm and scream but the tell-tale spot building at the peak of his bulging shorts betrayed his intentions. The stain widened as he selected a long winter scarf to bind Mouse's ankles together, spreading his thighs and exposing his hard-on.

"Mnn.."

"Not a sound," Sadao whispered as he lifted Mouse's bound feet up over his own head and sucked his fingers, moistening them. He eased Mouse's asshole open with his wet fingertips, pressing in. Mouse leaned his head back, closing his eyes and trying to relax - a difficult thing to do when excited out of his mind. God, did he ever have a thing for getting bound up by this man. Too many times he'd used memories of being chained up under his trailer table to beat off in Sadao's absence.

"Mmnf-!" Shit, the gag wasn't as sound proof as Mouse thought.

Sadao leaned in and bit his earlobe. "Not one fucking sound, I said."

Mouse opened his eyes and nodded vigorously. With his arms up over his head and legs over his lover's shoulders, he couldn't do much more than bite the gag and shudder as Sadao dragged a wet tongue across his chest, savoring each nipple, licking them stiff and sending goosebumps across his skin. Soon he made his way south to his dick, where he spent time exploring Mouse's length vein by vein until his whole shaft was lathered with spit. Sadao worked his head, easing it between his lips softly, kissing it and delicately licking the very tip, teasing the tiny hole, encouraging a squirt of precum.

The oozing release sent a wave of intense pleasure through Mouse. Tears built up under his eyelids with the need to moan as Sadao opened his mouth and took him deep into the back of his throat, holding him there, encased in heat, sucking softly.

"Pffff! Ffff-!" His struggling breath soaked the bandana through with saliva, making a flapping noise when he breathed.

Shhh!! Shhh!! Calm!! Mouse told himself. *He knows just how you like it, he doesn't need feedback, keep it together.* He tried to control his breathing - nice and slow - in and out, matching the pace of Sadao's mouth - up and down his dick, making it even harder to keep still.

Sadao sucked him silently, breathing at the same pace as Mouse to lessen any chances of gulping or slobbering noises. It was torture, this slow deliberate suck. His ass ached as Sadao's fingers stretched him open while his thumb worked his pearl, flicking it back and forth, hooking it and giving the jewelry a tug. Mouse couldn't help but rock his hips in encouragement and shudder whenever he felt the pad of Sadao's buried fingers press up against his prostate.

His dick was given a moment of cooldown as Sadao lifted his head to whisper in his ear again. "I wanted to get you off and just go to bed! But your ass feels so good..." he rasped, fingering his hole. "I won't be able to sleep until I've had you."

"Mmnn!" Mouse meant to say yes, yes, yes! But his voice came out as a desperate muffled groan.

"Kuso!" Sadao ripped the bandana off, rolled up a scrunchy wrist guard and stuffed it in his mouth and re-tied the gag. "I said fucking shut up!"

Sadao raised Mouse's ankles up over his head and tied them to his wrists, turning him into a naked ball of trembling limbs with his junk all poking out.

Who knew Sadao had a kink side? Woot!!

Sadao grinned in the darkness. "That's better. Now I can get at what I want!" He licked this thumb and ran it up over the tip of Mouse's cock, gathering the pearl of moisture there, smoothing it around the head before gliding downward to cup and squeeze Mouse's dangling balls, tugging them, just short of the point of pain. Mouse couldn't do anything but toss his head and bite the ball of material between his teeth. Jesus, was he ever turned on.

"One more thing…" Sadao whispered and reached for the other elastic wrist guard. He took it, doubled it and slipped it snugly down over Mouse's hard dick to the base. Immediately, Mouse felt his cock get hotter and thicken with the restriction.

Well, I did want the weird stuff after all …

Tied up now, head to tip, Sadao spread his butt cheeks and went down on him mercilessly. He ate up his ass, licking and probing his bung with his tongue and fingers. He bit his inner thighs and sucked his balls, gripping Mouse's dick and jerking it through his fist, twisting to increase the friction.

Mouse arched, screaming with excitement into the improved gag as Sadao fucked his asshole good with his fingers, nailing his gland, making it convulse and quiver but nothing was coming up, nothing was coming out of him as the urgency built up and up.

"Mmnngh!" His heart pounding and dizzy with need, Mouse felt the angry head of Sadao's cock demanding entrance. Bound hand and foot, Sadao held the back of Mouse's knees and pressed his dickhead into the clenched muscle. Properly loosened, and slathered with spit, the rim soon gave way and Sadao sank himself in, eyes closed and mouth open, breathing hard, until he they were locked solid.

He blinked there in the dark a moment, savoring the feel of being fully encased in Mouse's body. "Nothing…" he breathed. " … has ever been better than this." His voice was rough. "Not riding my first motorbike, not winning my first race, not even my first fuck can compare."

He leaned in and licked the tears from Mouse's cheek. "How can that be? It's just flesh against flesh," he said with a jerk of his hips that forced the air out of Mouse's lungs. "How can it make me forget everything else?" Thrust! "How can it make me want to give up everything else?" Thrust! "The first time I saw this ass, high in the air begging for my cock, I had to take it. I had to take it again and again until I couldn't even crawl."

"Mngh mmn mgh?" Mouse tried to answer. But it didn't matter, his miracle butthole was in control now as Sadao lost hold of himself and began to pound wildly into him. Eyes screwed shut and jaw set - the groans Sadao was fighting to hold back were making the tendons on his neck stand out. He sped up, taking Mouse so forcefully between his thighs that the bed began to squeak and they weren't even on it! The air-filled tires under the trailer floor were responding to his passion as he powered toward climax.

Eerk eerk eek.…

"Mmmm??" Mouse pleaded but his muffled cries were no match for Sadao's lust. At this point he was likely little more than an ass life support system.

Does he even remember he's tied a fucking band around my dick? What happens if I come and it's still there? Do my balls shoot off across the room? Okay, better not come, just don't come ... not a good idea right now ... ignore the fact the man you love to pieces is losing all his marbles over you right now. Don't look at how hot he looks right now all tensed and muscly, banging the hell out you. Hang in there little buddies! Stay with me!

His whimpers brought Sadao to half of his senses and somehow between brutal thrusts, he managed to rip the band up and off his cock, sending a euphoric wave of sensation so sweet through Mouse's body, he never wanted to be freed from bondage again.

*Oh God, Jesus, fuck, he's right on me. I'm gonna come so good ... ohh shiiiittt ... I'm gonna come so...*One glance down and Mouse realized he was staring right down the barrel of a loaded gun. His own gun. *Shit, I'm gonna come in my face!!*

"Ggggmmghghh!!"

Load after load of hot sticky release erupted all over his nose, chin, face, hair, possibly the ceiling ... God, he couldn't stop it. Eyes ... now it was in his left eye. Great, half blind now. And still getting nailed up the ass. The rug burn is real ...

"Hah-!" It wasn't so much a sound as an explosion of air as orgasm wracked through the man who'd gotten them into his mess. Sadao convulsed into Mouse two, three more times, heating him up inside, grinding his dick in good, drawing out every ounce of pleasure he could.

"Mmm?" Mouse asked when he'd slowed, giving a final twitch. Sadao's eyes blinked open. He took in the sight of Mouse all wound up in a ball and coated in spooge like he'd just realized the extremes he'd gone to. With quick moves he released Mouse's ankles, wrists and gag, and checked his skin for hurts with worried eyes.

"I'm okay, baby," Mouse smiled, wiping his face with the do-rag. "You've done worse."

Sadao held his head tenderly and buried his tongue in his mouth, tasting blood from where he'd bit himself to stay quiet.

"Thank you," he whispered, kissing him softly. "For knowing me so well, and loving me anyway."

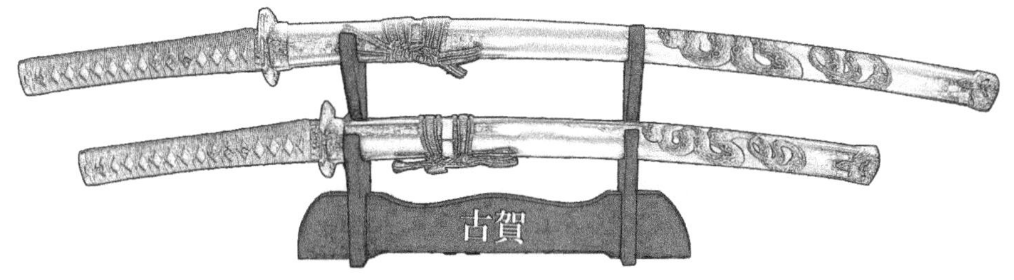

Chapter XXI

Whiteout

"Holy Santa Maria, gringo! Could you two go one fucking night without … *fucking?!*"

Mouse felt his face flush as he drove the Jeep up the winding forest trails to the summit of Garibaldi with Lupe in the cab and his snowbike in the rear. It had needed a last minute adjustment to the front brake. With an uncomfortably narrow ice bridge to cross in a few short hours, Mouse wasn't taking any chances with his best buddy's neck.

Tagata wasn't pleased with his delay and had already gone up with his team leads on the ski lifts at first light to check the trails via snowboard. Mouse was supposed to deliver their last bike and rider to the starting station at the summit and head down as soon as he could to catch up with them.

"You … heard us?"

"I heard *you*, gringo. And don't tell me it was the wind. I know your whimpering when you're getting nailed and that trailer's rocking motion in storms. It don't go up/down and right/left all at the same time, unless there's fucking going on."

Mouse bit his lip. All morning, flashes of the prior evening had been running through his head unchecked: Sadao binding him up like a ball and pinning him to the floor, spreading him open and fucking the stuffing out of him. Sadao had been so turned on, he was in him and out before he could catch his breath. It was the fastest, hottest fuck they'd ever had. Just thinking of it gave him a boner.

"Sorry?" he managed.

"No, what you should be sorry about is sticking me with the ex. Thanks a whole enchilada for that. I woke up to her staring back at me from the sofabed like I was supposed to do something about it!"

Mouse snorted in glee. "Really? We had a full audience? Not the kids, I hope? I didn't hear them."

"'They're lucky they're kids. They sleep through everything. Anyway, I said 'fuck it,' rolled over and put the pillow over my head. You can stop laughing. Between you, your old man and your old man's ex-girl in my crib, *and* the kids - I don't get no pussy until spring now!"

"I'm so sorry…!" Mouse gasped, wiping tears. "But you two out there … staring at each other. That's so funny - I really needed to hear that! Um… And I owe you a pair of wrist guards."

"I don't even wanna know what that shit's about. Can't even respect my stuff? Damn! Your day's coming, man."

"I know! I know! I owe you! Everything - twice!"

"What's your old man's deal anyway, bringing her along? This isn't gonna become some fucked up three-way is it?"

"Hell, no! Madame Ho-bag is out of here soon as the weekend is over. Sadao feels he needs to protect everyone with his own eyes is all. He thinks these masked assholes are after him and her and the whole damn team because of some bullshit that went down during his war days. He's been sleeping with the katana under the mattress for a week now."

"Huh? What kind of bullshit?"

"I dunno. He got all moody on me that night after he was attacked in the long-house. He told me this old story from his war days. He killed some little kid in the jungle, I guess. It's really messed with his head - for a long time now. Somehow, these douchebags know about that. Even though they weren't even born yet when it happened! Sadao was a kid himself! So I don't get it. But that's life with Sadao - you aren't supposed to 'get' half of it. I've stopped trying. I'm in it for the hot dick and cuddles."

"Hah!" Lupe punched his arm. "I think you're in it for a lot more than that!"

"Yeah, think I am…" A huge smile crept across his face.

"What…? Something else I don't wanna know?"

"He told me he loved me last night. That's why all the fucking."

"Just last night? Finally? Like, it took him three years?"

"You know, I always knew but, shit, it's nice to hear it."

"Good for you, man. Glad you're so fucking happy. Me, I'd be happy if some girl said hey, I'll pull your pork for five bucks!"

"It'll happen for you, Lupe. You're a great guy. Give it time."

"Shit - time's all I got, bro!"

As they drove up to the final switchback, they encountered a railed trail blocker - preventing them from getting to the summit. Race runners were stationed here, monitoring the access roads. Mouse pulled up to a guy with a radio.

"I've got an equipment delivery to make!"

The man shook his head. "Cut off for road access was over an hour ago!"

"I know but … we had a last-minute malfunction."

"No four-wheeled vehicles allowed any further up."

"Jesus, I only need to get up another mile…"

"If you cross this line, sir, your team will be disqualified. We don't want any damage done to the peak trails. They were groomed just this morning."

Lupe patted his shoulder. "It's cool, man. I can ride up from here."

Mouse turned to his friend. "You sure? We're not at the trailhead."

"Yeah, I'm cool. I know the way."

"Okay but, take my hand radio with you."

"How am I supposed to race with a radio?"

"For before the gun, dumbass. Toss it in the snow, I don't care. Just - I want to make sure you get where you need to go. Just buzz me, alright?"

"Yeah, alright. Fuck me if Boss get's pissed for dumping gear."

"I'll take the hit on this one."

Lupe winked. "You got it. Now help me get this *puta* out of the back."

"You are late!" Tagata snapped when Mouse caught up with him and his senior crew mid-mountain. They had snowboarded down to a narrow trail on the west side of the mountain, near where their planned racing route was going to pass through in under an hour.

"Sorry, you want racers and bikes at the summit station, don't you? Especially the good ones!"

"We need this Jeep to follow tracks!"

"Tracks? What tracks?"

Tagata motioned him to exit the vehicle. Mouse parked and hopped out, following him. "What is it?" Tagata pointed to two double rows of deep tire marks in the snow - fresh ones made after the storm had cleared about an hour before sunrise.

"This the truck from last night, you think?"

"Yes, so I think."

Mouse looked up mountain where the tracks had descended from. "How far up do they go? Did you see?"

"Storm came last night. Blew snow everywhere," Tagata said. He looked like he'd been up all night, chasing shadows. "Any tracks above treeline have been covered."

"They wouldn't let me up any higher than about 7000 feet. Did the crevasse look okay?"

"Eh?"

"Sorry uh ... the big blue hole...?"

"Big hole is good. Lots of new snow all around glacier peak. Safe to race on. Sasori racers will take the ice bridge."

"Good to hear, so ... what are we doing now, exactly?"

"We ride and follow where this truck go. I want to see what it carried."

Mouse got behind the wheel with Tagata in front and his men piled in the back with their snowboards. Although windy and overcast, there was enough light in the pines to follow the tracks quite a ways along the ever narrowing trail. It got so narrow in fact, there were places where bark and branches had been scraped off the trees to either side.

"I wonder why they didn't take a wider route." Mouse said as they bounced and dipped along in the crunching snow.

"I wonder this too. I think maybe they not want to be seen by race manager."

"Do you think they could have gotten to the top in the dark last night with all the wind - whoa! I see it!"

Mouse stopped the Jeep and all five of them got out, hands on their knives. Those that carried them, anyway. The truck was parked halfway off the trail, nose down in a rocky ditch.

"Looks like they ran into some trouble," Mouse said as Tagata ordered his men cautiously investigate the cab. It was empty. One of Tagata's leads pointed to boot prints marching away downhill. "And abandoned the truck."

Satisfied they were alone, the men untied the ropes holding the rear canvas down over the objects beneath. Mouse stepped forward as they rolled back the heavy material.

Inside was a mish-mash of empty sacks, some propane cans, rolls of wires and something with a long metal tube.

"Mouse, what do you think this is?"

"I dunno. I need a closer look," he said, climbing up into the bed to sort out the parts. His snow boots crunched on a white gritty material spilled from the sacks into the grooves of the bed. Mouse bent a knee to investigate. It was granular. He lifted some to his nose and took a tiny taste. "Oh! It's salt! Duh. You see enough of that around here. Maybe they were doing some extra trail grooming of their own?"

"Why fuel?"

"Well... that is odd. There's a lot of empty cans here. Propane, so not for vehicles but - hang on. This looks like a hose attachment and a valve." He lifted up a tube-shaped contraption with a grip release. "You've got here what might be a pressure washer or huh … whoa, hydrogen? That's an igniter - !"

Tagata banged on the edge of the bed to get Mouse's attention. "What is igniter?"

"I think this is some kind of custom flamethrower. A big ass one. And the salt? Oh shit! Wait-!" Mouse bent to examine a heavy roll of thick insulated cord - yellow and red - on a wide spool with a torn-off label. "Holy shit is this…?" He crawled around the deep end of the truck bed - there was crumpled waterproof packaging lying about. He grabbed a mass of it and straightened it out over his knee to read the label. "Oh, fuck, Boss! It's C-4 industrial grade explosive! And this yellow shit is detonator cord! If they hollowed out a hole in the ice with the flamethrower and then…"

Tagata and Mouse's eyes met. And for once Tagata's English was correct:

"The crevasse!"

"Look, Touchan! I made more fishies! There's a red one and a yellow one and a brown one and a green one and a all-colors one and this one has spots…"

Sadao looked up from the commissary sinks where he was trying to help Kei wash up 12 pairs of colorful finger-painted hands for lunch. The camp was on lockdown for safety reasons, and the strong winds blowing around outside kept himself and the little ones sheltered in the mess hall under a ring of heaters. A quick morning trip into Squamish's Hobby Mart by Kei's assistants rescued them from boredom with arts and crafts diversions. It wasn't long before they were up to their armpits in poster paint and glitter glue.

"That's lovely, hime! You're becoming quite an artist," he said, drying his hands and holding up her butcher paper masterpiece for inspection. Fish again. The girl certainly is consistent.

"Ta-kun says my spotted fishie is lame because fish can't have spots!" she complained, trotting after Sadao as he pinned it along the canvas walls with the others.

"Of course fish can have spots," he said, fastening it into place. "Mouse catches spotted trout from our lake, remember?"

"That's what I told him, but boys never listen!"

Sadao smiled at her frustrated expression. "Well, you don't have to convince me."

"That's because you're a grown-up," she said, reaching up for him with blue fingers. "You don't argue about everything."

"Come here," he grinned, lifting her up for a kiss to her glittery face. "Let's get you cleaned up for lunch, eh?"

Shinjyu wrapped her arms around his neck and pressed her cheek to his as he walked her to the sink. She was warm as a bun. He didn't want to put her down.

"Touchan, will you always carry me places?"

"Of course."

"Even when I'm big like you?"

Sadao sat her on the edge of the counter and turned on the warm water, lathering her hands. "How sure are you you'll get to be as big as me?" he said with a wink.

"Because ... I have to grow up someday!"

A little knife nicked his heart. "Not too fast or too big, hime. I want to be able to carry you for a long long time."

A huge smile lit up her rainbowed face. "I promise, not too big, Touchan! But you'll look silly carrying me on my wedding day! That's embarrassing! I think my husband should carry me instead."

The little knife tore right through his chest and out the otherside. *Why was loving a child so painful?*

"He'll have to fight me for the privilege," Sadao said sincerely, wiping her face clean with a damp cloth. "And I don't plan on losing."

Lunch was served. Sadao helped the chow crew serve up hot tomato soup and grilled cheese sandwiches - one of the few things Sadao had learned how to cook, thanks to Mouse. The kids gobbled it up fast and were getting restless again as they brought their dishes over to the scullery. Sadao had just gathered up the last of the dirty plates, when Shinjyu started screaming.

"My bucket!! My fishie bucket!!"

Sadao nearly dropped the dishware he was carrying. *"Shinjyu, donaranai no!"* He handed his dishes to the scullery boys and hurried to her side. She was standing over their crate of snow toys, sobbing.

"It's gooooooone!! My fishies don't have a hoooooome!!"

"Shinjyu, it's probably at the trailer with your fish. It's fine," he said, patting her head. "We'll find it later." Lately, the little bucket had been doing double duty as a snowball holder and snowman head molder. Sadao knelt down and helped her search the toybox. She snuffled as he shifted through the oddball items: bent pans, some hand shovels and balls ... was that an old license plate? Where did half this stuff come from, anyway?

"M-my bucket is goooone ..." she moaned.

"I'm sure it's back at the trailer," he said, wiping tears from her face. "I'm sure I saw it."

"I want it, Touchan! I want my bucket and my fishies - now!"

"Shinjyu, we will get them later, now it's time for read-"

"It's goooooone!! It's gone and you don't wanna tell meeeeee!!"

Kei came to his rescue. "Shin-chan, we are going to be reading your favorite story! Forest Families! You already know all the words, you can help me read to the younger ones so they'll take their naps. You're my very best reader!"

Shinjyu rubbed her eye. "Only if Touchan takes me to get my bucket from the trailer, first."

Kei and Sadao both eyed the rustling canvas walls for an indication of just how unpleasant that walk was going to be. "Okay, hime. We'll go find your fish." Sadao said, giving in. She stuck out her lip and nodded.

*She's training me so well…*Sadao kissed her head and stood up to get their coats.

"I'll settle her down at the trailer so the kids can get their nap in with less drama," he told Kei, but truthfully, he had wanted an excuse to get back for a peek at the TV to see how the Rally was progressing in the deteriorating weather. He had deliberately left the broadcasts off that morning so Shinjyu wouldn't drive him crazy begging to go see the racing live. He and Mouse had both agreed it was far too cold and risky to let the smallest ones out in this weather. And if one went, they all had to go.

He dressed her up like a confection in down coat, secured hood and mittens and opened the flap door. Outside, the wind smacked him hard in the face with how much the temperature had dropped in the last few hours. He fastened his coat up high on his neck and shoving on his gloves, bent to pick up his stuffed marshmallow who clung to his chest as they headed into the wind.

"Touchan! Hurry! I'm cold!"

The trailer wasn't more than 150 feet away but the windchill and blowing snow made it difficult to open his eyes long enough to aim straight for its black and grey outline in the white blur.

"You're going the wrong way, Touchan!" she shouted over the wind.

He had to course-correct himself more than a few times at Shinjyu's prompt to finally gain the trailer's sidedoor. With chattering teeth, he put Shinjyu on his good hip and inserted his key, but the lock wouldn't turn. He inspected the hole. Ice. Great. He blew on the keyhole to warm it and tried again only to have the door open automatically.

"Oi! Gisette! You startled me!"

"I don't know why," she said, backing up to let them in and shutting the door behind them to seal off the wind. "You're the one who demanded I stay here, after all!"

"Touchan! Why is she here again?" Shinjyu wanted to know as Sadao helped her out of her coat and gloves, brushing the snow from her boots.

"That is a good question," Sadao said, stamping his boots on the entry grate, trying to pump feeling back into his left leg. "I thought you'd still be out watching the races this afternoon."

"I was until the weather turned! The VIP deck was freezing! So I left to call my pilot but my satellite phone battery died and my charger is up the mountain at my cabin you won't let me live in. So I came here to use your hook-up," she explained. Indeed, her pink rhinestone-studded phone was blinking in the empty stand now that Tagata's team leaders borrowed Sadao's unit most of the time.

"Since there was nothing to see outside except white, I thought I might as well head home early. I got through to Vancouver but the tower won't let any Chinooks take off in this wind! I drove my SUV right through the camp, not a single one of Tagata's dreadful guards even noticed. I decided I'd rather stay warm and watch the Downhill broadcast in here."

"Turn it up," Sadao said, nodding to the TV panel over the lounge. "I'll put some tea on. Shinjyu - go look in your bunk."

"Hai, Touchan!"

"It's a difficult call for certain, Bill. Weatherman says the wind will be with us until sundown when the snow will begin descending down to 200 feet tonight. We are expected to get several more inches before dawn."

"The Downhill as we all know is a high risk race even in good weather. Starting gun is set to fire at 2 P.M. They have less than an hour to determine the risk factor on Mt. Garibaldi. Reports say the weather tower is measuring less windspeed at higher altitudes. Let's join Susan at the Summit Station, shall we?"

"Yes, Bill, as you can see the wind up here is fairly mild. These team flags behind me are just flowing gently in the breeze. Above the cloudline it's quite pleasant."

"I wouldn't call 4 degrees pleasant, Susan."

"You'll see I'm wearing my scarf, Bill…"

"Do you suppose they'll postpone it?" Gisette mused from the lounge where she sat.

"They'll fire on time," Sadao said, filling a teapot and setting it on the stove before starting his own hunt for lost buckets. "They just do this debating for audience ratings."

"They'll have trouble at treeline," Gisette said. "The trails will be hard to see in the blowing snow."

"They're hard to see regardless. It's not a proper downhill if necks aren't on the line. Drives up bets."

"Can you be any less bitter?" Gisette asked. "I have money on this race!"

"Doesn't matter to me. I'm not a betting man anymore. Just want our boys back safe."

"Ah, speaking of which, here comes your Mexican."

Sadao looked up from his rummaging. So far he'd found three fish and a pole with a fraying magnet. He set them on the table as the camera zoomed in on Lupe - geared up and ready to ride.

> *"We don't care about wind or snow, man! All we care about is that checkered banner!"*
>
> *"Can you tell us if the Sasoris have any surprise plans for their downhill navigation?"*
>
> *"Hell, yeah, we got plans, big plans! Can't tell you, though. Boss would boil us alive!"*
>
> *"Well there's rumors your team will be taking an unorthodox route from the summit. Some say through the glacier. Any comment you'd like to make on that?"*
>
> *"No way, man, you'd have to be loco to mess with a crevasse in this weather! I may be a racer, but I'm no pendejo!"*

"He's a real clown, your oddball," Gisette said.

"Touchan! I can't find iiiit! It's not up here!"

"Keep looking, hime!" Sadao bent down to peek under the dinette. "I recruited Lupe to paint, not to mug for the cameras. Can you move your leg? Idiot just announced to the whole world they're taking the crevasse route. Taga must be proud!"

Gisette bent in her seat to peer down at him. "What on earth are you crawling about under there for?"

"Bucket," Sadao said, standing up and brushing off his jeans. "Shinjyu's fishie bucket is missing."

"Did you just say, fishie?"

"She likes them," Sadao said as explanation. "And rocks…" A sudden thought entered his head.

Tink tink tonk! "Kuso!"

The kettle whistled. Sadao went to it and took it off the burner, shutting off the heat.

"Touchan it's not up here!" she cried, dropping down from the bunk and running over to hug his leg. "It's lost and my fishies don't have a home. Where can they go if they don't have a home?"

Sadao touched her hair. Her dark sad eyes were seconds away from tearing again. *Fuck, here I go back outside.*

"Tea will have to wait, unless you want to steep it yourself," he said to Gisette, reaching for his coat just as an especially strong gust of wind hit the side of the trailer, rattling it. "Keep an eye on my daughter. I'm going outside for a bit. Don't open the door to anyone you don't know."

"Outside?! Sadao, have you lost your head? Where are you going and on foot?"

Sadao pulled down his riding goggles and fixed them over his eyes. "The beach shore. Not too far. Shinjyu brought her bucket out fishing last night. She filled it with rocks. I haven't seen it since."

Gisette got up. "Well then leave it until the wind dies down at least so you can see."

"Can't, the snow will bury it. It's already starting to fall."

"Touchan - ! You have to save iiit!"

"Sadao, for Chrissakes, it's a bucket!"

"Yes, and I'm a father!" he said as he opened the door and stepped out, leaning into the white wind.

"Coyote One, Coyote One, do you read me?"

" … … "

"Coyote One, this is Little Mouse, can you hear me? Just pick up the fucking radio, Lupe! Shit!"

Mouse dropped the radio and grabbed the wheel of his speeding Jeep with two hands to narrowly avoid pitching Tagata and his team leads over into a ditch. The wind was blowing thick snow across the windshield, making the road hazards very hard to see.

"You drive!" Tagata yelled, reaching to grab the communicator from the floor. "I will use radio - go! Go!"

"I'm trying to!" Mouse hollered back, hitting the gas while the tires spun. "The rear is too heavy. We keep sinking into the damn snow!"

"Stop Jeep!" Tagata demanded.

Mouse hit the break while Tagata shouted orders to Nakagawa and his other three men banging around in the canvas covered rear. They looked relieved to be able to leave the cramped space. They climbed out the back, grabbed their snowboards and following some instruction from Tagata, took off into the woods.

"But … we need them!" Mouse protested as the figures vanished into the white.

"We need speed first. Men, I send to lifts - they will ski to summit station and stop race!"

"Okay - okay! But if you don't get Lupe on that radio in the next 15 minutes it's going to be too late!"

"I worry radio - you worry gas pedal!" Tagata ordered and fired off a series of loud screeches with the receiver before picking up where Mouse left off.

"Coyote One, Coyote One!"

Reaching Lupe by radio proved to be futile and they were too far from the camp towers to make a clear connection there, either. That, or whoever was supposed to be manning base communications had become too distracted by the Downhill race announcements. Mouse glanced at the dash clock. "It's 2 now!" he yelled, gunning the vehicle up the most direct trail to the top he could find. "We're not gonna make it in time! Oh fuck! More route monitors?"

Two men in safety vests on a snowmobile waving flares came riding over the hill to intercept the Jeep. "Go back! Go back! This is a live race course! It's off limits!"

"Fuck this race - the course has been booby trapped! We have evidence!" Mouse held the scrap of C-4 wrap out the window as one of the two men got off the snowmobile to come over and investigate.

"We don't know what this is all about sir, but you'll have to - "

Wham! Tagata had come around from the passenger's side with his snowboard and clocked the guy out cold. Dude was on his belly in the snow. Tagata made a threatening step toward the second guy and he was having none of it. Still on the vehicle, he gunned the engine and sped off. Tagata grabbed the spare radio off the prone guy, extended the much longer antenna and jumped back into the cab.

"Drive! I call emergency!"

Mouse had to admit, Tagata was proving to be quite fluent in English cursing as he hollered at the summit race radio officer who took his call. Mouse could overhear the conversation clearly, the dismissive nature of the asshole handling the call, as well as the cheering and firing of the starting gun in the background. Then the battery died.

"Jeep must go faster! Race is started!"

"I know! I know!" They'd come to the final turn in the mountain trail that ascended past the timberline. Here, above the clouds, the sky and snow cleared. Towering 2500 feet above them was the sister peak of Mt. Garibaldi, its brilliant glacial plain and the blue diamond shaped crack of the crevasse, grinning in the afternoon sunlight. Further in the distance, just above the eyeline of the peak was the white ridge of the traverse and on it were tiny moving dots. The wind carried a distant rumble Mouse knew like his own heartbeat - the engines of the Sasori snowbike fleet.

Mouse floored his accelerator to speed up and intercept. "If they've run that fucking detonator cord, I should be able to see it! Cut it or something!"

"May not be in the snow, I think. Early morning we search here. All snow, no cord. Like you say, they make hole under ice bridge and bury explosive inside. Can not see from above."

"How are they going to trigger it? Remote you think? Radio?"

"They can blow up mountain if they like," Tagata said. "As long as no Sasori racer is on ice bridge!"

"But you gave them the go ahead to take it, right?"

"Yes but, I will stop lead bikes! Drive close!"

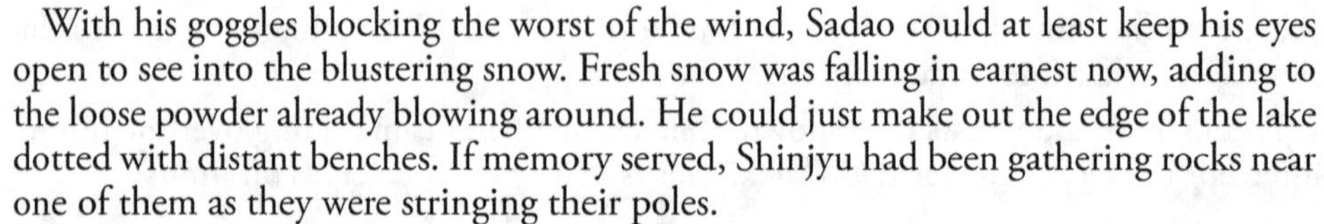

With his goggles blocking the worst of the wind, Sadao could at least keep his eyes open to see into the blustering snow. Fresh snow was falling in earnest now, adding to the loose powder already blowing around. He could just make out the edge of the lake dotted with distant benches. If memory served, Shinjyu had been gathering rocks near one of them as they were stringing their poles.

He made slow progress to the first bench at the edge of the gravel shore. Orienting himself, he stamped his boot around in the fluff in the general area of where she'd been sitting. But after several minutes of stamping down snow, hoping to hit a metal object, he began to question whether or not this was the right bench.

Sadao stood a moment, taking the weight off his numb leg, considering his choices. The park's picnic benches were set at about 60-foot intervals around the inlet's edge. *How far were we from the trailer?* He didn't think it was that far. But with his landmarks now shrouded in white, the whole inlet looked foreign to him. *Shit, better just go to the left.*

By the time he slugged his awkward way to it, he could see this bench had been dumped on its side. Definitely not the right one. He stretched his bad hip. It popped painfully in the socket. He couldn't feel his left foot very well even on a good day, but in the blowing cold it was like he was working with a wooden stump that was quickly icing up. He'd wrapped a scarf around his face but his nose was growing painful with each gust of bitter air. The sun was behind thick clouds, giving light but no heat.

Fuck, what am I doing out here? Must be 10 below in this wind! Big sad eyes lit up his mind. He couldn't bear to disappoint them.

So now what - go one more bench to the left or return to try the other direction? It couldn't be more than two benches out, that he was certain of. *Okay, one more this way, then turn around. Don't need to get lost out here and freeze a ten-minute walk from safety.*

Sadao had to admit it was no fun living someplace where the air hurt to breathe. Even inhaling through the thick scarf was making the back of his throat burn. He got to the next bench only to finally recall there had been a red brick cabin visible on the opposite shore directly across from their fishing spot. Blinking into the weather, he thought he could just make out smoke rising from the far shore, back in the direction he'd just traveled. *Just my luck. It was to the right!*

Kuso! Kuso! Going to lose a fucking nut out here!

By the time Sadao had retraced his steps to the first bench, he had to sit down a moment to cup his face and try to warm his cheeks and nose. The left leg was so cold now he couldn't feel past his knee. *That's not good. Just give it a rest and go get a hot shower before it falls off!* But Shinjyu's trusting face breaking with disappointment sank his heart and he had to give it one more shot. If he could believe the shifting billows of white, it looked like that chimney smoke was getting awfully close.

Going right meant going into the wind, and his steps were slower and more arduous as the snow drifts deepened. The shit leg was a nuisance now, refusing to move when he commanded it to and he took a tumble more than once into the snow.

Finally, he gained the bench and to his relief, he could still make out the outline of the large flat rock Shinjyu had been sitting on. He braced an arm on its surface and dug around in the snow until his good foot made contact with something that didn't sound like granite.

Tunk! *Youkatta. It's still here.*

He pulled the little bucket out of the snow and whacked it against the bench leg to knock out the frozen rocks. Just as he straightened up, he was hit in the face by one hell of a blast of wind. The force of it blew his scarf right off his face. He saw it go flying out over the ocean waves.

Fwap! Fwap! Fwap! Fwap!

The helicopter blew up the inlet from behind him. He'd been so focused on finding the damn bucket and the wind had been blowing so loud in his ears, he'd felt it before he even saw it. A big black transport chopper blocked out the the meager sun a moment before soaring over his head, heading toward the Sasori camp. He wiped his foggy goggles to observe the craft hovering over their mass of trailers and trucks.

Who the fuck is that? No sponsor flies without their colors.

All instincts told him something was very wrong and his heart pounded a warning in his chest to get his frozen legs moving inland as swiftly as he could manage. Between flurries, Sadao could see something being lowered from the belly of the black chopper as it hovered over a location near the peak of the mess tent.

Is that Gisette's pilot? Is she having him hoist her up by cable?! The fuck is going on here? Fuck this useless leg! Move! Move!

Sadao shouted into the snowfall to try and get someone's attention as if the sound of the rotating blades hadn't done so already. Tagata had guards watching over the camp still didn't he? The black mass at the end of the cable had just descended below the rooftops of their camp when he heard a scream, followed by a short burst of bullets.

"Shinjyu!! Gisette!!"

He could see figures in the snow running away from the helicopter and others climbing up the sides of trailers to the roofs, aiming rifles and shotguns at the craft, hovering with the cable still below its belly. He heard the sound of gunfire against metal and another short burst that flashed from the side of the helicopter. *They're shooting at us! Shooting!* He ran directly toward the sound of the bullets, oblivious to the fact he was clutching the little metal bucket in this gloved hand.

"Shinjyu! Run! Run to me!! Shinjyu!!"

He fell, spitting blood and snow out of his mouth. Screaming her name, he got up and ran again into the storm of shifting wind and snow until he saw the chopper rise above the range of the Sasori bullets back up into the sky. The cable was retracting and the lump of weight at the end seemed heavier. Its length grew shorter and shorter as the chopper soared away up above the cliffline. The doors closed at the base of the helicopter and the sound of its retreating blades was replaced by a succession of four massive explosions that sent rippling shockwaves down the cliff face, shattering the blankets of snowfall apart as it loosed 300,000 tons of freshly packed snow down onto the miniature trailers below in a rain of white death.

The impact blast of icy air knocked Sadao off his feet and blew him backwards. He hit hard on his ass in the snow where he lay for a moment's horror - witness to the rolling billow of falling, tumbling snow heading straight for him. He struggled to get up, but a large ice boulder hit him in the chest, knocking him breathless. His ears rang and then there was only white.

"Oh shit! They're coming over the traverse now! See them?! We're not gonna make it in time!"

Tagata already had his eyes on the colorful blurs as the Sasori racers popped over the cusp of the sister peak to speed down to the start of the glacial plain. Overhead, a broadcast helicopter flew over the snowbikes, giving chase. Red and black Sasori colors were seen among rival racers' livery. It appeared they weren't the only team who'd considered the crevasse route. The Marauders' signature purple grey and white camouflage was among the pack. Tagata suddenly opened the passenger's door and put a leg out - balancing himself half in and out of the Jeep.

"What are you doing?!"

"Drive close to edge of the ice bridge - but not too close! Have winch ready this time!" he yelled over the wind whipping outside. "I try to stop them. You watch and save who you can!"

He leaped out of the door and rolled in the snow. He popped up and regained his feet, running off to the west and towards the thin edge of the crevasse where the ice gap was narrowest but not strong enough to support the weight of a snowbike - or Jeep.

Oh fuck, is he gonna jump it on foot? Mouse wondered, but kept gunning the vehicle through the billows of snow until he heard ice begin to scrape and crunch under the Jeep's studded tires. *This is gonna be rough!*

The first racer hit the ice bridge just as Mouse was moving into position 30 feet below its downhill exit. The lead racer in green and blue tore across without incident and flipped Mouse off as he had to dodge the approaching Jeep to avoid an accident.

He was riding Canadian Division colors with two teammates hard behind him. They cleared the narrow span safely, offering similar hand gestures as Mouse exited the Jeep and moved to the front winch to wait for a signal.

Tagata soon came into view at his right on the opposite side of the crack. *Shit! He did jump it! How? Is he fucking deranged?!*

Mouse bent momentarily to unlock the cable lead when he saw the first Sasori leap over the cusp of the hill to attempt the bridge crossing. Mouse climbed up on the hood of the Jeep to try to wave him off. As he did, Tagata managed to cover most of the remaining distance on the opposite side, took an odd stance and pulled something from his braided hair that glinted as it was thrown 30 feet into the helmet of the Sasori racer's bike. The whack on the head distracted the racer and sent him into a debilitating wobble he was unable to recover from. Fearing a cavernous death, the kid ditched, pitching himself into the snow head-first while his snowbike continued on without him, swerved left of the bridge and plunged off the edge into the crevasse with an echoing roar.

A second Sasori was right behind him. Attempting to avoid a collision with his fallen teammate, he swerved, flipping end over end as he caught his lead ski on a rock. The broadcast helicopter began to hover more closely over Tagata. Its pilot began shouting something from the open side window. Mouse tried to get the pilot's attention himself but not before the next wave of racers bounced up over the ridge - two, three, five in quick alignment all came over at once - a mix of Sasori and Marauders running ski to tread. Another projectile flashed from Tagata's braids and hit a rival racer in the thigh, causing him to spin out with a cry of pain as he tried to kick off whatever hit him.

"Lupe!" Mouse screamed as he realized the rider hard on the knifed Marauder's ass was number 33. Lupe, helmeted and focused on the track immediately in front of him, did what any well-trained racer would do and pulled his throttle while simultaneously shifting his weight back to leapfrog over the obstruction - in this case, a bloody leg. He cleared his rival without a scratch, which unfortunately, was not Tagata's plan. When Lupe landed, his front ski was aimed dead on for the bridge's entrance, leading the remaining line of Sasori racers on course as planned.

Mouse dove off the hood of the Jeep and reached in the driver's side to hit the horn.

Hoooooooooonk! Honk! Honk! Honk!

At the same moment a shot was fired from the helicopter, hitting Tagata in the back, knocking him down with a rubber bullet from his co-pilot's shotgun.

Damn these idiots! "We're not saboteurs! You've got the wrong guys!"

Bam! Another rubber bullet took out Mouse's windscreen. But before he could even duck, a much more deafening explosion hit him so hard he was knocked sideways, landing on his back while above, he saw a rain of blackened ice, smoke and snow returning to earth, falling down over him and deep into the now bridgeless crevasse.

Lupe!!

When he regained consciousness, Sadao thought he'd been ill. Sick as he'd been in his early teens, lying motionless in a sanitorium bed, waiting for life or death to come claim him. Everything was dark and he could no longer feel his arms or legs. His chest seemed to be the only muscle that worked and it was straining hard under a crushing weight of blackness.

I'm dying this time. They couldn't save me. I was too old to survive Nagoya Fever.

Can you carry me?

Her sweet voice rang out in his mind and he struggled to open his eyes. They felt encased in concrete. He shifted his head, where he imaged it should be, to try and loosen whatever was shrouding his eyes. He tasted and smelled blood. His own, he surmised. His throat felt like he'd swallowed fire.

Touchan? Where are you?

Yes, where am I, hime? Am I close? I can hear you, princess. Come closer.

A weight slid away from above and there was a wedge of light coming in from up behind him. But he couldn't turn his head to see. *Is this sunlight? Where am I? What was I .. ?*

The ground had been rumbling. He'd tried to run, he was running …

"Shinjyu!!" He found his voice and the dark blanket over his eyes fell away. White, everywhere. Nothing but white. Endless piles and clumps of white. He was just a head sitting in it.

Where is my body? Am I dead? Was I screaming? He sounded like he was screaming.

"Over here!! He's over here!"

A voice rang out over the white. *Maybe they've come to collect my head. So strange I can scream without a body.*

"Whoa, he's in deep! Hey man, can you move?"

There were men, two of them wearing Canadian Division racing gear. They were leaning over him, talking.

"What's your name? Can you breathe? We're gonna get you out, okay?"

"Hey, this one's bleeding from the mouth! Bring a stretcher! And a shovel! He's in pretty deep!"

"I'm…"

"Bring that rope over here too! I think there's something pinning his legs!"

"I'm trying!" More voices were coming. He could hear digging and feel vibrations around him.

"Hey buddy, can you move your arms or legs you think? We're trying to figure out where you are under all this shit."

"Shinjyu…"

"Huh…? Oh shit, think he's foreign? Can you speak English?"

"Yes. My…" The words he was trying to make kept slipping out of reach. Too many confusing flashes of memory were echoing through his head. Glitter paints. The sink filling with water. He was washing … something…

"Yeah, he can understand but I think his head's all fucked!"

Well Bill you can see I'm wearing my scarf!

I ain't no pendejo!

Lupe, that fucking idiot Mexican…gave away the route…

Hey man, you saved my life. I love the shit outta you for that!

My fishies don't have a home!!

"I have to go … she needs me to find it…"

"Don't talk too much if it hurts, okay. We just about got your arm out, dude. Can you remember your name? Do you know what day it is? Who's Prime Minister?"

"Sadao … my name is Sadao. It's … Sunday or … last day of the Rally. I think. It's…"

Race. Snow. Wind. Rocks. Bucket. Shinjyu!

"Shinjyu!" Sadao cried out as they freed his arms and tried to haul him upright. "My daughter! Where's my girl?"

"What's he saying? Something about his daughter … oh fuck!"

"Dude, was she with you? How old?"

"She's my little girl. She's six. I think she's … where is this place?"

"Squamish Bayshore Park! You were camped here we think. Avalanche came down the cliffs covered everything! You're lucky to be alive but your daughter, uh, was she with you?"

"She wasn't with me. I was…looking for something … in the snow…"

Couple of his rescuers looked at each other as they finished digging out his chest. At last he could take a deep breath and ease the confusion in his spinning head. His ears were ringing and his face hurt.

"I was looking for her toy. Her bucket!"

"Looks like you're still holding it."

Sadao looked down at his gloved left hand still gripped around the metal handle. The dented bucket swung in the snowy breeze.

"Are you feeling any pain?"

"I - need to find her…! My girl! Shinjyu!!"

"Easy … easy … we're still getting your legs out. Relax - there's lots of people looking.

Do you know where you last saw her?"

"My trailer. It's big, long black and smokey grey. It was in the middle of the camp by the mess tent…" Sadao blinked around his line of sight as his right leg was freed. Not a pint of canvas or aluminum in sight. "Where's the camp? Where's the mess tent? There's a dozen children in that tent!"

"Okay, okay - we got it. We're looking!"

"I'll radio that in to S&R!"

"Medic! We got this guy out! He's over here!"

A man with a bright yellow vest was hovering over him. "Are you seriously injured anywhere?" he said looking into his eyes.

"He seems a little confused…"

"I am not confused! My name is Sadao Koga, this is British Columbia, Canada and I have to find my daughter!"

"Sadao Koga - hey, I know that name! Aren't you like, dead? I mean, like before now, drowned or executed or something…oh shit, aren't you that guy who kill -"

"Get me up! I don't know what you're talking about! Let me go!" He couldn't feel his legs to get them under him. He could see his boots lying in dug-out pits of snow, but all he could move were his arms.

"Please lie still. We need to check you out, sir and stop your bleeding."

"I don't care about that! I need to find my daughter!" He swung out with his numb arm and the pail came with it, knocking the EMT backwards. Sadao rolled to his belly and crawled out of the pit.

"I'd say let that one go, Mike. Fuck! You okay?"

Sadao stumbled on numb legs away from the shoreline where the wall of ice and snow had come to a tumultuous stop and pitched over into the sea. His face dripped blood, leaving a trail he was too cold to feel. Bucket still gripped in his right hand, he crawled over the jumbled mounds of broken snow, looking for something, anything familiar. The camp of hundreds of trucks and tents had all but been blown off the face of the earth. A bike wheel stuck just out of the snow, a rooftop of a short equipment trailer was just edging out of the frozen, clotted sea. Tears stung his eyes and clouded his vision every time her voice rang in his head, echoing.

Carry me, Touchan!

I will hime. I will … I'll never put you down!

"Shinjyu!!" Blood launched from his cracked lips. "Shinjyu!!"

A cry. Somewhere in the endless white he heard a child!

"Shinjyu!!"

He heard it again. A whimpering just under the dying wind. The sun was already sinking toward the peaks. Other voices of men scrambling over the buried wreckage called out across the inlet valley - straining for answers.

Sadao saw something flutter and then a hand, reaching up from the snow. He dove for it and grasped the small white fingers in his glove. "Shinjyu?!" he screamed. A little boy with a red scrape across his face was looking up at him from under a bent tent scaffold. Sadao ripped back the canvas and peered in. A twisted mess of poles, canvas and torn childrens' paintings tunneled out below him as he pulled the child out by the arm.

The mess! I found the mess tent!

He hung his face down into the wreckage and yelled. "Kei! Kei!"

Shadowy movement and children's cries and whimpers echoed below.

If they're crying, they're alive! Sadao wiped the blood and tears from his face and rose to wave his hands and shout at a cluster of rescuers. Fire trucks had arrived at the perimeter of the flow and orange vested men were heading his way.

"There's children down here! Twelve of them! Over here! This was the kitchen tent! It's caved in!"

The firemen waved back and hurried in his direction.

Sadao held the stunned child to his side and tried to keep him warm as he shouted back down into the hole. "Kei! Kei are you down there? Answer me!!"

There was a groan and a sound of hollow scraping metal. "H-hai Oyaji ... can't move...my ducklings..." his voice was weak but he was speaking.

"Are they all with you, Kei? It's too dark to see! I have Tama-kun!"

"I ... think so ... maybe ... please hurry ... my legs!"

"The men are coming! They're going to get you out! Kei, do you hear me? You and the children are going to be fine! Just hold on! There's lots of help coming!"

"Hai...."

Sadao held the little boy close and kissed his head. "You're all going to be fine. All of you."

A minute later the area was swarming with orange vests and Sadao handed the stunned but relatively sound child off to the first pair of arms that could take him.

"Sir, we should take you in too, you're hurt."

Sadao was deaf to their pleas. Now that he had the shoreline, the cliff face and the mess tent to navigate by, he knew with more than a blind guess where the trailer should be. The snow was harder here, icy-blue and jagged. It was dusted with black powder in places and cracked like glass. Sadao crawled over it, slid down it and fell again and again, shreading his jacket sleeves and gloves. His knees were exposed and bleeding by the time he came to the spot where he knew the vehicle should be and sure enough, Lupe's little barbeque grill had been uprooted and thrown into the snow heap a few feet to his left.

"Shinjyu!! Gisette!!" His voice was raw from screaming. He kept calling to them with each breath as he knelt in the snow and began to dig with the little metal bucket.

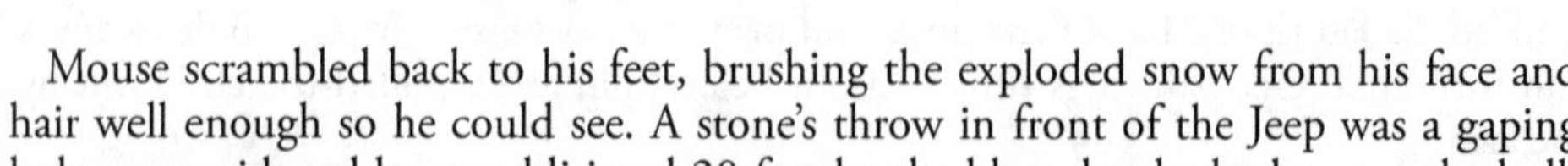

Mouse scrambled back to his feet, brushing the exploded snow from his face and hair well enough so he could see. A stone's throw in front of the Jeep was a gaping hole, now widened by an additional 20 feet by the blast that had taken out the bulk of the natural bridge.

"The bridge is gone!" Mouse shouted at no one in particular. Above him on the other side, a lagging pack of racers had managed to slow or leap from their bikes in time to avoid getting swallowed by the exploding glacier. A riderless bike, treads still running, rolled for the lip, slid over and fell deep down into the abyss, crashing off the sides until its motor died and it fell silent. Mouse spun around to see if any racers had made it across before the collapse, but the total paths of snow tracks leading away remained at two. "Oh, shit!"

Mouse ran for the edge of the gap and lying down on his belly, crawled forward to peer over the edge. Snow still crumbled and fell from the blast area far far down into the blue-black crack. "Lupe!" he screamed, hearing his voice echoing in the deep. "Lupe! Can you hear me? Lupe! Fucking answer me!"

"Gringo…? That you?"

"Lupe!! Where are you?"

"Down, *pendejo!* Look down!"

Mouse tightened his buns and scooted even closer to the hazardous edge on his belly. The ice made crackling sounds every time he inched forward. Once his head was beyond the edge he could look all the way down. Sure as shit, about 70 feet down, Lupe was there, lying on his side on a very narrow ice ledge.

"Are you okay?" Mouse shouted.

"I dunno, man. Can't move too well right now. Dizzy. Can you see my ride?"

"No. I - I think it fell!" It was dark and hard to see into the shadows where Lupe was caught by what most would call blind luck. Only the yellow stripes of his racing suit were clearly visible. "I'm gonna lower the winch! Hang on! Is there anyone else down there with you? Can you see anyone?"

"No ... I don't ... hurry, man! I don't think this shelf is safe!"

"Just - don't move!"

Mouse scooted away from the death gap and ran for the winch, flicking on the motor and letting out the cable as fast as it would roll. He grabbed the carabiner at the end and hooked it to his belt. Then he crawled back into position at the lip. "I have the cable! I'm going to throw the end of it at you! Can you catch it?"

"Hang on, let me try and stand…"

"Slowly, Lupe! Slowly!"

He could hear the ice cracking as his friend moved.

"Okay, I'm up! Go ahead and toss it!"

Mouse unhooked the carabiner and looping up a generous amount of cable, swung it out like a frisbee toward the ice shelf. It soared and disappeared into the dark. There was the echo of snow and ice chunks falling wherever it had landed. Overhead the sounds of a chopper could be heard moving in to hover close - the blades' velocity stirred up the loose snow, blinding Mouse.

"Fuck! Back off! Back off!" Mouse waved at the pilot who was invisible behind the tinted windows of the craft. He had assumed this was the broadcast chopper but that one had flown off. Far off Mouse could now hear sirens blaring. This helicopter was solid black with tinted windows. It hovered another moment like it was studying the situation, then as soon as it had appeared, it flew fast upwards into the air and off downhill toward the camps. *That was fucking weird*, Mouse thought as he rolled to look down into the crevasse again.

"Lupe! You get the cable?"

"Yeah, just, it's a little high to reach! Caught on something. I can't…"

"Lupe, don't climb! See if you can knock it loose with something! Throw a chunk of ice or something!"

"Shit idea, but okay."

Mouse could hear the sounds of ice knocking on ice, echoing in the deep. He took the cable by his shoulder in hand and wriggled it.

"That's it! That's it! I got it! Oh fuck, I got it!"

"Great! Great! Hook it onto your armor straps, man! Can you do that?"

"Yeah I - Oh shit, gringo! There's another dude down here!"

"Another what?"

"There's a racer down here - one of the other team's. Oh shit, man. I think he's dead!"

"Don't worry about him, Lupe! Those assholes blew the bridge! He can die down there for all I care! I'm gonna start the winch now, pull you up slow, okay? Can you climb some?"

"Yeah, sure! Just get me the fuck out!"

Mouse crawled back to the motor mounted to the front of the Jeep and clicked the reversing switch and power. The system hummed but didn't budge.

All equipment must be ready!

"Oh, shit! Oh, shit! I forgot to ice protect this thing! Fuck me! Fuck Lupe!" Mouse ran back to shout down - "Lupe! The winch is stuck. I gotta-"

There was a cry of surprise from below and the sound of ice cracking and falling. Lupe screamed as snow poured into the abyss. "Mouse pull me up! Pull me up! This cabron is trying to knock me off the ledge!"

Go down! It has to be down! Dig! Keep digging!

"Shinjyu! It's your Touchan! Can you hear me?" Sadao cried, shoveling bucketsful of snow behind him. "Hime, please!"

It may have been the wind but as he dug and yelled, he thought he heard a faint echo from below. It kept his bloodied blue hands swinging the bucket down into the snow and ice and flinging it up behind him. About three feet down he struck aluminum. He bent forward and wiped away the ice with his sleeve. He recognized the trailer's coloring - smokey grey - the same color as the day Gisette revealed it to him parked in the gravel lot at Training Headquarters half his life ago.

"Gisette! Shinjyu! Answer me!" he yelled at the siding, banging with his fists as he dug with his fingers to get at a point of entry along the seam. No answer. The trailer was completely engulfed in snow. And from the pattern of the grey paint, on its side.

"Someone help!!" He screamed. "I've found the trailer - come help me! My daughter's in here! Please! Bring a hammer! Bring a shovel! Shinjyu!"

He couldn't stop to wonder if the silhouettes in the white oblivion were moving his way or not so he kept clearing snow from the side of the trailer until he came to a window, cracked from the impact. He threw his shoulder against it - wham! And again until the safety glass gave in and he fell in with it, landing against the stove now lying at the bottom of the toppled vehicle.

He shook the stars from his eyes and yelled into the jumble of sleeping bags, shoes and mugs. "Shinjyu! Hime! Where are you? Please answer Touchan! Yell as loud as you can! Please!"

"Mnn…"

"Ah-! I hear you! Where are you?" he moved toward the cab, crawling through cooking pans, wooden fish and smashed plates. "Shinjyu!!"

"Not here…"

"Huh? What?" Sadao pushed over a loosed kitchen cabinet and under it lay Gisette, her face and chest covered with blood and her legs … somewhere under the heavy sofabed where she'd spent the last night. "Gisette! Where's Shinjyu?! Where is she?!"

Gisette's voice was distorted from the crushed appearance of her chest and the blood oozing from her mouth. "Taken…" she gasped. "I thought … it was my pilot…"

"Taken?! Gisette! Taken by who?" A shard of a memory hit him of fluttering blades. "There was a black helicopter! It had a cable!"

"She tried to tell me, 'the bad men,' she said. 'They're coming for me. Don't let them in!' But I didn't believe her. I thought it was only my…" A fit of coughing took her and blood erupted from her mouth. Sadao scrambled for a towel and swiped what he could from her face - so much of it, red everywhere, soaking into her white rabbit fur.

"I said we need help down here!!" he yelled, unwilling to leave her side. "There's men up there, Gisette, they're coming ... Shinjyu - who are they, who took her, do you know, Gisette?"

Her hand moved and Sadao took it in his own, bloody fingers.

"Kingoe…" she whispered. The name drained him of all hope. "Kingoe…came for her."

"I know this name. It's on her head! They branded her! Why? You know, don't you! You knew all along!" He squeezed her hand tight to bring her eyes back to his. "Answer me, Gisette! She's my daughter! I have to know!"

Gisette's lips moved but her voice was so weak he had to lay his cheek against hers to hear. "I'm sorry, my darling. I thought ... he'd be like you. I thought ... he'd be reasonable."

"Who? Gisette, I need to know who took my daughter! Where are they taking her?!"

"Not to worry my Sadao. She will be fine. She's going back to her family in Japan."

"She doesn't belong to them! She belongs to me!"

Gisette squeezed his hand and her eyes at last found his. "I'm dying, you know."

"Yes ... I think so," he said. "I'm so sorry Gisette, but she's my *musume*. My little girl ... I promised her I'd keep her safe!"

"Not even my last breath can stir your heart anymore…" she said with a weak red smile. "I should have just driven into a lake. Or walked off a ship into the ocean. I nearly did, you know. I wanted to see you again so badly. Just one last time. Even if it was under all that water. Clive stopped me. My poor dear sweet husband. He's all I have left in the -" Choking took her and Sadao leaned her head to the side so the blood could drain out to allow her a few more gasping breaths.

"You have a family now. But Clive is all the family I have. I had to do it to get him back home to me."

"Back? Back from where? Japan? You said he was in Japan!"

Gisette cringed. "They took him months ago. I thought he just had his head in his notebooks - chasing that damned virus all over Honshu."

"Gisette! Who has him? Kingoe? I need to understand! Did he threaten you? Why did he take my daughter?!"

Her fingers left his hand and traced the side of his face. "She looks a lot like you, how funny you never noticed. Kingoe said if I helped him get her back he'd let my Clive go. I do hope he keeps his promises better than you."

"You helped them *take* her? How could you do this? For fuck's sake, Gisette, she's my daughter!"

"But she isn't really ... she has a father."

"Of course, I know that!"

"It's *him*, Sadao. He's alive…" her words trailed and her eyes closed.

Sadao leaned in as close as he could to her mouth to hear. "Who's alive? I need a name! A real name!"

" … your little niece…her name is Hana … I've been told it means flower … "

Mouse could just make out the top of Lupe's head. He was standing chest flat to the ice on the narrow shelf with the slackened cable beside him. At his feet was another racer, helmeted and clawing at his legs.

"Pull me up, *pendejo!*"

"Lupe! Kick him off! I gotta fix the winch! It's stuck - oh fuck!!"

With a short scream, Lupe's leg slipped; there was a shadowy scramble and then the sound of his desperate voice between breaths. "Get me out of here, gringo!!!!"

Mouse ran back to the Jeep and pulled open the glovebox, tearing through it for a lighter, screwdriver, something…

"Shit shit shit!!! Fuck!! Nothing, why isn't there anything? Keys!" Mouse dove into his back pocket and pulled out the keys. One crank and the engine started. There was no way to speak to Lupe now, so he honked three times to prepare him and pulled the Jeep into 4-wheel drive reverse, slow.

Hang on, man. Hang on! He slowly pulled up the slack in the cable until he felt it catch. "Got him! I got you! Okay, but now I gotta pull you ... fuck, buddy, please be able to climb, please…" He gave the engine the tiniest bit of gas and it reversed smoothly. He rolled the window down, listening for something, any kind of sound. In his mind, he tried not to imagine Lupe's body being dragged bloody and broken up the sharp exploded walls of the crevasse. *Please be climbing, please be climbing….* Suddenly, the tension on the line doubled and Mouse hit the brakes, moved into low and inched forward. Then he reversed again and slowly attempted to back up. Same thing. Heavy and sluggish. *Something's wrong! Fuck!*

Mouse threw the brake and ran back to the edge of the crevasse. Looking in he could see Lupe dangling at the end of the line, thrashing his arms, trying to grasp at something. "Lupe!" Mouse screamed. "Are you okay?"

Lupe's head looked up. "Don't stop, gringo! He's got me! He's got my pant loop! I can't get him off! Fucking pull!"

Mouse sprinted back to the Jeep and got back in the driver's seat. Hands shaking, he eased the vehicle again into reverse. The sirens in the distance were getting closer. *Why aren't they here yet? Why?* He backed slow and steady until he heard a deep cracking sound and saw the lip of the crevasse break open and give way under the strain of the cable. A heavy chunk of ice sheared off the edge, dropping down into the chasm. *No! Nononono!!*

Once again, Mouse approached the newly reformed edge. He got down on his knees, one hand on the cable and the other guiding him forward to the jagged lip. "Lupe!"

Peering over, he could see Lupe wasn't all that far down now - maybe seven feet and finally in the sunlight. He dangled limply, with his head lolling to the side and his forehead dripping blood. "Lupe!" Below him was another racer with his gloved hand wrapped tight in Lupe's pant loop and his other hand around his leg. His purple and grey camo helmet was gone now as he raised his face to look up at Mouse standing at the edge. The sunlight caught his features and all at once, Mouse realized who this was.

"Kinjo? Kinjo!" The face was a little older and visibly scarred by Sadao's near-death beating two years ago. He'd been flown to a hospital where Mouse had assumed he'd died. Across his throat was a strip of something metal, like a collar but with a device in the center. It blinked when he spoke.

"*Konnichiwa*, Mouse-san," he said. He lips did not move. The device did all the speaking. Sadao must have crushed his throat to bits.

"Let go! I can't pull you both up at once - the edge is giving away!"

"No. I'll fall."

"Then you'll have to hang there until help comes! I can't pull you both up! The edge will break apart and kill you both! And probably pull the Jeep down in too! I'll pull forward and you can wait on the shelf-"

"I'll cut him loose," Kinjo's speaker said as he began to pull himself up by Lupe's armor straps, climbing up his limp body so he could reach the carabiner.

"Kinjo ... you fucking piece of shit!" Mouse screamed as the ice cracked under his feet. "What the fuck is your problem?! You're going to kill all three of us!"

The little collar blinked. "You are my problem. You and Koga-san have always been my problem. Before him we were Shiratori Team. Best racers in all the divisions," he said, loosening his tangled grip on Lupe's pant loop and rewinding his leather glove into the straps of his armor. "Shiratori-san was perfect leader! Perfect Boss! We come back now and ride for his memory, his glory!"

"That's why you raided the longhouse and took his shit? You think you're his successor?! You're not half the leader he was! You're pathetic! Using sabotage to win?! Even Shiratori knew there was no glory in cheating!"

"I may not be as great as he who chose death to save us. But I have been avenged. Koga-san is no more. His body lies silent now under meters of snow!" Lupe's armor straps shifted under Kinjo's weight as he slowly hauled himself higher up his body one inch at a time.

"Your English sucks, you shit! Sadao died at sea! It's meters of *water!*"

Kinjo laughed but to Mouse's ears it sounded like a child's toy running low on battery power. "I know water from snow! Water you swim. Snow you die. His French woman, she tell us where and when to find him. We watch and wait. Kingoe tells us when to strike! Kingoe gets his revenge and I get mine!"

Mouse's heart sank at the mention of that name. "Kingoe? Is that the asshole who's giving you money? Who is he? What the fuck does he have to do with us?"

"Koga-san knows. Koga-san always knows. But it is too late. Very bad idea to make a camp under the cliffs. Cliffs full of snow, many meters high! Not so high now."

"Fuck! What did you motherfuckers do? There's children in that camp! *Our* child is in that camp!"

Kinjo's gloved hand grasped the carabiner. "She was never yours. She is Kin-zzzzdt!"

Something fast wizzed by Mouse's head and planted itself deep into the voicebox at Kinjo's throat. Sparks flew from his device as it burst into flame. Kinjo screamed in a horrible pitch as he let go of the fastener to bat the fire sizzling his throat. His legs flailed, and with a sound of ripping fabric, he fell, the severed strap still in his hand, down into the gut of the crevasse. The flame lit the way as he tumbled end over end until even the light became extinguished by the impenetrable darkness.

"Now we are free of this *baka*." Mouse startled at Tagata's voice. He stood at the lip, his braids all askew from the lack of sharp little hidden knives holding it together. Blood oozed from his mouth and there was a large angry bruise on his chest from the rubber bullet where it had torn through his jacket. He pulled his lighter from his front pocket and held it out to a gobsmacked Mouse. "Fix fucking winch. I pull Lupe up!"

Sadao sat in the wreckage of his former home, numbly allowing a rescue worker to wrap his torn hands and knees as the medics worked over Gisette's frail body. In each second that passed, he could hear the beep of her heart slowing - between each squeeze of the airbag, until there was no longer a pause, just the wail of the monitor, screaming in defeat. He closed his eyes as they pressed on her crushed chest and forced air into her blood-filled mouth, praying for them to stop - praying they'd let her be at rest.

"I'm going to have to call it," the medic said, glancing at his watch. "14:56. Cause of death, blunt force trauma to the chest and … I can't even see her legs. Can we try getting the body out?"

"We can't move her. She's pinned under the sofa and the chunk of ceiling that came down with it."

"Jesus…let's get the other one out at least. We have the ladders yet?"

"Yeah, they're lowering it."

The young EMT wiping the bruises and cuts on Sadao's face with antiseptic nodded and tried to help him up. "Do you think you can climb a ladder, sir?"

"No," Sadao said as he watched the rescue team hurriedly stow their bloody tools in a case to carry off to the next victim. "Leave me."

"Sir, we can't leave you in here. This ... structure is not sound. We need to get you somewhere safe."

"Nowhere is safe…" Sadao said, refusing to take the young man's arm. When he insisted, Sadao threw off his hand. "I said go! I'm not leaving her here alone! There are others that need you! The children! Go help them!"

The one in charge stepped forward and touched Sadao's shoulder. He seemed to understand. "Try not to move very much in here. We will send men in with equipment to get her freed soon."

Sadao nodded as they filed out and up the rungs of an aluminum ladder. In another moment the ladder went away too, leaving him in the dim wreckage. All he could see was her pale hand, palm up in the beam of light falling through the broken window. Her ring, the one Clive had given her on their wedding day, was still on her finger. Sadao could remember how the diamond flashed under the stage lights when she sang.

"Your beautiful voice," he said, taking the cold hand in his, trying to warm it. "I'm so sorry, Gisette. We always used to outrun our enemies. I don't know how it all came to this."

Sadao sat, head down, holding her hand, still as stone. Above, the shouts and cries for help continued until the inside of the trailer became a cavern of twisted shadows.

Für Elise began to play somewhere nearby, tinny and muffled.

I'm dreaming, he thought. *This is just another nightmare. I should wake up and end it.*

There was a pause in the music and he closed his eyes, grateful for the silence until it started again - the same repeated bars over and over.

I'm losing my mind.

Sadao dropped the dead hand and crawled his way through the kitchen spillage and over a dam of cushions and children's clothes toward the sound. There was a light - back at the rear of the tipped trailer - flashing pink; Gisette's satellite phone. Sadao got to his feet and stepped over the remains of the bedframe. He reached for the phone, catching it just as it began to ring for the fourth time. He pressed "Talk."

"Hello?" he rasped. He could hear a sound like wind on the other end and a faint echo of his own voice. "Is someone there?"

The voice that answered sounded metallic, but with the inflections of human speech. *"Guess,"* it said in Japanese.

Sadao's slid down between the mattress and the dresser. The cracked vanity mirror lay on its side against the buckled wall that was once the ceiling. His ghostly face was reflected in the broken pieces. *"I don't know."*

"Guess…"

"I don't want to play games. If you are a friend of Gisette Hawthorn's - identify yourself!"

"Not a friend," the voice said. The tone wavered word to word - oscillating between a male and female pitch. *"An admirer. A secret one. I've watched her and you both for a*

while now. In news pictures and reels."

"This is no time for jokes. Gisette is dead."

"I know."

Sadao's heart thundered in his chest as he fought to keep his voice steady.

"Who are you?"

"Someone who has been searching for you for a very long time."

Sadao struggled with both hands to hold the phone against his pounding head. *"Kingoe…"*

There was a pause as the name took a few moments to bounce from satellite to satellite to the other end of the world.

"That is not how brothers should address one another, Onisan!"

"Ototosan," Sadao said slowly. *"Why her?"*

"She was precious to you?"

"Yes."

"Good."

Konezumi! Where is he? Is he safe? Don't say his name. Don't even think his name!

"I want my daughter back, kusoyaro! Where is she?"

"She's not yours, Onisan."

"Like hell she isn't! You abandoned her! You left her alone on the docks and we took her in and gave her a home she loved! Why did you send her here only to take her away again? What kind of a monster are you?"

"One just like you, Onisan. Blood of your blood."

"I know why you named her Hana - after my mother. And I know why you want to destroy me. I remember everything! How it must have seemed to you. I remember the slums! I remember the boy you were! I am sorry your mother died and left you alone. No one could have prevented that!"

"No one, Onisan?"

"Blame our father if you want to blame someone! Or blame me as you should! Blame my pride and ignorance! Bring Hana back to us and I will give you no resistance! Take me! Kill me if you want, if that will bring you satisfaction."

"I do not desire your death."

"What then? You've always envied my life - my home, my shoes, my name. If you want something - come take it! Leave these people in peace!"

"I have the one thing of yours I wanted. I wear it even now. Just like yours, Onisan, only smaller."

From where he sat Sadao could see the Katana - the end of the sheath was protruding from the mattress. He reached for it and pulled it into his lap. *"Our father's wakizashi,"* Sadao confirmed, remembering the matching hilt sticking out sickly from his young brother's throat. *"That night on the mountain has colored my nightmares for years! I thought I had murdered my own brother! A child! Is that what you want to hear? My life-long agony? My regret?"*

"No."

"Let Dr. Hawthorne go. Let him come home and bury his wife! Leave them in peace! Leave the Sasoris in peace! They have nothing to do with us! Bring Hana back to her brothers and sisters where she's happy - and you can take me in her place!"

"No."

"I'm injured! I'm defenseless! You know exactly where I am! If I am the one you want to punish, come take me!" Bloody spit flew from his mouth and ran down the mirror over his reflection. *"I give you my full surrender!"*

"No, Onisan. I do not want a surrender."

"What, then? Name it and I will give it to you!"

"I want a war."

The line died and was replaced with a solemn tone.

"Kusoyaro!!" Sadao threw the phone into the mirror, destroying it along with his reflection.

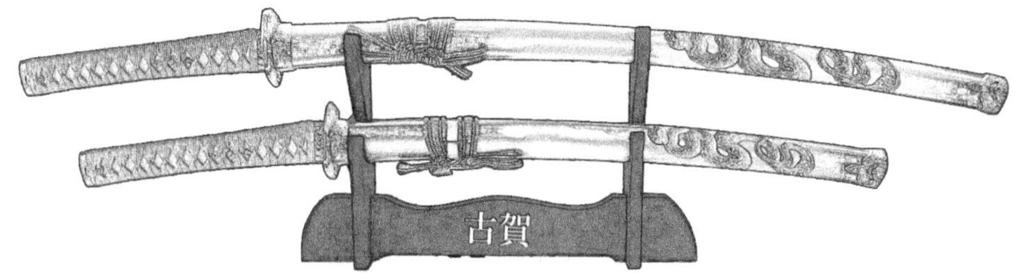

Chapter XXII

Nothing Else Matters

Sadao stood in the medical tent shower, letting the meager trickle of warm water run over his shoulder and down his bad leg to the foot where it hit in a splatter he couldn't feel. Minutes ticked by like hours now, slow and sluggish. His head and chest ached. Reality swam in and out of understanding. Gisette was dead. Her bloodied face still flashed in his mind along with the sound of her sick slow gurgles, struggling to breathe.

I never should have brought you into our camp … I should have seen this coming. I should have protected you.

Firemen had come back with jacks to set her free. They covered her disfigured limbs with sheets and carried her away. Strange to think she'd never appear unannounced at his door again. Bodies of the Sasori men who had stayed behind to guard the seaside camp were coming out of holes and crumpled aluminum in similar sheets. Very few had escaped death. The only structures and vehicles still standing had been those parked at the periphery closer to the Ski Lodge - the medical tent and the garage. Black streaks and exploded ice told the story - this was no act of nature. Investigative teams were already ribboning off the area and collecting samples. C-4, they suspected.

But the children were safe. Kei was safe … bruised, but ambulatory. The Squamish Ski Lodge took the children in and were keeping them warm by the fire with coco and away from all the death. Tagata had radioed down from the summit, hitting all frequencies for a response until Sensei picked up. There'd been an accident followed by an ambush, he'd said. Kinjo of all people was involved. They'd lost men from three different teams in the crevasse. But Lupe and Mouse were alive and heading down mountain in the jeep, carrying as many injured team members as they could manage. Some would go to the city clinic. Others would be airlifted out. It would be some time before they arrived.

Youkatta, youkatta…I should not feel so glad that he mistook you for my most beloved, Gisette. It was an easy mistake. Shinjyu … how will I explain to Mouse about Shinjyu? Our baby girl …

A wrap came at the thin shower door. *"Oyaji, daijyoubu desu ka?"*

"Daijyoubu…" he murmured. *"Let me dry off."* The medical shower was needed for others desiring to wash the caked blood and mud from their bruised bodies. The leg still felt numb past the knee, failing to come to life as it usually did in the presence of warm water. He shut the water off and stepped out into the small changing space under a single light. He toweled dry and lifted the bad leg to the bench for a closer look. The color of his left calf was not good and the foot, ghastly. Sickly greenish purple was the prevailing tone, growing darker from mid-foot to toes. He leaned over and pinched the skin. Nothing. His toes were already going cold.

This can't be good. But it also can't be helped.

Some work pants and shirts had been brought over from the garage lockers. He dressed quickly in a clean set, pulling a pair of long socks over his feet, hiding the difference in color. He stepped out, wrapped a spare blanket around himself, and collapsed on an open futon, wanting the blackness in his mind to swallow his consciousness for at least a short while. Around him he could hear the bustle and moans of the injured and Sensei and Michi's concerned efforts to ease their hurts.

Please save them. I can't save anyone anymore.

Sadao's head ached from what they told him was a concussion. His memory from the past few hours was still coming back to him in pieces - Gisette watching the race, him ducking under the table looking for wooden fish - his girl, his sweet dark-eyed princess, begging him to rescue her little bucket.

I'm sorry, hime … I guess I'm not much of a father, after all. Be safe. Be calm. I'll find you. If it takes the rest of my miserable life, I'll find you and bring you home. I promise.

Exhaustion took him under a short span of minutes until he woke to the sound of the approaching Jeep's engine. *Mouse!*

Sadao slipped into a pair of spare boots and keeping the blanket around himself, stepped outside. Snow was falling in light clumps, scattering the beams of the emergency lights. The night was aglow with it - flashes of red, orange and white - giving a false sense of security. The headlights of the Jeep approached and Mouse honked, squeaking the brakes. He got out and went around to the passenger's side to help Lupe out. The poor kid looked pretty beat up, scraped and bloody, but alive. Mouse led him gently to the medical tent and into Sensei's care before he ran straight for Sadao.

"Oh, God, baby! Are you okay?" he asked, surrounding Sadao and the blanket in a strong reassuring embrace. Sadao rested his pounding head on Mouse's shoulder.

"I fucked up," he gasped. "I really fucked up."

"Shh…" Mouse whispered, tugging him into the garage tent and out of the snowfall. He brushed Sadao's hair from his eyes, checking him over. "What are you talking about? Where's Shinjyu? Is she okay?"

"I don't know -" Sadao's head was so numbed with shock he couldn't speak clearly. "They took her."

"The medics took her?! Sadao, is our baby okay? Where'd they take her - oh God, is she hurt?!"

"No. The 'bad men,' the ones she was afraid of, they took her. Just before the avalanche. There was a helicopter. I - I left her with Gisette in the trailer and ..."

"Gisette? Why was she with our baby, Sadao? Why would you leave her with that woman?"

"She's dead..." Sadao's frozen leg gave out and his knees buckled. Mouse caught him on the way to the ground.

"Baby, oh God! You're hurt! Shh! It's okay; don't talk. Let's get you back into medical, come on...!"

"No..." Sadao pleaded. "I'll be fine ... just, let me sit and hold you a moment. Please."

Mouse's eyes were a storm of fear and worry but he was quiet for now, easing Sadao into his embrace. He stroked Sadao's hair as he calmed and warmed him against his strong chest, bringing a flicker of sanity back to his consciousness.

"I think I told you once, I had a younger brother..."

The snow stopped around midnight. Those who had lived were sitting or lying in the medical tent, staying warm, sipping various medicinal teas and trying to make sense of it all. Those who had died were being carried, sealed in plastic bags to the garage tent and lined up along the far wall side by side. Twenty-seven in all - mostly camp staff and teens in training. Nine racers were lost - six had been in camp, the others were assumed lost in the crevasse. There were a lot of questions. Most of them wondering where Tagata and his leads had taken off to. They hadn't radioed the medical tent in several hours.

Sadao was lying near a heater among the living at Mouse's insistence. Every time his eyes closed he'd hear Shinjyu screaming and he'd snap awake, heart racing. Eventually, the sound of a cruiser broke through the din of idling rescue vehicle engines. Curious, he got up to investigate. Tagata had just rolled in with Nakagawa behind him on Shiratori's Whitebird cruiser. Still intact, the machine's polished chrome shown brilliantly under the tent lights.

"Where on earth...?" Sadao began to ask as he stepped out.

"Sadao-sama, how is your health?" Tagata asked, dismounting and coming to him.

"Head's bruised and bumped. Nothing to be concerned about. Where did you find the bike?"

"Marauders' camp. I gathered my men still on the mountain and we organized a counter attack against our enemies. But when we reached their camp, the team was dead. Shot, everyone. High-powered, from above. Witnesses say a black helicopter came and killed them. The snow was red with their blood. Our deserted men were among them. I guess this too was the hand of Kingoe?"

Sadao nodded solemnly. *"I think so. I saw that helicopter as well. It fired on some of our camp guards as it stole my daughter."*

"I am sorry Sadao-sama has suffered so many losses today. The woman, your friend, I was told has passed too."

"Yes. Her estate has already come and claimed her body."

"It is very unfortunate. Miyagi, too, was found dead in my trailer with a bullet in his head that came through the roof."

"They did not want any witnesses. I doubt any of them planned to die this way. Kingoe promised them glory and revenge for our General."

"Yes, a revenge he would not have welcomed. We will pray for them all and mourn. But now, let us get out of the cold."

Tagata wheeled the bike into the garage tent with Sadao. Once inside, his eyes traced the line of bodybags. Mouse was out in the snow, helping the rescue crews bring in more bodies so they could be stowed until morning and transported back up the mountain to the Sasori property for proper rituals and cremation. Of all things, Sadao was thankful to get the cruiser back. The whole team was going to need the comfort of their shrine. *"So many … how will we burn them all?"*

"It will take time for the team to recover," Sadao said but he felt far from convinced by his own words. *"It is fortunate most of the racing members survived. You can rebuild. The Division takes care of those who have been sabotaged."*

"What will you do now?" Tagata asked, with genuine concern in his tone. Sadao was relieved beyond words to know, despite all his mistakes and misguidance, they were somehow still friends.

"You know what I have to do."

Tagata nodded, thoughtfully. *"Japan. My parents told stories of how they fled. How so many of our family did not survive the collapse. I fear what you will find returning to our homeland. I wish there was another way."*

"So do I. But it is time I returned to face what I left behind so many years ago. I have many debts to settle. And many fires to put out. I will not dream of returning until all of my past, all of my enemies are purged."

"I understand, but please know this," Tagata said, laying a hand on Sadao's shoulder. *"Sasori land will always be Sadao-sama's home. You and Mouse are always welcome here. Your enemies are our enemies. Do not doubt it. My only true regret now is how I will ever find another mechanic like him, or another friend as wise and loyal as you have been to me."*

Sadao struggled to speak. *"I … hope I can remain worthy of your regard. You have surpassed your predecessor in all possible ways. Live well and may your men bring you the glory you inspire in them, my friend."* He bowed low, lower than he ever had before to this young fierce man.

"Sadao-sama, we are in Canada," Tagata said in English, touching Sadao's shoulder. "And I am a Canadian. Here, we say goodbye, Canadian way."

Sadao rose and accepted Tagata's firm embrace.

"Sayonara, Oyaji," he said in his ear. *"Ki wo tsukete kudasai."*

Sadao worked the cabin's groaning sink pump firmly and waited for the water to come up and splash into the kettle. Once filled, he walked it over to the lit stove in the front room and set it on the top. Next, he prepared two mugs of loose leaf tea, scoop for scoop. He stirred the dry leaves - the spoon clinked against the inside of the ceramic mugs.

"Sadao! What're you doing?!" Mouse shouted from the bedroom where he was ransacking the dressers and cabinets aimlessly. After a cold night spent huddled in the medical tent, the dawn had come too soon and with it the long sad ride back up to the lake. Sadao and Mouse helped Kei and the children get settled back into the school room and trailer with cheery faces and many many hugs and reassurances that Shinjyu was okay - she was just away visiting relatives for a while. Which wasn't exactly a lie. And if it was, it was a lie Sadao had to keep telling himself if he wanted to keep from losing his mind.

"I'm making tea."

"What?! Are you crazy?! We have to pack!" There was more crashing about as Mouse knocked over a chair. "Shit!"

"Mouse. There's no point."

"Huh?" Mouse leaned out the bedroom door again. "Whatta you mean? We gotta get going, don't we? We need to go!"

Sadao took a slow breath and kept his mind calm. *I am the river…*

"Sadao…?" Mouse's voice became unstable as he glanced at Shinjyu's little bed by the stove. "We have to go, don't we? We have to … she's our baby!"

"Put the clothes down and come here, *Konezumi.*"

Mouse's eyes clenched shut. He'd kept up a brave face last night, but now that the children were safe and Sadao was seemingly okay, emotion caught up with him and he began to shake. Sadao went to him and put his arms around his love, holding him close, breathing soft reassurances in his ear. Mouse clung to his shoulders and let out a series of angry sobs. "Those assholes! Our baby … our sweet baby girl!"

"Shh *Konezumi*. I know ... my heart is broken, too."

When he calmed some, Sadao led Mouse gently to the table and sat him down. He fetched the mugs and poured the boiling water over them, stirring the leaves into mini hurricanes, staining the water light green.

He took the chair opposite Mouse and lay his hands down palms up for Mouse to grasp. Mouse's face was wet with tears and his breath uneven. He looked defeated, crushed inside and out - a feeling Sadao shared with him even if he didn't show it as well.

"I need you to listen, *Konezumi*. She is already very far away. Being hasty only puts us both in further danger and lessens our chances of finding her. Please drink some tea."

Mouse picked up his warm mug in both hands and took a couple of gulps. "But ... we are going to go find her, right? I mean, that's the plan, isn't it?"

"Of course," Sadao said, taking a sip.

"Then ... .we need to get out of here! We need to follow those fuckers back to Japan!"

"Japan is a bigger country than you think. We need some kind of a plan."

"How do we even get there, babe? There's an ocean! The biggest ocean! We can't fly there, can we? You need documents or something! And you don't exist! Shit, even I don't have documents. We'll never get through an airport!"

"Ship is the only way," Sadao confirmed. "And the slowest, unfortunately. It will take weeks to reach Tokyo and very few foreign ships are welcome in Chiba's port."

"Are we going to be able to do this?!"

Sadao squeezed Mouse's hands. "Have some more tea - you need to rehydrate and warm up." Mouse nodded and drank most of the rest of his mug. He was thirsty from their ordeal. Sadao wished he had time to feed him properly, too. But it was doubtful he'd really eat.

"There's a way to accomplish anything," Sadao said. "We just need to stay strong. And, I need you to trust me. Completely."

Mouse looked into his eyes and nodded. "Of course I trust you! I'm just ... scared. Whenever you talk about Japan it sounds horrible."

"It is a broken, war-torn nation - ruled by warlords and murderous clans. No one is safe there."

"How are we gonna find her?"

"The clan tattoo on her head is our biggest clue. That and the regional dialect Kingoe and his men spoke. If they are not still in the Kyoto-Osaka area, they at least originated from there. Locals will know something. But these are two large cities. It will take time to track him down."

"Are you gonna kill him?"

"Yes."

"But … we can't take an army with us! How are we going to get through his defenses?! We're gonna need help, Sadao!"

Sadao picked up his mug and sipped it. "He wants a showdown with me. He said as much during our call before he cut it off. He won't kill me until we are face to face."

"Face to face and surrounded by hundreds of his men! I don't like this plan at all! Fuck it! We just - go! We run and we go back into the U.S. - to the Arizona desert! Someplace where there's no one. We can live in the wastes. I know how to survive there! I can keep you safe! We can be happy! Please … we have to…"

Mouse pushed the chair back and made to stand but his legs collapsed under him and he fell to the floor. Sadao knocked his tea over jumping up to get to him.

"W-what's going on … spinning …"

"You're alright," Sadao said, kissing his brow and lifting him up into his arms. He carried Mouse back into the messy bedroom and lay him gently on the bed, sitting beside him. "You're going to be fine."

Mouse blinked and reached for Sadao's face. "S-Something's wrong … I can't …" he blinked his eyes to try and clear his head.

"The dizziness will pass soon," Sadao said. "Just close your eyes and relax."

"What? What's happening to me?"

"Sensei's special tea. I gave you some."

"Why?"

"You can't come with me."

Mouse's eyes widened. "What…? No…!!" The pain in his voice was hard to hear.

"You'll be safe here with the team. He doesn't know about you, yet. But he will if I stay. And I have to find our daughter. I promised Shinjyu."

"I'm coming with you…" Mouse insisted, although his voice was getting weak.

"You can't. Japan is no place for an American. Your blue eyes and light skin will give you away. Even in disguise, you can't speak the language. Word would travel. You'd become a target. They'd hunt you and capture you for ransom or worse. And if the war clans don't take you, exposure or disease will. You don't know my country like I do. You don't know what it takes to survive. I can't risk it. I can't find our daughter if I'm constantly in fear for you. Not in a hundred years would I ever want to put you in that kind of danger. Here, you'll be safe."

"Fuck…!" Mouse fought to keep his senses together but his focus was failing. "But you can't go now - you drank the tea too! How can you?"

"I've grown immune. Built up a tolerance, I'm afraid. See why I didn't want to go on pills? I didn't take in half as much as you."

"Please don't go…"

Sadao kissed his cheek softly. "I have to. You know I have no choice."

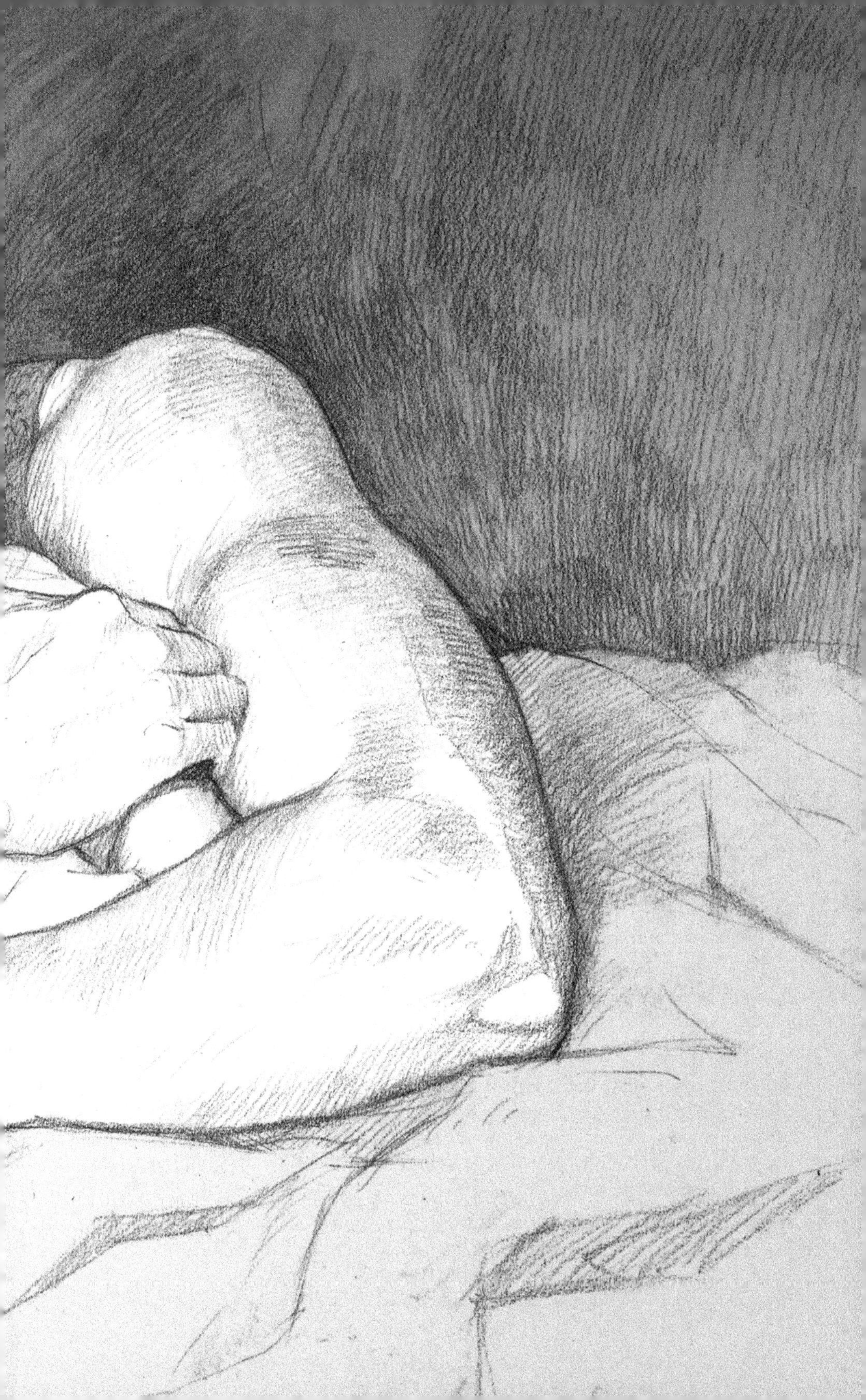

"But Japan … is so far away. What'll I do if you don't come back?"

"I'll come back."

"But …" Tears choked him. "If you don't, I'll never know what happened to you!"

"I'll come back to you."

"When?"

"Be patient. Be strong for me."

"I can't take it. You being gone again … I can't … "

"You are the strongest man I've ever met. You can take far more than you know."

"Baby, please … at least when you were in jail I knew where you were! I can't do this! Don't ask me to … " his voice was growing weaker as his eyes slid shut. Sensei's tea worked fast the first time around.

"Shh … You will fall asleep for a while. Once I'm away, I will radio Lupe to come look after you. I hid a key for him outside."

"Everyone always leaves me…" Mouse murmured as Sadao lay down beside him, covering them both in a blanket.

"I won't. Not for forever." Sadao spooned Mouse up close, surrounding him in his arms. "I promise you. You will always be first in my heart. No distance can change that."

Mouse tried to move his lips but no sound came out. Sadao kissed him and stroked his face softly. "I've made so many mistakes in my life. I have so many regrets," Sadao whispered into his hair.

"You're the only thing I've ever done right. I don't believe in your God, but I've come to believe in sin - the way it can weigh a man down and drag him out of heaven. This cabin was no place for a sinner like me. You, the girl, Gisette, the team - all punished for my crimes. If I can find a way to atone, I will come back to you. And I will stay with you for the rest of my life and the life after this life until my soul burns away."

Mouse didn't answer except to lightly squeeze his hand before he lost his grip and his body went limp in his arms.

Sadao held Mouse as he slept for a long time. Too long. He had to go but his arms wouldn't loosen their hold. His legs wouldn't shift him from the bed. Nothing else mattered but the feel of Mouse's warm chest rising and falling beside him. The winter sunlight was already beginning to fade into afternoon. Time was passing and he needed to get to the inlet before dark in order to spot a boat that could carry him out to sea and across the ocean.

His kisses fell softly on Mouse's cheek. One more. Just one more. Tears rose with how hard it was to stop pressing his lips to his fair skin, breathing in the scent of his tangled hair one more time, to burn him into his memory.

Your sweetness, my Konezumi, I would never want to be apart from it, but for her. I'm gutted with fear for her. Our child, Konezumi ... I can't be afraid for you both. I'm not like you - I don't have the strength.

"Stay safe," he said and kissed Mouse for the last time. "Leave a fire going for me. I promise I'll come back to you."

Outside, the wind was picking up, blowing the tears from his eyes. Sadao wiped his face on his riding gloves and fitted the goggles over his brow. He fastened a shoulder strap to the sheath of his father's ancient sword and slung it across his back before mounting the Kawasaki Vulcan. He inserted his key and pressed the start. The bike roared to life as he rolled out down the gravel drive, away from his home and into the thickening wood.

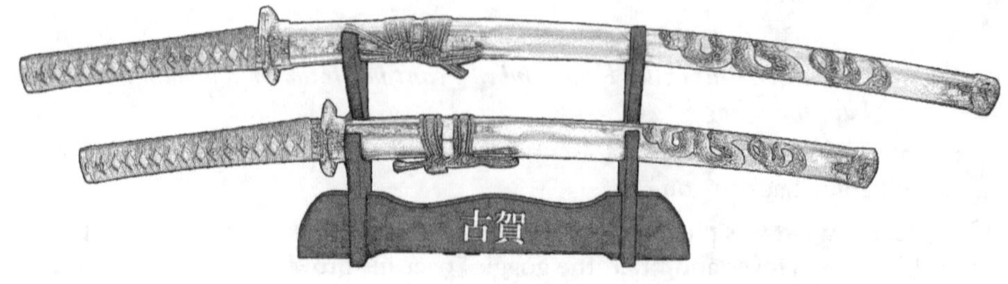

Epilogue

Grave of Red Stone

Blythe Arizona, 2059

Screeeeeeeeeeeeee!!!

Mouse woke with a start. The blue radio beside his cot had gone evil - screaming into the cluttered storage space at the back of the station office he called a bedroom. Not wanting to wake up all the way, Mouse yawned and fumbled at the big dial, hoping to hit a less annoying open channel. Screeches and bleeps for days, none offering the sound he craved - cool blissful static.

Scrrrreee!! Scriiiiiiitch! Scrooooch!!

Shit, what's up with this thing now?

Mouse shut the radio off altogether and sat up, scratching his messy head. The wall clock across the room over the desk displayed 3:55 A.M. *Fuck my life - it's early.*

Bang! Bang! Scriiiitch….!

Mouse jumped at the new sound. The wind was howling outside, rattling the garage bay doors across the hallway - that was typical. The bang-scritches on the roof, not so much. Mouse rotated off the cot and slid into his sneakers. He went over to his desk and flicked on the lamp.

"Fred? You up?" The old man answered with a snore from the sagging couch by the empty water cooler. "Fred? You alive? Wake up!"

"Uh? Eh? We gotta chase them dogs outta the chicken house again?"

"No, Fred. We don't have chickens, just empty gas pumps and potato chips. Can you get up? Something's come loose on the roof. I need to go check it out. I need a hand with the ladder."

"Yup, yup, you betcha, but first - be a champ and help your ol' uncle Fred find his pants."

Ratty pants on and torch in hand, Fred helped Mouse haul the stepladder out of bay door one and into the howling wind. Ground dust was scattering in whirls, scratching every surface it encountered. Far off across the empty desert, Mouse saw a flash light up the distant mesas.

"Looks like heck of a storm comin'!" Fred shouted over the wind.

"Yeah I know! I think the monsoon's arrived early!" Mouse said, steadying the top of the ladder against the storm drain that ran along the edge of the garage's tin roof. "Can you shine that light up here?" Fred complied and Mouse's concerns were confirmed. A stabilizing cable had come loose and was whipping around in the gusts. Its thrashings were causing the main radio antenna assembly to bend and sway dangerously off kilter.

"That don't look safe up there!" Fred shouted.

"Yeah I know, but I can't lose that antenna, Fred. That's the one Dad and I built! I've got to save it. Can you come hold the end of this thing? Put your foot down on the last rung, keep it flush against the drain pipes."

"Yessiree, you want the light?"

"Yeah, hand it here." Mouse took the flashlight and slipped it through a belt loop at his hip. Then he said a prayer, gripped the ladder in both hands and began to climb.

Crack! Boom!

A bolt of lightning hit the desert basin a few miles away, illuminating the saguaro and the outline of their rooftop. In the brief flash, Mouse was able to assess the problem. If he could bring up his tools in time, he might be able to reattach the cable before the storm came full in. He put his foot down on the snaking cable and wrapped the frayed end around an air vent.

"Hey Fred! Can you toss me up my belt kit and stuff a few fasteners in it?"

"Sure, where's it at?"

"I think I left it in the back by the lockers!"

"Yeah you got it! Uh, where do you keep them fasteners?"

"Old coffee can. Back of bay two by the sink - I think."

"Okay, hang tight."

Mouse clicked on the flashlight to examine the antenna's mast. It was bent about halfway up. Shit, that would be a pain to fix. He stepped closer, catching the antenna's arm as it swung his way. The whole frankensteined apparatus had been assembled by himself and his dad two summers ago to extend Mouse's listening range. On a good night he could tune into the racing commentary in far-off Phoenix. It was the second best thing to being there, which he hadn't been able to manage since his dad became ill. Fred was great for companionship, but fell short on the doctoring. Dad had taken a long time to die. There just wasn't ever enough gas or time.

As Mouse waited for Fred to locate his tools, the rain began to fall. Small droplets at first that felt good in the hot wind. But soon those few drops found some friends and began to bring down the rain in earnest. Fat wind-powered blobs soaked his T-shirt in 30 seconds flat.

"Fred! If you can't find the fasteners, forget it! It's raining like a bitch! I'll just take this baby down for now." Mouse knew Fred couldn't hear him very well when he was standing right next to him, let alone down in the garage under the sound of the storm hitting the roof. Mouse tried to pop the antenna loose from the mast, but it was stuck in fast. The roof was slightly slanted overall and it became slippery when wet. He had to plant his feet carefully between each twist and tug.

"Unngh! Fuck this thing!"

Another flash of lightning hit, brighter than the last followed by a rattling BOOM!

Ookay, now the thunder head's getting a little too close for comfort. Maybe I gotta just tie it down after all.

Crack! BOOM!

"Fred, my hair's standing up in the ozone here!!!"

"I hear ya, Mouse! Hang onto your britches!" Fred was coming up the ladder. The top of it was banging against the drain with each step.

"Fred! Don't come all the way up!" Mouse said, scooting gingerly across the tin roof toward him. "I'll come to you and you can toss me the belt, okay?"

"Sure thing. Just let me get my foot…"

Craaack!! Zzzzzzzt!!! BOOM!!

Mouse was temporarily blinded by the flash as lightning hit the old phone line across the road. His foot slid on the slippery tin and his legs shot out from under him. He landed hard on his side and started to slide. He scrambled for a grip to save his fall, but it was no good. Picking up speed, he flew off the edge of the roof and fell through the rain until gravity caught him and slammed him into the hood of the dumpster.

Wham!! Fuck!!!

Mouse saw more lights than just lightning bolts and then it all went dark.

When Mouse opened his eyes again there was a pack of ice on his head and he was surrounded by the long shadows of Doc Meadow's antique medical devices. A wave of deja vu hit him. He'd been here before, a long time ago lying on this same cot while his dad and the doc spoke in the waiting room just outside.

"Am I hurt?" Mouse asked the microscope.

"Huh? Oh, you're back with us," Doc said, raising his head from where he'd dozed off at the desk.

"Yeah, I guess. Head hurts, though."

"Do you remember what happened?" Doc asked, getting up and coming over to check his eyeballs with a pen light.

"Yeah, I did something stupid and slid off the roof on my ass."

"Head, actually," Doc corrected. "Gave yourself quite a knot. Fortunately, no blood - just scrambled your brains again, is all."

"Again? So I'm right. I did hurt myself before, when I was a little kid?"

Doc nodded with a kind smile. "Sure did. You took a tumble at the junkyard. Bumped your noggin. You shook it off pretty fast, though. Made of rubber."

Mouse smiled despite the throbbing in his skull. Something else was bothering him. He closed his eyes a moment to try and recall it. Something about the radio - his favorite blue radio that had started all the trouble tonight. "I found my favorite radio that day," he said, looking up at Doc.

"Um, yes I believe you did have a radio with you. Wouldn't let go of it. But then you almost always had a radio with you when you were a youngster."

"I think… I saw something… there was… lots of hoses or…"

Doc patted Mouse's shoulder. "Best get yourself some rest. I'll take you over to the 'Horse in the morning for pancakes. How's that sound?"

Mouse closed his eyes and smiled. "Sure, sounds good."

"That rusty station, boy, ain't doing nobody no good as she is. I admire you keeping your Pop's ol' place open, but we need to be realistic here," Sheriff Billy said. "Ain't no one driving that ol' highway no more."

Mouse glanced at the old man sitting across the long saloon table from him as he slathered fresh butter over a stack of Nana Marybelle's buttermilk pancakes. Billy was dressed in his Sheriff's uniform with an unloaded pistol at his hip and a silver badge his Dad had cast out of aluminum 30 years ago pinned to his ample chest. Billy was a tough old guy with keys to the crumbling jailhouse. He was Sheriff in name only, but deeply respected by the people of Blythe.

Mouse noticed that a few more folks than average had come out that Sunday morning for pancakes and eggs and they were among those who cared the most about him: Doc, Gloria, Widow Quelle, Nick the bartender, and some other townsfolk who had been loyal station customers since Mouse was born. They were gathered along the table with Doc Meadows, eating hotcakes with faces full of concern for Mouse and his bump.

"Besides, it's dangerous outside the town limits," Doc chimed in, blowing on his coffee. "You know we got loners and thieves crawling all over this desert, running off with whatever they can grab. You and Fred need to move closer in. We've got dozens

Dillon
"Ain't nothin' so broke it can't be fixed"
A GOOD FRIEND & DAD
2001-2059

of nice empty homes within a block of this saloon. Ennis and his brother says they'll get any one of 'em cleaned up and painted for you. Some have big ol' garages too."

Mouse turned to Fred who was seated at his left, downing a beer as fast as he could. He kept his eyes on the bottom of the glass. It was guilty drinking - he knew the real reason for this gathering and wanted no blame for it. Wasn't his way.

"Look guys, ladies …" Mouse said. "I appreciate your concern. And the offers and everything. You all just want to make sure I'm okay - I know. But I'm fine. I'm fifteen now. The station is fine. Fred and I are fine. We're doing just fine right where we are."

"But it's dangerous, honey," Gloria pleaded. "It's not right, you out there alone like that."

"I've got a shotgun and a rifle and plenty of trip wires and I know how to use them! Right, Fred?"

Fred frowned at his empty beer glass and Nick got up to fetch him another. "I'll do whatever Mouse wants to do," he said. "Dill left the place to him fair and square. Don't seem right to just leave it."

A cloud of arguments rose up. Some were saying the station made for a good lookout - others felt that Mouse was still too young to make this kind decision on his own and should become a ward of the town. Others said they wanted to sack the station for supplies and fixtures.

"Hey!" Mouse shouted over them. "This is my home we're arguing about! I learned to walk in that oil pit and I intend to keep the open sign lit for as long as I'm breathing!"

"Here - here!" Someone in the back shouted.

There were more grumbles but Mouse stayed firm, chewing his breakfast.

"All I ask then," Sheriff Billy said, "is you radio the jailhouse and saloon every night at sundown and at sunup, you hear me?"

"Yes sir," Mouse said, relaxing a bit. "I appreciate the breakfast company and advice, but if you all don't mind, I've got work to do back at the station."

Mouse drank the last of his coffee and tried to walk out, but Doc caught up with him at the doorway.

"I know you don't like being told what's right. And I admire you for wanting to keep your pop's business running. But times is changing around here, hard. I couldn't live with myself if you or the old man came to any harm by man or nature out there. It ain't right. And I can't be every place at once in this town."

Mouse reached up and clapped his shoulder. "Don't worry, Doc. Fred and I got this. Like you said, made of rubber."

Doc wiped his eyes and nodded as Mouse stepped out into the morning light to mount a spare dirtbike and roared away from the center of town.

Mouse walked around in the desert scrub looking for a rock. Arizona's desert floor was a color mosaic of blue-grey and red sandstones. He strolled about, kicking a stone now and again until he found the right one. It was a good handful in size and flat on the bottom and top with a brilliant rust red color in between.

"Gotcha!" he said and followed his footsteps back to the spot where he had parked his bike.

Salvation Hill was a bald rocky rise that overlooked the southern end of town. Consecrated when Blythe was founded in 1886, its leaning wrought iron gates and uneven fencing circled about 200 hundred some-odd crumbling tombstones and carved slabs. Mouse knew most of the names on the stones, the ones that could still be read anyway. He knew most of their surviving family too: Quelle, Meadows, Jamison, Fitzgerald … all good families, all good people gone into the ground while their descendants scraped out a living in the remainder of the once great town below.

He walked past the older fading names and entered the area with newer stonework where outlines of desert rocks marked the perimeter of each grave. The newest one, down at the end of the shallow slope by the dirtbike had a freshly carved headstone that read:

Dillon
"Ain't nothin' so broke it can't be fixed."
A GOOD FRIEND & DAD
2001-2059

"Got you a really bright one today, Dad!" Mouse said, setting the rock atop the stacks that defined the plot his father was laid to rest in just over a year ago. At first when he came each day to lay down a new stone, there would be many more new ones helping to build the formation. But as the months passed and new graves were dug, those anonymous stones had dwindled day by day until now, all Mouse could see were his own rocks, one by one, slowly keeping the plot intact.

People got to get on with living sometime, Doc was often fond of saying whenever a patient of his lost the battle to stay breathing. It was true, Mouse supposed. But it made his heart hurt to know that someday even he might stop bringing rocks to Dad's graveside.

Mouse sighed and took a seat on the low wall of his father's grave, looking back toward town. The recent rain had stirred the scent of the desert sage and darkened the red dust for miles out across the basin.

"I'm sorry Dad," he said. "I know everyone's worried about me. All I did was bump my head, but everyone wants to make sure I keep eating and growing and doing whatever is it I'm supposed to do! So I'm doing it. I'm doing the best I can. And Fred's doing it with me. We're both sticking together in this. Don't you worry."

A memory of his dad and him setting up the radio antenna over the garage bays for the first time flashed through his head. It was a blistering hot day. The network of welded vanes wasn't heavy, but it was awkward to lift and hold in place while his dad welded the base to the roofing beam so the apparatus wouldn't fly off in the wind. It was going well until Mouse lost his balance and started to slide.

If it weren't for his dad, he'd have shot right off that hot as fuck corrugated tin roof. No dumpster back then to break his fall, either. It could have gone really bad. Dad burned his left hand, grabbing onto a sun-baked riveted joint to reach out and stop Mouse from sliding. Mouse could remember chipping rusty ice out of the Coke machine to help soothe his blistered burns.

"I'm sorry, Dad," he'd said then, too.

"Don't you worry about it. It's a father's job. I'd take a bullet to the head if it would stop you from getting hurt."

I know you can't be here anymore to catch me, Dad. But it's okay. I bounce. Even if I fall far, I bounce.

The desert view below him blurred and he wiped his eyes to clear it. People often said the desert was a barren place, but they were wrong. The desert was filled with life. Beautiful life. Mouse loved the tall saguaro that stood out on every peak around their town, mile after mile - motionless sentinels of the desert. They watched over the bushy grey-blue scrub and dark scruffy bark of the mesquite trees. They watched over the powdery blue needle-tipped agave, the paddle-shaped prickly pear cactus, the short fat barrels with bright orange and yellow blooms amidst sharp spikes and the endless red dusty earth between.

He closed his eyes and inhaled the sweet musk of the desert sage. No sounds, no wind, just the occasional skittering of lizards racing with whip tails between the colorful rocks. No one but him was on this hillside to appreciate the sum of nature out on display. He could never leave this place, he realized. Never. Someone would have to hogtie him and drag him away before he'd leave.

Mouse often liked to imagine someone kind, sitting close to him, putting an arm around him and gazing out over the expanse, quietly sharing the desert view. The thought of this faceless man flooded him with peace.

"Be patient, boy," Dad would say. "Nothin' worth having comes easy."

Someday, Mouse thought, *he'll come for you. He's out there and when you meet him, you'll know it.*

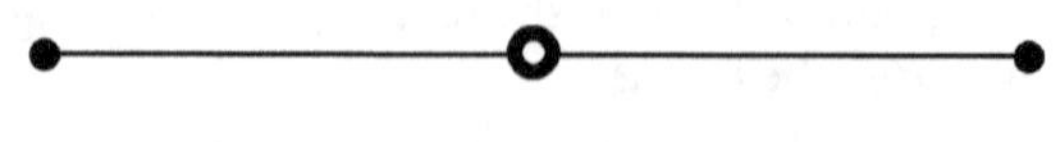

End

Extras

Extra Scene

An Unplanned Dip

Sometimes not every scene I write makes the final cut. I tend to write out of order and on odd days, just write sex scenes with no real idea where or how they will be used in the final novel. I knew at some point Mouse and Sadao would have to share their trailer space in Squamish along with Gisette and Lupe and as it turned out, a pack of kids too. This little nature walk was supposed to play out at some point during their full-house days. I was really fond of it, but in the end, it just didn't move the plot foward, so it had to go. Fortunately, printers require you to hit certain folio numbers for printing price breaks so we had a few extra pages to fill. So fill it, I shall. Enjoy!

--Itoshi

Sasori Squamish Seaside Camp - 2073

Although the sun was out, the temperature was still hovering just above zero as Mouse and Sadao slipped out of the insanity of camp to take a walk along the waterside. The air was calm and the short steep banks of the rocky inlet were still lined with bits of ice and snow from the recent storm. Mouse walked snug up against Sadao's side, borrowing as much body heat as he could. Soon they passed into the shade of a pine grove and the temperature abruptly dropped 10 degrees. Mouse stepped ahead and quickened his pace when he saw a bright patch of sun approaching.

"Come here!" Sadao didn't approve of this short separation and grabbed Mouse by the wrist, pulling him back.

"You are feeling your oats today, aren't you?" Mouse said as he was tugged into Sadao's chest. The man wrapped a firm arm around his waist and ground his crotch up against his - packed to please. Mouse slid a hand down to inspect the goods bulging the denim. "Damn, you get hard fast!"

"Can't help it," Sadao said, grasping Mouse's chin. "Too much excitement recently.

There's no privacy in my trailer anymore. Too many unexpected guests. I've been hard all day!"

"Really? Mmpf--!" Sadao caught his mouth in a firm kiss. Lips slid over his own with a tickle of beard. Mouse was a bit sorry he'd trimmed it. But long or short, the beard was a manly piece of Sadao that when encountered sent a shock of want right up Mouse's dick. Frantic with lust, Sadao was all over him from lips to ass - sucking, squeezing and caressing Mouse through his jeans like a dog with a favorite squeak toy. Mouse just held on and hummed in approval as he let Sadao walk them back into a tree.

"Mmnpf! We're outside in the elements, if you haven't noticed," he said as Sadao palmed his hardness and began battling his belt.

"We're far enough from camp," Sadao said, licking an earlobe. "Wildlife won't mind a little spring mating."

"Ah, it's dead of winter, you know…"

Sadao lifted his head and searched Mouse's eyes. "You're asking me to wait a few months?"

Mouse shook his head vigorously. "NO … no, now's good. Now will do fine. Um … how will we be doing *now* exactly?" The tree trunk at his back was a tad abrasive and far too close to the water for his taste. Plus, it was fucking freezing!

"We'll improvise," Sadao said grabbing Mouse's knit cap and tilting his head back for a gobble at his throat.

"Oh, babe…"

Mouse was out of protests by the time Sadao's fingers worked his shirt up and his mouth was sucking hard on a firm nipple. Mouse's dick was so stiff it felt like it might bust a seam.

Exhibitionist, much? he mused. Yeah they were far from camp, but the bright of midday shown down through the trees and they were in plain view of anyone out on the inlet. *Was it fishing hours?* Mouse tried to glance over Sadao's busy head but all he saw was calm blue water and the smoke rising from distant cabin chimneys. His breath blew out in little clouds but for once he was starting to not feel the chill. Sadao's intensity, mixed with the stark fear of getting caught in a compromising position, was making his head spin and his blood warm. He wound his fist in Sadao's hair and pulled him off his nipple, now peaked and reddened from the effort.

"Dick … needs suck … now…" he gasped. Sadao smiled, sinking to his knees.

"I like it when you lose your grammar," Sadao said, pulling his fly loose. Mouse's penis popped out of the top of his waistband for a look around. Sadao murmured something approving in Japanese and gave the head a good lick.

"Aaagh!" Standing up during a blow job always got Mouse crazy aroused. But adding the fact Sadao was down on his knees all leather jacket and hungry for Mousemeat was making him rub his ass up against the damn tree in anticipation. "Hurry…" he whispered.

Sadao looked up with an evil grin. "Sucking you off is not something I like to rush," he said, slowly drawing Mouse's dick out of his underpants and running a warm palm up and down its length. "Just lean back and relax. Enjoy the ocean view."

"Ooohh," Mouse moaned as his dick slid into the heat of Sadao's mouth. The inlet was beautiful today. Light danced across the water. Loons called to each other from opposite shores. The sounds of nature on a lazy afternoon mixed with Sadao's throaty groans as he ate up his shaft was Mouse's idea of outdoorsmanship. Sadao's fingers slid under his balls and started to roll them in time with his deep sucks. Mouse's eyes rolled shut and his head fell back against the tree. It was so hard to stay upright when his hips felt like they were coming unhinged.

"Hold onto the tree," Sadao advised as his mouth released his cock long enough to suck up a testicle. The captured gonad bulged out his cheek like a squirrel gathering, well ... nuts.

Enough nature metaphors! Enjoy this. Enjoy your man worshiping your sac like you're a Squamish thundergod!

"Aaagh!!" It was obvious Sadao wanted to treat him to a slow torturous ball wash, but Mouse's dick was getting painfully cold exposed to the elements. Mouse grabbed a handful of his dark hair and tugged. Sadao looked up at him and obeyed, running a hot tongue up and down the length, warming it up again fast. Slurp slurp.

Eyes locked on his own, Sadao slid his lips around the bright swollen head and sucked and sucked - popping him out to work the underridge with a deft series of flicks. It was just too goddamned lewd and he was just too goddamned turned on. Orgasm flushed through his groin.

"Oh, fuuuck!!!" Hot shots of spooge dashed across Sadao's face, icing him from cheek to eartip as Mouse rode out the spasms.

Oh, shit! He's gonna kill me - I got it in his hair! The spurts kept coming, and Mouse was helpless to stop the hosedown of his lover, who licked him fondly through the rush. *Jeeze was he bottomless?*

"Oh, shit, babe ... I didn't see that coming! I'm sorry..." Sadao didn't seem sorry - in fact, he seemed quite pleased with himself. He licked up what he could from his cheek with his tongue and the back of his hand. A shake of his head sent the lob of goop stuck in his hair flying into the leaves.

"Shame to waste it," Sadao said, admiring the spotted foliage. "Never knew a man who could produce quite like you."

Mouse was panting, gripping the tree behind him with both hands and rubber knees so he wouldn't fall bare-assed into pine needles. "You ... inspire me."

Sadao got to his feet, stretching the bad leg. "And you inspire me," he said. He grabbed Mouse by the waist and flipped him around, pushing his chest into the bark. "Now, give it up! I've got a hard-on the size of honshu!"

The man wasted no time pulling down his jeans and shoving his brand-like barb right up against Mouse's crack. No lube, no cum. *This is what you get for the hair gelling,* Mouse thought as Sadao backed his ass away from the tree so he was bent over, hugging the trunk with his arm.

Smack! Sadao never could start a fuck without an ass smacking warm up. *What was up with that?* Smack! squeeze squeeze....

"Spread your legs and show me my prize!" he growled. In the distance, Mouse could begin to hear the sound of a boat engine.

"Oh, shit, not now!! Somebody's coming!"

"Somebody's going to be coming alright - and he's standing right here!"

Smack smack!

Oh God, no no no....I know this is the kind of shit I get myself into for being a horndog, but ... ouch! Does there have to be witnesses?

Smack!

From Mouse's position he could see the water off to his left if he turned his head slightly. Sadao on the other hand, had his back to the inlet and was too far gone with animal lust to notice if a cruise ship pulled up full of retirees with cameras. He had both of Mouse's cheeks firmly in hand and was working his dickhead into the target ring with tight little shoves.

This is going to wind up on a cable channel for sure ... Racers Gone Wild!

"Aaanngghh!" Mouse bit his lips shut, wary of the approaching boat. Sadao was in. The first thrust was always the worst, or best, depending on how you looked at it. That first rush of heat, filling him up - the rough plunge and delicious sound Sadao would utter deep in his throat from the feel of being 'all in.' It was, in a word, painfully exciting. His lover didn't waste much time savoring it either, and pitched Mouse's hips up and his head down, scraping bark across his shoulder as he began to thrust in nice and solid. "Nnngh!"

Rrrrrrrr ... from the sound of the approaching motor, this was a small troller - hugging the coast with baited lines dragging the water, hoping to lure in some hungry halibut. *They're gonna catch an eyeful of something they can't unsee in a minute,* Mouse mused, holding onto the pine as best as he could while Sadao's hips pummeled him into the bark. *And I may lose my shoulder alignment.* The way they were angled this might not look so bad if Mouse could just reach down and pull up his pants from down around his ankles...

Smack! "Stop squirming!" Sadao barked, quickening his pace. The tree's needled branches rattled in protest. Probably the first time the conifer had been commandeered for sex-furniture. Sadao, oblivious, showed it and Mouse's asshole no mercy.

"I - ugh! Need - pants!"

Smack! Squeeze! Smack! "Why?! This is a fuck, not a tea party!"

What reason would Sadao-in-mid-rut most likely accept? Splinters? Woodchucks? Pinecones were falling to the ground at Mouse's feet.

Fuck, could he at least slow it down a bit?

Rrrrrrr putputput….any second now they'd be comin' around the bend.

"Because we've got fucking company is why!!"

"Good," Sadao growled, slamming in solid, knocking Mouse's lungs flat up against the trunk. Ugck! Mouse lost his grip on the tree and both of them pitched forward, Sadao falling on top of him, sending them sliding down the steep embankment. Mouse pitched headfirst into the freezing water right into the path of the fishing boat.

"Whoa! Slow up!" A voice yelled out just as Mouse's head broke surface and narrowly missed getting beaned by the fiberglass bow. His arms paddled the icy water, as he struggled to free his legs from his pants and Sadao was … all zipped up and laughing his ass off from the bank. He'd managed to arrest his slide a half foot from taking an unplanned swim.

Did that asshole come? Mouse wondered as a hand reached down to haul him out of the water. Mouse spilled into the boat - free and breezy and very very cold.

"Son, you seem to be missing some clothes."

Two grizzled bearded faces stared down at him in confusion. Pants and shoes were somewhere among the rocks at the bottom. Mouse covered himself with a shivering palm, feeling the tell-tale drizzle of Sadao's gratification oozing from the other side. He clenched more than his chattering teeth.

"I told him not to piss so close to the edge!" Sadao offered.

"He *pushed* me!" Mouse shouted back as a halibut leapt into the boat and smacked him in the leg.

Thanks, idiot. See if I cook you dinner tonight!

Sketch Gallery

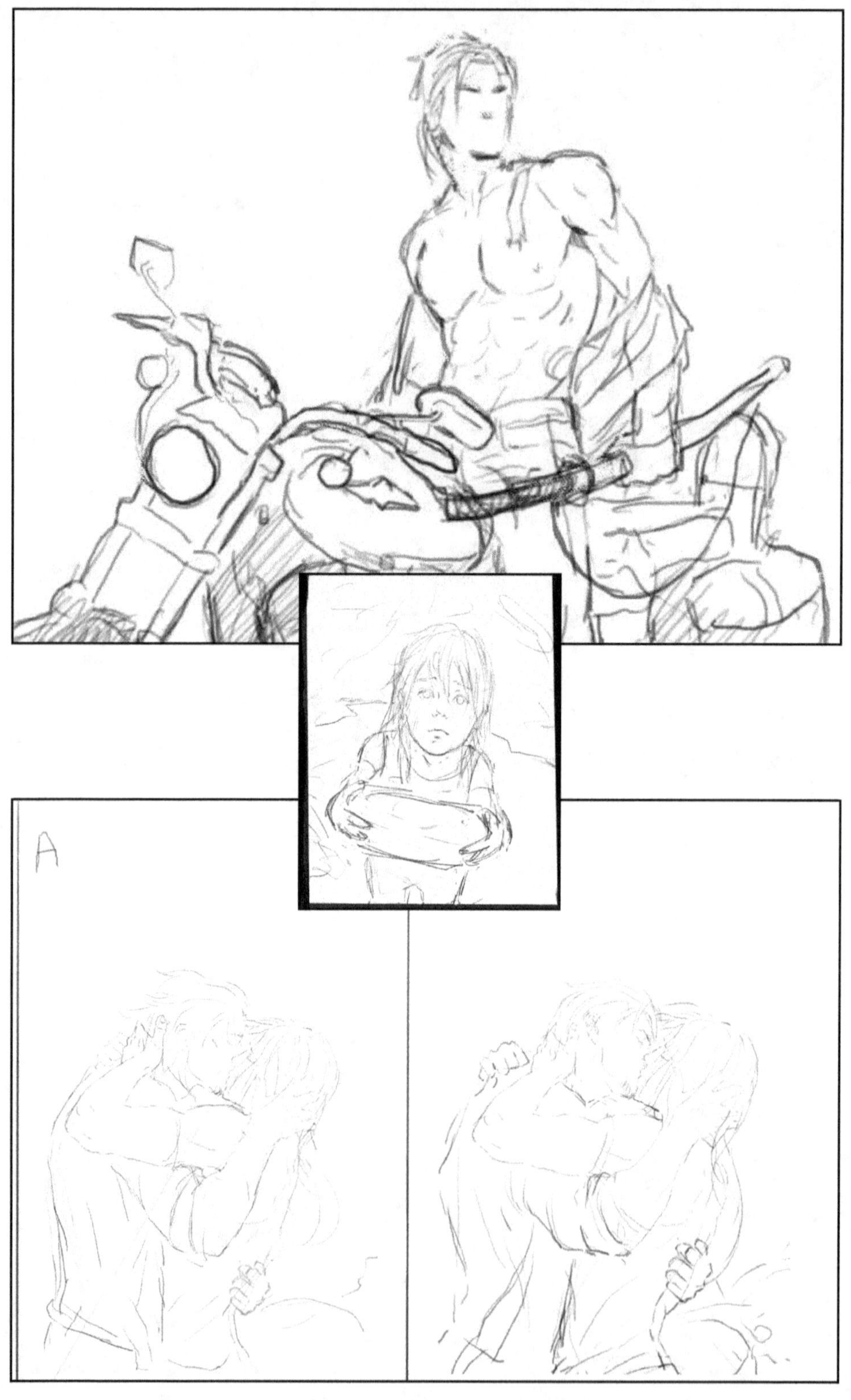
A

Aldaria gives me lots of
poses to choose from! It's
hard to pick sometimes.

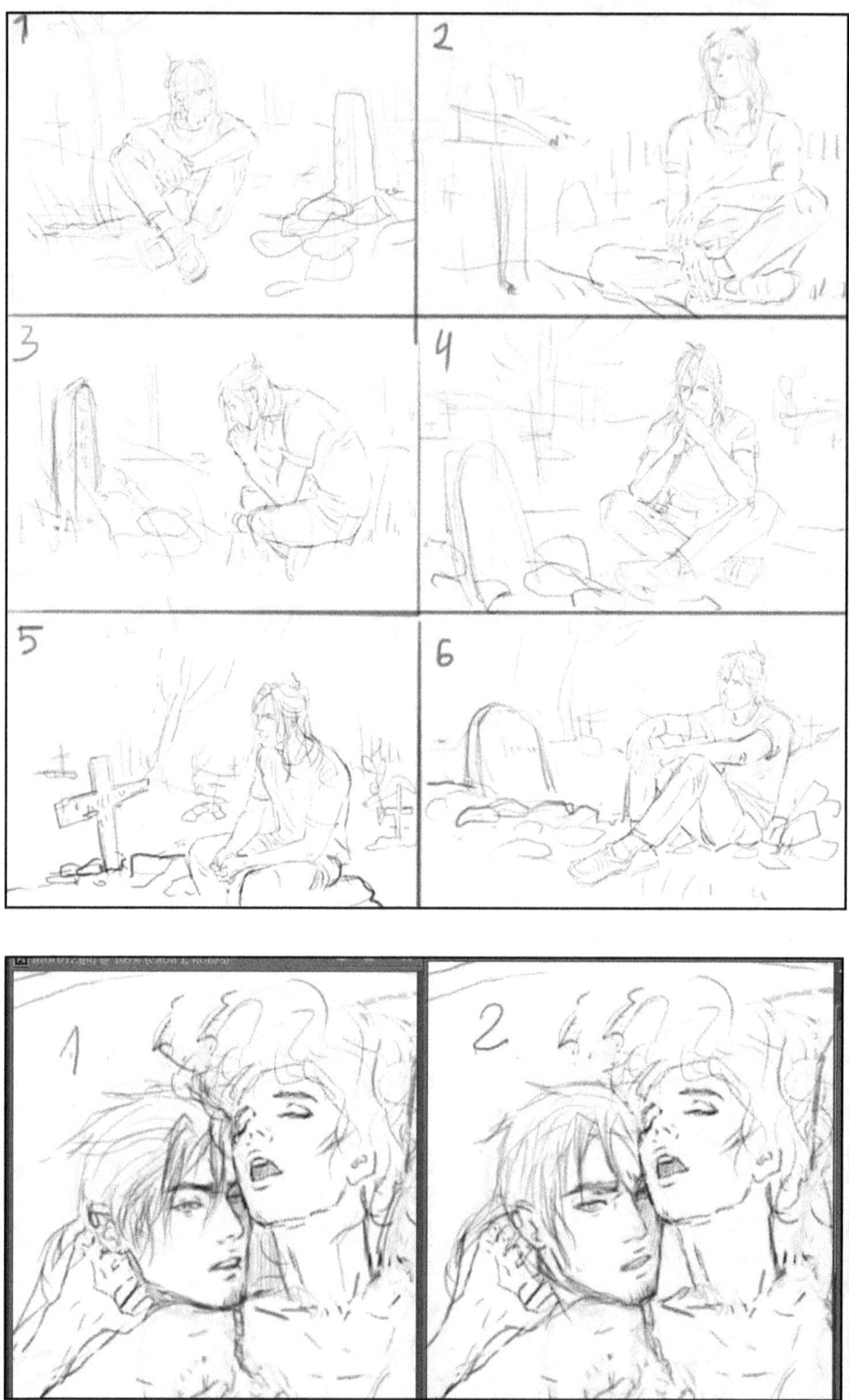

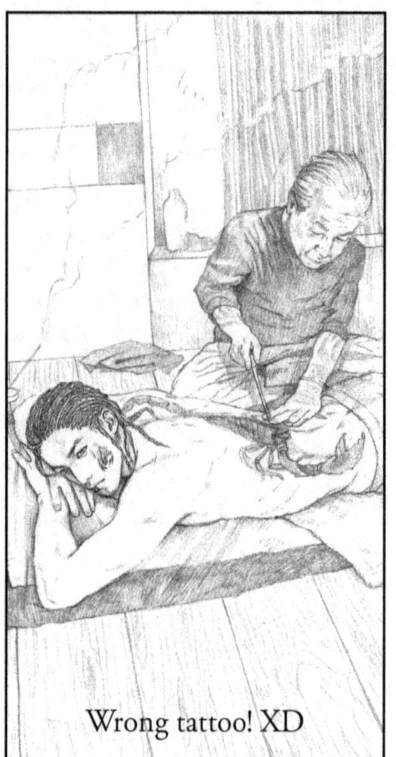

Wrong tattoo! XD

Orochi no Yaiba

by Itoshi

Art by Aldaria

Publisher/Typesetting: Sharon Barela
Associate Publisher: Emie Butcher
Editor: Murjani Sowell
Marketing Assistant: Nicole Le
Additional Artwork: Chris Barela
Special thanks to: Kaori, Geraldina, Charlotte, & Cindy!

Second Edition: March 2018
ISBN: 978-1-943695-11-9

www.yaoi-revolution.com
www.facebook.com/YaoiRevolution
twitter.com/YaoiRevolution

Inquiries: yaoirevolutionnow@gmail.com

The Orochi Series by Itoshi

Art
by
Aldaria

and

Orochi no Saido

coming in 2018

Visit: yaoi-revolution.com
for ordering information

www.ingramcontent.com/pod-product-compliance
Lightning Source LLC
Chambersburg PA
CBHW060755210726
48292CB00013B/154